Thieves, Spies and Other Lovers

John Patrick Blackheart; acknowledged
security consultant—unacknowledged cat
burglar. He does his best work at night!

Daniel Avanti; prominent businessman—
an expert at "intimate surveillance."
He does his best work in bed!

Matt Cavanaugh; international
playboy—international spy.
He does his best work under cover.

Thieves, Spies and Other Lovers

They'll steal your heart!

Relive the romance....

By Request™

*Three complete novels by your
favorite authors!*

About the Authors

Anne Stuart—Author of over forty-five romance novels, Anne had her very first work published by *Jack and Jill* magazine at the age of seven. She's been writing ever since and has won several awards, including Romance Writers of America's prestigious RITA award. Anne currently resides in an old farmhouse in Vermont with her husband and two children.

Dawn Carroll—Dawn, a native Californian, wasn't born wanting to become a writer. In fact, her first loves are singing and drama. But when those pastimes started to intrude on her family life, Dawn needed something she could do at home that would still satisfy her creative urges. Once she'd penned her first novel, Dawn knew she'd found her niche.

Lynn Erickson—Carla Peltonen and Molly Swanton, a.k.a. Lynn Erickson, have been writing together for almost nineteen years. With more than twenty books under their belts, these prolific authors are now experiencing "empty nest" syndrome and hate to admit that they're loving it. Both women currently live in Colorado where they're working on their next book.

THIEVES, SPIES AND OTHER LOVERS

ANNE STUART
DAWN CARROLL
LYNN ERICKSON

Harlequin Books

TORONTO • NEW YORK • LONDON
AMSTERDAM • PARIS • SYDNEY • HAMBURG
STOCKHOLM • ATHENS • TOKYO • MILAN
MADRID • WARSAW • BUDAPEST • AUCKLAND

HARLEQUIN BOOKS

by Request—Thieves, Spies and Other Lovers

Copyright © 1995 by Harlequin Enterprises B.V.

ISBN 0-373-20109-5

The publisher acknowledges the copyright holders
of the individual works as follows:
CATSPAW
Copyright © 1985 by Anne Kristine Stuart Ohlrogge
CODE NAME CASANOVA
Copyright © 1989 by Dawn Carroll Boese
IN FROM THE COLD
Copyright © 1989 by Molly Swanton and Carla Peltonen

Printed in U.S.A.

CONTENTS

CATSPAW   9
Anne Stuart

CODE NAME CASANOVA   217
Dawn Carroll

IN FROM THE COLD   371
Lynn Erickson

An expert thief can steal anything—
even a lady's heart!

CATSPAW

Anne Stuart

Chapter One

Ferris Byrd didn't want to be in that plush, silent elevator carrying her inexorably toward the top floor of the San Francisco town house that held Blackheart, Inc. She'd argued—oh, so gently—manipulated, dragged her heels and flat-out refused. And still she was here.

The elevator doors whooshed open, exposing a small, charming hallway with white plastered walls, stripped oak woodwork and several doors. All belonging to Blackheart, Inc. And they were all closed. No one had seen her arrive—she could turn around and head back down to street level and tell Phillip Merriam and the Committee for Saving the Bay that someone else could deal with their chosen security firm. God knows why everyone had insisted on Blackheart, Inc.

No, Ferris knew very well why everyone had insisted on Blackheart. He had cachet, he had charm, he had a sly sort of fame that most people found irresistible and Ferris found offensive. She hated feeling judgmental, disapproving, stiff and pompous. But she also hated what Blackheart represented.

What she hated most of all, however, was cowardice, particularly her own. Phillip had talked her into it, the committee had insisted and here she was. She had no choice but to carry through.

"May I help you?" The office was a perfect example of San Francisco remodeled, with stripped woodwork, antique oak furniture, masses of plants and the obligatory stained-glass window. The only thing that didn't quite jibe was the receptionist. She was young, in her mid-twenties at the latest, with

short-cropped red hair, distrustful blue eyes, a pugnacious tilt
to her chin and a small, compact body dressed in modified
army-navy surplus. The polite greeting had been uttered in a
surprisingly hostile tone, and the look she passed over Ferris
left little doubt as to her opinion. As if to emphasize it, the receptionist, whose desk plate identified her as Kate Christiansen, sniffed disapprovingly.

Ferris had little doubt what the woman would see through
her flinty blue eyes. She'd see a woman of elegance, her custom-made leather shoes worth more than Kate Christiansen's
entire wardrobe. Ferris's soft wool suit was Liz Claiborne, and
it draped artfully to conceal the rounder parts of her figure. Her
long legs were encased in real silk, her dark hair was clasped in
a loose bun at the nape of her neck in a style that showed off
her elegant bone structure. And the face itself wasn't bad, Ferris thought dispassionately. She knew her green eyes were cool
and assessing, her mouth, with its pale-peach lip gloss, had
curved in a polite smile, and the discreet gold hoops in her ears
added just enough color to her warm skin tones. She looked
rich, understated and well cared for, from generations of such
pampered elegance. And only she knew how hard that look was
to come by.

The thought pleased her into widening her smile. She could
afford to be generous, she was so close to her goals. "I'm Ferris Byrd," she said, her pleasant, well-modulated voice another triumph. Its slightly husky note was the only part she'd
left of her original mid-western twang. Now she sounded bored,
upper class and slightly naughty—and it was this voice, over the
telephone, that had first charmed Phillip Merriam. "I have an
appointment to see Mr. Blackheart."

Kate Christiansen did not look pleased, and Ferris wondered whether it was jealousy that caused that glower, or
something else. She was almost tempted to inform the pugnacious young lady that John Patrick Blackheart was the last
person she wished to entice, but then she controlled herself.
That had been her worst trial, overcoming the sudden, unbidden urges to do something outrageous. But she had conquered
the temptation, and it was only a passing fantasy, quickly dismissed.

Kate Christiansen scowled. "He'll be with you shortly. You can go in." With a jerk of her head she indicated the door on the left, then turned back to the sheaf of papers on the oak desk in front of her, effectively dismissing the upstart.

Ferris allowed herself her first real smile of the morning as she settled in a low-slung chair by John Patrick Blackheart's empty desk, her long, slender legs stretched out in front of her. Here she'd arrived, determined to disapprove, and instead she'd been made to feel the outcast. It served her right, but it didn't make her any more comfortable. Why hadn't she been able to talk them into hiring someone less . . . less unorthodox?

There was nothing about the office to suggest the history of the man who ran it. The walls were the ubiquitous white plaster, the stripped woodwork and oriental rugs as discreet and tastefully anonymous as Ferris herself, and probably manufactured with as much care. The only sign of personality was in the choice of paintings. They were a strange mélange: a romantic watercolor of the bay, a passionate oil of a storm at sea, a rigidly logical geometric painting that just might be a Mondrian. And most surprising of all, a Roy Lichtenstein silkscreen comic strip, with a cigarette-smoking, beret-clad lady holding a machine gun that went, according to the balloon, "crak-crak-crak." Ferris looked at it for a moment, a reluctant smile curving her deliberately pale mouth. It was an odd, jarring combination of artistic styles that somehow worked.

"Ferris Byrd?" The smooth, friendly voice made her jump, and the body that went with it was just as much of a shock. He was an immensely tall, almost ridiculously handsome man, with a mop of blond curls atop his high forehead, steely blue eyes, a thousand teeth shining forth in a tanned face, and the broadest shoulders Ferris had ever seen. He held out a hand the size of a small turkey that easily enveloped hers. "I'm Trace Walker, Patrick's associate. How can I help you?"

Ferris immediately decided that the toothy smile was charming, the steely-blue gaze warm and friendly. It was only Blackheart himself that she distrusted. With luck maybe she could deal with this affable giant entirely. "I represent the Committee for Saving the Bay, and we're in need of security consultants."

He smiled that dazzling smile of his. "How convenient. We just happen to be security consultants. I talked with Senator Merriam yesterday—he said it has to do with the Puffin Ball?"

Ferris controlled the little spurt of irritation that sped through her. Phillip never did trust anyone else to get a job done. His hands-on approach aided him immeasurably in his political career, but it irritated the hell out of his administrative assistant and brand-new fiancée. She smiled again, a little more tightly. "Exactly. We've added a new touch this year. The Von Emmerling emeralds, to be exact. The raffle last year was such an astonishing success . . ."

"You're raffling off the Von Emmerling emeralds?" Trace Walker echoed, aghast.

"No, of course not. They're not ours to raffle—they're only in San Francisco on loan. We're raffling off the chance to wear them at the Puffin Ball. The first prize winner gets to wear them for two hours, second prize one hour, third prize half an hour."

"Oh, Lord," Walker groaned. "And you want us to protect them? The most famous emeralds in the world, and you're going to be handing them out to just anybody to wear in a crowded ballroom?"

Ferris smiled. "Crazy, isn't it? But people seem to be going wild about it. We've already sold a huge amount of tickets, and the committee's had to order up another printing. It was an absolute brainstorm."

"Yours?" he questioned glumly.

She shook her head. "I'm too conservative. I'd be just as afraid as you are that someone might decide to keep them. Originally we were thinking of auctioning off the wearing time, then decided against it. If someone knew ahead of time, they could have copies made, and it would be simple enough to make an exchange in the bathroom or something. We thought with a raffle it would be safer—the winners won't know until they arrive at the ball."

"You're going to end up with a lot of women dressed for emeralds," Walker pointed out with a fair amount of gloom. "You realize this is going to be practically impossible?"

"I imagine it will be difficult," Ferris allowed. "But not impossible. At five hundred dollars a shot the guest list will naturally be limited, and we'll have our own security there to make sure there are no gate-crashers. Your only worry will be the emeralds. As long as Carleton House is secure and someone's on the scene, I expect it will be all right."

"Carleton House!" Walker groaned. "On the point? That rambling old mansion will take weeks to burglarproof."

Ferris smiled sweetly. "You have one week. The Puffin Ball is next Friday. I'm afraid we only just decided we'd need extra help for the jewels themselves. Of course, if you don't think you can handle it…" She was no longer certain she wanted him to give up. On the one hand, it would certainly make things easier for her, dealing with the firm that handled the regular security for Carleton House. On the other hand, Blackheart, Inc., had a certain appeal. Fortunately, it didn't seem as if John Patrick Blackheart busied himself with the mundane details of the workaday world. And Trace Walker had a puppy-dog charm that even a securely engaged woman like Ferris could appreciate. It really might work out very well indeed.

"Don't browbeat him, Miss Byrd." Another voice entered the fray, and Ferris cursed the silent doorways and the even quieter footsteps of the man walking toward her. Obviously her hope had been in vain. The man walking toward her with that amused expression on his face could only be the heretofore absent John Patrick Blackheart. The most famous living cat burglar in the world.

BLACKHEART HAD BEEN cursing quietly under his breath as he climbed the steep hill toward the town house that held his offices. Not that the hill was bad for the dull ache in his leg, but the dampness of the San Francisco weather certainly didn't do it any good. The knee had tightened up again, and it took all his willpower not to favor it. It had been three years since he'd conquered the limp, three years since the last operation and the physical therapy and rigorous exercises. And now his right leg was as good as anybody else's, could do what anyone else's could do. He could dance, if it was a slow one and he had a nice rounded body to hold on to, he could walk briskly without any sign of strain, he could even manage a sedate run along the beach north of the city when the mood hit him. The one thing he couldn't do was scramble up the side of buildings and over rooftops, couldn't cling like Spiderman to the back walls and sneak into fifteenth-floor windows. Not anymore.

He paused long enough to admire the discreet brass plate on the brick front of the town house, a wry smile lighting his face. It still amused him, two years later, that he'd be making his living from the same people who'd served him in the past. He'd taken his considerable experience and talent in the field of breaking and entering and used it to keep other people from following in his footsteps. And he did a damned fine job of it. Because, unlike the more traditional security firms in the city, he understood the mind of the thief, knew how his thought processes would work and how to circumvent him. If his job didn't net any disappointed felons for the city jails, neither did it come up with any valuables missing. Blackheart was never completely sure if it was his ability or honor among thieves that kept his jobs successful. He imagined it was a little of both.

He was late for his appointment, and Kate would give him hell. He viewed that certainty with not the slightest chagrin. From the very beginning he had been deliberately lax about appointments. His change in life-style was too radical as it was—he couldn't be expected to be punctual on top of everything else. Most of his wealthy clientele viewed it as a lovable foible, one they'd never accept in any other employee.

It was a woman, a friend of Senator Merriam's, who was coming in. From his knowledge of Merriam, he knew the woman was bound to be good-looking, so there really was no need to hurry. Trace would be sniffing at her heels, all but drooling over her. He'd be just as happy if Blackheart didn't show up too promptly.

They made good partners, Trace Walker with his handsome, open face and friendly manners, Blackheart so much the opposite. He had no illusions about the image he presented to the world. Just slightly devious, with secrets lurking in his shadowed face. Women seemed to find it irresistible, which was an added bonus. And the ones who didn't lean toward him were just as entranced with Trace's beefy good looks.

Trace would have never made it as a cat burglar, or any form of breaking and entering, for that matter. For one thing, he was too big, for another, he was too good-hearted. He could never hear the tales of Blackheart's illustrious career without worrying about the victims.

He'd been one of the victims himself, long ago. The one attempt Blackheart had made after his fall was Trace's apartment, and it had been a fiasco all around. Blackheart had made it a practice only to prey on the extremely wealthy and well-insured. Trace put up a good front as an antique jewelry dealer, but his openness and good-heartedness had proved bad for business, so that by the time Blackheart fell clumsily in his bathroom window he was on the far edge of bankruptcy. There were no jewels in the large apartment with its rent overdue by three months, there were no expensive artifacts. There wasn't even a camera or some portable stereo equipment, not that Blackheart would have stooped so low. There was only Trace Walker, glowering at him, more than happy to have someone on whom to take out his financial frustrations.

In retrospect Blackheart realized he hadn't needed to be so rough with him. Sure, Trace outweighed him by forty pounds at least, towered over him by five inches, and had fists the size of hams. But he would never have gone far in such an uneven fight. Unfortunately, he didn't realize that the fight was uneven in Blackheart's favor. Blackheart had some frustrations of his own—not the least being the sloppy attempt at burgling Trace Walker's apartment and his nagging feeling of guilt—so in less than a minute Trace was flat on his back, breathing heavily, staring up at Blackheart's fierce face with an expression of complete amazement on his open features. And then, slowly, that amazement had broadened into a grin, and he'd held out one of those hamlike hands to his would-be thief.

They'd been friends ever since. Trace seemed to think Blackheart needed looking after, and Blackheart felt the same about Trace. The two of them had an uneasy alliance that had served them well in the last two years, both professionally and financially. And Blackheart was more than willing to let all the pretty young debutantes of San Francisco end up in Trace's office and eventually Trace's bed. He'd gotten tired of perfect bodies and empty souls.

"There you are," Kate grumbled. "Trace beat you to it."

"Any need for me to go in?" He gave the proffered mail a cursory glance before attempting a winning smile in Kate's direction. As usual, it failed to get any response.

"Probably. Trace had a besotted look in his eye last time I saw him. And she's more than the usual type."

"How so?"

"I can't really tell. Everything looks right—the Rolex watch, the suit, the discreet little gold touches. There's something more there, but you know Trace. Everything at face value. And he sure seems to like her face." If her voice was slightly disgruntled, Blackheart was kind enough not to notice it. He knew what was going on with Kate's chronic bad temper, even if his obtuse associate didn't. And he knew there was no way he could interfere.

"Where are they?" he said, sighing.

"Your office. You can't miss 'em. He's the one looking like a lovesick calf and she's the one that stepped out of *Vogue,*" Kate grumbled.

He moved with the silence that had gained him access to a hundred hotel rooms. Kate was, as usual, right. Ferris Byrd looked as if she stepped out of *Vogue,* and yet there was something that wasn't quite right. Maybe it was the glint of humor in those incredibly green eyes, maybe in the scarcely disciplined curve of her pale mouth. Too pale, Blackheart thought critically. And the hair should be loose, flowing, a brown-black cloud around that arresting face of hers. She wasn't really beautiful, at least not with a pink-and-white prettiness. She had something more than beauty, and he wondered whether a predictable man like Senator Phillip Merriam could appreciate that something. From the look of the diamond ring on her left hand, it appeared that he did.

But the very last thing he expected, watching her bait Trace with the lightest of touches, was the look of hostility in her green eyes when they turned to his. Miss Ferris Byrd did not like John Patrick Blackheart one tiny bit. And despite his general indifference to the opinions of his fellow man, Blackheart found himself intrigued.

Chapter Two

He wasn't what she expected. Which was silly of her, since she'd seen photographs of him, heard enough to have a fairly accurate expectation of what he was like. But it was all shot to hell the first time she looked at him.

John Patrick Blackheart had to be somewhere in his mid to late thirties, and he'd lived every one of those years to the fullest. He was above average height, probably about five feet eleven, but next to Trace Walker he looked smaller. There was nothing particularly remarkable about him. His eyes were cool and brown and assessing, his dark brown hair a little too long, not styled, but rather like the hair of someone who hadn't managed to get to a barber recently and didn't give a damn. He had a light tan, and he was dressed all in black—black denims, a black turtleneck hugging his lean torso, black leather boots on his feet. He didn't look like a world-famous criminal, but he didn't look like an ordinary mortal, either. It might have been that genuinely amused curve to the sensual mouth, or the glint in the cool brown eyes. Or it might have been in the slightly tense way he held his lean, muscled body, poised for flight, poised for attack, poised for something. Ferris came to the unhappy conclusion that he was remarkable indeed, and she knew she was in trouble.

"Patrick!" Trace greeted him exuberantly, with only the faintest expression of guilt marring his open features. "I didn't know whether you would make it in this morning, so I thought I could get started . . . that is, Miss Byrd was here and I . . ."

Ferris watched the smaller man take pity on his partner, smiling at him with a charm that was nothing short of dangerous. She decided then and there to be prepared if he chose to use it on her. "Don't worry about it, Trace. You know I'm always late." He turned to Ferris, and for the first time she felt the full force of those tawny brown eyes. They weren't cool as she had thought, they were warm and subtly caressing, even as that mobile mouth of his curved in what was definitely a mocking smile. Ferris didn't like to be mocked.

"I'm Ferris Byrd." She rose, holding out her hand with determination, carefully putting this man in his place. She'd had to deal with men trying every sort of intimidation; she'd faced sexual intimidation often enough to recognize it and fight it. She waited for him to take her hand, and when he did she realized her tactical error. His hand was rough with calluses, strong and warm, and it caught hers with just the right amount of pressure. Like an equal, none of that pumping, caressing stuff that always made her skin crawl. "I've already explained the problem to Trace, and I—"

"Senator Merriam spoke with me this morning," Blackheart said gently. He had a soft, low voice that nevertheless commanded instant attention, and the quiet tones that should have been comforting were instead unnerving.

"Senator Merriam's been busy," she said, unable to control her start of irritation. "Then you know the problem?"

"The Puffin Ball, the Von Emmerling emeralds, and Carleton House? Yes, I know."

"Do you think we can handle it, Patrick?" Trace asked eagerly, obviously more than happy to try.

"I'm wondering what Miss Byrd thinks," Blackheart murmured.

He must have sensed her disapproval. She certainly hadn't gone to any pains to hide it, but the thought of his reading her so accurately bothered her. "I think the Carleton security staff would be just as capable," she said coolly, meeting his dare.

"Do you? I have the impression that Miss Byrd doesn't approve of us, Trace."

"Oh, surely not, Patrick," Trace protested, looking like a very handsome, very wounded moose. "We've been getting along like a house afire."

"I stand corrected. Miss Byrd doesn't approve of *me*," Blackheart said with a gentle smile. "Isn't that so?"

Damn him, he was playing with her like a cat with a mouse. A fat, succulent little mouse. Well, she wasn't going to cower away from him. "That's so, Mr. Blackheart," she said in dulcet tones.

"You've never heard the saying, 'It takes a thief to catch a thief'?"

"Certainly. The question is, what does the second thief do once he's caught the first one?"

Blackheart smiled. "I expect he splits up the booty, like any sensible thief. Is that what you're afraid of? That we'll run off with the Von Emmerling emeralds ourselves?"

"Oh, no, Patrick!" Trace's protest was explosive. "She wouldn't think that we—"

"Yes, I would," Ferris said sharply.

"Yes, she would, Trace," Blackheart said sweetly. "So the question is, how do we get Miss Ferris Byrd to trust us enough to enable us to do our job properly?"

"Are you taking the job?" Ferris questioned. For a moment she'd thought she'd driven him off.

"Oh, most definitely. I never could resist a challenge," Blackheart said. And Ferris had the melancholy suspicion that he wasn't talking about the Von Emmerling emeralds.

"That's just as well," she said briskly, squashing down the strong sense of unease that washed over her. "The Puffin Ball is only a week away, and we'd have a hard time making other arrangements at this late date."

"In that case, why don't I accompany Miss Byrd out to Carleton House to get a good look at the place?" Trace suggested eagerly. "I haven't anything on for this morning, and I'd be more than happy to make the preliminary study."

"Have you forgotten your report on the Winslow collection? Kate's going to have your head on a platter if you don't let her close the files."

"I'll close my own files." It was the closest Trace ever got to sulking, and he did a credible job of it, but Blackheart was unmoved.

"I can wait," Ferris offered helpfully. "I have some errands to run in town. I can come back in a few hours when you've finished the report and take you out there, Trace."

Trace's face lit up for a moment, then darkened as he cast a beseeching glance at his partner.

Blackheart shook his head slowly. "You're undermining discipline, Miss Byrd. Trace has got a full day's work ahead of him. Besides, he usually concentrates on the physical side of the job, not the planning stage. He's got too much energy to be a mastermind."

"I've got too little patience, you mean," Trace said sheepishly. "He's right, Ferris. Anything I did would just have to be done over by Patrick. You're better off with him."

Ferris controlled the disbelieving snort, turning her gaze, in curiosity, to Blackheart's. She'd expected smug triumph, not the very real amusement that lingered there. "All right," she said, knowing it was graceless and not really caring. "I don't suppose you'd rather go there by yourself?"

"I don't suppose. Senator Merriam assures me you know more than anyone about what's going on with this benefit. He promised me you'd be invaluable." Blackheart smiled sweetly, but Ferris wasn't fooled.

"Let's go then," she said, caving in. "We may as well get it over with."

"Charmingly put," Blackheart replied, almost purring. "Let me give Kate a message and I'll be ready. Soothe Miss Byrd's ruffled feathers, Trace, and tell her I'm not half as bad as she thinks."

"Patrick's great," Trace said earnestly, obeying unquestioningly as Blackheart's lean figure disappeared out the door with the same uncanny silence with which he had entered. "Really, Ferris, you have nothing to worry about. I'd trust him with my life."

"But would you trust him with your jewels?" she drawled.

"If he agreed to protect them, I would."

"And if he didn't agree?"

A frown creased Trace's broad, handsome face. "I'm not sure," he said honestly. "But I wouldn't work with him if I didn't trust him, and didn't think other people could trust him too."

"And I'll just have to take your word for it."

"I expect you'll have to," Blackheart had returned, damn him, still on silent cat's feet. He had pulled an ancient Harris tweed jacket over the black turtleneck, and Ferris remembered belatedly that he was half British. He didn't sound it—he sounded soft and menacing and American. But the coat looked as if it had belonged to some country squire. He probably stole it, she thought cynically.

"I expect I will." She rose, ignoring the hand he held out to her. She couldn't help but notice it was a well-shaped hand, with long, dexterous fingers, the better for plucking jewels out of someone's bureau drawer; strong wrists, the better for hanging off buildings; and broad palms, the better for vaulting over rooftops. It also looked warm and strong and more than capable of caressing a bare shoulder. Damn, but the man was trouble. "Let's go," she said.

Blackheart only smiled.

"We'll take my car." It was a challenge, one Blackheart didn't rise to.

"Certainly," he murmured. "I walked to work anyway."

Ferris gnashed her teeth as she yanked open the low-slung door of her Mercedes 380SL. The navy blue had pleased her discerning eye, the classic lines enhanced her image—and if she had a hidden craving for a red Corvette, she suppressed it admirably. Corvettes were tacky.

"Nice car," Blackheart said, gripping the seat as she tore into the traffic without looking.

"I worked hard to get it," she snapped, tires screeching as she rounded a corner and started down one of San Francisco's precipitous hills.

"And I wouldn't know anything about hard work?" Blackheart questioned softly.

"I didn't say that." She yanked the wheel sharply, and tires skidding slightly as she turned another corner and headed out toward the bay.

"The inference was clear. Tell me, do you always drive like this, or is it simply for my benefit?" He was completely unmoved, watching her with that damnable half-smile on his face.

She pressed harder on the accelerator. "A bit of both," she said in her sweetest tone of voice. The Mercedes had far too much power, and they were speeding full tilt down Nob Hill when his boot-clad foot slid over to her side of the car, hooked under her ankle and pulled it back off the accelerator.

She swerved in surprise, almost losing control of the car. Skidding to a stop, Ferris turned off the key with shaking hands. "What the hell," she said in a dangerous voice, "were you trying to do? You could have gotten us both killed."

"Not if you hadn't been driving so fast. I don't like speeding in the middle of the city. It attracts a great deal of unnecessary attention, and I have an aversion to the police." It was all said in the most reasonable of voices, and her lip curled.

"I just bet you do," Ferris snarled.

"We're not going to get very far like this, Miss Byrd," he said gently. "I think we should call an armed truce, at least for the next week. Senator Merriam is counting on you to give me every assistance."

"He is, is he?"

Blackheart's smile widened, opening up that dark, shuttered face. "So he told me this morning. You wouldn't want to let him down, would you?"

"I have no intention of letting him down," Ferris snapped.

"Then you'll be giving me every assistance?"

"To the best of my ability." It galled her to say it, but she had no choice.

"And I give you leave to disapprove of me all you want," he added magnanimously, that wicked smile lighting his eyes. "As long as it doesn't interfere with my work. I have my professional pride to consider."

Nobly Ferris swallowed the retort that rose to her lips. That left her with nothing to say, and she stared straight forward at the busy street ahead of them.

She could feel Blackheart's eyes on her, and they were far too astute. "A truce, Miss Byrd," he said, holding out his hand. And she had no choice but to take it, dropping it as quickly as she could.

"A truce, Mr. Blackheart. And you may as well call me Ferris, since we'll be working together."

"I might. But I don't like it. Do you have any other names?"

Ferris controlled the unexpectedly nervous start. "Frances," she said sullenly.

"I don't like that, either. I'll just have to make do with Miss Byrd until I find something that pleases me," he murmured.

"Do you mind if I continue driving?" she asked pointedly, but Blackheart was unruffled.

"Please do." Leaning back, he shut his eyes, but Ferris could see his hands clenching the leather seat as she pulled back into traffic. She drove sedately enough, and finally his eyes opened, those warm, all-knowing brown eyes that constantly unnerved her. "Are you going to tell me what you have to do with Senator Merriam? And the Committee for Saving the Bay?"

She wasn't sure if it was a peace offering, but the subject was innocuous enough. "I'm Phillip Merriam's administrative assistant. He's trying to move up from the state senate to the U.S. Senate, and I was working on his election campaign when he decided to lend me to the committee to help them with the Puffin Ball." She was quite pleased at her even tone of voice. Even the observant Blackheart couldn't guess how disgruntled she was at being out of the action, shepherding a bunch of bored debutantes and society matrons.... But she couldn't allow herself to think like that. If all went well, if things went her way, she could be one of those society matrons, safe and secure in her giant house in the heart of San Francisco.

"Administrative assistant?" he echoed. "In my experience, administrative assistants are either people who know nothing and do nothing, or know everything and do everything. Which are you?"

Her foot began to press down harder on the accelerator again. "Guess."

"Not so fast, Miss Byrd," he said gently. "We aren't in any hurry. We have plenty of time to get to know each other."

She took the corner too fast, but then made a concerted effort to slow down. She wouldn't put it past him to put that strong, rough hand on top of hers and pull her over. "That's what I'm afraid of," she said gloomily.

Blackheart laughed.

IN THE BRIGHT, glaring light of the small, secret workshop hidden behind the false wall of a closet in the basement of his jewelry shop on Geary Street, Hans Werdegast admired his handiwork. The Von Emmerling emeralds had to be his greatest creation, his masterpiece, his chef d'oeuvre. And there was no one to appreciate his genius, his craftsmanship.

Sighing, he shook his head, rubbing his lined forehead with a wrinkled linen handkerchief. That was the problem with his chosen avocation, he thought. No audience.

However, the money made up for it. He made a comfortable amount from the small, elite jewelry store above him, supplementing it with a few custom-made pieces in the upstairs workshop where his assistants had free access. But the secrets of his hidden workshop more than paid the bills, they bought him the luxuries and pleased his soul at the same time. He could no more give the workshop up than he could fly.

He was getting to be an old man, though. And he wouldn't like to be caught. There was no way he would ever submit to being imprisoned again, behind bars and barbed wire, locked away. He glanced down at the faded, almost unreadable tattoo on his wrist. Months went by without thinking about it. Maybe he should stop being such a foolish old man and think about it more carefully.

The Von Emmerling emeralds were admittedly magnificent, the replicas so close to the real thing that anyone without a jeweler's loupe would be fooled. Maybe it was a good place to stop. His customer was paying through the nose—the Von Emmerling emeralds were a fitting swan song.

Sighing, the old man dropped the glittering almost-jewels into a plastic bag, sealing it with a twist tie. It wounded him to treat his prize creations so shabbily. They deserved velvet as much as their authentic counterparts. But that would make the package too bulky, and he had to be ready to pass them to his customer later that evening with a minimum of fuss. A shoddy fate for a masterpiece.

He climbed down off the stool and shuffled back toward the hidden doorway to his storeroom closet. He'd miss his workshop, miss his secrets. But it was time to retire, and best to retire at the top of the game. For a moment he wondered what had possessed his customer to tackle such a monumental job. But he knew. As enamored as he was of the phony emeralds, he knew the real ones would be far more enticing. Particularly once you held them in your hands. No, he didn't blame his customer. And he would make sure that he profited by them, just in case the elaborate scheme didn't succeed. Elaborate schemes had a high risk factor, and Hans Werdegast had almost been burned too many times.

Yes, he thought with a sigh, shutting the back wall of the closet behind him and shuffling into the deserted storeroom. It was time to retire. He'd spend his time in the upstairs workshop from now on, and look back with satisfaction on his memories. Particularly the Von Emmerling emeralds.

Chapter Three

Carleton House was an impressive old mansion overlooking the Pacific Ocean on a point of land to the west of the magnificent Golden Gate Bridge. Once, years ago, it had been a private residence, until the bankrupt sea captain left it to the Daughters of the Pacific. In the last decades it had played host to any number of charity balls, garden fetes, debutante dances, ladies' luncheons and even a discreet conference or two. The multitude of cavernous, elegant rooms, the expanse of beautifully maintained gardens, the dozens of bedroom suites on the third and fourth floors made it an admirable facility for any kind of social affair. It also made it utter hell to protect. That thought pleased Ferris no end.

"There you are, Ferris, dear." The blue-haired lady in the Davidow suit greeted her with a warm smile. "And you've brought Mr. Blackheart. How good of you to come, Patrick! I knew we could count on you."

Ferris had her first look at Blackheart's celebrated charm as he kissed Phillip's mother's hand with a panache that would have done Errol Flynn proud. Had Errol Flynn ever played a cat burglar? He would have been good at it, Ferris thought dismally. And that explained, in part, why Phillip had been so insistent on Blackheart, Inc. Regina Merriam was clearly entranced with the cat burglar.

Ferris knew an escape when she saw one. "Regina, why don't you show Mr. Blackheart around while I check on the decorations committee? You know Carleton House as well as anyone."

Regina smiled at her future daughter-in-law. "I'd adore to. I had to sneak out from the flower committee—the air was getting a little thick in there. Too many boring old matrons. Come along, Patrick, my boy, and I'll show you what an impossible job you have ahead of you. How's Trace? Will he be coming later? Olivia has been pestering me all day."

"Trace will be here." Ferris could feel those eyes of his following her as she made good her escape. "Later, Miss Byrd," he called after her, the words a warning and a challenge.

She hesitated for a moment, contenting herself with a cursory nod before disappearing into the nearest reception room. She could hear Regina's amused voice drifting after her. "Heavens, Patrick, call her Ferris. She's the dearest girl. Far too good for my son."

Ferris stopped dead still just inside the door, straining to hear his answer. But they'd moved away, out of reach, and only the soft murmur of his voice carried to her ears.

God, she was in trouble. Blackheart was far more dangerous than she'd imagined. The only thing she could do was call Phillip and beg him to let her come back and work on his campaign. He'd thought the Puffin Ball would be good experience for her, outside the political arena in the social world where a politician's wife spent so much of her time. She was getting to know the major names in San Francisco society, she was becoming good friends with her future mother-in-law, but all those benefits seemed to pale next to the seemingly very real threat of Patrick Blackheart.

Not that there was anything he could do to hurt her. He couldn't read her mind, know the deep, dark secrets of her soul that she trusted to no one. He was no threat to her, she had to remember that.

In the meantime, she was too busy that day to think much one way or the other about John Patrick Blackheart, apart from avoiding him whenever she saw him coming. He had the uncanny habit of sneaking up on her, his booted feet silent on the marble floors of the old mansion, that damned, bland smile on his face. She would find him waiting patiently behind her shoulder as she listened to a thousand and one questions, complaints, and impractical suggestions from the busy ladies of the Committee for Saving the Bay, and the only clue that he had reappeared would be the sudden, fatuous expression on the speaker's face.

She couldn't get through to Phillip till late in the afternoon, when most of the members of the committee had drifted away. The sound of his deep, mellifluous voice had its usual effect, soothing and warming her. It was one of his greatest political gifts, that rich, mellow voice, and Ferris was no more immune to it than his besotted constituents. Especially when she knew what a basically decent, nice person resided behind that warm voice and those patrician good looks.

But the soothing tones offered her cold comfort indeed. "It will only be a week, Ferris. Surely Blackheart can't be so bad— my mother adores him, and I trust her taste implicitly. After all, she thinks you're too good for me."

"Blackheart isn't bad, Phillip. I'm just not comfortable around him. Things are coming together beautifully—your mother knows as much as I do about everything. Couldn't I please come back?" She let her voice sound mournful and pleading, hoping she might appeal to his protective instincts.

Phillip was too smart for her. "No, Ferris. There's nothing you can't handle, be it a hostile constituent or a retired cat burglar or the combined forces of the Committee for Saving the Bay. I'm counting on you, darling. This is the kind of experience for you that money can't buy, and it will all be over by Friday. I'll be there to take you to the ball, and we might even consider making our formal announcement."

"I thought we were going to wait till after the primary." Why was she suddenly reluctant to have her triumph made public knowledge? Enough people had seen the diamond on her left hand and given her a knowing look; it was no longer a secret.

"I was considering it, but I've decided you might bring me more votes," he said frankly.

That was the problem with their relationship, Ferris decided suddenly. His election always came first, for both of them, and their engagement was more a useful adjunct than an emotional commitment. The thought was suddenly depressing.

"Let's wait and see," she temporized. "Will you call later?" Her voice was no longer mournful, it was brisk and efficient.

"Sunday at three, same as always. You'll stick with it, won't you, Ferris? Mother's capable, you're right, but I don't like putting so much responsibility on her after her stroke. You can do it, can't you?''

Ferris sighed, well and truly trapped. She may as well acquiesce gracefully. "Of course I can, Phillip. I just miss you."

The deep, rich voice, like chocolate custard, breathed a sigh of relief. "I knew I could count on you, Ferris. I love you." The last was hurried, almost by rote, and Ferris repeated it the same way.

They would deal well together. She would be the perfect politician's wife, charming, reserved, very clever, with just the right amount of public deference and private encouragement to aid Phillip in attaining whatever office he was seeking. The public acclaim was not part of her own particular fantasy—she'd be just as happy if Phillip had remained a lawyer. But Phillip was an ambitious man, it was an integral part of his nature, and she wouldn't have him any other way. It was ambition that had gotten her where she was now, and she wasn't going back if she could help it. She would support Phillip completely, follow him . . .

"What's that determined look on your face?"

Ferris dropped the phone with a nervous shriek, cursed, and rounded on Blackheart. "Must you sneak up on people like that?" she demanded indignantly.

"I can't help it." He favored her with that charming smile that melted all women within a ten-mile radius. Ferris did her best to remain stonily unmoved, but it was an uphill battle. "I can't change years of habit overnight, Miss Byrd. Are you ready to leave?"

The last thing she wanted to do was get back into the cramped quarters of her car with him. That lethal charm was beginning to work on her, much as she fought it. Why did that smile of his have to be so damned infectious? And why did his brown eyes glint with hints of amber as he looked at her? And why couldn't she trust him?

None of that really mattered of course, with Phillip in the picture. "I'm not quite ready to leave," she said coolly. "Perhaps you could get a ride with someone else."

He seemed to have the uncanny knack of reading her mind.

Slowly he shook his head. "That won't do, Miss Byrd. Everyone's gone. I'll just have to wait here, all alone with you in this
big old house, while you finish whatever you're doing."

"I'm ready," she snapped, interpreting the smiling threat
correctly. "It'll take me a few minutes to lock up. I'll meet you
at the car at ten past."

"That'll give me just enough time to check in with my office," he said sweetly.

"Why?" Her suspicions were instantly aroused.

"To see if my burgling tools have arrived," he drawled. "Go
ahead and lock up, Miss Byrd."

She hesitated for a moment, watching as he picked up the
telephone. "If I'm the last one to leave, I have to lock up, Mr.
Blackheart. Once I do so, you won't be able to leave without
tripping the alarm."

He laughed then, a rich, full laugh that was even more at-
tractively unnerving. "You really think so?" he questioned
gently. "You do underrate me, Miss Byrd."

For her dubious peace of mind she could be grateful he was
waiting at the car for her. She had little doubt that he could
leave the house with its locks intact, but her sense of responsibility would have insisted that she go back and check, and
Blackheart would have been bound to follow, smiling that
damnable smile of his. What she wouldn't give to wipe it off his
face for just one moment, she thought with wistful violence.

It was a foggy day in late February, cool and chilly and dis-
tinctly unfriendly. She couldn't wait till she was back in her
small, cozy apartment, her shoes off and her long legs curled
up underneath her, a real fire in her working fireplace and a
snifter of brandy in her hand. *God bless gourmet frozen dinners,* she thought with a blissful sigh.

"What occasioned that erotic moan?" Blackheart drawled
from beside her, and she jumped. For a brief, heavenly moment she had almost forgotten he was sitting beside her as she
raced haphazardly back into the city.

She allowed herself a short glimpse of him, and her tense
shoulders began to relax a trifle. In less than five minutes she'd
be free of him, in ten minutes she'd be home. A tentative smile
lit her face. "I was thinking about food," she confessed.

He was staring at her, his expression arrested. "Do that again," he said, his low, drawling voice suddenly husky in demand.

"Do what?" She couldn't summon more than a trace of irritation as she screeched around the corner toward his office.

"Smile. I didn't think you could."

It was with a great effort that she kept another, answering smile from her mouth. "And you, Blackheart, smile too much. 'A damned, smiling villain,' Shakespeare said. He must have had you in mind."

"You think so?" He seemed genuinely pleased at the notion. "And who are you?"

"Lady Macbeth," she snapped, pulling to a stop in front of the old brick town house that housed Blackheart, Inc.

He made no move to leave the car, just looked at her out of those translucent eyes of his. "No, I don't think so," he murmured. "I haven't got it yet, but I will."

"Be sure to let me know when you think of it," she said sarcastically.

He smiled at her. "I will. You really detest me, don't you, Miss Byrd? Think I'm the lowest of the low?"

She said nothing, neither denied nor confirmed it. "Good evening, Mr. Blackheart."

Reaching for the door handle, he pulled himself out of the Mercedes with a graceful swoop. Leaning down to close the door, he looked in at her. "I'm not really that bad, you know," he observed gently.

"I'm sure you're not," Ferris said, sure of no such thing.

He grinned, a glint of wickedness in those tawny brown eyes. "At least I always go by the same name." This was said in the sweetest of tones, and the door closed before she could respond.

There was nothing she could say. There was a sick burning in her stomach, her hands were clammy with nervous sweat, and she felt a nasty headache coming on. Without another word, without a look in his direction, she screeched the car away from the curb, directly into the traffic. Horns blared in protest, and then she was gone, tearing down the hillside with a blithe disregard for traffic and stop lights.

HANS WERDEGAST HANDED the plastic Baggie over with a sense of real regret. He would never see them again, what he had fondly come to think of as *his* Von Emmerling emeralds. They were even prettier than the originals, if he were any judge, and he was. To be sure, the stones were fakes, beautiful ones. But he'd executed the delicate filigree settings with an even lighter touch than the original master who'd designed them. And now they were being shoved into the pocket of someone who'd done nothing more than glance at them through the filmy plastic.

The old man took the creased envelope stuffed full of old bills and shoved it in his pocket with all the care it deserved. Money was nothing, compared to art. "This is the only time," he said heavily, hating the sound of the words, knowing he had to say them. "No more. Tell the man who sent you."

"Why?"

"I'm getting too old for this sort of thing. You'll have to find someone else for your next job."

"No one else is as good as you."

"That's true," the old man agreed sadly. "But that's the way of the world. There are no craftsmen left, only technicians."

"You won't reconsider?"

He shook his head. "You have in your pocket, my friend, my last hurrah. Treat them with respect."

His customer grinned. "I'll put them to very good use."

HE COULDN'T HAVE KNOWN, Ferris thought as she undid the three locks and let herself into the maze of rooms that constituted her apartment in the marina section of San Francisco. There were six of them, with steps up and steps down, a small terrace with an impossibly windy view of the bay, the tiniest kitchen this side of a Winnebago and a bedroom so small it only held her queen-size bed and the television set. The largest room in the mélange was the bathroom, with a marble bathtub the size of a small swimming pool, a double marble sink, mirrors that would put a whorehouse to shame, and a towel rack directly over the radiator that gave Ferris deliciously heated towels in the morning. She loved the hodgepodge of space, but nothing pleased her that evening.

It must have been a shot in the dark. He knew she went by the name of Ferris, but she'd openly admitted her first name was Frances. And that was the truth, or mostly the truth. Her first name was a variant of Frances. And it was none of Blackheart's damned business if she chose not to use it. She didn't have any criminal reason for wanting to hide it.

There was no sign of her disreputable gray alley cat. Blackie must be out on one of his sabbaticals, wreaking havoc in female feline hearts. He might not be back for days. She kicked off her shoes, her bare feet padding comfortably over the hardwood floors as she trailed through the living room, dining room, kitchen and bathroom, finally ending up in the cramped confines of the bedroom. She took a delicious dive, ending up in the middle of her unmade bed, a trail of clothes leading toward her destination. She'd pick them up later. For now all she wanted was a moment of peace.

It was hours later when she opened her eyes. Blearily she peered at the digital clock residing on the floor beside her bed. Almost twelve-thirty. Damn! She'd never get back to sleep, not for hours. It was always a mistake when she let herself nap before dinner.

With a groan she pulled herself from the bed, scampering across its wide length to the bathroom. A long, hot shower would help, so would the glass of brandy she'd forgotten all about. It was too late for dinner. She'd curl up in front of the television and watch an all-night movie with her favorite vice.

Her flannel nightgown had seen better days, but the cotton was so thin that its comfort was practically transcendental. She poured more brandy into the Waterford snifter than was proper for savoring its bouquet, but once she got settled she didn't want to have to scramble back to the kitchen again. With a desultory attempt at housecleaning, she picked up the trail of clothing and dumped it in the hamper, then allowed herself the delight of opening her freezer. Oh, blessings, there was Heavenly Hash.

She must have made a ridiculous picture, tromping across her bed to the mound of pillows at the head, an overfull snifter of brandy in one hand, a small mixing bowl of ice cream in the other, mismatched socks on her narrow, chilly feet. With a sigh of pure pleasure, she collapsed against the pillows, spilling a tiny bit of the brandy on her nightgown.

Setting her goodies carefully on the floor, she dived under the bed in search of the remote control for the TV set. She had misplaced it for two weeks once, lost in the welter of clothes and papers and magazines and single shoes that lived and multiplied under her bed. The remote control had been a sinful extravagance, but there was no way she was going to clump back and forth over the bed every time she wanted to change the channel. She could only be thankful she didn't live with some man who had the right to complain about her life-style, which could only charitably be called casual. Her sisters had told her she was a walking disaster, but she liked it that way. At least if the earthquake that everyone had been promising came, no one would know the difference in her apartment.

Aiming the remote control, she settled back, reaching for her ice cream. If hot milk was supposed to help you sleep, cold cream should do almost the same thing, she thought righteously, digging in. Peter Sellers was on, the movie was just starting, and she settled back with pleasure to enjoy the travails of Inspector Clouseau. A moment later she sat back up, a low wail of anguish emitting through the Heavenly Hash.

"Oh, no!" she moaned, as a black-clad figure edged his way over the rooftops. She didn't need a movie about a cat burglar, tonight of all nights.

Quickly she flicked through the channels. Talk shows, John Wayne war movies, Betty Grable musicals. Peter Sellers was unquestionably the cream of the crop. With a sigh, she turned it back to the *Pink Panther*, reaching for her ice cream again. Some of the chocolate had melted and spilled onto the sheet, and she made an ineffectual attempt at rubbing it away. She'd have to remember to sleep on the right side tonight.

Finishing the ice cream, she pushed the bowl under her bed and reached for the brandy, settling back to concentrate on the movie. Maybe she'd learn something about how to deal with Blackheart. Taking a contemplative sip, she let the liquor burn through the ice cream coating on her tongue, swirling it around with absentminded pleasure. And maybe Phillip would change his mind and rescue her before Blackheart stumbled any closer to the truth. Somehow she doubted either of those things would come to pass.

"*A votre santé*," she toasted the good inspector, raising her brandy glass high. "And heaven help me."

Chapter Four

The alarm rang obscenely early. Ferris opened one eye, groaning as the sunlight beamed into her curtainless bedroom from the terrace. She fumbled around on the floor for her alarm clock, pulling back in disgust when her hand encountered the empty ice-cream dish. She had no choice—she opened the other eye and levered herself off the side of the wide bed to search for the recalcitrant alarm clock.

It was under an issue of *Time* Magazine at least six weeks old. How the magazine could have migrated over to cover the clock after she'd set it last night was beyond her imaginings, but she shrugged her shoulders, pulling herself upright with a weary sigh. She had long ago learned not to worry about what was where in her apartment.

There was one major blessing to this day. Nothing was going to be happening at Carleton House. It was Saturday, the ball wasn't until the following Friday and the jewels weren't due to arrive until Monday. The flowers had been argued over and ordered, the decorations planned, the security hired and left, thank God, to their own devices. The only duty she had to perform today, other than the onerous weekly task of mucking out the accumulated mess that was her apartment, was to run over to Carleton House and retrieve her briefcase.

Not that she'd forgotten it in the first place. She'd left it behind on purpose, part of her distrust of Blackheart extending to her personal papers. And she loved Carleton House when it was still and silent, its cavernous rooms spacious and secure in wealth and status. She would wander through those rooms this afternoon and pretend she was Grace Kelly, cool and patrician, born to the people.

As usual, the mess took longer than she expected. It was her weekend to do the full job, even taking a broomstick under the queen-size bed to roust out the dead panty hose, week-old *Chronicles,* empty boxes of Yodels, a silk blouse she'd thought she'd lost, and three Nikes, all for the left foot. She was a strange housekeeper, she thought as she washed the dirty dishes that had an amazing capacity for reproducing like rabbits. Like a secret eater, it was a case of binge and purge. Every night her clothes would be strewn over the apartment, the kitchen would be littered with every pot and pan, even when she utilized dear Mr. Stouffer's concoctions, the papers and magazines grew in piles that threatened to topple over every available surface. And every morning she would wash the dirty dishes, straighten the piles, hang up all the clothes that hadn't somehow snuck under the bed, just as she transformed herself.

At night she wore fuchsia silk kimonos, impossibly soft flannel nightgowns, skimpy French underwear, designer jockey shorts, anything that took her fancy, and her thick brown hair that was almost black hung in a wavy cloud around her face. In the morning she shrugged into her Liz Claiborne and Ralph Lauren suits, fastened her hair back in a loose bun, and became Ferris Byrd, young urban professional. It was an amazing creation, considering what she started out with, she mused. It was a shame no one but her sisters could appreciate it. And some of them were more offended than appreciative.

With a sigh she withdrew her hands from the sudsy water, letting it drain out of the tiny sink that could hold a service for one. It was fortunate that her messiness wasn't downright dirtiness—if she ever got so lax as to let the dishes pile up for days, it would take her a month to wash them all.

Stripping off the chocolate-stained sheets, she tossed them in her overflowing hamper. Making the bed was her one holdout against compulsive cleaning. When she was gone all day, the only appreciative audience for a neatly made bed was Blackie, the peripatetic alley cat, and much as she loved the stubborn feline, that was going too far. The bed was made when clean sheets were put on it, and that was that.

And where was Blackie this morning? He'd been around just yesterday, demanding kitty gourmet goodies as she'd tried to dress for her fateful appointment at Blackheart, Inc. She should be used to his travels, occasioned by feline randiness or a case of the sulks. Blackie had very strict standards when it came to food and attention, and Ferris had fallen woefully short yesterday. It would take nothing less than creamed herring or his particular craving, overripe Brie cheese, to get him to forgive her.

With a sigh, she emptied a tin of Seafood Supper and set it by the open door to the terrace before getting dressed. Sooner or later he'd have to return, even if it meant settling for cat food. Blackie, like all good San Franciscans, was a true gourmet.

On the weekends, when Phillip was off on the early campaign trail and Ferris had no one to answer to, her wardrobe was more her own. Always keeping in mind that she might run into someone who mattered, she allowed herself jeans and sweaters, braided the thick hair in a loose plait that fell just below her shoulders, and returned to her Nikes, granted she could find a matching pair. She dressed that way now, in faded Levi's rather than the Gloria Vanderbilts Phillip admired, leaving off the discreet gold jewelry that was her mark of caste. The apartment was clean, Phillip was out of town, and she was free, blissfully free.

She stifled the quick wave of guilt that washed over her. Neither she nor Phillip would want smothering togetherness. Any woman with a mind of her own would need time to herself. And she wasn't about to contemplate the unpleasant fact that she seemed to appreciate that private time more than she did the hours she spent with Phillip.

A reluctant grin lit her face as she sped her car along the freeway toward Carleton Point. Blackheart had been so determined not to be fazed by her driving. She'd made strong men weep before, and no pleas or threats from Phillip had made her improve her headlong, headstrong pace. Her driving style was the one thing that still belonged to the twenty-nine-year-old woman who hadn't been born Ferris Byrd, and she held onto it stubbornly.

The fog had lifted somewhat by the time she pulled up in the empty circular drive in front of Carleton House, but it was still a gray, chilly day, typical for late February in the Bay Area. She'd left her briefcase in the downstairs cloakroom, but she was in no hurry. Nothing much would be growing this time of year, but she was especially fond of the grounds anyway. The formal Japanese garden overlooked the Pacific, and she headed straight toward it, glad that she'd pulled a thick wool sweater on over the lighter cotton one. She shoved her hands in the pockets of her jeans, tucked her head into the stiff breeze and strode past the tall windows that overlooked the flagstoned terrace.

She never tired of looking at the ocean, even from a high perch like this one. The ever-changing variety of the ebb and swell of the deep-blue waves fascinated her, the never-changing vastness of it soothed her soul. A wide, four-foot-high stone wall separated the wide expanse of lawn from the rocky cliff beyond, and she leaned against the cool, damp stone, staring out dreamily into the windy day. There was a long, sleek yacht out there, slicing through the rough water with silken ease. For a long moment Ferris had the surprising wish that she were on it, sailing away from everything that surrounded her and weighed her down. And then she pushed away from the wall and headed back across the lawn to the French doors.

The ring of keys weighed close to five pounds, and it could unlock every single one of the thirty-seven outer doors of Carleton House. It took her twelve minutes to find the right one for the French door off the ballroom, another two minutes to rattle the rusty catch loose. And then she was inside, in her magic kingdom, with the wind and the constant hush of the ocean shut out behind her. With a sigh of pure satisfaction she surveyed the empty ballroom.

Ferris had fought the idea of using Carleton House for the Puffin Ball, fought it with all the considerable logic and wit at her disposal. Olivia Summers had been on the opposing side, determined that the Puffin Ball would take place nowhere but Carleton House. Ferris had been more than irritated when Olivia had prevailed, but that irritation had changed to delight when she first wandered through the old mansion. Her only wonder was that a cold-blooded bitch like Olivia Summers could appreciate it.

As a matter of fact, apart from the uncomfortable presence of Blackheart, Inc., Olivia Summers was the only cloud on her horizon. And she could thank Olivia for Blackheart, too. It was Olivia who'd first mentioned Blackheart's name, eagerly seconded by Regina Merriam and voted by the Committee for Saving the Bay with an almost lustful enthusiasm. And she supposed she couldn't really blame Olivia; Blackheart was the obvious choice. He was society's darling, his checkered past only adding to his desirability. She should have known any argument would have been quashed completely.

It still didn't help her feelings toward Olivia. Granted, Olivia had once been engaged to Phillip herself, before breaking it off to marry Dale Summers. And Olivia had her own political aspirations, coveting Phillip's senate seat with her blue, blue eyes. She never for one moment forgot that she was the granddaughter of Ezra McKinley, one of the founding fathers of the city, who was in turn the descendent of Abraham de Peyster, one of the founders of New York centuries earlier. Despite the fact that her family's money had long ago run out, her indisputable blue blood, her racehorse-elegant body, her patrician bearing and WASP blond hair kept her firmly in the forefront of any social gathering. She also had brains, charm, ambition and a seeming regret that she had dismissed Phillip three years ago. And Ferris hated her.

Olivia had always been unfailingly polite, and the blue-haired ladies doted on her, her peers vied for her attention and even Phillip seemed bemused in her presence. It seemed as if only Ferris could see the calculating look in those perfect blue eyes, could watch her clever manipulations with awe and dislike. Olivia Summers had the indisputable talent for making Ferris feel like an employee, and the interloper she knew she was. It was all done with admirable subtlety—a tone of voice, a condescending smile, a graceful gesture. If and when Olivia did run for office, Ferris was determined to work for the opposition, even if it was Richard Nixon himself.

There was no hurry to get the briefcase. She'd tucked it down beside the radiator; it had doubtless survived the night and would survive a few more minutes. With her own careless grace, she sank down to sit cross-legged in the middle of the empty ballroom floor. They were talking about white roses, Regina said. They'd do the gilt and rose-colored ballroom proud. With baby's breath, and just a hint of pink somewhere . . .

"Fancy seeing you here," Blackheart drawled from directly behind her, and Ferris screamed.

She rose to her full five feet four, never as tall as she would have liked, and her eyes were blazing. "Don't you ever," she said furiously, "do that again. Clear your throat, stamp your feet, belch, I don't care what. But don't sneak up on me."

Blackheart looked completely unmoved by her rage, and for a moment she could see why the combined force of the Committee for Saving the Bay had fallen beneath his spell. The black denims had been replaced by blue Levi's so faded they were almost gray, and the khaki field shirt rolled up to reveal strong forearms made his brown eyes almost amber. Ferris had always had a deplorable weakness for field shirts, with their epaulets and their myriad pockets, and she had to steel herself not to react. He was wearing running shoes, which would account for his silent approach. Except that he'd been just as silent in leather boots.

"What were you doing, sitting there in the middle of the ballroom with that erotic expression on your face? I wouldn't have thought a chilly room like this would arouse your fantasies."

"They weren't erotic fantasies," she protested.

"I was watching you wandering around the gardens. You're much more of a dreamer than I took you for, Miss Byrd," he continued in that low, warm voice of his. "You seemed so coldly practical yesterday. Today you look much more—" his hand reached out and gently tugged her braid "—much more human."

She batted at his hand, but he'd already removed it. She didn't like the words, coldly practical, but she was damned if she was going to call him on it. He just wanted a rise out of her, and she wasn't about to give him that satisfaction. And then the meaning of his presence there in the deserted mansion struck her, and she cheerfully jumped to the attack.

"What are you doing here, anyway?" she demanded fiercely.

"My job."

"How did you get in? The Carleton House security team was supposed to let me know if they gave out any keys."

He smiled that devilish smile, and her heart gave a little moan at its remembered effect. "I didn't need a key."

Her lip curled. "Of course you didn't. How could I have forgotten?" she mocked.

The mockery bounced right off. "I asked about you," he said conversationally, and immediately she was wary.

"I doubt you found out anything very interesting." She managed an admirably cool tone of voice. "I haven't led a very exciting life. Who did you ask?"

"Phillip, for starters." She didn't like that phrase, "for starters." "He told me all about your glorious career at Stanford, your rapid rise to your position as his personal assistant, your wit and charm. I had to take his word on the latter, of course."

"Of course."

"And he told me the touching story of your life. How you were raised by your patrician aunt on Beacon Hill in Boston after your parents were killed in their private plane. How you excelled at the exclusive little boarding school but were always just a poor little rich girl who had to throw all her energies into her studies, missing the comfort a real family could offer. It was very touching."

She held herself very still, hating him. "I'm sure you're not about to offer your sympathy."

His mouth quirked upward. It was an attractive mouth, she had to give him that, even as she longed to punch him in it. "And I'm sure you wouldn't accept it if I was."

"Very astute. What do you want from me, Blackheart?"

"You know, I rather like the way you say that," he mused. "Most people call me Patrick."

"Blackheart suits you."

"'What's in a name?'" he quoted softly, that devilish light in his eyes. "Ferris Byrd doesn't suit you one tiny bit."

"I like it," she said stubbornly, refusing to give an inch.

"Of course you do. I'm finished for the day, Ferris Byrd. Let me take you out to dinner and I'll pry all your secrets from you."

"Go to hell." She had turned to leave, consigning her briefcase to another night in the cloakroom, when his hand caught her arm. She had noticed the perfect beauty of his hands before, feeling the gentle force of one on her arm burned the impression of it into her flesh. If she yanked, he would have released her. She stood still.

"Come away with me, Francesca," he said, and his low, sweet voice was a silky caress along her nerve endings as he used her real name. "Your secrets are safe with me. I'll even tell you a few of my own."

"Blackheart," she said, and she never thought she'd plead with any man. But she was pleading with him. "Let me go."

Without a word, he dropped her arm. Without a word she turned and left him, her Nikes squeaking on the polished dance floor. She closed the French door quietly behind her, turned into the windy afternoon, and ran like hell, leaving Blackheart to stare after her, thinking God knows what.

Now THERE WAS NOTHING left to do but wait till the Von Emmerling emeralds were delivered, thought the thief, wait that interminable length of time until the night of the Puffin Ball. It was a shame the old man had finished with the copies so soon. There was nothing left to do, nothing left to plan. Everything was ready, all that was needed was for the time to pass. And it was passing damnably slow.

The old man was right, the fakes were beautiful. They'd look stunning against a silky white neck. Their glow was almost luminous—there was no way the originals could be any more glorious. It was a shame the Werdegast emeralds would have to be sacrificed for state's evidence. An ignominious fate for such craftsmanship, but now wasn't the time to be sentimental. Too much was at stake, it had taken too long to get to this point, with just this perfect opportunity. Rank emotion couldn't be allowed to enter in at this late date.

The Baggie with the emeralds was resting prosaically between the mattress and the box spring. So far it hadn't interfered with a good night's sleep. After all, "The Princess and the Pea" was nothing more than a fairy tale.

Ferris Byrd was a nosy complication, but she could be dealt with. That net of circumstance could drag her down, too. The

thought was amusing, infinitely satisfying. The poor girl would
never know what hit her.

Maybe it would be a good idea to check on the Werdegast
emeralds. It had been hard to resist the temptation to sit and
gloat over them. Maybe just for a moment, before anyone came
in. It wouldn't do any harm—in another week they'd be gone,
and the real ones would be in their place. Such a soothing,
pleasant thought. And one more peek wouldn't hurt.

Chapter Five

It had been *Raffles* last night. Ferris had told herself she wasn't going to watch. The last thing she'd needed was to be presented with the spectacle of David Niven cavorting as a debonair cat burglar in London of the 1930s. What she did need was to lose herself in a long, fascinating book, forget that Blackheart ever lived, forget that name that he'd uttered so charmingly. Francesca, he'd said, and she could no longer hide from the fact that he knew far too much about her.

But *Raffles* had been irresistible, and she had given up the pretense of ignoring it after the second dish of French vanilla. There was still no sign of Blackie, and the apartment had seemed curiously empty. She drifted off just as the sermonette was drifting into a test pattern, her lush body stretched across the queen-size bed wearing purple satin boxer shorts and a matching sleeveless T-shirt, her clothes in a tangle at the foot of the bed, the sink full of dishes. And when she woke the next morning, the first thing she saw was Patrick Blackheart, leaning against the doorjamb, surveying her sleeping form amidst the clutter with great interest.

Ferris usually awoke slowly, in stages, each successive cup of coffee bringing her into the real world. One look at Blackheart, however, and the adrenaline shot through her veins and she was suddenly completely awake. She sat bolt upright, ignoring the fact that she was wearing nothing at all under the thin satin undershirt and her full breasts were heaving with outrage and indignation. Blackheart's gaze dropped to their level, however, reminding her, and she quickly pulled the sheet around her.

"I hate to be redundant," she said in a voice strangled with rage, "but what the hell are you doing here?"

"Demonstrating my expertise. I thought I should convince you just how good I am at my job. I can get in or out of the most burglarproof apartment. If it passes my inspection, no one can get in."

"Apparently my apartment didn't pass your inspection. How did you get in?"

He gave her that cool, almost angelic smile. "You aren't hiring me, Francesca. Phillip is. Check with Kate for my rate for apartments." He moved out of the door, heading back down the three steps to the kitchen. "Want any coffee?" he called out over his shoulder.

She was after him in a flash, the huge sheet wrapped toga-style around her body. "I want you out of my apartment," she warned him, trailing him into the kitchen. "Now."

It had been a mistake. She had forgotten how very small her kitchen was, not much larger than a closet. There was barely room for the two of them to stand, much less without touching. Blackheart seemed amused by her predicament, but she stood her ground. She wasn't about to let Blackheart drive her out of her own kitchen.

"Do you take it black?" He reached overhead for one of her mismatched mugs, filling it from the pot on the stove before she could protest. She'd forgotten she had that pot—she usually made do with instant, much as she hated it. And damn him, he'd washed her dishes! They sat in the drainer, clean and shining. Ferris gnashed her teeth.

"No," Blackheart mused, "you'd take too much sugar and too much cream. Except that your cream is sour, and you're out of nondairy creamer. You'll have to drink it this way."

He held out the mug, and she had a hard time controlling the strong desire to splash the steaming liquid all over him. He was wearing jeans and a faded flannel shirt, and it would have hurt very much. With real regret she accepted the coffee.

"Thank you," he said in that gentle voice. "I wouldn't have liked having a bath in hot coffee."

"It's nothing less than you deserve," she grumbled, taking a sip for lack of something better to do. Even without the gobs of cream she usually added, it was substantially better than what she drank most mornings. "I still want you out of here."

He reached out a hand and touched a strand of her thick cloud of hair. "I like it better loose."

There was no room to whirl away from him—she would have come slap up against the refrigerator. One hand was holding the cup of coffee, the other clutched the sheet around her, and she had to content herself with a warning glare. Her regret when he dropped the hair and levered himself up on her kitchen counter, away from her, was inexplicable.

"So tell me, Francesca Berdahofski, what are you doing today?" he inquired casually. "I need some help, and I thought you'd be the perfect candidate to assist me."

"You bastard. If you think you can blackmail me into helping you steal the emeralds you must be out of your mind," she spat at him. The force of her noble outrage was weakened in the face of his astounded amusement.

"You really do have a vicious opinion of me, don't you? How am I going to convince you I've given up my sordid past? I assure you, I no longer have what it takes to be a cat burglar, more's the pity. I have to get my jollies where I can, stopping other people from doing what I used to do so well."

She suddenly felt like a complete idiot, standing there clutching the sheet around her like an outraged virgin. Except, of course, that she was. What else did he know about her, besides her name? "What do you need help with?" she said, stalling.

"My first step is to make sure that no one from the outside can get in to steal the emeralds. If I can narrow it down to the four hundred and some ticket holders, it will be a minor improvement. There are alarms on every window on the second, third and fourth floors, except for the Palladian window in the back of the second floor hallway. I presumed no one bothered because only one narrow section opens, and the entire thing is in full view of the downstairs hallway."

"And?"

"And, I'm not convinced that someone might not be able to manage it. I don't think the view is unrestricted at all, I think there's a blind spot. I want to see whether I can get in without you seeing me.''

"Why don't you just have another alarm put on that window, too? Why go to all that effort?"

Blackheart shook his head. "That's my reward for working a nine-to-five job. I get to try a little B and E in the name of business."

"B and E?" She took another sip of the wonderful coffee, and the hold on her sheet relaxed somewhat.

"Breaking and entering, it's called by the men in blue. A very unimaginative term for what can be a form of art. Of course, most B and E is crude and unimaginative. Junkies in search of stereo equipment and the like."

"You're really proud of yourself, aren't you?" she demanded, outraged. "You see yourself as some sort of hero, better than some poor junkie."

He shrugged. "I had standards."

"Standards!" she scoffed.

"I never robbed anyone who wasn't obscenely wealthy. I never kept anything that was uninsured, and I never kept anything that was overinsured. I only stole gems, beautiful, shimmering jewels." His voice had taken on an unbearably sensuous thread. "I never touched money or any of the other glittering toys rich people tend to have lying around. Just jewelry."

"Very noble," Ferris mocked, leaning against the refrigerator.

"So you'll come with me, Francesca?"

"Stop calling me that! My name is Ferris."

"Your name is Francesca. You never changed it legally," he retorted calmly.

"I don't like the name."

"Tough. It suits you, with that cloud of midnight hair and your magnificent breasts heaving in rage. What in the world are you wearing under that sheet? Those scraps of purple satin certainly look enticing, but not at all the sort of thing one would expect from the future Mrs. Senator Phillip Merriam."

"Damn you, you are trying to blackmail me."

"No," he said, the smile leaving his face. "I'm not."

"Then why did you check up on me?" she demanded.

"I could tell you I had Kate run a routine check on all the major people connected with the Puffin Ball and the Von Emmerling emeralds, and that would be true. When you're dealing with something worth that much money, you check out all the angles. But I didn't tell her to rush the others."

"And you told her to rush mine. Why?"

In that tiny, confined space, with him perched on the narrow length of kitchen counter and she as far away as she could be, leaning up against the mini-refrigerator, they were still within touching distance. A dreamy, sexy look came into his warm brown eyes, and a lazy smile curved that mouth that looked suddenly quite irresistible. He was going to reach out and touch her again, he was going to pull her body against his and kiss her senseless, and she was going to let him. The sheet was going to fall at her feet, and she'd be standing there in the circle of his arms wearing the ridiculous purple satin boxer shorts and she wouldn't care at all. The thought made her slightly dizzy.

"Because," he said finally, and his voice was a seduction, "I thought you were my prime suspect."

She stared at him in absolute amazement, and then he did reach out one of his strong, beautiful hands, placing a long finger under her chin and closing her mouth. "You'll catch flies, Francesca," he murmured, that devilish light in his eyes.

"I—I—" Her outrage was so great that words failed her, a fact that seemed to please her uninvited visitor.

"Since you're feeling so modest in that sheet, why don't you go get dressed? I brought some croissants, too. Once you feel you're safely attired, we can discuss what we're going to do at Carleton House."

"You're going to get Trace to help you," she snapped.

"Trace is otherwise occupied; so is Kate. Sorry, lady, you're drafted. You wouldn't want Phillip to hear you've been uncooperative, would you?"

"There's a lot you could tell Phillip," she said gracelessly.

"But I wouldn't," he said, and she trusted him. That far, at least. "Go get dressed. And don't wear one of those damned suits. We may need to scramble a bit."

She took as long as she possibly could, even doing the unheard-of and making her bed. She was sorely tempted to wear a suit anyway, but gave up the idea. Blackheart was outrageous enough to take it off her if he so chose. She settled for jeans and a silk and wool sweater that barely hinted at the ripe curves underneath. Scraping her thick hair back from her face, she pinned it into a ruthlessly tight bun and shoved Phillip's tastefully large diamond on her left hand before rejoining Blackheart in the kitchen.

He was munching a croissant, managing it with far more neatness than she ever could, but at the sight of her a frown creased his brow beneath the long dark hair, and he put the pastry down, advancing on her with a determined air. It took all her willpower, but she stood her ground.

"Very nice," he murmured, his long arms reaching behind her head, "except for this...." With speedy dispatch he removed the hair pins and the hair tumbled to her shoulders. "...And this." Tossing the hairpins on the counter, he caught her left hand and took the ring from her finger before she was even aware that he'd touched her. She stared at him with reluctant amazement. The ring was still slightly tight that time of month, and yet he'd removed it as easily as if it had been two sizes too large.

He gave the ring a dismissing glance before dropping it on the counter with as much care as the steel hairpins, and Ferris felt compelled to defend it. "That's a very nice ring," she protested. "You needn't sneer at it."

"Completely unimaginative," he said. "But then, Phillip Merriam has never had the reputation for creativity. You should wear emeralds to match your glorious eyes. Or rubies."

"Diamonds suit me fine," she said repressively, part of her getting caught up in the fantasy against her will.

"Then a huge yellow diamond, the size of a robin's egg," he mused. "But not a damned bland white diamond any banker's wife would wear."

"Did you want me to come with you or not? Because you're treading on very thin ice, Blackheart."

"Because I think you should be showered with precious jewels? I'd better watch my step."

"You'd better." She turned away, but not before a reluctant smile lit her face, and he caught her shoulder and turned her back, very gently.

"You can smile," he said softly. "I find that very reassuring."

"Then I'm no longer on the top of your list of suspects?" she said lightly.

The hand tightened for a moment on her shoulder, and she felt him lean toward her. And then the moment passed, and she breathed a small, uncertain sigh. "I'll trust you, Francesca," he said, "when you trust me."

"And that will be a cold day in hell. Let's go if we're going."

"I don't know, Francesca," Blackheart mused. "There are times when I think you're cold enough to freeze hell, and then some. Don't glare at me—I'm coming."

Chapter Six

Damn, but he was getting himself in trouble, Blackheart thought. Deeper and deeper, eyes wide open as he walked directly into the mire. At thirty-six he should have known better. It must be his restless streak acting up again. If he couldn't risk life and limb scrambling over buildings, he could risk the far too secure tenor of his life by messing with the bundle of contradictions by his side.

When it came right down to it, he disapproved of Miss Ferris-Francesca-Byrd-Berdahofski as much as she disapproved of him. He disapproved of her uptightness, of that proper image she'd created and wrapped around that surprisingly luscious body like an invisible cloak, of the snobbery that made her hide her roots, and most of all he disapproved of the fact that he wanted her so much it was a constant ache in his loins whenever he was around her. Of course, there was an obvious answer to the problem—stop being around her. But he couldn't resist—the danger pulled him like a magnet, and that cool, to-hell-with-you expression on her face was a challenge he couldn't resist.

"This isn't the way to Carleton House." He also liked that husky note in her voice, and the snotty way she called him "Blackheart," as if she thought the name suited him.

"No, it's not," he agreed, glancing at her averted profile as he continued heading toward the bay. She'd taken one glance at the disreputable-looking Volvo station wagon that had seen many better years, and the disbelief in those green eyes of hers had been worth it. She sat now in the front seat, seat belt firmly fastened, hands clasped loosely in her lap, trying to convince him she was at ease. Her knuckles were white.

"Are you kidnapping me?" she asked lightly.

"Would you like me to?" he countered. She appeared to consider it, then shook her head, the cloud of black hair swirling around her fine-boned face.

"We're stopping by my favorite deli to pick up something for a picnic." He took pity on her hidden curiosity.

"It's too cold for a picnic. And I didn't say I'd eat with you, I said I'd help you with ... I don't know that I actually agreed to a damned thing," she said crossly.

Damn, but he liked her. He liked the way she struggled to keep angry with him, he liked the ramshackle apartment with its piles of books and magazines over every available surface and the clothes tumbled on the floor, still smelling of Cabochard. It was a fitting perfume for her—it meant "pigheaded." And that was one thing that could be said about her; she was definitely a very pigheaded young lady.

Kate had warned him. She knew him and Trace like the back of her hand, had recognized that speculative look in his eyes and taken him to task for it. It was her thankless duty to try to keep Blackheart, Inc., running reasonably smoothly. Given Trace's susceptibility to the pretty debutantes and beautiful matrons that abounded in most of their jobs, given Blackheart's determination not to adhere to timetables or rules, she had her work cut out for her.

The last six months had added a new fillip to her problems. Kate had, apparently, always been uninterested in romantic entanglements, preferring to keep to herself. Until last year, when she'd suddenly become extremely secretive. Blackheart had suspected a married man, but he'd done nothing to verify it, respecting Kate's privacy. Whatever it seemed, it seemed to cause her more grief than sorrow. First there was a two-week period of swollen eyes, sniffling, and heart-felt sighs, and then Kate had pulled herself together, back into her usual pugnacious competence. And it had taken Blackheart months to notice that her usual bullying maternal attitude toward her co-workers had undergone a change. In Trace's direction.

Blackheart had been too respectful of Kate's privacy to inquire into it. He knew Trace had taken her out drinking a couple of times when she was recovering from her recent troubles. But he also knew that Trace thought of her as a buddy, one of the guys, having been lectured early on that she wasn't interested in him that way. But it looked to Blackheart that she'd changed her mind, and Trace hadn't the faintest idea.

He pulled himself back to the present with no difficulty at all. There was nothing he could do about Kate's tangled love life, and he didn't think he would interfere, even if he could. Years of being a loner were hard to break. In the meantime, he had his own tangled love life to work on right now. And that was just what he wanted it to be. Tangled—in her sheets, in her limbs, in the cloud of hair.

"Speaking of erotic daydreams," she snapped, "stop looking at me as if I were a piece of strawberry cheesecake."

"Cannoli."

"I beg your pardon?"

"I see you more as a cannoli. Rich and Italian and full of sweetened ricotta cheese," he mused.

"You may as well go all the way and call me a blintz. I'm half Polish as well as Italian," she said sharply. "So I look like something stuffed, do I?"

"You look," he said quietly, "absolutely delicious."

"Get that rapturous expression off your face, Blackheart. We're going to break into Carleton House, I suppose we'll eat something, and then you'll take me back home. And that's it."

"Yes, ma'am," he said with mock humility.

She turned those magnificent green eyes on him. "Why do you always try to goad me, Blackheart?" she questioned in a deliberately calmer voice. He could guess how much that effort cost her, and he applauded it silently.

"Because I like to make you mad."

"Why, for heaven's sake?"

"It shakes you up and keeps you from looking down that very pretty nose at me. It also makes you forget that you're trying to be Regina Merriam or Olivia Summers."

"Not Olivia," she said sharply. "And I don't look down my nose at you."

"Sure you do. I'm still not quite sure why. Just a law-and-order complex, or is it something deeper? Were you molested by a cat burglar when you were a child?"

She turned to look at him then. "You're the one who's so knowledgeable about my past. Didn't they tell you about that?"

"A molesting cat burglar? No, that somehow slipped past my informants."

"What did they tell you?"

"That you come from a very large, very poor family from a small farming community outside of Chicago. Your father was Polish, your mother Italian, and you're one of eight children. There was never much money, but it sounds as if there was plenty of love."

"Maybe too much love," Ferris said slowly. "And I'm one of nine children. I had a younger sister who died when she was twelve. Of kidney failure."

Blackheart was silent for a moment, digesting this. "Do you think if you'd had money she wouldn't have died?"

He was astute, she had to grant him that. "I don't know," she said. "I think if we'd had money I wouldn't have to wonder about it."

"Do you blame your parents?"

"Of course not. I loved them. They worked themselves to death before they were seventy, Mama from having too many children too fast and Pop from a form of emphysema called farmer's lung. Maybe money would have helped them, too, maybe not. It wouldn't have hurt." She looked at him then, with a sudden, savage pain in her green eyes, turning them from a distant sea color to a deep forest hue. "Do you know how many nieces and nephews I have? Twenty-two. Twenty-two from seven brothers and sisters. And one of them's a priest. And every single one of them either had a baby on the way when they got married or had one within a year after the wedding. My older brother Paul made it through one year of community college before he had to quit and get a job in a factory to support his three children. And he was only twenty-one years old."

"And you decided that wasn't going to happen to you?"

"You're damned right. I wasn't going to be trapped in that cycle of babies and poverty like everyone else. I finished high school a year early, got a scholarship to Stanford, and haven't looked back."

"Do you ever see your family?" he asked lazily.

"Of course I do. You think I'm ashamed of them? I'm not, not at all. But when I see how they're weighed down by poverty and too many children and no ambition, it makes me even more determined not to let myself get weighed down the same way."

"So there won't be any children for you?"

"Of course there will be. But they'll be wanted, they'll come from choice and not by accident," she said with great certainty.

"That makes sense." His voice was cool, nonjudgmental. "That still doesn't quite explain why you disapprove of me so heartily."

She looked at him for a long moment, considering something, he wasn't sure what, and then she leaned back in the seat, eyes straight ahead of her. "When I was eleven years old," she said slowly, "I wanted to be a Spanish dancer. I couldn't take lessons—even if we'd had the money, there was no one in our small town who could teach it. So I'd watch every movie I could, and practice out in the barn, humming to myself. I even made myself a costume out of one of my older sister's party dresses. All I needed was the shoes. I didn't even know what kind of shoes I should wear, but I knew they were important." There was a dreamy note in her voice, bringing back a nostalgic, painful past, and Blackheart listened intently.

"One spring afternoon I'd walked into town, and there in the local five-and-dime was a pair of red shoes. They were made from a sparkly, shiny kind of stuff, they were two sizes too big, and it was the only pair they had. And I wanted those shoes. I wanted them so badly that it made me ache inside. I wanted them so badly that I stood there in the store and cried. Every day after school I'd go in and look at them, every day I'd try to figure out how I could find the money to buy them. And then one day I went in and no one was there. The grain store had caught on fire, and everyone was out watching it burn. I was alone in the store with my book bag and no one to watch me, and the shoes were sitting right there, waiting for me." She closed her eyes, the lashes fanning out over her lightly tanned cheeks.

"I didn't take them. I stood there, rooted to the floor, staring at them, and all the while the fire engine was racing down the street outside and people were rushing toward the grain store, and I didn't even touch them, much as I wanted to. I just stared at them, and then I turned around and ran out of the store, ran all the way home."

He didn't say anything. He didn't know what to say. The sound of pain in her voice was fresh and new, from a wound that had never healed.

She opened her eyes again, turning her head against the seat to look at him. "No one, in the history of the world, has ever wanted anything as much as I wanted those red shoes. No one. And if I didn't take them, if I turned around and left without touching them when I wanted them that much, then there's no excuse for what you did. None at all."

"Did you ever regret not taking them?" he questioned curiously.

She sighed. "Every day of my life for the next five years. Until my baby sister died, and I had something more important to think about. Getting out."

"And you got out. Very effectively." She hadn't even noticed that he'd pulled over in front of the deli and was watching her, had been watching her for the last few minutes. "What does Merriam think about this?"

"I haven't told him. I've never told anyone about it."

"Apart from your family."

"Not anyone," she said distantly. "It didn't concern them. It concerned you." She closed her eyes again. "I'm going to take a nap. Go in and get the food. If I have a choice I like Beck's dark."

He wanted to lean over and kiss her on those soft lips, like Sleeping Beauty and the Prince. God, he must be going crazy! "Beck's dark," he agreed. "At least we have something in common." Sliding out of the car, he closed the door quietly behind him, careful not to jar her. If he had any sense, he'd turn around and take her straight back to her apartment. Francesca Berdahofski was going to interfere with his carefully made plans, and if he wasn't a complete idiot he'd stop the involvement that was entangling him before it was too late.

But he wasn't going to take her back to her apartment. He was going to get a six-pack of Beck's dark beer and a feast, he was going to wine and dine her on the floor of the empty ballroom at Carleton House, and then he was going to do his absolute level best to strip all those layers of clothes and defenses and armor away from her and make love to her on that hard, shiny floor, make love to her until she wept, till she cried away all the years of hurt that kept her heart locked away behind Ralph Lauren suits. And then he'd make love to her again, slowly, achingly, until...

Damn, he must have that look on his face again. What did she call it? Rapturous? Maybe they'd have cannoli in the deli.

THEY WERE an unlikely partnership, the three of them. Not what one would have expected, to pull off a caper of this magnitude. But their very unexpectedness would work to their advantage.

It was hard being a mastermind. Being responsible for your assistants' weaknesses, having to foresee every possible disaster when there were so many that could befall them. But it was a high, an ego boost unlike anything else. It was only unfortunate that no one would ever know the depth of the brilliance behind this particular little jewel robbery. It would be chalked up to Patrick Blackheart, others would be implicated as accessories, and the three of them would get off scot-free. And very, very much richer.

Quiet, self-satisfied laughter echoed through the room. *Yes, I am very clever,* the mastermind thought. *Very clever, indeed.*

Chapter Seven

This was a ridiculous thing to be doing on a chilly, rain-swept Sunday afternoon, Ferris thought, leaning against the newel post on the long, curving staircase in the front hall of Carleton House. She should be home, watching old movies on TV, eating Double Rainbow ice cream and waiting for Phillip's phone call. Every Sunday afternoon, precisely at three o'clock he would call her, and every Sunday afternoon she would be there, awaiting him. But not today. She hadn't even thought of it until Blackheart had left her alone, and then it had been too late. Only briefly had she contemplated the notion of having him take her back home. And then she'd dismissed it, without daring to figure out why.

She hadn't even had a chance to look at a clock before he'd dragged her out of the apartment, but she figured it had to be sometime in the early afternoon. Not three yet, but there was no way she could get back in time to receive his phone call. And no way she could get in touch with him—he could be anywhere from San Diego to Santa Cruz. So why wasn't she more worried?

Maybe it was the usual restful effect Carleton House had on her. She always preferred it when it was empty, no chattering magpies born to the purple cluttering up its clean architectural lines. And it might as well have been empty; after stationing her midway up the winding staircase, Blackheart had disappeared out the front door. He'd been unnaturally silent the rest of the trip out here, and Ferris had kept her eyes firmly shut, pretending to sleep. But there was no way she could sleep with that lithe, slender, jean-clad leg inches from hers in the rattling old Volvo, no way she could relax so close to him. Why had she told him that embarrassingly sentimental story about her childhood? She'd never told a soul before, and a retired cat burglar was hardly the choice audience for such a confession. God, she was a fool.

Well, now she could relax. Blackheart was supposed to make his way through the windows with their elaborate alarm system, pilfer a scarf he'd placed in a second-floor bedroom, and end up back in the ballroom without her seeing him. There was no way he could do it—she'd watched the upstairs hallway like a hawk, determined to catch him, and there'd been no sign, no sound, no hint of his presence. And he had to get down to the ballroom without leaving the house—he couldn't just exit through the window.

Games, she thought dismissingly. He was a little boy, playing at a game he couldn't possibly win, but she was content enough to humor him. Nothing would please her more than to catch him—

A quiet sound caught her attention, and she whirled around, ready to flash him a triumphant smile. He was standing in the doorway of the ballroom, the silk scarf in his hand, that damned smug grin on his face.

"How did you do it?" she demanded flatly.

"Never ask a magician to reveal his tricks."

"You must have cheated. You went back out the window and came in through the French doors. Though I can't even guess how you managed that."

"I didn't leave the house once I entered it," he said calmly.

She moved slowly down the steps. "This is supposed to reassure me as to your trustworthiness? You've now demonstrated just how easily you can burglarize a burglarproof house, you won't even tell me how, and yet you expect me to trust you."

"No, I don't expect you to trust me. That, it appears, would be asking too much." He held out his hand. "Come and have some lunch."

Ignoring his hand, she moved past him into the cavernous ballroom. He'd started a small fire in the huge fireplace at the far end, spread a blanket on the shiny wood floor, and set the goodies from the deli in place. "Where'd you get the blanket?" she questioned suspiciously.

"Same place I got the scarf—the upstairs bedroom."

"And you carried it back down here without me noticing?" She didn't know whether to be infuriated or awed. Perhaps she was a little bit of both.

"I'm very light on my feet."

"You and Dracula." She sank cross-legged onto the blanket, reaching with resignation for a beer. "If I didn't trust you I wouldn't be here, Blackheart."

Sitting down a decent foot or so away from her, he took the chilled bottle from her hand, opened it and handed it back, his tawny eyes sober. "Up to a point."

"Up to a point," she agreed, tilting back her head and swallowing a quarter of the beer. "Since you know all about my less than patrician history, I suppose I have to." Stretching her legs out, she leaned back on the blanket, a suddenly carefree smile playing about her lips. Phillip was out of touch, the echoing silence of the deserted ballroom seemed a magic place and the man opposite her a magician, a creature from some elfin world where people appeared and disappeared at will. And for a brief moment she was willing to be enchanted. The dark, rainswept afternoon let little light through the row of French doors, and the small, crackling fire lent a small pool of warmth and brightness to the shadow-filled room. "What are you going to feed me?" she questioned, that slightly husky note in her voice more pronounced.

"Knockwurst and blintzes. And Beck's dark."

Ferris laughed then, and once she started, she couldn't stop. Rolling onto her back, she let her delicious laugh ring out in the room, wrapping her arms around her waist to hold in the pain. Tears were in her eyes as the mirth bubbled forth. "That's...the most...ridiculous thing I've ever...heard," she gasped. "I thought you were on the make. Everyone's warned me about Blackheart, Inc., and its reputation for keeping bored ladies busy. With all that experience you should know that you can't seduce a woman with knockwurst and blintzes."

"You can if you pick the right woman," he said, levering his body forward. And then his mouth stopped her laughter as he covered her with his lean, lithe frame.

He couldn't have picked a better time. She was soft and vulnerable and relaxed from her laughter, with the warmth of the room around her, and his mouth on hers was right and natural, delicious with the taste of the dark beer. She started to put her arms around his neck, her mouth softened and began to open beneath the gentle pressure of his, and then sanity returned.

"No!" With a convulsive start she shoved him off her, rolling away to end up crouching like a cornered creature of the forest, staring at him as if he were the devil himself.

He'd landed on his back, and he made no move to right himself, just lay there looking at her out of enigmatic eyes. "You needn't act like a Sabine about it, lady," he murmured gently. "It was only a kiss."

"I don't want you kissing me," she shot back, and he politely said nothing, the small, eloquent quirk of his mobile mouth signaling his disbelief.

"All right," he said finally, pulling himself upright and catching her abandoned beer before it toppled onto the blanket. "Come here and eat knockwurst and I won't even be tempted."

Ferris felt the tension drain from her body, felt the absurd disappointment flood it in return, like the ebb and flow of the blue Pacific. She hesitated for a moment, then, with a wary look in her eyes, rejoined him on the blanket, a good two feet away from him. "Is that why you bought it?" she questioned, accepting the beer from him again. "As a medieval form of birth control?"

"You don't get pregnant from a kiss, Francesca."

"Is that all it would have been?"

His eyes had darkened in the shadowy room—as they looked at her they were warm and gentle and subtly promising. "If that's all you wanted."

Ferris swallowed. He was so damned attractive, sitting there. And that infuriating smile of his was half the attraction. It was no wonder the female half of San Francisco society was at his feet. "And if I wanted more?" Why the hell was she asking such a question? Was she out of her mind?

Blackheart's smile broadened. "Why then, I'd be happy to oblige. Ever the little gentleman, you know."

Ferris gave a snort of disgust. "Hand me a knockwurst, Blackheart. I think I need all the protection I can get."

"We're going to need something to roast them with. I forgot to bring any sticks."

"I thought you were on top of everything." The moment the words were out of her mouth she could have cursed herself.

Bless his heart, he didn't even smirk, though the light in his eyes showed his appreciation. "I try to be. Things don't always work out that way."

"I know where the kitchen is. I imagine they have skewers of some sort." She rose swiftly. She could feel her cheeks were flushed, she could still feel the warmth of his mouth on hers, his bones pressing into her softer flesh. She needed to get away, and fast. "You build up the fire."

She got as far as the door to the hallway when he caught up with her. His hands were gentle but so very strong on her shoulders as he turned her back to face him. "Don't be afraid of me, Francesca," he said softly. "I'm not going to hurt you."

She met his gaze steadily, making no move to break free. "Then let go of me," she whispered.

"Oh, love," he murmured. "I can't do that." He pulled her against his taut body, slowly, giving her plenty of time to escape. She made no move to break free. His head dropped down, his mouth catching hers in a deep searching kiss as his hands slid down her shoulders, down her back, molding her body to his. Slowly, carefully he kissed her, his tongue teasing her lips open, the rough texture exploring her quiescent mouth.

She didn't dare move, didn't dare react, or she would be lost. She stood there passively in the circle of his arms as he kissed her, willing her mind to think of other things, willing her body not to respond. But then his head moved away a fraction, his eyes were blazing down into hers with a slumberous, intense passion that she could no longer resist.

"What's the matter, Francesca?" he whispered, a note of laughter in his voice. "Cat got your tongue? You're supposed to kiss me back." And when his mouth caught hers again, she was lost. Her arms slid around his waist, holding him close against her, and she couldn't tell if she was trembling or he was. Maybe they both were. Her tongue shyly met his, sliding along the rough-textured intruder with a shudder of delight. His narrow hips were pressed up against her rounder ones, and she could feel him hard against her. Those strong, beautiful hands of his were gentling her back, soothing her fears, just as his mouth was melting her brain. She couldn't think, couldn't fight, couldn't do anything more than react to the overwhelming sensual stimuli he was using. She could feel the last restraints begin to slip away, her conscious thought fading before the sensual onslaught of his mouth and hands and her sudden, overwhelming, unbearable wanting, and she wanted to sink to the hardwood floor and pull him with her, pull that strong, lean body of his over her and into her and around her and—

"My, my, we seem to have come at a bad time." Olivia Summers's coolly amused tones broke through the haze of passion like a bucket of ice water, and Ferris tried to break away in sudden horror. But Blackheart held on to her, allowing her a few inches distance as his strong hands caught and held her there.

"What are you doing here, Olivia?" he questioned, and as sanity rapidly returned, Ferris could appreciate what he was doing. Guilt and panic were exactly what Olivia wanted, and she had almost made the mistake of giving them to her. She took a deep, calming breath, and Blackheart gave her arms a subtly reassuring squeeze before releasing her.

"Actually, I had a few measurements to make. I appear to have lost my notes, and Dale was a perfect lamb and offered to bring me over. It appears I interrupted a . . . conference?" she queried delicately, and it was all Ferris could do to control a snarl. "And such a charming spot for one," she added, her patrician nose raised in amused disdain. "Honestly, Patrick, you're up to your old tricks again. Do you and Trace always have to have a new conquest with each job? And you really shouldn't pick on poor Ferris. She isn't as sophisticated as I was—she might think you really mean it."

Ever the little gentleman, he'd called himself. He proved it then, Ferris thought, with that distant, polite smile. "Maybe this time I do."

"Oh, Patrick, I doubt that." Olivia laughed her soft, condescending laugh. "And if you have no pity for poor Ferris, think of Phillip. You really mustn't play fast and loose with people's emotions. You should save yourself for someone who's better able to handle you." There was little doubt who Olivia meant, and not for the first time Ferris wondered how someone who looked like Grace Kelly could act like Attila the Hun.

"Olivia, I think there's someone here." Dale Summers's rich, fruity voice came from the hallway, preceding his lanky form. "I don't think we ought to—" Spying Blackheart and Ferris, he came to a halt, and a blush came over his long, bony face.

His obvious embarrassment only made Ferris more miserable. But there was no way she was going to leave Olivia with the upper hand. "Go ahead with whatever you were planning, Olivia. Blackheart and I were just finishing."

"Really?" Olivia raised one exquisite eyebrow. "It looked to me as if you'd just begun."

"You do have a mouth on you, Olivia," Blackheart said softly. "You might consider washing it out with soap every now and then."

"So charming," Olivia purred.

"I do my best. What are you two doing here? I can't imagine you needed any measurements that couldn't wait till tomorrow. And why do you have a key? You aren't one of the people listed as having one."

"Dear Patrick, you are becoming professional all of a sudden. And you've caught me, I'm afraid. I borrowed Regina's key last week and had a copy made. I didn't really relish going to dear Ferris every time I needed to get in. It smacked too much of boarding school." She cast Ferris an appraising glance out of her china-blue eyes. "Though I must say you're looking a great deal less schoolmarmish than usual, Ferris."

"You still haven't answered my question, Olivia," Blackheart persisted, that deep, quiet voice of his embedded with steel. "Why did you and Dale come here today?"

Dale had blushed even a deeper red, and his prominent Adam's apple worked convulsively. Ferris watched him with distracted fascination, almost missing Olivia's indulgent little laugh.

"Why, Patrick, you taught me about the erotic possibilities of empty mansions. I'll never forget the costume ball at San Simeon. I thought I'd bring Dale along and see if I could recapture the old magic." Her perfect lips curved in a smile. "I figured anything was possible."

Ferris had finally reached her limit. "Then I think we should leave you two to your privacy," she said quietly. "We were just about to head back to town anyway. I'm expecting a phone call from Phillip." She said it defiantly, eager to show she had nothing to hide from Olivia's beautiful blue eyes.

"Does he call you every Sunday? How sweetly predictable of him," she cooed. "He used to call me every Sunday when we were engaged and he was campaigning. Of course he used to call me earlier. Three o'clock, every Sunday afternoon. I'm glad to know he keeps in touch." She took a step toward Ferris's still figure, leaning forward in a confiding fashion. "Listen, darling, I'd never realized that we had such similar taste in men. Why don't we trade men for the afternoon? I've missed Patrick's—shall we say, enthusiasm. And you'll find Dale can manage a creditable performance when properly inspired."

Ferris's hand clenched into a fist. She would have given five years off her life to have driven that fist directly into Olivia's perfect little teeth, but the strong hand on her back would have moved fast enough to stop her. She gave up the notion with great sorrow, promising herself that sooner or later she'd have her revenge. "I'm going out to the car now, Blackheart," she said calmly, congratulating herself on her even tone of voice. If she couldn't have revenge, she could at least have dignity.

With a cool nod at Dale, she strode past them, ignoring Olivia's amused smile. By the time she reached the broad front steps she was shaking with rage, by the time she reached the car she was swearing and cursing in words taught to her by her brothers in deepest secret. Yanking open the car door, she slid inside and sat there, waiting, counting until Blackheart joined her.

He got there by seventy-three, and the surface of Ferris's white-hot rage had cooled to red. He slid into the front seat beside her, turning to look at her before turning the key in the ignition.

She met his gaze accusingly. "How could you?" she demanded in a furious undertone.

"How could I what?"

"How could you sleep with that slimy bitch?"

Blackheart shrugged, and she could see the amused light in his eyes. If it had reached his mouth, he would have been the recipient of her fist instead of Olivia. "I had nothing better to do at the time," he replied. "You want to tell me about your past love life?"

"I would have thought that would be part of your report."

"It should have been. Kate couldn't find out anything of interest, apart from a high-school football player."

"Damn you, Blackheart, leave me alone!" she snapped, enraged. "Tommy Stanopoulos has nothing to do with this."

"Nor does my past affair with Olivia Summers," he said calmly, starting the car.

"You're right about that. Your affairs have absolutely nothing to do with me. As long as you have the energy left to get the job done you can sleep with every single socialite, married or otherwise, that you can get your hands on. I won't say I don't admire your prowess, but—what are you doing?"

Blackheart had started out the driveway, but as her words escalated he'd slammed on the brakes, turning to her with the first anger she'd seen from him. Part of her was gratified she'd goaded him beyond that smiling calm, part of her was terrified. He put those strong hands on her, yanking her against him, and his mouth effectively silenced her.

It was a long kiss, deep and searching, and she was helpless to do anything but respond. When he finally released her, they were both breathless. She fell back against her seat, staring at him as he slowly put the car in gear and started back out the driveway. His breathing slowed, the hands clenching the steering wheel loosened, and the tension in his wiry shoulders relaxed. "That seems as good a way as any to shut you up," he said meditatively. "For your information, I don't happen to want to go to bed with anybody but you. Not right now, at least. My reputation is based more on rumor than fact; Olivia Summers was an unpleasant mistake that I don't care to make again. And if you want any more excuses, you can damn well do something to earn them."

The rest of the ride was finished in complete, absolute silence. He didn't bother to turn the car off when they arrived outside her apartment, and he kept his face averted. Without a word she climbed out of the car, without a word she grabbed her purse and without a word she slammed the door as hard as she could. She heard the tinkle of glass with real delight, and ran into her building before Blackheart could respond. Forgetting that when he was ready, locked doors weren't about to keep him out.

The angry squeal of the tires as he drove away was balm to her outraged soul. "Take that, Blackheart," she murmured, climbing the flight of stairs to her second-floor apartment.

DALE SUMMERS TURNED to his wife, the high color fading somewhat. "That was close."

Olivia was staring out the window, watching the Volvo start, stop dead, and then start up again. "Too close," she murmured. "But every cloud has a silver lining. I've just had the most delicious idea."

Dale looked at his wife's serene little smile with worried doubt. "You wouldn't . . ." he began, but the icy expression in her blue eyes stopped him. "I just hope you know what you're doing," he said plaintively.

Olivia smiled her tranquil smile. "Oh, I do, darling. I know precisely what I'm doing. Come along."

Chapter Eight

Rough Cut hadn't been enough to hold her interest past one that night. She clicked it off with a determined snap, burrowed under her tangled covers, and tried to will herself to sleep. It hadn't been the best day of her life, starting with Blackheart's appearance in her apartment and ending with Phillip's querulous phone call. Even Phillip's querulousness was gentle and charming, and Ferris felt like every kind of traitor as she soothed his ruffled feathers. A traitor because she'd responded to Patrick Blackheart's kisses far more enthusiastically than she ever had to Phillip's restrained necking. Of course, Phillip respected her, planned to marry her. Blackheart didn't respect anything or anybody, whether it was someone else's diamond necklace or someone else's fiancée. And he probably went after both for the same reason—the sheer, mischief-making challenge of it.

Ferris was still trying to sleep when she heard the restrained batting against the door that opened onto her terrace, and she dived further under the covers, trying to escape the determined daylight and that nagging little sound. But consciousness had taken hold, and as the tap-tap renewed, she tossed the covers back with a glad cry to survey the fierce-looking gray beastie outside on her terrace.

"Blackie!" she cried, flopping across her bed and reaching for the door handle. It only opened a scant three inches against the oversize bed, just enough to let the furry creature slither through, hop onto her bed, and survey her with his usual haughty disdain while she slammed the heavy door shut again.

"Where have you been, old man?" she demanded, stroking him on his grizzled gray head. "I thought you'd left me for good this time."

Blackie the alley cat expressed his thoughts with a feline sneer, batted at her hand, and headed for the kitchen. Ferris, knowing her duty when she saw it, headed after him, shivering a bit in the early morning chill. An ice-blue Victorian teddy wasn't the warmest of sleeping apparel.

"You've been gone three days this time, Blackie," she informed him as she opened a can of cat food. "I'd almost given up on you. I met your namesake while you were gone." Blackie sniffed at the can, gave her a reproachful look and sat back on his haunches. "I know, you'd prefer herring in sour cream, but I ate it last night. I'll buy you some more if you promise to stay around."

Blackie continued to stare at her, unblinking. "No, I don't suppose you will. Any more than your namesake. He's far more elegant than you are, old man. And far quieter. You sounded like a herd of elephants outside the door this morning. Come on, Blackie old boy. It's Dixie Dinner, your favorite."

Blackie considered this, his gaze alternating between her beseeching face and the dish of Dixie Dinner. Taking pity on his poor mistress, he bit daintily into the food, slowly enough to show his disapproval. Ferris knew full well that the moment she turned her back he'd scarf it down in record time. "I should have left you in that alley," she said ruefully.

And that was just where she intended to leave Patrick Blackheart himself. She must be out of her mind, to risk everything she'd worked so hard for, jeopardize her relationship with an undemanding gentleman like Phillip Merriam. She was going to be a senator's wife, and with Phillip's genteel ambition, who knew where that would end? Short of the White House, she devoutly hoped, but not too far short of it. She'd have wealth, security, and her own kind of power. Why was an amoral felon having any effect on her whatsoever?

It took her longer than usual to whirl through the apartment, straightening the mess she'd made the day before. Blackie followed her, weaving between her legs and doing his best to trip her. He seemed to take exception to the white linen suit she was wearing, and even Ferris had to admit it was a little severe. Just the thing to keep Blackheart in line, to keep herself in line. Although she may have accomplished just that objective when she'd inadvertently smashed his car window.

She made it to Carleton House at more than her usual breakneck speed, frightening even herself once or twice. She had almost forgotten—the Honorable Hortense Smythe-Davies was arriving that very morning, with the Von Emmerling emeralds in tow. They were being kept at a local bank until the night of the Puffin Ball, but the elderly Honorable wanted to see for herself that the emeralds would have the proper setting. And the ladies wanted to see the emeralds.

Ferris couldn't remember whether she'd informed Blackheart, Inc., of the occasion. It would be just too bad if they didn't know. Maybe it would be enough to take them off the case, and the major problem in her life would be resolved. Then all she'd have to do would be to change her cat's name.

The parking lot was filled with cars. Predominantly Mercedes, with a Bentley, several Porsches, and a Ferrari mixed among the Hondas, Cadillacs and woodpaneled estate wagons. There was even a Volvo station wagon or two, but none of Blackheart's vintage. Ferris smiled triumphantly. He wasn't there.

None of that mitigated the fact that she herself was late. She scampered up the steps two at a time, entering the ballroom in a rush. Thankfully no one noticed her arrival—all the women were clustered three deep around an immensely tall, immensely skinny old lady with a crown of white hair, an aristocratic nose and an extremely British accent. Regina looked up and caught her eye, giving Ferris a broad wink before turning her attention back to the Honorable Miss Smythe-Davies, and Ferris allowed herself to relax for the first time that morning.

She made no move to get any closer to the famous gems—she'd see them soon enough, and she didn't fancy trying to elbow past Olivia Summers's regal figure, which was blocking almost everyone's view. Leaning back against the white-and-gilt paneled wall, she prepared to listen to the old lady's lecture delivered in tones loud enough to reach Oakland. And then she recognized the short, sturdy figure of Kate Christiansen, clad in modified combat wear, and her spirits flagged somewhat.

Well, she should have known Blackheart would be more efficient than he appeared. He was probably wandering around right now, preparing to pop out at her when she least expected it. That was resignation she was feeling, not pleasure. *Do you hear me, mind?*

"The Von Emmerling emeralds changed hands several times during the last three centuries," Miss Smythe-Davies was declaiming. "My great-great-grandfather, the Earl of Borsbury, won them in a game of whist, and they have been in my family ever since, with the exception of a two-week period in the early nineteen-seventies."

"What happened then?" Ferris could recognize Olivia's sculptured tones.

"My dear, they were stolen. The only time in their history, as a matter of fact. My father was livid, of course—it nearly brought on a fatal apoplexy."

"How did you get them back?" That was Regina's voice.

"We paid a king's ransom for them. I told my father we shouldn't, but he was adamant. Fifty thousand pounds we paid the miscreant, far less than the actual worth of the gems, but steep enough. Since then we've been more careful."

"It was only fifteen thousand," Blackheart whispered in her ear. "And it was dollars, not pounds."

She turned to stare at him, for once more startled by his words than his sudden appearance. "You didn't!"

He smiled that charming, self-deprecating little smile that seemed to have the most insidious effect on her stomach and its nearby regions. "I did," he confessed.

"Oh, my God."

"Don't worry about it, darling. The thrill is gone, the challenge has been met. I make it a policy never to steal the same thing twice. Unless it's a kiss."

"Keep away from me," she warned in an undertone.

"I wasn't talking about right now," he said, much aggrieved. "You know, you look like a nun out on parole. Isn't that outfit just a trifle severe?"

"I am a trifle severe. I don't dress to please you."

"That's for sure." His gaze turned back to the old lady, and Ferris gave in to temptation and studied his profile for a moment. It was a nice profile, with a strong, straight nose, good cheekbones, warm, deepset eyes, and that demoralizing mouth of his. The khaki shirt hugged his wiry torso, stretched across his shoulders, tapered into his faded jeans. "Have you seen the gems?"

Guiltily she pulled her eyes upward. His pants were too tight, she thought grumpily. Or maybe she had that effect on him. More likely it was his proximity to jewelry that was turning him on. "Not yet," she said. "I'll see them soon enough."

"They'd go beautifully with those eyes of yours."

"No, thank you. Bland diamonds are more my style." Of course she'd forgotten to wear her ring today, blunting the effect of that particular barb. She clenched her left hand, drawing Blackheart's attention to it, and he smiled.

He was leaning against the paneled wall beside her, entirely at ease. "I'm afraid I disagree. You'd look magnificent wearing the Von Emmerling emeralds and nothing else. Have you ever made love in nothing but an emerald necklace?"

"No."

"Well, I have. Of course, I wasn't wearing the necklace—I'm not that kinky. The lady of my life at the moment obliged. It was very uncomfortable. I don't recommend it."

"That's fortunate, because I have no intention of attempting it," she snapped.

"Of course, pearls might be a different matter. I can just see you, draped in yards of huge baroque pearls. We could try that. I'd have to find the pearls, of course, but I imagine I could put my hand to some."

"I imagine you could. No, thank you."

"You mean it's just going to be skin to skin when we make love?" he inquired, a thread of laughter in his soft, warm voice. "I thought I was going to have to be very inventive when I got you in bed."

"You're going to have to be fast on your feet when you try," she shot back. "Or you'll be walking funny for a week."

"Such a romantic. Humor me, Francesca. What's your most memorable erotic encounter?"

"Don't call me Francesca," she hissed.

"Then answer my question. I could always raise my voice, you know. Olivia would be fascinated—"

"You wouldn't!"

"No," he said regretfully. "I wouldn't. But I'm tempted. Come on Fra—Ferris. What did you do the last time you made love?"

Things were getting out of hand, as they always seemed to when she was around Blackheart. "I told Tommy Stanopoulos that I wouldn't."

"I beg your pardon?"

"I said that the last time I made love, I didn't. I'm wearing white on my wedding day, Blackheart. Well-deserved white." Why in God's name was she telling him, she wondered.

Blackheart went very still, and she couldn't read the expression in those beautiful eyes of his. It looked like an odd combination of amazement, wonder and belated anger. Why was he angry? It was a long moment before he said anything. "So if you can't give Phillip Merriam a patrician background you can at least give him an honest virgin on his wedding night."

"You bastard."

"Actually, I was never certain of that," he said calmly. "My father never told me, and I didn't want to pry, out of respect for my dear departed mother. I hope you enjoy your fairy-tale life, Ferris. You may find it's not quite what you expect." And without another word he turned and walked away from her.

So why did she feel bereft, watching him go? No, she wasn't bereft, she was relieved. She'd seen the last of Blackheart, heard the last of his taunting comments, and she was well rid of him. But why was he so angry?

"What'dya say to him?" Kate Christiansen had ambled away from the group of entranced women. "Must have been something hot. He doesn't often lose his temper."

"What makes you think he lost his temper?" Ferris questioned coolly.

"The way he was walking. He must've lost his temper last night, too. His car window was broken. I had to give him a ride out here today."

"Then I can thank you for getting him here on time."

"No, you can't. I don't want your thanks for anything. I just want you to leave him alone."

"What?" It came out in a little shriek, and Olivia turned her regal head to glance at them, a smug expression in her blue eyes.

"I said, leave him alone. He doesn't need you playing games with him. You're going to marry Merriam, aren't you?"

"Yes."

"Then leave him alone."

"Did it ever occur to you that it might be the other way around?" she questioned coolly, still aware of Olivia's fascinated gaze.

"It occurred to me. But you're not his ordinary type of squeeze. I don't think he needs a broken heart." That was pain in Kate's flinty eyes, and the pale mouth in her freckled face trembled slightly.

"Are you in love with him?" Ferris couldn't quite believe it, but neither could she fathom the emotion she was eliciting from Blackheart's assistant.

"Don't be ridiculous," Kate snapped. "He and Trace are my buddies."

The light dawned. "Oh, it's Trace you're in love with," she blurted out with less than her customary tact.

She was rewarded for it. Kate sent her a look of such murderous hatred that it made Blackheart's temper seem mild in comparison. "You go to hell, Miss Berdahofski." And she stomped out in her boss's wake.

"What have you been doing, Ferris?" Regina glided up with the unconscious grace that had taken Ferris months to perfect. The Honorable Miss Smythe-Davies had ceased her lecture; the magpies were chattering and Olivia was still watching her.

"Winning friends and influencing people," Ferris replied morosely.

"Don't worry about it, darling. Did Phillip manage to track you down yesterday? He called me hoping I'd know where you were."

"He got in touch with me a little after seven," Ferris said.

"Phillip was very upset that he couldn't find you. I told him not to be such a baby, but I'm afraid he's a little spoiled. I must be to blame, though I don't know how I let it happen." Regina's lovely brow wrinkled in worry.

"Everyone spoils him, Regina. He's so charming and so handsome that people can't help it, both women and men."

"Well, don't you do it," Regina recommended. "Your married life will be hell. I suggest you make a habit of not being around when he calls. It doesn't do him any good to be too sure."

"Regina, we're engaged. Don't you think people should be sure of each other if they're planning to marry?"

"Are you sure of Phillip?" Regina asked gently. "And your feelings about him?"

When it came right down to it, there were times when Ferris thought she liked Regina Merriam even more than she liked her very likable son. She liked her too much to lie to her. "Regina, I have a miserable headache. Do you suppose the entire Puffin Ball will collapse if I go home?"

"I think you're so marvelously capable that you've ensured that things will run smoothly even without your presence. Go ahead home, darling, and take your phone off the hook," Regina said.

"Bless you, Regina."

"What should I tell Patrick when he asks?" she queried slyly.

"Blackheart won't ask," Ferris said grimly, her head pounding. "If by any chance he does, tell him I've moved to Siberia." On impulse she leaned over and gave the slender lady a hug. "I don't deserve you, Regina."

"Nonsense. It's the Merriams who don't deserve you. I hope for our sake that we get you, but I want to make sure you know what you're doing."

That was too loaded a statement for Ferris to question. With another squeeze she headed back out into the cool San Francisco sunlight.

Olivia watched Ferris go, a cat's smile curving her perfect mouth. Things were looking very promising, very promising indeed. It always helped to be open to possibilities. Ferris Byrd would provide an admirable scapegoat if her first choice didn't work out. The more possible culprits the better.

She took another longing look at the Von Emmerling emeralds. When it came right down to it, the glass and gilt reposing beneath her mattress was prettier. Perhaps that yappy old lady would appreciate the substitution. Perhaps not. That was scarcely Olivia's concern.

She liked the choker the best. That one central emerald was really magnificent. The old lady said it had come from a Hindu idol and had a curse on it. Perhaps. Olivia had the notion that it would prove cursed indeed for several people. But lucky for her. Very, very lucky.

Chapter Nine

Blackheart still couldn't understand why he was so mad at her. If he had any sense at all, he ought to be pleased that Ferris had resisted the countless importunate young men who must have thrown themselves at her magnificent feet. There was no doubt, no question in his mind that he would have her sooner or later—why wasn't he obscurely pleased that he'd be the first?

Part of him was. Part of him reveled in the fact that whether Francesca Berdahofski knew it or not, her first lover was going to be a retired cat burglar and not the society blue blood she'd set her matrimonial sights on. Quite a comedown for such a ruthlessly ambitious young lady, and better than she deserved. Without any conceit on his part, he knew that he'd be a far better lover than someone of Phillip Merriam's limited imagination. Besides, there was no way in hell that the good senator could want her any more than Blackheart did. He must want her a lot less—if Blackheart was engaged to her, she would have long ago left her pristine state.

Maybe it was the very fact that she'd clung to her virginity for so long that bothered him. A part of him wondered whether she was holding onto it for bargaining power—forcing Merriam into marriage if he wanted to have her. No, that didn't seem likely. If Merriam was that hot to trot, he could have found a score of willing young ladies, with more easily traceable pedigrees. He wouldn't marry her just to get her into bed.

So why did the thought of her still being a virgin bug him so much? He had the unpleasant feeling that it was because he was afraid. Afraid of Francesca, of the depth of her feelings, of the entanglement that would result if he broke through twenty-nine years of defenses as he knew he could. And if he was willing to go through all that trouble, was he willing to pay the price likely to be demanded? He still wasn't quite sure.

He hadn't come to terms with his abrupt change in life-style yet, and it had been years since he'd made his living out of rich men's pockets. Well, no, that wasn't completely true. He still made a very handsome living from the upper classes—the only difference being that now they had some say in the matter. It hadn't always been so, he thought as he let himself into his apartment without turning on the light and flung his body down into the overstuffed sofa, stretching his stiff leg out in front of him.

There were three things his father had taught him, three things that were basic to the precarious profession of jewel thief. One: Never pull a job by the light of the moon. Two: Never feel sorry for the people you steal from—they can afford it far more than you can. And three: Never get caught.

He'd broken the first two prime rules, that night in London, and that, of course, had led to his breaking the third. His father later added a fourth rule to that list of sacrosanct commandments. Never trust a woman; they're seldom what they appear to be. It was the breaking of that particular rule that had set the seal on his fate, and one would have thought he'd learned his lesson. But here he was, five years later and five years smarter, about to do the same thing all over again.

Francesca Berdahofski was a bundle of contradictions, as far removed from his varied lives as anyone could be. And he had the uncanny feeling that she could bring him down as effectively as Patience Hornsworth had.

Patience hadn't been bad-looking, in a long-toothed, receding-chinned, sharp-eyed British sort of way. And of course, the diamond necklace her elderly husband had bestowed on her on the occasion of their seventh wedding anniversary, not to mention the tasteless but quite valuable sapphire and ruby collection belonging to Lord Hornsworth's socially ambitious and extremely ugly sister, only added to Patience's myriad charms. She hadn't minded cuckolding her husband in his own house, indeed, had been doing it on a regular basis since the end of their honeymoon, and Blackheart had done his best to tire the energetic creature out before he set off on his nightly rounds.

It was one day past the full moon, and Blackheart knew better. But the opportunity was too good to miss—the Hornsworth town house was chock-full of friends and relations, there for some boring but mandatory charity ball. Among the both elegant and seedy guests present in the rambling old mansion there were at least three other likely suspects when the jewels turned up missing, and Emmie Hornsworth had been far too tight and far too smitten with a rather myopic young fortune hunter to remember to see about locking up those hideous pieces her maiden aunt had left her. They would be lying on her dresser, and even if she were in the same room, accompanied by young Feldshaw, they wouldn't see or hear him. He'd had too much experience to be more noticeable than a shadow or a breath of wind.

No, the damning light of the moon could be dealt with. The odd diffidence that had been attacking him more and more frequently was another problem. He'd been brought up to steal, brought up to think of the idle rich as nothing more than ripe and deserving victims for a poor man's son. His father had thrown a whole lot of Irish nationalism at him at the same time, half convincing him, when he'd started out, that robbing the fat British upper classes was a political act for the oppressed minority. It had been a while before he'd noticed that the only oppressed minority who benefited from the influx of priceless jewels were his father and himself. By that time it was too late— he'd grown accustomed to the rich life, and the last thing he wanted to do was to turn his back on it. The fact that the precarious profession he was in had killed more than one member of his family made little difference—it even added to his self-justification. He'd risked his life for the jewels—the greedy owners had done nothing more, in most cases, than inherit them.

But even that constant litany wasn't helping anymore. He was beginning to feel sordid, sleazy and, worst of all, dishonorable. Honesty and honor were two different things to him, and always had been. He'd tried to keep the latter in mind, while consigning honesty to perdition as a luxury he couldn't afford. But honor was beginning to slip away, leaving him feeling like the lowest sort of criminal, and his self-proclaimed image as a latter-day Robin Hood somehow vanished beyond recall.

He'd have to give it up, he'd told himself as he'd shoved the tacky ruby and sapphire necklace and earrings in the black velvet pouch he'd inherited from his father for just such a purpose. Or find some way to rid himself of these absurd feelings of guilt. Because what in hell could he do as an alternative profession?

The rooftops of Hornsworth House were crenellated, gabled, full of interesting little twists and turns. He always preferred plying his trade in Europe—the boxlike structures that held most of moneyed America made it far too difficult to maintain an adequate hold. He'd done it, of course, and reveled in the challenge, but for pure esthetic pleasure you couldn't beat the stately homes of England or the châteaus of France.

He'd shut the window behind him with a soundless click, leaving Emmie Hornsworth happily entwined with a snoring Feldshaw. Blackheart had taken a moment to grin heartlessly at the happy couple. *Better him than me,* he thought wryly. Emmie had been after him for more than a year now, but he drew the line at skin and bones and wrinkles. If he'd wanted to support himself with his talent as a swordsman, he might as well just be a gigolo. For one last time he tried to tell himself that what he did had more class, and for one last time he failed to believe it.

The moon had risen as he made his way back across the steep expanse of slate to Patience's bedroom, and his silhouette was black and mercilessly visible against the silvered roof. He moved as swiftly as he dared, not giving up an iota of silence for the sake of speed. If it had only been two weeks later, he could have made enough to keep him comfortably for a year or more—the amount of jewelry adorning the wattled necks of the Hornsworths' guests was estimable even in those overtaxed days, with a surprisingly small percentage of copies among the real thing.

But that wasn't to be. He'd already risked far too much on a moonlit night, and he wasn't as sure of Patience Hornsworth as he'd like to be. When he got back to the safety of her bedroom, he'd have to wake her up and make sure that she was too besotted to even think he could have left her bed for a rooftop stroll to her sister-in-law.

It was with a rough start that he realized that for the first time in almost seventeen years of making his living he must have made a mistake. The window that he'd left open just a tiny crack was solidly locked. He must have miscalculated—Patience's room must be on the next section of roof.

But the moonlight made it more than clear that there were no wide dormers over there, nor were there any back the way he had come. He wouldn't have, couldn't have made such a mistake on such a brightly lit night. This was definitely Patience's room, and the window was closed and locked.

He was used to thinking fast, and this time he didn't even hesitate. He'd go back the way he had come, sneak out through Emmie's bedroom and...

And then what? Should he take his chances that Patience didn't suspect anything, had just woken up with a chill on her soft white shoulders and shut and locked the window? He could tell her he'd gone for a late-night brandy and take the chance she'd believe him. But then, he'd had the foresight to grab those very pretty diamonds that had been sitting in plain view on her bedside table. He hadn't taken the time then to check the rest of the room, planning on doing so at his leisure. Would there likely be enough to warrant the risk of going back? It wouldn't take him long, once he made his way back there through the rambling old house.

Or should he just get out as fast as he could? No one would see him go—he could be out of the house and out of the country before anyone realized that John Patrick Blackheart wasn't quite who he appeared to be. It would be an abrupt end to his career, at least in the British Isles, but he could always pick a new alias, a new identity, and start again. Or he could retire.

Suddenly, that thought seemed so beguiling that all hesitation left him. He spun around, planning to head back toward Emmie's room and, through that, to the sort of freedom he'd never really known, when he heard a clicking at the window.

He was fast on his feet, and tonight was no exception. But Patience Hornsworth was faster. The casement window crashed open and Patience shrieked in fury, lunging out after him, her pale blond hair hanging around her white face, making her look like one of Macbeth's three witches. He could have withstood that shock if it hadn't been for Emmie by her side, her improbably red hair a tangle, screaming imprecations. And for the first time in his remarkable career, John Patrick Blackheart fell.

IT HADN'T BEEN a pleasant time. He might have wished he'd suffered more than a smashed knee—unconsciousness would have been a great relief. As it was, an enraged Patience had directed her servants to drag him inside and lock him in the cellar, to await his fate like an eighteenth-century servant. And it had taken that bitch three days to bring in the police.

There were still times when he remembered what it had been like down there. The ghastly pain in his leg that had him rigid and sweating in agony, the hunger that began late the first day and was a gnawing in his guts by the time they let him out. The thirst had been worse—when the minions of the law had first shone their torches down at him, he'd been unable to do more than croak at them.

But worst of all had been the darkness. He had no idea where they'd dumped him—even the Hornsworths didn't possess dungeons in their London house, though he wouldn't put it past them to keep a covey of skeletons in the house in the Lake District. But that damp, impenetrable darkness had shut in around him, leaving him alone with his pain and his hunger and his fear, and only the sound of some curious rodent penetrated the thick silence.

In comparison, prison had been a snap.

There wasn't a whole hell of a lot they could do to him. After the weeks and months in the hospital, the operations just to enable him to walk, a goodly amount of time had been spent. And even if the entire British judicial system knew that John Patrick Blackheart was a burglar par excellence, even if they knew he'd been thumbing his nose at the police for more than a decade, and his family before him, there wasn't enough proof to do more than slap his wrist with a six-month sentence.

Emmie and Patience Hornsworth did their best, of course, elaborating on the hideousness of his crimes so that, if they'd had their way, he would have been on trial for rape, sodomy, grand larceny and bestiality besides. Fortunately, the little velvet pouch had never materialized, and the witnesses for the prosecution were taken severely to task for their foray into vigilante justice, not to mention creative testifying.

And at the end of his six-month sentence he had limped through customs and entered his mother's country and site of half of his own dual citizenship. There was no way the United States could refuse to take him, much as it would have pleased the customs officials to reject a convicted criminal. And the proceeds from the combined Hornsworth jewels would at least go far enough to pay for the best orthopedic surgeons on the West Coast. It would have pleased his sense of justice to have thrown it all away on wine, women and song, but finally he had his priorities straight. First he had to be able to walk straight again, then he'd see about making a living. He'd be far too busy to think about any kind of revenge, subtle or otherwise. The loss by Patience Hornsworth of her diamond necklace was revenge enough.

The only thing Patrick resented, the only thing that still grated against his sense of tentative well-being, was that it hadn't been his idea. He'd been on the verge of renouncing the life as it was—he hated like hell to let infirmity and the British judicial system make that renunciation for him. His anger at fate's manipulation had driven him to breaking into Trace's apartment so long ago, it pushed him into afternoons like yesterday, when he had to test his expertise against the solid bulk of supposedly impenetrable houses. And a part of him always wondered whether sometime he'd have to do it just one more time, succeed at it just once, before he could let it go forever.

Well, he hadn't listened to his father, and he was still paying for it with his peace of mind. He'd robbed by moonlight, he'd identified with his victim and he'd gotten caught. And worst of all, he'd trusted a woman, Patience Hornsworth, who wasn't the trusting, randy socialite he'd expected her to be, but an avenging Valkyrie.

And here he was, about to trust another woman who made it clear she wasn't to be trusted. If he had any sense, he would keep as far away from her as possible. *It was Monday now,* he thought, getting up from the sofa and moving across his darkened apartment to pour himself an amber whiskey, the ache in his leg slightly more pronounced than usual. If he kept a minimum of common sense, he wouldn't have to have more than a few words with her in the next couple of days. The question was, had he lost his common sense along with his ability to climb around on roofs? He was rather afraid he had.

OLIVIA WAS PLEASED, very pleased indeed. Things were falling into place with delightful ease. If things went as they should, she would be able to close up that little room, get rid of all that electronic equipment, and live the life she wanted.

Of course, enough people would remember her lucrative sideline. Distribution of certain damning videotapes and the high prices commanded by them would be bound to leave an indelible memory in certain embarrassed gentlemen of wealth and power. Which was all to the good. When Olivia made her move, ran for office, there would be plenty of people who still owed her. The paying off of huge sums to cover up a video-taped indiscretion didn't wipe out one's memory, did it? And she knew all their wives so well—a deliberately careless word here or there could do untold harm.

No, she would have a lot of people eager to help her. And all the money she needed, once the emeralds were liquidated. If things just continued to go her way.

Olivia smiled dreamily. Fate wouldn't dare do otherwise.

Chapter Ten

It was probably just as well that Blackheart was keeping such a low profile, Ferris thought. He seemed to have had an uncanny knack of avoiding her during the past three days. Every time she walked into a room he'd find a reason to leave, every time she had to seek out a member of Blackheart, Inc., Trace Walker would appear, a beaming smile on his affable face. Patrick was there in an advisory capacity—if she had any questions, Trace was more than happy to answer them. He was more than happy to drape one of his heavy, muscled arms around her slight frame, more than happy to invite her out to dinner, more than happy to flirt outrageously with a stricken, sullen Kate Christiansen looking on.

Fortunately he took no for an answer with equanimity, his enthusiasm not the slightest bit diminished by her constant refusals. She only wished there was some way she could steer him in Kate's direction. At her one mild suggestion that he feed Kate instead of her, Trace had stared back at her in honest shock. "Kate's my buddy," he protested. "Besides, she's got a broken heart and she's not interested in men right now, except as friends. Did I tell you about this little Vietnamese place I know...?"

Thank God it was almost over. It was Wednesday night, late, when Ferris fumbled through her keys. The ancient locks were more recalcitrant than usual—she had enough trouble using a key. How had Blackheart managed to get in so easily on Sunday morning? She should talk with her landlord—see about getting the antique locks replaced with something a little more reliable. Something hefty, burglarproof, fireproof, bullet-proof. But could they find any that were Blackheart-proof?

It was well after midnight—she'd had a late supper with Regina and several of the other stalwart members of the Committee for Saving the Bay, she'd had one brandy too many and she was tired, just slightly tipsy and edging toward depression. The only consolation was that it would soon be over. Phillip was murmuring something about announcing their engagement at the Puffin Ball, and in another four months Francesca Berdahofski would be Mrs. Senator Phillip Merriam. Damn it, no. Ferris Byrd would be Mrs. Senator Phillip Merriam. *God, Blackheart, what have you done to me?*

Success was finally hers. The last key clicked into place in its lock and she stumbled in the door, closing it quietly behind her and leaning her forehead against the cool panel. She fumbled with the locks, with the latch and chain, feeling weary, depressed and very sorry for herself. In her current state even Double Rainbow ice cream wouldn't help. She was going to go collapse on her bed and sleep the sleep of the just. She wasn't even going to turn on the television. They were still running those damned caper movies, and night after night she watched cat burglars and their kin romp through millionaires' homes and museums, and when she fell asleep she would dream of Blackheart. Last night it had been *How to Steal a Million,* and she'd been awake till four in the morning. Not that she was ever going to be Audrey Hepburn. And Blackheart was no Peter O'Toole in his prime. But God, she'd love to be kissed in a closet.

Slowly she raised her head from the door. Her blouse and jacket were off, her skirt a pile on the floor, when she heard the thin, distant thread of sound in her rambling apartment. There was also a pool of light coming from her bedroom. She stood very still, the last traces of the brandy leaving her brain, her hand on the locks. Didn't they tell you that if you came home and surprised a thief in your apartment you weren't to confront him? You were supposed to run as fast as you could.

Of course, the purveyors of that sage advice hadn't taken John Patrick Blackheart into account. She wasn't going to find some drug-crazed junkie looking for her cash. She was going to find what *San Francisco Nightlife* had termed one of the

area's most eligible bachelors. It was that article that had
prompted her to christen her cat in his honor. But it was a very
righteous indignation that prompted her to storm down two
stairs, across the hallway, up three stairs and into her bedroom.

He was lying stretched out on her bed, a pile of pillows
propped behind him. He was barefoot, with faded jeans hugging his lean, muscular legs, a white cotton shirt open and loose
about his chest. In the middle of his chest was a large patch of
fur. Better known as Blackie, the wandering alley cat.

The human cat smiled up at her lazily. "There you are. We
wondered when you were going to get home. Out with dear
Phillip?"

"With his mother. What—"

He joined her in perfect unison. "—the hell are you doing
here, Blackheart?" he mimicked. "Watching *Topkapi* and
waiting for you. Does Phillip know you wear sexy underwear
next to that virginal body of yours? What color is that? Peach?
It's very erotic next to your skin. But I suppose you still
wouldn't be so pure if the good senator did know. There are
some things that can't be resisted."

It was too late for her to run screaming for a bathrobe. Besides, the hip-length silk chemise covered more than what she
wore on the beach. "Blackheart, get out," she said wearily,
leaning against the doorjamb.

"Not on your life, kid. This is my favorite movie, and my
TV's broken. I'm watching it here. You can join me," he added
generously. "We won't mind."

"I'm going to call the police."

"No, you aren't," he said. "It would make too big a scandal, and a clever lady like you knows better. You're going to
climb on the bed and watch *Topkapi* with me. And I promise
on my honor not to make a pass at you. I doubt your feline
friend would let me."

He was right, of course. She couldn't call the police, much
as she wanted to. She couldn't even call Phillip—as usual she
had no idea where he was. She only knew he would arrive at her
apartment in less than forty-eight hours to escort her to the
Puffin Ball.

"Please, Blackheart," she said, hating the sound of pleading in her voice, unable to help herself. "I'm tired, I had too much to drink and I don't want to fight with you. Please go home and let me get some sleep."

Smiling, he shook his head, patting the bed beside him. "I promise, Francesca. I won't try to have my wicked way with you."

Was she demented in her old age? Or drunker than she thought, to be actually considering his suggestion. "Can I trust you?"

That mocking grin twisted his mouth, and she wanted to kiss it away. "For tonight you can," he said. "I can't promise you more than that."

And she believed him. Or was too besotted to know the difference. With a sigh she flicked off the overhead light and crawled across the huge bed on her hands and knees till she reached him. Blackie took one look at her, a disgruntled expression on his face, and left, stalking with all the dignity of either a Winston Churchill or a very old alley cat.

Ferris ended at the top of the bed, just within reach of her unwelcome guest, but he made no move to grab her, and slowly she began to relax. "He's a great cat," Blackheart said gently. "We had an interesting time waiting for you. What's his name?"

"Blackie."

"Very original. Except that he's not black—he's a dark gray."

"I know that, I have eyes."

"They're not functioning too well tonight. How much did you drink? Not that I'm meaning to criticize—far be it from me to pass moral judgments on other people," he said lightly. "I was just interested."

"Not enough to make me trust you," she snapped.

"Ah, but you're on the bed, aren't you? You must trust me a tiny bit. So why did you name your cat Blackie when he's gray?"

Yes, she was sitting on the bed, scarcely dressed. May as well be hanged for a sheep as a lamb. "I named him after you. I'd read about the infamous retired cat burglar in *San Francisco Nightlife* and thought it was a good name for an alley cat."

"I'm flattered. Come here, Francesca."

"You said you weren't going to make a pass." She eyed him doubtfully.

"And I'm not. I want to watch this movie, and I'd feel a lot more comfortable if you put your head on my shoulder and curled up, instead of glaring at me balefully. You'd feel more comfortable, too."

"No."

"Yes." He was stronger than she realized. One steellike hand caught her by the wrist, dragging her off balance, and she fell against him. His other arm came around her, his hand catching the nape of her neck and holding her against the hollow of his shoulder. She struggled for a moment, then gave it up, the fight draining from her body. His hold loosened, and she relaxed against him. It really was comfortable, lying there next to him. His shoulder was surprisingly cozy, considering that it was composed of bone and muscle and not an ounce of soft fat. She sighed peacefully.

"That's not so bad, is it?" he murmured softly, one eye on the movie in front of them as his hand began threading through her loose bun of hair. A moment later it was free, a cloud around her sleepy face.

"Not bad," she murmured, snuggling closer. "Why did you retire, Blackheart?"

She could feel the grin that widened his face. "I thought you weren't sure that I did retire?"

"I'm not. I'm taking your word for it tonight. Why did you? Was it because you were caught? I wouldn't have thought your prison sentence was long enough to account for such a radical change of heart. It was only six months, wasn't it?"

"You know a lot more about me than I would have thought. I'm flattered." His voice rumbled pleasantly above her ear. "And I haven't had a change of heart."

"Then why did you quit? And why did you start in the first place?"

"And what's a nice boy like me doing in a place like this?" he paraphrased with a soft laugh. "It's a dirty job, but somebody's got to do it."

"You aren't going to tell me."

"I'll tell you, if you really want to know."

"I really want to know."

"I became a . . . how shall I phrase it—"

"A thief," Ferris supplied sleepily.

"That's a little crass, but I suppose it's accurate enough. I became a thief because it was the obvious thing to do. I was merely following the family tradition. My father was one of the most famous . . . thieves in the history of society burgling."

"I didn't know there was a history of society burgling. I can't even say it."

"My father was a member of polite society in London in the thirties and forties and even into the fifties. He was known everywhere, accepted everywhere, liked by everyone. By day he'd play cards and gamble and ride with his friends, at night he'd rob their wives of their jewelry."

"A charming friend," Ferris grumbled against his shoulder. He smelled positively delicious. Of warm flesh, and Scotch, and something else. She realized belatedly it was the dregs of Dixie Dinner. Blackie must have enticed him into feeding him. With a sigh, she burrowed closer.

"Oh, he wasn't too bad. No one was seriously injured by his pilfering. He knew his victims well enough to know who could afford to lose a diamond or two. I think he did it more for the excitement than the money. He made as much gambling, I think."

"What happened to your parents?"

"My mother died when I was twelve. Some complications after gall-bladder surgery. My father died four years later." His voice was even, his eyes trained on the television, but that strong, beautiful hand of his was stroking her thick dark hair with a steady, soothing beat.

"How did he die?" Ferris asked quietly.

"Occupational hazard. He fell one night. His partner was counting on him, and I took his place. He'd shown me a few things, but I mostly learned on the job." His calm, matter-of-fact voice allowed for no pity, and Ferris swallowed the sudden surge of sympathy. It wouldn't have been welcome.

"And what made you quit? You must have been at it a long time—ten years?"

"Closer to fifteen. And I didn't retire—it retired me. Same thing as my father. I fell."

She felt suddenly sick. "What are you guys, the Flying Wallendas? How many other members of your family died that way?"

"Just an uncle."

"Damn."

"And I didn't die. I just had a smashed leg. Unfortunately, my fall attracted a bit of attention. It was . . . several days before I managed to get help. By that time infection had set in, and . . ." He shrugged, the gesture bringing her body temporarily closer.

"Is that when you went to prison?"

"Yes." The short syllable was neutral, neither inviting nor discouraging further confidences, but Ferris persevered with brandy-tinged tenacity.

"And you can't rob places anymore?" she asked.

"It's difficult. I've had enough operations to make my knee comparable to that of a retired professional quarterback. Good enough, as long as I don't ask anything exceptional of it. No skiing, no ballet dancing and no cat burglary."

"Do you miss it?" she asked in a small voice.

"Sometimes. Not often. Not right now. There's no place I'd rather be than lying in bed with the virginal Francesca Berdahofski," he said lightly.

"Don't tease me," she said sleepily. He was still stroking her head, gentle, soothing strokes, and if he stopped she would die.

"I can't help it. You're so teasable." His other hand reached up to touch her face gently. "So now I've told you my deep, dark secrets. Your turn."

"I've already told you more than you need to know," she grumbled.

"You haven't told me how you managed to be the only twenty-eight—twenty-nine?—year-old virgin left in captivity."

"Twenty-nine. And maybe no one's captured me."

"Not for want of trying. What about Tommy Stanopoulos, for starters? Why didn't you go to bed with him?"

"I didn't want to."

"I don't believe you."

Ferris sighed. It was much more comfortable to put her hand on his shoulder, to snuggle closer against his warmth, to tell him what he seemed determined to know. "We were all set to," she said. "We'd been going steady a year, been necking and petting and getting pretty passionate. He was going away to the university and I was going to follow him the next year, and we decided to 'go all the way.' We waited till his parents were out of town for the weekend, we lied to my parents and I thought we were all prepared. But he wasn't.''

"He wasn't?" Blackheart sounded perplexed, and his attention had shifted from the television screen with the low murmur of voices to her sleepy, troubled face.

"He didn't have any protection. He said we didn't need it, that I wasn't going to get pregnant the first time. I told him I didn't want to take chances, not with my family's track record, and he said, 'What's the big deal? We'll be married as soon as you graduate from high school, you'll be pregnant and have to drop out of college before the first year is over. I'll make more than enough to support you—you don't have to go to college.' ''

"And did you then proceed to emasculate him as he deserved?" Blackheart questioned lightly.

"I should have. I told him I wouldn't sleep with him if he didn't use protection. He told me I didn't love him enough to trust him. I told him I guess I didn't. And that was that.''

"So what's happened in the intervening years? You must know that there are ways for a woman to stop conception even more effectively than a man.''

"Believe it or not, things just never came together at the right time. Whenever I felt like going to bed with a man it was a spur-of-the-moment thing, and neither of us was prepared. By the time I had a chance to do something about it, the notion had passed. Until Phillip.''

"And you haven't even slept with Phillip?'' The hand had left her hair, was now gently stroking her shoulders, and she curled into him like a contented cat.

"Nope. I was all set to, but when he found out I was still a virgin, he decided we should wait till we were married. He figured if I'd waited that long I could wait a little bit longer and do it right. Phillip's very traditional at heart.''

"Phillip's an idiot," Blackheart mumbled against her forehead. "So you're going to be married in white lace.''

"You can come to the wedding," she murmured sleepily.

"I think I'll pass on that one. We're getting to the good part of the movie, Francesca. Don't you want to see them lower the mute down through the window?"

"Nope. I've seen enough caper movies in the past week to last me a long time. I'm going to sleep. Wake me when you leave." She shut her eyes, nestling closer still, and one slender hand closed around his shoulder. A moment later she was sound asleep.

Blackheart looked down at the woman lying in his arms, the wonders of *Topkapi* forgotten. He'd kept away from her as long as he could, far longer than he wanted to. And now he really didn't know why.

Someday he'd tell her about Patience Hornsworth and the rat-infested cellar. Sometime he might even tell her what he had never told another living soul—that he'd begun to hate what he'd been doing and who and what he was.

But not now, not yet. For now she was going to have to go by her seldom-used instincts and trust him. And despite all evidence to the contrary, despite that wary, mutinous look that came over her usually serene face, he knew that she would trust him. She couldn't help herself.

He didn't bother to think about why it should matter. He didn't even bother to think about where this was leading. Silently, carefully he pulled her sleeping body closer against his, flicking off the remote control for the TV before putting his other arm around her. It was a moonlit night again, and he'd long ago given up fighting his regrets. He was trusting a woman who wasn't what she said she was, and he had the uneasy feeling that his distant crimes were once again going to catch up with him. His father must be spinning in his grave.

Patrick hadn't been sleeping well these last three days, but the comfort of the bed beneath him and the soft body in his arms were producing an erotic sort of lassitude. A wry grin lit his face. He'd promised her he wouldn't make a pass at her tonight.

The sooner he fell asleep the sooner tomorrow would come, and he'd made no promises about tomorrow. Shutting his eyes, he willed himself to sleep.

Chapter Eleven

Ferris was aware of several things, all shifting and drifting in and out of her consciousness. It was another gray day—the early morning light filtered through the glass door and tried to pry her eyelids open. There was a heavy weight on her feet—Blackie, most likely. And another heavy weight across her breasts, which definitely couldn't be Blackie. And the mouth and tongue nibbling at her earlobe, nuzzling through her tangled hair had nothing to do with a cat. Or did it?

She opened her eyes, whipping her head around to stare at the man in bed with her. He just barely managed to miss getting knocked in the jaw by her forehead. "What are you doing here?" she asked in a shocked whisper. There was no need to raise her voice—he was more than close enough to hear her. She was lying curled up in his arms, her long bare ankles tangled with his, her breasts just touching his chest through the thin silk chemise. He was still wearing his shirt, and she felt his warm skin, his heart beating with surprising rapidity against hers as he stared quietly into her eyes.

"Waiting for you to wake up," he whispered back. He had just a fine covering of hair on his chest—not too much, not too little—and it tickled and aroused her sensitive skin. She found her own heart had started beating more rapidly, in time with his.

"Did you want to say goodbye?" she questioned breathlessly. It was such a big bed, why was she entwined so closely with him? Why didn't she want to move?

He shook his head. "I wanted to say hello," he said, his
mouth so near that the soft breath tickled her skin. His lips
reached hers before she could protest. And then protest was the
last thing on her mind as his mouth caught hers, gently forcing
her lips apart. Slowly, thoroughly, he began to kiss her, his
tongue teasing past her teeth, exploring the soft, trembling
contours of her willing mouth.

She made a quiet little surrendering sound back in her throat
as his rough, dexterous hand slid up one smooth thigh, under
the silky chemise, across her flat stomach and up to gently catch
one full breast. It seemed to swell in his touch, and Ferris
whimpered slightly against his mouth, trying to edge closer.

His mouth left hers, pausing long enough to nibble lightly on
her lower lip before moving back to her earlobe, as his other
hand caught her shoulder and turned her closer against his
body. Her hands were trapped between their bodies, there was
nothing she could do but spread them against the warm, enticing skin of his chest, threading her restless fingers through the
fine, crinkly hair. He felt so good to her hands, so strong and
warm and alive, and she wanted to feel all of him, wanted no
barrier of faded jeans or silk chemises. His hand slid its relent-
less way underneath the light material, and then it was his
strong, long fingers on her skin, the texture rough and arousing.

With a low moan she sought out his mouth herself, losing
herself once more in the heady delicious thrust and parry of
their tongues. Her hands slid lower, encountering the frustrating barrier of his jeans, and she had just reached for the zipper
when his hand caught hers, holding her still against his arousal,
his thumb and fingers like steel around her wrist, keeping her
captive. His mouth moved away from hers, reluctantly, and his
eyes were black as midnight as they looked down into her love-
dazed ones.

"Are you sure you want this, Francesca?" he asked quietly,
his voice slightly hoarse with controlled passion.

She looked up at him, at the passion-dark eyes, the tangled
brown hair that was rumpled endearingly around his face, the
mouth that was still damp from her kiss. He felt hard and
strong against her captive hand, and she knew how much he

wanted her. As much as she wanted him. Slowly she shook her head.

"I don't want this," she said coolly, calmly, a part of her shrieking in disbelief.

His hands released her, and she rolled away, pulling the skimpy chemise around her exposed body. Unfortunately the oversize bed wasn't made for dignified exits. She had no choice but to scramble across it, trampling on an outraged Blackie, who remained directly in her path, finally ending up at the doorway, rumpled, tousled, breathless and embarrassed.

Blackheart hadn't moved from the bed. He lay back, crossing his arms behind his head, and surveyed her with a calm she knew was completely false. She could see his chest rise and fall with the effort at controlling his breathing, and the state of his jeans hadn't changed appreciably since her escape.

"You're blushing," he drawled.

"You told me you wouldn't do that."

"Wouldn't do what?"

"Wouldn't try to make love to me," she said in a strangled voice.

"I said I wouldn't last night. I never made any promises about the morning."

"I trusted you."

"No, you didn't," he corrected her mildly. "You didn't trust me one bit. You were just tired and a little drunk and willing to play with fire. And I just proved to you how trustworthy I could be. I let you go."

"You didn't...you..." Her outrage suddenly deflated. "Yes, you did. Thank you, Blackheart."

His self-deprecating smile was only slightly mocking. "I could say my pleasure, but that wouldn't be entirely correct. I can't say I was happy to do it, either. I guess we'll have to settle for 'you're welcome.'" He continued to eye her from his position on the bed. "In return you might do me a small favor."

Ferris looked at him warily. "What?"

"Put some more clothes on. I could always change my mind," he murmured.

Ferris fled.

AND HE CALLED Merriam an idiot. What did that make him, calling a halt when she was lying in his arms, trembling, responsive, ready to be loved as she needed to be loved? If Merriam was an idiot, John Patrick Blackheart was the king of fools.

It didn't look as if he'd won any points for that magnificent bit of self-sacrifice. She'd looked at him out of those wonderful green eyes of hers like he was the devil incarnate, she wouldn't even stay in the same room with him, and her hands trembled when she handed him the worst cup of coffee he'd had in months. And he'd used every ounce of his willpower not to tease her, when what he'd really wanted to do was say to hell with it and drag her back into the bedroom.

And she would have gone with him. He knew from that slightly dazed expression on her face that she hadn't quite recovered from her near escape and wasn't sure if she wanted to. There'd been no questions about protection—for the first time in her life she'd forgotten all about it.

Well, he could wait. And that was what he was intending to do. But sooner or later he was going to have Miss Francesca Berdahofski exactly where he wanted her. In his arms, in his bed, in his life. And for now he was going to ignore the fear that he'd never want her to leave.

In the meantime, he had things to do. The San Francisco morning was cool and damp, and his leg ached slightly. Not enough to bring the almost forgotten limp back, but enough to slow him as he climbed the steep hill toward California Street. Francesca could wait until after the Puffin Ball. Could and should wait, until he could give her his undivided attention. She needed to be handled very carefully indeed. But he wasn't going to wait much longer than that.

There were things he had to check out. Something didn't feel right about this job, something was in the wind. He'd relied on his instincts during the past fifteen years, and they'd seldom failed him. Trace often scoffed at him, but Blackheart had seen the secret look of awe in his eyes. He'd laughed when Blackheart told him there was something funny about the Puffin Ball.

"You're getting spooked in your old age, man," Trace had said, clapping a heavy hand on Blackheart's shoulder. "This job is a piece of cake. Just a bunch of sex-starved ladies and their fancy party. There are no professionals in the city—we would have heard of them. And it would take a seasoned professional to handle something like the Von Emmerling emeralds in the long run. We have nothing to fear from amateurs. Not with your magic."

"Something smells funny about this," Blackheart had insisted. "I want you to be doubly observant."

Trace had looked hurt. "Don't you trust me to keep my eyes open?"

"Yeah, but I also know that pretty ladies have a habit of getting in your line of vision. I just want us to be extra careful."

Trace hadn't looked mollified. "You don't have to act so high and mighty. I've noticed you've been more than a little distracted on this job yourself. You should know better than to mess with Senator Merriam's lady. She's out of your league, old man."

"You were trying to mess with her pretty hard yourself, old man," Blackheart had replied mockingly.

"It's expected of me," Trace had said righteously, and Blackheart had let out a hoot of laughter.

"Well, for once, don't live up to people's expectations. Trust in my instincts. There's something going on."

"I always trust your instincts, Patrick. Even though they give me the creeps. I won't even blink Friday night."

"I knew I could count on you. Listen, don't mention this to Kate, okay? You know how she worries."

Trace had given him a funny look at that one, but agreed without question. Blackheart still wondered why he'd said it. Kate never worried; Kate was stern and unflappable. But she'd been more uneven in the past few months, and he didn't want to take any chances. He wouldn't even allow his mind to speculate how trusting someone who was as close to him as Kate would be taking chances. He felt enough like a traitor.

It was going to take some time today. He had to track down the man who'd installed the alarm system at Carleton House and have him tie in two more windows that had been considered impregnable. Blackheart had good cause to know they weren't.

And then he had another, more personal job to take care of. Miss Francesca Berdahofski could wait until after the Puffin Ball, but not long after it. Maybe an hour. And if he didn't want to be tossed aside like—what was the kid's name?—Tommy Popandopoulos or something like that, then he'd better be prepared. In more ways than one.

What had she called that expression that must be wreathing his face at the very thought? Rapturous. He had every intention of putting just such a look on her face as she lay underneath him, that mass of brown-black hair spread out around her.

Tomorrow night. The Puffin Ball was a fast job, worth a great deal of money and not an untidy amount of good publicity. And never had he wanted a job to end sooner. He had no choice but to put Francesca out of his mind for the time being, or a troop of Girl Scouts could march into the middle of the ball and carry off the emeralds under his nose. Business first. And then pleasure, he promised himself. Pulsing, pounding, delirious pleasure. For him, but most especially for her.

And a wicked smile wreathed his face as he topped the hill and started down the other side. Most especially for her, he thought.

"ARE YOU SURE we ought to go through with this, Olivia?" Dale questioned with that well-bred whine that was one of his most irritating characteristics. "I mean, we're taking a pretty big chance, and—"

"Don't be tiresome, Dale. If you haven't got any guts, don't come bleating to me about it. We're taking no chance at all—I've looked at it from every possible angle, taken care of any possible loophole."

"What about our unwilling partner? Don't you think Blackheart . . . ?"

"Blackheart, Inc., will go down the tubes once they're implicated in the theft," Olivia said coolly. "No one is going to believe their protests of innocence. The police will know someone had to be paid off. They simply won't be able to find out who did the paying and who did the collecting."

"But what if—"

"Enough 'what ifs,' Dale! It's too late for cold feet. You wanted this as much as I did."

"No one wanted it as much as you did, Olivia," Dale said, with more force than he usually used with her. Her glare was enough to whip him back into servitude. "All right, Olivia. I won't come up with any more objections. Just remember when they're carting us off to jail that I told you so."

"Don't worry, darling. They'll know at once I was the mastermind. You couldn't think your way out of a paper sack. You'll just face accessory charges. And you can always tell them I brainwashed you."

"You are a cool bitch, Olivia," he said slowly.

"Yes," she said, "I am. Be thankful for that, or we'd be in real trouble right now, courtesy of your little habits."

He looked at her for a long moment. "I suppose you're right," he said finally, unconvinced.

"Of course I am. Now why don't you go downstairs and see what's keeping our confederate? I don't want cold feet to be catching."

"Yes, ma'am," Dale muttered under his breath.

Olivia watched him go with a cool smile on her pink lips. She'd have to get rid of him sooner or later—he was too great a liability. It was a fortunate thing divorce was now allowed in politics—even the President had been married twice. There was no way she was going to spend the rest of her life carrying his dead weight.

She stretched her small hands, shaking them slightly to release the tension. Tomorrow night. And then it would be over, and she'd be so very much richer. And someone, she didn't really care who, would be in deep trouble. She smiled, quite pleased with herself, and lit another cigarette.

Chapter Twelve

The apartment was very quiet. For once Ferris hadn't gone through her usual binge-and-purge cycle of housecleaning. She hadn't dropped her clothes all over the floor when she'd walked in early that afternoon, she hadn't shoved her empty ice-cream dish under the bed. She hadn't even had any ice cream. When she fed the demanding Blackie—she had to change his name!—his can of Savory Supper, she tossed the lid and the can into the almost empty wastebasket. Even her bed was made, with fresh sheets, and the dead panty hose and year-old magazines had been routed from under it. The rabbit warren of an apartment was close to spotless, and for a very good reason. Phillip was coming.

She could just imagine his fastidious horror if he ever looked under her bed. Not that he'd been anywhere near her bed. But assuming that she was going to marry him, and the discreet diamond on her left hand suggested that she was, and assuming they would sleep together, sooner or later he would find out her deep dark secrets. She often wondered which would bother him more—her haphazard approach to housecleaning or her less-than-patrician background?

Of course, with Phillip's inherited money she wouldn't have to worry about housecleaning. Someone could follow her around and pick up the clothes as she dropped them, someone could whisk away the ice-cream dishes when she finished them, even bring them to her in the first place. Sheer, luxurious heaven it would be. Why did the thought depress her?

If she had the energy after her grueling week, she could summon up worry about his reaction to her background. But she knew she'd be manufacturing problems. Phillip Merriam was no snob. He might be disappointed that she hadn't been frank with him, but even he would admit she had never told him an outright lie. As for her Italian-Polish background, Phillip was a suave enough politician to know that would aid rather than hinder him in garnering votes. Once she told him, he might very well want to move the wedding ahead a few months. Though he'd probably insist she change her name back.

Well, that wouldn't be too great a hardship. She'd chosen "Ferris" off the top of her head, and she had come to dislike the cool, distant sound of it. Recently "Francesca" had taken on a certain charm. It was probably only coincidental that it was Blackheart's soft, compelling voice wrapping around it that had made it suddenly appealing.

She'd had too much coffee and Diet Coke that day—the caffeine was giving her an uncustomary case of the jitters, and there was absolutely no need for it. Everything was in order, everything in place—all the committees had proved responsible. The Puffin Ball was set to begin in a few short hours, preceded by a state dinner, and there was nothing left for Ferris to do but enjoy it in the company of her fiancé. And try to avoid Blackheart's knowing eyes as she'd been avoiding his presence the last two days.

Everything was set for Phillip's arrival. The Brie was at the perfect stage of ripeness, the imported British wafers exactly the ones he liked. She had his favorite Scotch, the Dubonnet she'd affected early on in her transformation and had since grown to hate, and everything was in readiness.

Ferris controlled the temptation to take one last look at her reflection. There was no way she was going to improve on coolly calculated perfection. She was exactly what Senator Phillip Merriam expected to see, she was a work of art created by a master. Even if she was no longer so proud of her efforts, she could at least appreciate the results.

The dress was a slight departure from her usual boring good taste. When she went shopping, everything she tried on looked like something Nancy Reagan would wear, and there was a limit to how far she would go in her quest for upper-class anonymity. Looking like Nancy Reagan was beyond that limit. Her final choice was a deceptively simple white sheath, as demure as she cared to make it, which was very demure. It was made of a clingy, silky material, with cunning drawstrings that could raise the side slit from below the knee to halfway up her thigh, could move the neckline from somewhere near her waist up to the polite vicinity of her collarbone. She had opted for the most coverage available, piled her silky hair atop her head and put on strategic gold museum jewelry. An Egyptian collar from the Metropolitan Museum in New York, an Abyssinian slave bracelet from a small college museum in the Northwest and round gold-disk earrings from the Roman collection at the Palace of Fine Arts in San Francisco. She had deliberately not taken a raffle ticket for the emeralds. The last thing she wanted to do was parade around in priceless jewels in front of Blackheart's avaricious eyes. He might well find her irresistible, and then where would she be? In deep trouble.

Carefully, Ferris reclined on her camelback love seat, the closest thing to a sofa that would fit in her tiny apartment. Phillip was late, an almost unheard-of circumstance, and for a moment she considered sneaking into the kitchen and pouring herself a neat glass of his Scotch. Her nerves were on the screaming edge, and sitting around waiting didn't help matters.

Five minutes passed, with her longing for a drink and Blackie weaving his fat gray body around her crossed ankles. At one point he looked up, uttering a plaintive "mrrrow?"

"You couldn't be hungry again, you pig!" Ferris said. "You scarfed down all of the Savory Supper and got into the Brie besides. You're just lucky Phillip wasn't here. He barely tolerates you as it is, and if he knew you'd been munching on his precious cheese you'd be in big trouble." Blackie replied with another plaintive "mrrow," and Ferris rose to her feet.

"All right, I'll give you some more. I may not be back till very late, and God knows what you'll do to the apartment if I don't leave you enough food." She kept up the conversation as she followed Blackie's furred chubby form into the pocket-size kitchen. "But no more Brie. You'll have to make do with Seaside Surprise and be grateful. I don't—'' Raising her head, she looked directly into John Patrick Blackheart's amused eyes.

"Merciful Mary in heaven!" Ferris said, falling back against the refrigerator. "You scared me half to death! You've got to stop sneaking up on me like that. And what—"

"—are you doing here?" he chanted in unison with her. "Really, Francesca, you're going to have to think of something more original to say every time I break in. It's getting redundant."

"Your breaking in is getting redundant. Don't you know there's a law against—against—"

"Breaking and entering is the legal term for it, remember?" he supplied politely. "Or B and E, as they call it in the trade. Who says I broke in? There's no sign of forced entry."

"You're too smart for that. I bet Blackie let you in when I wasn't looking."

"No, but I could always train him. He knew I was here long before you did."

"Damn it, Blackheart, you have to get out of here. Phillip's due any minute."

"Good. I haven't seen the senator in months, apart from talking to him on the phone about you."

"About me?" she squeaked, horrified.

"You remember," he said kindly. "He called and told me you'd take good care of me."

"God, Blackheart, you scared me!" she breathed, the panic never leaving her body. "You've got to get out of here," she said again. "I don't want Phillip finding you here."

"Why not?" He was leaning against the kitchen counter, in no mood to move, and his arms were crossed over his chest. A very elegant chest it was, in perfect evening dress, obviously tailored just for him. There was nothing prettier, Ferris thought with an absent sigh, than a gorgeous man in well-cut evening clothes. Unless it was a gorgeous man in nothing at all.

She shook herself, trying to regain a semblance of sanity in the face of incipient disaster. "Have pity on me, Blackheart. I don't want Phillip suspecting anything."

"What would he have to suspect?" Blackheart countered mildly, and the simple words made a tiny dent in her panic. "I mean, what have we done that's so awful? Shared a kiss or two?"

"Four," she corrected.

"I beg your pardon?"

"Four kisses," she elaborated, and then flushed in the face of his delighted grin.

"Bless your heart, Francesca, I didn't know you were counting."

"So I happen to have a photographic memory," she said defensively. "Anyway, how would you like it if someone kissed your fiancée once or twice, not to mention four times?"

"I wouldn't like it one tiny bit. But then, I wouldn't have left her in the first place with prowling wolves like me around."

"Alley cats," Ferris corrected him in a dulcet tone.

He grinned. "And I wouldn't have left her a virgin for so long."

"Come on, Blackheart." She grabbed his wrist and started dragging him toward the door, ignoring the little thrill that ran through her at the feel of his warm flesh against her fingers. "I really don't want Phillip to find you here. Be kind for once."

He stopped in the arch that separated the living room from the tiny dining alcove, and she couldn't budge him any farther. "I'm always kind, Francesca," he murmured, his voice a sinuous thread. "To you, at least. You just don't recognize it."

She gave a useless yank on his arm. "Please, Blackheart. You have to leave."

He was as still as a statue, his eyes alight with mischief. A moment later the wrist that had been so lifeless in her hand twisted around, capturing hers. Slowly, inexorably he drew her body toward him. She could have fought him, might have twisted away, but she didn't. She was mesmerized by those devilish eyes, that smiling mouth, and a wanting that all the sense in the world couldn't banish. And when his mouth reached hers she met it hungrily.

The hand on her wrist pulled her arm around his lean waist, her other arm followed of its own accord, and suddenly she was clinging to him as if he were the only safety in the world, the only reality that existed. A reality that was promptly shattered by the intrusive shrill of the doorbell.

"Damn!" She tore herself out of his arms in sudden panic. "Get out, Blackheart. I don't care how you do it. You managed to get in here without using the front door, you can leave the same way. I don't want Phillip seeing you."

"Don't you think he'll notice?" Blackheart said lazily, not moving from his perch against the arched doorway.

"Notice what?" she demanded, harried, as the bell rang again.

"That you've just been thoroughly kissed. If I were he and found my fiancée looking like you look, with your cheeks flushed and your eyes shining and your hair coming down, I'd be very suspicious."

"Damn," she said again. "I'll get you for this, Blackheart. I swear I will. At least wait on the terrace until we leave. He's late, we shouldn't be here long."

"Sorry. I told you I wanted to see the good senator. That's just what I intend to do." He moved then, striding past her horrified eyes, straight for the front door.

"No!" she gasped, diving for him in a vain effort to stop him. She may as well have been trying to tackle a tight end for the Forty-niners. He merely proceeded to drag her the rest of the way, opening the door before she could do more than moan in despair.

Trace Walker smiled down at them with impartial benevolence. "Sure took you long enough, Patrick. Are you guys ready?"

If her cheeks had been flushed before, it was nothing compared to the scarlet mortification that washed over her then. Slowly she detached her stranglehold from Blackheart's neck, slowly she tried to right her dress and brush the tumbled hair away from her face.

"Hello, Trace," she managed serenely, and Blackheart burst out in unrepentant laughter. "What are you doing here?"

"Didn't Patrick tell you? The Senator was delayed in Santa Barbara—he'll meet you at the dinner. He asked Patrick and me to pick you up. Didn't you tell her, Patrick?" Trace's handsome face creased in confusion.

"I didn't get around to it," Blackheart replied innocently.

"You—you unspeakable piece of garbage," Ferris said in a low voice. "You miserable, slimy piece of crud. You—" His hand caught her wrist just as she was about to hit another human being for the first time in twenty years.

"I know a very good way of stopping your mouth, lady," he said lightly. "And I don't mind if I have an audience."

"You two got something going?" Trace inquired curiously. "Kate told me you did, but I thought that Ferris was engaged to the senator."

"We have nothing going," Ferris said icily. "Apart from dire enmity. I'm glad to know Blackheart, Inc., is so sure of themselves that they can leave the place they're supposed to be guarding with easy minds. You haven't bothered to wonder whether someone might not break in ahead of time, or any other mundane consideration, have you?"

"Not to worry, Ferris," Trace said jovially. "Patrick and I have got it all under control. The general security staff is watching things right now, Kate is sitting on the emeralds with three large men surrounding her, and the alarm systems are fully operational. Everything's fine. You ready?"

Blackheart was still holding onto her hand, but the iron grip had softened, the thumb absently stroking the inside of her wrist and sending melting little tremors up and down her spine. And she was standing there like a fool, reacting to it.

Quickly she snatched her hand out of his loose clasp. "I'll be ready in five minutes. I have to repair my makeup."

Blackheart grinned. "I guess you do. I'll feed the cat for you."

As long as Trace was such an interested observer, Ferris had to content herself with an answering glare. Without another word she disappeared into the bathroom, determined to stall as long as possible. She didn't care if she jeopardized the Von Emmerling emeralds, the Puffin Ball or her engagement. She needed time to compose herself before she had to face Phillip's trusting blue eyes. Especially when she knew the greatest betrayal wasn't Blackheart's, it was the gnawing longing in the pit of her stomach, the ache in her heart, the hunger in her loins. And she wasn't leaving that bathroom until she conquered it. At least temporarily.

Blackheart was right. She did look thoroughly kissed. Staring at her reflection in the mirror for a long moment, Ferris let out a deep, trembling sigh. "Damn his soul to hell," she whispered. "What in God's name am I going to do?"

"ARE YOU READY? Olivia, do you hear me?" Dale's querulous tones were definitely getting on her nerves. She would have to be circumspect in divorcing him. He had a vindictive streak—if she pushed him far enough he wouldn't mind destroying himself just to get at her.

"I hear you, Dale." She turned from the window, icy cool and elegant in a pale-blue silk dress that matched the wintry blue of her eyes. "I was just wondering how our friend was handling things."

"Oh, I don't think there's any problem. You have an innate talent for putting the fear of God into anyone. Things will be just as you planned."

"I do hope so," she said mildly as he draped a silver fox stole around her narrow shoulders. "Because not only would I be very displeased if something went wrong tonight, I would also have to bring the two of you down with me. And none of us would like that, would we?"

"No, Olivia."

His agreement was mumbled, but Olivia thought she could see a furtive flash of hate in his milky blue eyes. Good. Hate and anger kept you on your toes. As long as Dale was actively hostile, she didn't worry about him. It was when he grew affable that he became careless.

It was their third, unwilling partner who troubled her. The partner that was right now in place, eagle eyes trained on the Von Emmerling emeralds. Olivia had managed to drown all objections and doubts with her forceful personality, but from now on she had to rely on the residual force of her orders. There was no way she could be on hand, reminding her minions of what was expected of them.

She took a deep gulp of the damp, chilly fog that blanketed the city. *A good night for a jewel robbery,* she thought, a little cat's smile curving her lips. She could only wonder whether John Patrick Blackheart might agree.

Chapter Thirteen

Ferris stood off to one side, half hidden by the heavy damask
draperies that shut the fog-ridden night away from the gaiety
of the crowded ballroom. The Puffin Ball was a smashing success, socially, artistically, and financially, and yet Ferris had
never felt worse in her life.

The third winner of the Von Emmerling emeralds, a stocky
brunette with the build of a fireplug and the voice of a sea gull
was whirling around the dance floor in the arms of her equally
unprepossessing husband. She'd chosen an unfortunate shade
of chartreuse chiffon for her dress, succeeding in making the
garish old emeralds look almost tacky in the candlelight.
They'd fared better earlier. The first winner had been a slight,
feathery blonde in pure white. Blue-blooded to her fingertips,
she'd done the jewels proud for the two hours she'd worn them,
giving them a stately elegance. As had the second winner, a
fashionably blue-haired matriarch. And even if number three
hadn't quite the style or grace, she more than made up for it in
enthusiasm, Ferris thought wearily, leaning back into the
drapes. Who was she to sit in judgment?

Damn, would she like to sit, though. From the moment she'd
arrived she'd been on display, an ornament on Phillip's very
urbane arm. She'd smiled till her jaw ached, her teeth felt
windburned and her eyes were permanently crinkled. She'd
shaken hands and chatted and danced and ate, and right now
all she wanted to do was crawl under a blanket and hide. Her
head hurt, her feet hurt, everything about her was a mass of
pain. She would have given ten years off her life to go home

right then, but she knew it was out of the question. Phillip had
let her escape, reluctantly, when she insisted there was some
important lady in need of her. That important lady had been
herself, but Phillip didn't need to know that. He was still holding forth, this time on gun control, and part of her longed to
stay and watch with real admiration as he told each listener exactly what he or she wanted to hear. But there was a limit to her
endurance. She would have to be there until the last possible
contributor to Phillip's campaign remained, she would have to
stay until the Von Emmerling emeralds were safely stowed for
the night.

If only the Honorable Miss Smythe-Davies had been up to
the rigors of the Puffin Ball, a good many of Ferris's worries
would have been over. Somehow she knew that she wouldn't
have a moment's peace until the damned jewels were no longer
even remotely her responsibility. And then there would be no
reason ever to see John Patrick Blackheart again.

She looked down at her slender wrist. There was a bruise
there, just above the bone, a smudge of darkness against the
lightly tanned skin. Would he regret it if he saw it? She'd make
sure he'd never have that chance.

Phillip had been waiting when they arrived, long arms outstretched, that smile that could charm old ladies into giving up
their Social Security checks beaming down on her and her
companions. Blackheart had relinquished her readily enough,
almost too readily, his eyes almost black in the romantic candlelight as his mouth quirked up in wry amusement.

But there'd been no sign of amusement from then on.
Whenever Phillip drew her into an admiring circle of men,
Blackheart would be nearby, glaring at her. Every time one of
Phillip's political cronies danced with her, and the times were
far too numerous to count, Blackheart's expression darkened,
and when Phillip finally drew her to the floor, executing turns
and dips to the fatuous pleasure of almost everyone there but
Olivia Summers, his face was nothing short of thunderous.
Ferris had smiled, moving closer to her fiancé's stalwart form,
each time she had caught sight of that unrestrained fury. Until
she finally pushed him too far, and he'd cut in during the last
one.

Phillip had relinquished her with a graceful smile and a hearty clap on Blackheart's back, not noticing that Ferris's smile was forced.

"You don't have to crush my wrist," she'd hissed at Blackheart when he'd swung her into the dance. The band was playing "I Can't Get Started," and the sound was slow and sad and sensuous. If Blackheart's tumble off the side of a building had hindered his career of thievery, it certainly didn't put a crimp in his dancing. He was smooth, graceful and more than able to concentrate on other matters as his body and hers did his bidding.

"Are you enjoying yourself, Miss Byrd?" he inquired acidly, the fingers biting into her wrist.

"Definitely, Mr. Blackheart." The more she strained against his imprisoning hand, the tighter the fingers held her.

"Do you think plastering yourself against the good senator sets a proper example for his constituents?"

"No one seemed to mind," she replied coolly, ignoring the memory of Olivia's pale anger. "I don't know what your problem is."

"Don't you?" His hand tightened for a moment, then loosened, and the grim look faded from his face. "No," he murmured, half to himself. "I won't do that."

"Won't do what?" Surreptitiously she flexed her aching wrist.

"Won't drag you closer and show you in specific, physical terms what my problem happens to be," he replied.

It took her a moment to understand his meaning. "You're sick."

"On the contrary, I'm a very healthy male, with healthy reactions, particularly to long-term frustrations. I've been in somewhat the same state since Wednesday morning."

"That's no one's fault but your own," she snapped.

"I wouldn't say that. You had something to do with it, willing or not," he continued in a musing voice. "Actually, I suppose if you'd been willing . . ."

"Could you please change the subject?" Ferris's voice was a little strangled.

"Certainly. If you'll move three centimeters closer to me. I'm not radioactive," he said gently. His thumb was absently stroking her abused wrist, the gentle caress sending shivers down her spine.

She looked up at him then, met his gaze directly. "As far as I'm concerned, you're even more dangerous."

His eyes were dark with a distant humor and something else, something she vainly hoped no one else would recognize. What in heaven's name would people think if they saw Senator Merriam's fiancée in the arms of an ex-cat burglar looking like that?

Of course, not that many people knew they were engaged, despite the discreet rock on her left hand. And not that many people would be able to decipher the mixed emotions in Blackheart's tawny eyes. But Ferris could, and it made her knees weak.

His temper, at least, had improved. "Do you want me to waltz you out onto the terrace for a little polite necking?" he murmured against her flushed temple.

"For one thing, Blackheart, we aren't waltzing," she said caustically. "For another, it's cold and damp and foggy out there, not at all conducive to necking, polite or otherwise. And finally, don't you think you might give at least a tiny portion of your attention to the Von Emmerling emeralds? After all, we're paying a rather exorbitant sum to have you protect them—I would think you'd like to earn your keep."

"Oh, but I am. As the only guest here under an assumed name, you're still my chief suspect. My assistants are watching the emeralds themselves."

"Don't be absurd, Blackheart. You know as well as I do I wouldn't steal those damned jewels. I didn't even take a raffle ticket."

"Maybe you still regret not taking the red shoes," he said. "Maybe you've been secretly acting out your aggressions, stealing here and there to make up for that one act of self-control," he continued, unmoved by her anger.

"I wish I'd never told you that," she said in a deceptively quiet tone of voice. "I should have known you'd use it against me."

"I wouldn't use it against you, love," he said softly, all the teasing gone from his eyes.

"You'd use anything to get your own way." She was horrified to feel sudden tears springing to her eyes.

There was no way he could miss them. "Francesca, love, I'm sorry," he said, stricken.

"Go watch your damned emeralds," she said, pulling out of his arms and moving with lowered head across the dance floor. She could feel curious eyes on her, but when she raised her head, the only face she saw was that of Olivia Summers, that cool-bitch smile on her perfectly shaped lips.

But if Blackheart had regretted his words, his actions the rest of the night didn't show it. To be sure, they kept their distance by unspoken mutual consent. But those dark eyes followed her, watching her when she least expected it, and she could no longer read their enigmatic expression.

And she watched him, from over Phillip's tall, broad shoulder, past Regina's stately coiffure, beyond the punch bowl and over the champagne. And every now and then his eyes would meet hers, and sparks would shoot through her body, and she'd wonder how Phillip could miss her very strong physical reactions.

Some of her tension must have penetrated, for at the end of the last dance he'd sent her upstairs. "You're wound up as tight as a spring, Ferris. Why don't you go upstairs and lie down for a few minutes? I can carry on without you. You've had a grueling week, I'm sure."

"So have you, traipsing all over the state," she replied conscientiously.

"Yes, darling, but I'm used to it," he assured her. "And I haven't got a tense bone in my body. I thrive on this sort of thing. I thought you did, too."

It would be useless to deny it. If she could say one thing for Phillip, it was that he was abnormally perceptive. "I usually do," she admitted. "I suppose it's been a little much for me tonight."

"Well, you go on upstairs and lie down for a bit. Try some deep breathing, all right?" He gave her his most winning smile. "You're as nervous as a cat."

Ferris couldn't help it, she winced at the simile. "All right, I will, Phillip." Reaching up on tiptoes, she kissed him on his smooth, scented, clean-shaven cheek. "I'll be back before too long."

"Don't hurry, darling. I can hold down the fort."

With a smile, she turned to leave. And there was Blackheart again, that still, unreadable expression on his face. He'd seen her kiss Phillip, and Ferris told herself she was glad. She was only sorry she hadn't given him a more enthusiastic embrace, just to make certain Blackheart understood how things stood.

But the problem was, Blackheart probably understood far better than she did. "There you are, Phil," he said lightly, ignoring her. "Dale Summers was looking for you."

"Thanks, Patrick. See that my lady gets upstairs for a rest, would you? She's worn out on her feet and refuses to admit it."

"Be glad to," he said blandly. "Come on, Ferris." He held out his black-clad arm.

There was no way she could avoid it. Phillip was watching her, concern clouding those big blue eyes that were a major asset in his political career. She put her hand on Blackheart's arm, and she could feel the steel of clenched muscles beneath her light touch. One strong, well-shaped hand covered hers with unnecessary force, and Phillip turned away.

Without a word he led her to the hallway, past a throng of merrymakers, up the stairs, both of them ignoring the curious glances cast their way. He stopped halfway up the wide, curving stairs, removing his warm, angry hand from hers, pulling his arm from her light grasp. "I think the senator's lady is more than capable of finding a bedroom on her own. You've made it clear you don't want my help."

She stared at him, a sudden, unwary delight filling her face. "You're jealous," she said, her voice soft with wonder.

His black expression didn't change. "Damn straight. I'd like to go back and rip Phillip's tongue out. If you marry him and spend the rest of your life as Mrs. Senator Ferris Byrd Merriam, you'll deserve it."

"How about ending my life as Mrs. President Ferris Byrd Merriam," she taunted. She shouldn't have, she knew it, but this unexpected fury was so flattering it went straight to her head. She wanted more of it, more proof that she mattered to him, no matter how dangerous it was seeking it.

"How about Mrs. Francesca Berdahofski Blackheart?"

That effectively wiped the smile off her face. "What?" she managed in a choked voice. "Are you serious?"

"That look of pained disbelief is hardly flattering," Blackheart drawled. "No, I wasn't serious. Never trust a cat burglar, Ferris Byrd. You've made your bed; you can lie in it." Without another word, he turned and left her on the stairs.

That was when her headache had started. For a brief moment she watched him go, wondering whether he really would rip Phillip's silver tongue out, whether there was any molecule of seriousness when he'd asked her to marry him. Of course there wasn't. She shook her head, trying to clear the mass of confusion, and continued up the stairs.

How did the man manage to move so silently, she wondered. It didn't seem to matter what he wore on his feet—he'd crept up on her in dress shoes, Nikes and Tony Lama boots. Could she ever learn to move about as silently?

The second floor was far too brightly lit and noisy. Practicing her quiet moves, she continued on up the broad staircase, passing only one or two curious guests. If she could only perfect it enough to sneak up on Blackheart and scare the spit out of him, just once, she'd die a happy woman. If you stepped just the right way on the ball of your foot, she discovered—

"Darling." A woman's voice sighed deeply, and she heard the rustle of clothing.

Ferris froze in place. The third-floor hallway was dimly lit, the open door to the bedroom was a pool of light on the floor. She had better than average eyesight, even in those less than perfect conditions, and she had no trouble at all recognizing Olivia Summers clasped in a fevered embrace. And the man holding her was distinctive enough. She'd know Trace Walker anywhere.

Never in her life had Ferris been so embarrassed and so fascinated. Cool, snotty Olivia wasn't just kissing Trace Walker, she was climbing all over him, her greedy hands pawing at him. He seemed to be enduring the attention with good humor, even if Ferris suspected his heart wasn't in it.

And then her hackles began to rise, as she recognized which bedroom the two of them had chosen for their tryst. The third-floor front bedroom was where the Von Emmerling emeralds were to be kept when they weren't on display or hanging around some lady's neck. And sure enough, that's exactly where they were, clasped around Olivia's skinny throat, the bracelet encircling the wrist that was traveling down toward Trace's lean buttocks. They looked prettier than Ferris remembered them, more delicate, and the emeralds shone more brightly.

Of course, it was probably a coincidence. Trace had been keeping the emeralds company, and Olivia had decided to keep Trace company, since Blackheart seemed to have no time for her. But Ferris couldn't stand around and let them use a fortune's worth of jewels as an erotic toy. She was going to have to interrupt them, no matter how embarrassing just such a move would be. And she'd better do it soon—Olivia's hands were getting positively indecent. Ferris caught the flash of the two-carat emerald ring before Olivia's hand slid down in Trace's front, and she could feel her face flushing. Damn them both, for putting her in such a position. It was just lucky that she'd come up here when she did.

She was about to clear her throat when she noticed the small dim figure by the far door. It was Kate Christiansen watching the embracing couple. She was wearing an unflattering floor-length dress of peach chiffon that made her short body look dumpy, and the expression on her face was a mixture of anger and such pain that it hurt Ferris to see it. She just stood there, her anguished eyes dark in her freckled face, too distraught to notice Ferris standing there like a voyeur.

Slowly, imperceptibly, Ferris backed away. Kate would interrupt them in another moment or two. Even if she wasn't sure she could trust one of Blackheart's associates, she knew that between the two of them the jewels would be safe. And there was nothing to worry about. Olivia came from a family as old as the San Francisco hills, and the Summers fortune was equally legendary. She had no need to filch the Von Emmerling emeralds. As well suspect Regina Merriam of trying to run off with them.

By the time Ferris reached the stairs she could hear the voices from the bedroom, low, slightly embarrassed voices. There would be no problem.

THE TWO WOMEN watched Trace Walker leave the room, an embarrassed angle to his shoulder. She'd played it well, Olivia thought. Trace was so embarrassed at having been caught in such a compromising position that he'd put the responsibility of the emeralds low on his list of priorities. He hadn't liked the expression on Kate's face one tiny bit. As she'd suspected, there was something more there than poor little Kate recognized. Her grand passion might not be as unrequited as she supposed. But fortunately for Olivia, neither Kate nor Trace had any inkling of the other's feelings.

Kate was glaring at her, her lower lip thrust out unattractively, her eyes wide and angry. Really, the whole thing was laughable.

"Don't glare at me, Kate, darling," Olivia said easily, unfastening the clasp of the phony emeralds. "Have you got the real jewels?"

Chapter Fourteen

Her apartment was still and silent as she let herself in. Phillip waited by her door, a pleased smile on his tired, handsome face. "You're dead on your feet," he observed kindly. "I won't come in."

She hadn't invited him in, but perversely she was annoyed. "I probably won't be able to sleep anyway."

"Sure you will. It's almost four in the morning. Just pour yourself a glass of Dubonnet and you'll be dead to the world," he assured her, and immediately Ferris was determined to stay awake till dawn. "I was glad to see that you and Patrick managed to get along," he added. "They did a great job, don't you think?"

"I suppose so. No one stole the emeralds, and that's the main thing." It had been with mixed emotions that she had watched the assembled staff of Blackheart, Inc., drive off with the beautiful gems safe in their possession. Now that it was all over, the Von Emmerling emeralds had suddenly taken on an added luster. She hadn't liked them much when she first saw them, but now that the responsibility was gone she found they were much prettier and more delicate than she'd first thought.

Blackheart must have lost his touch, though. He'd barely given them a cursory glance as he'd shoved the velvet cases into a briefcase that resembled something out of a James Bond movie. Ferris had little doubt that if some unauthorized person tried to open it, it would shoot poison darts at the very least. And he'd driven away from her, out of her life, without a backward glance.

"You'll have to admit that Patrick isn't so bad," Phillip persisted.

Ferris looked up at him then, suddenly curious. "He was no major problem. Why are you so concerned, Phillip?"

Phillip was a consummate politician. Even when he was avoiding a direct answer, he looked you straight in the eye. But this time he made no effort to avoid it. "Something my mother said," he replied lightly.

"She told you Blackheart and I were involved?" Ferris questioned, horrified that they had been so obvious, horrified that Regina Merriam would have said something to her son.

"Exactly the opposite. Apparently you two fight like cats and dogs. I've never known you not to get along with someone, no matter how offensive you find them. My mother was concerned, and so was I. You know how much Mother adores you. She's always considered you far too good for me. She wants what's best for you—my interests come second."

"Don't be ridiculous, Phillip, your mother worships you."

He grinned, that engaging grin that had melted the hearts of women from eight months old to eighty years. "Of course she does. How could she help it? But that doesn't mean she'll sacrifice your happiness for my well-being. Think about it, Ferris."

"Think about what?" she said irritably. "I don't happen to get along with Patrick Blackheart. I don't approve of him—does that make it a federal crime?"

"You've got a bleeding heart, Ferris. You approve of ax murderers when they're properly repentant. There's something else, and—"

"Phillip, I think you're the one who's overtired," she interrupted ruthlessly. "You're making a mountain out of a molehill. If you want to talk about this, in depth, we can do so tomorrow when I've had more rest. All right?"

He gave her his charming, rueful smile. "I'd like that, darling, I really would. But I've got to be in Santa Cruz for the next three days, and then Sacramento, and then—"

"Never mind. I'll be coming back to work for you now that the Puffin Ball is finished." Something in his expression alerted her. "Won't I, Phillip?"

"Yes," he allowed. "Though perhaps not in the same capacity. But we can always—"

"Why not? I like being administrative assistant." Her voice was getting a little shrill, and she quickly toned it down.

"Of course you do," he said soothingly. "And I love having you there—there's no one I count on more. But Jack Reginald has a son in need of a job, and—"

"And Jack Reginald is making substantial contributions to your upcoming campaign," Ferris said lightly.

"You understand the political facts of life as well as anyone, Ferris. You scratch my back and I'll scratch yours, and that sort of thing."

"I understand completely," she said, her voice calm and accepting. "And you're right, I am dead tired. Why don't you give me a call this week when you have a chance, and we can work something out?"

"I'll call you Sunday at—"

"I won't be in Sunday," she broke in. "I have other plans."

"When will you be in, then?" He managed to look both hurt and forgiving at the same time. A talented man, was Phillip Merriam, she mused.

"I don't know. You'll just have to keep trying till you get me."

He stood there, still in the doorway, half in her apartment, half out, half in her life, half out, and Ferris fingered her diamond ring, considering her options. She'd never been a fool, and practicality told her not to make a move she might later regret. Even though deep in her heart of hearts she knew that move would have to be made, and soon, tonight was not the night. She left the ring in place. For now.

"Well," he said finally, his usual urbanity wiping out his temporary frustration. "Well. You get some sleep, then, darling. I'll somehow manage to squeeze a few days out toward the end of the week, or maybe early next week, and we'll go someplace. How does that sound?"

"Just fine."

"Do have a glass of Dubonnet. It will help you relax."

She looked up quite fearlessly into his clear blue eyes. "I," she said, "don't like Dubonnet."

"Well," he said. "Well. Good night, then." He still seemed uncharacteristically uncertain, and Ferris felt a moment's sympathy. Reaching up on her toes, she kissed that sweet-smelling, smooth-shaven cheek. And there was no way she could fool herself into thinking it wasn't goodbye.

"Good night, Phillip."

His footsteps clattered down the two flights of stairs. She stood there at the open door for a long moment, then shut it after the disappearing sound of his departure. She looked at the three locks for a moment, reached for them, then dropped her hand, shrugging. Nothing would keep Blackheart out if he wanted to get in. Not that he would, ever again. It had been a dangerous few days, and part of her had found it irresistibly attractive, playing with fire. But it was safely over now, and she could go back to living her life.

Blackie had no intention of spending the fogbound night in her apartment. She met his look of haughty demand with an affectionate scratch behind the ears, and then he was out on her terrace and gone a moment later. For a moment she considered leaving the door open a crack. It was cool—about fifty degrees outside—but the air was refreshing to her flushing cheeks. She could always huddle under a blanket for warmth.

She kicked off her heels and let her bare feet sink into the carpet. Phillip was right; Phillip was always right. What was she going to do without him telling her what she needed? She did need her bed, and she needed a drink to take the edge off the nervous energy that was still sparking through her. Whenever she closed her eyes she could see Blackheart's eyes, watching her, following her, wanting her? Damn, but he gave up easily.

She must be more tired than she thought, to have regretted his sudden lack of interest. She trailed out into the kitchen, and poured herself a small glass of Drambuie and wandered back into the darkened living room. Without bothering to turn on the lights, she curled up on the sofa. Like a fool she'd left the Brie out when she'd taken off with Trace and Blackheart hours earlier, and Blackie had made a hearty meal of most of it. He'd even been piggy enough to sample a few crackers, but obviously found them less than entrancing.

Reaching forward, Ferris took a non-felined cracker and bit into it, following it with a sip of the sweet, rich Drambuie. A trip to her sister Cecilia's might be a good idea. Cecilia could be counted on for her good sense, her warmth and her marvelous ability to give a person space. A week spent at her ramshackle farmhouse, surrounded by half a dozen nieces and nephews in all shapes and sizes, with the soothing example of Cecilia's and Joe's love for each other and their numerous offspring, and she should be able to view her life with a better sense of reality.

The sound of the buzzer startled her out of her pleasant reverie. Leaning back she stared at her blank white door for a long moment. Of course it could be Phillip, come back to have his wicked way with her. He'd looked more than faintly disgruntled when he'd left, maybe he thought it was time to show her who was boss. This time she would give him his ring.

Or maybe it was the police, come to tell her that Blackheart, Inc., had never showed up at the Mark Hopkins suite of the Honorable Miss Smythe-Davies and was now wanted for grand larceny.

Or maybe it was Blackheart himself, come to tell her he loved her and renew that whimsical offer of marriage. No, that was the one person it wouldn't be. He wouldn't bother to ring the bell, he'd just come right in.

The bell rang again, interrupting her lazy thoughts. Whoever it was, she wasn't about to get up from her comfortable perch on the love seat. If she could help it, she wasn't going to stand on her feet for twenty-four hours. She could crawl into her bed.

One more ring. She considered it, then shrugged. If it was a rapist-ax murderer, he would doubtless find a way to get in anyway. Right now she really didn't give a damn. "Come in," she called in a throaty voice. "It's open." And she took another sip of her Drambuie.

There was a long pause on the other side of the door, and then it opened. And Blackheart stood there, a package in one hand, a furious expression on his face.

IT HAD BEEN a struggle for him, all night long. Blackheart wasn't used to being consumed by jealousy, he wasn't used to giving a damn. He wasn't so egocentric that he had to have every woman who didn't want him. When he was turned down, as every man was now and then, be he Mortimer Snerd or Robert Redford, then he usually shrugged his shoulders and looked further. But the more Francesca Berdahofski dodged, feinted, refused, insulted, fought, and struggled, the more determined he became.

He still couldn't figure out why he'd said that to her on the wide, busy staircase. Just to see the shock widen her eyes? Except that he'd been even more shocked. He'd never proposed to a woman in his life, never even been tempted. And the moment the words were out of his mouth, he hadn't wanted to recall them. In fact, he'd wanted to throw the troublesome wench over his shoulder like something out of an Errol Flynn movie and carry her out of that house, and be damned to her charming senator and her idiotic pretensions.

Phillip Merriam hadn't made things any easier. He'd been so damned decent, so revoltingly good-fellowship that Blackheart really had been tempted to rip out his tongue. If Blackheart was anywhere near the decent human being he tried to be, he would have then and there renounced his designs on Francesca Berdahofski's luscious body. But decency was in short supply nowadays. He could keep his hands off the Von Emmerling emeralds, but he couldn't keep his hands off Francesca.

He'd left Kate and Trace at the Mark Hopkins. Neither of them was looking particularly happy, but he racked that up to their tangled relationship. If he were the meddling kind, he'd drop a hint in Trace's inattentive ear. But then, maybe Trace knew, and figured that ignoring it was the kindest way to deal with Kate's languishing glances. Maybe.

He'd swung by his apartment, changing out of that damned monkey suit. He hated full dress nowadays. For so long it had been his working costume. He couldn't put on a tuxedo without remembering other nights, long ago, and his hands would start sweating.

He still hadn't decided how big a fool he was being. He'd probably get to Francesca's ridiculous little apartment and find Phillip Merriam in that oversize bed. And then what would he do? Slink away into the fog like a beaten dog? Or maybe rip out Phillip's tongue.

Tonight wasn't a night for a touch of B and E, just on the off chance that the good senator had finally chosen to initiate his virgin bride. He took the two flights of steps slowly, silently, unaccountably nervous. Would she be asleep already? Would she glare at him out of those green eyes? Was he being ridiculously sentimental? Maybe he should turn around, give it a few days.

Damn, he was acting like an adolescent boy on his first date. His hands were sweating for sure now, and shaking just a tiny bit as he reached for the bell. There was no way he could wait any longer. Push had come to shove, and he wasn't going to sleep until he knew that she was irrevocably in love with the good senator. Not that he could blame her. Any woman with good sense would be. The man was handsome, rich, charming, friendly, and possessed of a great mother. What did a man with a past like John Patrick Blackheart have to offer in comparison? As he rang the bell again, the box beneath his arm suddenly felt very heavy. Where the hell was she?

BLACKHEART HAD CHANGED his clothes, Ferris noticed. He was wearing jeans again, and his boots, and the black, body-hugging turtleneck beneath a corduroy jacket. She had never liked turtleneck shirts on men, but on Blackheart the effect was absolutely demoralizing. She wondered what he was angry about now.

"Why didn't you lock your door?" he demanded crossly, shutting the heavy door behind him and snapping each lock, including the chain. "Don't you realize there are dangerous criminals out there, waiting to prey on people like you?"

"It didn't seem worth the trouble. In the past four years the only person who's broken into the place has been you. And I knew those locks wouldn't keep you out."

"Certainly not these flimsy ones," he scoffed. "A stoned-out junkie with a credit card could get through those locks."

"Why would a stoned-out junkie have a credit card?" Ferris inquired prosaically.

"That's beside the point. Where's the good senator?" He moved toward her then, with his usual feline grace.

"Not here. What do you want, Blackheart? I thought we were finished with our dealings. Did the emeralds get safely back to Miss Smythe-Davies?"

"I wouldn't be here if they didn't."

"No, you wouldn't," she mused. "What's in the box?"

Blackheart pulled it out from under his arm, looking at it as if he'd never seen it before. "A present for you."

"From whom?"

"From me, of course. Don't just recline there like Cleopatra waiting for an asp," he snapped. He tossed the box to her, and she caught it expertly. "Open it."

She held it in her hand, weighing it, and her green eyes were extremely wary. "What is it? A time bomb? I don't hear any ticking."

"I sent the time bomb to the senator," he said. "May I have a drink? It's been a long night."

"Help yourself." She still didn't move, just stared down at the rectangular box. "My feet hurt too much to get up."

A moment later he was back, a glass of whisky in one hand, and he tossed the jacket across a chair before sitting down beside her, at the opposite end of the love seat. She had to pull her feet up, and she eyed him with a mixture of suspicion and wariness. If she didn't know better she'd say he was nervous. Maybe it *was* a time bomb. Or a rattlesnake. She shook the box again, but only a quiet thud rewarded her straining ears.

"It won't bite, Francesca," he said quietly. "Consider it a farewell present. Open it."

"You going somewhere?" she inquired in a desultory voice as she pulled at the wrappings.

"I hadn't planned to. What about you? Have you and the good senator set a date yet?" He took a sip of his drink, and his hand shook slightly. He was nervous, Ferris thought with amazement.

The brown paper came off, and the box underneath it read Ramon's. She looked up at him. "Ramon's what?" she queried lightly, mystified.

"Open it," he said again.

It was a pair of red shoes. The most beautiful red shoes she'd ever seen, made of shiny, metallic crimson, with high stacked heels, diamond buckles and no toes. There were little metal taps on the heel and toe, and she turned to look at Blackheart, her face very still.

He cleared his throat. "The taps are for when you dance. You're supposed to click them against the floor, and—"

"I know what the taps are for." Her voice was very quiet in the darkened room. "Why?"

He didn't pretend to misunderstand. "I thought you ought to have something to remind you of Francesca Berdahofski when you're Mrs. Senator Merriam."

The shoes lay in her lap, and she stared down at them. She was used to tears. She cried when she was frightened, she cried when she was unhappy. But she couldn't understand why she felt like crying right then, why the tears were stinging her eyelids, burning the back of her throat, taking control of her body so that she sat there and shook, imperceptibly, as Blackheart watched her out of distant eyes.

She felt him rise from the love seat, saw the strong, beautiful hand place the empty whiskey glass on the coffee table in front of her. "Good-bye, Ferris," he said gently, leaning over to kiss her cheek. "Have a good life."

His lips brushed her cheek gently, and he could taste the dampness on his lips. He drew back, startled, as she turned her tear-streaked face up to him. "Don't call me Ferris," she said with great, hiccuping sobs. "I hate that damned name."

"Francesca..." She could feel his hand on her shoulder, the fingers strong and warm on her bare skin.

She raised her head. "And don't you dare leave me," she added, her voice raw with tears. "Don't you dare?"

It was too dark in the room to see his face through her blur of tears, but his voice was clear, with a thread of warm laughter running through it. "Oh, love, I wouldn't think of it." And he drew her weeping body off the couch and into his arms.

Chapter Fifteen

She tumbled into his arms, the tears coming faster and more freely. She could feel the tender laughter shake his strong body as he held her there, the two of them in a tangle on the floor, trapped between the love seat and the coffee table. Gentle hands held her, cradled her against that smooth black chest, as she wept furiously.

It was a very long time before the storm of tears abated. One long finger reached up and brushed her tears away, and when they had finally slowed he shifted to a more comfortable position, holding her shivering body in his arms as he kicked the table away from them and leaned back against the sofa.

"Such a great many tears," he whispered against her cloud of hair. "Did the good senator jilt you?"

She managed a watery chuckle. "Pig," she said comfortably. "I'm about to jilt the good senator. How do you do this to me, Blackheart?"

"Well, first I get you off balance, then I pull you into my arms, and then—" his mouth feathered hers "—I kiss you. Not too hard—" he did it again, lingering a moment "—just enough to get your motor started. And then I move my hand, like this. . . ." His strong hand moved up to cup her chin, holding it gently in place as he kissed her again, and this time, when his soft, tempting lips left hers, she emitted a tiny moan, her tears forgotten. "And then, when I think you're ready for it, I kiss you again. A little longer, a little deeper." And his mouth dropped once more onto hers, nibbling, tantalizing, the gentle pressure of his fingers on her jaw opening her mouth beneath his.

Slowly, delicately, his tongue slid into her mouth, gently exploring the secrets of the soft interior, and for the moment she lay quiescent against him, glorying in the feel of him. And then, with the gentle prompting of his tongue, she began to kiss him back, sliding her bare arms around his neck and meeting him thrust for thrust, the glorious hot wetness of their mouths causing tremors of desire to twist and turn through her body.

She could feel his hand fumbling in front of her, and a moment later the neckline plunged to its lowest level, the silver cord loosely entwined in Blackheart's clever fingers. Reluctantly he pulled his mouth away from hers. "There," he said, his voice rich with satisfaction. "I've been wanting to do that since I first saw you tonight. Covering up all that beautiful flesh is a crime against nature." Leaning down, his hot, wet mouth traced random, teasing patterns along the tops of her almost exposed breasts as his hands cupped their bountiful fullness.

Ferris moaned, deep in the back of her throat, and arched against his hand and mouth. The silky covering was frustration beyond bearing, but she didn't know how to tell him.

There was no need. Another gentle tug of the silken cord, and the dress tumbled to her waist. His warm, damp mouth followed, catching one rosy peak with practiced care as his hand tended the other. His tongue swirled, teased, enticed, and she could feel a knot of wanting so strong that hurt twisted deep inside her, between her legs. She could feel him beneath her soft hips, hard and pulsing against her tender, silk-covered flesh, and the knot twisted again, so that she cried out with the pain of it.

She wanted him with a longing she'd never felt before. She wanted his warm bare skin beneath her fingers, smooth and hot and hard beneath her mouth, she wanted him above her, beneath her, around her and in her, she wanted to melt into the golden wonder of his body and never escape. She wanted him and she didn't know what to do.

Slowly, reluctantly, his mouth moved from the delectable feast of her breast, leaving a warm wet path across her exposed skin as he reached for her mouth again. And this time she was more than ready for him, kissing him with all the passion and aching love that had been locked away for too long.

When he finally broke away he was as breathless as she was, and his heartbeat thudded against her hand. His eyes were staring down into hers with dreamy desire, a desire that matched her no longer controllable need.

"Will you go to bed with me, Francesca?" he asked, the words slow and quiet and very distinct.

She wanted to sink against him with a helpless sigh, she wanted to fill his mouth with hers so that there'd be no more room for words. But she owed him more than that. "Yes, Blackheart. Please. Take me to bed and show me what it can be like."

He was very strong indeed. He lifted her effortlessly in his arms, rising from their cramped position on the floor with fluid grace. He moved through the darkened, twisting apartment with the eyes of a cat, with never a misstep. The first gray light of dawn was spreading over the city as he drew her down on the gigantic bed, and his hands were gentle as he settled her among the tumbled pillows.

Slowly, deftly, his hands withdrew down the length of her body, bringing the silky gown with him. He tossed it on the floor with a disregard worthy of Ferris at her most slothful, and stood there at the foot of the bed, watching her out of warm, wanting eyes.

She could feel the intensity of his gaze washing over her, her long legs, the skimpy swathe of silken panties across her hips, the smooth torso with its gently curved stomach and her full, aching breasts.

He stripped the turtleneck over his head with one swift move, kicking off his boots as he did so. She looked away as he reached for his belt buckle, and the sound of his soft laughter mingled with the rasp of the zipper, the rough slide of denim against flesh.

"Such a chicken," he chided, and in the morning twilight she dared a furtive peek at him. "Haven't you ever seen *Playgirl?*" He slid into bed with her, dropping his jeans within easy reach beside the bed.

With sudden nervousness she nodded, keeping her eyes firmly fastened to his face and nowhere lower.

"Well, I'm just like them," he said, and his hands began a warm, reassuring stroking along her bare arm.

"There seems to be a lot more of you," she said gruffly.

Leaning over, he kissed her gently on the mouth. "Nothing more than you can handle, I promise you."

"Are you sure?" Her voice was plainly doubtful, and she cast a nervous, scuttling glance downward before returning to his face.

Slowly, carefully, so as not to frighten her, his hand slid down her arm until he reached her wrist. He brought her hand to his mouth, kissing each trembling finger, one by one, letting his tongue gently caress her palm. And then he placed her open, relaxed hand on his chest, letting her become accustomed to the feel of his flesh against her, the muscle and hardness. Slowly he moved her hand downward, sensitive to her slightest hesitation. Her eyes met his, mesmerized, as he brought her hand down to meet his swollen maleness.

The quick intake of breath was his own, and when he opened his eyes again she was smiling at him. "There," he breathed. "That's not so bad, is it?"

She shook her head. He released her wrist, but her hand stayed where it was, the fingers cool and curious on his fevered skin. Slowly she encircled him, tugging gently, and he moaned softly.

She pulled away, suddenly skittish. "Did I hurt you?"

With a lazy smile he shook his head, recapturing her curious hand. "It feels very good," he whispered against her lips. "Too good." And he moved his hands to her waiting body, encircling her slender waist with his long deft fingers. They slid across her gently rounded stomach, slid inside the skimpy bikini panties and drew them downward over her unresisting legs.

"Oh, love," he breathed, "you are so very beautiful." Gently, carefully he nuzzled her full, straining breasts as his hands moved back up her legs, sliding inexorably toward their ultimate goal.

And then he found her, one large, strong hand reaching the damp, heated core of her, and she bit back a cry of part frustration, part joy, part unadulterated panic. Her legs instinctively clamped together, and her hands left the delights of his body to ward him off.

He was prepared for her panic. One hand caught her wrists in a gentle but unbreakable grip, and he threw a strongly muscled leg over hers, pulling them apart. She whimpered, struggling for a moment, and then she saw the stark whiteness of the scar along the length of his leg. There were two of them, running parallel from mid-calf to mid-thigh. And suddenly the fight left her. This was Blackheart, her nemesis, a man who had somehow managed to get closer to her than any human being outside her family ever had. And he was about to get even closer.

"Let go of my hands," she whispered. He must have felt the change, felt the tension leave her. He released her wrists, and she twined her arms around his waist, pulling herself up close to him, pressing her breasts against the smooth planes of his chest, pressing her trembling hips against that frightening, enticing arousal, pressing her mouth hungrily against his, giving and receiving a kiss that was a release in itself. And this time when his hand slid down over the gentle curve of her hip she turned for him, opening her legs at his gentle urging.

She hadn't known it could be so sweet. His hands were clever, so clever, and she could feel that burning need within her escalate out of control, until she knew she'd explode if she had to wait any longer. She touched him, and he was as damp as she was. She looked up through a haze of desire, puzzled, and his warm laugh shook against her swollen breasts.

"It's just me, wanting you," he said softly, his lips brushing hers, and she smiled against his mouth.

"Me too," she whispered. "Now, Blackheart. Please." Her voice was plaintive, polite, and he kissed her again.

"In a moment." Once more his hand reached down, the gentle, insinuating strokes preparing her for a more overwhelming invasion. She arched against his hand, her eyes closed, her senses slipping away.

And then his body covered her, and she could feel him against her, hard and strong and needful. She wasn't expecting the pain, the sharp burning of stubbornly resisting flesh. Her quiet moan turned into a whimper as he pressed against her, and she could feel his hands against her hips, holding her still for his steady invasion. When he came to rest, deep inside her, he was panting, beads of sweat sparkling against the dark planes of his face, and his tawny brown eyes were sorrow-filled.

"I didn't want to hurt you," he whispered, and she could feel the tension in his body, the rigid control in his muscles as he held himself above her.

Already the pain had begun to recede, in its place a wonderful lassitude that overlay that still-burning need that she didn't quite understand. She smiled up at him, love and longing all mixed up in a dazed, dreamy expression. "It's okay," she murmured. "It's more than okay. It's...very...nice..." The words drifted in a gasp of pleasure as he began to move, as his iron control began to melt within the heat of her body. The hands that held her hips slid down and wrapped her legs around him, and his mouth caught hers in a searing kiss.

And she was lost, lost in the tumble of flesh, pulsing heat and aching want that somehow coalesced through the shifting, pounding rhythms of his body and hers. She was there, floating, dreaming, awash in a current of slumbering sensual wanderings, when suddenly it peaked, and she was gone, lost in some starry universe with only Blackheart for safety.

In the distance she felt him collapse against her, felt the shudders rack his body, heard the distant echo of his voice. What had he said to her, when she was consumed in that fiery tumult? She could no longer hear the distant echo of the words.

But the vast sense of well-being had washed over her body and now enveloped her in a cocoon that was too strong to be denied. Her low wail of despair when he gently extricated himself from her embrace was greeted with a low, loving laugh.

"I'll be right back, love," he whispered. She was too sleepy and too peaceful to open her eyes, to ask him where he was going. She heard the water running in the bathroom, and then he was back beside her, traversing the huge bed with far more grace than she usually managed.

"What're you doing?" she murmured sleepily.

"Administering first aid." A cool, wet cloth was placed between her legs, and then he drew her into the circle of his arms, her head resting naturally against his shoulder. "Poor angel," he murmured. "Are you feeling battered?"

"Gloriously abused," she said against the smooth skin. "Are you going to make a habit of this?" The moment the sleepy words were out of her mouth she could have bit her tongue. She had been determined not to make demands her body and soul and heart craved. But it was hard to be strong and independent when you were lying in your lover's arms.

If Blackheart felt her withdrawal, he didn't comment on it. "As often as I can. Would you fancy a pair of green shoes next?"

She should have been furious. Instead she giggled.

His strong hand reached up and brushed the tumbled hair away from her flushed, sleepy face. "I like to hear you laugh. You should do it more often." He kissed her nose. "Do you have any regrets?"

"Fishing for compliments, Blackheart?"

"Just curious."

"You're asking me if I should have surrendered my virginity on my wedding night to a rich, handsome man who happens to love me, rather than lose it to a sneak thief who's offered me nothing." She said it baldly.

"Don't forget the shoes," he said lightly, but she could feel the tension in his arms. "Answer me, Francesca. Are you sorry you didn't give the good senator his pound of flesh?"

She smiled against his sweat-damp skin. How unlike Blackheart to need reassurance. She never would have thought he'd suffer from a guilty conscience. "No."

"No?" he echoed.

"No, I don't regret it. No, I don't wish I'd waited for Phillip. I'm content. Blissfully content." She snuggled closer, and felt the tension leave his body as his arm drew her even closer.

They were silent for a while, and Ferris was almost asleep when his warm, sweet voice broke through her lethargy. "You forgot to ask."

"Forgot to ask what?" she murmured.

"You don't want to end up like your brothers and sisters, do you? Or did you do something about it?"

"No." Ferris was suddenly wide awake, pulling her protesting body out of his arms in sudden horror. "Oh, God, no! I forgot all about it."

Blackheart laughed, a heartless laugh. "That must be a first for you."

"This isn't a laughing matter, Blackheart. It's just the wrong time of month, and I—"

"Hush, love." He was still laughing, and his hands were gentle as he pulled her back to him. "There's nothing to worry about. I took care of it."

"You did? Why didn't I notice?" She nestled back against him, still doubtful.

"You were, uh, otherwise occupied. Don't worry, sweetheart—next time I'll let you help me."

"Are you sure . . . ?"

"I'm sure, love." Reaching down, he rummaged through the jeans he'd dropped beside the bed, and a moment later half a dozen silver packets rained down on her. "Satisfied?"

"Silly question," she murmured, her hand drifting lazily downward across his stomach. She watched with interest as the muscles contracted. "Blackheart?"

"Mmmmh?"

"Thank you."

He looked down at her, a lazy smile lighting his face. "My pleasure, love. My pleasure."

SHE DIDN'T want to hear the pounding. She felt too good, lying curled up against Blackheart's warm skin, nestled in the cradle of his body, his arm possessive around her sleeping body. She didn't know when they'd gone to sleep the final time— there wasn't a clock in sight and she hadn't really cared. Her body ached in a thousand places, she ought to get up and have a long soak in the tub, but she had no intention of moving until she absolutely had to. The last thing she wanted was for reality to intrude.

But the damned pounding continued, and she felt Blackheart stir beside her. "Who's that?" he whispered against her ear, his tongue making tiny, darting forays that were stirring fires better left banked, given her physical condition.

"Nobody I want to see," she replied, moving closer and pressing up against him. "They can't know we're here. Let's just pretend we went to Australia."

Blackheart looked disturbed and overwhelmingly young in the late morning light. His long brown hair was rumpled around his sleepy face, and the white quilt they'd thrown over them sometime during the night made his tanned skin stand out in golden contrast.

But at that moment the pounding ceased, and Ferris breathed a sigh of relief. "It was the landlord, wanting to know if I had a man in here," she said, pushing him back against the sheets.

"And do you?" he questioned mischievously.

She slid her hand down across the flat plane of his stomach to brush against him tantalizingly. "I guess I do," she admitted with an air of wonder. "That's quite a surprise." She moved her hand back up, across the surface of his chest. "You're too skinny," she observed. "Very strong, but too skinny."

"I know the cause of that," he replied, nibbling on her exposed arm. "Not enough cannoli."

"Blackheart," she said, filled with an overwhelming emotion that felt uncomfortably close to love. "I—"

The pounding began again, louder than before, and Blackheart jumped, swearing, and pulled away from her. "I'm going to see who the hell it is," he said, grabbing his pants and crawling back down the bed. "And then I'll give you the attention you deserve."

"Blackheart, no!" she wailed, jumping up and heading after him. "You can't answer my door looking like that." She grabbed a robe and yanked it on, reaching the living room just as he was opening the last lock. His jeans were zipped but unbuttoned, his bare chest had a few artistic scratches that she hadn't realized she'd contributed, and there was little doubt as to what the two of them had been doing. "What if it's somebody?" she hissed.

The look he gave her would have quelled a sterner soul. "I expect it is," he said calmly, unhooking the chain and flinging the door open. Ferris held her breath, expecting Phillip, expecting Regina, expecting God knew who. But not expecting the small, dapper man who stood there, temper darkening an already overtanned face.

"Rupert," Blackheart said numbly, pulling the door open to let him storm in. "What's wrong?"

"What's wrong?" the angry man demanded. "What's wrong, you ask me? What the hell isn't wrong? You had to pick last night of all nights to do a disappearing act. Let me tell you, kid, your timing couldn't be better. Couldn't you have kept your pants on until the damned job was finished?''

Ferris flinched, looking anxiously from Blackheart's suddenly still face to the angry man in front of her. "Since no one's making introductions," she said with a last attempt at calm, "would you mind telling me who you are?"

"I'm Rupert Munz," he snapped. "And I'm this idiot's lawyer."

"Lawyer?" she echoed, her voice a little rusty. "Why were you looking for Blackheart?"

"Because, Ms Byrd, his partner was arrested last night for grand larceny. And the San Francisco police department are greatly interested in Patrick Blackheart's whereabouts."

"Grand larceny?" Ferris echoed, a horrid sense of déjà vu washing over her.

Blackheart had a grim expression on his face. "The Von Emmerling emeralds."

"There's nothing wrong with your thought processes," Rupert snapped. "And at least you had a good alibi. She'll testify?" A jerk of his head indicated Ferris, and Blackheart's eyes followed meditatively. She knew what her face looked like, mistrust and condemnation wiping out the last trace of warmth. He'd used her, and she hated him for it.

She could tell by the darkening of his face that he read her reactions clearly. Turning back to Rupert, he shrugged. "I don't know. Do you think it will come to that?"

Rupert frowned. "Who can say? They had a very nasty look on their faces when they questioned me about you. You may be about to have your first experience with the American penal system."

"No," he said sharply. "I told myself when I got out of prison in England that I'd never go back; I'll be damned if I let them pick me up when I haven't been doing a thing."

"I don't know if you'll have any say in the matter. Not if you want to help Trace," Rupert said heavily. "You can disappear for a while and leave Trace holding the bag, or..." He let the sentence trail off.

"Trace is as innocent as a lamb—he doesn't belong in jail, and you know it as well as I do. Has bail been set?" Blackheart snapped.

"Not yet. I was on my way back there when I thought I'd check here. Kate said you might be here. She's pretty upset, Patrick."

"I imagine she is." He was still staring at Ferris's shuttered face. "What do you want me to do?"

"Stay put. I'll check on what sort of evidence they have—they probably won't arrest you without something to go by. Unless they're so happy to finally be able to pin something on you that they don't bother with such technicalities. You don't need to worry—if they do, I'll slap a false arrest charge on them so fast their heads will spin."

"I don't know if that's reassuring," Blackheart said, his eyes grim.

"Don't worry about it. I'll see if I can get them to drop the charges before they actually arrest you. But keep out of sight. Let her answer the phone, the door, whatever."

She could feel those tawny brown eyes on her averted face. "I'm not sure if Ferris is willing to be Bonnie to my Clyde," he drawled. "I'll be in touch, Rupert."

Rupert opened his mouth to protest, then shut it again. "Don't let him answer the door," he ordered Ferris sharply. "Not if you don't want to see him in jail."

There was dead silence in the apartment when the door closed behind Rupert's dapper figure. Ferris kept her face averted, the old terry-cloth robe pulled tightly around her as she turned to head down the two narrow stairs to the kitchen. Her sense of betrayal was so strong that it tore at her body, engulfing her in pain that left her numb and shaken. Blackheart didn't move, but she could feel his eyes intent on her narrow back.

"Rupert was making too many assumptions," he said finally.

Somewhere she found a rusty semblance of her voice. "What was that?"

"That you don't want to see me in jail. I get the feeling you'd be very happy to see me locked up right now, with the key thrown away."

She couldn't even trust herself to look at him, much less deny his gentle accusation. "Would you make me a cup of coffee before I go?" he said suddenly.

She had no choice but to turn at that, and the look on her face was cold and angry. "You're going to abandon Trace after all," she accused him. "You're going to run off and leave him bearing the blame."

She had never seen such a look on any man's face. It was as cold and still as death, and she stumbled backward against the kitchen door in sudden panic.

An unpleasant smile curved his mouth. "I won't hit you, Ferris," he drawled. "Much as you deserve it. And you can believe what you want to believe. I'm not going to sit around and wait for the police to find me, and I'm not going to give you the chance to turn me in. I'm going out to find out who did take the emeralds, and when I find them I'm going to shove them down your throat." He brushed past her on the way to the bedroom, and she controlled the urge to flinch away. Just as she controlled the urge to fling her arms around his sleek, muscled body and beg him to tell her he was innocent.

She was still standing there when he emerged, black turtleneck pulled over his tousled head, boots on his feet, his jacket slung over his shoulder. "No coffee?" he drawled. "Nothing to send the weary felon on his way? Not even a goodbye kiss or a simple question? Such as, did you do it, Blackheart? Not that I'd find that element of doubt reassuring, but it would be a hell of a lot better than instant condemnation."

"Did you, Blackheart?"

He stared at her for a long moment. "Be damned to you," he said succinctly.

The buzz of the doorbell shattered the tension. The two combatants stood there in the narrow hallway, motionless, condemning eyes watching the other. Ferris couldn't move, couldn't breathe, could only watch him with sudden desperation shattering her heart.

The bell buzzed again, impatiently, followed by a steady pounding. A wry smile lit Blackheart's bleak face. "It would appear the police have found me."

She ran a nervous tongue over suddenly dry lips. They felt bruised to the touch, bruised from Blackheart's mouth. "It might be someone else."

"Who else would be so vehement?" Blackheart murmured. "Don't answer the door, Francesca."

His use of her real name almost convinced her. "They know we're here," she whispered.

"They probably don't have a search warrant. Just give me enough time to climb out over the terrace. Come on, lady, don't be such a damned prude. Let me go. I don't want to end up in jail for something stupid like this. It's a matter of honor."

"Honor?" she echoed, her voice rich with bitter accusation. "You call it honorable to let your best friend take the blame for your robbery?"

He froze, and the last bit of emotion died from his eyes, leaving them cold and brown as winter leaves. "Answer the damned door, lady," he said savagely.

"I didn't say I wouldn't—"

"Answer the damned door. Or I will."

She couldn't move. She could only stand there under the force of his rage and inexplicable pain and wonder if she had made the very worst mistake of her life.

"Then I will." He moved past her, careful not to touch her body, and the locks melted beneath his practiced touch.

And still she stood there, as she heard the words drift past her. "You have the right to remain silent. If you give up that right..." And when she was finally alone again in her small apartment, when Blackheart had been marched away, those awful handcuffs on his beautiful wrists, when he'd gone without a backward glance, she'd stumbled back into her bedroom and fallen on the tumbled sheets, her heart and her eyes burning with pain and disillusionment. And a doubt so horrifying that she pushed it resolutely away.

Chapter Sixteen

"Really, dear, I couldn't be more distressed," Regina Merriam murmured. "I can't imagine how such a thing could have happened. I've known Trace Walker for years now, and he's incapable of dishonesty."

"You can't say that about Blackheart," Ferris said in what she hoped was a desultory voice. They were having tea in a small coffee shop in the Mark Hopkins after doing their best to placate a semihysterical Miss Smythe-Davies, and Ferris wished they'd opted for the bar instead. In the three days since the robbery and the arrests, all hell had broken loose, for the Committee for Saving the Bay, for Senator Merriam and his staff—which included Ferris, in her own nebulous position, and his worried mother—and most particularly Blackheart, Inc. In the two years since Blackheart, Inc., had become society's darling there hadn't been a whisper of scandal about them. That halcyon reputation had come to an abrupt end.

"I wouldn't say that," Regina replied. "Despite his earlier manner of earning a living, I'd trust Patrick with my life."

"Yes, but would you trust him with your jewels?" Ferris countered. It was only through constant vigilance that she had kept her inexplicable feelings of guilt at bay, and if Regina had noticed her unusual hard-heartedness, she tactfully ignored it.

"Absolutely. And if you thought about it, so would you. If he had taken the jewels, he certainly wouldn't have hung around waiting to get arrested. If he were the kind of man the police and you seem to think he is, he would have taken off the

moment the theft was discovered and let poor Trace rot in jail
all alone."

"I don't imagine Blackheart chose to get arrested," Ferris
murmured cynically.

"Let me assure you, that if Blackheart had wanted to avoid
getting arrested he would have. And even the police found they
had nothing to hold him on. I think they just arrested him because they'd always wanted to. They just took the least little
excuse they could find—"

"The disappearance of a fortune in emeralds is not a little
excuse," Ferris said sternly.

"No, I suppose not. But I know in my heart of hearts that
Blackheart didn't have a thing to do with it. And so would you
if you were any judge of character. I just thank God he didn't
have to spend the night in jail." Her patrician cheekbones were
pink with indignation, and Ferris leaned forward to pat her
hand.

"Sorry, Regina. I'm afraid when it comes to Blackheart I'm
no judge of character at all." She sighed, taking a sip of her
too-cool Hu Kwa. "Have you heard from Phillip recently?"

"Last night. He's distressed, of course, but handling it with
his usual aplomb. He told me to tell you he'd be in touch next
Sunday. He thought it would be best if he kept out of the Bay
Area for the next week or so. That way he won't have to answer any impertinent questions."

Ferris smiled wearily. "But he's so good at dealing with impertinent questions."

"Better than Blackheart, certainly. I gather he punched a
reporter from the *Chronicle*. Very unwise of him," Regina
mused.

"Why did he do that? I'd missed that installment in this ridiculous soap opera."

"I gather the man was brash enough to ask Blackheart where
he was the night of the robbery. Apparently he wasn't arrested
till the next afternoon, and various people are wondering if he
was off stashing the jewels someplace and leaving Trace to take
the blame. They haven't turned up, you know."

"They will," Ferris said, with more wishful thinking than
any grasp of the situation. She could remember the look on
Blackheart's face when she'd suggested that he was going to

abandon Trace, and knew with sudden clarity that when Blackheart had taken a swing at the reporter he'd been seeing her accusing face. She swallowed. "And then I'm sure it will become clear that Trace had nothing to do with it."

"And Blackheart, too," Regina said sharply. "I certainly hope so. In the meantime—"

"I was hoping I'd find you two ladies here," Olivia Summers's cool, arch tones broke into their conversation, and it was all Ferris could do to control the glare she wanted to direct in the tall blonde's direction. "Miss Smythe-Davies didn't seem any happier to see me than she was to see you. I thought I'd help placate her, but I didn't seem to get any further than you did."

Regina gave her a distant, welcoming smile. "Join us, won't you, Olivia? I expect Miss Smythe-Davies's shattered nerves are beyond mending. I'm afraid we were less than a success. It was sweet of you to try your luck."

"Forgive my frankness, Regina, but are you sure you picked the right committee?" Olivia slid into the seat with her customary smooth grace. "Not that you wouldn't be welcome, but given the circumstances I would have thought Miss Byrd would have been a less than wise choice."

Regina didn't even try to hide the amazement that washed over her beautiful, lined face. "What in the world are you talking about, Olivia? What circumstances?"

"Didn't you know?" Olivia managed an expression of embarrassed concern that was just a shade too perfect. "I realize the details of Patrick's arrest didn't make the papers, but I assumed since you were so intimately involved . . . I'm sorry, I've been indiscreet. Forget I said anything."

"I think I should," Regina snapped. "You know I don't care for malicious gossip, Olivia, particularly about my friends." Tossing the linen napkin down, she rose to her regal height, and even Olivia managed to look paltry. "I have things to do. Are you coming, Ferris?"

Ferris's wary green eyes went from Regina's disapproving expression to Olivia's sly smile. "I think I'll share a cup of tea with Olivia. Call me, Regina?"

"Certainly, dear." She kissed Ferris warmly on her cheek. The look she gave Olivia would have withered a less self-centered person. "And you, young lady, watch your tongue."

"She's a dear soul," Olivia said with a bite of acid as they watched Regina thread her way gracefully through the closely set tables. "It's a shame she has to be disillusioned."

"Does she?" Ferris sat very still, waiting for Olivia to strike.

"But of course. Even if she won't listen to me, someone, at some time, will tell her."

"Tell her what?"

"Tell her about Francesca Berdahofski," Olivia murmured. "Tell her where Blackheart spent the night when he was trying to establish an alibi and where he was arrested the next day. And then I doubt her fondness will extend enough to cover those particular transgressions. She's a sweet old lady, but I don't expect she'll enjoy being lied to. It has the tendency to make people feel like fools, when they've been tricked. Most unwise of you, Miss Berdahofski." Her pink mouth curved in a pleased smile. "Tell me, does Phillip have any idea? I wouldn't think so, but the man has surprising depth. I would be surprised if he'd overlook the night of the Puffin Ball, however. I still can't imagine what Blackheart was doing there and not Phillip. Or were they both enjoying your rather earthy charms?"

That had pushed it too far. Up till then Ferris had sat there, misery and guilt washing over her. But belated pride made her snap her head up, and the look in her green eyes daunted even Olivia for a moment. A few little pieces of the puzzle had begun to fall into place. The unexpected arrival at Carleton House last Sunday. A tryst with more witnesses than she had expected. The Von Emmerling emeralds clasped around her skinny neck. Ferris smiled, a dangerous smile indeed.

"Nothing for me," Olivia told the waiter who'd just made his appearance. "I'm leaving." She rose, stretching gracefully, but Ferris wasn't fooled. Every muscle in her slender body was tense. "You might remember not to trust every ex-felon who tumbles you into bed, Francesca. I never got my recreational sex confused with real life. As good as Blackheart is in bed, security is better. And you've just lost both."

Ferris gave her more than enough time to leave. She sat there, sipping at her cold tea, thinking with careful deliberation. She had jumped to too many conclusions in the last three days—she should have enough sense not to jump again.

To be sure, only Blackheart had known her real name. He was beyond anger when they'd arrested him three short days ago. Would he have hit upon Olivia as the perfect revenge? But for all her doubts, Ferris had never suspected Blackheart of being vengeful. No, Olivia must have found out some other way.

Nothing would keep that mouth of hers quiet. But Ferris didn't know that she cared, one way or the other. Who and what Ferris Byrd was and what she'd done seemed of little importance right now, compared to the burning question that had left her with little sleep and no appetite. If it hadn't been Blackheart, who had taken the emeralds?

She got only that damned recorded message when she called Blackheart, Inc. And when she called the K. Christiansen in the phone book, she got no answer. That left her one place to check.

Blackheart's apartment was within walking distance, a pretty classy neighborhood for a retired cat burglar. If she called him, he might very well hang up; if she showed up, he could only slam the door in her face. But she couldn't wait any longer. More and more pieces of the puzzle were falling together. The only other person who knew about Francesca Berdahofski was Kate Christiansen. And Ferris needed to talk with Blackheart, to find out if her sudden, overwhelming suspicion was only wishful thinking.

It was a small narrow building on one of the cross streets. The disreputable Volvo, complete with a new passenger side window, was parked way down the street, and Ferris felt a sudden tightening in the pit of her stomach. Not an hour had passed in the last seventy-two without her remembering, her body feeling once again the silken slide of flesh within flesh, and her skin began to tingle.

Dammit, she wasn't going there to get tumbled into bed again, she reminded herself angrily. They were past that now—too much distrust had shattered what had always been too fragile a relationship. But she had to know whether she was manufacturing a scapegoat because she couldn't stand the thought of being used by him, or whether there was any chance that what she had begun to suspect was true.

The elevator was small and silent as it carried her up to the fifth floor, and it moved much too swiftly. She hadn't had time to get her composure in order before it spilled her out in the minuscule hallway. She stood there in front of 5B, hesitating, wondering if she shouldn't turn around and leave, when the damned door opened and Blackheart came out.

He didn't see her at first. When he did, his reaction wasn't promising. His eyes were shadowed, he looked as if he hadn't slept in days and his mouth was grim. He was wearing faded jeans, and she wondered briefly if they were the same pair that had resided by her bed so recently. The look he gave her was wary, unwelcoming, and she couldn't blame him.

"What are you doing here?" he demanded roughly. He hadn't closed the apartment door behind him yet, and Ferris thought she could see movement behind him. And it looked like a woman.

Pain sliced through her like a knife. "Absolutely nothing," she mumbled, turning back and punching the elevator button. But the hall was too small for her to escape, the elevator had already stopped on the second floor and Blackheart just stood there looking at her.

"You must have had some reason for coming," he said coldly. "Did you want to see what hideous mark five hours of American prison left on my recalcitrant soul?"

"It doesn't matter now," she muttered, pushing the button again.

His hand closed over hers, pulling it away from the wall, and it was all she could do to control the little rush that went through her skin at his touch, no matter how impersonal it was. "Leave it alone," he said. "The elevator will come when it's ready. Have you come to apologize? Because if you have, you'd better save it. I'm not ready to accept it, so it would just be a waste of time."

"I didn't come to apologize," she shot back.

"All right, then what did you come for?"

She hesitated, trying to peer past him into the apartment. It couldn't be Olivia—not that fast. "Nothing important. Forget it."

"Don't be a pain, Francesca," he grumbled. "I'm going out for beer and sandwiches. Go on in and hold Kate's hand for me till I get back. She needs someone to talk to."

Kate, Ferris thought, relief washing over her, followed swiftly by determination. "All right."

"And when I get back, you can tell me what made a saintly character like you enter this den of thieves."

"I may not be here when you get back," she temporized, not liking the command in his hostile voice.

"You'd better be. Or I'll find you. And in case you don't remember, locked doors don't keep me out."

The elevator finally chose that moment to arrive, and Ferris considered shoving him out of the way and bolting for it. But he was stronger than she was, and probably faster, and it would be an embarrassing waste of time. "I'll be here," she muttered gracelessly. And with a short nod he left her.

"Oh, no, just what I needed!" Kate greeted her from her curled-up position on the sofa. "What made Patrick think you could be of any help?"

Ferris paused just inside the doorway, surveying the room and its inhabitant with real curiosity. If she'd had to imagine how Blackheart lived, she never would have guessed with any degree of acumen. It was uncomfortably like her own apartment, from the haphazard piles of books and magazines to the rich, deep colors of the Oriental rugs on the hardwood floors. His furniture was bigger, and seemed a great deal more comfortable, and the paintings on his walls were modern and original, not copies of old French masters. But the room was surprisingly welcoming, warm and comfortable and aesthetically pleasing. Despite the lump of angry female flesh smack dab in the middle of it.

Kate had commandeered the blue sofa. She had a thousand used tissues scattered around her, a half full box in her lap, a cup of coffee with a cigarette floating in it on the table beside her and red swollen eyes above her belligerent pout. The look she gave Ferris was more than baleful, it was positively filled with hate. It was such an overreaction, as a matter of fact, that

Ferris wondered if that was fear beneath the petulance. Or was she still just looking for what she wanted to see?

Kate's unprepossessing greeting didn't augur well for the time while Blackheart was gone, but then, Ferris didn't particularly care about Kate's comfort, or her own for that matter. What she cared for was the truth.

Closing the door behind her, she advanced into the room. "I don't imagine he thought I'd be much good at all. He doesn't have much use for me right now."

Kate laughed—a coarse, humiliating laugh—as she dabbed at her reddened nose. "Oh, he has a use for you, all right. But I don't think it's what you have in mind, Miss Prissy Pants. Women like you make me sick. All your gold jewelry and your designer suits and you think that makes you better than the rest of us."

Yes, it was definitely fear lurking in the back of those red-rimmed eyes. Ferris sat down in the rocking chair opposite Kate, crossing her slender ankles and leaning back. "You know as well as I do that I wasn't born to gold jewelry and designer suits. You needn't have such a chip on your shoulder."

"What do you mean?" Kate was definitely edgy now, and the tissues lay forgotten in her lap.

"Blackheart had you check me out before he took the case. You must have been the one to tell Olivia Summers about my background," Ferris said easily, wishing she smoked—it would help her nervous edginess if she could toy with a cigarette. "I don't understand why you told her where Blackheart spent the night, though."

"I don't know what you're talking about. I don't even know Olivia Summers," she said staunchly.

"Certainly you do. You were watching her wrap her skinny little body around Trace Walker just three nights ago."

"What?" Kate looked ghastly, her face papery white around her red-rimmed eyes.

"You didn't notice that I was there, too. You weren't surprised at the little scene you interrupted, but you weren't unmoved, either. I saw your expression, Kate. You were mad as hell."

"I still don't know what you're talking about." Kate's voice was hoarse with pain and fear.

"What I don't understand is why, if you hate her so much, did you help her steal the emeralds?" Ferris said. A movement beyond the sofa drew her attention, and she saw that Blackheart, with his customary silence, had returned.

Kate must have felt his presence, for she swiveled around on the sofa, tears falling afresh.

Here it comes, Ferris thought. *Now he's going to kick me out for sure.*

Blackheart moved forward, taking Kate's plump hand in his, and his tawny eyes were dark with sadness. "Yes, Kate. Why did you help her?"

She fought it for a moment. "You can't believe what that stupid lying woman says. She's the one who turned you in to the police, remember? She's just jealous, trying to distract you so you won't think—"

"Why, Kate?" he repeated calmly, and her last bit of self-control vanished. She burst into loud, ugly sobs, her face crumpled in pain and shame. Ferris sat very still, wishing she were any place but right there as Blackheart moved around the sofa to take Kate in his arms. She was embarrassed, and she was stupidly, painfully jealous. Ferris wanted Blackheart's arms around *her,* she wanted to weep against the white cotton shirt and feel his soothing hands sweep down her back. Maybe he had some cigarettes lying around.

For a moment, Blackheart's eyes met hers over the weeping figure. She couldn't read their expression: She could only tell that it wasn't condemnation or dismissal. He seemed to want her there, though she couldn't imagine why. So she stayed.

"I was going to tell you," Kate snuffled noisily. "I never thought Trace would be blamed, or you either. She told me no one was even going to catch on. The copies were so good that it was impossible for anyone to tell."

"They were good," Blackheart said. "Too good. They're much prettier than the real Von Emmerlings—I know from experience." He was capable of a wry smile in the midst of all this drama.

"If only she hadn't come . . ."

"I knew, Kate. I always knew. I just didn't know how you managed it, and I still don't know why. Was she blackmailing you?"

Kate shook her head miserably. "There were a hundred rea
sons. One was the money. She was offering a lot, and I needec
it. Another was blackmail. I—I did something I shouldn'
have . . . a few years back. She was going to make sure certair
people found out about it."

"How did she know?"

Kate's flush turned her already red face an ugly mottlec
shade. "She was involved, too. She helped me out at the time—
lent me some money when I needed it. When she first asked me
to help her, she said it was for old times' sake."

"And when that didn't work she threatened you," he murmured. "And by that time you were so mad at Trace you didn'
care who you hurt."

"I cared. But that big moose can't see two feet in front of his
nose. I would have died for him."

"You don't have to die for him. You just have to come down
to the police station and tell them the truth. How Olivia got in
touch with you, how it was planned, exactly what you did. . . ."

Kate was shaking her head. "It won't do any good. She's got
an airtight alibi. And no one's going to believe me anyway. The
moment I start making accusations, some very nasty photographs get sent to the newspapers. You see, I was in some—
home movies, you might call them. With a few influential
businessmen and politicians, and we weren't exactly fully
dressed, if you know what I mean. And you can take that look
off your face, lady," she snarled at Ferris. "Senator Merriam
wasn't one of them."

"I'm sorry," Ferris stammered. "I didn't mean to be disapproving."

"Hell, you can disapprove all you want," Kate said wearily.
"I was young, just dropped out of college, and I was into some
things that I should have been smart enough to leave alone.
And now it's too late. The *Chronicle* wouldn't print the pictures, but plenty of others would sure the hell jump on it. And
anything I said to implicate a blue blood like Olivia would be
laughed at. I don't even know how she was involved. I just
know that she seemed to know everything that went on."

"So you won't testify?" Blackheart asked, no surprise or
shock clouding his expression.

"If it will help you and Trace, I will. But Olivia covered her tracks too well. The only way for her to be caught is with the stuff right on her."

"And is it? Does she have the stuff in her apartment?"

Kate shook her head. "I don't know, Patrick. She didn't tell me or Dale a thing."

"Dale was in on it with her?" Ferris couldn't keep still a moment longer. "But why?"

Kate cast her a withering glance. "Gambling debts. And he does everything Olivia tells him."

"How did you do it, Kate?" Blackheart questioned, handing her a tissue as she snuffled noisily.

"It was easy enough. You trusted me." She dissolved into fresh wails. "Olivia got the copies made, and I carried them in a little bag sewed inside my dress. Olivia had the dress made for me. I looked like a stuffed cabbage in it."

Blackheart's mouth twisted up in a reluctant grin. "It wasn't the most flattering dress."

"I hated it. Olivia must have gotten it on purpose. That's the kind of person she is."

"So you were the courier? When was the switch made?"

"Just after the last raffle winner."

"But what did Trace have to do with it?" Ferris couldn't help but ask. "Why did she throw herself at him like that? He didn't need to be distracted—he trusted you to look after the jewels."

Kate flinched at the memory of that betrayed trust. "That was just the icing on the cake. I told you Olivia was that kind of person. She knew that I—I cared about him, and she decided to amuse herself by showing me just how out of reach he really was. Well, she showed me." She blew her nose heartily into the tissue.

Blackheart leaned back wearily against the sofa, stretching his legs out in front of him and shutting his eyes. "That answers most of my questions," he murmured. "But it doesn't answer the most important one. What has she done with them?"

"Does it matter that much?" Ferris ventured.

The look he gave her held withering disdain, and she realized with despair that now she had proof that he'd done nothing, that her accusations had been groundless. And he despised her all the more. "Of course it matters," he said patiently. "They can't arrest Olivia without some proof. At this point it's only Kate's word against hers, and Olivia McKinley Summers's word holds a great deal more clout. We need proof. And it's a waste of time to go to the police without it. They'll just assume I'm trying to foist the blame on someone else. They dropped the charges against me very reluctantly."

"But what can you do?" Ferris questioned anxiously.

His smile was mocking. "Not what can *I* do, Francesca, my trusting one. What can *we* do? And the answer is absurdly obvious and quite, quite simple."

Ferris knew a sudden sinking sensation. "All right, I'll bite. What are *we* going to do?"

He smiled seraphically. "We're going to break into Olivia Summers's apartment."

Chapter Seventeen

"You have to be out of your mind," Ferris snapped.

"Not in the slightest." Blackheart was placidly grinding coffee beans in the warmly lit kitchen of his apartment. It was much larger than her kitchen—there was even room for a butcher-block table and several stools in the middle of it. She had been hard put to control the sigh of covetousness that had filled her when she first saw it. The gleaming copper pots and pans had just enough discoloration to prove they were there for hard use, not decoration. The butcher-block countertop was scarred and pitted from a thousand knife strokes, the food processor was artistically battered, and the electric coffee grinder was buzzing its overworked heart out. If she had a kitchen like this, she just might give up her allegiance to Le Menu frozen dinners.

"You can't seriously expect me to help you rob Olivia Summers's apartment. For heaven's sake, it's a twentieth-floor penthouse!"

"The very best kind," he said sagely, dropping the pulverized coffee into a filter. "High enough to be out of sight, not too high. We've gone over this already, Ferris. And you're coming with me."

He was still very angry with her, she could tell. Despite his calm tone of voice, his use of that hated name tipped her off. And if he weren't mad, he wouldn't be trying to punish her by dragging her into a life of crime.

"But why?" she wailed.

Blackheart sighed. "Reason number one—it's your reputation and future that's on the line as well as mine. Number
two—if I do it alone, what's to stop me from running off with
the emeralds and never being seen again? Number three—with
my bad knee I don't know if I can do it without help. And
number four—you're the one who accused me of it. You can
damn well find out for yourself whether your charming lack of
trust was justified." He poured the hot water over the grounds,
his face bland, his voice easy.

"What did you expect from me, Blackheart?" she said,
suppressing her justifiable guilt. "The circumstances were
pretty damning."

"Sure they were. I don't know why I would have thought the
night we'd spent together might have earned some vague sort
of loyalty, not to mention commitment. But what I really don't
understand is why you've suddenly chosen to believe that I'm
innocent. Kate could be wrong, you know." Together they
watched the water level descend in the coffee filter. "I wouldn't
be surprised if you suddenly decided that I was in on it with
Olivia, the mastermind behind it all. You could ignore the fact
that if I were interested there were a lot bigger scores available
in the last two years. Not that the Von Emmerling emeralds
aren't worth a substantial amount, but I could have done better." He poured her a cup of coffee, black and dark and rich,
and she looked at it distrustfully.

"I don't think I ought to have any," she demurred. "I've had
too much caffeine as it is."

Blackheart smiled that wry smile that was now completely
devoid of tenderness. "Haven't you seen the ads on TV? This
is decaffeinated. Just what us artistic types need before a big
job."

"Blackheart, you can't blame me," she said suddenly, ignoring the innocuous topic of conversation. "It looked like a
setup. I couldn't hide you from the police, it would have been
aiding..."

Blackheart walked out of the kitchen, and her words trailed
off. Well, he'd told her he wasn't ready for an apology. And she
still wasn't completely convinced he deserved one.

Looking down at her inky cup of coffee, she sighed. She
didn't need any more sugar—she was too wired as it was. She

wondered if she could fling herself at Blackheart's feet, beg him to let her cry off? It wouldn't do any good, and she would be damned if she'd tell him . . .

But why did it have to be twenty floors up? Why couldn't Olivia be sensible and have a basement apartment? Only Blackie knew of her weakness, it was only for Blackie's sake that she'd venture out on her unused, windy second-floor terrace. It wasn't paralyzing acrophobia; if she had to, she could tolerate high places. She just didn't like them much. Her family's trip to the Grand Canyon when she was fifteen had been torment, she'd never even taken a close look at the Coit Tower, and the only way she managed the steep hills of San Francisco was to drive as fast as she possibly could. And now Blackheart expected her to traverse twenty-story buildings without a qualm.

Well, she wasn't going to tell him. She'd be more likely to get mocking disbelief than compassion, and nothing would make him let her off. It was his revenge, and if he was innocent, then he had every right to it.

And if she didn't go, if she somehow managed to cry off, then what? Then she would never be certain of him. There'd always be room for doubt, and she'd never know if she was the lowest slime bug in creation or a painfully good judge of character. And that uncertainty wasn't something she could live with.

The living room was in shadows when she finally trailed in after Blackheart. He was sitting on the sofa in the twilight, his feet up on the coffee table, hands clasped loosely around the mug of coffee, eyes trained on the skyline. He didn't move when she came in the room, didn't turn. Kate had left hours ago, with stern instructions to stay in her apartment and not answer the telephone or the door unless it was on Blackheart's prearranged signal. The solitude of the apartment pressed down on Ferris, and she idly wondered what Blackheart would do if she gave in to her irrational temptations and leaped on him. He probably would have dumped her on the floor.

Sighing, she took a chair opposite him. "When are we going to do this?"

"Nine-thirty."

"Nine-thirty!" she shrieked. "That's four hours from now."

"Three hours and forty-five minutes," he corrected. "And that's when Olivia and her husband should be well settled in at Regina Merriam's. If we leave earlier they might decide to be late, or even worse, not go at all. If we go later they may decide to come home early. Regina's going to do her best to keep them, but there's nothing she can do, short of force, if they make up their minds. She's a redoubtable lady, but I can't see her barring the door."

"Regina's in on this?" Ferris couldn't control her astonishment.

Even in the gathering darkness she could see the flash of teeth as he smiled his ironic smile. "Regina trusts her own judgment, and she trusts me."

"Was this her idea or yours?"

"Oh, mine. She just offered her assistance."

"And does she know I'm going to be part of this?"

Blackheart turned his head to look at her then, and she wished she could read his expression in the gathering darkness. "Don't worry, Ferris. Your secret is safe with me. None of the Merriams have the faintest idea that you ever had doubts about my perniciousness. I imagine if all goes well, no one will believe what Olivia has to say about my whereabouts the night of the ball. And once the police are convinced of my innocence, I imagine they'd have no reason to tell anyone where I was when they arrested me. Rupert had a damned hard time keeping it out of the papers as it was, but we've been fortunate so far. If you're cool-headed and lucky, you should be able to carry it off and have your white wedding after all."

"Don't, Blackheart." Her voice was very still in the dark room. A long silence ensued. Despite her tightly strung nerves, the sleepless nights were beginning to take their toll. In the dark, silent living room she found her eyelids drifting closed, and the half-empty mug of coffee tilted in her hand.

"Come here," he said suddenly, and despite the softness of his voice she jumped, spilling coffee on her camel-colored skirt.

"Why?"

"Because we have hours before we have to leave. You need to sleep. You may as well curl up in the corner of the couch."

"Why don't I just go home and take a nap?"

"Because I don't trust you to come back," he said simply.

There was no way she could argue with that. "What about the bedroom?"

"I keep that for sex," he drawled. "Come here, Francesca. I promise you, you're entirely safe."

She should have been offended by that snotty tone of voice, but at least he'd called her Francesca. It could have been a slip of the tongue, but for some reason Ferris felt cheered. Without a word she set down the mug of coffee and moved over to the sofa.

He was right, there was more than enough room for her to curl up without touching his body on the far end. "What are you going to do?" she asked sleepily, trying to make herself comfortable.

"What I usually do before a job. Empty my mind of everything."

Ferris couldn't control a sleepy giggle. "I guess meditation has a thousand uses."

"It does," he agreed softly. "You're at the wrong end of the couch."

She lay very still, her nerves atingle. "I thought the bedroom was for sex."

An iron hand closed around her wrist and she was hauled upright and over to his side of the sofa. A moment later she was curled up by his side, her head resting against his shoulder, his arm around her. "It is. Go to sleep, Francesca."

A thousand protests sprang to mind, but she uttered not a one. He smelled of coffee and Kate's cigarettes and Blackheart, and she hadn't realized how much she missed him, how much she missed the feel of his body against hers. She wanted to turn her face against the smooth cotton of his shirt, put her arms around his waist and tell him how sorry she was. But he was right—it was too soon. He wasn't ready to forgive her, not yet. But the feel of his arm around her body, holding her comfortably against him, told her that he was getting there. With a sigh she closed her eyes.

FERRIS HAD BEEN half hoping that she'd awake to find herself stretched out along the wide couch, safe in his arms. When she awoke she was alone in the darkness, the light from the bedroom a small pool of brightness in the inky room. She lay there for a moment, hoping she could pretend to be asleep, hoping against hope he'd go without her. Without any warning her heart had begun a steady, violent thudding, and her palms felt cold and damp.

Blackheart's shadow blocked the light, and then he moved across the room. She lay there absorbing his approach. As usual she couldn't hear him, and once he was out of the lamplight she couldn't even see his silhouette. But she could feel him, feel the displaced air as his body moved closer. Maybe he'd lean down and kiss her. Maybe brush the hair away from her sleeping face. Maybe even—

The pile of clothes hit her with a whoosh. He must have dropped them from quite a distance, and the force of their landing made her sit up with a startled squeal. "Damn you, Blackheart!" she snapped. "Haven't you heard about waking people up gently?"

"I don't have the time," he drawled, leaning over to turn on the light. "Besides, you were awake."

Ferris didn't bother to argue with him—Blackheart always knew too much. She looked up at him, silently impressed. He was dressed for work, that much was obvious. The faded jeans had been traded for soft black denims, the black turtleneck covered him from wrist to chin, even his running shoes were black. A pair of thin black gloves was tucked into his hip pocket, and a black sailor's cap balanced the other side.

"You look very effective," she said, and her voice was slightly strangled. He also looked devastatingly attractive, and the thought didn't help her inner turmoil.

"Put those on." He nodded toward the clothes. "They're the same sort of thing. I can't see you climbing over rooftops in a business suit."

The very thought made her stomach lurch, but she managed a brave smile. "No, I suppose not. Whose clothes are they?"

"Mine," he said without batting an eye. "You'll have to roll up the pants, but they should fit well enough." He cocked his head to one side. "They may be a little tight in the hips."

"Pig," she said, too nervous to be as insulted as she should be. "What do I do for shoes?"

"That may prove a problem." He gave her high-heeled sandals a disapproving glance. "I'll check and see if I have anything that will do. We may have to stop on our way over to Olivia's. I think black ballet slippers would be the best."

"Won't I look funny walking around in ballet slippers?" she questioned caustically.

"This is San Francisco, remember? Everybody looks funny. Hurry up. Are you hungry?"

The very thought of food made her knotted stomach twist, but her panicky brain reminded her that food would take time. "I'm famished," she said brightly.

"Too bad. I never eat before a job."

Ferris looked up at him, a sudden, furious suspicion entering her mind. "You're looking forward to this, aren't you?" she demanded. "You're excited, you're glad to be breaking into a twenty-story building."

He smiled at her with more benevolence than he'd shown in the three days since the emeralds were stolen and he'd been arrested. "Damn straight. Wanna make something of it?"

As the sinking feeling filled her heart, she realized there was nothing she could say. "No."

"Then change your clothes and let's get going."

Heartless, the man was completely heartless, she thought, struggling into the clothes in the small confines of his apartment-size bathroom. And damn his soul, the soft, faded black denims *were* tight in the hips. Sucking in her stomach, she pulled the zipper up, then turned to admire the back view in the mirror. Even if they were tight, they looked very enticing. Maybe she'd do her best to precede Blackheart up a ladder. Oh, dear God, what was she thinking?

Blackheart was waiting impatiently by the door when she finally emerged, and his expression was critical, not admiring. "You'll need to tie your hair back," he said, his eyes running over her body with a professional eye. "Maybe we ought to cut off those pants, rather than roll them up."

"Don't you think you might need them again?" she said sweetly.

Blackheart didn't rise to the bait. "If I do, I could afford to buy new ones. B and E is a lot more lucrative than security work. Come on, we're running late." He tossed her a wool hat and a pair of thin kid gloves. "Keep those stowed until we get up on the first roof."

"First roof?" Her voice came out in a tiny squeak, and his smile was chilling.

"I've been thinking about it. There are two ways we can get in. One way is from the bottom, but the security on Olivia's building is very tight. Our alternative is to go from the top. There's a building on the corner that's fairly accessible, and the rooftop route is straightforward enough. No peaks, at least. We'll scout around a bit before we actually do it."

"Don't you want to try starting from the bottom?" she said wistfully. "It sounds a lot more direct."

"And a lot more dangerous. Five hours in jail is just about my limit. Much as it would please me to drag you along with me, I think I could do without another arrest." He peered at her, and his sadistic smile widened. "You aren't afraid of heights, are you, Francesca?"

She managed a creditable shrug. "Of course not."

"That's good," he murmured. "Because if you were, you wouldn't like tonight at all. Not one tiny bit." And his smile was nothing short of sinister.

"Don't try to scare me, Blackheart. I'm tough enough to take anything you have to dish out and more," she snapped, her backbone stiffening. "What do I wear on my feet?"

"I found these in the back of my closet. They should do." He tossed her a pair of dark-brown moccasins, a size too small for her size-eight feet.

"Whose are they?" she queried, then cursed herself for opening her mouth.

Blackheart smiled. "Let's just say they came from the bedroom. Are you ready?"

He wasn't going to goad her. "Ready."

"Well, I'm not." He'd been standing a few feet away, watching her. Before she could realize his intent, he'd crossed those few feet and pulled her into his arms, his mouth coming down on hers with a hungry fierceness that washed everything away, her panic, her doubts, her guilt.

Twining her arms up around his neck, she opened her mouth for his plundering tongue, lost in the sudden swirl of wanting that washed over her. He'd caught her hips in his firm, strong hands, pressing her up tightly against him, and she whimpered softly as his tongue met hers, seeking a response that was there for the asking. His hands slid up her black-clad sides, around in front to cup her breasts, and the fingers were enticingly rough and arousing. She pressed herself against those hands of his, her own traveling up his strong, narrow back, the feel of the soft cotton turtleneck frustrating when she wanted silken skin. His blatantly aroused hips ground against hers, and for one brief, mad moment she considered tripping him up and jumping on him. Anything to avoid heights, she told herself righteously, pressing closer to his enticing body.

His hands left her breasts, caught her arms and drew her away from him, slowly, deliberately, being very careful not to hurt her. His breathing was labored, his eyes glistening in the darkness, and she could hear the rapid thudding of his heart in counterpoint to hers. "Now I'm ready," he said finally, dropping her wrists and turning away. "Let's go."

Chapter Eighteen

It was a cool, damp night, with a low-hanging mist that just might obscure the deadly drops between buildings, Ferris thought hopefully. It might also obscure her footing, but she was resigned to that. She was going to end up smashed on the sidewalks—she'd prefer not to have to see anything as she fell.

Blackheart was right, as always. Nobody gave them a second look as they strode arm in arm, two black-clad cat burglars out for a stroll, she thought bitterly. She kept casting nervous glances up at the jagged roofline that looked like sharks' teeth, with Blackheart constantly pulling her attention back to the earth. Where she'd so much rather stay, please God.

"Where are we going now?" she whispered angrily as they casually strolled past Olivia's building for the second time. It was a stately, post-earthquake building on Nob Hill, heavily doormanned, as Blackheart had warned her. She cast the uniformed guard a longing look. Maybe she could entice him into a back alley while Blackheart slipped upstairs alone. Without her archaic virginity to protect, she'd choose additional dishonor before death any day.

But Blackheart had dragged her past the building without allowing her more than a wistful glance. "Forget it," he'd ground out in her ear. "I've already checked everything. The only way we could get into that place is with a Sherman tank or the Pope by our side—and even then they might still want IDs. And I'm afraid anyone connected with Blackheart, Inc., is strictly persona non grata around here."

"But maybe I could distract him...."

His laugh was heartlessly derisive. "You're starting to see yourself as a Mata Hari after one night of passion? If you managed to get past him, there'd still be the elevator operator."

"Oh."

"Oh," he echoed cynically. They plowed onward, Ferris's hand numb on her arm. "We're here," he said finally, and her heart plummeted to the too-tight moccasins.

It was a small building, a little seedier than its sisters on the neat upper-class street, its facade smog- and pollution-stained. "What is it?"

"A hotel. Look sultry." He began to steer her in through a tawdry lobby, and the woman behind the desk looked up with absolutely no expression on her tough, tired face. Her hair was an improbable shade of blond, her eyes were dead, and the stub of a cigarette hung from a coral-lipsticked mouth. Ferris stared at her for a moment, wondering how she managed to smoke so far down without burning those overripe lips of hers.

"We'd like a room," Blackheart announced, still maintaining a tight grip on Ferris's arm.

"So what else is new?" the woman returned, shoving the register at them. "Mr. and Mrs. Smith, I presume?"

Still clamping the defiant Ferris to his side, Blackheart signed in a dark, sprawling script. The desk clerk turned it back, peered at it, then glanced up at the two of them suspiciously. "Berdahofski?" she queried.

"Mr. and Mrs.," Blackheart said sweetly.

"Any luggage?" She dropped her cigarette butt in the disposable cup of congealed coffee by her side. She didn't bother to look or wait for an answer. "No loud noises, no screaming, no breaking the furniture. Twenty bucks."

"We'll be discreet," Blackheart assured her, dropping thirty on the desk. She pocketed it without looking up, tossed them a key and jerked her head in the direction of the elevators.

"She didn't tell us the checkout time," was all Ferris could find to say as they traveled upward in a creaking elevator that had served as a urinal in the not-distant past.

"That's because she doesn't expect us to stay more than an hour or two," Blackheart said patiently, finally freeing her arm from that iron grip.

Ferris's eyes opened wide. "Why?"

"This place caters to the hot-sheet trade, darling. They get quite a turnover, if you'll pardon the expression." The elevator doors creaked open, and Ferris wrinkled her nose.

"How could such a sordid place be so close to Olivia's?" she demanded. "Isn't there such a thing as zoning?"

"They don't zone places like this. And the neighborhood's on the upswing. I'm sure this place hasn't got much time left." He slid the key into the fifth door down from the elevator, opening it with a flourish. "After you, *madame.*"

Ferris cast him a worried look. "You don't seriously expect me to—to—"

He shoved her inside, switching on the light, and closing the door behind them. "No, I don't seriously expect you to—to—" he mocked. "I can think of pleasanter places and better times. This is hardly my idea of romance." He gave the sagging bed with its rose chenille bedspread a withering glance. "Make yourself comfortable, Mrs. Berdahofski. We have a wait."

"But why? I thought Olivia would have been gone for hours now. We don't want to run into them coming home." She plopped herself down on the bed, alternating relief and panic washing over her. On the one hand, she was in no hurry to end her life in a fall from a San Francisco rooftop. On the other, the longer she put it off, the harder it was going to be. She didn't want Blackheart to have to drag her, kicking and screaming, up there. She had no doubt at all that he would.

"I don't want to run into her, either. But the desk clerk was watching the elevator when we went up—she'll probably keep an eye on it for a while. I wouldn't put it past her to head up this way. I want to allay her suspicions."

"She wasn't suspicious," Ferris protested, bouncing slightly on the loose springs. "She didn't give us more than a second look."

"She wouldn't have done that if you hadn't been giving her that helpless white-slave routine. If I hadn't kept a grip on you, you probably would have bolted. And if I were you I wouldn't sit on that bed—you never know what might be crawling around."

She was off it in a flash, casting a dubious glance back. "How long do we have to wait?"

Blackheart smiled, that sinister, heartless smile. "It's time. Come on, chicken. We're going a-thieving."

Even through her panic Ferris had to admire him. He picked the lock to the roof with practiced ease, using a small collection of tools that resembled a manicurist's weapons. No one would have been faster with a key, and for a moment she wondered whether she could get him to teach her. Then she abandoned the idea as tactless. Besides, when would she have cause to break into a place? But still she paid close attention—anything to keep her mind off what was awaiting her.

The breeze was stronger up on the roof, but the reality of it was far less threatening than her imagination. The adjoining building was gloriously flush with the hotel, and a mere two feet higher.

"Put your hat and gloves on," Blackheart instructed, doing the same himself. He looked different like that, she thought as she hastily complied. He looked like a cat, lean and lithe and dangerous, with his eyes aglow and his nerves tightly strung.

"You sound like my mother on Sunday morning," she grumbled. The gloves were too small, the hat too big, with an unfortunate tendency to slip down over her eyes. She smiled up at him brightly. "I'm ready."

He paused, looking down at her with a wry smile. "Okay, Poncho," he said, pushing the hat back off her forehead. "Remember to do everything I say, without hesitation, backtalk or panic. Look ahead, look up, but never look down. You got that?"

She didn't like the sound of that, but she nodded. "Good girl," he said, kissing her on the forehead with unexpected warmth. "Let's get going."

Ferris scampered after him, up onto the adjoining building, her feet silent and just a tiny bit slippery on the tarred roof. *This isn't so bad,* she told herself with a hint of pleading. *I'll be fine.*

In the misty darkness the huddled shapes of the heating vents made eerie obstacles, but she kept her eyes trained on Blackheart's narrow back, unconsciously imitating his catlike grace. He was waiting for her at the far end, and this time the neighboring building was a good two stories higher. He was standing by a rusty wrought-iron ladder.

"You first," he offered kindly.

"Very convenient of them to have left a ladder," she grumbled, glad now for the tight gloves. They gave her better purchase than her cold, wet palms.

"Most buildings have them. Didn't you ever watch 'Starsky and Hutch'?" She had paused three rungs up, and he put his hands beneath her black-denimed rear and shoved. "Or any other cop show, for that matter?" he continued, following her upward, and the sound of his voice was blessedly distracting. "They're always chasing around on roofs, and there are always convenient ladders."

"And if there aren't?" Her voice quavered slightly as she neared the top. She nearly collapsed on the next roof in relief, but with a superhuman effort she maintained her balance. Not dead yet.

"Then we're in trouble," he said with callous cheer, dropping down on the roof beside her, making no noise at all. "You're doing okay, partner. Ever thought of taking up mountain-climbing?"

"No," she snapped. "How many more buildings to go?"

"Only three," he said, with genuine sadness, the swine. "And we're just beginning to get the feel of it. I hope it's not all as tame as this. You won't get any proper taste of it."

"I don't want a proper taste of it," she said through clenched teeth. "I want to get the damned job over with and get home."

"You have no soul, Francesca," he murmured, peering past her through the murky darkness. The tangle of antennas stretched against the cloudy night sky like bare tree limbs, and a look of inhuman delight lit his face. "Ah, now that's more of a challenge."

"Wh-what is?"

"No ladder."

She swallowed the yelp of panic. "How are we going to get up?"

"Leave it to me."

She only wished she could. She only wished she dared turn around and head back down, back to street level to disappear into the fog and never be seen again. South Dakota could be very pretty in February. If you liked the Arctic.

She'd thought those clothes of his fit like a second skin, but somewhere beneath them he'd managed to hide a thin coil of rope. Sudden dizziness assailed her, and she sat down abruptly on the rooftop, taking deep, covert breaths as she watched Blackheart size up the wall.

He looked back at her for a moment. "Sitting down on the job, Francesca?" he inquired.

"Just for a moment. I figure I may as well relax while I wait," she said with deceiving calm.

Except that when had she ever deceived Blackheart? Maybe now, when he was distracted. She could only hope so. Her heart was thudding so loudly that surely he could hear, if he weren't so busy trying to figure out how to kill them both. She wouldn't look any closer, she wouldn't. But she had to.

Slowly she rose, edging toward the next building. Her quiet little moan was swallowed up in the night air. There was a good two feet between the two buildings. Enough for her body to bounce down, ending wedged in some narrow alleyway.

Blackheart had taken a small cylinder from his pocket and was unfolding it into something that resembled a cross between an umbrella and an anchor. From somewhere in the murky mists of memory Ferris recognized it as a grappling hook, the kind used by mountain climbers. She watched him attach it to the end of the thin rope with practiced ease. He tossed it expertly, and it caught on the next building, some twelve feet higher than their current uneasy level.

"You want to go first?" he offered courteously, yanking on the rope a few times to ensure that it was sound.

"No, thank you," she said, choking. "After you."

He went up easily enough, though she could see that he was favoring his right leg. What would happen if he fell, she wondered. He'd done so once, and his father had died from a fall. Would it be better or worse if it was his body smashed against the pavement and not hers? She really didn't know.

"Come on, chicken heart," he called softly from the roof above her. "Time's a-wasting."

I can't do it, she thought suddenly. *I simply can't do it.* Taking a few steps back, she shook her head. Blackheart was up there, waiting patiently. "Come on, Francesca," he said softly, and his voice was a siren's lure. "I can't leave you alone on the roof. Either come with me or I'll have to take you back, and it will all be for nothing."

Good, she thought, still not saying a word. She no longer cared about Trace Walker, the emeralds or anybody's reputation. But Blackheart was looking down at her, and through the misty darkness she could see those calm, laughing eyes, daring her to come up. And she knew that if she turned and left she'd never see him again.

Some things were worth dying for, she thought dazedly, grabbing the rope. Was Blackheart one of them? Was the truth one of them? Would she ever find out?

"That's right, love," he crooned down at her, his voice soothing. "Just don't look down. The rope's more than strong enough to hold you—I'm up here to catch you when you get in reach." He kept up the calming, gentle litany as she climbed, hand over hand, her moccasined feet bouncing off the opposite brick wall. Her face felt chilled, and she realized that tears were pouring down unbidden, tears of pure, simple terror. She couldn't take her hands off the rope to wipe them away, and it would have done no good. They just kept coming, silent, copious, slipping down her face as she moved up the rope.

His hand on her wrist was like a vice, biting, blessedly painful, as he hauled her up the rest of the way. She kept herself stiff, not falling into his arms as she longed to do. If she did, she would start to howl and scream and he'd never get her to move another foot.

"Is this it?" she inquired, her voice calm, her face wet with the tears.

"One more," Blackheart said. "We'll have to jump."

She thought she'd reached the apex of terror, but she had been mistaken. She looked at him with shock and disbelief, but he just shrugged his shoulders. "Don't think about it," he advised. "Do it before you have time to be frightened." He hadn't released her wrist, and she felt herself being dragged to the opposite end of the roof.

There was a yawning abyss between the two buildings. A vast chasm of perhaps thirty inches. She couldn't do it—she'd reached her limit. If that same space was flat on the sidewalk she would have made it with feet to spare. But if she tried to jump those thirty inches, twenty stories above the street, she would die. It was just that simple.

Blackheart jumped first, making it look ridiculously easy— a child's hopscotch game. He stood on the other side, waiting for her. "Come on, Francesca," he said. "Prove that you love me."

"But I don't," she said, and knew it was a lie.

He smiled, unfazed. "Then prove that you don't. Jump. For once in your life, trust me."

It was rotten and unfair of him, and it left her no choice whatsoever. And she knew if she hesitated one more moment she'd never move in the next five hundred years. She leaped, not preparing herself, and her shins hit the edge of the opposite building as she began to tumble downward.

Of course Blackheart caught her. How could she ever have had any doubts about it? One moment she was sliding down the outside of a building toward certain death, in the next his hands had clamped around her wrists and she had been hauled onto the roof before her knees had even made contact with the building. They tumbled onto the rough surface, his arms locked so tightly around her that she couldn't breathe. She didn't think she wanted to, anyway, and she hugged him back, closing her eyes and willing the dizziness to fade.

"Damn you," he muttered in her ear. "Damn, damn, damn you. I ought to wring your neck. Why the hell didn't you tell me you were scared of heights?" There was no way she could answer, first because the arms crushing her didn't give her enough breath to do so, then because his mouth had come down over hers, stopping any effort at speech.

She considered protesting for a brief moment, then decided against it. She'd really rather be kissing him than breathing anyway. Especially since he had just ensured that she would be breathing in the near future, she could give up a few moments of air in a good cause. And his mouth was so very delightful. There was a faint, windy sort of humming in her ears, and little blue and pink stars in front of her eyes, and she wondered if she was going to come just from being kissed, and then realized that no, she was more likely simply going to pass out from lack of oxygen, when he released her. The return of her breathing almost made up for the absence of his mouth. Almost, but not quite. She lunged back for him, but he held her at arm's length.

"None of that, wench," he cautioned sternly. "We have work to do."

"Oh, no, Blackheart," she wailed. "No more rooftops."

"No more rooftops. Everything is downhill from now on. We're on Olivia's building. See those trees down there? That's her terrace."

The tops of the trees looked bizarre twenty stories up, but Ferris took his word gratefully. "How do we get there?"

By this time she was past fear. Very slowly, very carefully he lowered her down the eight feet to Olivia's flagstone terrace, very carefully he leaped after her, landing lightly on his cat's feet.

"Blackheart, there's a light on in the apartment," she hissed, ducking behind a potted Douglas fir.

He caught her arm and dragged her back out. "Do you think Olivia worries about the electric company? It is—" he peered at his watch in the darkness "—ten forty-five. I don't expect them back before eleven at the earliest."

"Blackheart!" she moaned.

"More likely midnight. Regina promised she'd stall them. Come along, darling. You'll reach street level by the service elevator."

It sounded too good to be true. "Do you mean it, Blackheart?" she breathed as he busied himself with the terrace door. He was using an American Express card, and the door opened immediately and soundlessly.

"How did you do that?"

He grinned. "I never leave home without it. And yes, you'll leave by the elevator, or at worst twenty flights of stairs wouldn't be so bad, would it?"

"It would be sheer heaven. But what about the people in the lobby?"

"It's a lot easier going out than in," he explained patiently as he stepped through the sliding glass door, beckoning her to follow. "Even so, we'll probably leave through the basement. It should be deserted this time of night."

The apartment was still and silent, the bright lights lending a false sense of security to the whole operation. "You take the bedroom," he ordered. "I'll start in here. Use your gloves, and don't disturb anything. We just want to make sure the emeralds are here, we don't want to take them."

Ferris nodded obediently, heading into the bedroom and shuddering at the strong reek of Olivia's perfume. Shalimar. Wouldn't you just know it? The room was spotlessly, compulsively neat, even the makeup and perfumes on the glass-topped dressing table in alphabetical order. The clothes in the closets and drawers were arranged by color and season, each shoe had its mate, and though the jewelry looked very valuable to Ferris's untrained eye, there wasn't an emerald among them.

Nothing between the mattress and the box spring, nothing under the bed, not even dust or a missing paperback novel. The woman was definitely sick, Ferris decided righteously.

The bathroom was an equal washout. Nothing secreted in the back of the toilet, hidden among the color-coordinated towels, concealed in the extra roll of toilet paper. There was one advantage to the demented neatness, Ferris conceded. It made searching surprisingly easy.

"Any luck?" Blackheart appeared in the doorway, and Ferris told herself she could see the pleasure and excitement jumping in his veins.

"Nothing. Except I can't open that door." She gestured toward the locked door hidden beneath a row of curtains.

He gave it a critical look. "Piece of cake. Does Olivia have anything as mundane as a nail cleaner?"

"Olivia's nails don't get dirty," she said dourly. "Will this do?" It was a narrow emery board, and he nodded his approval.

"Go to it, kid."

"Don't be ridiculous, Blackheart. We don't have time for games."

"This is a learning experience. You can do it, Francesca. And we're staying right here until you try," he said blandly, leaning against the doorway.

And she'd thought she was over being scared for the night. Gracing him with an obscenity she seldom used, she set to work, jabbing at the keyhole in a fine temper.

"Don't be so rough," Blackheart advised. "You have to coax a lock to open, tease it open. Treat it like a lover, talk to it."

"Go to hell, Blackheart!"

"Of course, since that happens to be the way you talk to your lovers, it might be better if—"

"Oh, my God, I did it," Ferris breathed, sitting back on her heels in amazement as the knob turned with a well-oiled click.

Blackheart strode past her, giving her an approving pat on her capped hair. "Of course you did. I knew you had the makings of a felon in that heart of yours." He stepped inside the room and stopped dead still, blocking her entrance. "Well, well, well."

"What is it?" She pushed past him, curiosity getting the better of her.

"I think I've discovered how Olivia knew what Kate had become involved in. And how she's been making money for the last few years."

Ferris looked around, her forehead wrinkled. "It just looks like a lot of electronic equipment."

"Exactly. Videotape machines, a video camera, a small pile of tapes. I think Olivia and Dale have been involved in experimental filmmaking for very high profits."

"What makes you think they haven't just been bootlegging movies? Isn't there a big profit in that, too?" she questioned curiously, roaming around the small, dark room, trailing a gloved hand over the shiny equipment.

"Not as big as the profit in blackmail," Blackheart drawled. "I wouldn't have thought Olivia would be so enterprising. Though she always was a little kinky."

"What do you mean, kinky?" Ferris demanded, her interest in the videotape machines vanishing.

Blackheart smiled seraphically. "Never you mind, Miss Innocence. Let's just say that Olivia's not particularly my cup of tea. Why don't you go ahead and check her drawers one last time? I'll give this place a quick once-over and see if I can come up with anything."

"You think they might be in here?"

"They might," Blackheart said. "They might be anywhere. And we're running out of time as it is. Hurry up, Francesca. The sooner we get out of here, the better."

Ferris left readily enough as he pushed her out the door. The small silver clock by the spotless king-size bed said five past eleven, and once more Ferris was struck with the difference between this compulsive neatness and the squalid mind that conceived of blackmail as a way to make a living. Poor Kate, enmeshed in Olivia's schemes. And poor Trace, set up like a clay pigeon. And poor Blackheart, and poor Ferris, more unwilling pawns. Damn her soul to hell.

She found them by accident. All her mental energy was spent on her fury with Olivia, and her search was desultory, mindless, instinctive. She hadn't bothered to check the wastepaper basket the first time around—the idea had been too absurd. But this time she was going by instinct, not ideas, and the solid weight of the supposedly empty tissue box tipped her off.

She was kneeling on the floor on the far side of the bed, the box held loosely. With shaking hands she opened it, and the Von Emmerling emeralds tumbled into her lap.

She stared at them for a long, speculative moment. They looked garish, ornate, and tacky in the electric light, and sudden doubt assailed her. She didn't even look up when Blackheart reentered the room, carefully locking the door behind him.

"Nothing in there," he said. "Not even any videotapes. She must have them stored someplace else. Though from the dust on the machines I don't think she's been using them for quite a while. Maybe she decided theft was more lucrative than blackmail. I expect it's safer."

"I think I found them," Ferris said quietly.

"What?" She had his full attention now, and he materialized by her side immediately, squatting down next to her. "You've got 'em, all right," he said, a rich note of satisfaction in his voice as he looked at them. Reaching forward, his long slender hands lifted them, holding them up against the light, tender as a lover stroking satin flesh.

And what was she doing, being jealous of a few rocks, she wondered, miserably aware that that was exactly what she was feeling. "How do you know they're the real ones? Didn't Olivia have copies made?"

"The police have the copies," he said absently, never taking his tawny gaze from the jewels. "Don't you remember, we tried to pawn them off on Miss Smythe-Davies? No, these are the real things. You can tell by the shimmer of blue light in the heart of the big emerald.'' He held it out for her admiration, but like any jealous woman, she only gave it a cursory glance, controlling an urge to sniff contemptuously. ''What makes you think they might be fake?''

''They look so...so tacky,'' she said finally. ''I remembered them being a lot prettier.''

''Jewelry usually looks prettier by candlelight, particularly those that were designed when that was the main form of light. But that's your proof right there. The Von Emmerling emeralds are famous for being vulgar. The fakes were much prettier. If I'd had my mind on my business and not on—something else the night of the Puffin Ball, I would have noticed immediately when the substitution was made.''

''What did you have your mind on, Blackheart?'' she asked quietly.

''Sex,'' he said bluntly. ''Put them back, Francesca. We found out what we came for. The sooner we get out of here the better.''

''Shouldn't we just take them?'' She was wrapping them reluctantly and shoving them back in their box. ''I mean, they may find out we've been here. Wouldn't it be safer if we took them to the police ourselves?''

''And you think they'd take the word of Patrick Blackheart against the likes of Olivia Summers?'' he scoffed. ''They were overjoyed to have finally managed to arrest me—it just about broke their hearts to let me go. Even if they couldn't make any charges stick, they still knew exactly what I was doing for the last fifteen years of my life, and most people figure six months at a minimum-security British prison wasn't punishment enough. They'd love to get something new on me. If I showed up at the police station with the Von Emmerling emeralds and some cock-and-bull story about the Summerses, I don't expect they'd waste too much time listening.'' He shook his head, rising to his full height. ''No, we'll leave them right where we found them. Olivia's foolish enough to think she's home free. Tomorrow morning Kate and I will make a visit to our local police station in the company of Rupert and set our case before their impartial judicial eye.''

"And then they'll believe you?"

"Of course not. They won't believe me until they get a search warrant and find the jewels themselves, and even then they might not be certain. Come along, darling. This isn't the place for postmortems. That's the second rule of thievery, right up there after don't look down. It's don't stop to count the loot while you're still at the scene of the crime."

"Yes, sir." She stuffed the box back in the trash. "How are we getting out?"

"Service entrance just off the kitchen." He headed for the door, and Ferris paused for a moment. Had the bedside light been on or off? She couldn't recall, but what was more important, would Olivia remember? She was about to call after Patrick, but he was already gone.

Well, she'd just have to chance it. Flicking it off, she sped across the thick wall-to-wall carpet in search of the kitchen. Blackheart was standing in the open door, looking impatient.

"Off with the hat and gloves, Francesca," he ordered. "You don't want to advertise what we've been doing."

Sudden guilt assailed her at the memory of that bedside lamp. "Blackheart, I don't remember—"

His hand suddenly covered her mouth as he pulled her back against him. The only sound was his heavy breathing. And the rattle of the lock being turned on the front door of the apartment.

Chapter Nineteen

They were halfway down the twenty flights of stairs when reaction began to set in. One moment she was racing after him, the too-tight moccasins flying down the narrow metal steps, the next she was clinging to the railing as a sudden wave of dizziness assailed her.

He was half a flight ahead of her when he realized she was no longer following him. In a flash he was back beside her, gently prying her clutching hands from the railing and rubbing an elbow over the section of metal to wipe out her fingerprints.

"You go on ahead," she said in a choked voice. "I just need a minute." She tried to break free of his grip, but he held fast.

"Francesca, love, we can't hang around the scene of the crime. That's rule number three, darling. Rule number four is don't touch anything once you take your gloves off."

Her knees were trembling so much she doubted she could stand much longer, and there was a shocked look to her face and eyes. "I'll be along in a moment, Blackheart," she pleaded.

"Rule number five, and most important. Do as the senior partner says, without question. Come on, my fledgling felon. We're getting out of here."

"Blackheart, I can't," she whispered, sinking down to sit on the narrow steps.

Her rear hadn't even made contact before she was hauled up again, his fingers digging painfully into her arms as he gave her a hard, teeth-rattling shake. "The next step is a slap, Francesca," he informed her coldly. "Do you want that?"

The shocked expression was leaving her face, her cheeks were filling with color and her eyes with fury. "Don't you dare!"

"Then stop whining and come on," he snapped, dragging her on down the steps. She stumbled after him, gritting her teeth and concentrating on the cold anger that was filling her.

Five minutes later, when they ended up in a deserted alleyway that looked as if it belonged more to the Bontemps Hotel than to Olivia's classy condo, that anger was still rampant. Blackheart finally released his grip on her hand, leaning back against a brick wall and taking in slow, deep breaths of the foggy night air.

For a brief moment Ferris considered flinging herself down and kissing the blessed ground. She contented herself with a surreptitious caress with her moccasined foot, while she continued to glare at Blackheart's shadowy figure.

"Don't give me that look, Francesca," he drawled out of the darkness. "You know as well as I do that you couldn't afford to stop on the stairs like that. If I hadn't dragged you you'd still be there, just waiting for someone to find you."

The fact that he was probably right didn't help her nerve-induced temper. "I was just wondering, Blackheart. We had no trouble leaving by the basement, ending up in this deserted alleyway. Why didn't we go in this way? And don't tell me the service door is locked—I've seen the way you deal with locks. They melt beneath your fingertips."

Blackheart shrugged. "What can I say? There's not much challenge in unlocking a service door and climbing twenty flights of stairs. Besides, there's usually an alarm system wired into those service entrances, and I'm not familiar enough with American current to dismantle it."

Ferris held herself very still, outrage coursing through her veins. "Was there an alarm system?"

"No."

"Then we could have gone up that way?" Her voice was low and dangerous in the aftermath of her fright.

"Yes."

There was nothing she could say in the face of that bald confession—rage left her momentarily speechless. That was one she owed him—and by now they were almost even.

"What about the hotel?" she asked finally, her voice a semblance of normalcy. "Aren't they going to wonder when we don't return the key?"

"Nobody wonders about anything at places like that," he replied, taking another deep breath of the cool night air. "I left the key on the dresser—someone will find it and figure we had a fight before we made it."

"Maybe I should have messed up the bed?"

"A made bed would get more attention than an unmade one, but no one's going to give a damn. Trust me—the Bontemps Hotel is the least of our worries."

"And what's the greatest of our worries?" she asked after a moment. Some of the rage had left her, some of the panic, but her blood still sang with nervous energy.

"First, getting back to the apartment without being seen. Second, getting the police to issue a search warrant. And third, making sure the Summerses are caught red-handed."

"Do we have to worry?" she asked in a very small voice, and through the misty darkness she could see his wry smile, like the Cheshire cat.

"We always have to worry. Come along, my intrepid mountain-climber. Let's get the first worry out of the way. Hold on to my arm, look up at me as if you adored me, and we'll go out for a stroll."

"I don't know if I'm that good an actress," she bit back, taking his arm in her slender hands. The muscles were taut and iron-hard beneath her hands, telling her he was far from relaxed, despite that drawling tone of voice.

"You can manage, I'm sure," he returned, moving out of the shadows with her clinging to his side. His hand reached up and covered hers, and the touch of his skin was comforting. He probably did it just for that reason, Ferris thought, knowing she would pull away, knowing that was the last thing she wanted to do. He must be right—it would look more believable if she snuggled up against him as they walked.

It was a long walk. Blackheart made no move to get a taxi and Ferris made no move to request one, as they made their circuitous way back to Blackheart's apartment. The long, leisurely walk, up and down the hills, skirting Chinatown, started to sooth her shattered nerves. They stopped once, and Blackheart bought her a Double Rainbow coffee ice-cream cone; later he bought her a bag of coconut-and-macadamia-nut cookies and then proceeded to eat most of them. The night was getting cooler, the fog was fitful, but Blackheart's body next to hers was a furnace. She wanted to curl up next to it, to luxuriate in its animal heat, to get as close as one human being could possibly get to another. It was getting harder to remember this was an act, to fool passersby into thinking they were just a couple in love, out for a walk on a foggy winter's evening. As she looked down at the strong arm she was holding, she found herself wishing she still believed in fairy tales.

Blackheart's street was deserted. The Volvo was still parked down the street from his entrance, the streetlights provided pools of light to keep muggers and their ilk at bay. With a start Ferris realized that she and Blackheart qualified as "their ilk." They had broken into someone's apartment that night, and even if their motives had been pure and their victims evil, even if they hadn't taken a thing, they were still technically criminals.

That knowledge appeared to affect Blackheart in the strangest way. He seemed positively lighthearted as they climbed the front steps of his apartment building, and if the arm beneath her hand was still iron-hard with nervous tension, his spirits were soaring.

When they reached the front door of the building, she quickly detached herself. "I'll see you tomorrow," she murmured. "It's late."

Blackheart smiled then, that ironical, laughing smile that always made her feel like a fool. "Don't be an idiot, Francesca. You don't want to wander around town in my clothes. Besides, you've been limping for the last three blocks. Come in and change and I'll call you a taxi."

If that wasn't what she wanted to hear, she would have gone to the stake rather than admit it. But her feet did hurt, and the sooner she retrieved all her possessions from his cool, airy apartment the sooner she could get him out of her life, where he belonged.

She'd thought the elevator was small when she rode up alone. With Blackheart's warm, black-clad figure sharing the space with her, it was practically a coffin. Or a bed. Her nerves were still jumping, the blood pumping through her veins, and her hands were trembling slightly. But she could be just as cool as Blackheart, she told herself as he unlocked the three professional-looking locks on his door.

"Your locks look a great deal more solid than mine," she said, striving for a calm she was far from feeling. With a sudden sinking feeling she knew she'd have to change and get out of there fast, before she threw herself at his feet.

"They slow me down more than most when I've forgotten my keys," he replied, almost absently, as he swung the door open and gestured for her to precede him. "Those pieces of tinfoil on your door wouldn't stop an eight-year-old."

"I'll get them replaced." He hadn't bothered to turn on the light, and as he closed the door behind them they were plunged into a thick, velvet darkness.

"Do that," he murmured, and she could feel his soft breath on the back of her neck, his long fingers in her hair, deftly releasing it from the hairpins. She stood motionless beneath his touch, afraid to say a word and break the sudden spell that had come over her. The hair tumbled down onto her shoulders and his hands ran through it, caressing it with a feather-light touch. And then suddenly she was trembling all over again, her knees weak, her heart pounding, her breath rapid in the thick darkness.

"Will they keep you out?" She struggled for a last brief moment. He was only touching her hair, and that was so gently she might almost be imagining it. If she were abrasive enough he might move away, turn on the light, and watch her go with that enigmatic expression in his tawny eyes.

The hands lifted her hair up, and his hot, wet mouth touched the vulnerable nape of her neck in a slow, lingering kiss that melted the last hope she had of escape. "Nothing will keep me out," he whispered against her sweetly scented skin.

The small, lost wail that came from her mouth could have been despair, could have been surrender, could have been protest, could have been all three. "Don't, Blackheart," she murmured brokenly. "Please, don't."

His hands caught her shoulders and turned her around to face him, and she could feel the tension running through his strong, lean body. Her own tension matched it. "Why not,

Francesca? Give me one good reason to leave you alone and I will."

"Phillip . . ."

He shook his head. "That's not a good reason. Try again."

"We don't have anything in common."

"No good, either. We have a great deal in common, and well you know it. And you're a born cat burglar. If I'd met you five years ago, there would have been no stopping us."

"Don't be ridiculous, Blackheart." Her words were brisk, her tone breathless as his hands gently brushed the hair away from her face. She couldn't help herself, she turned her face into that hand and kissed his palm.

"Give me another reason, Francesca," he said, his voice low and husky and unbearably seductive. "Just one."

She was struggling hard; her Catholic mother would be proud of her. "I don't trust you," she said. "Do you want to go to bed with a woman who doesn't trust you?"

"No," he said, his hands cupping her face and holding it still. "But I saw you jump tonight, Francesca. You couldn't have done it if you didn't trust me." His lips feathered hers, lightly, tantalizingly, and she found herself reaching for more. "Could you, Francesca?"

"No," she murmured against his mouth. "Yes." She no longer knew what she was saying, but she liked the sound of the latter. "Yes," she said again, kissing him. "Yes, yes, yes."

She was glad the lights were out, glad she wouldn't have to see the look of cynical triumph that must be on his face. It was all an act, a sophisticated, manipulative act to get one more notch on his list of bedmates. So why were his hands shaking as he pulled the close-fitting turtleneck jersey over her head and tossed it in the corner? Why was his heart pounding as fast as hers, his lips traveling over her face as if he wanted to memorize her features with his mouth? And why was the tightly strung tension in his body transmuting into a pure sexual tension that trapped her within its threads?

Somehow she had gotten pressed up against the wall, the grainy texture of the plaster cool and rough against her bare back. He'd unfastened her bra and disposed of it, and his mouth traveled down her collarbone, his tongue slipping over her satin skin, enticing, arousing, worshipping, as his hands caught the zipper of her black denim pants and drew it downward. His hands pulled the jeans off her hips, sliding them down her long, trembling legs, and she was grateful for the support of the wall behind her. She stepped out of the crumpled jeans, and it wasn't until his hands reached her hips again that she realized he'd taken her panties with him, and she was naked.

His hands cradled her hips, the long fingers easily encircling their ripe contours, as his mouth moved slowly, sensuously across her bare stomach. She felt like a pagan goddess with Blackheart kneeling in front of her, slowly worshipping her body with his mouth and fingers. She felt decadent and sinful and gloriously alive, and when his mouth sank lower to the tangled heat of her femininity, her heart and soul emptied in a rush of pleasure so heady that she had to brace herself against his strong shoulders or lose her balance.

This was new to her, and unbearable, sweetly glorious. Her body trembled against his mouth, and the world began to slip away, bit by bit, until it finally shattered in a tumbled rush, and her body convulsed in a white-hot heat of love.

She was falling, falling, and she cried out. But he was there, warm and solid and loving, catching her against his hard body, and she hid her face against his shoulder, frightened of her sudden vulnerability.

He held her until the trembling ceased, held her until she somehow found the courage to lift her head and look at him, half fearfully. There was no trace of cynical triumph in the shadowy darkness of his face, no cool calculation. There was nothing but love and desire in those tawny eyes of his, a love and desire that mirrored her own.

A moment later she was swung up high, and he was carrying her through the darkened apartment with the sureness of a cat. He laid her down on the bed, stripping off his clothes with thoughtless grace before stretching out beside her. She felt lazy, sensual and well loved, but the sight of his strong, slim, absolutely beautiful body sent the slow-burning embers of desire glowing into a brighter flame. With a shy sort of boldness she reached out for him, relearning the planes and hollows of his body with a wondering delight. In the darkness there were no rules, no pride, no ego and no fear. No safety, either, but the most elemental trust. He needed her on every level that existed, and that need was her delight.

He moved to cover her, lean and strong and powerful, and she reached up, wrapping her arms around him, drawing him into her heart, into her life, into her body. Her sigh of pure pleasure met his, and then his mouth covered hers as he suddenly turned deliciously, playfully rough, arousing her to a fever pitch that left no room for anything but the heated, pulsing, shattering intensity that swept between them like wildfire.

Their love was fast and furious, a celebration and a culmination of the tension and danger they had shared, washed clean by love and sweat. She was reaching, reaching for a summit that was somehow beyond her, and he was there with her, holding her, helping her as they reached it, and together they fell. He collapsed against her, and for the first time that night she felt the tension drain from his body.

Ferris wanted to cling to him forever, wanted to keep her arms and legs wrapped around him, holding him tight against her. But he began to stir, restlessly, and she knew she had no choice but to let him go.

He rolled away from her, leaving her alone in the darkness. A moment later he was lying back against the sheets, and his breathing was still uneven. Ferris realized suddenly that he hadn't said a word since he'd begun to make love to her. It had all been silent and intense, and she had the sudden, age-old need for reassurance.

Blackheart wasn't the man to give it. They lay together in the darkness for a long time, not touching, and then Blackheart reached out and turned on the bedside light. Ferris blinked at the sudden brightness. When she could focus, she wished she'd kept her eyes shut. On Blackheart's face was the cynical expression she'd dreaded.

He yawned, stretching, and gave her a distant, cool smile. "There's nothing better than a little quick sex after a job," he drawled. "The perfect way to wind down, don't you think?"

She stared at him for a long moment as a tiny part of her heart started to wither and die. And then her head snapped up, her backbone stiffened and she pulled herself into a sitting position, doing her level best to ignore her nudity.

"Cut it the hell out, Blackheart," she shot back, determinedly unmoved. "You don't fool me with that crap."

If she expected to shock him she was disappointed. Blackheart was unshockable. But that cold look vanished from his eyes, and the smile warmed up several degrees. "What crap?" he inquired pleasantly. His nudity was a lot harder to ignore than her own, but gamely she persevered.

"Don't try to pretend you took me to bed to wind down," she said severely. "That's hogwash, and you know it."

His smile broadened. "Then why don't you tell me why I did take you to bed? Not that I approve of that terminology. Whether you like it or not, it was mutual."

"Did you hear any complaints?" Ferris said dangerously.

"No. So why did we have sex?" He crossed his arms behind his head, prepared to be entertained, and for a moment she contemplated mayhem. It had been a long time since she'd hit anybody, but now might be the time to start.

Well, maybe she deserved it, she thought forlornly. But she wasn't going to give up without a fight. "We didn't have sex, Blackheart," she said flatly. "We made love. There's a difference."

"And that difference is very clear to one of your great experience?"

She sat there, looking at him out of frustrated eyes for a long moment. "Blackheart," she said wearily, "I'm in love with you. You know it—you've probably known longer than I have. So stop playing these stupid games."

Blackheart just watched her, and she couldn't read the expression in his tawny eyes. "And what does this mythical love entail?" he said finally, in a bored voice. But Ferris knew he was far from bored.

"For God's sake, Blackheart, give me a break! I've given you my virginity after fighting off scores of determined men, I've turned to a life of crime for your sake, I've leaped tall buildings in a single bound. What more do you want?" she demanded, desperate.

He grinned at her, and sudden relief washed over her. It was going to be all right. It might take some time, but it was going to be all right. "So you love me, do you?"

"Yes."

"What about the good senator?"

"The good senator will have to look elsewhere for a suitable . . . senatress," she said finally.

He still watched her out of those distant eyes. "Scores of men, eh?"

"Hundreds," she replied.

He cocked his head, as if weighing her. "All right, wench. If you love me, come here and prove it."

She sat very still. After all, there were limits. "You come here," she said sternly.

And he did.

Chapter Twenty

Ferris liked sheets. She'd never noticed before, not really. To be sure, she'd bought pretty sets for her huge bed, dribbled chocolate and ice cream and even spaghetti sauce on them on occasion. But she'd never noticed their erotic potential.

Mind you, having Blackheart's sleeping body between them, pressed up against hers, helped. He had particularly nice sheets, she thought dreamily. Navy blue, with white piping. It made his skin look gloriously golden, and she wanted to touch the rumpled brown hair against the pillow.

He'd look nice in charcoal-gray sheets, she mused, snuggling closer with the subconscious hope of waking him. Or maybe beige. He'd even looked glorious against the tiny blue-and-white flowers that had decorated her bed. If she had a lover, she thought lazily, or a husband, she wouldn't waste money on sexy nightclothes that would end up on the floor before long. She'd buy sheets. All colors and patterns, deep rose and black and purple and yellow. Flowers and stripes and solids, cottons and satins and flannels. The very image made her giddy with anticipation.

Was she going to have a husband or lover? Blackheart looked angelic when he slept, but he'd given her no clue last night. She'd presented him with her heart and soul, and he'd accepted them willingly enough. But he hadn't offered anything in return. Not yet. Would he?

It was too early to wake up. Dawn was just creeping over the rooftops, the sun fighting its way through another gray, misty day. It hadn't been that long ago when Blackheart had fallen asleep. If she was going to be worth anything, she'd better try to sleep herself. She and Blackheart had a long way to go. She'd need all her wits and her energy to get there.

He was so warm under the cool blue sheet. Turning over, she pressed up against him. One arm came around her waist, pulling her back against him. "Love," he murmured in her ear. She tensed, waiting for something else. But the rhythm of his breathing told her he was sound asleep, and his murmured word could have meant nothing. Or something too important to bear. Ferris sighed, closing her eyes against the brightening sunlight, and drifted off.

FOUR HOURS LATER he looked down at her, sleeping so peacefully in the center of the dark blue sheets. She looked good there, with her thick mane of hair spread out around her. She looked like she belonged.

And he belonged there in bed with her. The last thing he felt like doing right now was trying to convince a stubborn SFPD that Olivia Summers was the jewel thief, not he. And despite what he'd said last night, he wasn't any too certain he was going to be able to do it, even with the jewels in place.

The last thing he felt like doing was returning to the precinct that had held him with such unrestrained glee a few short days ago. If it were up to him, he'd never set foot inside a police station again.

The last few days had brought home the hard-learned lesson of his life. Never again could he stand the suffocating, demoralizing, slow death of prison. He'd flirted with the idea that he could go back to the rooftops any time he wanted, as long as his leg could support him. Last night had proved beyond the shadow of a doubt that he could scramble over all the rooftops he wanted. The magic touch was still there, and his body still did his bidding.

But his luck was gone, and his options with it. He'd lost his innocence as surely as the woman in his bed had lost hers, and things would never be the same. And it was past time for him to face up to things.

When it came right down to it, when he looked at his life devoid of any illusions, it was more than clear to him that he no longer wanted to make his living from other people's possessions, and hadn't for a long, long time. The fall and the shattered knee had been an excuse, a welcome one. The prison sentence had done more harm than good—he'd stubbornly refused to let someone else make that decision for him. But if it hadn't been the fall, it would have been something else, sooner or later. John Patrick Blackheart had been more than ready to settle down, and last night was his last fling.

How would Ferris-Francesca react when he told her? And he'd have to tell her, sooner or later. Though he hated like hell to give her that trust when she was still withholding hers. If it hadn't been for her sudden excess of morality, he could have gone through life with only that one arrest marring his career. But then he might have gone through his life never having faced the welcome end to his inherited profession. In the last few days he'd finally faced who and what he was, and who and what he wanted. And the woman in his bed was part and parcel of that wanting.

Kate was meeting him downtown. Trace would be with her, she'd said, and Blackheart's interest had been piqued. Had she already told him? How would he react to Kate's treachery? Knowing Trace, he'd be surprised if the big moose was anything less than sympathetic. Trace never blamed anybody for anything, just accepted people, warts and all. Pray God things went as they should, and he wouldn't have to pay for his trusting nature.

And once that was settled, then maybe he could figure out what he was going to do with Francesca-Ferris Berdahofski-Byrd. He didn't for one moment believe that she loved him. Her religion and her working-class upbringing had taught her that you have to love the man you sleep with. He had given in to overwhelming temptation, seduced her and *voilà*, true love! It would take care and time to elicit the real thing from her.

But that was exactly what he intended to do, once he got Olivia Summers sorted out. Because even if he didn't trust Ferris's protestations of true love, he knew exactly what he was feeling. For the first time in his life, in thirty-six misspent, fairly promiscuous years, he had fallen in love. And he wasn't about to give up without a fight.

Neither was she. The memory of her drawling, cutting temper last night still made him grin. He thought he was going to keep her at arm's length, maybe teach her a lesson or two. She should know what it felt like, to make soul-shattering love and then have your partner look at you with complete distrust. It still smarted, even though part of him couldn't blame her. Things had looked suspicious. But damn it, she should have trusted him.

Well, she trusted him now. Now that she'd seen the proof with her own eyes, heard it from Kate. And she'd trusted him enough to follow him up on that roof when she was petrified of heights. If he'd had any idea, he wouldn't have made her go.

But she'd gone, without a word, and he loved her for it. And he loved her for her messy apartment, her temper and her lop-sided morality. He could go on, making a list of all the things he loved about her. But now wasn't the time. He could save that for some night when he was alone and couldn't sleep for wanting her. That time would come sooner than he wanted. Francesca Berdahofski wasn't going to give up being Mrs. Senator Phillip Merriam without a struggle, no matter what she said in the heat of passion. He'd just have to take every unfair advantage he could think of, to make sure she ended up with him and not in Washington. It was all for her own good, he thought righteously.

She needed her sleep, but he couldn't resist. Leaning down, he kissed her on the soft curve of her jaw, trailing his mouth up to her high cheekbone, glancing off her brow and ending on one closed eyelid. The eyelid fluttered open, and she smiled up at him, shyly, sleepily, and he almost jumped back on top of her.

"I'll be back," he said, trying to keep a disinterested tone in his voice. "I'm not sure when."

"I'll be here." She frowned sleepily. "If that's all right?"

"You stay. If you're gone I'll find you." It came out sounding almost like a threat, and he could have cursed himself. Ferris didn't seem to mind in the slightest. Smiling, she closed her eyes and fell back asleep.

If you're gone I'll find you, he echoed to himself grimly. *Fine. Real cool, Blackheart. That's just the way to keep a distance from her. Next you'll be proposing again, and then where will you be? Up a creek without a paddle. And without Francesca. Damn.*

It was all he could do to keep himself from slamming the door behind him. He'd have to do something abut her apartment. He didn't want anyone else breaking in there. It was his domain, and she was his woman. It might take some time, but sooner or later she'd come to terms with that. Please God it was sooner, or he still might have to rip out Phillip Merriam's tongue.

It WAS PAST NOON when she finally decided to wake up. Each time she opened her eyes earlier she'd reached out for Blackheart and he hadn't been there. She could think of no reason for getting up without him, though she probably would have been even more loath if he'd been with her. But high noon was getting just too decadent to be believed, and her stomach was putting up a noisy protest.

"Damn," she said out loud to the silent apartment, throwing back the cool blue sheets and staring around her. Her stomach replied with a grumble, and she moaned. Every muscle in her body ached, both from the unexpected romp over San Francisco's rooftops and the romp that followed. She needed a hot bath and a huge amount of food, not necessarily in that order. And then she needed Blackheart.

There was a pot of coffee keeping warm on a hot tray, half a loaf of moldy bread in the bread box, and a six-pack of Beck's dark in the fridge. And not even a cannoli in sight, she thought with a groan, sagging against the open refrigerator door. The hell with the long hot bath—a shower would have to suffice. And then she'd be bold enough to go out and buy enough food to feed them both, and to hell with him if he thought she was being encroaching. She was, and he'd have to put up with it. After all, he'd started it.

The shower went a long way toward making her feel more human; two aspirins helped, and a cup of rich, strong coffee almost completed the job. All she needed was food in her stomach and she'd feel like a new woman.

The light wool suit and high heels felt tight and restricting after the freedom of Blackheart's black denims, and for a moment she considered raiding his closet for something more comfortable. Then she dismissed the idea. The last thing she wanted to be caught doing was rummaging through his apartment. She'd just managed to convince him that she did trust him—and she didn't want to risk blowing that fragile belief.

He'd left an extra set of keys on the hall table. Tossing them in her leather purse, she let herself out of the silent apartment and headed for the nearest food store.

It took her longer than she expected. The first place she stopped had fresh croissants and Häagen Dazs ice cream, a good enough beginning for the day, but as she was leaving she developed a sudden craving for cannoli. They weren't to be found for seven blocks, and by that time several other delicious ideas had come to mind. It was one of those rare, brilliantly clear days that San Francisco so seldom got, with a chilly little breeze that made her glad for the wool suit, if not for the tottery high heels. By the time she was back on Blackheart's street her arms were aching, her ankles were tired and her stomach was knotted. So preoccupied was she in getting back to the apartment that she almost didn't notice the small dark Porsche parked illegally by the curb. It was a pretty car, oddly familiar. But even more familiar was the slender figure strolling casually down Blackheart's front steps.

Even half a block away Ferris could recognize Olivia Summers's greyhound elegance. Ducking quickly behind a large American car, she watched with dawning horror as Olivia made her way back to the Porsche, sliding into the front seat with a pleased expression hanging about her pale lips. Every blond hair was in place, and her patrician blue eyes were glistening with triumph. Triumph that didn't allow her to notice Ferris's watching figure as she drove off down the street, gunning the motor.

Ferris ran the rest of the block to Blackheart's apartment. The elevator was in use, and after slamming her hand against the buttons and cursing, she dashed to the back of the hall and ran up the five flights of stairs, pausing only long enough to yank off her obstructive shoes.

Blackheart's door looked the same—no sign of forced entry. But what the hell did she expect? Olivia Summers carrying a crowbar beneath that elegant suit she was wearing? With shaking hands Ferris fiddled with the three locks. They all turned beneath the key, and Ferris's blood ran cold. She'd only locked two of them.

The apartment looked exactly as she'd left it, silent and deserted, the lingering smell of the warming coffee lending a false air of coziness to the place. And with a sudden, horrifying clarity Ferris remembered. The light beside Olivia's bed had been on when they'd broken in. And she had been stupid enough to turn it off when they left.

It was a small enough thing, but anyone with Olivia's compulsiveness would notice it. And know that someone had been in the apartment.

What had she done? Why had she sneaked into Blackheart's apartment when no one was there? There could only be one reason. To find some way of incriminating him, rather than herself. Olivia could feel the noose tightening around her, and she needed another scapegoat. Trace and Kate weren't enough. Blackheart was a big enough prize to divert attention from the Summerses permanently. And this time, when the police came after him, they'd hold him a great deal longer than five hours.

Ferris quickly, methodically, began to tear the apartment apart. Somewhere was something incriminating enough to send Blackheart to prison for a very long time. It might be something as easily overlooked as a receipt for copying the jewels. If forgers gave receipts. Or it might be the Von Emmerling emeralds themselves.

Nothing but clothes in his drawers and closets. Nothing but papers in his desk. She tried to take the time to see whether anything was incriminating, but panic was beating down around her like bat's wings and she couldn't concentrate. Nothing under the couch, unlike her own apartment, nothing under the bed or between the mattress and spring. To her horror she found a handgun, complete with ammunition, in his desk, and she slammed the drawer shut on it with absolute terror.

No, you can't do that, she told herself sternly. Olivia might have planted a murder weapon. *Not that anyone's been shot, much less murdered. But you have to check.*

She opened the drawer again, staring down at the ugly black thing with a shudder of distaste. Slowly, reluctantly, she picked up the cold gray metal and brought it to her nose, sniffing for the smell of gunpowder. It smelled of metal and oil, and if it had been fired recently there was no way she could tell. With a shudder, she dropped the gun back in the drawer, slamming it shut.

She was mumbling under her breath as she upended sofa cushions and dropped them back haphazardly. "Where is it? Where the hell is it?" Inspiration struck, and she dived for the ice bucket. Nothing in it but three inches of cold water.

"The kitchen," she murmured under her breath. "Check the kitchen. Lots of drawers. Maybe in the freezer."

The first drawer spilled onto the floor as she yanked it out, and she refilled it with shaking hands. Cabinets, drawers, refrigerator, oven—all were empty of anything remotely suspicious. The bags of recently purchased groceries were in a pile on the floor, the croissants and cannoli probably crushed, the Häagen Dazs melting. The coffee had heated down to a thin layer of sludge in the bottom of the pot, and she reached over and turned it off, her mind still intent upon her search. There was a two-pound bag of coffee beans out on the counter. How odd that a coffee snob like Blackheart hadn't put the beans in the freezer with the other two-pound package. And why did he have two packages, when beans were better fresh roasted? He certainly didn't stock up on anything else.

And the bag in the freezer was half full. With shaking hands she reached for the bag. Did it feel heavier, was there anything bulkier than coffee beans in it? She upended it on the counter, and the small dark beans scattered over the butcher-block surface, raining over the floor like marbles. But it wasn't two pounds of beans. In the midst of the pile lay a plastic-wrapped package of tawdry silver and green. The Von Emmerling emeralds.

Damn her, Ferris thought savagely. *Damn her soul to hell.* Her fingers were trembling so badly she had trouble dialing the phone. Which precinct, damn it, which precinct? She got lucky on her third try. Patrick Blackheart was there, all right, but he was in conference. Would she care to leave a message?

What the hell kind of message could she leave, she thought savagely after she'd hung up. The stolen jewels are in your apartment, but don't tell anyone. Damn and double damn.

They'd arrive at Olivia's, search warrant in hand, and would find exactly nothing. And it wouldn't take much effort on Olivia's part to put the shoe on the other foot. Even if Ferris re-hid the emeralds, what in heaven's name was she going to do with them? And how would anyone ever prove that Olivia had masterminded this whole plot?

She had no choice. And no time to hesitate, to panic, to have second thoughts. Her course was clear, and she had to take it.

"Darling, what's wrong?" Regina responded to her breathless phone call. "You sound in an absolute panic."

"Regina, can you do me a huge favor? Can you somehow get Dale and Olivia to come over to your house? Right now? You could tell them they left something—"

"They're not home, Ferris," Regina broke in.

"They're not?"

"Blackheart called me from the police station a while ago to tell me they were being brought in for questioning. I don't like Olivia Summers, but I still can't believe—"

"Good-bye, Regina." Ferris slammed down the phone. So it had already started to happen. Would the police search their place while they were at the station? Or would they question them first? She'd have to count on it being the latter. Damn, why didn't she know more about criminal law? If Olivia had the right to be present when her apartment was searched, she'd doubtless insist on it. Ferris didn't fancy being caught red-handed by some of San Francisco's finest.

She wasted precious minutes changing back into Blackheart's burgling clothes. She found an old zippered sweatshirt hanging on the back of the bathroom door. The pocket was large enough to hold the bulky packet of emeralds. In the other she slipped Blackheart's lockpicks and trusty American Express card. Pray God she remembered enough from last night to retrace his steps.

It was with a sinking sense of horror that she realized she'd have to traverse those rooftops once more. Blackheart could have made short work of the service door to the basement of Olivia's building, but Ferris was still a rank amateur. It would take all of her concentration and a fair amount of luck to get through the simple locks of the night before. She had no choice but to take the high road. And to hope that she made it in time.

Chapter Twenty-One

"You, again?" It was a different cigarette dangling from the desk clerk's lips, a different shade of fuchsia on those lips, and her unlikely blond hair was up in curlers. But those same hard eyes flitted over Ferris's figure briefly, then went back to the magazine she was reading. *Cosmopolitan,* Ferris noticed. One hand with red chipped nails pushed the register at her. "Twenty bucks," she said flatly.

She hadn't signed her name Berdahofski in years. For a moment she hesitated, then wrote in bold, black letters. She pulled a twenty out of her wallet and dropped it on the desk. The woman just looked at her, and belatedly Ferris remembered. Another ten floated to settle on top of the twenty, and the woman took it, tossing a key back at her. "He meeting you up there?" she queried in a bored voice.

"Uh . . . er . . . yes," she finally managed.

"That'll be another five," the blonde said flatly.

"Another five?"

"For the inconvenience. Not to mention the security problems," she said with a straight face. Another five followed, and the woman nodded. "I gave you the same room, seeing as how you didn't bother to use it last night. This time, sweetie, wait till after to have your fight. And next time bring me back the key," she called after her, as Ferris scurried toward the elevator.

She didn't even bother to open the hotel room door. Getting off on the ninth floor, she headed up the stairway to the roof, the emeralds weighing heavy in her pocket. She felt like she was playing Dungeons and Dragons. Her first obstacle loomed ahead—the locked roof door.

It seemed to take hours. Her hands were slippery with sweat, but she didn't want to bother with the gloves just yet. She concentrated fiercely, poking with the little tools, sweat pouring off her forehead. She broke one, snapping the end off, and she cursed. Just one more try, she kept telling herself grimly as the stubborn lock held. One more, and then I'll give up. One more try.

She almost missed it when it finally worked. The tiny click was almost too good to be true. Reaching up, she turned the greasy knob. It opened with the lightest of touches.

That gave her enough confidence to carry her across the first two roofs. It was better in the daylight, with the blue sky overhead. It gave her something to concentrate on, rather than the inky blackness of certain death below. The ladder between the second and the third building looked more rickety in the daylight, but she reminded herself that it had held both of them last night. It could hold just her slight, shaking weight with no trouble.

It took her three tries to get the grappling hook safely attached to the fourth roof. Each time she yanked it to test its purchase it would clang back at her. When it finally held, she almost wished it hadn't. She had no choice but to go ahead, and the longer she hesitated the worse it would be. She pulled on her gloves, knowing that her sweat-slick hands could easily slide right down that thin nylon rope.

"Hail Mary, full of grace," she muttered under her breath, and swung out between the two buildings.

It was over in a minute. She was lying flat on her stomach on the pebbled roof, the sun-heated asphalt hot beneath her face. The worst was yet to come, and she had to force herself up to face it. But not yet. She needed a brief silent moment to regroup her scattered bravery. Just to the count of sixty, and then she'd move on.

It had looked like the Grand Canyon last night when they'd made their final jump to Olivia's building. This afternoon it was more like the Pacific Ocean. There was no way she was going to make it without Blackheart there to catch her. She was going to tumble down between the buildings, bouncing off the sides and ending in an ignominous, very dead heap on the sidewalk.

If there was any justice in the world, Olivia would be beneath her when she fell. And she'd taken too long as it was—she couldn't stand there and stare at the great chasm waiting to swallow her up. This time she'd take a running leap, and if she didn't make it . . .

Well, she would make it. She wasn't going to die a tragic death and leave Blackheart to chase after bored socialites. He needed taking in hand, and she was the one to do it. She moved backward, slowly, carefully, until she was a good ten feet from the edge of the roof. And then, before she could think about it any more, she ran and leaped.

"Ooooh, damn!" she cursed in a muffled shriek, as her knee hit the pebbled roof and she sprawled in a graceless bellyflop that knocked the wind out of her. She lay there like a beached whale, struggling for breath, hugging the rooftop like a crazed creature.

Her breath came back in a sickening whoosh. Her knee felt smashed in a hundred places, her gloves tore and her palms were scraped by the rough roof, but she had made it. This time she did kiss the roof, her fingers caressing its rough surface. She'd made it.

Jumping down onto the Summerses' terrace was a piece of cake compared to everything else. Her knee almost gave way as she landed, but she caught on to a wrought-iron chair that held her upright. No sign of life beyond the sliding glass window. No men in blue staring back out at her.

Reaching around in her back pocket, she panicked once again as she came up empty. She didn't find the card until she checked her front pocket for the third time, and by then her nerves were screaming once more. She'd taken Blackheart's American Express card for luck. Her hands were shaking again as she jammed the thin plastic between the two doors. It had looked so easy when Blackheart did it. One little push, and the door had slid open. Why couldn't it be as easy for her?

She jammed again, and the card made an ominous cracking noise. Ferris was mumbling and moaning under her breath, prayers and curses tumbling forth. What had Blackheart told her last night? So many things, and right now they were all jumbled in her panicked brain. *Caress it open,* he'd said. *Treat the lock like a lover. Tease and soothe it.*

She pulled the card out, swearing at the splintered end. Reversing it, she gently slipped the undamaged end between the two doors, using the lightest possible touch. Like a lover, she thought with a rueful grin, Blackheart's smiling eyes dancing in her mind. The door clicked open.

The apartment was still and silent, blessedly so. Ferris took a deep breath before stepping inside, her moccasined feet silent on the thick wool carpet. She had made it, in time. Reaching into the sweatshirt pocket, she drew out the plastic-wrapped emeralds and headed for the bedroom.

The door was open, the tape equipment and cameras and stacks of videotapes gone, she noticed with a sudden surprise. A desk had been moved in place, with a typewriter and a pile of correspondence, everything bright and businesslike. *All clean and nice and normal,* she thought with a twisted smile. Olivia certainly knew they were coming.

The empty wastebasket was her next shock, and it stopped her for a moment. Of course the tissue box would be gone, along with the trash. And she couldn't very well just dump the plastic bag in there without any covering. It took her a moment to realize it didn't have to be where Olivia had originally left it. Anywhere reasonable would do the trick. The police would be politely thorough if...when...Blackheart prevailed on them to get a search warrant. Olivia would be unlikely to raise more than a token objection, being blissfully secure that the jewels were residing among her nemesis's coffee beans. It would be interesting to see how she planned to turn the tables. Of course she wouldn't get the chance.

Underneath Olivia's silky lingerie would be the best bet. With her fastidious tastes, she wouldn't like strange men pawing through her panties, and she'd dislike even more the thought of someone planting the loot there. Did she know her secret room had been breached last night? Maybe she hoped they'd come across the jewels before they found her lucrative sideline.

She would have given anything to be a fly on the wall when they found the jewels. But that was far too risky, just as standing around dithering was. With exquisite care Ferris slipped the bulky jewels beneath the pastel silk lingerie, careful not to disturb the neat piles. This time she had to leave no sign that she'd been there. It had been her own stupid fault that Olivia knew they'd broken in the night before. If she'd just remembered about the damned light none of this would have been necessary.

Her knee and shin were beginning to throb. The sooner she was out of there, the better. It was going to take some time getting down those twenty flights of stairs. And this time she was going to stop and rest if she needed to. Her leg was stiffening up, and there was no longer any need to push it. She'd make her way slowly, carefully down those narrow metal stairs, maybe get a taxi and head out toward Oakland, just in case anyone happened to be watching. In another hour or two she could end up back at Blackheart's and receive the praise and love due her. With a weary sigh, she let the kitchen door shut quietly behind her and headed down the first flight of deserted stairs.

"DID YOU SEE the expression on her face?" Rupert demanded for the third time. "I thought she was going to have a fit."

"Very satisfying," Blackheart drawled in agreement as they climbed the front steps to his apartment an hour and a half later. "What I can't figure out is why she looked so damned surprised. And why she'd moved them from her first hiding place. Hiding the emeralds under her underwear seemed just a bit too obvious for someone like Olivia."

"Her husband certainly thought so," Rupert chortled. "It was just like 'Perry Mason.' The accomplice takes one look and starts ratting on the other. The police couldn't even keep up with him to take notes. I love it, just love it."

"There's still something that doesn't seem quite right about it," Blackheart murmured, punching the elevator button. "I can't get rid of the feeling that something more was going on. Why did Olivia look so surprised, when she'd been so smug beforehand? And why was that room cleared out, if she wasn't expecting the place to be searched?"

"The less you tell me, the better," Rupert warned him. "I don't want to know what you were doing last night."

"Rupert, you're my lawyer," Blackheart drawled, gesturing for the shorter man to precede him into the tiny elevator. "You're allowed to hear privileged information."

"Well, I don't want to. I'm too cheered by how things worked out. Stop raining on my parade, will ya? For once just appreciate that everything worked out and stop trying to find problems. Jeez, you're such a downer, Patrick."

"Sorry," Blackheart murmured, unmoved. "I can't help it." He began unlocking the three locks. If only there was some way he could rid himself of that nagging feeling that something had gone wrong. Over the years he'd learned to rely on an almost mystical instinct, and that instinct was clanging loudly inside him, and had been for hours now. He'd been almost as surprised as Olivia when the jewels turned up. He'd taken one look at that smugly opened inner door and been prepared for the worst.

The apartment was dark and silent when he opened the last lock, and his feeling of foreboding increased. She'd said she'd be there waiting for him. It was getting darker—she must have been gone for some time. Where the hell had she gone?

Without betraying his uneasiness, he flicked on the light. "I don't know where Ferris is, but I imagine she'll be back in a while. Do you want to meet us for dinner? I imagine love's young dream will want to be alone."

Rupert laughed. "Kate and Trace were pretty funny, weren't they? He seemed almost glad she'd helped with the robbery. I've never seen so many meaningful glances in my life."

Blackheart shrugged. "They're in love. Trace is the most tolerant man I know—he doesn't give a damn what she did, he only cares about what she's feeling now. I guess he was so busy being her buddy that he didn't realize he was in love with her. And of course, given her earlier standoffishness, he didn't think he had a chance with her. You can tell it's the real thing—the two of them look absolutely ridiculous together."

Rupert snorted. "Ain't love grand?"

Blackheart grinned. A month ago, ten days ago, he would have echoed Rupert's cynicism. But that was before Francesca Berdahofski had argued her way into his life. "Yes, it is," he drawled. And then stopped short, as that instinct began clanging loudly inside his head.

"Something wrong, Patrick?" Rupert was quick to pick up the sudden tension.

"The apartment's been searched."

"Oh, surely not. It's a little messier than usual, but no one's trashed the place."

"No one had to," he said grimly, taking in the cushions still askew, the desk drawers left haphazardly open. "She had plenty of time to go through it—she didn't need to dump everything on the floor."

"She? Surely you don't think Ferris . . . ?"

Blackheart turned a bleak face to his lawyer and friend. "Of course it was her. I left her here, with a set of keys. Anyone else would have had to break in."

"Think about it, man. Why would she do such a thing? What could she expect to find? She knew the emeralds were at Olivia's. Maybe she was just curious. Women are like that sometimes."

"Simple curiosity wouldn't involve a thorough search like this. And she wouldn't have been so clumsy. I think maybe she wanted to see if I was involved after all. Maybe see if I had some jewels left over from before. Maybe she didn't think it was before, maybe she thought I was still working even if I didn't do the Von Emmerling job. Damn her." His voice was furious.

Rupert stared at him for a long moment. "Listen, Patrick, give her a chance to explain. There may be a perfectly logical reason for this."

"There is. She didn't trust me," he said bitterly, flinging his tired body onto the sofa. "Get me a drink, will you, Rupert? Something strong. And get something for yourself."

Rupert paused, looking at his friend. "Okay," he said finally. "But you think about it before you start making accusations. You want me to stay in the kitchen?"

They could both hear the fumbling with the unfamiliar locks. "I don't give a damn," Blackheart said. "Do what you want."

"See you in a while," Rupert said hastily, vanishing into the kitchen as Ferris finally opened the door.

She looked tired, Blackheart thought, feeling not an ounce of pity. She dumped his keys on the hall table and looked up, and the exhaustion on her face vanished, replaced by a look of intense joy as she moved toward him, limping slightly.

"Blackheart, you're back," she cried happily. "What happened? Did…" Her voice trailed off, and the joyful look on her face disappeared, leaving a wary expression in its place. He just sat there on the sofa, looking up at her with a cold, bleak expression. "Didn't they arrest Olivia?" she asked.

"They did. Caught red-handed, and Dale started blabbing and nothing could stop him. There'll be no problem. The charges against Trace and me were dropped, and Rupert says Kate will probably get off with a suspended sentence." His voice was clipped and dry.

"Then what's the problem?" Ferris demanded, relief warring with the wariness. "Everything's wonderful. Blackheart, I have to tell you what I did. I—"

"You don't have to tell me," he interrupted in a savage voice. "It's more than clear."

She had started toward him, but the cold words stopped her. "What is it you think I did, Blackheart?"

If he'd bothered to look at her, he would have recognized the pain and surprise that washed over her face. But he kept his eyes on the skyline. "You searched my apartment. Couldn't quite trust me, could you? Despite all those pretty words, when it came right down to it you had to make absolutely certain that I wasn't still a felon. Didn't you?"

"Didn't I what?" she asked very calmly.

"Didn't you search my apartment?"

"Yes," she said.

"And did you find what you were looking for?"

"Yes," she said again. She stood there for a long moment, not moving. "Good-bye, Blackheart."

He didn't turn his head until he heard the door shut quietly behind her. And then he began to swear, steadily, obscenely.

Rupert appeared from the kitchen, two dark drinks in his hand. "You got rid of her, I see. Didn't listen to my advice, did you?"

"When I want your advice I'll ask for it and pay for it," Blackheart snapped.

"I do think I ought to mention something to you," Rupert said casually, handing him the drink and sitting down opposite him. "Your kitchen is a mess. She was in a bigger hurry when she got to it."

"So?"

"So, there are coffee beans all over the counter and the floor, and the bag that held them is ripped apart."

Blackheart just looked at him. "This is supposed to be edifying? Maybe she didn't like my kind of coffee."

"It wasn't your kind of coffee, Patrick. You drink Sumatran coffee exclusively. This was a bag of Colombian beans."

He'd finally gotten Blackheart's interest. "I don't like Colombian coffee."

"Exactly."

"And what does your analytical mind tell you, Rupert?" Blackheart was genuinely curious.

"Oh, I wouldn't jump to any conclusions, unlike you who thinks he knows everything. But I will mention that the police noted one curious thing about the emeralds. There was a coffee bean wrapped up in the plastic wrap."

Dead silence filled the room as Blackheart looked at his friend in horrified comprehension. "I'm an idiot!" He slammed his drink down and was at the door two seconds later. There was no sign of her—she was long gone. He turned to look for his keys, and swore again. Sitting there on the hall table were his butchered lock picks and a shredded American Express card. And a key to the Bontemps Hotel.

Chapter Twenty-Two

Blackie greeted her at the door when she let herself in. The apartment had that faintly stale, musty odor places get when they've been closed up for a while. It hadn't been that long since she'd been home, she thought wearily. Only a lifetime ago.

Seaside Surprise wasn't compensation enough for her outraged gray tomcat. The look of contempt in his yellow eyes was unnervingly like Blackheart's, and Ferris hastily rummaged for a tin of people tuna. Blackie gave her a look that said, Don't even try.

"Well, what do you want?" she demanded, harassed. He raised his tail with supercilious grace and she gave in, reaching for the leftover bit of Brie. She wouldn't be entertaining Phillip again, anyway, so there would be no one to begrudge its absence.

Very carefully she stripped off the black denims, dropping them in the middle of the kitchen floor. Her fall had scraped layers of skin off her shin and knee, and the blood had crusted over, sticking to the denim. She moaned softly as she pulled the cloth away, and Blackie looked up from the cheese for a moment, offering a questioning "mrrrow?"

"It's nothing, kid," she murmured, peeling the turtleneck over her head and dropping it on top of the discarded jeans. "Just a battle scar." Clad in her underwear, she limped into the bathroom. For the time being she wasn't going to think about Blackheart, wasn't going to tear her heart out over him. She was going to sink into a hot, soothing bath and soak all the aches and pains out of her bones. And then she was going to eat everything she could find in the house, short of Seaside Surprise. And then maybe she'd feel like thinking about Patrick Blackheart.

SHE WAS IN THE KITCHEN when the doorbell rang. She was clad in a pair of powder-blue ladies' jockey shorts and matching tank top, and for a moment she considered ignoring the summons. If it was Blackheart he could find his own way in there. And she didn't know whether she felt up to facing anyone else. Especially if her afternoon's activities weren't as discreet as she had hoped, and someone had seen her clambering over the rooftops.

The bell rang again, and she reached for her old terry-cloth bathrobe, padding to the front door on bare feet. Peering out the tiny peephole, all she could see was a huge basket of red roses.

"It's me," a tinny voice said. "Mrs. Melton from next door. These were delivered for you earlier today and I took them in."

She controlled the immediate pang of disappointment, hastily opening the door to let the little woman in. "You were out," Mrs. Melton continued, eyeing Ferris's bathrobe as if she knew full well what lay underneath and disapproved of it heartily. "I told them they could leave them with me, but they ought to be watered."

"Who are they from?" The question was desultory. If they arrived this afternoon they couldn't be from Blackheart, complete with heartfelt apology.

Mrs. Melton drew herself up to her full height of four feet eleven inches, bristling with outrage. "I haven't the faintest idea, Ms Byrd. I wouldn't think of looking. I'm not a nosy neighbor."

Mrs. Melton was an extremely nosy neighbor, but Ferris let that pass. She was rummaging through the roses, looking for a card, when her neighbor spoke again.

"It's in the back," she said, and blushed. "I didn't read it, I just happened to notice it was there."

Ferris gave her her nicest smile. An overwhelming curiosity about one's fellow man surely wasn't the worst trait in the world to possess. The card wasn't sealed, and there was a smudgy fingerprint on it.

The roses had to be from Phillip. But the card was a definite surprise.

"I understand," it read. "Love, always. Phillip."

What did he understand? Mrs. Melton was craning her neck, trying to read the card, but Ferris tucked it back in the envelope. "Do I owe you any money?" she inquired tranquilly.

"What for?" She was still looking forlornly at the card.

"Did you give the messenger a tip?"

Mrs. Melton sniffed. "Of course not. He's paid for delivering things, isn't he?"

Ferris controlled the smile that threatened her. "Of course. Thank you again, Mrs. Melton."

There was nothing the woman could do but leave. Ferris watched her go, refastening the ineffectual locks with an abstracted air. Phillip understood, did he? The note sounded like a farewell. A farewell that was long overdue, but she had expected it was going to be more of an ordeal.

Well, maybe things were improving. She'd send Phillip back his ring, and perhaps that would be the end of it. She only hoped she could remain friends with Regina. She'd always liked Phillip's mother a tiny bit more than Phillip himself. It would grieve her more than she liked to admit to lose that relationship.

Phillip's ring was nowhere to be seen. She searched over every available surface, under the bed, in the drawers, in her pockets. *Don't panic,* she told herself. *It'll turn up. You never lose anything for good. When did you last see it?*

The memory wasn't reassuring. She didn't remember seeing it since the night of the Puffin Ball. Had Olivia somehow managed to get her slender, patrician fingers on that, too?

It was late, after midnight, when she gave up and finally headed for bed. She'd been avoiding that room like the plague. It was ridiculous—she'd lived in the apartment for three years, and after one night it had taken on all sorts of unshakable memories.

There was no way she could summon up a great deal of self-pity, she thought with determined fairness. She'd condemned Blackheart without a hearing the moment the theft was discovered. It served her right to have the same lack of trust thrown back in her face.

The red shoes were sitting on top of her dresser. She slipped them on her feet, giving her reflection a wry grin. Powder-blue jockey shorts and red high heels. Too bad Blackheart wasn't here to enjoy it. Flopping down on the bed, she grabbed a pillow and tucked it underneath her as she flicked on the TV. And flicked it right off again. Channel 12 was still running its series of caper movies, and the last thing she was going to do was lie on her big empty bed and watch *To Catch a Thief*.

She lay there, staring at the sheets for a long moment. They were new, a deep wine color. Blackheart would look beautiful on them.

Damn, there was no way she was going to get him out of her mind. She may as well watch the movie—his memory was going to drift in and out like the Ghost of Christmas Past as it was.

And damn Blackheart. Cary Grant he wasn't, but there was still no way she could lie there and watch and not be inundated with the memory of Blackheart. The sound and smell and feel of his supple flesh, the memory of his laughing eyes and mocking, arousing mouth.

She was lying at the opposite end of the bed, the shiny red shoes on one of the pillows, her head at the foot, watching the television set intently. Hugging the pillow as Cary Grant sank onto the couch with Grace Kelly and the fireworks flashed overhead. She moaned miserably into the sheets. Maybe ice cream would help her forget her sorrows.

"Where did the flowers come from?"

She kept very still, her fingers still clutching the pillow beneath her. Maybe that low, warm voice was a figment of her imagination. Maybe she'd died and gone to heaven. Slowly she lifted her head, to look straight into Blackheart's tawny, rueful eyes.

"From Phillip," she replied breathlessly.

"Did he have anything interesting to say?" Blackheart was determinedly casual. Blackie was reposing in his arms, and one long-fingered hand was stroking the furry gray head.

"I guess he was saying goodbye." She tried to summon a tentative smile. "He beat me to the punch. You can get rid of them, if you want." She held her breath, waiting for his response.

"I already did." Blackie jumped out of his arms then, stalking back toward the living room without a backward glance.

"I'm going to have to find Phillip's engagement ring to send back to him," she said, still not able to gauge Patrick's mood. "I looked everywhere for it, but I couldn't find it."

"Are you accusing me of stealing it?" he asked, and she flinched.

"No, of course not. I wouldn't think—"

"Because I did," he continued smoothly.

"—of accusing you of . . . You did?"

His smile was entrancing. "Guilty. I couldn't resist. It was just sitting there, abandoned, and my palms started itching."

She stared at him for a long moment. "What did you do with it?"

"Sent it to Phillip. I neglected to mention that it came from me and not you. I didn't think it mattered," he said gently.

"Why did you take it?"

He shrugged. "I guess I can't resist. Every now and then something comes along and all my good intentions go out the window. I really need someone to keep me in line."

"What sort of someone?"

"Well, I'd prefer another cat burglar. Someone who could climb over rooftops with me if the need arose. Someone who could even do it by herself if she had to."

Ferris held her breath. "Wouldn't that be encouraging you?"

"Oh, I don't think so. She could make sure I only broke into places that I had to. Maybe she should be afraid of heights. That way she won't be into doing it at the drop of a hat."

"Sounds logical," she said softly. "Does she need anything else?"

"An American Express card. Mine got mysteriously shredded. I don't know how I'm going to explain it to the company. Not to mention getting certain slightly illegal tools replaced. I suffered a lot of losses today."

"Did you?"

He nodded, moving into the room with his usual catlike grace. "I lost my secretary to my assistant. It looks like they're going to make a match of it."

Ferris grinned. "That's wonderful."

"And my tools of the trade suffered considerable damage," he continued. "I've probably earned the displeasure of Regina Merriam, not to mention half of San Francisco society, for my part in Olivia and Dale Summers's fall from grace."

"I think you're more likely to win appreciation for that one."

"Maybe." He shrugged again, and Ferris suddenly realized that cool, sophisticated Patrick Blackheart, cat burglar extraordinaire, was nervous. Nervous as a cat. "Most people knew about their gambling debts, so I don't think it came as too great a surprise."

"What else did you lose today?"

"The respect of my lawyer, for jumping to conclusions. And I may have lost the woman I love. I'm sorry, Francesca."

Slowly she closed her eyes as relief washed over her. When she opened them, he was staring down at her intently, and she smiled, a tremulous, loving smile. "You haven't lost her," she said. "You haven't even discouraged her a little."

He still didn't cross the last few feet of space. "Trust is a funny thing," he said meditatively. "It's a gift that's given, it's something you earn, and yet it's so damned fragile. And without trust, love isn't worth a damn."

Ferris pulled herself into a sitting position, looking at him intently. "Blackheart," she said steadily, "there's trust and there's trust. I trust you with my heart and my soul and my life. If I find that I can't trust you with other women's jewels, I'm just going to have to accept the fact that I'll be spending a lot of time returning them when you're not looking. At least I'm not without experience."

Those beautiful hands of his caught her bare shoulders, and he was drawing her slowly up to him, almost into his arms, when a startled look came into his eyes. "What the hell are you wearing, woman? You have the strangest taste in nightclothes."

"You can always take them off me," she murmured, moving the rest of the way. His mouth met hers in an open, searing kiss that weakened her already abused leg. She sank against him, and slowly he lowered her to the bed, following her down. His hands were eager, hurried, but oh, so gentle as they stripped the ridiculous clothes away from her body. Slowly, carefully he loved her, his body tuned to her every need, anticipating them and satisfying them with an almost mystical cleverness that left her reaching, longing, aching, and then blissfully sated.

She lay in his arms, cradled against his warm body. He did look beautiful against the wine-colored sheets, his skin warm and firm and faintly tinged with dampness.

"I suppose it's only fair to tell you," he murmured against her cloud of hair.

"Tell me what?"

"That I've decided I don't need to replace my tools of the trade."

She lay very still against him, holding her breath. "Why not?"

"I think I've broken into enough places in my misspent life," he drawled. "I held on to the lockpicks just in case I wanted to go back to the life. I've realized in the last few days that I never want to go back. My fall and the prison term were only an excuse to put a stop to it."

"Won't you miss the excitement?" She had to ask.

She could feel the smile that creased his face as it rested against her temple. "Not with you around." His lips brushed her damp forehead. "I don't suppose there's any chance of your making a similar sacrifice?"

"Hell, no," she replied lazily. "I intend to keep on breaking into places."

"I wasn't talking about B and E," he said with mock severity. "I was wondering when you felt like facing Francesca Berdahofski."

She bit him, lightly, on the smooth skin of his bony shoulder. "I did, Blackheart. Days ago. If you'd stopped to buzz my apartment, you would have noticed the new name on the mailbox. Ferris Byrd bit the dust the night of the Puffin Ball."

"I'm glad. I have a reputation to consider, after all. I wouldn't want it known that I was consorting with someone living a double life."

She bit him again, a little harder, her mouth nibbling at his warm, enticing skin, and he growled an approving response.

"There's one major problem with all this," he said as his hand reached up to stroke her neck.

"What's that?" She wasn't going to fall for one of his teasing ploys this time. There were no major problems that would stop her.

"If you marry me and change your name, you won't be able to call me Blackheart in that deliciously scathing voice of yours. Not when you share the same name."

She grinned up at him. "Of course I can. You don't think I'd settle for anything as tame as Patrick, do you? You have a wicked, black heart, and your name suits you better than anything your parents might have saddled you with."

"I thought so, too," he said complacently.

"What do you mean?" She was suddenly wary.

"Just that you aren't the only one who changed their name. John Patrick Blackheart is a much more fitting name for a cat burglar than Edwin Bunce."

"Oh, no," she groaned, hiding her face against his smooth silky chest.

"Oh, yes. Still want to marry me?"

She eyed him. "Can I marry Patrick Blackheart? I'll accept Francesca Berdahofski, but Francesca Bunce..."

"Changing my name was one of the few legal moves I made in my formative years," he murmured, kissing her lightly on the nose. "You can be a Blackheart, too, but you'll have to make it legal."

"Whenever you want, Blackheart. I have to warn you, though. I expect I'm out of a job. Phillip won't want his ex-fiancée as an administrative assistant."

"Kate's out of a job, too. I don't suppose you'd be interested in whipping Blackheart, Inc., into shape?"

"Along with Blackheart himself? That might prove very...challenging."

His mouth dropped onto hers, his tongue tracing the soft contours of her lips. "Why don't we start now?" he whispered.

"Because we're coming to the best part of the movie," she murmured limpidly. "And I want to see how Cary Grant manages those rooftops. Professional curiosity, you know. Just because you're giving up a life of crime doesn't mean I intend to follow suit." Rolling away from him, she grabbed the remote control and turned up the sound.

A moment later the little box was wrenched gently from her hand, the television went black, and the room was plunged into darkness. "I'll tell you all about it," he drawled. "If you come here."

"Well, it's a tough choice," she said in a low note of laughter. "But I guess they'll rerun the movie."

His code name is Casanova—
he's earned it!

CODE NAME CASANOVA

Dawn Carroll

Daniel scowled as the full implication of Lucretia's unexpected call dawned on him. "Lord, when I think of the megabytes of data stored in that computer of yours, it scares the hell out of me. Next you'll tell me we share the same blood type."

Lucretia gave her rusty imitation of a chuckle. "No, but we show every indication that you'll be compatible. *Do* you know her?"

Daniel searched his memory briefly. "I know of her, but I've never met her. Classique is one of my largest accounts, but most of our business is conducted by bookkeepers and secretaries. I heard she inherited the business from old Gus Anders when he died. My secretary said there was quite a scandal when they got married. Seems Gus was nearly old enough to be her grandfather."

"You see?" Lucretia sounded triumphant. "You already know something about her. Getting closer should require very little effort. And you wouldn't have to neglect your beloved business in the least. The perfect setup, right?"

"Wrong!" Daniel surged to his feet, then remembered his considerable height wouldn't give him an advantage over the phone. His handsome features hardened in a frown as he sat down again and tried to control his temper. It was a weakness Lucretia had taken advantage of too often in the past. That and the guilt. "Look, I'm not going to waste time arguing with you. The answer is no, and it always will be. Goodbye, Lucretia, dear." He started to hang up, when her voice rang out, naming an amount of money that made him jerk the receiver back to his ear.

"I thought you said the job was surveillance. That kind of money usually means heavy trouble."

Lucretia laughed, the dry, humorless exclamation of a hyena. "Retirement is making you overly suspicious, my friend. Did you consider that the lady might simply have some very wealthy friends in high places?"

"Someone you owe a favor, no doubt."

"Not really. Think of it more as a hands-across-the-sea gesture. Liaison for a foreign cousin. I can't tell you more than that, for now, but I do have some fascinating background on the lady in question. I can have the dossier on your desk in thirty minutes."

There had been a time when special agent Casanova would have considered her an irresistible challenge, but Daniel wasn't hooked until he flipped to the second glossy photo in the stack. This portrait was a tribute to the thoroughness and competence of Lucretia's photographer. That he had caught his subject in an unguarded moment was immediately evident.

Although the second picture was a close-up head shot, like the first, a shocking vulnerability had replaced the continental sophistication of the previous photo. Something intensely private was exposed on that chemically treated piece of paper: a raw flash of emotion totally at odds with the cosmopolitan poise of the woman in the other photo. Seeing it affected him like a blow to the heart. He'd seen that look before on another lovely face. Angelina's face. The passage of time had dimmed exact recall of her features, but nothing could erase the memory of that look.

Damn Lucretia. She couldn't have found out about Angelina. Only his immediate family and a few old friends such as Alita Spencer had witnessed that painful episode. But then, Lucretia was well known for her instinctive knowledge of a man's weaknesses. Had she anticipated his reaction? Was she capitalizing on the fact that the great Casanova, purportedly heartless when it came to women, had ultimately been destroyed by a backlash of guilt?

Daniel impatiently drummed his fingers on the desktop as he considered his options. He could just relock the briefcase and forget the whole thing. That would be the rational thing to do, if he wanted to keep Lucretia and her memories in the past where they belonged.

He gazed around, taking in the wood and leather elegance of his private office. The office he'd inherited from his father, along with an auto-repair service that cosseted some of the most valuable automobiles in the state, maybe in the whole country. The paneled walls were lined with photographs of the rich and famous who entrusted Avanti's with the care of their exotic machines. This was important to him now, along with the careful mending of the precious family ties he'd so ruthlessly severed seventeen years ago. He'd be a fool to let Lucretia into even one tiny corner of his life. And yet . . .

He looked again at the exotically beautiful face frozen in a moment of utter defenselessness. What was her name again? He

shuffled the papers until he found the basic stats sheet and read,
Subject Name: Kerith (pronounced Care-ith) Marie Anders.
Maiden name: Braun. Below that was a personal note from the
investigator, stating the origin of the first name was unknown
and that Braun was the surname given to her by the nuns at the
orphanage where she'd been raised.

An orphan. That piece of news gave Daniel pause. He'd never
known an orphan before, and he was ill equipped to guess at how
it would feel to be one. Even during all those years of deliberate
separation from his family, he'd always had the certainty of his
roots, his heritage to fall back on in the lonely times.

If Lucretia's information was correct, Kerith Anders had no
one. Except, of course, for the rich and powerful friends who
wanted her watched, Daniel amended with a grim smile. Could
they be the cause of the sharp melancholy in that second photo?
Even if they weren't, it was still possible that their interference
wouldn't be in the lady's best interests. He knew a sudden,
forceful urge to protect Kerith Anders from Lucretia and her sort.
And the only way he could do that would be by accepting the
assignment and finding out what the hell was going on.

He held up the two pictures, side by side, and studied them,
feeling again a sympathetic ache in the region of his heart. "Well,
Kerith Marie Anders," he murmured softly. "I think you've just
acquired a champion. I hope I don't live to regret it."

With that decision made, he sat forward and reached for the
telephone. His first order of business would be getting close to
this woman who obviously wasn't in the market for male company. And he knew just the person to arrange it. Ali Spencer was
a chauffeur at Classique. And when it came to matchmaking,
she was almost as compulsive as his mother. All he'd have to do
was drop a hint or two to Ali about his utter fascination with her
boss . . .

KERITH PROPELLED HERSELF out of the pool's refreshingly cool
water, her hands braced on the tiled coping. With fluid grace,
she came to a standing position on the brick patio and raised her
arms to the shimmering blue expanse of the morning sky. Water
sluiced down her golden nakedness like sunlight sliding over silk,
highlighting the becoming curves and hollows of her supple
body. Head back, eyes closed, spine arched, she offered herself

like a pagan to the warmth of the late-August sun. She remained like that, reveling in the freedom of the moment, her soul soaring like a captive bird unexpectedly set free.

And then the intrusive chime of the front doorbell brought her tumbling back to earth. Instinctively, her arms swooped down to shield her nakedness, but she caught herself at the last instant and straightened resolutely. *No one can see you*, she chided herself silently, her eyes sweeping the high brick walls surrounding her backyard.

Still, she retrieved a thick, white terry-cloth robe from a nearby chaise lounge and shrugged into it as she headed through the house to the front door, her bare feet leaving damp impressions on plush ivory carpeting. As she squinted to look out the peephole, she heard a car door slam and the roar of an engine accelerating away, but the porch and the street in front of her house appeared to be uninhabited.

Had she imagined the bell? But no, there had been the slamming door and the sound of that retreating engine. She opened the door a crack and checked the neighborhood. It looked deserted, which was normal. This quiet suburb was primarily inhabited by the night people of Las Vegas. People here were performers and dealers who began their workday as the moon rose and slept when the hot dessert sun burned over the city.

Satisfied she was unobserved, Kerith stepped out and nearly tripped over the potted plant someone had left on her welcome mat. With a muttered exclamation she bent to pick it up...then froze as her brain registered and identified the star-shaped flowers nestled among long, slender leaves. A casual observer might have dismissed them as common wildflowers. Not Kerith. She knew that this particular flower grew wild only in the Alps, but more importantly, to her they were an unwelcome reminder of a time in her life she had worked hard to forget.

"Edelweiss," she whispered in a stricken voice. Like a sleepwalker she rose and carried the plant inside, placing it on the coffee table before sinking onto the couch, unmindful of the damage her damp robe might do to the satin-brocade upholstery. "Edelweiss," she murmured again, reaching with one shaking finger to stroke the fuzzy, white petals that surrounded a bright yellow center. The flower bobbed gently on its stem and the colors blurred before her eyes as memories surged up with poignant clarity.

Her fifth birthday. That's when it had begun; when this small, unassuming flower had begun to carry a deeper significance in her life. She still remembered the day with painful clarity: the summons to Mother Superior's office; the long walk down a cold hallway on trembling legs; the grave expression on Mother's softly aged face . . .

"Come in child and sit down."

Relaxing a little at the lack of steel in the old nun's tone, Kerith had climbed onto the hard wooden chair positioned in front of Mother's ancient oaken desk.

"I have something to show you," the nun went on once Kerith was settled, her thin legs sticking straight out over the edge of the chair. "God has seen fit to bless you with a benefactor and I think you are old enough to know about it."

Of course, being five, Kerith had assumed the envelope handed to her had come from God Himself, in spite of Mother's vague explanations about anonymous gifts. It wasn't until much later that she began to wonder about the donor of the cashier's check inside the envelope. And wondering had led to wild hopes and fantasies that had inevitably given way to disillusionment and frustration, because her benefactor had remained a maddening enigma, despite her most determined sleuthing. Not even her occasional midnight forays into the orphanage's locked files had ever produced any information.

The check itself had been drawn from a numbered Swiss-bank account each year on her birthday. No names, no signatures, except the official scrawl of the bank president. The only clue she'd ever had was the blank piece of paper folded around the check, an expensive piece of vellum embossed with an edelweiss.

Kerith shivered and pulled her robe more securely around her. Edelweiss. For a time, she'd actually dared to hope that someone would come to claim her one day, just like Daddy Warbucks in *Little Orphan Annie*. But the years passed and no one came. Edelweiss had never offered more than monetary benefaction and the autocratic arrangement of her life. She shivered again as a phantom of the old pain touched her soul, followed quickly by the inevitable flash of resentment. Hadn't Edelweiss had enough of manipulating her life back then? Why this unexpected reminder after years of silence?

Twelve years, to be exact. Twelve years since the last check had arrived on her eighteenth birthday, along with a scholarship to a frighteningly foreign-sounding American university. It had been the final step in the long series of directives that had ruled her childhood and shaped her into the woman she was today. She'd taken the irresistible offer of a prepaid formal education at the cost of accepting, once again, the life-changing decisions of a person she had never even seen. What if she had turned the scholarship down . . . ?

The ivory phone resting on the end table near her elbow rang twice before the sound penetrated her troubled thoughts. Still slightly distracted, she reached for it and answered in the language of her childhood. *"Do isch Kerith."*

"Hello? Kerith, is that you?" Ali Spencer's familiar contralto quickly brought the present back into focus.

Realizing her slip, Kerith laughed self-consciously. "Sorry, Ali. I was thinking about Switzerland and automatically answered in German. What can I do for you?"

"I have a big favor to ask." Ali rarely wasted time on long preliminaries. "I promised to chauffeur a friend of mine and some of his relatives tonight, and this afternoon I fell and sprained my ankle."

Kerith groaned sympathetically. "How bad is it?"

"The doctor said to stay off it for a couple of days. That includes driving, since it's my right foot. Anyway, I checked with Charlotte and all of our drivers are busy tonight."

"Except me, the boss," Kerith put in wryly.

"Right." Ali's husky chuckle trailed off uncertainly. "I know it's asking a lot at the last minute, but this is really important. In fact, you might even think of it as good business relations. The friend I mentioned is Daniel Avanti, as in Avanti's Foreign Auto Service. His sister Annette is getting married tomorrow, and tonight Daniel and a few of his relatives are taking the groom out on the town. Sort of a bachelor party on wheels."

Kerith started to protest, but Ali quickly cut her off. "I know, it's not your run-of-the-mill contract, but you're always telling me how much you enjoyed chauffeuring before you took over administration, especially the unusual jobs. Think of this as an opportunity to brighten up one of your normally dull and lonely Friday nights."

"You'd better watch the subtle slurs on my social life, if you don't want your friends to walk," Kerith warned, reaching for the notepad and pencil she kept near the phone. "Now, where and when do I pick up these gentlemen?" Listening intently, she quickly noted Ali's instructions. "Okay, I've got it. Anything else?"

"Yeah, I agreed to drive the newlyweds from the church to the reception, and then on to the hotel where they're spending their honeymoon. I wasn't going to charge them the full rate, since I was invited to the wedding anyway, but you can take the difference out of my paycheck. They want to use the Rolls, which, if you'll recall, you agreed to when I asked two weeks ago."

"I also told you I haven't been using the Rolls much because I can't rely on it—thanks to your pal Daniel's service manager. He keeps sending it back saying it's fixed, and a few weeks later it breaks down again. If that happens during a contracted ride, my business reputation is on the line."

"I explained all that to Daniel. He said he'd look into it personally after the wedding. In the meantime, he's willing to risk the odds of the car not breaking down. You see—" Ali's voice faltered with sudden emotion. "Joe Avanti died six months ago, and Daniel's doing everything in his power to make up for the fact that Annette won't have her father to give her away at the wedding. When she mentioned her dream of riding in a Rolls-Royce, Daniel and I committed ourselves to making that dream come true."

Kerith smiled and brushed back the damp tangle of her bangs. "You and Daniel, hmm? Sounds like you're sold on this guy. Are you perhaps thinking of giving up your role as the swinging divorcée?"

Ali's startled laughter provided an answer before she spoke. "Daniel isn't that kind of friend. Although, lord knows, he's got everything a woman could want. It's just that we've known each other since we were kids—our dads were even in business together for a while—and I've never been able to think of him as anything more than a big brother." There was a significant pause. "He's definitely available, Kerith. He's also devastatingly handsome, financially secure and remarkably lacking in conceit."

Kerith was instantly on guard. "Take it easy on the glowing praise. I'm not interested."

"You never are, darn it, and you should be." Ali's voice was gently accusing now. "Gus would have been mortified at the prospect of you mourning him like this. There hasn't been one man in your life since he died, and it isn't for lack of trying on the male side of the population."

There hadn't been any men in her life before Gus, either, Kerith thought, pushing her damp bangs back from her forehead with an irritated motion. Except that near-disaster in college. But no one, not even Ali, knew that. Since Gus's death two years ago, people had attributed her lack of social life to lingering grief. Not that she didn't grieve. Gus had given her a brief taste of the dangerous sweetness of letting someone get close, of caring deeply. And then he had abandoned her in death, as surely as she had been abandoned at birth. She'd vowed not to repeat the experience.

Her eyes focused on the flowering plant sitting so innocently on her coffee table. *You see, Edelweiss? I've learned a lot since I escaped your influence.*

"You're not talking," Ali said with a nervous little laugh. "Are you mad at me for nagging? You know I only do it because I care. You're a dear friend, Kerith, in addition to being the nicest boss I've ever had."

Not going to let anyone get close, huh? a silent voice accused. Restlessly Kerith picked up the pencil, and began doodling a border of star-shaped flowers around the hastily scribbled instructions on her phone pad. Friendship with Ali was different than involvement with a man, she told herself. And even though Ali had been pushing the boundaries of that friendship lately, Kerith couldn't bring herself to halt it just yet. She'd allowed herself so few real friends in her lifetime.

"I'm not mad," she said at last. "But I wish you'd give up. My life is too busy for the kind of complications men seem to generate. And I've yet to find one worth the trouble."

"Daniel is," Ali responded promptly. "You'll see once you've met him."

"Don't count on it. I'm going to be his chauffeur tonight, and chauffeurs are generally ignored by their clients."

"Not when the chauffeur looks like you," Ali said with a knowing chuckle.

"Ali . . ." The single word was heavy with warning.

"All right, I'll quit. Especially since you're being nice enough to fill in for me. I don't know how I'm going to repay you."

"I'm willing to call it even if you'll just stop trying to sell me on the amazing Mr. Avanti."

Ali laughed again. "Don't worry, my promotion won't be needed once you meet him. He'll do all the selling himself."

WHEN DANIEL AVANTI opened the door to his trendy, two-story condominium that evening, it occurred to Kerith that Ali might have been right. The tall, raven-haired man before her looked like he'd probably be able to sell striped shorts to zebras. Not only was he blessed with the dark-eyed sensuality so typical of Latin men, but Daniel Avanti seemed to radiate the kind of innate charm that could reach out and beguile before his victim had time to react.

His eyes, the rich color of bittersweet chocolate, were meltingly intimate, his disturbingly masculine smile promised the world, and his strong, slightly aquiline nose suggested he was a man who delivered on his promises. The faint lines of experience etched on his lean, tanned face told her he was probably well into his thirties, but they only added to his compelling attractiveness. For the first time in her life, Kerith found she was unable to look away with cool disinterest.

"You must be Kerith," he murmured through that captivating smile. "I've been looking forward to meeting you."

As his deep voice caressed her ears, a soft evening breeze, still warm from the setting sun, wafted between them carrying the delicate perfume of night-blooming jasmine. Its intoxicating sweetness caused a sharp increase in her disorientation, and Kerith forced her eyes away from his face in an effort to break the spell. She quickly discovered looking at the rest of him didn't improve matters at all. He was unusually tall, probably four or five inches over six feet, and his body had the kind of lithe, toned muscularity that bespoke disciplined maintenance. Even in a simple, white sport shirt and navy slacks, he radiated urbane power and masculine confidence.

The silence between them had stretched uncomfortably, too long to repair. Kerith decided to ignore the warmth of his greeting and get back to basics. "I hope you'll enjoy your ride with Classique Limousine, Mr. Avanti," she said in her most formal chauffeur's voice. "I'll be waiting at the car whenever you're ready to leave."

Daniel watched in surprise as Kerith pivoted neatly on one heel and returned to the sparkling white Cadillac limousine parked at the curb. After the dazed once-over she'd given him at first sight, he'd expected either the subtle come-on of a woman well versed in sexual games or the flushing confusion of one of her less experienced sisters caught gazing too long at a man's attributes. Those were the reactions his appearance normally garnered. Instead he'd gotten cool dismissal, and it challenged him in a way nothing had in a long time. As he locked the door to his condo and started after Kerith, his pulse quickened in anticipation.

He walked slowly, taking time for his own detailed perusal of the woman waiting at the open rear door of the limo. Dynamite. Even better than her picture, he thought, enjoying the way the tailored gray trousers of her uniform hugged her trim waistline, and the saucy curve of her bottom. He had known she would be slightly above average height—five foot eight, according to Lucretia's report—and that she weighed around a hundred and twenty-five pounds. But not even Lucretia could have described how delightfully those pounds were distributed.

The view from the back was almost as enjoyable as the one from the front. The white shirt of her uniform was short-sleeved, an obvious concession to the extreme Las Vegas heat, but other than that it closely resembled the formal shirt worn with a tuxedo, including pin-tucked pleats and a neat, black-satin bow tie. Over it she wore a short gray vest, with a deeply scooped neckline that buttoned snugly under the rounded softness of her breasts. On her shining golden brown hair was perched a smart, gray chauffeur's cap. The entire outfit had been designed to promote an image of formal efficiency, but seeing it on Kerith's lush, womanly body made his senses stir with decidedly informal thoughts . . . like bedrooms and rumpled sheets and the musky scent of lovemaking.

A surprising thought filtered through Daniel's stirring senses. Where was that little shaft of self-disgust that normally checked his desire at this point, forcing him to continue in a more calculated route to physical satisfaction? Was it possible . . . ? No, he wouldn't jump to any conclusions just yet; he'd see where the evening led, first.

Kerith heard Daniel's approaching footsteps and purposely kept her eyes focused on the flowering ash trees lining his street. She was still reeling a bit from the aftereffects of her first real encounter with sexual awareness. Oh, she'd felt stirrings before, the unnamed urges that swept over one at certain times of the month, but never anything like this. Not even that time in college, when sheer curiosity had prompted her to foolhardiness, had she felt anything like this.

Looking at Daniel Avanti had brought on a dizzy breathlessness, like that experienced by the uninitiated in the high altitude of the Alps. And in this, she was uninitiated.

When he stopped in front of her and bent to peer into the back of the car, she felt as if her heart actually stopped for an instant before it shot up to a racing tempo. It pounded even harder, when he spoke.

"Hmm, looks lonely back there. Mind if I ride in front?"

Years of discipline was the only thing that kept Kerith from shouting a denial. While she struggled to form a gracious reply, he went on.

"I know it's irregular, but we're picking up five more guys tonight, and your backseat doesn't look big enough to hold more than that comfortably. Especially if one of them has my long legs." He glanced down at his limbs, and Kerith's eyes automatically followed. Even though dark slacks covered his legs, she could tell they were magnificent, lean and muscular and definitely masculine.

As was the rest of him, she thought, her gaze snagging for a telling microsecond on his fly. Belatedly, she realized what she was doing and jerked her eyes back to his face only to feel the betraying heat of a blush sweep her cheeks. Once again she fell back on professionalism to cover her loss of composure.

"You may sit wherever you wish, Mr. Avanti. I merely thought you'd be more comfortable in the back." She knew *she'd* be a lot more comfortable having him back there.

"I think I'll have a better time up here." Daniel's smile was dazzling as he allowed her to usher him into the front passenger seat. "And I wish you would call me Daniel. It's friendlier."

Kerith thought distractedly, friendlier! That was the last thing she needed right now. In fact, her strongest impulse was to put as much distance as possible between herself and Daniel Avanti's potent charm. Lacking that option, she said with polite determination, "I think Mr. Avanti would be more appropriate. You're paying me to be your chauffeur, not your friend."

"Ah, but I think I'd much prefer having you for a friend," he responded quietly, gazing up at her from the plush interior of the car. All playfulness had vanished from his expression, in its place was a vibrating intensity that had nothing to do with mere friendship. When his dark eyes slowly swept the length of her body, Kerith felt as if summer lightning had suddenly invaded her nervous system. Her first reaction was outrage over his blatant perusal. But then she remembered the embarrassingly long look she'd given him on his porch step, and the urge to put him in his place vanished. After all, she'd started it.

They remained like that for an interminable moment before Daniel finally sighed and broke eye contact. He checked the elegant gold watch that gleamed against the dark hair on his forearm and smiled regretfully. "Unfortunately, I'll have to settle for a chauffeur for now. We're running late and my relatives aren't patient men when it comes to partying."

Kerith let out an inaudible sigh of relief. It was enough just to have the electrifying moment over. She'd analyze her atypical reaction to the man later, when he was a safe distance away. Right now she had a job to do. With a formal little nod, she closed the car door and hurried to take the driver's seat. Unfortunately, she'd never realized before just how intimate the front seat of a limo could be.

2

FROM THE MOMENT Kerith slipped into the driver's seat of the limousine, she began to suspect her sense of relief had been premature. Dusk lent a peaceful, watercolor wash of mauve to the quiet residential streets, but her thoughts were far from tranquil as she skillfully steered the stretch Cadillac toward her second pick-up point. Thanks to years of chauffeuring experience she was able to maintain an outward appearance of calm competence, but inside she struggled against a riot of emotions and sensations, all of them stirred up by the man who now sat only inches away. She'd always scorned the concepts of sensual electricity and instant physical attraction, and having them swoop down on her unaware was demoralizing and a little frightening.

When Daniel turned toward her and spoke, she tensed, preparing to resist yet another round of sensual banter. But he surprised her. "Tell me what it's like to run a limousine service," he requested, drawing her into a completely neutral discussion of their respective businesses. Warmed by relief, she found herself gradually responding to the keen intelligence she soon discovered lurking behind his entrancing dark eyes. He was an adept conversationalist, changing subjects as smoothly as the large automobile changed lanes under Kerith's skilled hands. She'd almost forgotten her original wariness when he shifted into a decidedly personal topic.

"Ali told me you're from Switzerland originally, yet I can barely detect an accent. Have you lived in the States long?"

Kerith's grip on the steering wheel tightened noticeably. How had they gotten from comparing the relative merits of hiring an outside accounting firm to her personal history? Damn Ali. She talked too much.

"I grew up in Switzerland," Kerith admitted reluctantly. "But I attended college in Los Angeles on a scholarship. As for the accent... I've always had a knack for that sort of thing. It's the reason I chose languages as my major in college." She threw him a challenging look. "Most people think I was born here."

"I'd probably assume that, too, if it hadn't been for the time I spent in Europe doing liaison work for Uncle Sam." He gave a self-deprecating shrug. "I guess you could say I have a talent for noticing little nuances like that."

If he noticed small details, Kerith didn't want to think about what he'd seen in her response to him. "Exactly what kind of liaison work did you do?" She knew she was breaking her own rule about getting too close to the personal lives of others, but it was better than discussing nuances.

He didn't answer right away, choosing instead to point out the street where his brother-in-law lived. Once Kerith had negotiated the turn, he responded easily. "I was involved in cultural exchange, foreign affairs, that sort of thing. I specialized in sorting out misunderstandings between our government and whoever we happened to be dealing with at the moment. Sort of an international conciliator."

Envisioning him in that role wasn't hard. Kerith would have been willing to bet his incredible charm would work on almost anything that drew breath.

"Now it's your turn," Daniel went on smoothly. "How does a bright, beautiful, multilingual Swiss lady end up owning a limousine service in Sin City?"

It was his second subtle probe for personal information in less than five minutes, and Kerith decided it was time to establish some boundaries. "I doubt you would find the story interesting," she demurred. With an admirable economy of movement, she parked in front of an attractive adobe-styled home.

"On the contrary." Daniel caught her arm as she tried to get out of the car. "I'm completely fascinated."

His large hand was warm where it encircled the soft skin of her upper arm, and it caused an even warmer response in her bloodstream. Even as her body yearned toward that warmth, Kerith forced herself to resist it. She tried to pull away, but he wouldn't release her. "I don't see any need...."

"Come on, Kerith, don't tease me with mysteries." He was using his selling smile again. "They only make me more determined." The gentle, yet firm grip on her arm told her he wasn't bluffing. And since a group of men, obviously the rest of her party for the evening, emerged just then from the house and headed toward the limousine, she decided pacifying him with a little information now would be easier than having him pursue the matter in the company of others.

Letting her irritation show in a huffing sigh, she acquiesced. "I came here with some college friends to celebrate our graduation. They assured me the tab was being picked up by their parents, and when they didn't seem to have any difficulty charging things, I believed them. Then, after three days, my so-called friends disappeared, leaving me with the unpaid bills."

Kerith made a little moue of self-disgust and shrugged. "I needed a job, fast. Fortunately for me, Gus, my late husband, was looking for a chauffeur who could handle the occasional non-English-speaking client. I discovered I really loved the business and stayed. Eventually, Gus and I married, and I inherited the business two years ago when he died. End of story." She looked pointedly at his hand. "Now will you let me go, so I can do my job?"

Daniel nodded slowly, but didn't release her. "Betrayal by a friend, that usually causes some pretty heavy disillusionment," he said thoughtfully. "I hope it hasn't soured you on the idea of friendship." He paused and looked directly into her eyes. "I would never betray you, if you were my friend."

A new kind of alarm shivered to life inside Kerith. Even though she'd purposely delivered her story in an emotionless monotone, this man had immediately zeroed in on the feelings beneath. Coupled with his effect on the rest of her senses, Daniel Avanti's perception was a real threat. In defense, Kerith retreated behind the polite demeanor of an experienced chauffeur. "Thank you for the offer, Mr. Avanti, but I have all the friends I need at the moment."

Daniel saw Kerith's guard go up and knew it was time to let her put a little distance between them. He released her and watched as she left the car to assume her duties with the men outside. Progress had been made, despite her resistance. And while he'd once denounced the attributes that had served Casanova so well, he was gratified to know Kerith wasn't immune to them. Not as a matter of pride, but because of the depth and gathering power of his response to her.

With each smile, each word she uttered, the pull was stronger, drawing him toward feelings and emotions he hadn't experienced in years. It was like being reborn, exhilarating and just a little frightening, given that he still didn't know exactly what Lucretia and her cohorts were up to.

Instinct told him Kerith wasn't an agent, but that only opened up more disturbing possibilities. Maybe she'd had an innocent affair with the wrong person. She might have been involved with an agent from the wrong side, and these powerful friends of hers wanted to make sure she hadn't been converted. He'd handled that sort of case too often. To think of Kerith being involved in such a situation made his gut clench.

Had there been a lover? Perhaps before she left Europe? She would have been young then. Vulnerable. As she'd looked in that second photograph. Daniel's jaw tightened in a barely discernible show of frustration. Lucretia was going to give him some answers, if he had to wring them out of her.

The sound of the rear doors of the limousine opening brought him back to his more immediate goal: the seduction of one reluctant lady in the midst of a stag party for his future brother-in-law. The incongruity of the situation made him smile ruefully.

As KERITH GUIDED the fully loaded limousine through the neon-blazed canyon of the Las Vegas strip, she got a steely grip on herself and vowed to maintain a safe distance from Daniel Avanti for the rest of the evening. No more embarrassingly long looks. No more intimate conversation. She'd just drive the car and keep her eyes on the road.

Daniel, however, wasn't cooperating. While appearing to contribute to the partying in the back of the limo, he managed to maintain a quiet monologue meant for her alone, acquainting her with his boisterous relatives.

There was Frank Bonelli, a lanky, sandy-haired man in western shirt and cowboy boots, who was married to Sophia, the oldest of Daniel's three younger sisters. Jim Peterson, husband to the middle sister, Teresa, was a nuclear physicist at the nearby federal government test site.

Rounding out the party were two cousins, Armand and Tony, and the prospective bridegroom, Dominic Conte, a short, stocky man with a dazzling smile and an epicurean zest for life that sparkled in his dark eyes. Kerith wasn't surprised when Daniel told her Dominic owned Casa del Conte, one of the more elegant Italian restaurants in the city.

By the time she pulled up in front of the sparkling big-top facade of the Circus Circus casino, Kerith felt as if she had somehow been made a part of the close-knit group. But even the mood of easy camaraderie couldn't override the gathering tension in the near seclusion of the plush front seat.

Daniel continued to commandeer the spot next to her as they moved from one glittering establishment to the next, and even the time she spent waiting alone with the limousine wasn't sufficient for her to build any defense against his tantalizing presence. His slightest smile induced the craziest fluttering in her heart, and the deep timbre of his voice wrapped her in sensual warmth even though the conversation was light.

And then there was his scent, a heady mix of expensive aftershave and healthy masculinity that even the air conditioner's cool blast couldn't conquer.

You're imagining it, she told herself for not the first time that evening, as she sat in the waiting area reserved for limousines in front of Caesar's Palace. Caesar's was to be the last stop of the evening, and she eagerly anticipated the moment when she could escape Mr. Daniel Avanti and his dangerous charm. She hadn't felt so threatened, so out of control since the time when Edelweiss dictated her life. And while she'd learned long ago that facing trouble was far more effective than running from it, she'd also discovered sidestepping it entirely was the optimum solution. Yet, here she was toying with the idea of just driving off and leaving her clients to their own devices; a cardinal sin in the chauffeuring business.

She was still worrying the idea like a sore tooth when Daniel and his fellow revelers emerged from the glassed entrance of the casino. Shoving her misgivings aside, Kerith quickly started the limousine and pulled up in front of the gleaming black steps.

Except for Daniel, who appeared as self-possessed as he had when the evening began, they all gave evidence of being well past the legal drinking and driving limit. Shaking her head in amused exasperation, Kerith got out of the car just in time to see Dominic throw back his dark, curly head and burst into a soulful rendition of an Italian aria. She might have laughed if she hadn't noticed one of the doormen begin to signal for the security guards. In a flash, she was up the steps and reaching for the would-be opera star. In the process she nearly collided with Daniel, who'd obviously had the same idea. Even occupied as she was, Kerith reacted to the warm, hard strength of his forearm which rested alongside hers as they hustled Dominic into the waiting limousine.

The others, sensing they'd overstayed their welcome, followed close behind and within minutes were all safely inside, hooting with laughter at their near escape. Kerith didn't waste any time getting under way, but when the car reached the end of the circular drive, Daniel touched her arm lightly, making her hesitate before pulling out into the traffic.

She was coming to expect the little jump in her pulse each time he touched her. What she didn't anticipate was the rush of emotional communion she experienced when their eyes met, a shared glow of accomplishment and relief over their near miss.

"Thanks," he said softly. "That was quick thinking back there. I don't know what my sisters would have done if I'd let any of these clowns get into trouble. Especially Annie, who's going to marry old Pavarotti back there." He jerked his head toward the backseat, then winced as Dominic ran out of Italian lyrics and switched to hilariously ribald English.

A particularly shocking line about tender young maids and lusty men jolted Kerith out of her bemusement. Muttering a quick acknowledgment of his thanks, she turned her attention to the task of merging her long, cumbersome vehicle into the still heavy evening traffic. Dominic continued to serenade them, with the occasional, off-key assistance of the others in the back, and Kerith couldn't resist asking, "Does your sister know what she's getting into?"

"I think she has a fair idea," Daniel replied, his dark eyes sparkling with mirth. "Annie manages his restaurant. Did I tell you he sings while he cooks? Whenever he hears a familiar song on the piped-in music, his patrons are treated to an impromptu concert. He claims they love it."

"Not with those lyrics, I'll bet," Kerith drawled, barely restraining a smile.

"He is rather . . . loose tonight. I think I'd better take him back to my place to sleep it off. Annette will kill me if he's late for the wedding." He spared a glance toward his well-oiled relatives. "You'd better take the others home first, though. I don't want their wives to worry."

By the time they had dropped the others off and returned to Daniel's condo, Dominic had run out of songs and lapsed into snoring slumber. When they couldn't waken him, Kerith had no choice but to help Daniel move the somnolent man inside.

She had a brief impression of comfortable-looking contemporary furnishings in the darkened living room as they half carried Dominic to a long, sectional sofa that formed a U in front of a white brick fireplace. He murmured incoherently as they lowered him onto the ivory cushions, and Kerith was suddenly struck by the potential intimacy of the situation. With Dominic dead to the world, she and Daniel were, for all practical purposes, alone.

With a hastily uttered, "Goodnight, Mr. Avanti. I hope you enjoyed your evening," she turned and nearly ran down the short hallway and out the front door.

Daniel caught up with her on the sidewalk, his large hand encircling her arm at almost the same spot it had held earlier that evening. Kerith's arrested forward momentum pulled her around in a neat arc, and she slammed hard into his big solid body. Reflexively, Daniel wrapped an arm around her waist, steadying her as she stared up at him wide-eyed.

They remained that way for endless, tension-laden moments, and Kerith felt as if she were caught in a still frame of a motion picture, all action suspended except for the rapid pounding of her heart. Daniel's face was so close she could have counted, by moonlight, the heavy midnight lashes that framed his dark eyes. As she watched, his pupils dilated until the irises seemed almost black, and then they were shielded as his lids drooped and his head began to descend.

"Don't." Had that breathless, ineffective protest come from her? She wasn't given time to wonder further. In the next instant Daniel's mouth brushed hers, and it was like lightning touching down on dry desert grass. The flame was so quick, so intense Kerith couldn't think fast enough to fight it. She made a small sound—half gasp, half moan—and immediately felt the wet velvet of Daniel's tongue slide along her parted lips, teasing, tasting, tempting . . .

Another moan escaped her, and she felt Daniel's free hand slide under her hair to cup the back of her head and guide her more deeply into his kiss. He didn't plunge or dominate, but rather tempted her with a silken thrust that a more experienced woman would have found irresistible. For Kerith, however, it caused an overload in sensual circuits that had been pushed beyond normal limits all evening. In less than a heartbeat, she was three feet away from him and still backing up. Her golden eyes were enormous, her breasts heaving, her mouth quivering. "Damn you," she whispered raggedly, then turned and ran toward the limousine.

Daniel stood stunned, as much from the unexpected power of that one kiss as from its abrupt end. He realized he hadn't felt that kind of magic in years—if ever. And she hadn't even been kissing him back. Shaking off his amazement, he started after her, then halted when he realized he was too late. Kerith was already in the driver's seat and had the car started.

"Great strategy, Avanti," he muttered disgustedly, as he watched her power away with an inelegant screech of tires. "Spend most the evening trying to impress the lady with your charm and finesse, and then blow it with one, impulsive kiss." He winced as Kerith rounded the first corner with a scream of rubber on pavement. Actually, he hadn't intended to kiss her at all. He'd merely wanted to thank her for filling in for Ali, and for her extra help with Dominic. But the way she'd looked up at him with those sexy golden eyes of hers had driven all thoughts of restraint out of his head.

Casanova never lost control like that. The thought cheered him immeasurably. Casanova rarely felt anything. But Daniel, not Casanova, had agreed to take this assignment. And Daniel was feeling more vitally alive than he had in a long time. As he turned to walk inside he began to whistle softly, his agile mind already plotting how he would smooth things over with Kerith when he saw her the next day at the wedding.

THE FOLLOWING MORNING, tension was high at Classique Limousine's headquarters. More particularly, in Kerith's office.

"Are you positive there isn't anyone else available to drive the Avanti wedding today?" Kerith frowned, and dropped her copy of the weekly scheduling chart onto the wide expanse of her Danish modern desk. The entire office was furnished in the same design, done in satiny white oak, with a cool, turquoise-and-cream color scheme to promote a feeling of discreet elegance.

"I'm positive. I even called all the standbys on our list." Kerith's secretary, Charlotte McAllister shifted on the low chair facing the desk and reached for the discarded schedule. With her free hand, she absently shoved a pencil into her unruly mop of red curls. "You can blame the unseasonably cool temperatures we're having, and the strike in Atlantic City," she added, with a helpless shrug. "Everyone in town, including us, has more business than they know what to do with."

Kerith made a face and bit the end of the gold pen she'd been using to doodle on company stationery. Delicate edelweiss twined around Classique Limousine's gold-embossed logo, which only served to increase Kerith's ire when she realized what she had been drawing.

"Why don't you want to drive?" Charlotte inquired, confusion clouding her normally cheerful expression. "You're free this afternoon. And you're always telling me how much you love driving the Rolls."

"There isn't a big problem, really," Kerith hedged. Except for a tall, very persistent Italian. "I just . . . had other plans." The most important plan being to avoid Daniel Avanti like the plague. Just the thought of him, sent a rivulet of sensation down her spine. Last night she had lain awake for hours, staring at pale moon shadows on her ceiling, while memories of his strong, hard body and the unique flavor of his mouth painted bright sensual images in her mind. Ultimately, she'd resorted to swimming fast laps in her moonlit pool until exhaustion pulled her into a restless dream-laden sleep.

"Shall I call Mr. Avanti and cancel?" Charlotte offered reluctantly.

Cancel? Kerith's innate business sense balked at the thought. "Of course not. I'll do it, if no one else can." It wouldn't be fair to spoil Annette Avanti's wedding plans just because her brother had dared to kiss his chauffeur last night. She would handle Daniel Avanti somehow. Maybe he wouldn't even remember that kiss today. After all, any man who looked like Daniel probably had women lined up and waiting for his kisses. Not to mention all the other breathtaking activities in which he no doubt excelled.

"Kerith, are you all right? You look a little flushed."

Annoyed at the erotic direction of her musings, Kerith shook her head vehemently. "I'm fine. Just a little tired, after getting in so late last night."

"Well, if you're through with me, I think I'd better get back to typing the schedule for next week." Charlotte hopped up and bustled to the door, then turned back as a last thought struck her. "By the way, when I was refiling some papers in the confidential files this morning, it looked like you'd been searching for something. Did you find it?"

Perplexity, then concern brought Kerith's brows together. Only she and Charlotte had access to the locked file cabinet standing in one corner of Kerith's office. And since Charlotte's filing system tended to be dauntingly precise, Kerith normally let her secretary take care of any record-pulling or refiling that needed to be done. If something looked amiss to Charlotte, there could be cause for concern. Those files held some extremely personal information about Classique's high-class clientele.

Still frowning, Kerith shook her head slowly. "I haven't been in those files since the day you were out sick, a month ago. Are you sure someone other than yourself has been in there?"

Charlotte shrugged, but she was beginning to look uneasy, too. "I could be wrong."

"Nevertheless, I don't like the idea of anyone snooping. Some of our clients are extremely sensitive about their privacy. I think I'll have the combination changed, just to be safe."

"Maybe you should say something about it at the next staff meeting, too. You know, just a casual warning."

"I think I will. And thanks for telling me, even if it is a false alarm."

As Charlotte quietly closed the door behind her, Kerith made a note on her staff-meeting agenda, then did a quick mental inventory of the potentially dangerous information contained in the confidential files.

There were private phone numbers and addresses of at least fifty show-business personalities, and Kerith's notes on the preferences and idiosyncrasies of Classique's regular customers. Such as the married banker who wanted a limousine to meet him at the airport every other month, a well-chilled bottle of Mouton Rothschild and his current show-girl playmate in the backseat. Or the Bible Belt politician who had a weakness for the baccarat tables. Maybe they weren't earth-shattering secrets, but the scandal rags would probably be willing to pay top dollar for some of them.

Kerith also kept most of her personal records in that file cabinet, including the carefully preserved birthday envelopes from Edelweiss, and the stiffly formal letters from the president of the bank in Geneva, politely refusing her repeated pleas for information on her benefactor. Again, not urgent secrets, but things she preferred to keep to herself.

Pressing two fingers to the twin creases between her brows, Kerith sighed wearily and made a note on her calendar to have the cabinet's combination lock changed on Monday. Now, if only there were some way she could as easily rid herself of the other frustrating complications in her life: Edelweiss and Daniel Avanti.

She wasn't any closer to a solution several hours later as she stepped from the private bathroom in her office, dressed once more in her chauffeur's uniform. In fact, she was so busy composing herself for the coming ordeal of facing Daniel Avanti, she didn't notice the blond, arrogantly handsome man lounging against her desk until he spoke.

"My, don't we look stunning today," Arthur Kingston said in his clipped British accent.

Kerith jumped and swung toward him accusingly. "Arthur! You nearly scared me to death. What are you doing in here?"

"Sorry." He smiled guiltily and stood up as she moved toward him. "Charlotte was away from her desk, and I didn't think you'd mind my waiting for you in here."

Kerith realized she was partly to blame for that assumption. For although she maintained a definite personal boundary, beyond which no one was allowed, she encouraged an atmosphere of easy camaraderie among the employees of Classique Limousine, and made a show of joining in it herself. Occasionally it backfired. "Next time, I'd appreciate it if you waited for an invitation to come in."

"Of course. I never meant to overstep," Arthur replied smoothly.

Everything about Arthur was smooth, Kerith thought. His lithe body was shorter than average, but when he was dressed in Classique's distinctive uniform, he exuded an air of sophistication and punctiliousness that made him immensely popular as a chauffeur—especially with women. His thick, fair hair and sharp aristocratic features belied the fifty years he claimed on his employment application. He was also an exemplary employee, always punctual, and willing to work overtime when necessary.

In spite of all that, Kerith couldn't seem to overcome a slight uneasiness whenever she was around him. There was something about Arthur Kingston that just made her edgy. Perhaps it was the occasional hint of cruelty she thought she detected in his cool blue eyes. Or perhaps it was his rather cavalier treatment of the growing number of rich, lonely widows who vied for his attention day and night.

"I tried to call you last night, but you weren't home," he said casually. "Was it, as American teenagers put it, a hot date?" Kerith could feel his eyes on her as she moved to put the comforting width of her desk between them.

Hot date! A lightening-quick memory flared in her brain, of the heat that had swept through her body like wildfire as Daniel kissed her. She quickly ducked her head to head the blaze of color she felt rising to her cheeks. "You might say I had a whole carful," she said with a forced little laugh.

"What?" Arthur sounded slightly outraged.

"I said I had a whole carful of hot dates," she repeated, laughing genuinely when she caught his expression. "I was chauffeuring last night. Ali hurt her foot and couldn't come in."

"Ah! I might have known. Too bad, really. I had tickets to a show at the Flamingo. One of my . . . er, customers had to fly home on short notice and she gave them to me. I thought you and I might go together."

Kerith's eyes narrowed suspiciously. "Trying to add me to your long list of lonely old widows, Arthur?" That was another thing about him that disquieted her—his occasional attempts at elevating their friendly employer-employee relationship to something more personal.

"You wound me, Kerith. I merely wanted to share my good fortune." He leaned one hip on the edge of the desk and picked up the piece of stationery she'd been scribbling on earlier. "You're a talented doodler." He squinted interestedly at the gracefully twined border of edelweiss. "What are these, anyway?"

Quickly plucking the paper from his fingers, Kerith shoved it into a desk drawer and said, "Just flowers. Now, you'll have to excuse me, Arthur. I have a wedding to chauffeur."

"Charlotte mentioned that. Sorry I couldn't take it for you, but I'm booked till two this afternoon. You know I would if I could."

Kerith felt a twinge of guilt. Arthur really could be quite nice at times, in spite of his rather supercilious manner. As recompense for her earlier suspicions, she offered a warm smile. "Thanks, Arthur, I know you would. Want to walk out with me and see the Rolls? I'm using her for the wedding today, and Jamie has been polishing chrome all morning." A self-confessed admirer of Classique's elegant antique, Arthur accepted the invitation with alacrity.

The noon sun poured golden warmth over Kerith's bare forearms and face as she and Arthur crossed Classique Limousine's fenced back lot. Situated in a bustling commercial area west of the Las Vegas strip, the lot had ample room for a modern office building in front, a fair-sized garage in back and plenty of parking space in between for a modest fleet of stretch limousines.

At the moment the parking area was empty, except for the white Cadillac Arthur was due to drive and a majestically beautiful Rolls-Royce Silver Wraith limousine.

Bright sunbeams shimmered along gleaming silver-gray flanks, and sent piercing shards of reflected light off the winged hood ornament. The car's gracefully curved fenders and voluptuously regal silhouette had earned her the nickname "the Duchess" the day Kerith and Gus purchased her at an estate auction. A grand old antique, she personified romance and refinement, even if she did get fractious occasionally.

"Lord, but she's lovely. I just hope she doesn't make trouble for you today," Arthur said, giving voice to Kerith's thought.

"She shouldn't, Mrs. Anders." Jamie unfolded his lanky teenaged frame from where he had been crouched, polishing the car's rear license plate. As Classique's routine maintenance man, he was responsible for keeping the cars sparkling clean and tending to any minor repairs. "Avanti's service manager sent her back last week with a clean bill of health."

"He's done that before," Kerith pointed out with more force than she'd intended. Mere mention of the name Avanti had caused a distressing lurch in her stomach.

"It was pretty bad right after old Joe Avanti died," Jamie conceded with a nod. "But since Daniel took over six months ago, their work has been the best."

"I hope you're right," Arthur put in doubtfully. "Newlyweds generally dislike unscheduled walks." He lifted one hand in a casual salute to Kerith. "I've got to be off now. Good luck with the Rolls. If you get stuck and it's after two, don't hesitate to call."

"Don't worry, Mrs. Anders," Jamie said, as soon as Arthur was safely ensconsed in the other limousine. "Even if the Duchess does act up, Daniel will be there to help out."

Don't remind me, Kerith thought dourly. Another quake hit her stomach region, as she got into the car and started the engine. At least the Duchess was behaving so far.

Seeing her frown and misinterpreting its cause, Jamie rushed to reassure her. "Hey, Daniel's really an all-right guy. He even agreed to show me and a couple other guys at Avanti's some basic moves in martial arts. For free!"

"Martial arts?" Kerith echoed disbelievingly. That hardly fit the image of smooth urbanity she'd gotten last night. Although she might have guessed after seeing the fluid, muscular grace of that big body maneuvering in and out of her limousine . . . This time she felt as if her stomach had actually done a double flip.

"He said he picked it up when he was in the Marines," Jamie explained enthusiastically. "He's totally awesome—"

Kerith held up a hand to end what sounded like the beginning of a long diatribe of praise. "All right, I believe you. If the Duchess refuses to start, I'll have him give her a karate chop or something." Jamie laughed and closed the car door, then waved her off with an exaggerated bow.

SAINT ANDREW'S CHURCH was a modern, red-brick structure located in the affluent northwestern section of Las Vegas. Kerith parked the Rolls in front of the sweeping front steps fifteen minutes before the service was due to conclude. After a last-minute check of champagne and glasses, she settled herself comfortably on the pliant leather upholstery of the front seat and prepared to wait. To her annoyance, thoughts of Daniel Avanti immediately popped into her head.

What would he have to say for himself today? Would he try to pick up where they left off last night? Lord, was she ever going to be able to forget that kiss?

Scowling, Kerith fixed her gaze on the church's imposing bell tower, and made herself think about the weather. It was a gorgeous day; sunny, yet lacking the searing heat Las Vegas usually suffered this time of year. A perfect day for a wedding.

She and Gus hadn't been so lucky. A touch of melancholy pressed in on Kerith as she remembered that day, over four years ago. But even unhappy memories were better than thinking about dark-eyed Italians.

The wedding chapel had been small and tawdry, a chilling November rain adding a dank heaviness to the odors of stale cigarette smoke and cheap perfume. Not that she or Gus would have considered a church wedding under the circumstances. Not when they both knew the union would take place on paper only.

Gus, always the gentleman, had put on a good show for the shabby couple who ran the place. His blue eyes had twinkled, as he gave her a bear hug and a gentle buss on the mouth. Only Kerith knew it was more like the caress of a doting father, than a husband.

Oh Gus, why did you have to die?

A dark swarm of old regrets threatened Kerith briefly, but a movement at the front of the church caught her attention just then, breaking the mood. Thoughts of the past faded to insignificance as the large double doors swung outward, and Daniel Avanti stepped into the dazzling sunlight, resplendent in a dove-gray tuxedo. Given the business she was in, Kerith was used to seeing men in tuxedos, but none of them had possessed the breathtaking virility that Daniel brought to formal wear. He'd been potent enough in casual clothing, in a tux he was positively dangerous.

Kerith let out an explosive little sigh, and gathered her resolve as she stepped out of the car. Not one slip, she warned herself. Today she was going to maintain a chauffeur's poise if it killed her. By the time Daniel had loped easily down the stairs,

Kerith was waiting on the passenger side of the car, her expression purposefully remote.

"Hello, Kerith." His voice was pitched low, as though he were saying goodnight—from an adjoining pillow! His smile was incandescent.

Kerith gritted her teeth and resisted a reckless urge to smile back. "Good afternoon, Mr. Avanti."

When her eyes remained fixed on the tiny white rosebud nestled against the satin lapel of his jacket, Daniel bent down until they were almost nose to nose. He looked surprisingly abashed. "I guess you're still angry with me for kissing you last night, mmm?" His dark brows arched appealingly, as he let out a regretful sigh. "I'm really sorry I upset you. Normally, I make sure my attentions will be welcomed before proceeding. Last night I just seemed to lose my head." An amazingly boyish grin creased his handsome face. "I don't suppose you'd be willing to make allowances, if I told you I have a terrible weakness for women in uniform?"

Amusement and embarrassment warred for supremacy behind Kerith's carefully composed expression. She didn't want to remember that kiss, damn it. And while she knew she should acknowledge his apology as impersonally as possible, she was sorely tempted to grin back at him and give in to that wonderful charm. Common sense prevailed only when she happened to glance at the entrance to the church. "No allowances are necessary, Mr. Avanti. Consider the incident forgotten. Now, if you'll excuse me, I think the wedding party is about to descend upon us. And there's a pretty blond lady in a bridesmaid dress who's standing at the top of the steps glaring at you."

Daniel's gaze followed hers to the gaily dressed crowd spilling from the church doors and fanning out on the wide steps. Poised in the doorway, ready to make their dash through a shower of rice, were the bride and groom. When he spotted the scowling young woman in pink satin, who stood next to them, he groaned. "That's Claudia, the maid of honor. She thinks my being best man means I should be glued to her side for the day."

Kerith managed a nonchalant shrug and opened the rear door of the limousine. "Why are you complaining? She's very attractive."

Daniel braced an arm on top of the open door and watched her pull an icy bottle of champagne from the tiny refrigerator located in the back. "I told you," he said, as she straightened and began to uncork the bottle with unstudied skill. "I have a thing for women in uniform. Especially ones who fill them out the way you do."

Kerith nearly dropped the bottle of champagne, as tingling, electric heat zapped through her body, just as it had the night before when he'd so blatantly charted her physical assets with his eyes. She was trying to formulate a properly discouraging reply, when the newlyweds arrived at the bottom of the steps—breathless and laughing amidst a shower of rice—and the opportunity was gone.

For the next few minutes, Kerith had her hands full getting them settled in the back of the Rolls with glasses of complimentary champagne. She was only peripherally aware when Daniel sprinted back up the church steps. She did, however, have time to note that Daniel's sister Annette possessed a feminine version of her brother's stunning attractiveness.

Daniel reappeared, escorting a now-beaming Claudia, and he gallantly helped her onto one of the rear jump seats that folded down to accommodate extra passengers. Kerith was about to circle the car and offer him the adjacent jump seat, when something small and solid barreled into the back of her legs, tumbling her right into Daniel's arms. She stiffened immediately, half expecting him to take advantage of the situation. Instead, he acted the perfect gentleman, swiftly setting her upright almost before anyone could notice, using only one strong hand on her shoulder to steady her. When he spoke, his voice conveyed genuine concern. "Are you all right?"

Slightly dazed, Kerith nodded, while a funny glow blossomed in the region of her heart. Was it possible he sensed her abhorrence of losing her composure in front of others? "I . . . I think so. What hit me?"

"A pint-sized tornado, I'm afraid." Daniel smiled ruefully and nodded toward a small boy who was bouncing around them like a jet-propelled pogo stick. "Meet my nephew, Joey Peterson." He placed a calming hand on Joey's head. "Slow down, pal. I think you owe this lady an apology."

"Sorry, Mrs. . . .lady," came the sheepish response. The child was a darling, miniature version of his uncle, right down to his gray tuxedo and entrancing dark eyes. And when he raised those eyes to Kerith and pleaded for a ride in the Rolls, she began to wonder if all Avanti males were gifted with the ability to charm a woman's socks off with a single look. Of course, she agreed to let him ride.

"And you can call me Kerith," she added, helping him into the front seat. "Mrs. Lady seems a little formal."

"So you're a softy when it comes to kids," Daniel mused quietly, from behind her. "Perhaps I should have Joey plead my case the next time I kiss you."

The outrageous presumption of his calm statement touched off an automatic rebellion in Kerith. How dare he assume there would be a next time? Completely forgetting her resolve to maintain a professional demeanor, she turned and fixed him with a cool stare. "There's a name for people who use other people to gain what they want. It's manipulator. And I think you should know, I have no tolerance for them."

For several seconds Daniel appeared too surprised to respond. Then, when he did speak, there was an odd note of regret in his voice. "In view of that, I think there's something I'd better confess now . . ." he began, only to be interrupted by Dominic's voice coming from the interior of the limousine.

"Hey, Daniel, could you romance the chauffeur later? I'd like to get to my wedding reception before I celebrate my first anniversary."

There was a rifle of laughter from the small crowd gathered around the limousine, and Kerith wished that the earth would open and swallow her whole. Mortified beyond words, she gave Daniel a fulminating glare, then marched around the car to wait pointedly by the rear passenger door. He followed promptly enough, but before taking the remaining jump seat, he leaned close and whispered for her ears only, "I intend to finish this conversation at the first opportunity."

Not if I have anything to say about it, Kerith swore silently as she buckled herself into the driver's seat. But then another thought distracted her from her fury. Confess? What in the world had he intended to confess?

3

THE RIDE TO DOMINIC'S restaurant, where the wedding feast was to be held, should have been routine for Kerith, even considering the dozen cars that followed the limousine, honking wildly, and the steady stream of questions that poured from little Joey. Such things were only minor distractions to a seasoned chauffeur, yet when she finally pulled up in front of the white, Moorish-style building housing Casa del Conte, Kerith was hard-pressed to restrain a sigh of relief.

Having Daniel seated behind her and out of sight had in no way diminished Kerith's awareness of him. And even though Claudia brazenly attempted to monopolize his attention throughout the trip, each time Kerith glanced at the rearview mirror, she encountered the reflection of his dark, penetrating gaze. Confess? What could he possibly have to confess to her?

A large crowd of family and friends had gathered outside the restaurant, and they flowed forward in a warm familial wave, encompassing first the bride and groom, then Daniel and Claudia as they emerged from the back of the limousine.

Kerith helped Joey get out and tried to ignore the affectionate interplay; a discipline she'd learned as a child. There was no point in hungering after things you couldn't have. But for some reason her eyes kept returning to the happy crowd, where kisses and hugs were being exchanged with abandon. And as she watched Daniel bend to embrace an elderly woman whose smile matched his exactly, Kerith couldn't deny a twinge of curiosity.

How would it feel to be surrounded by people who had known you all your life; who had known your parents before you were born, and maybe their parents before them? What would it be like to know where you'd gotten your eye and hair color, your smile, or even your name?

A hollow ache began to spread in Kerith's stomach, and she closed her eyes briefly to fight it off. Self-pity was a wasted emotion. Years ago she'd come to understand there were some things she would never know, including the kinds of things a man like Daniel Avanti represented.

"Hey Kerith, are you okay? You look kinda sad."

Startled out of her silent reflection, Kerith looked down and found Daniel's nephew regarding her with a worried look on his cherubic face. "I'm fine, Joey," she murmured, embarrassed that he had witnessed her uncharacteristic self-indulgence. So much of her behavior had been out of the ordinary since she had met Daniel Avanti. The man posed a real threat to the carefully schooled thought processes that had protected her for years.

"You don't look fine," Joey insisted, his big brown eyes solemnly searching her face. "You look like you need a hug."

The idea surprised her into a smile. Hunching down until they were eye-to-eye, she chucked his soft babyish chin. "A hug, hmm? Sounds nice. Do you happen to have one you could spare?"

Joey's answering smile was adorably gap-toothed.

He was going to be a real lady-killer when he grew up, Kerith thought. Just like his uncle. Still smiling, she gathered his sturdy little body into her arms. Joey hugged with an almost fierce affection that brought a stinging pressure of tears against the back of her eyes. How long had it been since she'd allowed herself this kind of closeness with anyone? Holding, being held like this, how sweet it was—so achingly sweet. If only the price weren't so high . . .

Joey's small grunt of protest gusted against her ear, making Kerith realize her grip had grown too tight. She released him and smiled apologetically. "Sorry if I squeezed too hard. I haven't had much practice lately."

"That's okay. Uncle Daniel used to do that, too, when he first came back. Mommy said it was because he was so happy to be with us again, but I saw tears in his eyes sometimes. Just like you have now."

Kerith blinked hard against the telltale moisture and tried not to show her dismay. "Well, sometimes tears can be happy. Did you know that?"

"I guess so." Joey shrugged and stuffed his small fists in the pockets of his trousers. He studied her soberly for a moment, then his expression lightened, as if a happier idea had just occurred to him. "Would you like to get married, Kerith?"

Suppressing amusement as his abrupt change of subject, Kerith pretended to consider him seriously. "I'm not sure. Are you proposing?"

Joey chortled and scuffed one small black shoe on the pavement. "Nah, not me. I'm never gonna get married. But Mommy and Gramma Rosa say Uncle Daniel needs a wife, and I think you'd be a nice one."

This time she couldn't hold back her laughter, but it quickly died when an all-too-familiar male voice sounded behind her. "Good grief, sport, have they stooped to using you as a matchmaker now?"

With a silent curse against the unrelenting force of fate that seemed bent on putting her at a disadvantage with Daniel Avanti, Kerith rose slowly and met his twinkling gaze.

"Although I have to admit, Joey," he continued smoothly, "you have better taste in women than your mother and grandmother. What do you say, Kerith? Will you marry me?"

The outrageously casual way he said it—like a man requesting a luncheon date—gave Kerith an equally outrageous urge to laugh and say yes, just to see what he'd do. But instead she pulled a stern face and said, "I'm afraid not, Mr. Avanti. My chauffeurs aren't allowed to accept proposals of any kind while on duty."

"Well, then, at least say you'll come inside and help me celebrate my sister's marriage."

"You can't tell him that's against the rules," a husky feminine voice chimed in.

Kerith swung around and frowned suspiciously at the stunning brunette who was strolling toward them, leaning gracefully on the arm of a tanned, athletic-looking man. "Ali! What are you doing here? You're supposed to be home nursing a sprained ankle."

Ali's former years as a show girl were manifested in the dramatically pained smile she offered before responding. "I don't suppose you'd buy the idea of a miracle cure?"

"Dammit, Ali. I told you to wait until I could explain." Daniel stepped forward, positioning himself between the two women.

Like a referee in a fight, Kerith thought, her suspicions growing by leaps and bounds. Daniel's earlier need to confess came back to her with distressing implications.

"I know what you said." Ali shrugged impatiently. "But I discovered I have no taste for deceiving my friends. And besides, I hate skulking around." Her green eyes were imploring when she turned her gaze on Kerith. "I know it was a rotten thing to do, but I faked the sprained ankle so you'd have to chauffeur and you and Daniel would have a chance to meet. Given your normal reaction to meeting any of my male friends, it seemed like the only way. I even tried to call you and warn you last night, but you were already gone."

Ali's male companion, who had been listening with the bored incomprehension of a career jock, suddenly lit up. "You mean you had her chauffeur this guy on her own blind date? Out'a sight!"

Kerith spared him a scornful glance before fixing Ali with a look that should have set fire to her elegant, green silk dress. Greater fury than she'd ever known simmered in her veins, made worse by the underlying hurt of Ali's breach of faith. When she spoke, her voice vibrated with quiet accusation. "I thought you were my friend."

Ali flinched as if from a physical blow, then paled as she began to comprehend the extent of Kerith's wrath. "I was...I am.... Oh damn, I never dreamed you'd be this upset."

Upset? That doesn't begin to describe it, Kerith wanted to scream. But of course she didn't. Public displays of temper were unthinkable to her. So she contented herself with saying tightly, "I ought to leave right now and let you explain to the bride and groom why they won't be riding in the Rolls to their honeymoon retreat. I won't, however, because I assume they knew nothing about this little subterfuge. As for your part in it, Ali, we'll discuss it in my office tomorrow morning. Seven-thirty, sharp!"

As she walked away from the small stunned group, Kerith heard Ali's horrified whisper, "I think she's mad enough to fire me."

And Daniel's murmured response. "Let me handle it, Ali. I'm the one to blame. After all, I talked you into it."

A grim sort of satisfaction settled over Kerith as she circled to the driver's side of the Rolls. Firing Ali hadn't occurred to her up to that point, and even if it had, she wouldn't have seriously considered it. She wasn't the kind of employer who used the threat of dismissal to exact top performance from her employees, and she never used it to solve personal differences, unless the employees in question had performance problems, also. Still, it would serve Ali right to let her stew about it for a while. Maybe she wouldn't be so eager to play matchmaker next time.

She was reaching for the door handle when Daniel stopped her. "Kerith, I need to talk to you."

"Haven't you caused enough damage for one day?" She tried again for the door, but he put his hand on her shoulder, turning her until her back was pressed to the sun-warmed metal.

"Damage?" His eyebrows rose inquiringly. "Isn't that a little strong? I admit Ali and I shouldn't have lied to you about the ankle, but what actual damage has been done?"

"How about betrayal of a friendship?"

Daniel sighed impatiently. "I find it hard to look at it that way, when I know Ali was only trying to do something nice for two of her friends. And last night was very nice," he added with an intimate smile. "If you're honest, I think you'll admit you enjoyed it just as much as I did." When she didn't respond, he put one finger under her chin and tilted it up until she had to look directly at him. "Come on, look me right in the eye and tell me you didn't enjoy it."

Kerith fully intended to resist him, to jerk her head away, stamp her foot down on his highly polished dress shoe, or at least avoid looking into his eyes. But the deep, soothing cadence of his voice was having a decidedly calming effect on her fury, and when she encountered those meltingly dark brown eyes, all she could think about was the bedazzling fire of a moonlit kiss. "I thought we agreed to forget about...that," she said with as much steel as she could muster.

Daniel's smile broadened. "I was referring to the conversation and the company, but now that you mention it, the kiss was pretty spectacular. So are you. Can you blame a man for going to any lengths to have a little of your time?" His mouth tilted in wry humor. "Even when it means being chaperoned by five of his drunken relatives?"

"I told you how I feel about manipulators," Kerith said, stubbornly clinging to the remnants of her resistance. "Justifying what you did doesn't change the fact that you and Ali lied to me."

"Does that mean you're thinking of firing her?" His hands gripped her shoulders with sudden earnestness. "Please don't. I'm the one who's really responsible. Be angry with me if you must, but don't punish Ali for something I talked her into." Daniel might have argued further, but Claudia chose that moment to swoop down on them in a huff. "Daniel! For heaven's sake, will you come on? The photographer has everyone lined up for pictures inside and you're the only one missing."

Annoyance creased Daniel's features for a moment, but then he favored the scowling young woman with a heart-melting smile. "Tell them I'll be along in a minute, will you, love? I need to clear something with the chauffeur." Claudia hesitated, her blue eyes narrowing a bit suspiciously at the way Daniel's hands rested on Kerith's shoulders, but in the end she gave in and even smiled as she left to do his bidding.

As they watched Claudia swish away in her long skirts, Kerith couldn't resist commenting. "Did you take a course on calming irate women, or were you born with the talent?"

Daniel's soft laughter caressed her senses. "Did I calm you? Good. Maybe Ali won't have to go job-hunting after all."

"I never said I was going to fire her," Kerith retorted, shrugging out of his grasp. He was standing too close again; so close she could smell the delicate white rosebud pinned to his lapel, its fragile perfume in startling counterpoint to the more potent essence of the man towering over her. It reminded her sharply of her own vulnerability to him.

"Just because I'm calmer, doesn't mean I'm not angry with you," she said, giving him a challenging look.

"Yes, but you won't stay angry," Daniel answered softly. "Because under that cool exterior of yours beats a warm, generous heart. I saw it first with Dominic, then with little Joey today. That attracts me to you even more than the memory of how sweet your mouth tastes. It makes me want to—" He didn't get a chance fo finish, because another voice hailed him from the direction of the restaurant.

"Daniel! For Pete's sake, if you have to flirt with the chauffeur, could you at least bring her inside to do it?" The speaker was a petite, auburn-haired young woman, with a rounded, obviously pregnant tummy, and she was waiting impatiently by the restaurant's open door.

Daniel glanced toward her and swore softly. "That's my sister Teresa. I suppose my mother will be out next."

The spark of humor in his eyes indicated he wasn't really concerned about the possibility, but Kerith was horrified. She pushed hard against his ruffled, white shirtfront forcing him several steps back. "Damn you, Daniel Avanti. Do you have any idea what you're doing to my business image?"

Daniel sighed. "Does that mean you won't come inside?"

"Absolutely!" Kerith's temper was back in full force, fueled by a blaze of embarrassment.

"All right, I'll go. But I haven't given up on you. You'll be hearing from me soon. Count on it!" With those provocative words, he made his exit, heading toward his waiting sister. Halfway there he turned around and continued his progress backward long enough to offer Kerith a parting shot. "By the way, I love it when you call me Daniel, but you really should drop the 'damn.'"

The door of the Rolls took the brunt of Kerith's anger when she slammed it shut behind her seconds later. "Damn Daniel Avanti, that's a good name for him," she muttered wrathfully as she scanned the parking lot for a place large enough to hold the Rolls. Leaving it on the street was asking for trouble, and she had more than enough of that at the moment. She was further incensed when she tried to get the key in the ignition, and discovered her hands were shaking too hard to manage the simple task.

What was happening to her? Lately it seemed as though there was a conspiracy against the calm, safe world she had built for herself. First there had been the emotional bombshell of Edelweiss's possible reentry into her life. That alone might not have been enough to undermine her poise. But then Ali had to drag Damn Daniel Avanti into the picture, and things had been going downhill ever since. Even her own body was betraying her. How was it possible for her pulse to be altered by the mere presence of a man? And how could the mere mention of a kiss send pleasure winging through her like a herd of sun-drunk butterflies?

"What's it going to be next?" she groused, finally getting the key inserted. When she turned it, however, her reward was complete silence. She turned it again. And again. Nothing. Not even a click.

Letting her head drop forward against the steering wheel, Kerith groaned wearily, "*Et tu*, Duchess?"

She'd have to call a towing service. Visions of wading through the mob of Avantis inside the restaurant, or worse yet, having to ask Daniel for help, made her groan again. But after a moment her head snapped up defiantly. She'd be damned before she went into that restaurant. There were other phones in the businesses nearby. She'd use one of them, have the car towed, and get out of here without Daniel ever knowing about it. One of the other drivers—perhaps Arthur—could take care of the rest of this ride. Fate might be trying to throw her another curve, but that didn't mean she had to meekly accept it. She'd been taking care of herself for a long time now. She didn't need anyone. Not Daniel, not Edelweiss, not anyone!

THE EMPLOYEE LOUNGE at Classique Limousine was deserted when Kerith entered it on Monday morning. Only the mechanical hum of the compact refrigerator greeted her as she skirted the comfortable couch and chairs grouped around a small television set, and headed toward the counter spanning one end of the room. The counter held a microwave oven and automatic coffee maker, the latter of which lured her with the irresistible aroma of freshly brewed coffee. Today she needed the caffeine as much as the rich flavor. It wasn't easy to get up in the morning when one spent half the night in a pool trying to work off a restlessness that seemed to worsen with every hour. She refused to even think about the cause.

"Sneaking in for an early caffeine fix, huh?" Ali's voice came unexpectedly from the door, causing Kerith to jump and spill her coffee.

"Good grief, you scared me." Scowling, Kerith grabbed a paper towel and blotted the hot liquid.

"Sorry." Ali's classic features tightened into a grimace of regret as she came into the room, a hanger bearing her chauffeur's uniform slung over one shoulder. "And while I'm at it, I'd like to apologize again for the other business. I know there's no excuse for lying, but when Daniel told me how he'd seen you once when you picked up one of the limos at his garage, and how he hadn't been able to get you off his mind . . . Well, I just couldn't resist getting the two of you together somehow."

Kerith's scowl deepened, and Ali lifted her hands beseechingly. "I meant well. Look, Daniel hasn't shown much interest in women since he moved back here, and his family is getting concerned. They're hoping he'll settle down with a family of his own soon." Ali smiled ruefully as she helped herself to the coffee. "And since he's thirty-eight and never been married, I suppose they're entitled to worry. When he started raving about you, it seemed almost providential."

"I'm not the answer to their prayers. I'm allergic to familial ties."

"What about me and my daughter? At times, I think Cami actually forgets you're not really her aunt. And I've come to think of you as one of the family, too, especially after all the good times we had together." Ali reached to touch Kerith's arm tentatively. "I'd hoped you felt the same way. Please tell me I haven't ruined things with this business about Daniel. I think I'd rather be fired than lose your friendship."

Kerith shifted uncomfortably and busied herself straightening a stack of napkins. She had spent a lot of time with Ali and her adorable eight-year-old daughter since Gus died, although she'd never thought of it in Ali's terms. The question now was, did she want to continue the relationship, with all its inherent risk of emotional involvement, or should she back away?

For that matter, could she back away? This was Ali, the woman who'd shared the lonely vigil in Gus's hospital room the night he died. The one who had seen to it that Kerith had eaten and rested in the difficult weeks after his death. Ali was right, they had formed a sort of surrogate family. What must be decided now was, should it continue?

Kerith frowned and stared into the steaming, dark liquid in her mug. She should say no. What Ali was asking went against every self-protective instinct Kerith possessed. But when she turned and saw tears shimmering in Ali's sea-green eyes, the decision was made.

"You and Cami do mean a lot to me," Kerith conceded slowly. "But I'm going to need some time to forget this incident. In addition, you'll have to swear on your sweet daughter's life that you'll give up trying to arrange my social life."

Relief flooded Ali's expression and tears spilled over onto her cheeks. "I swear!"

Kerith pulled some tissues from a nearby box and handed them over. "You'd better go get yourself together. It's time for work."

"Thanks, Kerith. You won't regret it." Her smile was tremulous, but her step was jaunty as she headed for the changing rooms.

On the way back to her office, Kerith experienced a strange elation. She'd done the right thing, giving Ali another chance. Allowing one friendship to deepen didn't mean she was relinquishing all control of her life. As far as she was concerned the episode with Daniel Avanti was over now. And if he showed signs of pursuing the matter, she'd put him off as easily and effectively as she did other men.

That opportunity came sooner than she expected. Kerith had barely settled herself in the soft, cream leather of her executive chair, when Charlotte buzzed on the intercom to announce a call from Mr. Avanti on line two.

"Just my luck, he's the persistent type," she muttered to herself, glaring at the insistently flashing button on her telephone. Well, he wasn't going to get the best of her this morning. She punched the button and said with distant politeness, "This is Mrs. Anders. How may I help you, Mr. Avanti?"

There was a significant pause and then his deep, compelling voice came, stroking her senses to instant, tingling awareness. "It's Daniel, remember? Why did you run away yesterday?"

A sudden breathlessness caught Kerith unaware. Damn the man and his sexy voice. "What...what are you talking about?" she managed finally.

"The Rolls. It and you were gone when I stepped out to check on you yesterday, and some stiff-upper-lip British type was there to replace you. Then, when I came to work this morning, I found the Rolls sitting in my shop. When I questioned the tow driver, he said he'd picked it up in front of Dominic's restaurant Saturday. Why didn't you come in and ask for help?"

Drawing a steadying breath, Kerith said, "I had no desire to see either you or Ali again."

Daniel sighed regretfully. "Have you seen her yet today?"

"Yes, and I think we've managed to salvage our friendship, no thanks to you."

"I guess I deserve that. What can I do to redeem myself in your eyes?"

"Try leaving me alone," she replied promptly, then quietly hung up on him.

DANIEL SAT BACK, propped his feet on his desk and regarded the dead telephone receiver with disgust. *Well, you certainly handled that well. You must be losing your touch, Casanova, old boy.* How ironic that it should happen with the first woman he'd really cared about in years. Lucretia would die laughing if she knew. As it was she'd nearly crowed with triumph when he called her last night.

"I knew you'd come around, Casanova," she gloated. "Is the grease-monkey business beginning to pall?"

"Not at all. This is a one-time offer. I'm only doing it out of consideration for a valued business associate." If he had anything to say about it, Lucretia would never know of his rapidly deepening personal involvement with Kerith. "In addition, I'm running the show," he added firmly. "I don't want any more of your snoops nosing around the lady. I'll tell you whatever you need to know. I also want more information on the people behind all this, including a motive."

Lucretia hadn't been overjoyed by those terms, but when she found out he'd already made contact with Kerith, she didn't have much choice. "All right, you're running the show, within reason," she agreed reluctantly. "As for the details you're demanding, I'm afraid I don't have that much. I do know that the meeting with Kerith has been requested by Edelweiss, the former benefactor mentioned in her dossier. And that Kerith shouldn't be told anything until she's contacted by Edelweiss."

"Just a quiet little reunion, hmm?" Daniel laughed mirthlessly. "Come on, Lucretia, that doesn't sound likely, given the kind of money they're offering."

Lucretia's sigh was eloquent, even over the miles of long distance line. "You were never this suspicious when you worked for me before."

"I wasn't as smart, either."

"All right, there is a slight complication. Apparently, Edelweiss has a superior who's a stickler for security. He wants one of our people around as insurance against any embarrassing international incidents, and he's willing to pay well for that insurance."

"Good Lord, you mean Edelweiss is one of their agents?"

"Retired agent, actually. But still quite important to them. These people are big-time, Casanova. When they want something, we normally don't ask for detailed reasons why."

Daniel had been inclined to withdraw from the whole mess at that point, but something had held him back. Perhaps it was the memory of that look Kerith got in her eyes at times. When she was watching the loving interactions of his family, for instance, or when she thought she'd been betrayed by Ali. The soul-wrenching power of that look didn't diminish with remembering. Like it or not, he had to see the thing through. Lucretia had sounded triumphant when she hung up.

The receiver in Daniel's hand began to beep its off-the-hook warning, reminding him of the call Kerith had just ended so abruptly. Leaning forward, he hung up the phone and slumped back again. Now what?

Fingers steepled on his flat stomach, he toyed with several possibilities, all of which he discarded on the basis they would most likely spook Kerith irreparably. Maybe it was time for a little old-fashioned wooing. Flowers, candy, the works. Yeah, that just might be the ticket. A new spark of resolve lit his dark eyes as he reached for the phone once more.

KERITH SHOULD HAVE had no problem keeping Daniel Avanti out of her thoughts. She certainly had enough business to keep her mind fully occupied during the rest of the day. There were schedules to review, contracts to consider, calls to return, and in between it all, she interviewed several people who wished to train as chauffeurs. She didn't have time to think about Daniel, but that didn't seem to matter.

The harder she tried to concentrate, the clearer became the disturbingly alluring vision of his handsome face. It superimposed itself on paperwork and walls and once, embarrassingly enough, on the face of one of her male chauffeurs. Chagrin had given her cheekbones a warm apricot color when she caught the poor man's guarded look, and realized she'd been staring at him distractedly instead of answering his question.

Matters didn't improve at all when the flowers arrived mid-afternoon. Roses. Masses and masses of pale apricot buds, whose nectar-sweet fragrance filled her office, not to mention her head. The enclosed card had read:

> Their color reminded me of your lovely blushes, but their scent isn't half as enticing as yours. Forgive me. Aside from everything else, I'd like to be your friend.
>
>   Daniel

His words caused a strange stirring in her soul, and she knew she must put a quick end to this new approach. But when she called his office, fully intending to politely thank him for the flowers, and just as politely refuse his offer of friendship, his secretary told her Mr. Avanti was away on business for the rest of the day. Kerith suppressed a groan of frustration and declined to leave a message.

By the time she arrived home that evening she felt tense and irritable from the daylong struggle to keep her mind off Daniel Avanti. Dinner would have to wait, she decided, stripping as she headed for the bedroom. Within ten minutes she was doing rhythmic laps, the pool's refreshing water flowing over her naked body like a lover's caress, or rather what she imagined a lover's caress to be. Floodlights turned the pool's surface to rippling silver in the gathering twilight.

At the end of a particularly long underwater run, she surfaced to the sound of the phone ringing. Unsure of how many rings she'd missed, Kerith lunged out of the pool and grabbed the receiver. Her "hello" was understandably breathless, but her breath caught and held when she heard a familiar bass voice greet her.

"Hello, Kerith. It's Daniel. Did I interrupt your bath?"

"What makes you think I was taking a bath?" she demanded tartly, hoping he couldn't hear the betraying tremor in her voice.

"You took quite a while to answer the phone...and you sound wet and naked."

Kerith sucked in a shocked breath, and glanced down at herself. Her nipples had contracted until they looked like dusky little buds against her golden tan, and a heavy warmth seemed to swell in her breasts.

After a long, telling moment, Daniel's breath hissed in, too. "Sweet heaven, you really are, aren't you? I knew I should have dropped by unannounced."

His last words were light, teasing, but there was an undertone of raw desire that jolted Kerith's defense system back to working order. "How did you get my home number? It's unlisted, and Ali swore she wouldn't interfere anymore."

"You forgot, we're business associates. I have it on file at work," he replied smoothly. "I also know where you live."

Kerith shivered and hastily reached for her robe. "Is that some kind of threat?"

Daniel's husky laughter filled her ear. It was, she decided, the kind of sound that could dissolve even the stiffest backbone, and hers had been in a steady decline since she'd first met this man.

"I never threaten, I coax," he said softly.

"Then why did you call?" She had the robe on now, and some of her self-possession was returning.

"I was going to ask you that. My secretary said you called today, and gave your name but no message."

"Oh, that. I just wanted to thank you for the roses. Which, by the way, you shouldn't have sent. I thought I made myself clear, I'm not interested."

"You sound different. Did you put something on?"

This time his perception made her angry. "Damn it, if you don't stop talking so...so suggestively, I'm going to hang up on you."

"Please don't. At least not until you agree to have dinner with me tomorrow."

"Not a chance."

"Lunch then."

"I'm busy."

"We need to discuss the ills of your beloved Duchess."

Mention of the Rolls made Kerith sit down abruptly on the nearest chaise lounge. "What about the Duchess?"

"Uh-uh. Not over the phone. I'll see you at noon, tomorrow. Lunch is on me."

"No! Wait...." She was addressing a dead line.

THE FOLLOWING MORNING another gift from Daniel arrived at Classique Limousine. To make matters worse, the special messenger showed up right in the middle of the weekly personnel meeting, and the large gold-foil package he handed over caused a storm of speculation among Kerith's employees. She gave in gracefully to their pleas that she unwrap the box, and even passed it around to let them sample the expensive Swiss chocolates within, but the enclosed card she slipped into the pocket of her white linen blazer. No telling what Daniel had written this time.

Later, in the safety of her office she read his bold script:

They say chocolate is a sensuous food. Will you think of me each time one of these melts against your tongue?

Your friend,
Daniel

Something elemental shivered through Kerith, and it wasn't a craving for chocolate. How had he known of her utter weakness for that particular brand? And how could she possibly sit across from him at lunch, and calmly discuss the mechanical problems of the Rolls after reading that note?

The latter question hovered on the back of her consciousness like a half-finished melody as she moved through her routine morning business, which included several long-distance calls to arrange the final details on limousine service for upcoming conventions. She still didn't have an answer when Charlotte buzzed on the intercom to announce in a slightly giddy voice that a Mr. Avanti was there to see her.

Kerith barely had time to stand up and brace herself against her desk, before Daniel strolled in, looking cool and inordinately virile in a beige, summer-weight suit. Her senses started overreacting immediately, and she tried to compensate with drollery. "Do you always carry a purse for business lunches?" she inquired, her eyes dropping to the large wicker basket slung over his left arm.

"Always." Daniel grinned and winked at Charlotte, who returned his smile dreamily and left, pulling the door firmly shut behind her. "Nice secretary," he said, scanning the office with undisguised interest. "She was most helpful when I called about the flowers and candy."

"So that's how you found out. I'm going to have to do something about the spies in my ranks . . . What are you doing?"

Daniel looked up from spreading a red-checked cloth on the low coffee table positioned under one of the office's large, tinted glass windows. "I thought a picnic would be nice, and since you're not exactly dressed for the park . . ." His eyes moved admiringly over her white, pleated skirt and peach silk blouse. "Not that I'm complaining."

Kerith started to protest, then reconsidered. Maybe she would be better off here, with familiar surroundings to remind her of who she was, and why she shouldn't respond to this man. She watched in bemusement as Daniel's beige jacket and brown silk tie landed on a chair. And then he was striding toward her purposefully, rolling up the sleeves of his crisp yellow shirt as he came.

"But a picnic in an office?" she asked vaguely, her attention caught by strong forearms lightly brushed with black hair. "You must be crazy."

"Only about you." Daniel gave her one of his special smiles as he led her to the impromptu picnic area and settled her on the thickly carpeted floor.

"But why? I keep telling you I'm not interested. A man like you could probably have his pick of women any day of the week. Why bother with me?"

Daniel had eased down next to her, and now he leaned closer on one arm. "Because," he said, his gaze resting on her mouth for a moment, then lifting to delve deep into her eyes. "You're the first woman I've really wanted in over seventeen years."

Kerith burst into incredulous laughter. "Oh, come on. You expect me to believe you've never..." Realizing what she'd been about to say, she bit her lip and looked away. How did they get on this subject so quickly?

Daniel smiled and touched a blunt fingertip to the blush warming her cheekbones. "You're confusing wanting with lust. Wanting involves what's in here." He moved his fingertip to her temple, then trailed it down to the peach silk covering her left breast. Beneath it her heart pounded with a new, reckless rhythm. "And here." His eyes roved slowly downward and back up. "In addition to all the rest."

She felt certain he was going to kiss her then, but he surprised her by turning to the basket and busying himself with pouring a glass of chilled, sparkling mineral water for each of them. After slipping a slice of lemon into one crystal goblet, he handed it to her.

"I've only felt this way once before," he continued after a sip of his drink. "And that was a long time ago, with a girl named Angelina." One corner of Daniel's attractive mouth quirked with bitterness. "Unfortunately, my family felt she wasn't good enough for me."

The implications of what he had said startled Kerith into blunt inquisitiveness. "You mean they actually forbade you to see her? I didn't think families could do that anymore in the free world."

Daniel smiled sadly. "You obviously haven't had much contact with old-fashioned Italian families. My father wasn't a harsh man, really, just immovable when he thought he was right. He vowed to disown me if I married Angelina. Not that that would have stopped me, if things hadn't been taken out of my hands." Daniel shifted restlessly and began rummaging around in the basket again. "Here we are. Croissants with crab salad and crudités with herbed yogurt. Your favorites, according to Charlotte."

Kerith opened the packages of food he placed before her on the table, and they ate in silence for a few minutes. But she couldn't focus on eating, not without knowing what had happened to the young woman who'd had such a powerful effect on such a strong, confident man as Daniel. She was truly surprised, though, when she heard herself ask, "What happened?" Once the question was out, she averted her head. This level of communication always made her feel ill at ease.

Daniel, however, caught her chin and made her look at him. "Don't regret asking that. I want to tell you, because I think it'll help you get to know me better. And I want that very much. Almost as much as I want to learn about you."

He took a quick sip of water and continued in a low voice, "Angelina was pregnant. She didn't tell me because she knew I'd insist on getting married immediately, regardless of what my family said. I guess you could say she didn't think she was good enough for me, either." He closed his dark eyes briefly, and when they opened there was a memory of pain in them. "She couldn't afford a good abortionist—so I lost both of them, Angelina and the baby. And, ultimately, my family, too, for sixteen long years."

Daniel experienced an odd sense of release as he finished speaking. It was as though some lingering vestiges of the hurt and guilt and anger had finally been lifted from his soul. And he suspected the reason lay with the woman who was looking at him now with such utter compassion in her eyes. All her reserve seemed to have vanished, for the moment at least, and he knew an aching happiness mixed with a sweet surge of pure desire. Lord, how he wanted her.

Kerith sensed that leap of passion in Daniel as surely as she felt the nascent stirrings in her own body. And she knew he would kiss her if she didn't say something. What surprised her was her reluctance to break the spell of intimacy that held them in thrall. "Ali told me you've never married," she said at last. "Was Angelina the reason?"

A shadow flickered in Daniel's clear, dark eyes before he answered. "Partly, yes. After the initial shock of her death wore off, I discovered I was just as angry with Angelina for deceiving me as I was with my father for his obstinacy. Since then, I've known a lot of women, but none of them ever meant anything to me." He hesitated, his mouth a little grim. "And I made sure none of them got pregnant by me."

An awkward silence stretched between them, and he tried to break it with a rueful chuckle. "What a hell of a thing to tell you, just when I've been working so hard to win your trust, right? My only justification is that I want you to know you're different, Kerith. That's why no other woman will do. That's why I'm not giving up on you."

Kerith felt a little frisson of anxiety at the determination she read in his smile, but before she could say anything to disavow his claim, a sharp rap sounded on her office door. "I'd better see who that is. Charlotte must be out to lunch, otherwise she'd have buzzed me on the intercom."

Arthur Kingston waited for her on the other side of the door, his expression grave. "I'm sorry to interrupt."

Kerith thought she detected a brief flash of anger in his eyes when he looked past her to where Daniel sat casually on the floor, but Arthur's next words made her forget that worry.

"There's been an accident involving one of the limos, and our driver's been hurt. I thought you'd want to know right away." He handed her a message slip from the dispatcher.

Concern for her injured employee immediately took precedence over her other worries. "You were right. I'm glad you didn't wait to tell me." By the time she thanked Arthur and got the door closed again, Daniel had begun gathering up the remains of their lunch.

"I'm really sorry, but I've got to go see about this," she said, waving the message like a truce flag.

"I understand. I own a business, too, remember?" Daniel finished repacking the basket, scooped up his jacket and tie and joined her by the door. "You can, however, make it up to me by coming over to my garage tonight."

"Your garage? Whatever for?"

"Avanti's garage," he corrected with a wink. "I started working on the Rolls . . . I mean, the Duchess, myself last night, and I'd like to show you where I think the problem might be."

Given the tone of their last conversation, Kerith was instantly wary at the prospect of being alone with Daniel Avanti in a deserted building, especially at night. "I don't know..." she hedged.

"Did the story of my lurid past disgust you so much that you're afraid to be alone with me?"

She glanced at him, ready to laugh, then didn't when she saw he was serious. His unexpected vulnerability prompted her to offer a swift, forceful denial. "Of course not."

Daniel's smile brightened the room by several thousand candlepower. "Then come tonight and give me a chance to show you how talented I am—as a mechanic."

Some of Kerith's wariness returned. "No ulterior motives? I haven't changed my mind about not becoming involved with you."

"No ulterior motives. Unless you consider it a motive that I enjoy your company." He grinned and tapped her on the nose. "See you around eight. And wear something you don't mind getting dirty. I may put you to work."

For the rest of the day, as she waded through insurance forms and police reports from the accident, Kerith waffled over whether or not she should have accepted Daniel's invitation. In the end, she decided it would be safe enough to go. After all, as invitations went, it wasn't exactly full of sensual promise. He had said he was working on the Rolls. How erotic could a dirty old garage be?

4

AVANTI'S GARAGE was immaculate. Kerith noticed that the minute she stepped inside the vast, dimly lit building. She also felt
as if she were entering one of the few remaining bastions of ma-
chismo. Women's liberation and female mechanics aside, the
place was unquestionably masculine. The smell of gasoline, oil
and rich leather upholstery lent an accent of male power to the
air that made her feel at a distinct disadvantage.

"You must be Kerith." The young mechanic who'd admitted
her to the locked building offered a friendly grin. "I was just
leaving, but Daniel's still here. He's down in the last stall, where
the bright light is." Obviously anxious to be on his way, the
young man stepped outside, then turned and gave a casual wave.
"Nice meeting you." Before Kerith could respond, he was gone,
relocking the door behind him. Moments later she heard a truck
start up and drive off.

As the sound died away Kerith realized she and Daniel were
probably the only two people left in the huge building, and her
strongest impulse was to follow his mechanic out the door. But
even as the thought occurred, she discarded it. The door had a
dead bolt secured with a key from outside. She could get out, but
she had no way of relocking the door. And a quick glance down
the long center aisle told her a locked door was a necessity.

Lining either side of the aisle were work stalls containing some
of the most exotic and expensive automobiles ever invented. Just
like a stable, she thought, except the kind of horsepower housed
here was fueled by gasoline. Avanti's Foreign Auto Service
probably brought in a fortune in routine maintenance fees alone.
Knowledge of Daniel's financial power only added to her unease at meeting him on his own turf. In the safety of her office,
she'd convinced herself she could control the situation, now she
wasn't so sure.

As she made her way toward the bright light at the end of the building, however, she was oddly reassured by the sound of a soft-jazz radio station and a low, melodic whistling—obviously Daniel's. And then she saw the Duchess in the stall right next to the one the mechanic had indicated, and her anxiety eased a little more. The Rolls was elevated on a hoist, and Kerith was struck by how naked and vulnerable the venerable old car looked with its underbelly exposed. *Poor Duchess. I know just how you feel.*

She nearly jumped out of her skin a second later when the sound of metal striking metal rang out, followed by a pithy expletive. Cautiously, she stepped around the wall of the last stall and discovered a dashing, vintage sports car, its front wheels on a ramp to allow space for the male body lying beneath it.

Well, half a male body, Kerith corrected herself. Two long, well-muscled legs and a definitely male pelvis incased in blue coveralls were in full view. As she watched in utter fascination, one leg flexed at the knee, drawing fabric taut over the unmistakably masculine bulge at the junction of those magnificent thighs. Daniel's thighs. She recognized them as easily as she'd recognized his voice a moment earlier when he'd cursed. But it was the part of himself he was unknowingly calling attention to that held her eye.

Normally, she didn't look at men down there. Not that she was a prude. She'd seen nude men in art and movies, and had even looked at a few on the beach in France the summer she'd vacationed there. But looking at the evidence of Daniel's masculinity, even when it was appropriately shielded by cloth, caused a primal surge of heat in her blood.

"Oh, help!"

Kerith didn't realize she'd actually voiced the thought until she heard a startled, "Wha...," followed by a dull thud and a pained, "Ouch, dammit." Before she could think to move, Daniel slid out from under the car, his big torso riding easily on a mechanic's creeper. With one slightly grimy hand he rubbed his temple, with the other pushed himself to a sitting position.

"Kerith!" His pained expression shifted quickly to a welcoming smile. "Sorry, but I didn't hear you come in. Guess I had the radio too loud." He frowned slightly. "By the way, how did you get in? The door was supposed to be locked."

"It was . . . is," Kerith said lamely, wondering if he could see the flush on her cheeks. "One of your employees was leaving as I arrived, and he let me in. I...I'm sorry if I made you bump your head." Kerith took a step backward. Coming here had been complete foolishness on her part. Now she had to find a graceful way to get out—fast!

"I see you came prepared to work." Daniel's dark eyes held a hint of amusement as he perused her age-softened jeans and faded "I love Las Vegas" T-shirt. He got up with enviable ease and nodded toward the adjoining stall. "Come on, I'll show you what I'm doing with the Rolls."

As he moved toward her, Kerith's apprehension grew. Hastily, she backed away on the pretense of allowing him room to pass. "I don't want to interfere with your work on someone else's car," she said, glancing at the sports car he'd been lying under. "We can do this another time."

"No problem, that one's mine. I bought it and restored it when I was living on the east coast." He favored the car with an affectionate glance. "It's a 1952 Jaguar XK 120. Like it?"

In that, at least, Kerith didn't see any need to hide her true feelings. "I love it. I think I saw one like it at the Imperial Palace's auto museum." Using the car as an excuse to put more space between them, Kerith walked over and lightly stroked the gleaming white finish of one long, down-sloping fender. "Gus introduced me to the museum years ago, and I've been a fan of vintage cars ever since."

"Then that's two things we have in common," Daniel said, as he continued toward the Rolls. The car had been elevated to accommodate his height, and when he reached a point under the front end, he turned and beckoned to her with one finger. "Come over here, and you can learn something about your own antique."

Kerith started toward him warily. "If you think my interest in cars includes any ability to fix them, I'm afraid you're mistaken. Which means we have only one thing in common."

Daniel arched one black eyebrow, and let his gaze rest on her mouth for a telling minute. Immediately her lips were suffused with a tingling warmth. "Mechanical skill wasn't the other thing I had in mind," he said in a velvety drawl. "But that isn't why I asked you here. My purpose tonight is to convince you I'm doing everything I can to make sure the Duchess gets fixed and stays fixed this time." He grinned down at her as she joined him. "Of course, I'm also glad for the chance to see you."

Kerith decided it would be wisest to ignore his last remark. Looking pointedly up at the Rolls, she said, "Tell me what's wrong with my car."

Daniel promptly adopted a more businesslike tone. "I think your problem is a short somewhere in the electrical harness. That sort of failure is often intermittent and can be a real pain to trace. Which explains why my service manager kept sending the car back to you, claiming it was fixed."

He paused, and pointed to a cylindrical piece of machinery bolted to the side of the engine. "The starter motor is the most logical place to begin looking. Unfortunately, I won't be able to start on it until tomorrow. I can't get the motor out without help, and the guy who was supposed to assist me just left on a minor family emergency."

"You mean, you intend to work on the Rolls yourself?" Kerith eyed him incredulously. "I thought the boss was supposed to sit around and give orders."

"Normally, I do." Daniel's voice lowered seductively, and the smile he gave her made Kerith's knees feel weak. "But this is a special case, for a special lady."

"That isn't fair," she said, quickly turning her face away. "You're trying to make me feel obligated to you."

"Oh, for heaven's sake." Daniel gestured impatiently.

"Well, aren't you?" Kerith insisted, rounding on him. "How do you expect me to feel, knowing you're devoting your free time to fixing my car?"

Daniel made a frustrated sound. "I don't know—friendly, maybe? Look, if it'll make you feel better, you can help me."

"I don't know the first thing about fixing cars."

"You don't have to. I'll tell you exactly what to do."

Kerith started to protest further, but Daniel was already grasping her hands and tugging them upward. "All you have to do is put your hands up here and hold the starter in place while I remove the bolts. Once they're free, I'll be able to grab the thing and get it out myself. It's heavy, but as long as you hold it still, the drive pinion that connects it to the engine will take most of the weight. Whatever you do, though, don't let go once I get the first bolt out. I don't relish the idea of having the thing fall on my head. One bump a night is enough." His large hands felt strong and capable as they pressed against the backs of her smaller ones, positioning them on either side of the starter.

"Wait a minute," Kerith hedged. "Are you sure this is safe?"

"Relax. You don't have a thing to worry about." He paused to give her a wicked grin. "Unless you're allergic to getting your hands a little dirty. This isn't exactly the cleanest part of the car."

Kerith wasn't quite sure why she didn't lower her hands and walk away from him right then. Maybe it was the light challenge in his last words. Or maybe it was her stronger need to avoid being in his debt. Whatever the reason, she gave him an arch smile and said, "If you can take it, I can."

She rued those words a moment later, when Daniel pulled a wrench from his pocket and reached up to unfasten the first bolt. The action brought their bodies into breathtaking proximity. So close, Kerith could feel his warmth, even through the layers of their clothing. Standing there, with her abdomen separated from his by less than an inch, her arms trapped in an upraised position, she had never felt more sexually vulnerable in her life. Worse yet, the idea excited rather than repelled her. Biting her lower lip in chagrin, she tried to concentrate on watching Daniel's deft movements as he loosened the bolts overhead. But all was lost when his exertions, finally, inevitably caused his broad chest to brush against her breasts. At first contact, her nipples contracted with a stinging intensity that forced a soft gasp from her lips.

The sound caught Daniel's attention just as the last bolt came free, and he looked down at her inquiringly as the weight of the starter settled against her palms. Unable to move, she watched his eyes slowly darken in recognition of their enforced intimacy.

"Kerith..." Daniel's voice was a deep, sensual rumble. She saw his head begin to lower toward her and had time for one breathless, "No!" before his mouth caught hers with a fierce need.

For Kerith, the first instant of contact was volatile, causing an explosion of the pent-up feelings she had struggled with for days. Liquid fire invaded her bloodstream as Daniel's mouth ground against hers with a desperation that compelled her to open eagerly and accept the plunging invasion of his tongue. She felt his arms wrap around her, bringing their bodies into even closer contact. Her breasts were crushed against the unyielding strength of Daniel's chest, a wonderfully satisfying pressure that caused a wild quivering deep in the pit of her stomach.

This was what had been keeping her restless and wakeful at night for the past week, she thought vaguely. This hunger, this irresistible need. How could anyone fight it? Why would they even try? Insulated by a hot haze of sensation, Kerith wasn't inclined to analyze further, but a sudden sharp pain in her shoulders accomplished what years of caution could not. Uttering a low cry that ended up in Daniel's mouth, she was suddenly aware of the burden her arms still supported overhead.

"Daniel, please," she gasped when he released her mouth for a moment. "My arms . . . I can't hold this thing up much longer. My hands are getting numb."

It took only an instant for Daniel to comprehend and respond. "Oh, hell!" His arms shot up to take the weight of the starter motor, which had started to slip. "I'm sorry, love. Kissing you must do something to my memory. For a minute there I completely forgot this thing." He grinned apologetically and lowered the bulky piece of machinery to the ground.

So did I, Kerith thought with a rising sense of self-disgust. Numbly she noted the labored cadence of their breathing as she cleaned her hands with the rag Daniel tossed to her. How had it happened so fast? It seemed as if one minute she'd been standing there watching the man work on her car and the next she was leaning into his kiss, resenting the barriers of clothing separating their bodies. Wanting . . .

Kerith shuddered and chanced a look at Daniel, who was scrubbing at his hands with a second rag. He looked as aroused as she felt. Damn him. He'd probably counted on this happening. The entire business with the Duchess had probably been a ploy to get her alone.

"You planned this didn't you?" she accused in a tight voice. "You manipulated me into coming here just so you could . . . could . . ." She drew a quick angry breath. "I warned you, I don't tolerate manipulators. Goodbye, Mr. Avanti." She turned and stalked toward the door, refusing to give in to an undignified urge to run.

Daniel felt as if he'd been poleaxed. "Kerith, wait...dammit!" He nearly tripped over the starter in his haste to follow her. What had happened to his self-control? he wondered irritably as he broke into a jog. He'd promised himself—hell, he'd promised Kerith—he wouldn't rush things. But when he'd heard that sexy little gasp and looked down to see the glow of awareness in her eyes, it was as if a dam had burst inside him. His arousal had been painfully swift, demanding release. Was this a belated punishment for all the years he'd been in absolute control? Was he doomed to frustration now that he'd finally found found the woman who could inspire not only passion, but compassion in him? His temper flared. *No!*

"No!" he repeated aloud, as he caught up with Kerith, encircling her waist with both arms and swinging her off the ground. "You're not going to run away. Not until we get a few things straight."

"I was not running," Kerith retorted fiercely. The undersides of her breasts pressed softly on his arm, and her bottom bumped tantalizingly against his lingering arousal as she struggled against his hold. "But I'm not going to stay here and let you try to seduce me." Her heel connected sharply with Daniel's shin and the pain brought a flash of Italian temper.

"If I'd merely wanted to seduce you, sweetheart, I would have succeeded by now," he snapped, trapping one of her flailing legs between his hard thighs. He needn't have bothered, because in the next moment Kerith went still in his arms, her body rigid.

"Like all those other women you said you knew, but never cared about?" she inquired with cold fury. "You said I was different, but that was a lie, wasn't it? You're just like all the others, trying to control my life, using me for your own purposes, never caring about what I want, what I need."

She drew a shuddering breath, and Daniel was shocked to realize she was trembling. His anger vanished in a flood of concern. What had started as an argument over his motives had suddenly taken on much heavier connotations. He quickly set her down and turned her to face him, his hands gripping her shoulders firmly. When she refused to look at him he gave her a little shake. "What others, Kerith? Whose sins are being laid at my door?"

"Never mind. I shouldn't have said that."

"No, you're not going to stop now. Was it the orphanage? Did they treat you badly?"

Kerith's head jerked up. "How did you—"

"Ali told me," he interrupted. "Before you put the gag order on her, which seemed rather unnecessary since she didn't have much to tell. Mainly, she warned me about the high-tech defense system you've built around yourself. Who did that to you?"

She twisted against the restraint of his hands, but he wouldn't let go. "Why should I tell you? You don't really care." She looked directly at him then, and her golden eyes were filled with raw desolation—the kind of despair borne of believing no one does care. Daniel knew intuitively he was one of the few who had seen it in Kerith Ander's eyes. It made him want to spend the rest of his life convincing her she was wrong.

"I care," he said roughly, before pulling her into his arms. "I told you that in your office, today. Every time I see you I care more. Now tell me, who tried to control you and use you?"

Kerith stiffened, resisting his embrace, but she couldn't stop the trembling that seemed to vibrate her very bones. It sapped her strength and shook the walls of her reserve. She'd fought closeness for most of her life, but suddenly the struggle seemed almost more than she could bear. Her anger and wariness were replaced by a strange fatigue. She was so weary of always being on guard. How would it feel to let go, just once, and tell it all to someone? Someone who looked at her with warmth and compassion—as Daniel did?

No, no, no! She shook her head in silent denial.

"Kerith." Daniel caught her chin in an infinitely gentle grip. "What harm could it do to tell me? I'd never tell anyone else. Trust me."

She looked up and saw the inviting reassurance in his eyes, and an unexpected urge to comply temporarily overrode caution. "It started with Edelweiss," she began. The words, so long held back, came out sounding flat and lifeless. And the rest followed in the same manner, like a slow-moving stream in the first thaw of spring. The orphanage, the checks, the hopeless dreams of a lonely child, it all flowed out once she'd started.

"How long were you in the orphanage?" Daniel asked when she paused at last.

"Until I was twelve. Then I was sent to boarding schools—some of the finest in Switzerland." She tried to repress a shudder. "I hated them. Life at the orphanage wasn't ideal, but it was the only home I'd known, and the children there were all without families, like me. At school I was an oddity."

"Didn't you have any friends?"

Kerith laughed sharply. "Oh yes, I was quite popular when they found out I was an advanced student. I discovered friends could be easily purchased for the price of a difficult assignment completed, or the answers to a test. Unfortunately, the relationships never outlasted my usefulness. At first, I let it bother me, and there was . . . trouble. I was moved from one school to the next, until I discovered life was easier if I didn't allow myself to care."

She heard Daniel swear softly, and felt his hand reach to massage the tension from her shoulders, but she couldn't relax, not with the story half told.

"When I received Edelweiss's offer of a college education—with the stipulation that it be obtained in an American college—I refused to accept it at first. I spent an entire year traveling around Europe on the birthday money from Edelweiss, which had been banked for me over the years. But then I realized I had no real ties in Switzerland. And I really wanted the college education."

"But it must have taken a lot of courage, coming to a foreign country all alone," Daniel protested quietly.

Kerith shrugged dismissingly. "I survived."

"By not letting anyone get too close. That's a high price to pay."

His gentle pronouncement caused a tremor in the foundation of Kerith's self-possession, and she felt compelled to defend herself. "Not so high a price." Using her hands she forced a little distance between them. "Closeness merely invites manipulation, as you should know. Look what your family did to you and that girl you got pregnant."

Daniel looked pained. "That wasn't really manipulation. They thought they were acting in my best interest, just as Ali did when she agreed to help me meet you. True manipulation is self-centered." He smiled ruefully. "You may find this hard to believe after that kiss, but I invited you here tonight because I thought it would be a more neutral setting for getting acquainted. I don't consider a garage the ideal site for grand seduction. However..." He touched one blunt fingertip to her chin, urging her to meet his eyes. "We can't pretend that kiss didn't happen. And I suspect if you were completely honest with yourself, you'd admit you wanted it just as much as I did."

Yes, she had, Kerith thought desperately. And it was dangerous and foolish and... She didn't get a chance to finish. In the next instant all hell seemed to break loose, beginning with a loud crash just outside the building and followed immediately by the strident ringing of an alarm bell.

"Daniel, what—" She was cut off abruptly as Daniel shoved her into the shadowy darkness of a nearby service stall.

"Stay put," he ordered tersely. "Someone—or something—just tripped the security alarm. It's probably a dog or cat, but I don't believe in taking chances. We've had a few break-in attempts in the past. Don't move until I get back."

"Where are you going?" Kerith called over the clang of the alarm. A new anxiety gripped her. What if it wasn't a dog or cat? What if some criminal was out there, and Daniel...? Impulsively, she clutched his sleeve. "You're not going to do something dumb and heroic, are you?"

Daniel smiled reassuringly and put his hand over hers for a moment. "Don't worry, I'm just going to have a look around. If it's a false alarm, I need to notify the security company before they call the police. It's nice to know you care, though." He moved off with the stealth of a jungle fighter, and Kerith was left alone in the darkness to deal with those last unsettling words.

She didn't care for him, not in the way he meant, or so she told herself as she waited for his return with a pounding heart. But when the alarm cut off a short while later and Daniel reappeared looking unharmed, the surge of happiness she experienced went far beyond simple relief.

"Did you find anything?" she demanded, her whisper sounding unnaturally loud in the eerie silence enveloping the building.

"Just a trash can knocked over, most likely by some stray looking for a snack. The can must have bumped a window frame hard enough to trigger the alarm." Since he'd returned, his expression had been preoccupied, wary, now it softened. "Are you all right? You look a little shaky." He took her hand and drew her out into the soft light bathing the main aisle.

"I'm fine." Using the back of her free hand, she brushed back the tumble of golden bangs feathered over her forehead.

Daniel watched the gesture intently. "Such lovely, silky hair," he murmured. "I've wanted to touch it since I first saw it. He lifted one hand as if to do so, glanced at it and sighed. "Guess I'd better not until I've used some soap and water. In fact... Turn around."

"What?"

"Turn your back to me," he elaborated, then chuckled when she complied. "Your shirt looks like one of my shop rags. That alone should prove I didn't plan our passionate little interlude. I prefer lovemaking without grease."

Once again, the air between them was charged with sensual undertones, and Kerith kept her back to him while she nervously tugged at the hem of her sweatshirt. "I don't think you planned it, but that doesn't mean I think it should have happened." She gestured helplessly with both hands. "Every time I'm around you, I say or do something I shouldn't."

"Like going wild when I kiss you?"

Kerith ducked her head. "Like pouring out all the intimate details of my past. I've never done that before. And I don't think I should have done it tonight."

Daniel came up behind her and settled his hands on her shoulders. "Hey, no regrets. I think you needed to tell me almost as much as I needed to hear it. I want to be close to you, Kerith. And I don't mean in the physical sense alone, although I think we both know that's inevitable if we spend much more time together."

With an uneasy shrug, she stepped out of his reach. "You make it all sound so simple, when I know it's not. I . . . I think I should go home now." Home, where she could work it all out, alone and safe.

Daniel didn't argue further. He simply took her arm and said, "All right, I'll walk you to your car."

Nothing more was said until she had opened the door of her silver Mazda RX-7, then Daniel motioned for her to wait. "This isn't goodbye, you know. I'm going to give you a little time to think, but that doesn't mean I'm giving up. I want you, Kerith

Anders." He tipped her chin up until she could see the need darkening his eyes. "Remember this while you're doing all that thinking." His kiss was a dazzling, sweet demand, and disappointingly brief. When it was over, Kerith stared at him in bemusement for a long moment, inhaled sharply, and ducked into the safety of her car. When she pulled into her own driveway a while later, she could still feel the hot imprint of his mouth on her lips.

Over the next week, she was haunted by the memory of that kiss—and every other distracting detail of her encounters with Daniel Avanti. Again and again she ordered herself to stop thinking about him, but even though he kept his word about giving her time to think, she couldn't banish him from her mind.

And the dreams she had at night! Sizzling, Technicolor fantasies that left her lying wide-eyed and breathless in the damp tangle of her flower-sprigged bed sheets. She felt as if she were suffering through puberty again, except now she was mature enough to know, at least in theory, what her body craved.

"The man hasn't even called me this week, and all I do is think about him," Kerith muttered irritably as she stared out her office window. The cloud-darkened Nevada sky matched her mood exactly. Of course, there had been the T-shirt, a soft lavender one with "I love Las Vegas" imprinted across the front in iridescent rainbow colors. It had arrived by special messenger with a note from Daniel that said:

> This is to replace the one I ruined. Try it on and guess which letters I'd like to trace with my fingertips.
>
> Yours hopefully,
> Daniel

Just remembering it brought a hot flush to her cheeks and a frown of consternation to her brow.

"Oops! Something tells me you aren't as happy as I am to see Friday night." Ali stood poised in the doorway to Kerith's office, a tentative smile on her face.

Kerith sighed and waved her in. "I'm fine, but you may not feel quite so happy when you see the weather report. The forecast mentioned a possibility of thundershowers."

"A great night for a fireplace and free-delivery pizza. Want to join Cami and me?"

"No, thanks. After the week I've had I wouldn't be very good company. Besides, I have some paperwork to finish before I go."

Ali grimaced sympathetically. "It has been hectic, hasn't it? Especially with Arthur out the whole time."

Kerith smiled wryly. "Wasn't that ironic? You faked a sprained ankle and Arthur, who is the most coordinated man I know, actually manages to do it. Although I didn't quite believe his story about tripping over a cat. More likely he did it climbing out of some rich matron's window in the middle of the night, when her husband came home unexpectedly."

Ali gave a throaty chuckle and waved one hand. "Speaking of home, it's late and I'm going to head for mine. See you Monday."

Alone again, Kerith sat down at her desk. There was still at least an hour's work ahead of her. As if in protest, her stomach rumbled softly, reminding her she hadn't eaten since that morning's coffee and raisin toast. What she needed was a snack to hold her until she got home. Automatically, her thoughts went to the box of candy sitting in one drawer of the desk. Daniel's candy.

She'd been nibbling on it unrepentantly all week—one didn't waste gourmet chocolates, regardless of the source—and now it beckoned.

The rich chocolate coating began to melt against her fingertips as she lifted the piece of candy from the box. Raising it to her lips, she licked it delicately before sinking her teeth into the rounded center. The sharp piquance of cherry liqueur squirted into her mouth, followed immediately by the sweetness of the cherry center and the silky richness of dark chocolate. Kerith moaned helplessly, her eyes closing in near ecstasy as she slowly chewed.

"Lord, what I wouldn't give to be the one who put that look on your face."

The huskily voiced sentiment came unexpectedly, nearly causing Kerith to choke. Her eyes flew open and fastened on Daniel, who was moving toward her purposefully. "Mind if I try some?" He seated himself on the near corner of her desk and leaned toward her with his most charming smile.

Kerith swallowed quickly, tried to speak, and discovered she couldn't. Something had gone awry with her brain's circuitry from the instant she'd registered Daniel's presence, and the only message coming through at the moment was an overwhelming joy in seeing him again. So she merely nodded her assent and offered the box of candy.

Daniel had other ideas. Without warning, his head came down and his mouth captured hers, leaving her time for just one startled "Oh!" before his tongue gently pushed past her lips. He swept through her mouth like a greedy marauder, gathering up the lingering sweetness of the candy, rubbing his tongue sensuously over and under hers, stroking the slick softness of her inner cheek, and testing the sharp even edge of her teeth. When he'd finished, Kerith felt as if her mouth had been ravished.

Gasping, she collapsed against the soft backrest of her chair and searched for something to say. Daniel beat her to it.

"I don't think I've ever tasted anything sweeter. Come on, let's get out of here." He tugged Kerith out of her chair, scooped up her purse, and was halfway to the door before she dug in her heels and stopped.

"Not so fast, Mr. Avanti. Just where do you think you're dragging me?"

Daniel looked down at the stubborn set of her chin and grinned. "I wondered how long it would take you to come out of that daze. We're going for a ride, if you must know. I think I managed to find the electrical problem in your Rolls, and I need to test-drive it. I thought the least you could do is come with me, since it is your car."

Kerith's eyes narrowed consideringly. "A test run. Are you sure that's all it will be?"

"No." Daniel's expression sobered. "It's been a damned long week, Kerith. I'm starved for your company." One dark brow arched suggestively. "And judging by that kiss, just now, I think you're a little hungry, too." He carefully placed the purse in her hand and released her.

"You've had a whole week to think things over and I suspect your decision was made before I walked in here tonight. I won't, however, be accused of forcing you to do anything against your will." He walked to the door, then looked back at her, his hand held out invitingly. "Are you coming?"

A small lifetime seemed to pass before Kerith in the moments she stood there looking at Daniel's outstretched hand. A speeded-up review of the events and decisions that had made her what she was, and what she was not. As she weighed the evidence, she couldn't escape a feeling of deficiency—that she'd been cheated of something essential.

Before Daniel had arrived in her life, she'd found peace and security in her isolation. But with a few kisses, he'd given her a taste of the things she'd lost in her quest for safety. He was offering a chance to make up for that loss. Did she dare take it?

"I'm coming," she announced firmly, crossing the room to place her hand in Daniel's warm grasp. But as she followed him outside, she couldn't escape the feeling that she was stepping into an alien territory, from which there might be no return.

5

"JUST HOW LONG does a test run take?" Kerith asked, twisting to face Daniel from the passenger side of the Rolls's richly upholstered front seat. He had taken the wheel, with her permission, and for the past ten minutes the Duchess had been humming along under his competent hand. Now they were on Boulder Highway, which led out of the city in a southeasterly direction, and Kerith had begun to wonder when he would turn back.

At her question, Daniel gave her a guileless smile and said, "There isn't a set time or distance. I thought we'd run out to Hoover Dam."

"Hoover Dam!" Kerith couldn't hide her dismay. She'd committed herself to spending some time with Daniel, but this was more than she'd expected. "That's a forty-minute drive. And look at those storm clouds. We could get some really nasty weather tonight."

Daniel dismissed her objections with a careless wave of his hand. "You've lived in the desert too long. Every time anyone around here sees an overcast sky he thinks it's time to start building an ark. I'll bet you didn't react like this when you were in Switzerland."

"I don't want to talk about Switzerland. I did more than enough of that a week ago." Even now, the memory made her uncomfortable. Shifting uneasily in her seat, she turned her attention to the night-shaded view outside her window. The flat valley floor was gradually giving way to barren foothills, and beyond them she saw the sharp silhouette of the mountain range sheltering Lake Mead.

"Kerith, please don't withdraw from me now. I don't think I could stand it." Daniel's softly voiced plea brought her eyes back to his strong profile.

He was serious, she realized in surprise. And vulnerable, maybe as vulnerable as she was to him. "I'm not withdrawing, exactly," she responded quietly. "But I can't rush into...this. I'm not used to sharing my life with anyone."

Daniel reached out and gently squeezed her tightly clenched hands as they lay in her lap. "I understand. Unfortunately, that means you're stuck with hearing more of the boring details of my life."

Kerith laughed and pulled her hands from beneath his, ostensibly to stifle a fake yawn. But her real goal was to hide the shivering excitement his touch had caused. An excitement that seemed to grow even after the contact was ended.

Daniel didn't appear to notice. After returning his hand to the steering wheel, he proceeded to entertain her with some of the current exploits of his extended family. From there he went into a droll recounting of Avanti history.

As they climbed higher and higher on a road that twisted through rock-scarred slopes, Kerith was drawn deeper and deeper into the web of Daniel's charming narrative. By the time they'd reached the curving downward stretch of road leading to the dam, she'd nearly forgotten her reservations about being alone with him.

And they were alone, she noted, as Daniel drove the limousine past a succession of deserted parking lots, and a snack and a souvenir stand with a Closed sign in the window. When he reached the lot nearest the dam, he parked and turned toward her with a self-conscious grin. "Are you sorry for getting me started on my family? You've been kind of quiet, and you don't look very entertained."

Outside, the only sign of life was a few pieces of trash dancing across the pavement under the force of a gusting wind. But the interior of the car was alive with the familiarity that had been steadily growing between them. Knowing where that familiarity could lead, Kerith decided it would be safest to keep him talking about his family. "I wasn't bored," she said, with a small shake of her head. "I was just thinking about how much you seem to care for your family, and how difficult it must have been for you being separated from them all the years you were gone."

In the dim light from the parking lot's overhead fixtures, Kerith saw a flicker of pain tighten his features.

"Those were the emptiest years of my life," Daniel admitted in a low voice.

"Couldn't you have patched things up with your father, somehow?"

"Maybe." Daniel hesitated. How much could he tell her? Would she turn away in disgust if she knew of his life as Casanova? Most likely. And yet, he was suddenly seized by a compulsion to confess, to lay himself bare before her and hope for understanding. After the way she'd opened up to him the other night, it seemed only fair.

"That wasn't the only reason I stayed away," he went on carefully. "Before I wised up and stopped trying to make others pay for the mistakes Angelina and my father made, I got myself involved in a situation that nearly destroyed my self-image. For a long time I wasn't able to face myself, let alone my family."

A heavy, expectant silence settled over the interior of the car. Just like a confessional, Daniel thought ruefully. Then he heard Kerith draw a slow breath, and her question—when it came—held an unexpected note of sympathy. "What did you do?"

And when he looked into her lovely golden eyes and saw the genuine empathy there, he knew he was going to tell her, regardless of the fact that it probably was the riskiest step he'd ever taken. He couldn't tell her everything, of course, but he had to give her something to equal the confidences she'd offered a week ago, and the gift of caring she was offering now. It was the least he could do, in light of the deception he must continue until Edelweiss made an appearance.

He sighed and rubbed a hand over his face. "My job with the government wasn't as straightforward as I originally led you to believe. I did a lot of top-level security work."

"You were a spy?"

Daniel winced. "The accepted term is agent, but yes, I did some spying."

"Did it involve killing? Is that why you couldn't face your family?" Uncertainty vibrated in her soft query, and the sound cut deep into Daniel's soul. What he had done was bad enough, but to have her think him a killer was too much.

"I never killed anyone. At least not after I left the Marines," he denied quickly. "Sometimes, though, I felt as if I'd condemned a few." *Stop now*, an inner voice warned. *Only a fool would tell her the rest.*

Kerith looked confused. "Condemned? How?"

Daniel opened his mouth to speak and realized his heart was pounding at a rate normally reserved for moments of imminent physical danger. His palms were sweaty, too, and he rubbed them dry on his slacks before gripping the wheel of the car. "What would you say if I told you my code name was Casanova? And that I earned it seducing secrets out of unsuspecting women?"

A stunned silence followed, and he knew with a dreadful certainty that he'd gone too far. Blown it. No woman would welcome that kind of news about a man she was seeing, let alone a woman who had strong reservations about a relationship in the first place. How could he have believed otherwise? He'd be lucky if she let him have a ride back to town, at this point. On top of that, how was he going to tell Lucretia he'd blown his contact?

"What kind of women?" Kerith's low-pitched question barely penetrated the thick miasma of his self-disgust.

Daniel sighed heavily. "All kinds. Lady scientists who worked for unfriendly nations, idealistic young women who thought they could change our government by passing top-secret information to our enemies. You name it, I probably encountered it."

"Did . . . did you make love to all of them?"

"Not all." Daniel considered leaving it at that, then figured, what the hell he might as well tell the whole sordid story. "In the beginning, when I didn't care, there were quite a few. But toward the end, when I realized what I'd become . . . well, it just didn't happen. I became quite adept at getting the information I wanted before things progressed to the bedroom." He laughed harshly. "The funniest part was, as the bedding frequency went down, my reputation as a tireless lover grew." He chanced a look at Kerith, and found her regarding him thoughtfully.

"Does your family know about this?"

"No. They all believe I had a nice respectable job. You're the only person I've told." What was that look in her eyes? Disgust? Dismay?

"Why are you telling me?"

Daniel took a slow cautious breath. "Because I thought you had a right to know. I care very deeply for you, and I wanted honesty between us before we make love." *Please forgive me, love, that it can't be complete honesty,* he added silently.

"If you can't accept what I was, I'll understand," he continued out loud. "But I want you to know I've changed. And I'm trying to make up for the mistakes I made."

Kerith saw the anxiety tightening Daniel's expression as he waited for her response, and she felt a flutter of panic. She hadn't expected this kind of intimacy when she'd accepted his invitation. It disturbed her more than his confident assumption that they would make love. And yet, his confession seemed strangely appropriate, after her soul-baring of a week ago. She cleared her throat nervously. "I'm not sure I know what you want me to say."

"Just tell me whether or not my past is going to be a problem for you."

Kerith considered that, and finally shook her head. "My life hasn't been perfect. I wouldn't presume to judge yours. In fact, I think you're being a little too hard on yourself. What you did—it was supposedly done to help your government, wasn't it?"

Daniel snorted softly. "In my more forgiving moments I allow myself to believe that. Your vote of confidence means a lot, though." He smiled suddenly and grabbed her hand. "In fact, I feel better than I have in a long time. Come on, let's go look at the dam."

Kerith gasped in protest, as he flung open the car door and got out, tugging her out behind him on the driver's side. "It's cold and windy out here, and we're not exactly dressed for sightseeing."

As if to prove her point, a fierce gust of wind buffeted them, whipping at the hem of her pink linen coatdress, and raising the tails of Daniel's beige sport coat. Daniel didn't appear to notice. He simply laughed and wrapped an arm around her as they proceeded down to the walkway crossing the dam. Once there, he astounded her by bracing himself against the railing and bursting into a lusty Irish sea chantey.

When she laughingly questioned his sanity, he grinned and replied, "I always feel as if I'm on the bow of a great ship when I come up here. Makes me want to sing."

When Kerith looked out over the dark, choppy water, she had to admit it did feel like standing at the rail of a huge luxury liner. She started to tell him so, but all of a sudden the heavy clouds above them unloaded a deluge of rain, and they had to make a mad dash for the Rolls.

"It was your singing," she teased, as they scrambled into the front seat, dripping wet and laughing helplessly.

Daniel pretended to glare at her, while using both hands to comb back his wet hair. "I'll have you know some people think I have a very good singing voice."

And he did, Kerith thought, squeezing water from her own drenched hair. His singing perfectly matched the rich baritone of his speaking voice. "All right, Caruso," she conceded with a grin. "You can serenade me all the way home. Just get this car started so we can turn the heater on."

Giving her a cocky little salute, Daniel moved to comply. But when he turned the key in the ignition, he was rewarded with an ominous click. When he'd gotten the same result on the second, third and fourth tries, he leaned his head back against the seat and groaned. "To think I actually wished for this sort of thing to happen when I was in high school." He gave Kerith a worried look. "You don't think I planned this, do you?"

Kerith eyed their bedraggled clothing and laughed. "No. I would, however, like to know what you plan to do next."

"Look under the hood, I guess," Daniel said, sighing in resignation. "Do you happen to have a flashlight?" When Kerith produced one from under the seat, he grinned and added, "How about a raincoat and umbrella?"

"There should be a slicker in the trunk. Anything I can do to help?"

"No, stay here. There's no point in both of us being out in that."

But when he'd been tinkering under the hood for ten minutes, with no result, Kerith got out and joined him. "You can't accomplish anything, with it raining like this," she shouted over the roaring wind. "There's a public phone outside that snack stand we passed on the way down. I'll go call for help."

Swearing softly, Daniel gave in and slammed down the hood. "You get back in the car. I'll make the call. After all, it was my idea to come up here." He got her settled in the backseat, with a blanket he found in the trunk, then started up the hill at a slow, splashing jog.

A long twenty minutes later he was back, streaming water like Niagara Falls and trying not to shiver as he joined her in the backseat and closed the door. "Who would have believed the weather could get so bad so fast," he grumbled, accepting the small towel Kerith had borrowed from the mini-bar.

"Not I," she assured him, her eyes twinkling. "Did you find the phone?"

"Yes, and it actually worked." Daniel's reply came out muffled as he scrubbed his face and hair with the inadequate piece of terry. "My brother-in-law will be here as soon as possible. In this filthy weather, that could be an hour or more, so I guess we're stuck for the moment." He sneezed, and a shiver ran down his large frame as he shrugged out of the dripping slicker and his sport coat. Fortunately, his shirt and slacks appeared to be merely damp.

"You must be nearly frozen," Kerith said, instantly concerned. "Here, take the blanket. I'll be fine without it."

"Absolutely not. It's my fault we're in this mess. If you got sick, I'd never forgive myself."

"Don't be ridiculous. I chose to come." She pulled the blanket from around her shoulders and pushed it toward him. "Now take it."

"All right." Daniel accepted the blanket reluctantly. Then, before she knew what he intended, he grasped her waist with both hands and hauled her unceremoniously onto his lap. "But only if we share."

"Daniel!" Kerith's squawk of protest was cut off when the blanket settled over her head, cocooning her against his broad chest. His laughter rumbled beneath her ear, and when she tried to push away, his strong arms formed a warm prison.

"Quit fighting me, love," he said, still chuckling. "This is the only positive aspect of the entire situation."

"Positive for you, maybe," Kerith fumed. "I can't breathe under here." The truth was, she could breathe; the result was the problem. With each inhalation her nose was filled with pure essence of Daniel, and it was having an incendiary effect on her system.

"Sweetheart, if you don't stop squirming your sweet bottom around on my lap, I'm going to get a lot warmer than I intended."

Kerith's head came up so hard, she managed to break free of the blanket's smothering confines, but that only served to put her in most intimate proximity with Daniel's smiling mouth. "Do you know what I'd like right now?" he murmured.

"No, what?" Kerith's heart went into overdrive, and her mind did an instant replay of the kiss they'd shared in her office.

"Champagne," he replied, leaning over her to pull a bottle out of the Rolls's tiny refrigerator. Somehow, he managed to unwrap and pull the cork without loosening his hold on her.

"Very professional, sir. But I hardly think it's appropriate for our circumstances."

"*Au contraire, mademoiselle.* Champagne always tastes better in the middle of a storm at Hoover Dam." After some rummaging, he located a stemmed glass and filled it with the effervescent liquid. "Especially when I'm with a beautiful woman. Here, drink."

Given the choice of either drinking or having the chilly stuff dumped on her, Kerith wisely chose the former. The combination of icy cold liquid and tingling bubbles made her shudder at first, but only moments later the wine hit her empty stomach, resulting in an instant rush of warmth. Apparently satisfied with the drink she'd taken, Daniel lowered the glass and drank himself, resting his lips on the exact spot hers had touched.

"Mmm, champagne and Kerith Anders, two of my favorite flavors." He refilled the glass and offered it to her again. This time she didn't balk, not even when he insisted she down at least a third of glass.

"I think you're right," Kerith said a little breathlessly, after swallowing. "This champagne tastes better than any I can remember."

"Really? Let me taste." Without further warning, Daniel's mouth came down on hers with a hunger that had nothing to do with food or drink. And just as quickly Kerith felt an answering need rise within her, compelling her to open her lips to the bold thrust of his tongue.

He tasted of rain and champagne and the essence she craved most of all—Daniel. She was dimly aware when he reached to set down the champagne flute, and then his hand returned to add to the magic his mouth was creating. Slowly, he stroked the curves and planes of her body, warming her in spite of her cold damp clothing. And when his hand settled on her breast, Kerith was flooded by a heat that transcended mere physical warmth.

"Damn, I keep forgetting just how potent your kisses are," Daniel gasped, when he broke away last. His mouth brushed hers again lightly, as if he couldn't quite bring himself to stop. "When you agreed to come with me tonight, I told myself I wouldn't rush things, but self-control isn't easy around a woman like you."

"A man like Casanova out of control? I find that hard to believe."

"I'm not Casanova anymore," he said gruffly, and bent to press a kiss on the soft curve of her throat. "I'm just a man who happens to go a little crazy when he's with you." His fingers flexed gently on her breast, and Kerith moaned at the pleasure surging through her body.

"So incredibly lovely," Daniel murmured against her lips, as he deftly undid the front buttons on her dress and slipped his fingers inside to trace the satiny swell of flesh that strained against the low-cut cup of her bra. He found the tight bud of her nipple beneath the lacy material, and his descending mouth caught Kerith's helpless cry of need. This time, the stroke of his tongue was more eloquent, telling her of the ultimate invasion he desired. Beneath her thigh she felt the swelling heat of his arousal, and a quivering need pulsed to life between her thighs. She shifted impatiently, wanting more, wishing . . .

A sharp rap sounded against the rear window, startling them both to sudden awareness. Daniel swore softly, and hastily pulled his hand out of her dress. "We've got company love. Perhaps you'd better sit next to me until I find out who it is." He needn't have made the suggestion. Kerith was already off his lap and huddled in the far corner of the seat, embarrassment and dismay already cooling the fire of abandon.

When Daniel rolled the foggy window down a crack, she caught a glimpse of a security guard, who kindly inquired if they were having car trouble and offered aid. He didn't linger after Daniel assured him help was on the way.

"Nice to know someone is nearby," Daniel commented, as he rolled up the window. "But the timing was lousy." His easy grin faded when he saw the look on Kerith's face. "Hey, don't let it upset you. He couldn't see a thing with the windows steamed up the way they are."

"It isn't only that." Kerith lowered her gaze to her lap. "I was thinking of what might have happened if we hadn't been interrupted just then. What would that man have found if he'd shown up ten or fifteen minutes later?" She threw him a slightly belligerent look. "I wasn't thinking of stopping, were you?"

Her unexpected honesty charmed him into a smile, and he reached over and dragged her close for a hug, before she had time to resist. "I have to admit, I lost control for a while there. But I like to believe I would have stopped short of making love to you in the back seat of a car, even if it is a Rolls-Royce." He cupped her cheek tenderly and turned her to face him. "You deserve better than that. Our first time together is going to be very special."

"You say that as if it's a certainty," Kerith mumbled, suddenly reminded of her lack of experience. "I think I'd better warn you, I haven't had much . . . practice at this. I won't be able to measure up to the other women you've known."

Daniel twisted around to cup her face with both hands. "Don't even think of comparing yourself to them. What happened before meant nothing to me. I want you, Kerith Anders. I want you more than I've wanted any other woman. So much so, that at times I even forget the basic niceties of seduction."

"Are you going to seduce me?" she inquired in a shaky voice. The thought sent a thrill to the center of her being.

"No. Casanova seduced women. I'm going to make love with you." He planted a quick kiss on her lips and released her face, then drew her tightly to his side, with one arm. "And that precludes groping in the backseat of a car. Until we can get out of here, I'll have to settle for champagne and the pleasure of your company."

To Kerith's surprise, he did just that. Outside the storm escalated to a howling gale, yet inside the car there was an atmosphere of comfort and security she wouldn't have believed possible. The passion still glowed within her, but it was banked, put into abeyance. When Daniel's brother-in-law arrived a while later, his eyes twinkling at their predicament, she found she could actually laugh at his jokes about Las Vegas weather.

They arrived at Daniel's condo in the middle of a torrential downpour, and Kerith quickly agreed to Daniel's offer to drive her home from there, allowing the tow truck to proceed directly to Avanti's garage. By the time she and Daniel reached his front step, they were both soaked to the skin.

"Whew! I'd forgotten how fierce these desert storms can be," Daniel gasped. He quickly opened the door and hustled Kerith inside.

"Given our normally dry climate, it's easy to forget." She smiled as she skinned her wet hair back from her face, but her expression turned to dismay when she saw the huge puddle she was creating on the white tiled floor. "I think you'd better take me home right away. I'm going to cause a flood in here."

"A little water never hurt anything," Daniel replied easily. He bent and tugged off his sodden shoes and socks, then started unbuttoning his shirt. "And I don't intend to go anywhere until I have a hot shower and some dry clothes." He peered at her critically. "You look as if you could use the same."

Until that moment, she hadn't been aware she was shivering. "I . . . I'll be all right," she said quickly, her wanton mind instantly filled with pictures of them showering together. Contrarily, her body chose to betray her just then, with a sneeze.

"Sure, you will," Daniel agreed, taking her arm and urging her down the hallway to a small bathroom that contained a shower. "You can use this one. I'll take the one upstairs. I have a robe you can borrow until your things dry."

Kerith perused her dripping wet dress. "Unless you have a clothes dryer, that could take a long time. And I'll just get wet again when you take me home."

"I don't have a dryer," Daniel said quietly. His dark eyes were suddenly intent as he reached to cup her cheek with one large, warm hand. "I was hoping I might be able to convince you to stay, at least until the rain eases a bit." He must have seen the apprehension that instantly tightened her body, because he added, "I'm not going to ask for anything you aren't ready to give. If you like, we can just sit in front of my fireplace until it's safer to drive."

Such an uncomplicated offer, on the surface, Kerith thought. But she knew, even if Daniel didn't, that by agreeing to stay she would be taking the last step toward becoming intimate with him. It wasn't an easy step, after so many years of caution, but the touch of his hand against her cheek felt so warm, so right. And as she stared into the depths of his midnight eyes and saw the undisguised need there, desire came simmering up to the surface of her consciousness, burning away any lingering restraint.

"I think I'll accept the loan of that robe," she murmured, moving into the bathroom and closing the door behind her. "You can leave it outside the door."

When she stepped out of the bathroom twenty minutes later, she was warm and dry and bundled up in a navy velour robe that swamped her slender frame. Even her hair had been dried, courtesy of the blow dryer Daniel had thoughtfully left at the door with his robe. All in all, she felt a lot less vulnerable than she had expected as she ventured down the hall, looking for her host.

She found him in the living room, which opened off the hall to the right. He was sprawled comfortably on the couch, staring into the bright flames that filled the white brick fireplace. It offered the only light in the darkened room. His loafer-clad feet were propped casually on a glass-topped coffee table, and next to them stood two mugs filled with steaming liquid.

Some sixth sense must have warned him of her silent, barefoot approach, because he turned with a glowing smile and beckoned her to join him. "You're just in time. The cappuccino was getting cold."

Kerith settled herself cautiously on the cushion next to his and gratefully accepted the tall slender mug he offered. "I love cappuccino. How did you know?"

"I didn't. I guess it's just another of the many things we have in common."

"Maybe not so many," Kerith argued, glancing around. "This room, for instance. It's nothing like my living room." She didn't add that she hadn't decorated her living room. It had been professionally done before she married Gus, and she'd never felt the need to change it. Now, as she studied Daniel's decor, she decided she liked it better than the formal, brocaded furnishings in her place. The walls were pristine white, as was the tiled floor, but bright splashes of turquoise and gold had been added with mini-blinds and area rugs, and on the walls there were several vivid desert scenes painted by a Southwestern artist she admired.

"You don't like it." Daniel sounded a little hurt.

"Actually, I think it's fantastic." *And so are you*, she added silently as she surreptitiously studied him over the rim of her cup. He looked magnificent in the worn jeans and soft yellow sweater he'd donned after his shower. His hair, still slightly damp, had been combed carelessly back from his broad forehead and gleamed silky black in the firelight.

Physical attraction, she told herself, that's what they had in common. Of course, that didn't explain his ability to draw her into deeply personal revelations, but she didn't want to think about that now. She didn't want to think about anything but the sweet rush of returning desire that came just from looking at him—and how it would feel to have him satisfy that desire completely.

"I'm flattered you like the cappuccino, but you didn't have to drink it quite so fast." Daniel's amused comment drew her attention to the nearly empty mug she held.

Kerith blinked distractedly, the rich flavor of espresso laced with milk and amaretto just then registering on her taste buds. She smiled apologetically. "I guess I got carried away."

Daniel pulled a comically unhappy face. "And here I thought my charming presence had put that avid look in your eyes." He nodded toward her mug. "Would you like more?"

"No." Kerith's heart began to beat faster. Tell him what you want, she ordered herself silently. But the words wouldn't come.

"It's still raining pretty hard. I hope you're not going to ask me to take you home."

Before answering, Kerith carefully set her mug on the coffee table. Then, nervously clutching the thick folds of Daniel's robe, she boldly met his gaze and said, "I want to stay."

The dark brown of Daniel's eyes deepened almost to black, as comprehension dawned. A slight smile curved the corners of his mouth as he slowly reached out to draw her onto his lap. "Then why don't we see if we can find something to do to pass the time?" he murmured.

For Kerith, it felt as if she'd stepped out of an airplane at ten thousand feet. Tactile sensation swept over her like the rush of air in a mad free-fall. Daniel's fingers digging into her ribs with barely restrained force as he pulled her nearer. His mouth, warm and tender at first, then hard and hungry as his control suddenly gave way. His hands were almost rough in their urgency, as he sought her body through the thickness of the robe, then impatiently shoved the material aside, baring her breasts to the soft firelight. He touched her almost reverently at first, his voice coming in a rough growl.

"Even in my dreams I never imagined you to be this beautiful. Your skin is so lovely, like gold satin." He bent and touched the tip of his tongue to the tight bud of her nipple, and a trembling seized Kerith. And when he drew the tip of her breast into his mouth, suckling softly, then harder and harder, an ache blossomed in the pit of her belly and quickly grew unbearable.

"Oh, please," she cried, sinking her fingers into the silky depths of his hair to hold him nearer. But to her dismay, he raised his head, his breathing labored as he fought for control.

"Too fast," he managed after a moment, even as his fingers delicately tormented her throbbing nipple. "I can't believe what you do to me. One minute we're talking, and the next I can't think of anything beyond how it will feel to be deep inside you. You deserve more finesse."

"I don't want finesse," Kerith responded with a fierceness born of desperation. Her fingers tightened in his hair. Passion, so long held in check, was now in full control, demanding immediate satisfaction. And nothing—nothing—was going to stop it now. She brought her mouth to his and recklessly pushed her tongue inside, imitating the teasing movements he'd used on her. And when he groaned and took control of the kiss, she released his head and slipped her hands under his sweater, seeking the warmth of naked skin. She found it, swelled by hard muscle, roughened by masculine hair, and her touch elicited another groan from Daniel.

"Kerith, love, that feels so good . . . too good." He swung her up in his arms and stood suddenly, then placed her flat on the couch. The robe spread open around her, but she was beyond feeling modest, even when his eyes appraised her body with frank approval.

"You're tan all over. I used to dream about how you would look after I found out you swam in the nude. A golden lady...my golden lady." He knelt beside her, his hands smoothing over her skin, raising her excitement unbelievably high, until his fingers pressed into the soft, golden curls shielding her womanhood, and Kerith felt as if she'd received an electric shock. His fingertip probed delicately until he found the one tiny spot that burned for his touch. Her body arched upward convulsively, and she grabbed handfuls of Daniel's sweater, pulling until his reassuring weight was pressing down on her. Even through the material of his jeans, she could feel his arousal, hard and hot, nestled against the aching place between her thighs. Her hips flexed up, an instinctive entreaty.

"Daniel," she wailed softly. "I can't stand it. I need . . ."

"I know." His voice was heavy with reluctant acceptance, as his lower body lunged hard against her once. "We'll have to save the leisurely pace for another time." A moment later he was up and stripping off his clothes with hands that shook in their haste.

He stood naked before her for one eternal moment, his glorious body gilded by firelight, his phallus daunting, yet beautiful in full arousal. Then he was beside her again, naked flesh pressing warmly to hers, as his fingers sought and found the tight, moist readiness of her femininity. "Kerith, my love, relax. I don't want to hurt you."

"A-all right," she said, and then drew in a hissing breath, as his deft touch started a shivering that wouldn't stop. She squeezed her eyes shut and felt Daniel's hands urging her knees to bend and open to him. The couch cushions gave softly beneath her as he settled heavily, his manhood searching only briefly before finding its goal. And with one, long irrevocable thrust he drove home.

A startled cry escaped Kerith as her untried flesh resisted for one, painful instant—then gave way, and she was deeply, overwhelmingly filled. She felt Daniel hesitate; heard his muttered oath. But when she urged him on in a trembling whisper, he groaned and gave in to the raging need that would not wait. His hips drove forward, faster and faster, building a storm within her that exceeded the fury of the elements outside. Until at last it exploded, again and again, like a fireworks display gone wild. And in the midst of it all, she felt, deep inside her, the pulsing heat of Daniel's release.

Long moments passed as they lay together gasping, shivering and spent. Kerith was drifting dangerously close to slumber when Daniel's quietly accusing inquiry came. "How the hell did a woman as beautiful and sophisticated as you manage to keep her virginity this long? And why didn't you warn me?"

6

Rain lashed furiously against the windows of Daniel's living room, and a heavy boom of thunder echoed in the distance, but Kerith barely heard as a sweet lethargy dragged her toward oblivion. She couldn't remember ever feeling so peaceful, so content, so . . . complete. Daniel's weight shifted against her as he propped himself on his elbows. She forced her eyes open drowsily and found him watching her expectantly.

"Are you going to tell me?" he prompted, when she didn't speak. "At this point, I think I have a right to know."

The undeniably possessive note in his voice sounded a warning deep in Kerith's mind, but she felt too good to worry about anything at the moment. "I did tell you I wasn't very experienced," she said, smiling slightly. Did everyone feel this wonderful after sex? If so, it might just be worth the risk of all the emotional entanglements that seemed to accompany the act.

"That hardly covered the issue," Daniel retorted gruffly. "I could have—" He frowned, and framed her face with his hands. "Did I hurt you? I must have. Damn, why didn't you tell me?" His obvious distress sent an unexpected wave of tenderness through Kerith, and she reached up to smooth the lines of concern furrowing his brow.

"It wasn't that bad—just an instant really. And then it was fantastic." She lowered her eyelids, shivering in remembrance. "Maybe just a little scary at the end. I felt like I was shattering into a million pieces."

Daniel's deep chuckle vibrated against her breasts, as he bent to nibble gently on her earlobe. "It was fantastic, wasn't it? In fact, I'm still shaking from it."

He wasn't exaggerating. Kerith could feel the fine vibration everywhere their bodies touched. It gave her a gratifying sense of power. "Does that always happen?"

Daniel levered himself up again to smile down at her. "No. I've never felt anything like this. It's almost like a madness. I used to pride myself in being a slow, considerate lover, but the way I just treated you was closer to a neanderthal's tactics."

"Hey, quit punishing yourself. I told you I loved it." She stretched experimentally, then froze when she realized he was still inside her, and still very much aroused. "Um...are you...? I mean, I thought I felt . . ." Words failed her.

"Yes I did, and yes I still am," Daniel supplied, punctuating each word with a light kiss. "Once wasn't nearly enough, with you. However, before we start discussing an encore, there's a more serious subject that needs to be addressed, and that's your protection—or lack of it. I assume you aren't using any form of birth control. And I, in the heat of the moment, forgot for the first time since I was a reckless teenager." He used a fingertip to trace the elegant line of her cheekbone. "I'm sorry, Kerith. I won't be so careless again. And if anything should...happen, you don't need to worry. I'll take full responsibility."

A swift dart of alarm pierced Kerith's cloud of bliss, as the import of his last words struck home. He was talking about her becoming pregnant, about permanent consequences she wasn't prepared to consider. It couldn't happen that easily, could it? No, of course not. Most women had to try for months to get pregnant. Still, the possibility made her shift uneasily beneath Daniel's suddenly threatening weight, and she brought her hands between them to push at his chest. "Don't you think you're being a bit premature, pledging yourself to something so unlikely?" she asked irritably.

Obliging her bid for space, Daniel eased his body away to the side, but the moment he left her, Kerith wished he hadn't. An empty loneliness settled over her, and she was relieved when he pulled her around to face him on the wide cushions.

"I didn't mean to upset you, love," he said softly, his hand stroking comfortingly down her back. "I was just trying to be realistic. We don't have to think about it anymore, now."

"Perhaps you should take me home . . ." Kerith's voice trailed off in a moan as his caress strayed from comfort to sensuality. And the last of her unease fled as he gathered her against the inviting heat of his naked body.

"Oh no, not yet," he implored softly. "I have a lot of making up to do." He slipped one hand down to cup the damp curls shielding her femininity, and she immediately quivered in response. "If you're too sore to have me inside again, I know lots of other ways to love you. In fact, I probably won't have enough time in one night to demonstrate all of them."

He slipped off the couch and scooped her up, robe and all. "Come on, I want to show you what an attractive bedroom I have."

As Daniel crossed the darkened living room and started up a curved staircase, Kerith wrapped her arms around his neck and gave herself up to the delicious lure of returning passion. After all, what difference did it make at this point if she stayed the night? The risk had already been taken, she might as well get as much pleasure as possible out of it. Consequences could be dealt with tomorrow.

WHEN KERITH WOKE the next morning it was with a sense of disorientation. Wondering why her bed felt different, she stirred restlessly beneath unfamiliar blue sheets, and the soreness at the juncture of her thighs brought instant recall. This was Daniel's bed. And last night they had... Groaning softly, she turned onto her stomach and buried her face in the pillow.

"That bad, hmm?" Daniel's voice came from somewhere nearby, and when she whipped her head around to look, she found him seated on the edge of the bed, steaming mugs of coffee in his hands. "I warned you that last time would be too much."

"It's very ungentlemanly of you to remind me," Kerith complained, lowering her face to the pillow again. The memory of what he'd done to her—what she'd done to him!—inspired an urge to bury herself under the covers completely. And when she peered at him from behind the tawny disarray of her hair, she discovered a more disquieting side effect of the night before. A strange thrill stirred in the depths of her heart; not unlike the feeling one experienced at the top of an dangerously steep ski run right before pushing off. In skiing, she'd relished the sensation. Now, she found it vaguely frightening.

"I brought you café au lait," Daniel announced placatingly. "Will that redeem me?" He set the mugs down and propped two fluffy pillows against the headboard, then settled himself there. "I also think you look absolutely beautiful in the morning."

"Your eyesight must have deteriorated overnight," Kerith quipped, but the heady aroma of freshly brewed coffee overcame her reticence. Gingerly, she scooted up next to him, the sheet carefully clasped to her breasts.

Daniel had reclaimed his robe, and she had to admit it looked far better on him. Even with his hair rumpled and his face unshaven, he looked marvelous. While she, on the other hand, probably resembled a tornado victim. Accepting the mug he offered, she sipped and let out a reluctant hum of appreciation. "No one ever served me coffee in bed before."

"Not even Gus?"

Kerith sighed and rested the mug on her lap. She'd wondered how long it would be before that subject came up. Her eyes moved restlessly over the masculine oak furniture in Daniel's tastefully decorated bedroom. It was definitely a man's room. And Daniel was going to want to know why his was the first man's bed she'd slept in.

"Tell me about your marriage, Kerith. Tell me why I was the first, instead of your husband."

"Gus was a very special man," she began hesitantly. "He sort of adopted me when he found out I was an orphan. Then he discovered he had terminal cancer, and since he didn't have any living relatives, he decided I should be the one to inherit his business. Legal adoption would have been complicated, since my birth records were incomplete and registered in a foreign country. So he suggested a platonic marriage."

"Did you know he was dying when you married him?"

"Of course not!" She shot him hurt look. "What kind of woman do you think I am? He told me he was impotent—that I didn't have to worry about any demands for a physical relationship between us. But I didn't find out the cause was cancer until months after the wedding."

"Did you love him? Is that why you married him?"

Kerith closed her eyes against the pain his question brought. "No. I did it because he offered companionship and security—two things I'd never known—with no strings attached. He told me he wanted to be sure the business would be in good hands if anything ever happened to him, and I didn't allow myself to question his motives. I knew I didn't want a traditional marriage, and what he offered sounded good at the time. What I didn't count on was the depth of his feelings for me." She twisted her fingers into the folds of the sheet. "Sometimes I wish I could have . . ." Suddenly aware she was again revealing too much of herself, she turned away and set her mug on the night table on her side of the wide bed. "I think it's time for me to go. Would you get my things? I'm sure they're dry now."

"Not so fast." Daniel's arm wrapped around her waist, pulling her back. "What about the others?"

"What others?" She began to struggle ineffectually, as he slid down in the bed and snuggled their bodies together, her back hard up against his chest, her bottom nestled against—No, don't start thinking about that again, she ordered herself sternly, even as her mind was filled with vivid memories of the night before.

"I mean, all the other men in the world who saw you and wanted to make love to you. Why didn't any of them succeed?"

"Because . . ." Kerith drew a quick breath as his mouth brushed softly over her nape and down her shoulder, leaving a rapidly spreading trail of heat. "Because . . . I never . . . wanted . . . Oh, don't do that."

"What? This?" He tugged her over until she lay on her back, his tongue flicking out to taste the delicate skin of her throat. "So sweet, like honey and cream. Did I tell you how much I love to taste you?"

"Daniel, please stop," Kerith whispered faintly, her resistance slipping. She might have lost it completely if the phone on Daniel's side of the bed hadn't shrilled just then, startling them both. Daniel hesitated, obviously ready to ignore it, but on the third ring he gave in and reached for the receiver, swearing succinctly.

Kerith scrambled off the other side of the bed, dragging the sheet with her to use as a makeshift cover as she went in search of her clothes. The intrusion of the phone had served to remind her of the real world, with all its problems and complications, waiting for her outside the fantasy world she'd been living in since last night. And the biggest complication was, she actually felt reluctant to leave.

As she carefully navigated the stairs she told herself that nothing had changed. She'd had sex with the man, but she was still the same woman.

She stubbed her toe on the bottom step and swore. Who was she kidding? Everything had changed. Who would have guessed satisfying a simple physical urge could have such a strong emotional effect? It didn't happen every time. Not if the current popularity of one-night stands was any indication. So why did she feel as if Daniel Avanti had invaded not only her body, but her very soul? Every time she'd looked at him this morning, there'd been a scary tightening in the region of her heart.

Kerith's anxiety deepened to frustration as she searched fruitlessly for her clothing. There was no evidence of the missing articles in Daniel's neat, compact kitchen, nor were they in the adjoining dining area, which looked out over an inner courtyard and pool shared by Daniel and his immediate neighbors. Outside, the sun was shining brilliantly, as if the previous night's storm had been an illusion. But the clear brilliance of the sky didn't lighten Kerith's mood. Instead, a premonition of doom clouded over her, making her steps quicken with determination as she headed back toward the living room.

Daniel arrived at the bottom of the stairs just as she swept into the room. In one large hand, he held a hangar containing her dress, in the other was clutched her frilly underwear. Kerith felt something in her stomach give way. The hand that held those silky intimate articles so casually had known her with equal intimacy. How would she ever be able to forget that?

"You were looking for these?" he said, smiling.

"Yes, thank you." She hurried over and practically snatched her things from him. "I'd like to get dressed now."

"What's the rush?" Daniel inquired, bending to pluck the dragging ends of the sheet out of her way as she stumbled on up the stairs.

She didn't answer until she'd reached the door of the bathroom separating the two upstairs bedrooms. "I'm sure you must have things to do on your day off, as I do." She turned, deliberately blocking the doorway.

"As a matter of fact, I do. That was my sister on the phone, reminding me of my mother's birthday party this afternoon."

"Well then, I'd better hurry and change so you can take me home." She stepped into the bathroom and started to close the door in his face, but he pushed it open and followed her inside, his expression suddenly grim.

"If you don't mind, I'd like some privacy—" she began sharply, but he cut her off.

"Stop it, Kerith." There was an unsettling determination in his expression as he started toward her, and Kerith backed away until she bumped into the far wall.

"Stop what?"

The sheet had slipped a little and he caught her bare shoulders in a firm grip and gave her a little shake. "Stop acting as if last night was just a casual encounter, something you're going to walk away from without a second thought."

She refused to look at his face, staring instead at the tanned vee of hairy chest exposed by his robe. "Why should that bother you? It's what you're used to, isn't it?" It was a low blow, one she regretted the moment the words were out. But just looking at his chest made her feel week-kneed and far too vulnerable.

His fingers tightened painfully. "Dammit, Kerith, that was unfair. I told you how much you mean to me. Hell, I'm even tempted to skip that birthday party today, just so I can be alone with you a little longer. Considering I haven't been home for my mother's birthday in over ten years, I think that's pretty significant."

She threw her head back, prepared to meet the anger in his face, but instead she saw a combination of hurt and frustration that pulled at her heart. "I'm sorry, Daniel," she whispered, turning her head away. "But I think we both would have been better off if last night hadn't happened."

Daniel's hands relaxed, and he gently caught her chin and made her look into his eyes. "You're wrong, love. And I can prove it, if you'll just give me the chance."

"I don't want to become involved with you," she insisted, as he brushed his mouth tenderly across her forehead. Just that simple caress made her body start to go soft and languid.

"But you already are." His lips teased hers with the lightest of plucking kisses, until she tilted her head searching for more.

And, heaven help her, she knew he was right. When he wrapped his arms around her, she gave a small moan of resignation. "It'll never work," she protested uselessly, as his familiar manly scent tugged at her senses.

"Trust me. Stay with me today."

"What about your mother's party?"

"Go with me."

Alarm made her stiffen momentarily. "I couldn't. I abhor family gatherings. Too much noise and confusion."

"Please, Kerith. For me?" Daniel's fingertips began to coax the tension out of her back.

"I'll be terrible company," she threatened, but her resolve was weakening again.

"Let me worry about that." This time when he kissed her, there was no teasing, just a seductive need. By the time their lips parted, she couldn't bring herself to deny him anything.

"All right, I'll go."

His hug nearly squeezed the breath out of her. "You won't regret it," he assured her, his smile dazzling.

But he was wrong, she thought a while later, watching him draw a hot bath to soothe her morning-after aches. She regretted it already.

By the time they arrived at Rosa Avanti's comfortable ranch-style house that afternoon, Kerith's regret had darkened to a sense of foreboding. As a result, a headache had formed at the base of her skull, and it worsened when they went inside. The place was packed to the walls with laughing, shouting, gesticulating people. Worse yet, once in their midst, Daniel seemed to transform into one of them.

Kerith was jostled on every side as Daniel tugged her through the throng, introducing her to so many people in rapid succession that names and faces became a blur. Within five minutes her smile felt frozen in place and her headache had become a distinct throb of misery.

She wondered dismally how she could have allowed herself to be talked into this, as Daniel exchanged personal quips and joked with his relatives. Even amid the chaos she could sense a cohesiveness, a thread of unity that proclaimed them a family. And she didn't belong.

All her life she had known she was different, set apart by her lack of family, but she'd never felt it more keenly. Anger worsened the pounding discomfort in her head. She was angry at

Daniel for talking her into coming, and at herself for giving in to him.

The final straw came when he introduced her to his mother. Rosa Avanti's smile was gracious as she welcomed Kerith, but her dark brown eyes—so like Daniel's—sharpened perceptibly when he mentioned Classique Limousine. "Yes, I remember now," she said slowly. "You were married to Gus Anders. My late husband thought a lot of him. We were sorry to hear of his untimely death." Her hand was warm and firm when she offered it, but the look Rosa sent her son asked a multitude of questions.

"That's very kind of you," Kerith responded, feeling as if she'd just been tried and convicted. The woman was obviously wondering what her son was doing with a known gold digger like Gus Anders's widow. Fueled by a flush of embarrassment, the heat of Kerith's anger went up several degrees. She felt as if she were steaming beneath the white linen suit she'd put on when Daniel had taken her home to change. Her headache grew to migraine proportions, and only pride kept her from marching out right then.

She persevered another hour and a half, responding only when spoken to, wishing she were anyplace else in the world— or the universe. Finally, she told Daniel she had to leave.

"What is it, love?" He had to speak directly into her ear to be heard over a stereo, which had added the music of an Italian opera to the din. "You look a little pale."

"I have a headache," she said, holding her anger at bay. She didn't want to fight with him; she wanted to get away from him.

Daniel was instantly concerned. "It's probably hunger. You didn't eat much of the omelet I fixed for you this morning. Why don't you have some dinner? I think they're about ready to serve."

The thought of food sent Kerith's stomach into a tailspin. "No, please. I just want to go home."

Daniel hesitated, the inner battle of his loyalties apparent in his distressed expression.

"Look, you don't have to leave," Kerith offered stiffly. "I'll call a cab."

"No, you won't." Daniel swore under his breath. "Just wait here a minute. I should explain to my mother." He started across the crowded room, his progress slowed by numerous affection-ate bids for his attention.

There certainly wasn't any question over the prodigal's wel-come, Kerith thought impatiently. How could he possibly un-derstand her aversion to all of this? Even when he'd purposely distanced himself from his family, he must have known subcon-sciously he would return someday.

As Daniel started back toward her a few minutes later, Kerith eyed him critically. He looked as if he'd just stepped out of the pages of a men's fashion magazine. His navy blazer and gray slacks fit perfectly, and the pale peach shirt, casually open at the throat, was a compelling accent to his dark handsomeness. To her surprise, however, she discovered her reaction to him wasn't as overpowering, when filtered through a haze of pain and re-sentment.

They didn't speak as he escorted her to the gleaming black Pontiac Firebird he used for everyday driving. Kerith sank gratefully into the bucket seat and, closing her eyes, let her head drop back against the headrest. She heard Daniel get in and start the powerful engine, but the car remained parked. When she opened her eyes to determine the reason, Daniel was studying her with a frown.

Kerith sighed, and shut her eyes again. "Can we go now?"

"Of course." His response was clipped, and the tires squealed a bit as he started the car down the street. "Are you going to ex-plain to me what came over you back there?"

"I told you, I have a headache."

"Correction: you have a headache as a result of the way you reacted to the situation at my mother's house."

"I told you I can't abide the noise and confusion of family gatherings."

"It isn't that simple, and you know it. You were chilling over, pulling in on yourself even before we got there. You prepared yourself to be miserable."

Kerith's eyes popped open in surprise. The man actually sounded angry with her. How did he dare, when it was all his fault? "I'd challenge any sane person to have a good time in that zoo."

The car jerked forward as Daniel hit the gas with unneces-sary force. He was visibly upset, and it became evident he'd lost control of his temper when he spoke. "Are you jealous of my family, Kerith? Are contempt and withdrawal your way of dealing with the fact that you never had one?"

His assessment of her motives was so devastatingly accurate, Kerith felt as if she'd been laid wide open for all the world to see. Her own temper at last broke free. "Yes, damn you. It's called survival. I didn't choose the circumstances of my birth, but I learned to live with them. I was perfectly happy until you started trying to change things."

"You call that living? No emotional ties, no commitment, no love? You may have laid down those rules for Gus when you agreed to marry him, but I won't settle for them."

"No one asked you to." Kerith pressed her fingertips to her aching temples. "In fact, you won't have to put up with me at all after today."

"Like hell I won't," Daniel snapped, but he didn't argue further. A depressing silence reigned, until he'd brought the car to an abrupt halt in the driveway of Kerith's brick-and-stucco home. He sat rigid for a moment, his hands locked on the steering wheel, then his shoulders slumped and he twisted in the seat to look at her. "I'm sorry," he said in a low voice. "That got way out of control. Blame it on my Italian temper."

"I don't want to lay blame anywhere," Kerith responded dully. "I just want to be left alone." The few minutes of quiet had given her time to regain some of her composure. Now, she only wanted to put the entire episode behind her. "Goodbye, Daniel." She reached for the door handle, but his hand intercepted hers.

"Wait. I can't let you go until we have this settled."

"It is settled. I don't want to see you again. Ever."

"No, I won't accept that."

"You'll have to, because I really am too ill to argue with you anymore." She pushed his hand out of the way and opened the door, then glanced back to let him see her misery. "If you have any compassion at all, you'll leave and let me take care of my headache."

"At least let me see you to your door," he implored, as she slipped out of the car.

"No." She said it with a finality that stated clearly just how much his angry outburst was going to cost him.

Daniel felt a little sick himself as he watched Kerith disappear inside her front door. How could they have reached this point so quickly after their glorious lovemaking of the night before? He shook his head in despair, backed the car into the street and floored the gas pedal, leaving a trial of rubber that would have made any teenager proud.

After only a block, however, he backed off and proceeded at a more sedate speed. "A teenager," he muttered to himself in disgust. That was about the level of maturity he'd shown, blowing up at Kerith instead of offering understanding and support. He loved her. His entire being had been singing with the knowledge from the moment she'd welcomed him into her body with such sweet, hot fervor. The problem was, making love to her hadn't broken down the heavy walls of defense she'd erected over the years. If anything, it had probably strengthened them, because she now knew the utter vulnerability one experienced at the moment of climax.

If only he could tell her how much he loved her. But that wasn't possible, not until the business with Edelweiss was finished. He didn't want any shadow of deception between Kerith and himself when he confessed his love.

Edelweiss, Daniel thought with sudden venom, as he braked for a traffic signal. There was the real culprit in this whole mess. Why hadn't he heard anything about the proposed meeting? His mouth tightened in determination. Perhaps a call to Lucretia would speed things up in that quarter.

THE CLOCK on the dingy wall of the all-night drugstore read 10:45, as Daniel punched out a long-distance number on the pay phone. He propped one shoulder against the wall, using the other to hold the receiver to his ear. Warily he scanned his surroundings. The place appeared deserted, except for the overweight, frizzy-haired woman behind the cash register. Old habits die hard, he thought wearily, as he listened to the series of clicks routing his call. At one point, a flat, anonymous voice came on the line, demanding identification. When Daniel gave it, there were more switching noises, then Lucretia's voice, raspy with sleep.

"This had better be important, Casanova. Standard procedure is to call during normal business hours, and it's not quite three in the morning here."

Wicked satisfaction brought a smile to Daniel's face, as he automatically hunched over the phone for privacy. Even small moments of revenge could be sweet. "I was . . . uh, tied up earlier." Facing the rabid curiosity of my relatives, he added silently. There had been a minor inquisition waiting, when he'd returned to his mother's party without Kerith.

"What I want to know is when I can expect some action from Edelweiss. I've got a situation of my own to handle, and I need to get this assignment out of the way."

"What kind of situation could be urgent enough to justify dragging me out of bed?" Lucretia demanded crossly.

"Something personal. It doesn't concern you."

"It does if it involves the Anders woman. As I recall, you accepted this assignment out of concern for her as a business associate. Has that concern taken on more intimate aspects?"

Daniel ground his teeth in annoyance. He'd forgotten just how intuitive Lucretia could be. Quick, evasive action was required if he didn't want her to gain the upper hand. "You seem to have forgotten my mode of operation," he said coolly. "I don't get involved."

"There's always a first time. However, considering the lady's reputation as a cold fish, I'm inclined to believe you this time."

Kerith cold? Daniel nearly choked on that one. After last night, he couldn't imagine the word cold applying to her, in any context. "Could we get to the information I want, then?" he inquired, injecting just the right note of bored sarcasm.

"You probably won't like it. Evidently there've been more complications. No one's giving any details, but it looks like the whole project is shelved for at least a month, maybe more."

"What?" Daniel's exclamation echoed in the silent store, and when he glanced at the cashier she was staring at him nervously. He turned back to the phone, and lowered his voice to an angry murmur. "Who the hell do these guys think they are?"

"This isn't exactly a time-clock type of business, as you should know. You've handled delays before."

"That was before I had a real life to live. I don't like this. I don't like it at all."

"I could assign someone else," Lucretia suggested slyly.

Daniel barely kept himself from shouting "No!" That's all he needed, someone else from Lucretia's department messing things up. "I doubt they'd get to first base," he said, keeping his voice even. "I'm in, and I'll stay in. But I'd appreciate it if you'd light a fire under these people. And while you're at it, you might tell this Edelweiss character not to be too surprised if his welcoming committee isn't too enthusiastic. The lady has some bad memories involving the name."

"I'm not among the privileged who speak to Edelweiss, but I'll pass it along," Lucretia agreed, her tone implying she couldn't see any point in doing so.

"Good. I'll be waiting to hear from you." He paused and added meaningfully, "Let's hope it's soon." He hung up with barely restrained force, and strode toward the door.

On the way, he passed a row of Las Vegas's ubiquitous slot machines, and on a whim he stopped and fished in one pocket for a quarter. It clinked cheerfully, when he pushed it into the coin slot and pulled on the handle. The triple display spun into a blur, then clicked three figures into place—a lemon, an orange and a cherry. Useless. A big zero. Daniel made a disgusted sound and continued out the door, his hands shoved into his pockets. Luck seemed to be running full tilt against him today. Heaven help him, if it didn't improve when he tried to redeem himself with Kerith.

7

"YOU LOOK LIKE you were bitten by the same flu bug that had me under the weather all weekend." Ali Spencer stood in the doorway to Kerith's office and scrutinized her employer with a critical eye. "Is that the reason you left Rosa Avanti's party so abruptly?"

Kerith looked up from the accounting statement she'd been checking. Her mouth quirked in annoyance as she gestured for Ali to have a seat. "Who told you I was at the party?"

"Rosa did, when I called to apologize for not making it myself. She said you were with Daniel." Ali strolled over and draped herself elegantly in one of the turquoise chairs facing Kerith's desk. "Does this have anything to do with the reason you weren't home to answer your phone Friday night?" Uncertainty suddenly furrowed Ali's brow. "Or am I overstepping again by asking that?"

Kerith sighed and leaned back in her chair. "I'll tell you, but only because I want you to understand why the subject of Daniel Avanti is off-limits around here."

"Oh brother, this doesn't sound good."

"It was an unfortunate set of circumstances," Kerith corrected, tiredly massaging the back of her neck. Saturday's headache was only a faint echo now, but tension had taken up permanent residence in her shoulders. "Daniel and I took the Rolls out for a test run Friday night and got stranded in the storm."

Ali barely suppressed a smile. "The Duchess is still up to her old tricks, hmm?"

"With a vengeance. Daniel's brother-in-law rescued us and dropped us both at Daniel's place, since it was storming too hard to risk any unnecessary driving with the Rolls in tow. When Daniel invited me to wait out the storm with him, I agreed." Kerith dropped her gaze and felt a slight flush warm her face.

She'd intended to come across sophisticated and nonchalant about the whole thing, but apparently some subjects didn't automatically become easier with age. "It was a big mistake."

"You weren't . . . um, compatible?"

Ali's delicately posed inquiry made Kerith look up. Her friend's green eyes were filled with a gentle concern that put to rest any question of prurient interest, but there was a limit to what Kerith could bring herself to reveal. "Daniel Avanti and I come from totally different backgrounds," she said evasively. "Even if I were interested in having a relationship, it wouldn't work."

Ali drew a deep breath and let it out slowly. "Sometimes differences have a way of working themselves out, when genuine caring is involved. I think Daniel cares for you a great deal."

Kerith's newfound resolve tightened instinctively. Somewhere in the wee hours of Sunday morning, after a night of tormented soul-searching, she'd decided on a method of overcoming her susceptibility to Daniel. "I don't want our differences solved," she said resolutely. "In fact, I don't intend to see Mr. Avanti again, except when business makes it unavoidable."

"But—" The buzzing of the intercom interrupted Ali's protest.

"Mr. Avanti is here to see you," Charlotte announced cheerfully.

Kerith groaned softly. She'd been half expecting this, but now that the moment was here she couldn't bring herself to face it. "Tell him I'm not in."

"He already knows you are. He said to tell you he'd sit out here all day if necessary." Charlotte's voice lowered to an excited whisper. "He has roses, at least two dozen of them. They're absolutely gorgeous."

Realizing it would be better to face him now and get it over, Kerith gave in and told Charlotte to send him in. But when Daniel appeared in the open doorway, the force of her reaction dismayed her. Her pulse doubled, and within the depths of her being there was a shudder of recognition. The man had been her lover, even if for only one night, and it appeared she wouldn't be able to forget it quickly.

Kerith rose, thankful for the man-tailored rust suit she'd chosen to wear that day. It gave her a badly needed sense of fortification against the feminine weakness Daniel engendered. "Good morning, Mr. Avanti," she said with amazing composure. "How may I help you?"

At mention of Daniel's name, Ali was out of her chair like a shot and heading for the door. "Hi, Daniel. I was just leaving."

"There's no need," Kerith protested sharply. "I'm sure our business will be brief." But Ali was already zipping out the door, pulling it shut behind her.

"I guess she must be aware of what's going on between us," Daniel observed, smiling slightly.

As he moved toward her desk, however, Kerith saw that his handsome features were marred by fatigue. She stiffened every muscle in her body, resisting a pang of sympathy. "There isn't anything between us," she replied firmly.

Ignoring her denial, Daniel positioned himself just in front of her desk. The roses—a mix of apricot and pristine white this time—lay casually in the crook of his arm, a curiously appealing accent to his gray business suit. "You didn't return the messages I left on your home answering machine. That wasn't very polite."

"It also wasn't polite to fill the entire tape with the same message," Kerith countered. "Nor is it considered good form to pound on a person's door after it's apparent she isn't going to answer."

"I didn't pound."

"Knock repeatedly, then." Kerith sighed impatiently. "There isn't any point to this conversation. I told you I don't want to see you again. Why don't you accept that?"

"Because I can't." Pain flashed in the deep brown of Daniel's eyes. "And I don't believe you will, either, once you've gotten over being angry with me." He held out the roses, but she refused to take them, so he lay them on the desk, a fragrant peace offering.

"Anger isn't the issue," Kerith began, picking up the flowers and practically tossing them into his arms.

"I know. It's trust. And I betrayed yours badly when I selfishly forced you into a situation you weren't prepared to handle. I'm truly sorry for that, Kerith."

"I don't want your apologies. I want to be left alone."

Daniel shook his head almost regretfully. "That isn't possible anymore. You and I belong together; Friday night convinced me of that. Now all I have to do is convince you."

Frustration at his persistence caused Kerith's temper to erupt. "To put it in your words, 'That isn't possible.' Now, will you please leave and not come back?"

Daniel sighed unhappily. "I knew this wouldn't be easy. All right, I'll go, for now. But I'll be back. I won your trust once, and I believe I can win it again." He leaned forward and stroked her soft cheek before she could flinch away, then turned and left with a self-confident spring to his step that provoked her further.

"Stay away from me, Daniel Avanti," she warned fiercely. If he heard her, he gave no indication of it, but in the weeks that followed, it appeared he had, because she didn't actually see him more than once or twice. Which didn't mean he'd absented himself from her life. On the contrary, hardly a day passed without some contact, however subtle.

He began sending her a rose every day, which she promptly threw in the trash. But when Charlotte bemoaned the waste and pleaded for permission to keep the rejected blossoms in a vase on her own desk, Kerith relented a little and agreed.

Then there was the expensive espresso machine, delivered to Classique Limousine with a generous supply of gourmet coffee. That gift would have been sent back immediately, but Charlotte unknowingly unpacked it in the employee lounge, and the delight it generated in the morning assembly there seemed to preclude grand gestures on Kerith's part. Anyway, she reasoned defensively, if the man wanted to waste his money making her employees happy, he could go right ahead. It wouldn't have any influence on her feelings—as long as she didn't allow herself to think about cappuccino. And she still had the power to refuse to see him or accept his telephone calls.

When the notes began appearing, however, the situation wasn't quite as simple. The first one she found in mid-September, tucked in the visor of her car after it had been to Avanti's for regular servicing. Until that time, Kerith had considered maintaining business relations with Daniel to be a sign of her total disregard for what had passed between them. Aside from that, reputation-wise he was the only game in town when it came to keeping her fleet of limousines operational. But when she read the note he'd written, she began to wish there were other options.

Daniel's heavy, masculine scrawl nearly filled the small slip of paper. "I remember how lovely your golden body looked by firelight, and I ache."

Kerith closed her eyes and felt the heat of that fire sweep through her body as surely as if she'd still been lying before the flickering flames. Damn it! She should be over the whole thing by now. Why this lingering weakness?

She opened her eyes and glared at the spot where the note had been hidden. He must have put it there before his mechanic returned the car.... A new outrage occurred to her, and she scrambled out of the car and ran back to her office.

"Damn you, Daniel Avanti," she snapped, as soon as his secretary had routed the call to his office. "I don't wish to be the subject of your...your pornography. Especially when you leave it lying around for all the world to see."

"Kerith, love, how nice to hear your voice," Daniel responded, pleasure reverberating in each word. "If I'd known writing a note would do the trick, I'd have tried it sooner."

"What trick? Embarrassing me in front of your employees? Making me the topic of their shop gossip?"

"What are you talking about?" Daniel sounded more confused than happy now.

"Your mechanic, the one who picked up my car this morning and returned it this afternoon. How could you leave a note like that where he could find it?" The very idea made her stomach churn, something it had been doing with little provocation lately. She sat down at her desk and glared out the west window, totally unappreciative of the magnificent sunset gilding the distant mountainous horizon. Why did she feel so lousy all the time, lately? It was barely six o'clock, and she was exhausted already. Daniel's relieved laughter made her feel worse.

"Relax love, no one saw the note. I drove your car back this afternoon. I tried to see you, but as usual, your secretary said you were unavailable. Do you think it's fair to use her as a shield between us? The poor woman looks utterly miserable every time she has to lie to me." He hesitated, sighed, then went on in a more subdued tone. "I still want you Kerith, more than ever. Won't you give me another chance?"

The naked longing in his plea stirred an unwilling response in the depths of her soul, but she quickly suppressed it. "I learned a long time ago that wanting something doesn't necessarily make it happen. Don't you think it's time you accepted that fact, too?" She didn't wait for his answer. The ivory receiver hit its resting place with considerable force as she hung up. The incoming line on Charlotte's extension began to ring almost immediately, but Charlotte was gone for the day, and Kerith didn't give the clamoring instrument a second glance as she passed on her way out.

SEPTEMBER CAME and went in a blaze of scorching days that made it seem as if Mother Nature were bent on compensating for the relative mildness of August. Adding noticeably to the heat, were Daniel's notes, which continued to appear mysteriously in places only Kerith would find them: her purse, her locked desk drawer, the pocket of her suit jacket. Some were unabashedly erotic, reminding her vividly of their night together. Others had an emotional poignancy that almost frightened her. Strangely enough, the latter were the ones she began saving first—although after a while she found herself stowing even the "hot" ones in the small, locked chest where she kept her jewelry. In the beginning, she told herself she kept the notes as a reminder of her one foray into stupidity, but after a time, a more troubling motive occurred to her. Despite all her determined efforts, there was a chink in her armor, a soft spot. And it belonged to the man who had taught her the meaning of ecstasy.

OCTOBER BROUGHT cooling temperatures, and a sigh of relief from everyone at Classique Limousine. The milder weather sparked a general vivacity among Kerith's employees that made her more aware of the fatigue and general listlessness that continued to plague her. Hoping it was nothing more than a simple case of anemia, she made an appointment with her physician. When she left his office on a balmy day in mid-October, she knew her life course had been permanently altered.

"YOU'RE PREGNANT!" Ali popped to a sitting position on the chaise lounge from which she'd been dreamily contemplating a bright orange Halloween moon.

"Shh! Not so loud." Kerith sat forward on the webbed patio chair she'd been using and glanced nervously toward the sliding glass door leading to Ali's house. They were alone on the patio, but only two rooms away Ali's daughter was counting her trick-or-treat candy and watching a horror movie on the living-room television. With her was their neighbor, Sam, a somber bearded giant totally unlike Ali's usual boyfriends. Ali had been seeing Sam a lot lately, a surprising turnaround in her social habits. He had a quiet, easy way with little Cami that Kerith found reassuring, but that didn't mean she wanted to share her life's secrets with him. Telling Ali had been hard enough.

"This isn't a public announcement," she cautioned in a whisper. "I only told you because . . ." Kerith turned her head away abruptly and faced the dark expanse of Ali's backyard. "Because I just needed to tell someone. I haven't even decided what I'm going to do yet."

"Does that mean you're considering an abortion?" Ali asked in a low voice.

Kerith stiffened, her response instant and vehement. "No! Never!" The words echoed in the quiet night, as she slumped back and tilted her head to gaze at the night sky. "Adoption is out, too," she went on slowly. "I know what it's like to be unwanted."

"As I see it, that leaves you two options: marriage or single-parenting. Have you considered what Daniel's reaction will be?"

Kerith glanced at her sharply. "Why should I?"

"Oh, come on. You and I both know he's the only man you've been with lately. I think he has a right to know he's going to be a father."

"Well, I don't. And I trust you're not planning to change your hands-off policy concerning Daniel and me." Kerith jumped up and walked quickly to the edge of the concrete patio. "I guarantee, I won't be forgiving."

"I thought I'd proved myself in that area over the last few months." Ali's voice was etched with hurt.

Kerith turned back, her expression filled with regret. "I'm sorry, you didn't deserve that. Your restraint has been admira-

ble." Wrapping her arms tightly around her waist, she moved
back to her chair and sat. "You've never mentioned anything,
but . . . has he ever tried to get you involved?"

Ali shook her head. "Not unless you consider an occasional
phone call to ask if you're okay. Daniel may be an old friend, but
he's about as closemouthed as you are, when it comes to emotions. I do think, however, that the man has fallen in love with
you. If he knew about that baby you're carrying—"

"I wouldn't know a moment's peace," Kerith interrupted impatiently. "Which is precisely why I won't tell him."

"It's going to be pretty hard to hide after a few months," Ali
pointed out ruefully.

"I know that." Kerith hopped up again and began to pace. "I
could always tell him there had been someone else." She saw Ali's
skeptically raised eyebrow. "Or I could leave Las Vegas before
he knew. I'm sure I could sell Classique and start over somewhere else."

"Good grief, you'd go that far? What are you so afraid of?
Daniel is a kind, honorable man. Unless I miss my guess, he
probably would be happy to marry you, or at the very least share
the responsibility of raising his child."

"That's the problem." Kerith stopped pacing and threw her
hands out in frustration. "I don't want to get married. It's my
baby, my responsibility. I don't need his help."

"Are you sure? Even though my ex-husband was a louse most
of the time, I was glad to have him around when I was carrying
Cami. Pregnancy can make you feel incredibly vulnerable, at
times. Probably has something to do with hormones."

"You and Cami seem to have done all right since you've been
on your own."

Ali got up and walked over to place one hand on Kerith's
shoulder. "I thought so, too, until Sam came into my life." She
cast a fond glance toward the house. "In the last few weeks he's
shown me what I've been missing—what Cami's been missing,
too. Companionship . . . support . . . love . . . You can survive
without them, Kerith, but it isn't easy."

Kerith experienced a twinge of disappointment. Until that
moment, she hadn't realized how much she'd been counting on
Ali's support. Ali had always seemed to be the ultimate, liber-
ated woman, strong enough to walk away from a destructive

marriage and raise her young daughter alone, without losing the feminine warmth that made her such a good friend.

"I think I'd actually marry Sam . . . if he ever gets up the nerve to ask me," Ali continued with a wry smile. "Can you believe that, coming from me? Normally, I wouldn't hesitate to propose myself, but Sam inspires something traditional in me. I'm actually enjoying an old-fashioned courtship."

Tradition. Courtship. Marriage. Ali was beginning to sound like one of those flowery romance novels. Purposely stepping away from Ali's comforting hand, Kerith said stiffly, "If you're sure that's what you want, I'm happy for you. But don't expect me to jump on the bandwagon. I'm not like you. I don't need the things you're talking about."

"Don't you?" Ali's voice came quietly from the darkness behind Kerith. "You might find it's not so easy being self-sufficient, now that you have another life dependent on yours."

"I'll be fine," Kerith insisted, then quickly changed the subject. But only two days later something happened that made Ali's words sound prophetic.

THE COLLISION occurred in the middle of morning rush-hour traffic. Kerith never saw the other car coming. She just felt a tremendous jolt, right before the scenery started spinning. When her small sports car finally stopped, it was facing the wrong way on the other side of the busy intersection. According to the officer who appeared almost immediately, Kerith and the woman who'd broadsided her were lucky to have escaped without serious injury. Their cars weren't as fortunate.

As she surveyed the extensive damage to her RX-7, Kerith acknowledged the man's assessment with a vague nod, but the full realization of what might have happened didn't really hit her until she sat down beside her badly dented car to wait for the arrival of the tow truck.

I could have been killed, she thought. And then a heavier knowledge settled over her. Her life hadn't been the only one at risk. Another life—her unborn child—now depended on her for survival. The enormity of that responsibility made her begin to shake.

By the time she'd finished answering the police officer's questions, accompanied by the hysterical weeping of the woman who'd caused the accident, Kerith's endurance had almost run out. So when she heard a screech of tires and looked up to see Daniel's Firebird pulling up right behind his brother-in-law's tow truck, she felt relief rather than annoyance. He looked like a knight charging to the rescue as he lunged out of the car and raced toward her.

"Kerith, sweetheart, are you all right?" He crouched down in front of where she sat on the curb and took her trembling hands in his big, strong ones. "When Tom called me and said you'd been in an accident, I thought my heart would stop. Do you need a doctor? Have they called an ambulance?"

"I don't need an ambulance," she assured him quickly, the shaking already beginning to subside. "But the officer said I'll probably have a nasty bruise from the shoulder harness on the seat belt. And he suggested I see my doctor, just to make sure everything is all right."

"I'll take you as soon as you're finished here."

"You...you don't have to do that. I'm sure someone will come for me as soon as I contact my office."

"Not a chance, honey. I'm not letting you out of my sight until I know you're really okay. Now, do you feel up to walking, or should I carry you to the car?"

Kerith hastily opted for walking, but she couldn't talk him out of driving her to the doctor's office. Nor could she stop him from waiting for her there.

The doctor was encouraging. "You don't seem to have any serious injuries, although that seat-belt bruise may be a little tender for a while." He gave her a reassuring smile. "And you don't have to worry about your baby. Mother Nature does a pretty good job of protecting the little rascals. Just call me if you notice anything unusual."

When Kerith returned to the waiting room, Daniel was restlessly leafing through a magazine, and the worry in his eyes, when he looked up, gave her a moment's pause. How much deeper would that concern be if he knew of the child she carried? His child. Guilt nibbled at the edge of her conscience, but she quickly pushed it away. She couldn't afford such feelings. For that matter, allowing him just this small contact had been a mistake.

But Daniel wasn't so easily dismissed. He drove her to work, then insisted she keep the Firebird. "One of your drivers can drop me off at my place," he explained when she resisted. "Your car is going to need quite a bit of repair work, and Avanti's does provide loaners occasionally."

Kerith frowned and crossed her arms over her midriff as she leaned against the Firebird's gleaming fender. "But this is your car. What will you drive?"

"My Jag. I've been intending to use it more, now that the weather has cooled down."

"Daniel, I can't let you do this. It doesn't feel right after . . . after what happened." It also didn't feel right to have her heart tripping along at a dangerous clip just because he was standing so close and looking so damned attractive. Was there another man alive who had such meltingly dark brown eyes?

"There's no law against being nice," he said, a certain sadness clouding his gaze. "At least allow me that, Kerith."

Reluctantly, she agreed, thinking it would be easier to return the car later, when its disturbing owner wasn't around. A few nights later, however, she found herself heading for the Firebird yet again as she crossed the darkened employee's parking lot. "Face it, you enjoy driving the thing," she muttered to herself. But it went deeper than that, and she knew it. In truth, she was hooked on sliding into the deep bucket seat and inhaling the lingering scent of Daniel's aftershave. Anticipation of indulging herself again had her so preoccupied, she didn't notice Arthur lounging on the front fender until he spoke.

"Your Italian friend must think a lot of you, letting you use his car all this time."

Kerith's head jerked around as she paused, one hand on the Firebird's door handle. "Arthur! For heaven's sake, what are you doing lurking around out here? You nearly scared me to death."

"Sorry. I was merely enjoying a moment of fresh air." Arthur smiled apologetically and strolled closer, until he was so near she could smell the acrid licorice of the imported lozenges he favored. The scent nauseated her slightly, so she opened the car door and stepped behind it to put some distance between them. The man still made her uneasy, and lately there had been an intensity in his eyes when he looked at her that added to her wariness. His overtures toward her had remained casual and friendly, but the last few times she'd turned him down, his polite acceptance had seemed to mask a far more emotional response. His next words seemed to justify her suspicions. "You've been seeing a lot of that Avanti fellow lately." Arthur's smile twisted almost to a grimace. "Who would have dreamed you'd have a weakness for the Latin-lover type?"

His vehemence surprised Kerith into defending herself. "I don't have a weakness for anyone, Latin or otherwise, but I do think you have a lot of nerve calling names considering the number of rich, lonely ladies you currently have on a string."

"Hardly the same thing. Those women are old, no longer attractive. I'm merely being kind to them because no one else will. You're different, Kerith. You deserve a man who will take care of you; someone you can trust. Avanti could never be that for you, but I could."

The man's taken leave of his senses, Kerith thought. *And he couldn't be more wrong.* If she were inclined to trust any man again, it would be Daniel. He had proved his concern for her welfare and happiness repeatedly, without any encouragement from her. And while she still considered her brief venture into intimacy a mistake, she had to admit she couldn't imagine any man, other than Daniel, being able to tempt her to try it in the first place. Yet, here was Arthur, thinking himself the answer to her lonely widow's prayers. She couldn't stop an incredulous smile as she regarded his slightly condescending expression. "Arthur this is...absurd. I don't need anyone to take care of me."

Even in the dim light, she could see the disastrous effect of her amusement. Arthur's angular features became like chipped granite. "You're laughing at me," he accused with sudden heat. "You're choosing him over me, after all the time I've waited..." Suddenly, his hands were pressing her fingers into the top edge of the door.

The look in his pale eyes reminded Kerith of a wounded animal, and though the unexpected change in his behavior made her uneasy, a spark of empathy stirred in her heart. She knew how painful rejection could be.

"Arthur, I think I should remind you of something," she said very carefully. "Even if I were in need of someone, I would never become involved with an employee."

"You're too good for me, is that it?" Arthur demanded raggedly.

Irritation overrode her compassion. "No, that is not it. And would you please let go of my hands? You're hurting me." The sharp ring of authority in her voice seemed to bring Arthur back to his senses.

He hastily released her and stepped back. When he spoke, he sounded embarrassed and contrite. "I've really overstepped, haven't I?"

"Yes, you have," Kerith agreed, relieved to be in control again. "I try to maintain a friendly relationship with my employees, but that doesn't mean I welcome unsuitable familiarity. I have no use for a chauffeur who can't remember his place, whether it's with myself or with one of the people who use my limousine service." She saw Arthur stiffen in alarm, and relented a little. "You have an excellent working record, and I'd hate to have to terminate you."

"You...you won't find that necessary, if...if you'll only give me another chance," Arthur choked out.

Realizing how hard it must be for a man like Arthur to plead, Kerith relented even further. "All right. For now, we'll consider this little incident forgotten."

He nodded and thanked her awkwardly before turning toward his own car. Watching him go, Kerith decided she'd handled the situation in the best way possible. But over the next few days, she found she couldn't quite forget it. The part about trusting Daniel came back again and again, in annoying challenge to her self-proclaimed independence.

"You don't need him or anyone else," she told herself for the hundredth time, as she unlocked her front door late Saturday night. She pushed the door open, then hesitated. In the past, coming home to an empty house had never bothered her, but lately she'd been feeling edgy.

"Must be those overactive hormones Ali was talking about," she muttered, stepping inside.

The carved cuckoo clock she'd brought from Switzerland brightly announced nine o'clock as she entered the living room. She paused, savoring the homey sound, but when she turned on the light, her sense of security vanished.

Someone had been in her house! Everywhere she looked, there was evidence of the ruthless invasion. The edelweiss plant lay on its side, the lovely pot cracked in half, the soil spilling over the small table on which it had stood. Cushions lay helter-skelter, magazines and books were scattered and paintings had been pulled from the walls.

Fingers pressed to her lips to hold in a gasp, Kerith scanned the room with panic-stricken eyes. What else had they done? There! On shelves of her curio cabinet, more destruction. All the little knickknacks she'd collected over the years—so many of them depicting the edelweiss in some way—all were broken and scattered.

Who would do such a thing? Why?

The phone shrilled, startling a scream from her throat. She grabbed it and barely croaked a hello.

"Kerith? Is that you?" Daniel's deep voice wrapped around her like a comforting arm.

"Yes," she replied in a tremulous whisper. "D-daniel, some . . . someone's broken in . . ." Her voice failed.

"Kerith! I can barely hear you. What's going on?"

"They . . . they destroyed my edelweiss . . ."

"I still can't hear you. Did you say edelweiss?" His voice sharpened. "Is Edelweiss there with you?"

"N . . . no." She raised her free hand to the phone receiver and tried to think clearly. "I think—No, I *know* someone's been in my house . . ."

Daniel's startled oath cut her off. "Listen carefully, love. I want you to get out of there this minute. Don't stop for anything. Get in your car and drive to that little convenience store two blocks away. You know the one?"

"Yes." A random thought occurred to her. "What about the police? I should . . ."

"I'll take care of it. Just wait for me at the store. And lock your car doors!"

"But . . ."

"Go!" The force of that one word drove her out the front door without further hesitation.

KERITH WASN'T SURE how long she'd been waiting when Daniel drove his low-slung sports car into the parking lot of the brightly lit store, but it seemed like hours. And when he scooped her up into his warm, reassuring embrace, she knew a contentment beyond anything she'd experienced before.

"Kerith, thank God. I think I broke every speed record in the state getting here." He held her at arm's length to look her over. "Are you okay?"

She nodded, a smile pulling at her mouth as she took in his disheveled appearance. His rumpled dress shirt was unbuttoned and hanging free of his trousers, his feet were bare, and he'd never looked better to her. "You could have taken the time to put on some shoes," she teased unsteadily. "I don't think there was any real danger. I . . . I just overreacted when I saw how they . . . how they . . ." She faltered, remembering the pathetically wilted leaves of the edelweiss, the shards of broken ceramic and glass.

"To hell with shoes." Daniel pulled her close again. "I told the police to meet me at your place. Do you want to wait here or come with me?"

Kerith sighed, allowing herself the luxury of his embrace for a moment, then pushing resolutely away. "I'd better come. Dressed as you are, you might be mistaken for the burglar," she joked weakly.

She couldn't, however, manage any humor when they surveyed the damage done to the rest of the house. Her bedroom looked ravaged, drawers pulled out, clothes and personal items strewn everywhere, the sheets on her bed stained with red wine taken from her own pantry.

"Looks like malicious mischief to me." The investigating officer looked up from the notes he'd been scribbling. "Are you sure you can't think of anyone who might do something like this? A disgruntled customer or maybe an ex-employee?"

Kerith's memory briefly flicked back to her confrontation with Arthur, then just as quickly discarded the idea. Arthur had been a model employee, since that night. He didn't deserve to be dragged into this just because he'd formed an unfortunate emotional attachment to his boss.

She shook her head firmly. "Sorry, there isn't anyone I can think of."

The policeman sighed. "Probably was kids, then. Occasionally we have some trouble with the ones whose parents work nights at the casinos. Judging by the money and jewelry you said were missing, and the clumsy way the back door was forced, I'd say it was youngsters too inexperienced or scared to try fencing any really big items."

"But why the destruction?" Kerith asked forlornly, picking up the remains of a favorite Hummel figurine.

The uniformed man shrugged. "I leave that to the psychiatrists. Do you have another place to stay tonight? Regardless of who did this, you shouldn't stay here until you get that door fixed. For that matter, I'd suggest you have a home-security system installed." He glanced meaningfully at her expensive television-and-stereo unit. "Next time, you might lose a lot more."

"Don't worry, I'll see that it's done," Daniel announced forcefully. He stepped forward to place a protective arm around Kerith's shoulders, then glanced down at her challengingly as he added, "In the meantime, she'll be staying with me."

8

"I STILL DON'T THINK this is a good idea." Kerith stubbornly folded her arms across her chest and faced Daniel from the doorway of his guest room. It had taken hours, handling the police, picking up the debris from the break-in and packing the things she would need for the night. Now, she was almost numb with fatigue, but she still felt the need to protest Daniel's plan.

He turned from placing her suitcase on a low chest and smiled patiently. "That's the twenty-fifth time you've said that, and you're still wrong. This is the perfect solution to your problem. You need a place to stay until your house is safe again, which could take several days, since we can't even call for an estimate on the security system until Monday. I not only have the room, I also like knowing you're safe, just in case that break-in was something more than a kid's prank." He crossed the room to her and pulled a small packet of folded papers from his pocket. "I found these before the police came and figured you'd prefer not having them read."

His notes! Those sexy, romantic missives she'd hidden in her jewelry box were as incriminating as evidence presented before a jury. "I . . . I was only . . ." she faltered, feeling a hot rush of embarrassment from her head to her toes.

"Shh." Daniel's fingertips pressed gently against her lips. "Don't try to explain. Let me dream a little."

At his touch, her flush deepened to a sensual heat that raced through her veins like liquid fire. She experienced a sweet, melting sensation deep within, reminding her of the part of him she carried there.

"I can't stay here," she said, even as her body swayed toward him. "Because I don't intend to go to bed with you again, and sooner or later that issue is going to come up."

Daniel took advantage of her movement toward him, pulling her close. "Hey, didn't I tell you I wouldn't push on that? Right now, I'm just happy to have you here. If anything more comes of it . . . well, that's up to you." He gave her a little squeeze and set her away from him. "All I want, for now, is the chance to take care of you."

Take care of you. At that moment, with the picture of her vandalized home still clear in her mind, no words could have sounded sweeter to Kerith. She accepted, adding quickly the situation was only temporary.

ALMOST BEFORE she knew it, temporary stretched into a week.

"The home-security business is booming right now," Daniel explained after he'd done some checking. "Installation dates are backlogged three weeks at the least."

Kerith promptly insisted she had to find another place to stay, but as the days passed she found herself settling into Daniel's home with unbelievable ease. After a while, she reluctantly admitted the reason to herself. She and Daniel suited each other.

Whereas she and Gus had coexisted, making allowances for the differences in their habits; her living patterns seemed to mesh with Daniel's like the hues of a fine watercolor. Even the occasionally unannounced visits of his relatives stopped bothering her after a while. Taken a few at a time, they weren't so bad, and she simply absented herself on the one occasion his mother appeared.

Her only lasting concern was over the inescapable current of desire that grew stronger between them with each passing day. She saw it in the flash of Daniel's dark eyes as he sat at breakfast, his fingers absently caressing the fuzzy leaves of her rescued edelweiss, which now held a place of honor on his breakfast bar. She felt it as a provocative ache deep in her abdomen each time she saw him arrive downstairs in the morning, freshly groomed, or lying rumpled and relaxed on the couch at the end of the day, listening to a favorite tape. She heard it in the affectionate way he teased her about his superior cooking skills as they shared the task of preparing dinner in his small kitchen. But most of all, she sensed it in the electric, waiting tension that hummed in the air whenever they occupied the same room. Strangely enough, an invitation to Thanksgiving dinner brought the waiting to an end.

DANIEL HESITANTLY brought the subject up after dinner one night, two days before the holiday. "My mother called today," he began, toying with the stem of his wineglass. "She told me I won't get any pumpkin pie if I don't talk you into having Thanksgiving dinner with the family."

"Think of the calories you'll save," Kerith teased, smiling to cover the sudden panic squeezing her stomach. But when she saw the disappointment clouding Daniel's eyes, she sobered. "You know how I feel about big family gatherings."

"It won't be like the birthday," he hastened to assure her. "Just my mom, my sisters and their families and us. No more than thirteen people, including you. You've gotten along with them whenever they came over here, how much more difficult can a small dinner be?"

Kerith got up quickly and started gathering dishes. "I can hardly believe your mother wants me there," she said offhandedly. "I saw the way she looked at me when you told her I was married to Gus. She probably thinks I'm after your money now."

"What the—" Daniel broke off in astonished laughter. "That's the most ridiculous thing I've ever heard. Ever since she met you, she's been driving me crazy asking when I was going to bring you again." He caught Kerith's hand and pulled her toward him. "She wants you to be a part of our holiday, almost as much as I do."

His simple pronouncement flowed like a healing balm over her anxious heart, and a new feeling unfurled there like a sun-warmed rosebud. "All . . . all right. I suppose I could come. But I can't promise to enjoy it."

"Thanks, love." Daniel smiled and raised her hand, and pressed his lips against the soft center of her palm.

It was the first time he'd kissed her since their current living arrangement had begun, and Kerith felt the warmth and softness of his mouth throughout every inch of her being. She shuddered, stepping back abruptly, and Daniel let out a soft groan.

"Sorry," he muttered after passing a hand roughly over his face. "I thought a simple hand kiss would be all right."

"It . . . it's okay," Kerith stammered, busying herself with clearing the table. "You've been very good about keeping your word." Which made it totally unreasonable for her to wish he had less fortitude, she told herself sharply as she headed for the kitchen. But she did wish it. And she was more than a little disappointed when he made no further move toward her. After the dishes were done, he excused himself to go work out in the small gym contained within the condominium complex.

"Sister Agnes always said you were perverse," Kerith grumbled to herself as she prepared for bed a while later. "Always wanting what you couldn't have." Except, she could have Daniel—if she was willing to accept the emotional entanglements that came with him. The real obstacle was her lingering fear of those entanglements.

Still muttering to herself, she scurried down the hall to the bathroom for a glass of water. Her last ritual each night was taking one of the prenatal vitamins the doctor had prescribed. Not bothering to turn on the light, she quickly filled a glass and swallowed the large pink pill. She nearly dropped the glass, however, when the connecting door to the master bedroom swung open and the light came on to reveal Daniel standing there in nearly naked splendor.

Equally startled, they exclaimed almost in unison.

"Oh! I thought you were . . ."

"Sorry, I thought you were . . ."

Kerith smiled weakly and finished, "working out" as her eyes skittered nervously away from the towel fastened precariously low on his hips. His hair was slicked back, still damp from the shower, and there were a few diamond-bright droplets caught in the light furring on his chest.

She saw Daniel's biceps bulge slightly as he gripped the doorjamb and let his gaze travel slowly down the flower-sprigged length of her sheer cotton nightgown. When he brought his eyes up again, they rested for a breath-catching moment on the soft swell of her breasts not covered by the scooped neckline. He inhaled sharply and stared at the floor, the muscles in his arms tightening even more.

"I swear, Kerith, you are the most beautiful woman I've ever seen," he said in a low, anguished voice. "Having you here and not being able to touch you is the sweetest torture I've ever known."

Sweet torture. Yes, that's what it is, Kerith thought, her body pulsing with sensual excitement. And what had she gained denying it, except frustration and loneliness? Were those any better than the potential pain of being vulnerable again? "Daniel,

I . . ." She faltered, overwhelmed by the magnitude of the decision she was making.

"No, you don't have to repeat all the reasons you can't," he said, misinterpreting her hesitation. "I made a promise, and I'll keep it." He looked up, disappointment plain in his rueful smile. "But if you ever change your mind, I'll make sure you don't regret it." He stepped back into his bedroom, preparing to shut the door, but Kerith's voice rang out, stopping him cold.

"Is that a promise?" For a moment, she was surprised she'd actually spoken, but then she felt only certainty.

"You can count on it, love." A very different smile curved Daniel's attractive mouth as he watched her walk toward him. When their bodies were almost touching, she reached up and stroked one hand down the powerful curve of his chest, over the taut, smooth skin covering his ribs and further, until she was touching his flat, hard belly just above the knot of the towel. His breath sucked in, and the silky hair on his groin tickled her palm.

Daniel's eyes searched hers with a newborn urgency. "Will you consider me barbaric if I haul you right off to my bed? Because I'm almost at the end of my endurance. Even the workouts aren't helping anymore."

Laughing softly, Kerith shook her head, then let out a soft shriek when he immediately swung her up in his arms and proceeded to do as he'd threatened. The sheets of his neatly turned-down bed were cool against her back when he laid her on it, but his skin was hot beneath her fingertips as he stretched out beside her. His mouth came down on hers with the hunger of a man too long denied, and Kerith returned the kiss with all her own pent-up desire. They writhed and twisted, arms and legs tangling until Kerith's hand encountered the knot of Daniel's towel. After only an instant of hesitation, she tugged it loose, and the rigid heat of his erection filled her hand. With a soft murmur of appreciation, she stroked the satiny skin stretched taut over his iron-hard shaft...relearning...adoring... Too soon, he pulled away, gasping.

"Not so fast, love," he growled softly. "I have a few other things in mind first." His mouth sought the silken curve of her throat as he gently eased the wide neckline of her nightgown down. But she had to stifle a cry, when his strong hands molded her breasts.

Daniel's concern was instantaneous. "What is it, sweetheart? Was I too rough?"

Kerith froze. She couldn't tell him pregnancy was the cause of that unusual tenderness. "I . . . I'm just a little sensitive there sometimes. It's fine now."

"It doesn't hurt if I do this?" His fingers moved ever so gently, their skill tantalizing beyond belief. "Or this?" His mouth formed a soft, moist prison around her puckered nipple.

Kerith gasped in helpless pleasure. "That . . . that's wonderful. Please . . . please don't stop." And he didn't, although he drove her half mad with gentleness. She felt her nightgown being slipped off, felt his gentle hands and avid mouth tasting, praising, worshiping her body like a celebrant at a shrine. She was quivering and damp with need by the time he paused to take care of protecting her, and she nearly cried out in frustration that it wasn't necessary. But then he was back, surging heavily into the satiny tightness of her body, driving her to a shuddering explosion almost immediately. Kerith grabbed frantically for the solid strength of Daniel's shoulders, as pleasure rocked through her in waves. She was only vaguely aware when his arms gave out and he collapsed on her with a guttural cry of release.

A long while passed before Daniel found the strength to roll over onto his back, bringing Kerith's limp form with him. Never had he felt more drained or exhausted. And yet, within his innermost being there was a surging joy, a singing elation that paradoxically made him want to weep. How perfect lovemaking could be when the love was real—and what a travesty without it. If only he could tell Kerith all that was in his heart . . .

He brought himself up short. No, not yet. The specter of Edelweiss remained between them. Damn Lucretia! The last time he'd called in she'd been as vague as ever, regarding any kind of time schedule. And when he'd told her about the break-in and his new living arrangement, she'd been positively obnoxious.

"I knew you still had it, Casanova. There isn't a woman alive who could resist sleeping with you," she'd crowed triumphantly.

"I didn't say she was sleeping with me," he'd responded coldly. "I brought her here for protection."

Lucretia sobered temporarily. "Does that mean you think the break-in night not be simple vandalism? If there's any hint of trouble, I want to know."

"Don't worry about it. I checked things out before the police arrived. The place was vandalized, but it wasn't searched, not by anyone who knew what he was doing, anyway. It looked like the work of juvenile delinquents, to me."

"Keep your eyes open, regardless. And stick as close to the lady as possible. I have a hunch we'll be hearing from our foreign friends soon."

Soon being a relative term, Daniel amended, coming back to the present at a soft, contented sound from Kerith. It reminded him of the purr of a cat. *She* reminded him of a cat, with that sleek, golden body of hers and those sexy, up-tilted eyes. Did she understand how vital she was to his happiness? At least he could tell her that, even if the love part had to wait. "Are you asleep?" he asked quietly when she shifted in his arms.

"Mmm, no. But I'm not too sure I'm still alive. I feel like the victim of a cyclone."

Daniel chuckled softly and brushed the silky, golden tangle of hair back from her face. "I know what you mean. But I also feel more alive than I ever have before. You do that, Kerith. And it makes me want to hold on to you forever." He felt the caution tighten her body, even before she spoke.

"Daniel, I think you should understand something. What just happened, it doesn't come with any guarantees. I can't promise you forever, or even next week." She raised her head from his chest and looked at him, uncertainty creasing her brow.

"Then we'll take it one day at a time. I can be very patient when I try," he assured her, gently stroking the tension from her forehead. "Just allow me the chance to sway your thinking." He pulled her closer and teased the swollen softness of her mouth with a flick of his tongue.

"I should warn you, however," he added with a grin. "I can be very convincing."

Slowly, deliberately, she ran her tongue over her top lip, savoring the lingering taste of his kisses. "That sounds like a threat. What devious means do you plan to employ?"

"How about a little old-fashioned domination?" With a lunge, he turned over, pinning her beneath his hard body.

Kerith merely laughed and lightly trailed her fingernails over the sensitive hollow at the base of his spine. Daniel arched his back and let out a low, guttural sound. Almost at once, she felt a burgeoning hardness begin to press against her inner thigh.

"For a late bloomer, you certainly picked this up fast," Daniel accused, his dark eyes glinting with renewed fire.

Kerith laughed again and flexed her fingers against his tautly muscled buttocks. "I've always been a quick study."

"That may be, but I can make love in five languages." He gave her a teasing leer, then sealed her mouth with a deep, hungry kiss.

"I'm fluent in six," she gasped when he'd finished.

"Ah, but can you make love in them?" His mouth trailed down to her jaw and he nibbled her chin lightly.

She tried to answer, but could only manage a moan as he slid down to give loving attention to her breasts.

"*Que magnifique!*" he murmured. The velvet roughness of his tongue rubbed over her contracted nipple, and she began to quiver with the inner hunger only he could satisfy.

He moved lower and kissed the tender hollow beside her hipbone, then inched lower still. "*Je t'adore*", he whispered over the gentle mound of her womanhood. And then she felt his tongue caress her with a breathtaking intimacy that brought shimmering star bursts of release.

"*Je t'adore*," she echoed impulsively, urging him up until she felt the heavy pressure of his manhood seeking entry. And then he was surging into her, swift and deep, and her world shattered into bright prisms of sheer pleasure.

They didn't make it past French that night.

KERITH AWAKENED on Thanksgiving day with strong misgivings about her coming encounter with the Avanti family. But making slow, exquisite love with Daniel helped a lot. In fact, making love had become a panacea for a lot of her doubts.

Maybe that had something to do with why they did it so often, she mused, as she settled back in the Firebird's passenger seat. Daniel had taken the wheel for the drive to his mother's house, and she found it reassuring to watch his strong, competent hands guiding the powerful car. Just as they had guided her body, again and again . . .

She cut off the thought, faint color touching her cheeks. That certainly wasn't the kind of thing to think of now. Not when faced with the ordeal of interacting with the man's family.

"What are you thinking about?" Daniel braked for a traffic signal and glanced at her with eyes still glowing from the morning's activities.

"Nothing."

"Oh, yes, you are. I can see it in your eyes." He grinned and turned his attention back to the road as the light changed. "And if you keep looking at me like that, my mother is going to start asking me if my intentions are honorable."

Kerith flinched a little, remembering one of her main worries. "Does . . . does she know I'm staying with you?"

"Yes." Daniel caught her anxious expression and hastened to assure her. "I told her what happened to your house, and she said I did the right thing, moving you to my place." He gave her a teasing grin. "She might be harboring secret hopes, though. Mothers tend to be that way when they have unmarried sons my age."

Panic leapt anew in Kerith's heart. "Daniel, I don't think I can do this. What if she asks me if my intentions are honorable?"

Gentle laughter rumbled deep in Daniel's chest, and he reached to give her hand a comforting squeeze. "She wouldn't do that. My mother may be old-fashioned about some things, but she also has class. Stop worrying, love. Everything is going to be fine."

To her surprise, he was right. After a few awkward moments when they first arrived, the warmth and gaiety of Daniel's relatives swept over Kerith, drawing her in. Added to that were the rich, inviting aromas of roasting turkey and freshly baked pies. It soon became evident Rosa Avanti's only concession to old-fashioned ideas was an overloaded table.

In fact, the only uncomfortable moment came when Daniel chose to announce with a devilish twinkle in his eyes, that Kerith was quite fluent in Italian. Remembering how he had tested her fluency that morning in bed, Kerith nearly choked on a bite of pumpkin pie. Luckily, no one seemed to notice, and Rosa quickly drew Kerith into a lively discussion of Italy. Since Kerith had visited that country several times, talking about it was easy, and from there the day only got better.

LATER THAT NIGHT, as she lay cuddled with Daniel, pleasantly exhausted from yet another test of their linguistic skills, Kerith was struck again by how easy it all had seemed. Was it possible she'd been fooling herself all these years, thinking she was better off living without any emotional commitment? And the unborn child she carried, was it fair to deprive it of such a warm, loving family as the Avantis?

One way or another, she would have to make a decision soon. Her waistline was beginning to thicken, and Daniel was sure to notice before long. If she intended to stay with him, she would have to tell him about the child. The thought of how little time she had, made her squirm restlessly. At once, she felt Daniel's arms tighten protectively around her waist, and the instant comfort that unconscious gesture brought, made her wonder if the decision had been made already. As she drifted off to a troubled sleep, she resolved to talk it over with Ali as soon as possible.

But when Ali arrived at work on Monday morning, she had some unsettling news of her own.

"Congratulate me, I'm getting married!"

"What?" Kerith turned from the spectacular sunrise outside her office window and gaped at her radiantly smiling friend.

"I said, I'm getting married. Sam proposed over the weekend, and I accepted."

Kerith tried to hide her dismay. "Isn't this a little sudden?" she asked faintly.

Ali shrugged and joined her at the window. "Not really. We've been neighbors for ages." She grinned and toasted herself with the coffee cup she carried. "And he says he's been in love with me almost since the day he moved in next door. He was just waiting for me to settle down and notice."

Sunlight poured through the window, warming Kerith's back, but inside she felt a chill of uncertainty. So many changes had taken place in her life lately. When Ali married, their friendship would change, too, including the amount of time they spent together.

But you have Daniel now, an inner voice reminded her. *Or you could, if you'd stop hesitating.*

"Hey, in there." Ali waved a slender hand in front of Kerith's eyes. "You don't look very happy for me. I thought you liked Sam."

Kerith summoned a bright smile. "Of course I'm happy. And Sam's a wonderful man. Your news just took me by surprise." She took Ali's arm and urged her toward the couch. "Sit down and tell me your plans. I hope this doesn't mean you'll be leaving Classique. I can't say I'll be overjoyed at that prospect."

Ali laughed. "Don't worry, I'm not quitting unless I get really crazy and decide to have another baby." She glanced meaningfully at Kerith's middle. "Speaking of which, have you told Daniel yet? You're bound to start showing before too much longer."

"I'm still wearing my regular clothes," Kerith protested, one hand going self-consciously to her stomach. "The doctor said I could go another month like this." He'd also jokingly assured her that an active sex life wouldn't harm the baby as long as she didn't go in for chains and whips. Kerith grinned, remembering.

"How can you look so happy, while you're still deceiving that poor man?" Ali sighed irritably. "I've never seen you look more... I don't know... content."

Unsettled by Ali's perception, Kerith rose quickly and walked to her desk before speaking. "Actually, I am more content lately. And I've even considered telling Daniel about the child." Her mouth twisted in wry humor. "Unfortunately, I can't seem to come up with the right way to do it after holding back so long."

"Don't worry about the method, just do it," Ali urged, coming over to perch on the corner of the desk. "The man's so crazy in love with you, he'd forgive almost anything."

"Perhaps he would, but that doesn't help me with the other consequences of telling him." Kerith sat down in her executive chair and restlessly ran her hands down the smooth, leather arms. "He's a family-oriented man. And I'm still not sure I can handle a commitment like that."

"You've been living with the guy for weeks."

"That's a long way from marriage."

Ali slapped her hands down to her thighs in exasperation. "Okay, I can't tell you what to do with your life, but I do feel compelled to say this—Daniel Avanti is one fantastic man and, believe me, they are few and far between in this world. You'd better think carefully before you reject what he's offering. Speech ended." Ali stood up, straightened the razor-sharp crease in her uniform trousers, and walked to the door. "I have to go—early pickup today. But think about what I said."

Kerith smiled ruefully. "Rest assured, I'll probably think of little else until this is resolved. And by the way, I wish you and Sam and Cami all the best."

Ali smiled over her shoulder. "Thanks. I'm wishing that for you and Daniel, too."

If only wishes were enough, Kerith thought, picking up a sheaf of letters requiring signatures. Yet, deep inside she agreed with Ali. Daniel was a fantastic man.

For the rest of the day Kerith mulled it over, weighing pros and cons until her head spun. By the time she was ready to leave that evening, however, she'd talked herself into telling Daniel of his prospective fatherhood. With a determined step she headed for the door, but then the intercom buzzed, calling her back.

"There's a woman on line one who wants to speak to you, but she refuses to give her name," Charlotte explained apologetically. "She sounds kind of foreign—claims it's extremely important."

Kerith sighed, glancing at her watch. She'd probably be late getting home to Daniel, but being in business required catering to the eccentricities of a potential client. "I'll take the call. Who knows? It could be Marlene Dietrich or the Queen of England." Charlotte chuckled sympathetically and put the call through.

After politely announcing herself, Kerith waited, but the only response she got was the sound of a softly indrawn breath and then the hollow hum of an open line.

She tried again, with a little more force. "This is Kerith Anders. Who's calling, please?"

"I . . . I'm sorry." The woman's voice, although hesitant, had a melodious precision that demanded attention. "My name is Julia Robbins. We haven't met, but I know you, Kerith. I've known you for a long time."

A little frisson of apprehension ran down Kerith's spine, but she made herself respond calmly. "Your name isn't familiar to me. Have we done business before?"

"No, never." The woman made a sharp, frustrated sound. "I knew this would be difficult. Perhaps I should just state it plainly. I...I'm your mother. And I would like very much to meet you."

Kerith's first reaction was stunned disbelief. "Is this some kind of joke? I don't have a mother."

A deep sigh came from the other end of the line. "No, no joke. When we meet you'll see . . ."

"Why should I agree to meet you?" Kerith demanded, a sick premonition stirring to life in her stomach. "I have no way of knowing what you're saying is true. Can you prove it?"

"Quite easily." There was a brief pause, and then the cultured voice announced quietly, "I am Edelweiss."

9

IRREPRESSIBLE OPTIMISM put a spring in Daniel's step as he entered Kerith's office, a fragrant bouquet of mixed flowers in one hand. But his step faltered and his smile of anticipation faded when he found her sitting hunched over at her desk, arms clasped around her middle, features pale and stricken.

He rushed to her side, the flowers falling to the floor, forgotten. "Kerith, honey, what is it? Are you ill?"

She looked at him as if she hadn't even noticed his arrival until that moment. "Edelweiss," she murmured vaguely.

Daniel was instantly alert. "What about Edelweiss? Come on, Kerith, talk to me." He gave her a little shake which seemed to bring her back to her senses.

"I'm sorry, I guess the phone call gave me a bit of a shock."

"What phone call?" Daniel demanded sharply. But he knew, even before she spoke, and frustration swept over him in a boiling tide. Why now? After all the months of unexplained delay, why did it have to come just when he'd begun to make real progress with her?

"Edelweiss called me." Kerith laughed shakily. "Now, doesn't that sound like the shocker of the year? But it isn't. The real news is, I have a mother. I never was an orphan."

Daniel sat back on his heels in surprise, his hands falling from her shoulders. "Edelweiss told you that you have a mother?"

Kerith laughed again, a faint hysteria echoing in the mirthless sound. "Edelweiss *is* my mother," she announced, jumping up to pace over to one window and back. "Can you believe that?" she asked, eyes widening incredulously. "I never even thought of Edelweiss as a woman."

Daniel stood to face her. "Why not? Flower names are generally considered feminine."

Code Name Casanova

"But what kind of woman would treat her child as she treated me?" Kerith threw out her hands in exasperation. "She abandoned me!"

"Perhaps she had her reasons," Daniel suggested, thinking of Lucretia's allusions to Edelweiss's elevated rank. It could explain a lot. He'd heard a few horror stories about retaliation against the friends and relatives of top-level agents.

"I don't give a damn about her reasons," Kerith said coldly. "I told her I didn't want to meet her."

Dread settled like a millstone in Daniel's chest. At this point he didn't really care about his agreement to aid Edelweiss in arranging the meeting. What did distress him was the sudden detachment he saw in Kerith's eyes when she looked at him. The barriers were going up again, stronger than ever, and he sensed there might be only one irreversible way to do away with them—through Edelweiss.

Shoving his hands into the pockets of his slacks, he said carefully, "Don't you think you owe it to yourself to at least get a few answers before you tell her to get lost? I got the impression you've always wanted to know about your heritage." Her belligerent scowl wavered a bit, and he knew he'd scored a hit.

"What can it hurt to let the woman tell her story? No one can force you to change the way you feel." Silently, he sent up a fervent prayer that Edelweiss could, indeed, do just that.

"I don't know..." Kerith was shaking her head, but she looked uncertain. "I probably won't like what she has to say."

Daniel reached out and gave her shoulders an encouraging little squeeze. "You won't know that until you hear it."

Kerith looked up at him, apprehension unexpectedly adding an endearing childishness to her lovely face. "I don't think I could face her alone. What would I say to her?"

"I'll be there if you like. In fact, if it makes you feel better, you can ask her to come over to my place. That way, you'll have the advantage of familiar surroundings." *And Edelweiss will have her damned security. Very smooth, Casanova,* an inner voice mocked. His earlier dread became an oppressive weight. How the hell was he going to explain his role in all this to her?

The answer was, he couldn't. Not yet, anyway. Kerith didn't need that kind of news right now. He could only hope the meeting with Edelweiss wouldn't make matters worse.

"I suppose it wouldn't be too bad, as long as she doesn't expect anything of me," Kerith said reluctantly.

Hope welled up, easing a little the load on Daniel's heart. "You're a grown woman now. She can't control you as she did when you were a child."

A grim little smile tugged at Kerith's lovely mouth. "You're right. She said she'd call again tomorrow, just in case I'd changed my mind. I'll just tell her we're dealing on my terms now."

"Good for you." Daniel gave her a smile of encouragement, but he worried over the cool determination he saw in her eyes.

IT WAS STILL there the next evening, as they waited for the arrival of Kerith's mother. When the doorbell rang, however, Kerith turned to him in sudden panic.

"I'll get it," he offered, rising quickly from the couch.

He opened the front door, prepared to offer a cordial welcome, but the smile froze half formed at the sight waiting for him outside. It was like being zapped through a time tunnel into the future, he thought vaguely, as he stared in shock at the woman before him. Except for the deep blue eyes, and the delicate ivory skin tone, she looked exactly as he imagined Kerith would look twenty, maybe thirty years from now.

"Hello, Mr. . . . Avanti, isn't it?" she inquired, shifting the ornate cane she held to her left hand so she could offer the right one in greeting. "I'm Julia Robbins." She glanced over her shoulder at a craggy-featured man who stood behind her on the stoop. "This is my . . . friend Karl Barber."

Daniel wasn't fooled by the man's iron-gray hair and neat business suit. The guy was an agent. Extra protection, maybe? Yet, when the introductions were complete and Daniel invited them inside, he could have sworn he heard the man mutter, "Careful of the step, honey," as Julia limped forward.

Kerith heard their footsteps in the hallway, and jumped up off the couch to take a position by the fireplace. The cheerful blaze Daniel had built earlier did nothing for the chill in her hands, but standing gave her confidence a boost. Straightening her spine, she prepared herself for whatever was to come, then stiffened in surprise when Daniel and two strangers appeared in the arched doorway to the living room.

No, both weren't exactly strangers. There was something vaguely familiar about the woman, Kerith thought, as random impressions avalanched her mind: chic, black suit, rose silk blouse, shiny hair curving forward to frame a slightly exotic face.

What was it about that face...? The truth, when it hit her was an unwelcome shock. *I look like her,* Kerith realized, stricken. She'd been prepared to hate an anonymous stranger; it was another matter, to scorn a face as familiar as her own.

"Kerith, this is Julia Robbins and her . . . friend Karl Barber," Daniel said smoothly, breaking the awkward silence.

Then the woman moved forward and Kerith received another unpleasant surprise. The confident bearing and slim, supple body were marred by a painful limp. "Hello, Kerith," the woman said, her voice bearing the rich accent associated with England's upper class. "I've been looking forward to this day for a long time." She made a move as if to offer her hand, and Kerith almost recoiled.

"Please come in, have a seat . . . uh, Ms Robbins," she said quickly, wanting to avoid any physical contact.

The smile she got in response was rueful. "Thank you, but I'd rather stand, if you don't mind. We've been traveling for quite a while, and sitting is a little uncomfortable at the moment." She waved a graceful hand toward the couch. "You needn't stand, though. And please call me Julia. Heaven knows, the situation is awkward enough without unnecessary formality."

The men moved first to comply, and Karl stopped next to Julia long enough to lay a gentle hand on the silky hair curving against her nape before taking a seat at the far end of the couch. Daniel settled on the section that extended toward the fireplace on the opposite end. After a moment's hesitation, Kerith perched in the center of the long expanse of cushions between the two men.

Uneasy silence settled over the room as Julia slowly made her way to stand before them, a heavy stillness like that of an audience waiting for the opening curtain of an anxiously awaited play. It seemed to rob Julia of some of her poise, and she turned uncertainly to Karl. "Now that I'm here, I'm not sure how to begin."

Karl sat forward, his rather harsh features softening briefly in a smile. When he spoke, Kerith detected a slight Texas accent.

"Just start at the beginning, and tell it all straight through. I'm sure Mrs. Anders will let you know, if she has questions."

Kerith assented with a quick nod, and Julia began. "Have you heard of an organization called Interpol?"

At the back of Kerith's mind, a little warning light clicked on. "Of course. It's sort of an international law-enforcement agency, isn't it?"

Julia nodded. "I've been one of their agents since I was twenty-one."

An agent! Kerith barely suppressed a startled guffaw. What was this, some kind of weird joke? She threw Daniel a questioning glance, and the look he sent back unsettled her more. Why did he suddenly look as if he'd been convicted of a crime? Something didn't feel right here... She left the thought half formed as Julia went on.

"I can see you're having difficulty assimilating this, and I don't blame you. My career and my life have been a bit out of the ordinary. Perhaps I should explain how it began. You see, I was quite alone in the world when I was approached. My parents had died of influenza two years previously, and I had no other living relatives. I'd just left university, wasn't sure what I'd do next. The people who recruited me offered job security and what sounded like an enormous amount of money." Julia's mouth twisted in a wry smile. "More than that, they convinced me I could actually make a contribution to world peace, and I was quite an idealist at the time."

"You *have* made significant contributions," Karl put in gruffly, but Julia silenced him with a gentle shake of her head.

"My first assignment was in Germany, and I met and fell in love with your father there."

"Was he an agent, also?" Kerith asked, remembering the times in her childhood when she'd toyed with that particular daydream—especially after seeing one of the more glamorized spy movies.

"He was a courier for the British government. Although, by nationality, he was Greek." Julia dropped her eyes for a moment, and when she looked up again there was a haunting sadness in them. "You inherited your coloring from him. Your eyes..." She appeared to sag a little, and when she turned to take a step, she stumbled.

Karl was beside her in an instant. "Perhaps you'd better sit for a while, hon—" He cut off the endearment too late.

Julia resisted briefly, then gave in and let him lead her to a place near Kerith on the couch. "Your father's name was Jon," she continued, when she was settled. "I think I loved him from the first instant I saw him. It was like being struck by lightning."

Kerith felt a vicarious tug. Hadn't she experienced something similar with Daniel? But that couldn't have been love . . . Shaking off the thought, she quickly asked, "What happened to him?"

Julia lowered her gaze to her tightly clenched hands. "He...he was killed. I discovered later it was something to do with the East Germans. I . . . I found out I was pregnant two days afterward, so he never knew about you. If he had, I suppose we would have married. We'd discussed it, but as long as we were under assignment, it wasn't possible. He talked often about how it would be when we were both free. He called it our golden future. When he died, I felt as if my future had gone with him. All I had left was the past, the present and my work."

"And me," Kerith put in shortly. Up to that point, she'd been listening with a stunned detachment, but now the story began to take on a painful reality.

Julia nodded, her tawny hair swinging forward to brush her jawline. "Yes, there was you. When I told my superiors I was pregnant, they were furious. Relationships are strictly forbidden when you're in the field. They wanted me to have an abortion, but I refused. The thought of having a child terrified me, but you were the only part of Jon I had left, and I couldn't bring myself to destroy that."

"Then why did you give me away?" Kerith demanded, her voice tight with the betrayal that had haunted her for years.

"Because I believed it was my only option." Julia looked up, her blue eyes beseeching. "Please, try to understand. At the time I was torn with grief over Jon. I didn't know if I could take care of myself, let alone an infant. When my employer offered to keep me on, with the prevision that I give you up, I didn't have the will to refuse. My work seemed to be the only secure thing in my life just then."

Without warning, Kerith's tightly reined emotions broke free. "Then why didn't you really let me go?" she demanded, her voice raw. "Why didn't you release me for adoption?"

Julia flinched, and the delicate color of her face faded to stark white. "Because, you were all I had left of my future. In the hospital, when they came to take you away, I realized I couldn't let go completely. I had this dream of one day finding a way for us to be together. So I devised an interim plan for your care and education." She shook her head remorsefully. "By the time I admitted to myself the improbability of my dream, it was too late. You were long past the age when adoption is likely."

With a harsh sound, Kerith jumped up and stalked to the fireplace where she grabbed a poker and began jabbing viciously at a sputtering log. "Did you ever think of my dreams? Did you ever consider what it felt like, not knowing who I was or where I belonged? You say you provided for me, but you never gave me the one thing I really needed—a sense of belonging." Damn, how could she still feel the hurt so intensely?

Unable to hold back anymore, she let it all out. "You had it all your way, didn't you? Making sure I was always tied to you, yet protecting yourself from any emotional commitment by hiding behind your damned shield of secrecy."

"Now, hold on," Karl interjected, rising quickly from his seat to stand between the two women. He gave Julia an apologetic glance. "I know I agreed not to interfere, but someone has to state a few facts here." He turned on Kerith, his gray eyes fierce. "Your mother left out a few important details. First, she is one of the most important agents in our organization. Her gift for languages and her extraordinary memory are invaluable in our line of work. Which is why our people were so anxious to have her back after your birth. You can believe they did everything in their power to convince her to give you up. Second, being that important comes with a high price."

"Karl, please," Julia protested, looking pained. "It isn't going to make any difference."

"Maybe not, but I'm going to say it anyway." He glared at Kerith. "You think of her secrecy as an act of cruelty, but did you ever consider that it might have been meant to protect you? Your mother and I are in a dangerous business; sometimes we make enemies who aren't above taking their revenge out on the innocent."

His implication hit Kerith like a cold dash of water. She moved away from him until against her back she felt the cool, rough texture of the white bricks surrounding the fireplace. Edelweiss a protector? No, impossible! The concept challenged too many lifelong convictions. Yet, when she looked again at Julia, she experienced a whisper of uncertainty.

"Yes, look at her," Karl continued forcefully. "She's still recovering from the injuries she sustained on her last assignment. She shouldn't even be here."

"Then, why did you come?" Kerith asked Julia in a low, anguished voice. "Why now?"

Julia sighed, and absentmindedly rubbed a hand down the length of her injured thigh. "Because I've been forced to retire. And to do that, I must undergo a complete change of identity— including plastic surgery." She opened her eyes and gave Kerith a poignant smile. "I wanted you to see the resemblance between us before it's forever erased. And I wanted to tell you, just once, that I loved you."

Kerith reared back like someone dodging a blow. Being asked to acknowledge the extenuating circumstances behind Julia's actions was one thing, but accepting belated declarations of love was quite another. Eyes narrowed accusingly she said, "If you had really loved me, you wouldn't have been able to give me up in the first place."

Like a lion defending its mate, Karl turned on her. "Who are you to judge her? Can you be so sure you wouldn't make the same decisions if you and that kid you're carrying were in the same situation?"

Shocked silence followed his harsh inquiry, broken only by the dry snap and crackle of the fire. Then Daniel's voice came quietly. "What kid?"

Kerith scarcely heard him over the roaring storm of outrage sweeping her senses. "How did you know about that?" she demanded angrily. "Did this . . . this reunion require that you pry into my personal life?" The look Karl exchanged with Julia was answer enough. "I don't believe this. You actually had me investigated." Remembering her wrecked home, she grew even angrier. "I suppose it was necessary to ransack my home too, right?"

Karl looked confused. "Ransacked? What's she talking about?"

"A completely unrelated incident," Daniel supplied impatiently. "Damn it, Kerith, are you pregnant?"

Even in the midst of her turmoil, Kerith experienced a flash of guilt. Of all the rotten ways to have it come out . . . But before she could offer an explanation, Julia spoke up.

"You didn't know? We'd assumed you were being kept informed."

The urge to explain vanished, as a darker suspicion introduced itself. Daniel informed? But that would mean he was involved in this, too . . . One look at his face made it all disastrously clear. Of course, he was involved. He'd told her himself he was an agent—one who specialized in seducing women. What an utter fool she'd been, believing that story about his retirement, letting him get past her defenses until she had actually begun to care for him. When all along she'd been just another assignment to him, another victim of his infamous charm. The idea sickened her.

"Kerith, don't look at me like that," Daniel said, beginning to rise. "You don't understand."

"Oh, yes I do. I understand perfectly, now." Pressing one hand to her churning stomach, she started toward the door, but as she passed the couch, Julia waylaid her with an outstretched hand.

"You mustn't blame Daniel. He was brought into this for your protection. I couldn't take any chances, where your safety was concerned."

"Protection?" Kerith laughed scornfully. "He hardly qualifies for that job. He's the reason I'm pregnant."

Julia's mouth dropped open in surprise, and Karl made a rough sound of astonishment.

Apparently I wasn't the only one being kept in the dark, Kerith thought with some satisfaction. That knowledge alone seemed to restore some of her self-possession.

"You'll have to excuse me now," she said coldly, starting for the door again. "I've had enough lies and deception to last a lifetime." At the arched doorway, she paused and turned back for a final word. "I'm sure you'll be able to entertain yourselves without me. You can exchange techniques for manipulating people."

She heard them calling her name, as she ran up the stairs, but she didn't hesitate. She needed to get away, as far away as possible. But before she could do that, she had to find her purse and keys.

"IS THIS WHAT you're looking for?" Daniel inquired a few minutes later. He stood in the doorway to his bedroom, her small shoulder bag clutched in one hand.

"Yes, thank you." She stepped out of the closet and started toward him, then stopped short when he moved into the room and closed the door behind him. "I'm leaving," she announced decisively.

"Not until you let me explain." He looked implacable.

"I've had too many explanations already." She walked toward him, her hand outstretched. "The purse, please."

He simply hid it behind his back. "You'll have to listen, first. I can imagine what you're thinking, and you're not leaving until you hear the truth. I hated lying to you. I wouldn't have accepted this assignment if there had been any other way. I'm not Casanova, not anymore."

"Why should I believe that?" Kerith arched one brow skeptically. "It sounds to me as if I'm just another of Casanova's ladies. One of the gullible multitude who've been seduced by your charm."

"No!" Daniel dropped her purse and grabbed her shoulders roughly. "It wasn't like that with you, and you know it!"

"Do I?" She tipped her head back and glared at him. "You're just like those two downstairs. Living lies, telling half truths whenever it suits your purpose."

Daniel's dark eyes narrowed accusingly. "And what about you? Haven't you been doing the same? How do you think it felt, having a total stranger tell me the woman I love is carrying my child?"

The woman he loved. A small tremor ran through Kerith's heart, but it had no chance against her overriding sense of betrayal. "Don't talk to me about love," she snapped. "You and that woman down in your living room don't even know the meaning of the word."

"That's where you're wrong," Daniel countered. When she tried to twist away, he tightened his grip and herded her backward until she sat down on the bed with a bounce. "I concealed my involvement with Edelweiss, but I never lied to you about my feelings. On the other hand, I don't think you've been exactly honest with yourself in that area." He grabbed the valet chair standing near the closet and seated himself on it before her. As he gazed at her, his expression softened.

"I do love you, Kerith. I would have told you long before now, but I had to wait until there could be complete honesty between us."

Again Kerith felt a fluttering in her heart, only this time it was stronger. Unwilling to give in to it, she forced her attention to the deep blue velvet of the bedspread. But as her hand moved restively over the soft, thick nap, she had an unexpected memory of how it had felt against her naked skin as Daniel made slow, delicious love to her. No! Not love, lust. And yet, she found herself hesitating at the thought of simply storming out of his life. In the midst of her anger, a small voice tempted her to believe him.

Her hand clenched convulsively around a wad of the rich fabric. "I'd be a fool to believe you."

Daniel reached out and touched her cheek. "Kerith, look at me." When she complied, he smiled sympathetically. "I know you've had a lot thrown at you this evening. But I want you to stop a minute and think of how it's been between us for the last few weeks. I've never loved any other woman as I love you. And I'd begun to hope you might feel the same way some day. I want to share my life with you—" Deliberately, he lowered his eyes to her stomach, then looked up again. "—and our baby. But I don't think that's possible until you stop letting the past rule your life."

Again, Kerith experienced a small quake of uncertainty. Could he be right? She shook her head and looked away. "You don't know what you're asking."

"Don't I? From the first time you told me about Edelweiss, I knew this meeting wouldn't be easy. But I allowed myself to hope it would help you ultimately. I don't condone what your mother did, but I do think you should forgive her, for your own sake."

She turned toward him, her chin tilting defensively, a stubborn denial on her tongue, but when their eyes met the certainty of his love crashed over her like a tidal wave. And with it came a more fundamental knowledge—she had fallen in love with him. The feeling flooded her heart, overwhelming indignation and damaged pride. It also unnerved her completely.

"I . . . I can't think here," she exclaimed, springing off the bed like a frightened rabbit. "I need to get away for a while."

"Kerith, wait," Daniel called, rising to follow as she hurried toward the door. "You can't drive when you're upset like this; it isn't safe."

"Then I'll walk."

"It's dark outside. I don't like the idea of you being out there alone."

Impatiently she shrugged off his concern. "I did a pretty good job taking care of myself before you came along. Don't push me right now, Daniel. You might not like the outcome."

"All right," he agreed reluctantly. "But only if you promise not to go far."

"Whatever you say." Quiet and solitude, that's what she needed to sort this all out.

"And don't stay out too long," he added, as she dashed down the stairs and out the front door.

The night air had an invigorating chill that made Kerith grateful for the long sleeves of the white sweater dress she'd chosen for the meeting with Julia Robbins. Overhead a pearlescent slice of moon adorned the night sky, but offered little illumination. Remembering her promise, she decided to confine her walk to the landscaped inner courtyard shared by Daniel and his neighbors.

A brisk wind swished eerily through the branches of palm trees and huge hibiscus bushes as she strolled by them. She shivered, her mind straying to the firelit warmth of Daniel's living room. Warmth...security...love. He was offering all of that and more, but it came with a price. Could she afford to love him? Did she have any choice?

She paused in the shadow of the stucco-walled recreation center and stared at the shimmering surface of the swimming pool. It reminded her of the afternoon she and Daniel had splashed and played there, and of all the other wonderful times they'd had together lately. Loving. Being loved. As the images played slowly through her mind, a sense of peace settled over her, and she knew there really wasn't any decision to be made. Being with Daniel, loving him was worth any price—including forgiving Julia Robbins. Daniel was right. She'd been a victim of the past long enough.

An odd rustling in the nearby bushes made her start and glance around uneasily. The area appeared deserted, but she quickly decided it was time to go back inside.

"Too much talk of spies and danger," she muttered, heading for Daniel's backdoor. "You're getting paranoid." But an instant later she sensed a slight movement behind her, and before she could turn or cry out, a hard hand clamped over her nose and mouth. She struggled violently at first, but lack of air quickly took its toll. Consciousness had begun to fade, when a strangely familiar voice growled into her ear.

"Sorry if I startled you, but I was afraid you'd cry out. I'm going to let you go now, but if you try to scream, I'll have to tape your mouth."

She was released and shoved back against the rough surface of the wall. Then Arthur Kingston's arrogant features were crowding her face as he used his lean body to hold her immobile. "Arthur, what are you doing here?" she gasped, trying to push away from his surprising strength.

"I've come to join your party," he said, with a smile that chilled her blood. "Stop struggling, please, or I'll have to hurt you."

Kerith stopped pushing and glared at him, her breathing labored. "What party? What are you talking about?"

"Your little family reunion, of course. Didn't you know your mother and I are old friends?" He laughed, obviously enjoying her confusion. "No, perhaps not. She always was secretive."

"Arthur, you're not making sense." Kerith tried to put some conviction into the words, but it wasn't easy when the whole situation was becoming terrifyingly clear. This man she'd employed for almost a year was somehow connected with Julia Robbins. And the malicious gleam in his eyes didn't speak well of his intent.

"Come along inside, dear, and I'll explain it all." He stepped back, and she saw for the first time he was dressed completely in black, like a man who made his living skulking in shadows. When he took her arm, she instinctively pulled away.

"Still resisting, hmm? I believe I will use the tape. I wouldn't want you to announce our arrival. And perhaps we should have something for those lovely hands." She started to open her mouth to scream, but his hand was quicker, and within moments a wide piece of adhesive tape was sealing her lips.

"Most ungentlemanly of me, I know," Arthur murmured, twisting her arms back, and cinching her hands behind her with something that dug into her wrists. "But necessary. And just in case you decide to get balky, I think you should know I'm armed." He raised his free hand, and the faint moonlight glinted off an evil-looking handgun, its silhouette elongated by what she guessed to be a silencer.

Fear began to pulse heavily in Kerith's veins as she viewed the weapon. Dear Lord, this wasn't a joke. It was appallingly real—as real as the danger Julia had spoken of.

She looked at Arthur, unable to hide the terror in her eyes, and he laughed again. "I see you're beginning to understand. Good. I'd have no compunction about using the gun." He gave her a nudge toward the backdoor of Daniel's condominium. "Shall we join the others?"

10

"GOOD EVENING, everyone," Arthur said with mocking cordiality. Using Kerith as a shield, he paused dramatically in the doorway of Daniel's living room. The cold muzzle of his gun pressed into the soft underside of her jaw.

Kerith knew she'd never forget the expressions on the three faces that turned to face them from the couch. Surprise came first, then frozen alarm. Daniel paled visibly and started to rise; Karl swore and started to reach inside his unbuttoned suit coat.

"I wouldn't if I were you," Arthur admonished quickly. The hard nose of the gun forced Kerith's chin up, exposing the vulnerable curve of her throat. "That includes you, Avanti," he added as Daniel lunged off the couch. "I don't want to shoot this lovely lady, but you can change my mind with one suspicious move."

"Damn you. If you hurt her in any way, I'll kill you," Daniel snarled, but he remained where he was.

"There'll be no need for that, as long as you all cooperate. You with the shoulder holster, bring out your weapon slowly, drop it on the floor and kick it over to me."

"Who are you? What do you want?" Karl demanded stonily as he complied.

Arthur retrieved the gun and stowed it in the backpack he had slung over one shoulder. "Perhaps the lady on the couch can answer that for you." He smiled coldly and spoke in perfectly accented German. "*Guten abend, Edelweiss*. How pale you look. I had heard you didn't fare too well on our last assignment."

Julia's complexion turned chalky. "Reardon . . . Frank Reardon. No, it can't be. They told me you were dead."

"Grossly overstated, my dear. Although there have been quite a few changes in my appearance since you last saw me, thanks to the miracle of cosmetic surgery. And the name is Arthur now. It fits the blond hair better, don't you think?"

"Reardon!" Karl's fists clenched at his sides. "How the hell did you escape that mess in Singapore? Julia nearly died because of you."

"Will someone tell me what's going on here?" Daniel interjected forcefully. He pointed at Arthur. "This guy works for Kerith, are you telling me he's also one of your cohorts?"

"Was," Arthur provided, his thin mouth twisting. "After my last endeavor, I seem to be persona non grata with Interpol and a few other organizations. Julia can tell you all about it, but first I want you two gentlemen facing the wall, with your hands out where I can see them. Quickly now."

When Daniel and Karl were positioned to Arthur's satisfaction on either side of the fireplace, he pulled some odd-looking strips of perforated plastic from the backpack and tossed them to Julia. "You used to be quite efficient with riot handcuffs. Put them on your friends over there. And keep talking, while you're at it; I wouldn't want you plotting anything behind my back." He smirked and urged Kerith further into the room. "Why don't you start by telling your dear daughter, how close you and I once were? How I comforted you in your bereavement and the early months of your pregnancy."

"Any closeness between us was purely a figment of your imagination." As she spoke, Julia rose awkwardly and moved toward Daniel and Karl, the handcuffs in one hand.

Behind her adhesive gag, Kerith swallowed a soft sound of surprise. Where was Julia's cane? A quick look at the couch revealed nothing. Had she dropped it?

Julia stopped behind Daniel and went to work applying the cuffs. When she glanced back at Kerith, however, her eyes seemed to send an oblique message. But when she spoke, her voice held only remorse. "Please believe me, Kerith. I wouldn't have come if I'd known it would endanger you in any way. We were so careful with security."

"Your security was useless," Arthur scoffed. "I've known about your precious daughter all along." He shoved Kerith down on one end of the couch and waved the gun expansively. "Your mother and I worked together before you were born. An amusing little operation in Berlin. At least it was amusing until she got mixed up with the Greek. What was his name?" Arthur stroked his jaw with the tip of the gun. "Oh yes, Jon. Never could understand what she saw in him."

"He didn't have much use for you, either," Julia said scornfully. She finished binding Daniel's hands and shuffled over to repeat the process on Karl.

"Watch the sarcasm," Arthur advised, indicating the far end of the couch with a sharp gesture when she'd finished with Karl's hands. "And have a seat."

As she slowly obeyed, Julia's face grew taut with dismay. "How did you find Kerith? No one aside from me and my direct superior knew she survived the birth. There were no records, no ties. And you were already assigned elsewhere by the time she was born."

"You always did underestimate me." Arthur cautiously maneuvered himself around the glass coffee table to check Julia's handiwork on the men. He kept the gun trained on Kerith's heart. "I offered to take care of you, remember?" He waggled the gun at Kerith. "Including Jon's illegitimate offspring. But you thought you were too good for me."

"That wasn't it, at all," Julia protested. "I refused to marry you because I didn't love you."

"So you said, but I saw the scorn in your eyes." Arthur's features contracted in an ugly sneer. "A man never forgets something like that. Never. When I found out you'd lied about the child being stillborn, I began to keep track of her. Over the years, it became evident you intended to do the same, and I realized I'd found your weakness, your Achilles heel." Satisfied that Karl was securely bound, Arthur edged his way toward Daniel. "Did you know she has an almost fetish-like fascination with you, Edelweiss? She has every one of the birthday envelopes you sent her, and all the correspondence from that discreet bank in Zurich . . . keeps them in a special, locked file in her office."

Kerith's eyes widened in recognition. So he was the one. He probably did the break-in at the house, too.

Arthur's next statement confirmed her guess. "There was quite a collection of mementos in her house, too. I took great delight in smashing them, the night I . . . visited."

Evidently, that last bit of cruelty was too much for Daniel. With a low growl of anger he jerked around.

Daniel, my love, no! Kerith cried silently, struggling to rise. But she was too late.

Arthur, reacting instinctively to the sudden movement, swung the gun up in an arc and brought it down on the side of Daniel's skull with a sickening thud. Daniel pitched sideways into the wall, bumping his head again, and crumpled to the floor.

A sharp, keening cry echoed in Kerith's throat as she started to go to him. But Arthur stopped her with an aggressive movement of the gun. "Sit down," he snarled. "Or I'll use this gun as it was intended."

Unfortunately, Karl chose that moment to make his move, apparently hoping Arthur was too distracted to notice. Karl had barely taken two steps, before the gun gave a muffled report and the force of a bullet drove him back against the wall. He slid to the floor, knocked unconscious by the impact.

Julia echoed Kerith's cry and tried to rise, but Arthur cut her off with another gesture of the gun. "Stay where you are," he warned. "Both of your men are still alive, at this point. If you want them to remain that way, you'd better cooperate."

Blinking back tears, Kerith frantically surveyed Daniel's still form. His tanned, handsome face looked ashen and incredibly vulnerable, and her love for him made her heart feel as if it would break in half. What a fool she'd been to deny her feelings for so long. She was as irrevocably tied to him as she was to the precious, new life he had helped create within her. A second wave of understanding crested over her.

As irrevocably as she must have been tied to me, Kerith thought, her startled gaze going to the woman sitting at the other end of the couch. *Daniel was right, I haven't been honest with myself—or fair to her.* A new despair tugged at her heart as she gazed again at Daniel, lying unconscious on the cold tile floor. Why did it have to take a disaster like this to make her see the light? The way things looked at the moment, she might never have a chance to tell him of her love.

"Why did you wait until now, Arthur?" Julia inquired, breaking the tense silence. "If you wanted revenge, why didn't you do something sooner? We worked together twice more after Germany, yet you never gave any indication of how you felt."

Arthur sauntered around the coffee table and positioned himself between Kerith and her mother, clearly enjoying his role as dominator. "None of those occasions was right. I wanted you to suffer as I did. Your beloved daughter seemed to be the ultimate means to that end. I was almost certain you'd be retiring—with all that implies—after your narrow escape on our last assignment. So I came here to wait, hoping you'd give in to the urge to meet Kerith, at least once, while the resemblance between you still existed." He tipped the gun up and used its nuzzle to stroke his upper lip thoughtfully. "I must admit, you are strikingly alike. Although I think Kerith would make a more interesting bed partner, considering your injuries."

"You animal!" Julia exclaimed with sudden venom. "Leave her out of it. Just tell me what you want, and let's get on with this." Her mouth tightened with sarcasm. "I assume you do have some goal in mind."

Arthur resumed pointing the gun at Kerith. "My goal is quite simple. I want the documents you received from the Chinese gentleman just before everything fell apart in Singapore. As you know, nuclear arms information is quite valuable, at the moment. I could retire rather comfortably on the proceeds from selling it."

Julia looked stunned. "What makes you think I have that? You know I'm required to hand anything like that over to my superior."

"But you didn't, this time. If you had, Interpol would have immediately taken certain actions, and I happen to know they didn't."

A subtle change took place in Julia's attitude. Her elegant features assumed a crafty arrogance. "Suppose I did have them. Why would I give them to you?"

She was bluffing. Kerith knew it without bothering to reason why. And that same instinct told her Julia wasn't planning to remain passive much longer.

Arthur smiled, still confident of his superiority. "Oh, you'll give them to me, my dear. Because your lovely daughter is going to be my guest at a very secluded hideaway until you do. You see, I have a few scores to settle with her, too. Including the sprained ankle I got keeping an eye on her and the Latin-lover boy." He paused to give Kerith an assessing leer and ran his free hand over the tarnished gold of his hair. "Who can tell? If you take long enough, she might even come to enjoy my attentions."

Kerith saw the attack coming almost before it began. Julia yanked her cane from its hiding place behind a couch cushion and swung it at Arthur with amazing speed. Arthur was too quick for her, though. He was already aiming the gun at her when the cane hit his shoulder a glancing blow.

A wild desperation seized Kerith as she saw the gun jerk, then level with deadly accuracy. She lunged off the couch without a thought for the consequences. Only one thing burned in her mind. She couldn't let him hurt her mother.

She barreled blindly into Arthur's side, using all her weight, knocking him sideways onto the coffee table. There was a tremendous crack of breaking glass, and then Kerith heard the muffled report of the gun just as something slammed into her temple, bringing exploding pain and blackness.

THE DARKNESS held her suspended. She struggled against it, straining to see, fighting for a sense of stability in a world that reeled and floated. Gradually the black lightened to fuzzy gray and she began to hear voices—distant, then nearer and more audible. They were calling her name. She tried to answer, but couldn't make her voice work. A woman's voice, vaguely familiar, said, "I'll never forgive myself for this . . ."

Am I dead? she wondered, twisting in panic.

Then someone's hands settled on her arms, warm, wonderfully strong hands that made the world stop spinning at last. She gave a mighty effort, forced her eyes open and encountered Daniel's marvelous face, tense with concern and only inches away.

"What happened?" she whispered in confusion.

Daniel's face broke into a smile. "Thank God you're awake. No, don't try to get up. I want you to lie still until I can get you to an emergency room."

"Emergency room? Why?" Kerith looked around and discovered she was lying on Daniel's bed. How had she gotten there? The last she remembered, she'd been downstairs . . . "Arthur!" she cried, as the memory came into sharp focus. "I remember now. He was going to shoot my mother. Where is she? Is she all right?"

"She's fine, thanks to you. Right now she's downstairs helping Karl keep an eye on Arthur."

"But what about you?" Kerith anxiously levered herself up
toward him. "When he hit you, and you were lying so still, I
thought..." With a little cry, she threw her arms around his neck.
"Oh, Daniel, I love you so much. And I was afraid I'd never have
the chance to tell you."

His strong arms wrapped around her, pulling her closer as he
lovingly nuzzled her ear. "I'm all right, love. Just a bad headache and a large case of self-disgust. If I hadn't been so busy falling in love, I might have noticed something wasn't right about
that Kingston character. I was supposed to protect you, and you
end up having to do the job yourself. When I came to and saw
you throw yourself at that monster..." He shuddered, then raised
his head to peer at her questioningly. "That last part, did you
mean it?"

"The part about loving you?" She smiled tremulously and
nodded.

"Kerith, sweetheart . . ." Daniel started to gather her close
again, but a soft knock at the door stopped him.

Julia stood in the open doorway, looking nervous and exhausted. "I'm sorry to bother you, Daniel, but you're needed
downstairs. The people we called have arrived."

Daniel sighed and got up reluctantly. "It's all right. Kerith and
I will have time to talk later."

"What people?" Kerith inquired. "What's going on down
there? Was Arthur . . . ?" She paled. "Did I kill him?"

Daniel stroked her hair reassuringly. "No, he's not dead. Not
even badly injured. Although the two of you could have been,
when you crashed through that glass table." He tapped her temple lightly, and she winced at the resulting pain. "And you're
lucky his elbow didn't connect with your head just an inch or so
lower. As for the people downstairs, you might say they're a
special cleanup crew. When they're finished, Arthur will have
quietly disappeared."

Kerith's eyes widened in alarm. "Disappeared? Where?"

"Karl and I will be accompanying him back to our headquarters," Julia put in quietly. "Arthur has a lot of things to answer
for, and we're going to see that he's put out of commission permanently."

"But wasn't Karl shot?" Kerith persisted, still confused.

"It wasn't a serious wound," Julia assured her. "Although I did have a bad moment when that gun went off."

"I really should get down there," Daniel said reluctantly. "Julia, would you stay with her until I get back?"

Julia hesitated, her uncertainty painfully clear. "I will, if Kerith doesn't mind."

Kerith's heart went out to her. "Why would I mind? I think it's time I got acquainted with my mother."

Julia smiled then, but there was a mist of tears in her blue eyes, as she came forward to sit at the side of the bed. "We have so little time, and there's so much I've wanted to say to you."

"Do you have to go?" Kerith asked sadly. She reached out, took her mother's hand, and realized it was the first time they'd touched. So little time . . .

"I must. I won't be responsible for putting your life in jeopardy again. Daniel promised me he'd look after you. Are you in love with him?"

Kerith smiled and nodded.

"Good, then I can go with an easy mind about that at least. Now, what would you like me to tell you?"

THE MOUNTAINS to the east of Las Vegas were limned with the first pink encroachment of dawn as Daniel and Kerith stood at the living-room window and watched a nondescript gray sedan drive off. When it was gone, she turned to him with tears shining in her golden eyes.

"Did I tell you about my name? She chose it." Kerith bit her lip to stop its trembling. "My middle name, Marie, was her name before they changed it. And she took Kerith from the Bible. She...she said there was a brook named Kerith, where God hid His prophet Elijah during a time of danger." A few, bright tears escaped, and Kerith swallowed with some difficulty. "When I think of all the years I resented her for hiding from me, and all along I was the hidden one."

"Don't punish yourself anymore." Daniel hugged her close, rocking gently. "You made it up to her tonight. I only wish you could have had more time."

Sniffing back her tears, Kerith snuggled against his strong chest. And the pain eased a little.

"She said we might be able to arrange a secret meeting in a few years. And Karl told me there were ways to get messages to her occasionally, even though she wouldn't be able to reply." She looked up at him and attempted a smile. "Did you know she and Karl are going to retire together? It helps to know she won't be alone."

"But what about you?" Daniel asked, tracing the path of a tear with his fingertip. "You still won't have a family. And whether or not you want to admit it, I think you really do need one."

Kerith didn't have to work at smiling this time. He sounded suspiciously like a man promoting a cause. "I've been thinking of that lately. Would you be interested in sharing yours?"

He went completely still. "Do you mean having the same last name, children, the works?"

Kerith glanced down at her middle. "I think the children part is a foregone conclusion, but yes to the rest." Her breath whooshed out a second later as he swept her up into his arms with a happy shout.

As he looked down at her, his smile rivaled the brilliance of the morning sun peeking over distant mountains. "You're going to love being an Avanti," he proclaimed exuberantly. And when he kissed her, she knew he was right.

Epilogue

KARL BARBER paused outside a private room, one of a select few at the exclusive clinic hidden high in the Alps. His hand went self-consciously to the dark brown hair now adorning his head as he checked his appearance in one of the gilt-framed mirrors lining the plushly carpeted hall. The face looking back at him belonged to a stranger. *So many changes.* He shook his head and rapped on the door.

The voice calling for him to enter belonged to the woman he loved, but the face he saw when he went inside wasn't Julia's. She was still lovely, but in an entirely different way. *Thank heaven they can't change the inside,* he thought, bending to give her a kiss. Soon, even their names would be different, although he had the comfort of knowing they would be sharing their new last name.

"Hello, darling." Julia's smile was still a little uncertain, on the new mouth they'd given her. "I was just enjoying the view." She crossed to a window where lacy curtains stirred on a pine-scented breeze. "Kerith told me she used to love the summers here."

Karl followed her to the window, one hand reaching into his trousers pocket. "I have something for you." He withdrew a small envelope and handed it to her.

She sank down onto the velvet-cushioned window seat and quickly tore it open. "You bought me a card?" she inquired, drawing out the folded paper. "But it isn't my birth..." She stopped, seeing for the first time the pink-cheeked baby depicted on the front. Inside was a formally lettered birth announcement. It began: Mr. and Mrs. Daniel Avanti proudly announce the birth of their daughter, Amanda Marie.

Tears welled in Julia's newly shaped eyes as she held the note to her heart and looked up at him. "Marie," she whispered. "Her middle name is Marie. It...it was my name once." The tears overflowed, rolling down the altered line of her cheeks.

Karl used his thumb to gently wipe them away. "Congratulations, Grandma," he said, grinning broadly.

Her answering smile reminded him of the bright splendor of the edelweiss blooming outside the window.

Risking his life—that's his job.
This time he's risking his heart!

IN FROM THE COLD

Lynn Erickson

PROLOGUE

It WAS HOT in the jungle.

Matt Cavanaugh followed the man in the camouflage shirt. The man's shirt was black with sweat, and his pack dug cruelly into his shoulders. The pack was heavy; it had a machine gun strapped on top of it and many rounds of ammunition.

Matt's pack wasn't so heavy, but it still dug into his shoulders, aching, chafing, dragging.

It was hot. It was a lethal heat, and he was too damn old to be doing this sort of thing.

"Señor Smith," the leader of the group said, calling over his shoulder from the front of the line. "We stop here. *Pocos minutos.* A few minutes for a rest."

"And none too soon," Matt muttered thankfully under his breath. Señor Smith. He'd almost forgotten his alias. Of course, he'd had so many over the years: Smith, Jones, Brown. He slapped at a mosquito absently. This was the last one, he thought, the last undercover job. He didn't care what Ned had to say about it. Thirty-eight was too old to be slugging through a crawling, wet jungle. He was losing his edge.

They rested for a few minutes, the men speaking softly in Spanish to one another in the shade of a guanacaste tree.

"One hour more, Señor Smith," the leader said to him, passing Matt a field canteen, "and we will be at the camp. We are lucky this was an uneventful journey."

Yes, lucky, Matt thought, tipping the canteen up, his throat working as he swallowed the tepid, metallic-tasting water. But in the jungle you had to drink, because you lost so much water sweating. In fact, he mused, none of the men, himself included, had needed to relieve themselves—the oppressive heat sapped a body dry. He sat back against the tree and tried to re-

lax. Only another hour. He could make it. The most challenging part of his job was still to come—the meeting with Juan
Ramirez.

He leaned back and closed his eyes for a moment, recalling
what Ned had said in the briefing about this assignment. Juan
Ramirez, a man from a wealthy family of Costa Plata, a rebel
leader now, fighting a guerrilla war against the official president of Costa Plata, General Raoul Cisernos, who, as the entire world knew, was a corrupt dictator and a pawn of the
Soviet Union via the Cuban connection.

Costa Plata. A tiny Central American banana republic, like
so many of the nations in the area, caught in a never-ending
spiral of coup and hope and corruption and disappointment.

But this young rebel leader, Ramirez, had been educated in
the States. He had, apparently, the brains and determination to
lead Costa Plata, but most importantly, he was a firm ally of
the United States, a believer in free enterprise and an enlightened populace. He promised his followers a republic, with
elected officials, voting rights and an end to Cisernos's brutal
police state.

At present, Ramirez was holed up in a camp in the interior
jungle of his small nation, surrounded by Cisernos's troops,
only venturing out on small hit-and-run missions. The United
States could not officially supply the rebels with money and
weapons, but they *could* send a representative to assure
Ramirez of their support if—and when—he became president
of Costa Plata. And to advise him to hang on, that General
Cisernos was in trouble and would soon, in all probability, be
toppled from his seat of power.

Hence the presence of Matt Cavanaugh, alias Matt Smith, of
the U.S. Foreign Service, Section C, for covert operations.
C-section, as his boss, Ned, liked to call it jokingly.

It was hot. Matt wiped the stinging, oily sweat from his
forehead, pulled the bandanna from his neck, rolled it and tied
it around his head.

"Vámanos," the leader said, rising. "Let's go."

They followed a narrow path that snaked through the jungle. It was damp, full of bugs and smelly. The leaves of the un-
dergrowth were limp and faded green like old paper dollars.

The jungle screeched and cackled and rustled and wrapped itself around the puny men as if it were not going to let them go. A giant stomach, heaving and grunting, trying to digest them in its hot juices.

Matt stuck his thumbs under the straps of his pack to ease the strain. The skinny guy ahead of him with the RPG-7 machine gun sweated but didn't falter or complain. He trudged in his U.S. army issue boots, the pack a welcome burden, like the gun, a gift for the cause.

This mission was a vital one, vital but unofficial. If Matt was captured by the general's forces and discovered to be an American, the United States Foreign Service would disavow all knowledge of him. He would be on his own, a civilian breaking the law of Costa Plata.

It was a good thing this hike had been uneventful. He always chuckled to himself when Ned repeated the warning about being on his own if he was discovered. It reminded him of *Mission Impossible*, the old television program. "And this tape will self-destruct in five seconds," he would say to Ned, mock-solemnly.

"Get serious, Cavanaugh," Ned would growl.

"Never," Matt would reply with exaggerated insouciance.

But maybe, at thirty-eight, he should start getting serious. Or at least start thinking about it. And he would, after this assignment.

The jungle was a suffocating tangle around him, alive, a mass of hairy green vines catching at him, drooping, crisscrossed, thick with screaming birds and monkeys.

Brightly colored butterflies sat on overgrown hothouse plants, on ferny limbs, fluttering in the seams of green light. The trees grew thickly, stubbornly, viciously, heavy with creepers. Flowers hung like bright rags or had blossoms oddly shaped like shuttlecocks.

The smells. Stink and perfume. The green hum of something gone bad. The glorious whiff of heaven. The tropical brew that attacked the olfactory nerves—too strong, too sweet, too rotten.

The sounds. Cackling and clicking and howling. The buzz of insects excited by the proximity of hot blood. The drumming and ringing of howler monkeys. The rattle of branches moved by an unseen hunter.

It was hellishly hot.

Matt had been in jungles before. In Java and Angola, in Brazil. He'd also been in bitter-cold places: Iceland, Tibet. He'd been in primitive villages and sophisticated cities on assignment. He'd been on yachts in the Mediterranean. He'd been around. And it was time to quit, time to come in from the cold, to get a regular job with the Foreign Service, to take vacations, to settle down.

Alone?

And would the service ever let him come in, knowing all that he knew? But more than that, Matt was good at his job, terrific at it. He'd been recruited straight out of George Washington University, a twenty-two-year-old wise-mouthed brat, a bulletproof kid with a wild reputation already, a lost kid who couldn't have known it at the time, but who was in need of a home and security.

Well, the service had provided it all. And Matt had quickly made his mark in undercover work. Who would have thought a kid with a pocketful of trust fund money was the eyes and ears for the service? In all his travelings, in all those part-time, goof-off jobs he'd taken, not once, in sixteen years, had his cover been compromised. Of course, it had meant no close relationships, not with women, college friends or co-workers. Relationships were luxuries. And his family? Given the Cavanaugh clan, except for his long-suffering mother, they were all too ready to write him off.

"We arrive soon," the leader called to him. "You are very strong, Señor Smith. I was afraid this trip would take much longer."

"Thanks," Matt replied, "but I'm as anxious as you are to get there."

"Yes, I understand." The man nodded, turning away, leading the dozen of them deeper still into the maw of the jungle.

There had been a time, Matt thought, when he would have been thrilled at this assignment. It would have been an adventure. He would have drunk it all in: the discomfort, the heat and bugs and wildness, the wet itch of hairy vines. His job had been a challenge, and an escape, too; an escape from his family, from his alter ego, Matt Cavanaugh—beach bum, trust funder, sometime bartender, apparent drunk, a useless human being.

And all the time he was laughing inside, laughing at those ignorant people who saw only his cover and never knew he was a secret agent for the Foreign Service, a valued employee of the United States government, a man who risked his own life to save their butts.

It was ironic, and he laughed at those ignorant souls. And he cried inside, too, because the one person in the world who needed to know the truth about Matt couldn't be told. But then, his father had disapproved of Matt long before he'd gone to work for Section C, so he guessed it wouldn't have mattered much what he did.

His shoulders hurt, his legs throbbed, he was getting blisters on his feet. And after seeing Juan Ramirez, he had to walk back out of this hellhole. Well, he'd done harder things before, and he supposed he'd do it this time, too, but he was glad they were almost there. He had to be back across the border in three days' time so that the helicopter could pick him up at the rendezvous spot. He'd make it, no problem, and then he'd be flown home in air-conditioned, Pan Am comfort to report to Ned.

If he wasn't caught on the way back across the border, that was.

The leader had stopped ahead and was holding up a hand. He called out something, a password, Matt supposed, then waved his squad on. The clearing appeared miraculously. Matt stepped past some thick brush in the trail and into the encampment. He could have sworn there was nothing ahead except jungle. But there were tents and sandbagged gun emplacements and the entrances to underground bunkers. There were also clothes hanging on lines, rifles stacked against trees, a low-smoke cook fire going in the center of the clearing and lots of uniformed men lounging around, smoking, talking, mending, eating, reading.

"Come, Señor Smith, I will take you to Juan," the leader of the expedition said.

He led Matt across the clearing, waving to individuals, ex-changing greetings. He smiled for the first time since he'd met Matt at the drop zone. He was home.

The camp was large. Matt tried to size it up for his debrief-ing. There were dozens of tents, hundreds of men. And this, he knew, was only one of many secret fire bases the rebels con-trolled. The soldiers' equipment looked to be well taken care of. Discipline was obviously strict. He tucked the knowledge away for future use.

Juan Ramirez sat behind a folding table in a roomy tent. He was a slim man of Matt's own age, with short, fine black hair and strange hazel eyes that met Matt's when he looked up from the papers he was busy reading. Heavy eyebrows, a thin high-bridged nose and a delicate mouth completed the picture. An ascetic. An idealist with the fire of conviction in his yellow eyes. A dangerous man, so Matt had been told.

"Juan," said the man who'd brought Matt there, "here is Señor Smith."

Juan Ramirez rose, came around the desk, tall and straight and graceful, holding out his slim-fingered hand. "Well, Mr. Smith," he said in unaccented English, with a hint of Boston in it, "welcome to Camp Hiawatha." A thin smile slanted his mouth, mocking his surroundings, himself, even Matt.

"And thank you, Diego," he said to the other man. "You did a good job guiding Mr. Smith here."

"*Gracias*, Juan," the man said, breaking into a smile, back-ing out of the tent.

"Mr. Smith," Juan Ramirez mused, with obvious emphasis on the "Smith."

"Just Matt, if you don't mind."

"Good. And call me Juan. And please, take that pack off, sit down. You must be exhausted. The camp activities are car-ried a bit overboard, aren't they?" Juan grinned. "Would you like a drink? Believe it or not, I happen to have a bottle of Cutty Sark. Alas, there's no ice or soda."

"Sure, I'll have a small one. Lots of water," Matt said. He was looking around the tent, taking everything in, preparing all the while for his debriefing back in Washington. There were maps on the canvas walls, a neatly made-up folding cot and a state-of-the-art shortwave radio set.

Juan was filling two tin cups with Scotch and then pouring water from a canteen into them. "Boiled," he said, gesturing to the water, then he handed Matt the well-diluted Scotch.

"To peace," he said, holding his cup up.

"To peace," Matt repeated. The liquid was warm and a bit rusty looking, but it was relaxing, somehow taking the edge off the primitive surroundings.

"So, Matt," Juan began, "you are here. You walked a long way through the jungle to visit me. Your government wanted this meeting. I'm very interested in what you have to say."

Matt studied the man for a minute, his senses alert, his feelers out. Was Juan Ramirez afraid? Overconfident? Hotheaded? Too careful? Was he a liar, only accepting American aid until he achieved power, then condemning the capitalist pigs for interfering? It was Matt's job to report on his intuitions as much as facts. He cleared his throat, felt the alcohol soothe away some of his fatigue and started in. "As you know, the United States has promised to recognize you as the legitimate head of Costa Plata in the event of your victory. Cisernos is a Communist puppet and a bad leader, as well."

"Yes, that we can agree upon," Ramirez said carefully.

"However, the obstacle here is, naturally, your victory."

Ramirez's mouth twisted ironically. "That, too, we can agree upon."

"I was sent here to inform you of a significant development in General Cisernos's status." Matt leaned forward. "Costa Plata is deeply in debt. The economy is falling apart. Cisernos had to take out some enormous loans a few years back. Loans from the World Bank."

Ramirez nodded slowly.

"Those loans will be called in when they come due this fall. Principal *and* interest. The total amounts to several hundred million U.S. dollars."

Ramirez fixed his yellow eyes on Matt intently.

"What that means is that the treasury of Costa Plata will be bankrupt. Cisernos will have no money to pay his army. His regime will fall." Matt paused, then continued. "There must be

someone on hand to pick up the pieces, someone to take over
from Cisernos. A leader with popular support and, of course,
an interest in keeping the United States as an ally. It's May now.
Before the new year, Costa Plata will need a new president. My
government would prefer it to be you." A droplet of sweat
trickled down Matt's cheek, tickling, but he ignored it, holding the rebel leader's gaze in the sultry silence.

"Well," Ramirez finally said, "this *is* news." He smiled
thinly, and Matt could almost see the wheels of his mind turning. "And are you a political man yourself, Matt?" All very
friendly, mundane, while the man digested Matt's revelation.

Matt gave him his time. "No, not really. I'm merely an employee. I try never to discuss religion or politics."

"Wise of you." He looked Matt in the eye, a sharp glance.
"So Cisernos is about to take a fall. Interesting." He leaned
back in his chair and turned the tin cup in his fingers. "And
what, may I ask, is your source of information?"

Matt shook his head. "Top secret."

"I need to judge whether your information is correct."

"You'll have to take it on faith," Matt said.

"The World Bank is an independent entity. It does not do
the United States' bidding. I have heard that the president of
the World Bank is nobody's lackey. How can you be so sure the
bank will call in these loans?" Ramirez asked skeptically.

"I am sure," Matt said quietly. "Evan Cavanaugh is the head
of the World Bank, and he doesn't like red figures in his books.
His job is to keep the bank solvent."

"But, still, how do you know what is in the mind of this
Evan Cavanaugh?"

Matt smiled sardonically. Oh, he knew all right. What he
couldn't tell Ramirez was that the president of the World Bank,
Evan Cavanaugh, was his father.

CHAPTER ONE

NICOLA GAGE LOOKED IDLY out of the bedroom window, out over the misty green expanse of the Cavanaughs' estate in Westchester County, New York. The driveway swept into sight over a hill, past a half-tumbled stone wall covered with dark green, glossy ivy, traversed acres of emerald lawn, then curved into a circle in front of the Tudor-style house.

A lovely scene on this hot, humid June morning: peaceful, secure, bucolic.

The warm breeze wafted in through the open window, fragrant with the smell of newly mown grass and honeysuckle, and with it came the throaty, humming noise of a well-tuned engine.

It was a white Ferrari, a sleek beauty, the top down, the dappled sunlight filtering through the leaves of the locust trees and racing across its shiny hood. The driver pulled up alongside the far wing of the mansion and hopped out of the car without opening the door, a quick, agile movement that impressed Nicola and teased her memory. Somewhere, someplace, she'd seen that movement before.

My Lord, Nicola thought, her eyes riveted on the man, *it's Matt, the prodigal son. Well, well.*

She watched as he stood beside his vehicle and removed his aviator-style sunglasses, casually eyeing the old homestead, the multimillion-dollar brick and stucco and beamed house that had once been home to him. Matt Cavanaugh. A face from the past. Oh, she'd seen him briefly—six, or was it seven years ago?—at Thanksgiving dinner. Right here. Thanksgiving had always been a command performance at the Cavanaughs': close family and twenty or so of their nearest and dearest friends. Nicola had been there because she'd just finished hotel and restaurant management school in Michigan and hadn't yet landed her first real cooking job up in Vermont. And Matt had breezed in late, clad in a tuxedo, a bottle of champagne under one arm and a glitzy, half-bombed redhead under the other.

Evan Cavanaugh, Matt's father, had had a fit, Nicola recalled, and the normally reserved, dignified Maureen had held back her tears when the two men, her husband and oldest son, had gone directly and without hesitation at each other's jugulars.

Oh yes, she'd seen Matt that once—if only for ten minutes before he'd left. Just as she'd seen him several times before that, since she'd moved in with the Cavanaughs; although his appearances at the family home had been few and far between. Matt was twelve years her senior. She'd been a tall, gawky kid when he'd graduated from George Washington University's foreign affairs school, come home for two days and had a terrible fight with Evan about his future. Bartending, she remembered. He'd had the nerve to tell his ambitious father he was taking a job *bartending* on a Greek island, and he'd been booted out of the house, Evan yelling after him that he should have expected Matt to pull a stunt like that!

Oh Lordy, Matt was here. Better get ready for the fireworks.

And Nicola had seen him again after that Greek isle scene. It had been one of those few times he'd graced the Cavanaugh home with his presence, around the year Nicola had graduated from high school. He'd shown up on a cold, snowy winter night, when the wind had been howling down the four chimneys and the driveway had just about been drifted over. Matt had sashayed in, back from a skiing trip, or something equally as recreational, out in Squaw Valley, California.

Nicola could almost remember Evan's greeting. "Still bartending? Or are you just plain living off the trust fund my father so unwisely left you?"

"Oh, I take on odd jobs, mostly bartending, but I like to move around a lot. A rolling stone and all that." Matt had shot his father an insolent grin, and the family members, Maureen and Matt's brother, T.J., had winced. Once again the battle lines had been drawn between father and oldest son, and the war had come shortly thereafter.

"You're a bum!" Evan had shouted from behind closed library doors. "The only son I have who's got the brains and the know-how to run the family bank, and you turn out to be a no-good wastrel! Get out of here! I mean it, Matt, and don't come back until you're ready to act like a Cavanaugh and a man!"

Matt had rolled his eyes at his mother, who had been waiting in the living room with T.J. Then he'd smiled at her with true affection, hugged her warmly, and he'd given T.J. a commiserating punch to the arm. As far as Nicola went, he'd grinned at her, too, flicked her heavy dark braid and said, "Hang in there, kid, the old man's not really as tough as he sounds." He'd left then, not twenty-four hours after his arrival. He'd gone back out into the blizzard that raged in the Hudson River valley and had left behind a weeping mother, a confused, sullen brother and Nicola, who could only stare after him and wonder why it was that fathers and sons so often tore one another to shreds.

Nicola stood at the window now and wondered if fathers and daughters fought like that, too. She had no way of judging, because her own father had ignored her so completely that she'd never even had an argument with him. Wentworth Gage, the famous chef, a wealthy and respected and popular man, beloved by all. Beloved by his only daughter, Nicola, even though he rarely saw her.

It never ceased to amaze her, either, that she'd actually enrolled in hotel and restaurant school with the intention of becoming a chef, just like Dad, so the man—who had not even sent her a birthday card in five years—would finally notice that she was alive.

Dumb, Nicola, really dumb.

Oh, she'd sent him copies of her grades and letters from professors—she'd sent them to Evan and Maureen, too—but he'd never acknowledged them. At graduation in Michigan, he'd finally, *amazingly*, sent flowers and a note.

Dear baby,
Congrats.
Come and see my new French restaurant on Third Avenue. Dinner's on me.

Love, Dad

Love, Dad?

She could have screamed. She could have held a seven-inch chef's knife up to his throat. But instead she beat her pillow and sobbed and missed him so much it ached. If only there had never been the divorce in the first place....

When Nicola was ten, Went had told her mother that he wanted a divorce. Suzanne had had a nervous breakdown over it and had been sent to an expensive private nursing home. Went, good fellow that he was, footed the bill. But he hadn't had time for his daughter, his scared, *terrified*, bereft child, whose whole world had collapsed in a terrible emotional holocaust.

It had been Suzanne's best friend, Maureen Cavanaugh, who had offered to take care of Nicola. Maureen and Evan had become her legal guardians and had provided the only stability in her life from the time she was ten.

It was very odd, too, that Nicola had been able to have such a good relationship with Evan when he was so hard on his two sons. It was as if he could relax his rigid standards because she was not his blood, or was not a boy, or whatever. She saw Evan's faults, but she loved him, anyway. She saw Maureen's too-passive nature, but she loved her, too. And she hadn't stopped loving her own father.

Went Gage never complained that someone else was raising his only child; he loved his freedom and his women too much. Suzanne had been in and out of the private nursing home since the divorce, had been diagnosed as being clinically depressed and even now lived in a Thorazine haze, a pretty, vague woman, who always cried when her daughter visited her in the expensive home.

Some family.

Nicola stepped to one side to cloak herself from Matt's gaze in case he should look up toward her window. But he only began to cross the circular driveway toward the front door. The years had been kind to him, she thought. He'd lost none of those good looks or the indolent grace of his lean, six-foot frame. From what she could see as he approached the front steps, his eyes—those bright blue eyes of his mother's—still sparked with devilry, and his curling brown hair was as unruly and thick as ever. She wondered if he was going to press the doorbell, but he smiled instead and opened the door as if it hadn't been so many years. As if he'd be welcome.

Quickly Nicola realized that she was only half-dressed and was expected—uh-oh, ten minutes ago—on the patio below.

"I don't like Mr. Reyes," Nicola had said to Maureen the day before. "He gives me the creeps every time he kisses my hand and shoots me one of those slick Latin looks."

"Evan can handle him," Maureen had replied. "You know Evan, when it comes to the affairs of the World Bank, he'll put up with worse than Mr. Reyes."

Oh yes, Nicola knew that Evan could handle anybody. He was a powerful man, president of the New York based World Bank, the institution that provided loans to Third World countries for large development projects. And he was an attractive man, too, who kept himself trim and in great physical condition. He had smooth, tanned skin, regular features, thick salt-and-pepper hair and black eyebrows over large, dark brown eyes.

Oh yes, Evan Cavanaugh had the world by the tail. He also had all the right connections, and Señor Reyes was merely a nuisance, the finance minister of a Central American country, Costa Plata, a small nation that was apparently in deep financial distress. Thus Reyes's visit to Evan Cavanaugh. He was discussing money with Evan, his country's treasury, in fact, which was on the verge of bankruptcy, Maureen had told Nicola. It was all tied in with past due moneys and loans owed to the World Bank that could be called in—unpleasant stuff. Evan, it seemed, was not telling Reyes what the man wanted to hear. But then, that was Evan's job.

As for Nicola, she'd rather cook good food and see folks enjoy it. Basic, simple fun.

Nicola's thoughts drifted back to Matt, and his sudden, unannounced arrival. What a scene *that* would create at brunch, and in front of Reynaldo Reyes, too. Still hurrying, she tossed the sheets up onto the canopied bed, tried to tidy the room, buttoned up her thin, white cotton blouse, tucked it into the matching skirt and slid her feet into open-toed sandals. This was as dressy as she got, as dressy as she wanted to get. She rushed down the elegant, curving staircase and across the floor, her heels tap-tapping on the marble.

Where was Matt? On the patio already? Lordy, Lordy, were *they* all going to be shocked.

She went through the living room, past the wing chairs and across the Persian carpet. She could see the patio now through the drapes, but apparently Matt wasn't out there yet.

Where was he? In the kitchen, talking to Lydia, the old cook? Rambling around the mansion, reacquainting himself? Sprucing up in a powder room? She couldn't see him doing that. Oh no, not Mr. Swashbuckler himself. Men like him didn't need mirrors; they already knew that charm oozed from every pore like hot drops of lava.

"There you are," Maureen chided when Nicola, out of breath, crossed the stone veranda toward the pool. "We're ready to sit."

She wanted to warn Maureen, to shield her from what was to come, but Reynaldo Reyes stood up, his tall, slim, white linen-draped frame bent over Nicola's hand, and Evan was winking at her as if to say, "Put up with his oily behavior for just a short while longer," and T.J. was nodding in her direction—quiet, introverted T.J., who was still, as always, a stranger to her.

Without warning the scene altered. As if an invisible director said, "Places, action," the expressions of the characters and the mood of the setting changed. It was hot out, hot and close with humidity, but goose bumps rose on Nicola's arms as heads turned toward the French doors leading out to the veranda. There was an abrupt, waiting silence. For a split second, just a fraction of time, everything and everyone froze. But then Matt seemed to draw strength from the utter silence and began to move toward the surprised entourage.

"What?" he said lightly. "Have I suddenly grown another head or something?" He kept moving confidently; if a man can be graceful, then he moved gracefully, self-assured, smiling that infernal smile of his, the ironic grin that seemed to lift the corners of his mouth permanently as if he were laughing at the bad joke that was life. And, for widely varied reasons, he caused pulses to quicken.

"Matt," Maureen breathed, tears forming in her eyes.

"Well, if it isn't my big brother," the six-foot-three-inch T.J. offered guardedly.

"Hi," Nicola got out.

"This must be your eldest," Reyes said with less certainty than usual.

Evan remained coldly still.

"Just in time for breakfast." Matt came up to his mother and pulled her into his embrace, kissing her short, blond-gray head first and then her cheek. Nicola could see Maureen's slim, straight body tremble as her firstborn held her close with unaffected love.

Introductions were made to Reyes, of course, who bantered lightly with Matt, while the older son tried out his fair Spanish on the minister. Maureen looked at her husband through pleading eyes, and T.J. stepped nearer to his mother, Nicola noted, and she wondered at the gesture. Was T.J. being protective? Was he jealous of his outgoing, purportedly brilliant brother? Could T.J. actually have thought Matt had come home to weasel his way back into Evan's good grace and usurp T.J.'s position as the future president of the Cavanaugh family business, the First Bank of Westchester?

Once Reyes had released her hand, Nicola had slipped back into the shadows beneath a tree. It wasn't that Matt intimidated her—not at all. It was rather that he was the sort of man who repelled her. Matt Cavanaugh reminded her too much of her father.

From her safe spot she watched the drama unfold. Maureen was still smiling, tentatively and hopefully; T.J. regarded his wisecracking brother without expression but was dragging deeply on a freshly lit cigarette, a nervous habit of his. Evan, too, was staring at Matt, his face closed, suspicious, a hint of anger just showing through. And all the time Matt seemed impervious to the roiling emotional impact his unannounced arrival had caused his family. He kept right on chatting with Reyes, his manner relaxed.

"How's the drought situation in Costa Plata this year?" he was asking. "That's good to hear. And the old El Libertad Hotel in San Pedro, is it still standing...? Oh sure, I've visited your country. I even had a job there once, on the coast. I bartended for a private party one of your cabinet members was throwing. Quite an affair.... Oh, I got the job through a local man I met." Matt shrugged.

Yes, he was handsome and devilishly charming, and by the sound of it, there weren't many places in the world he'd missed. What an aimless existence, Nicola thought derisively. What a waste of a disarming personality *and* a good brain. And there was T.J.—Thomas John—inwardly motivated, reserved, dull. He was not a bad-looking man at thirty-six, tall and fair and somewhat debonair, but let's face it, she mused, he lacked spark. He was dutiful and capable but so introverted that no one, save Maureen, had a clue as to what went on behind those deep-set blue eyes.

Nicola breathed a sigh of relief when Maureen finally announced that if Señor Reyes was to make his flight back to Costa Plata that morning, they simply had to sit down to brunch. At least Nicola was going to be spared that dose of Matt Cavanaugh charm.

She was wrong, however. She began to move from beneath the shadows of the tree and was heading to her place at the table, when she was suddenly stopped by his hand on her arm, gentle yet firm.

"Nicola." He said her name in a kind of quiet caress that surprised her, taking her off guard. They were barely acquaintances, after all. "Boy, kid, I hardly would have recognized you." He turned her around then and gave her a big brotherly hug, a friendly peck on her cheek.

"Hello, Matt," she said, uncomfortable, aware of the eyes of the others on them. "Nice to see you again."

"I can't get over it," he was saying. "You've really grown into a beauty."

God, thought Nicola, growing more ill at ease by the moment. Why on earth was he trying to charm her, too?

He shot her one of those magic, crooked smiles and continued to hold her. "Little Nicky. The kid."

A beauty, indeed, she thought, smarting. Who was he fooling? Oh, she had passable looks, with long black hair and white skin. And she was trim, able to eat what she wanted, but only because she was so active. But she'd always considered her eyes to be a dull, muddy brown and too expressionless, almost sad looking, she'd been told, and her lips were too full, too pouting to suit her frank, curious nature. Then there were her teeth. A touch crooked because her dad had been too cheap to spring for braces. At five foot eight, her limbs were okay, but as for her small breasts... Height and full bodies didn't exactly go hand in hand.

A beauty. *Take a hike, Matt.*

"And I can't believe you're here," Matt was saying, still smiling despite her skeptical expression.

"It's only a vacation," she replied, wanting to add, *Some of us work, you know*.

"Well, vacation or not, maybe we could get to know each other at last. Heck, you're practically my little sister."

"Um."

"Say, what're you working at now? Weren't you a...a...?"

"I'm a chef. I cook food."

"I knew that," he said with the quirk of an eyebrow and the deepening of a dimple in one cheek. "Where are you cooking?"

"I work for a sportsman's outfitter in Colorado in the summer and a ski lodge in Wyoming in the winter."

He regarded her with interest. "All by yourself, kid?"

"Sure, all by myself." She started to bristle, but he looked impressed and his expression was so winning...

"Are you two going to sit down?" came Maureen's pleasant voice, heightened slightly, Nicola noted, by her barely suppressed anticipation. "Come on, now, Señor Reyes only has a short time left."

Finally Matt released her but kept his warm hand at the small of her back as they walked to the table. She was mildly surprised that she even noticed his touch, that strong hand on the thin cotton of her blouse. His fingers pressed against her gently, guiding her, leading her toward the only two empty chairs—side by side.

She sat down and put her peach-colored linen napkin in her lap and thought, *Boy, is he a flirt.* And that jaunty smile, those flashing white teeth, the blue-blue eyes—a girl could get lost in those eyes of his . . . a naive girl, that was.

Through the years Nicola had heard all the gossip about Matt. If it was Tuesday it must be Paris and Francoise; if it was Wednesday, it was Rome and Maria. She had listened to Evan complain about his eldest son's philandering life-style and Maureen's excuses. "You don't know that, Evan. He's just sowing his wild oats. He'll settle down. I'm certain he will. Matt's a smart boy."

But Matt, it appeared, had not settled down. Was this Saturday and Nicola's turn?

A stream of smoke curled up around T.J.'s head. "Put that damn thing out," Evan said roughly. "You're at the table, boy."

Dutifully T.J. crushed his cigarette in an ashtray.

Matt poured himself a cup of coffee. "Hey, T.J.," he said offhandedly, "you running the family bank yet?"

T.J. looked at his father for a breath of time, then back at Matt. "Not yet. I'm into some other ventures right now. Short-term mortgages, that kind of thing."

"He's with a small firm, but he's doing very well," Maureen put in smoothly, and Nicola caught the sharp glance she let fly in Evan's direction. "T.J. has gained more experience on the outside than he ever would if he'd gone straight into the family bank."

"He better be learning," Evan said while the omelets were being served by the stooped and uncomplaining Lydia. "If he thinks he's going into the bank still wet behind the ears—"

"Dad," T.J. said, interrupting, "let's not get into this now."

Evan nodded, then turned to Reyes. "You have children?"

"Ah, yes," Reyes replied in his smooth, well-oiled voice. "I have three sons and two daughters."

"Um," Evan said, "then you know how difficult it is. I don't believe in just handing them a living on a silver platter. They have to earn it. I did. And so can they."

"So true, my friend, so true."

Unspoken words that Nicola had heard too often seemed to hang in the air. What Evan had not said in front of his guest might have gone like this: "Oh yes, I made my own fortune. I built the First Bank of Westchester into what it is today. It was no accident that I was offered the position of president of the World Bank, either. But my father, my very *unwise* father, was shortsighted and left a large trust fund to Matt, enough so that the boy I'd put all my hopes into turned out to be a bum. Thank God," Evan would have said, "T.J. wasn't born yet when my father died, or he would have been provided for, too."

Nicola swallowed her fresh-squeezed orange juice past a lump in her throat. As soon as Reyes was gone, Evan *would* say those things.

"So, Matt," T.J. was saying, "where have you blown in from this time?"

"Here and there. Actually I just drove up from Haig's Point, in South Carolina. I had a good job there, on one of the new golf courses."

"Bartending?" Evan asked, his expression held tightly in control.

"Sure. I met a lot of your old buddies there, Evan. You know, it's a haven for the conservative Washington crowd."

"So what exactly happened to your job?" Again, Evan spoke.

Matt leaned back in his seat and clasped his hands behind his head nonchalantly. "I didn't get along with the boss. He canned me."

"I see." Evan's ruddy color heightened.

"Oh, T.J., dear," Maureen said, "would you pass Señor Reyes the muffins?" Then, "My goodness, *señor*, it's nearly eleven. I don't know where the time went this morning."

"So—" Evan was barely hiding a scowl "—it's been six years, boy. Six years and no more than a dozen calls to your mother here. Don't you think—"

"Hey," Matt said, "the time just gets away from me." He grinned, unconcerned.

"Are you staying?" T.J. asked.

"Maybe."

That got a rise from the group, Nicola saw. The idea of Matt coming home for any length of time was inconceivable. Leopards did not change their spots, after all.

Why, she wondered, did it always have to be this way? It was a household swollen with intensity, expectant, ever the apprehensive calm before the storm. Yet it hadn't been that way when she'd first come to live there. Back then Matt and T.J. had been away at college, and Evan had been busy building his Westchester bank into a monumental financial institution. He'd been good to the insecure waif newly come to his home. No, more than that. He'd loved her like the daughter he'd never had. He still did.

Nicola sat there noting the charged air and recalled when she'd had trouble with her algebra in ninth grade. Evan had sat up with her and helped, night after night. And he'd been nicer to Maureen then, too. There had been kitchen and maid gossip in those days of an affair on Evan's part, though, but if it was true, he'd hidden it beautifully. Now, however, Evan and Maureen seemed to be marching to the beat of different drums. They were polite to each other, but gone was the excitement and growth of their marriage. Instead, it appeared that the affection in the home flowed between Maureen and T.J., and Evan stood on the perimeter, looking in with suspicion. Now here was Matt, barging into this already precarious situation. Why, Nicola asked herself, couldn't Evan treat his boys as he did her, with caring and understanding?

Despite the discord she felt so strongly, Nicola believed that this was truly her home. She could talk to Maureen, *really* talk to her, and with Evan she'd been able to laugh and tease and recapture bygone days. Where had her own parents been these past sixteen years? No place that Nicola could reach, that was for darn sure.

Matt moved back to the food, leaning forward in his chair, elbows on the table, his khaki trousers brushing her leg. She inched away unobtrusively.

Matt Cavanaugh. She played with the omelet on her plate, her appetite gone, and glanced at him out of the corner of her eye. He *was* a good-looking guy. And to top it all off, he had charisma; it surrounded him like a circle of delicious candy. She could see the ladies eating their way through the layers just to get at him.

Nicola felt like laughing at herself. Only a chef would come up with a mental image like that! And what did she care, anyway? He was not her type. He was too much like good old Went, her father.

"Ah," came Reyes's accented voice, breaking into her thoughts, "such a lovely home, Evan. So American, many styles borrowed from the Old World, yes?"

"My idea," Maureen interjected. "I couldn't decide on English Tudor or French Provincial. So the outside is English, and the interior more sweeping, more open."

"The gardens are lovely, Señora Cavanaugh. A gazebo on the lawn, so quaint, a small hedged maze . . . enchanting."

"Thank you," Maureen said graciously.

"Mom sure has a green thumb," Matt put in then, a childish but calculated statement, a rude hand slapping to Reyes, who obviously was polishing the apple.

"Ah, yes," Reyes managed to say, "a green thumb. How clever of you."

"Oh, it's nothing," Matt replied, grinning. "I've always had a way with words."

If looks could have killed, then the one Evan shot his son was lethal. What in heaven's name did Matt have against Reyes? Why, he hadn't even been home long enough to know who the man was or why he'd come. How bizarre, Nicola thought, shooting Matt a look herself.

"Oh my," Maureen was saying as she glanced at the diamond-studded watch adorning her slim, tanned wrist, "Señor Reyes, you did say the limo would be here at eleven?"

"Why, yes. The time has flown." He dabbed at his lips with the napkin and set it on the table, rising. "If you'll excuse me, I'll ready my suitcase. Your hospitality has been most gracious." He nodded courtly at Maureen and Evan, then seemed to hesitate. "Señor," he began, "perhaps you would allow me a moment more of your time? In the library, if you will, in, say, five minutes?"

"Of course," Evan replied, and Reyes disappeared across the flagstone terrace and into the house.

"Oh, Evan," Maureen said in a hushed voice, "what can he want now? For three days he's been badgering you so. Doesn't the man know what the word no means?"

"Apparently not," Evan said in disgust.

Matt pushed himself from the table, patted his stomach over his polo shirt and stretched his arms over his head. "What's it all about, anyway, Evan?" he asked, sounding mildly bored.

Evan grumbled something, finished his juice and muttered, "Money, what else? Costa Plata owes the World Bank two hundred million. They haven't made an interest payment on their loans for eighteen months. I'm recommending they be called in."

"You've decided for sure?" T.J. asked.

"I think we're close to a consensus," Evan said. "I'd say there's little chance of renewal."

"What if they come up with some interest money?" Nicola put in.

Evan shook his head. "They won't. They're flat broke. Even the Soviets don't want to throw good money after bad."

"Um," Matt said, "calling in those loans is going to topple the government, isn't it, Evan?"

"Not my problem," the man replied.

"I read terrible things about Costa Plata in *Time* magazine," Maureen said. "It's a police state. Innocents just disappear off the streets every day, and no one has the nerve to question it."

"Since when were you concerned about human rights, Mom?" Matt asked lightly.

"For your information," she returned, "I'm a very informed woman, kiddo. I keep up."

"I'll bet you do," Matt said, then leaned over and kissed her cheek.

"Oh, do stop," she said, but clearly Maureen was delighted. Even Evan had to smile at his son's antics, as did Nicola. But she noticed T.J.'s face then, and was surprised to see open jealousy there. My Lord, Nicola thought, her smile fading, T.J. was too old for sibling rivalry, wasn't he?

"Well, I suppose Reyes is waiting," Evan said, then stood and excused himself.

"Do check on the man's limo, will you, dear?" Maureen asked T.J. "I just hope it hasn't had a flat tire or something, and we're stuck with the man."

"How hospitable of you," Matt said.

"I don't like him."

"And neither do I," Nicola added. "He's been nothing but . . . but *slimy* ever since he got here. I wouldn't trust him as far as I could throw him."

"Obviously," Matt said, "the Latin lover flopped badly with you two."

Lydia cleared the table with Nicola's help, while Maureen and Matt sat there talking, comfortable, their faces looking young and relaxed. It heartened Nicola to see mother and son reunited; she only hoped that Evan would curb his disappointment in Matt and let sleeping dogs lie.

It wasn't long after the dishes had been cleared that T.J. reappeared, his hands thrust deep in his white trouser pockets as he strode in long-legged steps back to the table. "Well," he said, his brow creased, "Reyes is gone. But I'll tell you, Dad's cooking."

"Oh my," Maureen breathed just as Evan came banging out of the French doors, growling mad.

"Uh-oh," Matt said.

"Can you imagine!" Evan thundered as he began to pace the terrace. "That no good . . ."

"What happened?" Maureen asked quietly, troubled.

"*What happened!* I'll tell you what happened! That pompous ass offered me a million dollars to renew the loans!"

Matt let out a deep chuckle. "Hey," he said, "it's probably drug money."

"Matt," Maureen warned, "this is not the time—"

"Oh," Evan interrupted, still flaming mad, "the boy's finally using his head. I have no doubt that any money still lying around the treasury is illegal. That pompous . . ."

"What did you tell Reyes?" Nicola finally ventured.

"I told him exactly where he could go!"

"And what did he say to that?" It was Matt who spoke, and Nicola had to turn and look at him, never having heard such a sober tone of voice come from the man.

"Now *that's* the kicker," Evan replied, pacing even harder. "He had the nerve to threaten me!"

"What exactly did he say?" Again, Matt posed the question.

Evan waved his hand in the air as if in dismissal, but Nicola could see that he was troubled. "It's ridiculous, absurd. Who does that Reyes think he was talking to, anyway?"

"What did he say?" Matt reiterated.

"He said—" Evan turned to face them all "—that if I didn't renew the loans, I was a dead man."

CHAPTER TWO

NICOLA WANDERED into the kitchen to grab a snack before she was to go horseback riding with Evan and Maureen. Despite the unsettling words between Evan and that ingratiating, calculating Reyes, not to mention the tension caused by Matt's abrupt arrival, she was really quite famished. So what if it was only one o'clock? She hadn't swallowed a bite of solid food since last night.

T.J. had just left for the city. He'd told his parents he had an appointment with a client, and he'd gracefully bowed out of the ride. But maybe there *was* no client, Nicola thought; maybe he was just too uncomfortable around the whole family, afraid the war would break out between Evan and Matt, afraid that he'd be drawn into it. One never knew what went on in T.J.'s head.

The poor guy, she mused, opening cupboard doors, browsing. Trying so hard to emulate his father, waiting to be taken into the family business, wanting to be trusted by Evan, to become financially independent, no doubt. Not an easy life, nor a particularly happy one.

Nicola shrugged, opening the double-doored refrigerator, searching for something that tickled her fancy. Sure, T.J. had his problems, but then so did everyone. Nicola herself had plenty: a load of guilt over her mother, even though her mother's condition was none of her doing, an empty emotional hole where her father was concerned, a certain questioning of her future beyond career, an insecurity that frightened her at times. Well, everyone had their bugaboos, but they lived with them.

Hmm. Salami cut paper-thin, mayonnaise, mustard. Sprouts, lettuce, tomato. Ah, a jar of green chili peppers. She hummed as she layered a fat sandwich on good New York kosher rye. Iced tea with lemon and lots of sugar would be the perfect accompaniment.

Evan hated the way Nicola piled sugar into her coffee or tea, on her cereal. "Use honey," he would admonish, "or nothing. Sugar'll rot your guts and your teeth. Not to mention playing havoc with your blood sugar level!" But she always laughed at him until he subsided, glowering at her from under his thick black brows.

It was affectionate, their teasing, their easy no-holds-barred relationship. Through the years, she'd found she could say just about anything in front of Evan—except swearwords—and get away with it. With him she felt secure. Too bad she couldn't feel that way with more men, but then, considering the way her own father had treated her, that innate distrust and shyness of men was hardly surprising.

I do okay, though, Nicola thought. Certainly she was around enough men in hunting and fishing camp and on long horseback rides for the Colorado outfitter service to know that she could pull off being one of the guys. Maybe it was because she had no interest in men sexually. Maybe her body language or attitude or something gave off a loud and clear message: *Hey, fellas, hands off. This girl isn't interested.* Whatever. But they seemed to like her, especially her cooking, and she'd learned to keep a safe distance, holding secret their manly boasts, allowing them their off-color jokes, fading into the shadows when she needed to.

It would have surprised Nicola, however, to learn that the men saw her quite differently; they saw a capable, pale-skinned young woman with gorgeous long black hair and winsome, bottomless dark eyes that challenged a man to probe their depths. They saw a woman who could ride or hike or fish with the best of them, but who required gentling by a trusted hand; a vulnerable woman who only needed the right man to unlock the secrets of her heart and to heal the wounds left by a self-serving father. But then Nicola could hardly recognize these things about herself.

She leaned back against the counter, holding the bone china plate in one hand and the messy sandwich in the other, and took a bite. She chewed thoughtfully. Not bad. It would have been better with a sharper mustard and pickles on the side. Maybe some sliced turkey, too. She'd have to keep the combination in mind for her job at the outfitters. Those men liked to *eat*. No sparing cholesterol, not for them. They liked to play macho hunters out in the wilderness. No nouvelle cuisine, either. Hot and tasty food, sticking to the old ribs, was the ticket.

She pulled an errant lettuce leaf out of the layered sandwich with her teeth, then took another bite. Um, she was starved, and dinner would be late, she knew. Maureen would want them all to go out somewhere to celebrate Matt's being home. Of course, Evan would grumble, T.J. would be so quiet he'd almost disappear, and Maureen would try desperately to make the disparate souls under her care get along. Oh yes, Nicola knew all the games the Cavanaughs played with one another.

She shifted her weight against the counter, uncrossed one booted leg and crossed her feet the other way, chewed, took a quick swallow of sweet-tart cold tea to wash it all down, and was staring unfocused out the window overlooking the green-green lawn when the swinging door from the dining room opened.

It was Matt, looking surprised and glad to have discovered her and casual all at the same time. "Found you," he said. "Do you spend a lot of time in the kitchen, Cinderella?"

The last of the sandwich was posed halfway to her mouth. "Oh." She swallowed. "Were you looking for me?"

He nodded. "Actually I was. Mom sent me to tell you they can't go riding this afternoon. Evan just got a call." He never referred to his father as anything but Evan, she noticed, while T.J. always called him Dad. "Some head of state is in town for a few hours. You know, the usual. They have to meet him for a late lunch in the city." Matt raised his eyebrows facetiously. "'It's an absolute must,'" he said, imitating Evan's intonation so perfectly it was eerie.

"Oh, darn," she said. "I was looking forward..."

"Ah, fair maiden, do not despair. I'm going in their stead."

"Oh."

"Hey, kid, it could be worse. It could be Godzilla."

"Oh, I didn't mean that. I just was looking forward to, oh, well, you know...."

"No, I don't know. I can't say I've ever been bereft at my revered father's absence. He tends to go for my throat."

Nicola looked away. "He's not always like that, you know."

"With me he is. But really we don't want to discuss the boring subject of father-son competition, do we?"

"I guess not."

"So, we'll have a nice, long ride and relax, and I'll be so sore tomorrow I won't be able to walk."

"Well, maybe..."

He held a hand up. "I promised Mom. You know she hates anyone to go riding alone. Says it's too dangerous."

"You *do* ride?"

"Let's say I *have* ridden. It's been a while. Do they still have Brownie in the stables? He was always my favorite."

"Brownie died years ago. He was ancient."

"Hmm, I see. Time flies."

"I guess you really haven't been in touch much," Nicola said carefully.

"No, not much."

She put her plate in the sink and drained the iced tea from the glass. "Well, I'm all set then."

"Good. I'll just run up and change. Meet you at the stables. Pick out a nice calm one for me, will you? No fire breathers."

As she walked out to the stables, Nicola couldn't help wonder at Matt's wisecracking. She used sarcasm at times to mask her true feelings, but not *all* the time. What lay beneath the surface of his mockery?

The stable boy had three mounts saddled and ready when she got there.

"Oh, I'm sorry, Alonzo. Didn't they phone from the house? We only need two horses," she said. "Mr. and Mrs. Cavanaugh couldn't make it. Why don't you put Sally back? I'll ride Lark, and we'll keep Lucky for Matt, okay?"

Lucky was twenty years old and had been a terror in his time, as well as a champion jumper, but now he had settled down, a tall, almost white horse near to his retirement. Perfect for an occasional rider like Matt. Her own mount was a dark bay mare called Lark, a handful but a challenge. She had run away with people consistently, until Maureen refused to let anyone but a selected few ride her.

Nicola stroked Lark's smooth neck and checked the girth for tightness. She looked up to see Matt striding toward her, carrying a grocery sack. He was wearing tall black leather boots and riding britches, as she was, and a white short-sleeved polo shirt.

"Thought I'd dress the part," he remarked. "Country squire and all that." As he said it, he mocked the very concept of rustic squires and the country and himself, but oh, he looked so dashing, slim and straight and young for his thirty-eight years, with a smile that curved adorably. "Here." He held up the bag he carried. "I brought snacks and a bottle of wine. Mom insisted."

She couldn't help smiling back; his good humor was infectious, all-encompassing. Nothing could get Matt down—not his father, not his aimless existence, not even Nicola's apparent reluctance to join him on this ride. "This is Lucky," she said, patting the old gentleman's neck. "He's yours."

"Great. I'm ready if you are. Alonzo, do you have a saddlebag handy? That's it, perfect. This place is so damn well supplied. Makes you sick, doesn't it?" He threw the bag over Lucky's withers, gathered the reins and swung a leg up.

Nicola mounted Lark, keeping an eye on Matt, just to make sure he wasn't going to fall off or something equally embarrassing, but he looked fine on the horse—easy, comfortable and, as always, athletic.

They left the stable yard at a walk, down the lane through the lines of white-painted fences, across the slanted meadow to the bridal path under the huge elm trees along the bank of the Hudson River.

"I wish Maureen and Evan could have come. It's too bad," Nicola said, "isn't it?"

"Oh, I don't know. I kind of like the way things worked out."

She shot a sidelong look at him and saw his mouth twitch a little. Baiting her, that's what he was doing. Lark fluttered her nostrils and shook her head, jingling the bridle. Nicola had put her hair back in a ponytail, but it still clung to the back of her neck in this heat. She tossed her head and swept it aside with a hand. "Hot, isn't it?"

"Not so bad," Matt replied easily. "I've been in worse."

"Like Haig's Point, South Carolina?" she asked. "Or Costa Plata?"

"Maybe."

"You *do* get around."

"This is true. I like it that way. There's a big world out there, and I'm lucky enough to be able to see it. I like new experiences and new places."

"And new faces," Nicola added pointedly.

"That also is true."

She waited for some masculine bragging, but none was forthcoming. She'd have thought Matt would jump at the chance to tell her a few stories, but he didn't.

"Forget my wanton existence. I'll bet Mom talks about me, so you know all the gory details. She does, doesn't she?"

"Well, sure, some."

He nodded and twisted his lips. "You know, kid, you're good for Mom. She needs someone to talk to. She's so lonely, stuck in that great monument to Evan's success. I'm glad you're in touch with her a lot."

She was surprised at the genuine feeling behind Matt's statement, so unlike his usual insouciance, but then, she hardly knew him. Maybe he cared more than he let on.

"I hope so," she said quietly. "I know she isn't happy...."

"Evan leads her a helluva life, doesn't he?" he asked, his words tinged with bitterness.

Nicola couldn't say anything. She knew that Evan and Maureen had a troubled relationship. Divorce was out of the question apparently, due to Evan's position or Maureen's timidity or whatever. And she couldn't really discuss it with Maureen—that was too personal and none of her business, besides.

Matt made a gesture with his hand, causing Lucky to throw his head up and show the whites of his eyes. "Let's talk about you for a change. I'm fascinated. Tell me about your work. Last time I was home, I think you had just finished school. Am I right? And you were skinny."

She ducked her head. "Yes, skinny, and my hair was short that year, not very becoming at all, and you were too busy with the, ah, redhead to notice me."

He threw back his head and laughed. "The redhead. Lord, I forget her name! I thought Evan would appreciate her, but he failed to get the joke."

"You must have known he wouldn't."

"Sure I did. But I keep trying to enlighten him. So—" he eyed her deliberately up and down, his gaze as intrusive as a pair of hands, from her smooth black hair down her neck and over her breasts and waist and hips, down the one leg he could see to the tip of her black leather boot "—tell me more. What exactly do you cook?"

Nicola kept her eyes glued to the path. "Well, I've ended up as sort of a specialty cook. Seasonal. I've worked for ski lodges in the winter, first up in Vermont, then out in Wyoming. And that's how I met Ron Mitchell, who runs the hunting and fishing outfitter in Colorado."

"You just rustle up some grub over the old camp fire, is that it?"

"Not exactly. The ski lodge I work at is four-star, so beans and bacon don't exactly fit the bill," she said dryly.

"I catch a note of irritation. Sorry, kid. I wasn't being patronizing. I'm truly interested."

"Okay. So, in the summer I cook for fishermen or hikers or pack trips, whatever Ron has booked. I'm in charge of everything from ordering supplies to cleaning up. It's hard work but it's fun, and lots of times I get to go along on the trips, so I've learned a lot about the great outdoors. Then in the fall, of course, the hunters arrive. First bow and arrow. Deer, elk, bear, a few, very few, get licenses for mountain lion or bighorn sheep."

"And you're handy with a gun, too?" Matt asked.

"I've gone a few times. Never bagged anything, though."

"A tough lady," Matt said under his breath.

"What?" Nicola asked, not sure she'd heard him right.

"Oh, nothing. You've been around, kid."

"Seems you have, too."

"Just resort hotel to resort hotel. As a matter of fact, I thought I might give Colorado a try myself this ski season. You know, work in a bar at night—something not too taxing—ski all day."

"I seem to remember your mother telling me you were a good skier."

"Sure, we all are. You know Evan. He took us up to Canada every year, come hell or high water, for helicopter skiing. We had to learn."

"He still goes. Every year, in January. He loves it. It must be wonderful up there. All that powder...."

"You ski?" Matt asked, urging Lucky into a faster walk to keep up with Lark. The horse swished his tail in irritation and laid back an ear.

"Oh yes, I love it. I've been skiing at Jackson Hole, since I work near there. It's a great mountain."

"Is there anything you *don't* do, Nicola?" Matt asked.

"Sure, lots of things."

"Hmm." He turned and gave her an inquisitive look. "What, for instance?"

"Well, I don't sing or dance or play the piano. I'm a lousy writer, and I don't paint or draw or act. I don't sew my own clothes . . ."

He laughed. "Okay, okay."

"And I don't do windows," she concluded.

He was silent for a time. She could see his white knit shirt sticking to him, as her own blouse was. His back was straight and, even under the fabric, she could see the curves of muscle, the lines of his ribs.

"Do you have a boyfriend?" he finally asked.

She stiffened. "No."

"What, a pretty girl like you? And all those men around? Hunters and skiers and such?"

"I'm just one of the guys when I'm at work," she stated.

"What about when you're *not* at work, little Nicky?" His tone had turned soft and fluid, insinuating.

Too long a pause passed before she could find a witty reply, a way to sidestep the question. She should have lied to him, immediately, easily, and told him she dated a few men here and there. Or she could have tossed her head coyly and said it was none of his business. But nothing came out. She could feel his gaze still on her, interested, perhaps amused by her discomfort. She pretended she hadn't heard him and looked down, seeing Lark's muscular neck, her dark shoulders alternating forward and back. A dampness broke out on Nicola's forehead and upper lip. Why was he teasing her? Did he act like this with all females? And how many unsuspecting women had fallen for his charm and good looks?

The path wound down from a hill to the broad, slow-moving Hudson River. Thick greenery lined the way and hung out over the dark, sluggish water. Every so often a monumental granite outcrop, a cliff or hillock of solid gray stone with shiny flecks, would lift from a meadow, the bare bones of the earth breaking through its verdant skin. It was hard to believe that only a few miles downstream lay Manhattan, sweating and convulsing and cursing with seven million tongues.

"You know, it's strange," Matt said, breaking the gravid silence, "but this is probably the longest we've ever spent together. Funny, being raised in the same house by the same parents."

"It is odd," she said, finally able to clear her throat.

"We're strangers to each other."

"I guess so."

"I think we should remedy the situation, don't you?"

Nicola hesitated, then decided to be frank. "I'd say there's not much chance of that. You aren't around. Our paths really don't cross."

He looked at her appraisingly. "Well, there's a rejection if I ever heard one. Hell, Nicola, I'm not used to that."

"I'll bet you aren't."

"Well, well."

"Oh, come on, Matt," she chided. "We're just going on a ride. Don't feel obligated to impress me or . . . or ask me out or anything like that."

"Whatever made you think I was going to ask you out?"

Oh, what Nicola wouldn't have given to have wiped that sly grin off his face! "You were coming on pretty strong. Maybe I was wrong." She shrugged and patted Lark's neck.

"Just habit." He paused, then added, "*Bad* habit."

"Okay, just so we know where we stand."

"Sure, you're right. I'll practice my big brother routine."

"Come on, let's canter a little. You up for it?" she suggested, not liking the way the conversation was going. She had always been better at action than words, anyway.

"Hit it, kid."

She touched her heels to Lark's sides, and the feisty mare took off down the shaded path so that the bushes whipped by and Nicola had to duck to avoid low branches. Behind her she could hear Lucky pounding along. The wind felt refreshing on her face, the horse surged powerfully beneath her, and she could gallop along forever, free and full of the joy of uncomplicated, pure physical sensation.

But eventually Nicola had to pull Lark up and walk her to cool down. The mare was breathing hard, and her satiny coat was wet with sweat. "That's a girl," Nicola said, patting the horse's damp neck. "Good girl."

Lucky was blowing hard, too, his white hide splotched with dark sweat. "It's too hot to do that today," Matt said. "Us old guys like to take it easy."

"We'll stop up ahead. I know a nice spot. Then you 'old guys' can rest," she said.

They tied the horses' reins to a low branch under an enormous old maple tree and loosened the girths. Matt pulled the saddlebag off and took out a bottle of wine, plastic glasses, crackers and a round of Brie cheese. "Good, the wine's still cool. Want some?"

Nicola sat on the thin grass in the shade of the tree, leaned her back against the trunk and looked at Matt, shading her eyes. "Maybe one glass."

"Good. Live a little, I always say." He sat beside her and poured, handing her a glass. He lifted his. "*Santé,*" he said.

"*Santé.*" The wine was cool and velvety, a rosé zinfandel, a little sweet and fruity. A nice vintage. "Um," she said. She closed her eyes and felt the wine warm her belly and the breeze cool her flushed cheeks.

Out beyond the circle of shade insects clicked and buzzed, and the sun came down hard on the tall grass. Nicola could hear the horses swishing their tails at flies and jingling their bridles.

"Nice," Matt said quietly.

"Um."

She heard him moving around then and opened her eyes. He was taking his polo shirt off, pulling it inside out over his head, wadding it up and putting it under his head as he lay down.

"That's better," he said, sighing, closing his eyes, balancing the wineglass in the hollow of his stomach.

She couldn't help looking. He was whipcord thin, his torso ridged with ripples of muscle. He wasn't the weight-lifter type at all, being much too slim in build, but he must have done something to keep in shape. A fuzz of brown hair spread across his chest, and a faint line ran down to his navel. She could see his face, too, relaxed, eyes closed, and the stubble of his beard.

It was a good face—a handsome, manly face—his nose generous and slightly curved downward, a bit like Evan's, only larger. But it was that mouth of his, that wide, mocking mouth, that made him appear as if he always had a secret or, perhaps, could read your mind. And then there was that dimple in his cheek, negating the cynicism.

Matt had great eyes, too. Like Maureen's, his were a bit heavy lidded, and they tilted down at the corners, where they met laugh lines. The color, though, set them off from most blue eyes—his were as blue as sunlit tropical waters, clear and almost turquoise.

She studied him from her spot resting against the tree. How could she help it? She could see a drop of sweat from the curling hair behind his ear run down slowly onto his neck, then disappear under his head. Matt Cavanaugh....

He looked young and healthy and in top physical condition. How did his apparently aimless life as a lush and a bartender tally with his glowing health and the obvious care for his body? Shouldn't he be puffy, with circles under his eyes, flaccid muscles and broken veins on his nose?

Strange.

Also, curiously, his face and neck and forearms were very tan, but his torso was pale. A workingman's tan on a beach bum?

Even stranger.

Nicola suddenly had the distinct feeling there was an awful lot she didn't know about Matt Cavanaugh, and what she *did* know was only the tip of the iceberg. Nine-tenths of him was unseen—and dangerous.

She nibbled on a few crackers and sipped her wine. She could smell the dusty aroma of sun-kissed grass, the musk of dry dirt and the faint perfume of wildflowers carried on the soft, damp air. When the breeze blew into her face, she could smell the horses, warm and familiar. And Matt. A vague, foreign scent of male sweat and skin and shaving soap and leather boots. Something inside her belly melted, a soft warmth that curled and sighed in a lassitude of pleasure.

He *was* dangerous, a jarring note in her well-guarded serenity. A man. An attractive man. An irresponsible charmer like her father. And she knew what men like that could do if you let them. They destroyed whatever—whomever—they touched, leaving forlorn lost women behind them, a trail of tears, broken lives, shaky hollow women like her own mother.

Well, it wasn't going to happen to Nicola.

Matt rolled onto his side, facing her, drained his wine and set the glass down. He picked a blade of grass and chewed on it, eyeing her thoughtfully until she looked away.

"You are gun-shy, aren't you?" he asked.

"I'm careful," she said, "about my friends."

"Hmm. And I'm apparently not one of them. Has my father's opinion of me rubbed off on you?"

"I hope not."

"So do I."

"Why should you care what I think of you?"

He shrugged, chewing on the grass, studying her.

She tossed her head, throwing her ponytail off her neck, uneasy under his scrutiny. She would have left if she could have, but there was nowhere to go. Desperately she searched for a neutral subject, but what came out of her mouth surprised her. "Why isn't your chest as tan as your face?"

He looked surprised, then amused, and he glanced down at himself as if seeing it for the first time. "Sunburn," he explained. "I get burned on the beach. I always wear a T-shirt."

"Oh." She shouldn't have asked. Now he knew she'd been looking at him. She felt her cheeks flush. Oh Lordy.

A shrill whistle made her jump. Matt had stretched the blade of grass between his thumbs and blown on it. His eyes met hers over his hands, and they were dancing devilishly.

"Scared you, didn't I? I always was a champ at silly things like this. Always blew louder than T.J. He was a dud at grass whistling."

"I'll bet he tried, though."

Matt laughed. "Until his lips wouldn't pucker anymore. Poor kid."

"It must have been tough having you for an older brother," she said. "Maureen says you were so good at things. Track and skiing and school."

"Oh, T.J. did all right. He's a plodder, but he gets there. We're not real close, you know, so I don't think I bothered him that much. And now, well, he's probably secretly gloating that I'm the black sheep of the family."

"I don't know. T.J. is hard to read. He keeps things to himself."

"He sure does. Sometimes I wonder what goes on under that calm exterior," Matt mused.

Nicola waved a persistent fly away, then she sat, chin on her knees, watching Matt break a piece of Brie off and pop it into his mouth. "How're your folks?" he asked, chewing. "I know your mother's not well. Do you see her often?"

Nicola folded her arms around her knees and stared off into the distance. "She's in a home, not far from here. I don't see her often because I'm not around much anymore. When I visit her, she cries."

"I'm sorry." He said it with such genuine sympathy she was surprised. "I didn't realize ..."

Nicola shrugged. "Clinical depression." She still stared out over the bright meadow, but now she was frowning. "And my father, well, he's busy. You know. And I hardly ever spend any time with him." She recalled the last time she'd seen him, having gone to his Manhattan penthouse on an impromptu visit almost three years ago. He was in his silk pajamas, hair mussed, being catered to by a gorgeous brunette who wore his bathrobe. At two o'clock in the afternoon. But she wasn't about to tell Matt *that*.

"Good old Wentworth. Mom told me he was going to get married again last year."

"Guess not. I suspect that he enjoys women too much to tie himself down," she said, trying to keep the bitterness from her voice. And the sadness. She shifted her chin to the other knee. "I really do have to visit my mother before I leave. I've been putting it off. Maureen said she'd take me, but..." Why was she telling him this?

"It's tough, isn't it?"

She nodded, feeling a lump in her throat, the same lump she felt whenever she thought of her mother. And in reaction to that lump of misery, she felt anger as well, anger against her mother, who was too sick, too weak, too helpless to take care of her daughter. Anger, at least, was easier to bear than misery.

She raised her head then and forced a smile. "Let's lighten up, what do you say?"

"Sure. No use dwelling on the bad stuff. When are you leaving for Colorado?"

"In a few days. There's still snow up in the high country until mid-June, so we have a long off-season."

"Heck, maybe I'll see you out there this fall, kid."

"Maybe, but not if you keep calling me kid."

"Sorry, it just slipped out," he said, grinning, his dimple making a shadow on his tanned skin, his blue eyes crinkling. He rolled over onto his back again and stuck another stalk of grass into his mouth idly. An inadvertent thought eased into her mind: he looked as if he'd just woken up. His brown curling hair was tousled, a lock or two sticking up above an ear boyishly. And his eyes, half-closed, had that lazy, sultry look to them, as if he'd ... he'd just made love. Oh yes, she knew that look. There'd been the handsome, rakish cowboy up in Wyoming, a rodeo rider. Not surprisingly, he'd had Nicola in

Jackson Hole and Laura in Laramie. Too bad it had taken her nearly a year to find out.

Drowsy eyed and languid, smiling slightly and crookedly, sure of himself after a good performance—like Matt right now. Wasn't there a man out there for her somewhere, an honest man?

Lark shook her head, rattling her bridle. The sun sent shafts through gaps in the maple's foliage, mottling the ground. A butterfly settled on Matt's boot tip, bright blue, like a bit of the sky come down to earth. It *was* an idyllic afternoon, Nicola reflected, hot and lazy, tranquil. And despite her better judgment, she found herself still curious about this sexy, philandering man. *Darn.*

She couldn't help liking him when she was with him—he certainly had a way about him. She would dearly love to believe that there was something under his lighthearted surface, something serious, something he cared about other than living it up. Once in a while she thought she saw a sadness in his expression. Wistfully studying his face as he lay there so relaxed, she searched for the truth about Matt Cavanaugh, but she couldn't be sure she saw anything.

The silence lasted a long time. She hugged her knees tighter. "Why are you a bartender?" she asked finally.

He opened his eyes, looked at her from under dark brows and burst out laughing. "I can't believe *you're* going to start on me! Have you been taking lessons from Evan?"

"Seriously," she pressed, "why?"

He stared at her for a moment, making her shift her feet and draw aimless patterns in the dust with a finger. "It gives me freedom. I come and go as I please. It's a great excuse to hit all the world's hot spots. Simple."

"Maybe, but what about the pain you've caused Evan and Maureen?"

Silence came as easily to Matt as laughter. He shrugged and didn't answer, content to lie there, arm behind his head, one foot crossed negligently over the other knee, sweat shining on his bare skin. And he kept watching her, his blue eyes never leaving her face. She crawled with discomfort, frantically searching for a way to change the subject.

"What did you think of Reyes?" she asked. "I didn't like him a bit. He threatened Evan—can you believe it?"

Matt frowned. "Nasty fellow."

"You know about the position Evan's in now, don't you? He's got to make a final decision on calling in those loans to Costa Plata. It'll ruin the country. He's really unpopular, Maureen says. He's had hate mail, calls from congressmen who want to keep the status quo down there. He's gotten threats, too, phone calls, letters. This morning was only the latest."

"Was it?" He looked away, chewing on the stalk of grass.

"Yes. You know Evan. If he thinks it's good for the World Bank, he'll call in those loans, regardless. And he refuses to take any of the threats seriously. Maybe he should have protection. Maureen is worried."

"Is she?"

"Yes. She wants him to hire bodyguards."

"Bodyguards? My father? He's so cocksure, it would never occur to him that anyone would dare try to hurt him." Matt gave a short laugh.

"I know." She drew a spiral in the dust, watching an ant follow the curving line. "Do you think you could talk to him about it?"

Matt tilted a brow. "I am probably the last person on earth Evan would listen to."

She looked down. "I was afraid you'd say that."

"Now, don't you worry about Evan. He can take care of himself," Matt said with finality.

She sighed. "I hope so."

It was a glorious day. They rode back through the slanting gilded light of the afternoon. A few fluffy white clouds slid across the sky, chasing their own shadows along the contours of the terrain. Grasshoppers buzzed, the serenade rising to a crescendo, then falling, as one after another took up the refrain, then dropped it. A perfect afternoon, Nicola thought, except for Matt Cavanaugh's curious, unwanted interest in her and the slight tension between them, as if they were past lovers who had met again after years and still felt a spark of attraction for each other. But that, of course, was ridiculous.

The horses perked up their ears when they turned into the lane between the white fences that led to the stable.

"I'll race you," Matt announced abruptly, grinning a challenge at her. "T.J. and I always used to."

"Sure." She flashed him a smile, kicked Lark and raced away. She heard Matt yell something at her, and then Lucky was pounding along behind her as she lay low over Lark's neck.

There was a ditch across the path; Lark took it, flying, stretching out, but Lucky was there—she could hear him breathing hard at her shoulder.

Nicola won, pulling up in the stable yard in a flurry of hooves and dust, laughing and panting. Matt reined in next to her. "You cheated!" he yelled across the horses' dancing forms.

He dismounted and came around Lucky to help her down, but she was already halfway out of the saddle. "But I won," she said. "Doesn't that count?"

He put his hands on her waist as she dropped to the ground and turned. They lingered there a heartbeat of time too long, scalding and hard on the damp fabric of her blouse, and she felt a deep, shivery exaltation at his nearness. The horses were still sidling and blowing, excited from the race, and she was imprisoned between their hot, lathered bodies, staring, paralyzed, into Matt's eyes as the beasts moved restlessly, pinning them together. She felt him press against her, saw his face close to hers; she smelled horseflesh and leather, dust and hay, Matt's man odor. She felt her own rapid pulse pound in her temples.

"Nicola," he started to say, but Alonzo ran up to take the horses, and the moment was forfeit.

CHAPTER THREE

THE COLD WATER ran in rivulets down Matt's back and chest,
icy, sensual fingers that soothed him while he cooled down and
showered off the dust and sweat. He'd be sore tomorrow, he
knew, because it had been years since he'd used those muscles
sitting astride a horse.

God, but it felt good to be away from the questioning eyes of
his family and the *looks* he'd been getting that afternoon from
Evan. The bathroom was a safe haven.

He and Nicola had returned from the ride to find everyone
home once more. Maureen had complained of a headache,
"That DuPlessy woman always gives me one," she'd said, referring to the wife of a French representative of the World
Bank, whom Evan and Maureen had gone into the city to meet.
So Maureen was napping, Evan had conveniently disappeared
into his library, and T.J. was lounging quietly on a float in the
pool, sipping on a gin and tonic.

Matt was thinking—and hiding out.

He stepped out of the shower, wrapped a thick blue towel
around his middle and searched his shaving kit for his razor.

Sure, he thought, scraping at his whiskers in front of the
mirror, it was easy for him to act outgoing, and he'd always had
a wise mouth on him. But this charade he was enacting with his
family was starting to make his gut churn with doubt. It had
been sixteen years that he'd been playing the errant son, the
footloose trust funder, the *bum*.

How had it all started? Better yet, why had he let it start?

The answer was right there, staring back at him from the
mirror. He'd been recruited by Ned Copple of the U.S. Foreign Service, right out of college, and he'd gone straight undercover for the service, working for the little-known Section

C. And from day one, Ned had made his function very clear. "You're to become the playboy, the ex-college kid who's got just enough money to travel on and only needs to take a job when pressed for extra cash. You'll move, on my orders, at a drop of a hat. You'll overhear conversations on golf courses, in swank bars, on yachts that will in due course help your country set foreign policy. The things you'll hear, the circles you'll run in, will provide us with inside info we couldn't possibly get over a negotiation table."

"A spy?" Matt had asked dubiously.

"An intelligence gatherer," Ned had corrected tactfully.

Matt had liked the work. He'd drifted into the "in" circles with ease and grace and moved around the world so many times he'd lost count. And just to make it all look right, he'd taken those jobs occasionally, bartending mostly, overhearing things that made even Ned's head spin. It was truly amazing, Matt had discovered, what a man'll tell his bartender after three martinis.

He'd worked private parties on yachts from the Potomac River in Washington to the Persian Gulf. He'd taken on jobs in the Swiss Alps at exclusive ski lodges, folded towels at the Istanbul Hilton, washed dishes on a kibbutz in Israel, waited tables in Hong Kong, slung gin on a Caribbean cruise ship. You betcha, it was amazing the things a man could overhear.

And there'd been women. Matt had learned how to charm and flatter. There had been senators' daughters and foreign diplomats' secretaries, all needing a sympathetic ear. Oh yes, there had been plenty of them. He had a rule, though. No rolling in the hay with an attached female. There was no better way to blow someone's trust than to bed his woman.

He was tired of it all, true enough. But he'd actually done some good in this old, used-up world of his. There was that time in Beirut when he'd gotten wind of a supposed terrorist raid on an Israeli school. He'd reported in on Ned's scrambled phone line, and the terrorists had been caught not fifty yards from that school. And the time he'd been a tour guide living in Bangkok, Thailand, and been able to quietly arrange the release of some American POWs shot down over Cambodia.

He'd helped, okay. The trouble was, at first he'd enjoyed throwing his purported uselessness in Evan's face. Evan, who had demanded and pressured, presumed and controlled for much of Matt's life. Yep, being a bum had definitely been a tool with which to punish his father and give back some of the man's own. But the years had passed, and Maureen deserved more from her oldest son. It just might be time, Matt thought, to come in from the cold and find out who he really was beneath the carefree, sarcastic facade.

"Jeez," he muttered as he started to get dressed, "why all the sentimentality?" What had gotten into him this past year? And why had he been so eager to take on this latest job for Ned— the Costa Plata Caper, Ned had dubbed it. Had Matt said yes because it meant sticking close to his family for once—particularly to Evan? He'd known immediately when Ned had suggested he gather some information on the meeting between Evan and Reynaldo Reyes that there would be problems in his showing up unexpectedly at home. Yet he had jumped at the chance.

Why?

"You're getting old, man, slipping," he said as he put on his loafers with no socks.

He stood now, dressed in loose, pleated white pants and a black shirt, in the middle of his old bedroom and thought about Reyes. Was the man capable of carrying out his threat? Of course, Evan, the stubborn old coot, would never see the real danger he might be in. Oh no, not his dad; he thought he was above it all, bulletproof.

Coming home hadn't all been bad, though. He'd been expecting the usual recriminations, and instead, he'd discovered a face from the past, a darn pretty face, at that.

Matt heard voices below his bedroom window, around the pool. Idly he pulled back the curtain and glanced out. T.J. was still lounging on the float, drink in hand, and there she was, as sleek and toned as a cat, walking out on the diving board.

Despite himself, Matt's pulse began to pound. She was long limbed and lean, smooth skinned and, oh, that midnight-black mane of hair that swung free over one shoulder...

She was wearing a dark bikini, a string job that left little to a man's imagination. Her hipbones showed, sharp and pointed, and the nice, muscular curve of her fanny. Her belly was flat, the line of her whole upper torso almost as flat, in fact. Small, faintly curved breasts—enough, though, to rev up his imagination. Damn, but those bikinis were provocative. They just about left a woman naked, but not quite; there was only enough material there to drive a guy out of his mind.

She sprang off the board on one foot and did a passable swan dive—not great, but graceful. Then her white body with those scanty dark strips slipped through the clear blue water and came up by the steps. She was laughing and panting and slicking her black hair back with both hands, her breasts straining against the two dark pieces of triangular material.

"You're rocking my boat," T.J. said as his floating lounge bobbed up and down in her wake.

"Oh sorry," Nicola said, and looked as if she might splash him teasingly, but she hesitated; instead she climbed the steps.

That's right, Matt thought, leaning against the windowsill, *T.J. isn't the type to take a joke.*

Matt found himself ambling on down to the terrace, fixing himself a light cocktail and heading on over to the pool. He should have stayed away.

Nicola dived in and out several times more, did a few laps, then declared it was enough. And who was there with her towel when she finally came up the steps for good? Just the idea of touching that satiny, glistening white flesh was too tempting.

"Oh," she said, "thanks, Matt." She shivered deliciously and looked away, blinking the water from her eyes. "Wow, it's sort of chilly."

"Um."

"That looks good," she said, nodding toward his drink. "What's in it?"

"Soda. Some vodka."

"Maybe I'll—" Nicola began.

"*Some* vodka?" T.J. interrupted, using his hands to propel himself to the edge of the pool. "Knowing you, brother, it's probably half the bottle."

Oh boy, Matt thought, *here it goes, the sibling rivalry.* And he couldn't very well tell T.J. that he rarely drank any booze at all.

He chose to ignore him. "You want me to fix you one?" Matt turned to Nicola.

"Sure. But really light. I mean, just a splash of vodka. I'm a cheap date."

While Matt strode to the outdoor wet bar, Maureen made an appearance. "I thought I heard you all down here," she said.

"Did we wake you?" It was T.J. who spoke, his fair brow wrinkled in concern. "I tried to be really quiet, Mom."

"Thank you, dear," Maureen said, sitting herself down by the pool, "but I was awake, anyway. Lord, but that Claudine DuPlessy gives me a migraine."

"Maybe we should skip dinner in the city," T.J. offered.

"Well . . ." Maureen began.

"Really, Mom," T.J. said, "we can go another time."

"But Matt's here and . . ."

"Hey," Matt said, "don't worry about me. I'm happy staying home."

"Are you really?" Maureen asked, and the double and triple meanings dripped from her voice.

"Yes," Matt replied slowly, "I'm as happy as a clam." He let her take his hand and squeeze it affectionately, then he turned back to Nicola with the drink, but not before he noted the envious expression on T.J.'s face before he covered it up. *Whoa there, brother. I'm not the enemy.*

"Oh, thank you," Nicola said, taking the sweating glass, sitting down near Maureen.

"And you won't be disappointed if we stay in tonight?" Maureen asked her.

Nicola shook her head. "No. In fact, maybe I'll drive on over to Fenwick and visit Mom." She shrugged as if it were no big deal at all. "I've been meaning to do it for almost two weeks now."

"Are you sure?" Maureen asked carefully. "Nicola," she went on in a very quiet tone, "I saw Suzanne in May. She's not . . . clear right now, dear. You might only upset yourself. I'm so, so very sorry."

But Nicola took it like a champ. "Oh," she said, forcing a smile, "I know how it is. Sometimes Mom's very lucid, other times...well, it's those awful antidepressant drugs, you know."

"Yes, dear, I know." Maureen frowned. "You must eat, first, though. I'll have Lydia—"

"Tell you what," Matt chimed in, "I could drive Nicola on out to Fenwick, and then we could grab a bite to eat somewhere."

"Oh," Nicola was quick to say, "I'll be fine. I'll borrow Maureen's car, if it's okay, that is."

"My goodness," Maureen said, putting a hand to her brow. "My car's still in the shop." She straightened and looked at her watch. "Oh, dear, it's five already. Evan was supposed to remind me."

"He was pretty busy today," Matt said. "I can drive you tomorrow to get it. Okay?"

"I guess. Oh, thank you, Matt, that will be fine. So," she said, "you'll still be here tomorrow?"

"Long enough to get your car," he replied evasively. In truth, he had no idea what Ned had planned for him. Maybe, because of Reyes's threat, Ned might want him to hang around and play bodyguard.

Nicola was looking at Matt. "You really don't mind driving me?"

If ever there was an understatement... "Not a bit. I'll see if I can keep the Ferrari on the road for you, too."

"How gallant of you," Nicola replied flippantly.

After finishing her drink, she changed into a red-and-white knit sundress that was sleeveless and midcalf length. It was clinging and sleek looking, showing off her long, elegant limbs and that rather cute bottom he was getting to know. It swung around her legs and hugged her slim waist, caressing all the sensual promise it concealed. He couldn't help watching her, finding new surprises in her face, her movements. She had a fine-drawn, delicate grace, a little sad but wonderfully alluring. She wore little makeup, he saw, just some pale lipstick and mascara, and round white earrings completed her outfit. Simple but suitable.

When Nicola had headed up to change, Matt had done something quite out of character. He'd gotten on the telephone and meddled in her life. He'd told himself that he was just being a friend, that he was only going to be a companion to her during a difficult time. But he'd wondered as he'd dialed the Sansouci Restaurant in the city—Wentworth Gage's place—and made reservations for two. Wasn't he being too pushy, too protective? No, this meddling was not one bit like him. It smacked too much of giving a damn.

He was curious about Went Gage, too, and was indulging his curiosity. What exactly was the man's relationship with Nicola?

They almost made it to the car, almost, before Evan stepped outside and tried to take control.

"We'll eat right here tonight," he said when Matt told him their plans.

"I already made some reservations." Matt stood his ground, holding his slubbed silk Armani sport coat casually over his shoulder.

"Cancel them. Your mother isn't feeling well. We're going to stay in."

"*You're* going to stay in, Evan, we're not."

Nicola cleared her throat. "Evan," she began, stepping between the two men, who faced each other as stiffly as growling dogs, "I'd like to eat out tonight, if it's okay with you."

He gazed at her for moment, grumbled something, then relented. "If it's what you want, Nicola."

Amazing, Matt thought, but he could see now that Nicola was like a late-life child to Evan, a daughter to boot. Apparently Evan did have a soft spot or two. Incredible.

"See you, Evan," Matt said, shooting him a sly smile and helping Nicola into the Ferrari.

Nicola pulled her hair back and fastened it with a clasp while Matt revved up the engine. It purred and sang to him.

"Expensive item," she noted, settling into her seat.

"Hey," he said, putting on his aviator glasses, "what's money for?" The truth was, the service provided it as part of his cover.

"Oh," Nicola said airily, "money can do things like educate kids or buy a home. You know, silly little things like that."

"Why, Nicky," he said, giving her a flashy grin, "you're almost as sarcastic as I am."

A home and family, he mused as he kicked up gravel on the driveway and sped around the circle. What would it be like to have a little house, a little wife and some curly headed little kids?

Nicola would make some man a good wife, he decided. She had always been a cute girl and not a bad teenager, kind of sassy. She was athletic, smart and had grown up to be terribly attractive in an old-fashioned way. Heck, a man could drown in those dark, melancholy eyes of hers.

And there was that vulnerability, too. He liked that. It made him feel all masculine and protective and angry at her folks, who had screwed her up so damn bad in the first place. What right did parents have doing that, anyway? Like Evan, for instance, forcing his sons to be competitive, making them vie for his love and attention, holding himself above them, God-like, unreachable. Evan hadn't learned a thing in the past twenty years. He was still, as ever, an SOB.

We're one of a kind, he thought as he drove, *me and Nicola. Messed-up adults because we had parents who never should have brought children into the world.*

Pretty, young, vulnerable Nicola. He'd like to pull off onto that grassy shoulder over there and reach out for her, bring those small, soft breasts up against his chest and stroke the length of that spectacular mane. He'd like to hold her and keep her from pain. He'd like to take her to see her mother tonight and then her father, and when it was done she might cry for a while, but he'd be there all the time, listening, caring, holding her....

Who was he kidding? He'd be willing to bet she was put off by him already, well, by his type, that was. And he couldn't tell her it was all a cover. He couldn't tell her that he wasn't a lush or that life wasn't as funny as he pretended it to be. He couldn't even tell Nicola that he was as worried about Evan as she was. He'd blow his cover to bits. It was all top security stuff, and, if Matt was nothing else, he was loyal to the oath he'd sworn.

Above the Ferrari the trees formed a canopy, that East Coast, lush green ceiling that cooled the roads. Late sun, a golden profusion of shafts, seemed to rush by overhead, spearing the dark green leaves. Tidy stone walls lined the curving road, and beyond them horses grazed.

Matt pushed the Ferrari to the limit when the road straightened, then downshifted and took the narrow curves with ease. His black shirt flapped against his skin in the wind as did Nicola's skirt, rippling against her bare legs. He'd have loved to bend over and run his mouth across that knee or to press his lips to the bone in her shoulder, to taste her—all women tasted differently, some ordinary, some as sweet and succulent as a ripe peach. He already thought he knew what Nicola would taste like.

Fenwick Estates, a very fancy name for essentially a sanitarium, sat east of the Hudson River, on New York's Route 9, not too many miles north of the city. It was a beautiful old place, expensive as all get out, a one-time country manor on thirteen cleared acres behind the ubiquitous stone wall. Dr. Fenwick evidently had decided back in the 1920s that not all mentally disturbed patients belonged locked in cages—especially the ones with bucks.

Matt had no way of knowing just how much Went Gage laid out a year for his ex-wife's comforts at Fenwick, but he'd wager it was twenty-five thousand minimum, on top of a hefty initial investment. Suzanne had been in and out of Fenwick, mostly in, for sixteen years. Sansouci Restaurant had a good reputation—even Evan used Went to cater larger affairs—but it was still a steep bill. Did Went have the grace to feel guilty for driving Nicola's mom nuts?

"It looks smaller," Nicola said when they pulled up to the gate and identified themselves.

Matt turned to her and rested an arm over the steering wheel. "How long's it been?"

"It's been almost two years since I've seen Mom. Oh, I write, and I've called lots, but I never know how I'll find her. I always feel like I make her worse when I come."

"What did the doctor say you could expect this evening?"

Nicola rubbed her arm. "He said Mom was doing very well. What he meant, I'm sure, is that she's on a new drug that's got her less depressed."

"Um." Matt put the Ferrari in gear and drove on up to the parking lot. Maybe this wasn't such a good idea; maybe Nicky should have come alone, after all. He felt out of place. He also wondered if she could bear to see Went tonight, as well.

Nicola insisted that he come along. "Mom doesn't say much," she said. "And, to be honest, I'd like the support, Matt. She'll remember you. You are kind of family."

But not the kind of family he'd like to be.

One thing was for sure: Fenwick Estates spared no cost when it came to accommodations. Every patient had his or her own room and porch, spacious rooms, light and airy. The communal rooms—dining, television, game—could have been those of a luxury hotel. At least Nicola had that knowledge as comfort.

He could see Nicola taking a deep breath as they approached Suzanne's room, a nurse leading the way. Matt was following the women, and Nicola suddenly reached behind her and caught his fingers in hers, giving them a quick squeeze. Touching her hand was like dipping his fingers into a brook of bubbling water, but water that was as pure and hot as a flame. He felt the heat flicker at the root of his being.

Suzanne was sitting, very nicely attired in a lemon-yellow shirtwaist dress, next to her empty fireplace. Behind her, a summer breeze lifted filmy curtains, and Matt noted the scent of lilacs, a sweet, cloying scent reminiscent of bygone days.

Yes, he remembered Suzanne Gage. She'd gone to a private girls' school with his mother, and they'd been close then. Afterward, it had been the University of Rochester for Maureen and a finishing school in Geneva for Suzanne, who was, as Maureen had put it, a dreamy girl, soft and gentle and not terribly in touch. Suzanne had met Wentworth, a native New Yorker, while he'd been apprenticing with a French chef in Paris. It had been reportedly a whirlwind courtship. Later, while Maureen had been busy having her boys, Suzanne had been busy not having children, afraid of the responsibility trying to keep her girlish figure for a husband who already had a roving eye and was trying to save enough cash to open his dream restaurant, Sansouci, the home of the Broadway stars and the New York elite. Twelve years of marriage had passed before Nicola began to grow in her mother's womb, a surprise, disaster. True to form, Went had found other women when Suzanne was occupied with Nicola, kept apartments for them in New York, finally keeping the ultimate apartment right here at Fenwick for Suzanne.

And where had Nicola been all this time? Raising herself, pampering her unhappy mother, doing somersaults in the air to get her dad to notice her.

"Hi, Mom." Nicola walked cautiously to the wing chair and stopped. "It's Nicola, Mom."

Matt was no judge, but this woman's eyes—the same sad, dark eyes of her daughter—were so glazed that a body could swim in them. It seemed nothing short of a miracle that she recognized her daughter at all.

"Nicola," she breathed, remembrance expressing itself on her calm face. "Why, Nicola, they told me you were coming, dear. How nice. Do you like my new dress?" She patted her lemon skirt. "I ordered it from a catalog. I do love the catalogs, don't you?"

It went just like that for a good forty-five minutes. Suzanne, still an attractive woman at fifty-eight or so, with short dark hair and pale skin, seemed to have no sense of time or space. She was not unhappy—the drugs saw to that—but she was so far out in left field that Maureen's description of *dreamy* would have been laughable in any other situation.

Nicola stuck to safe subjects. "Remember the swing set we used to have out back...? Remember Tinker, that big orange cat you found on the road...? I'm in Colorado. Remember, I told you on the phone last summer."

"And you're going back soon?"

"Yes, Mom, I still work for the same people."

"And how is Maureen? Why, I just saw her. She brought me some hothouse flowers."

"She's fine. Mom, this is Matt, her son. You remember him."

Suzanne looked up to where he was still standing near the door. "Oh, my, yes. Of course I know Matt. Why, he was a big, strapping boy when you were just a baby, dear. Come into the light, Matt.''

But by the time they were saying their goodbyes, Suzanne stared at him as if for the first time and said, "Oh, Matthew, has it really been twenty years since I've seen you?" And she started crying silently, tears oozing out of her eyes.

"It's those drugs," Nicola said as they walked back outside. "If they'd quit giving her so much, then maybe—"

"Hey." Matt caught her arm. "They give her the drugs because she's clinically depressed. You can't have it all, kid. Without the little white pills, she'd be . . ."

"I know. Suicidal."

"That's right. This way she just looks at her catalogs and stays out of harm's way."

Nicola seemed to tremble then with the chill of her misery. "Damn," she said, trying to gather herself.

By then, Matt had decided that Sansouci was a terrible idea. No way was he putting her through any more of this hell. She probably wasn't the least bit hungry as it was. He wished to God that he could take this lady up to his room and lie down on the bed and hold her all night. She was so precious to him at that moment, so in need, that he could almost thank the Gages for giving her all those insecurities—it had kept her, so far, from finding happiness in the arms of another man.

Matt led her over to the car and opened her door. "Want the top up? It's getting cool out."

"Sure," she said, but her voice was threatening to crack. "What a mistake I made coming here. What did I expect? A miracle cure?"

"You expected love."

That got her attention. Suddenly Nicola looked up through glistening, dark eyes and stared at him. "Why, Matt Cavanaugh," she said, "of all people to figure that one out."

"Hey," he said, getting into the car, "I'm human, you know. Well, almost."

Surprisingly Nicola declared that she could use something to eat. "I really don't want to go home yet."

"You sure?"

"Yes."

It was time to come clean. He felt like ducking his head. "Listen," he began, "I did a stupid thing. While you were changing, I made reservations at, ah, Sansouci. Dumb, I know. You can bite my head off, if you want."

Nicola turned and studied him for a moment. He'd expected anger from her but instead got curiosity. "Are you trying to play big brother or what?" she asked. "I mean, if I want to see my own father while I'm here, Matt, I don't need a bodyguard, you know."

"Well, I . . . Hey, I slipped. It was a lousy idea. So," he said, "where would you like to eat?"

"You said you had reservations."

"Yes, but after seeing your mother, you may not want to go there."

"Why don't you let me be the judge of that," she said.

"You really want to see him?"

"Sure, why not? Who knows when I'll make it east again? And one thing's for certain, he'll never come see me."

"You've got guts, kid, I'll say that for you."

"Nicola. Nicky, if you must. But quit calling me kid."

Matt drove the parkways and crossed the river into Midtown Manhattan, enjoying the ride, enjoying the comfortable silence between them. At that hour of night, eight-thirty, there was little traffic heading into New York City, and they made good time.

He was thinking a lot about this woman sitting next to him, her eyes staring straight ahead. He'd like to know her better. But he had no right to even approve of his own thoughts. What could he offer her at present? He couldn't even tell her that he wasn't quite the bum she thought he was. And yet a part of him wanted to woo and charm her that night, to catch her with her guard down. He felt like a single cell dividing itself, tearing apart, as if he were becoming two separate entities, conflicting beings. And all because of a job and an oath he'd sworn many years ago. Well, he was fed up with the work, with the question bobbing around in his head continually now: *If I weren't the footloose trust funder, then who would I be?* Maybe he really was playing himself; maybe he really was a wisecracking wastrel. He owed it to himself and to his family to find out.

He parked in a secure garage a block from Sansouci, took his jacket from the back and locked up. It had rained lightly in the city earlier, and the air was as soft and tangible as spun silk. There was something special about dusk, a feel to it, a peaceful ending to the day.

"It's pretty out," he commented, and took Nicola's arm. "I love it after an evening shower."

"Me, too," was all she said as they crossed Third Avenue and headed east.

Just touching her, seeing the last light catch in her hair, smelling the faint scent of her honey sweetness, lent him a kind of shaky elation. It couldn't last—he wouldn't do that to either of them—but for now he'd accept those feelings and enjoy them.

Nicola stopped beneath the striped canopy and took a deep breath. "Boy, I think I'm just asking for it tonight," she said.

"You want to find another spot?"

She shook her head, determined.

Inside Sansouci it was dark and elegant. The gold damask walls were covered with signed photos of the rich and famous. The booths were plush red velvet, the linen the finest. Chandeliers twinkled, waiters flourished, soft classical music hung on the air. Even the carpet seemed to give beneath their feet.

"Nice," Matt said, then gave his name to the headwaiter.

"It looks the same," Nicola breathed. "I guess Dad's done pretty well for himself."

"Even better, I'd say."

On their way to the table, Matt touched her arm lightly. "Would you like me to tell the maître d' who you are? I'm sure your father..."

Nicola smiled. "No. Went always makes the rounds of the tables. You know, 'How is the sauce? The veal?' That kind of stuff. He won't be able to miss us."

They had a cocktail, then ordered their meals and chose an expensive bottle of Bordeaux. Nicola studied the menu carefully, commenting on this and that, the new items, the always popular entrées. No nouvelle cuisine for Went's place; every dish was swimming in his famous sauces, lots of clarified butter and garlic and heavy cream. The vegetables, lightly steamed or sautéed, were as rich as the entrées. Wonderful tasting foods did not go hand in hand with limited calories.

"I thought everyone ate light nowadays," Matt said, leaning his elbows on the table and catching her eyes over the candle.

"Not Dad's customers evidently. I guess they still splurge once in a while."

"Maybe he's smart," Matt said, "and lets everyone else in the business lighten up their menus. This way, he's the only game in town."

"No one ever said Went was dumb." Nicola sipped her drink casually, but he noticed her eyes kept glancing over his shoulder toward the swinging kitchen doors.

"How long's it been?" Matt asked a few minutes later over their tender Bibb lettuce salads.

"Since I've been here? Well, I'll bet it's been six years. The place wasn't even that established yet."

"Nervous?" Just then the wine steward arrived, the white towel over his arm. Matt sniffed the cork on the bottle, nodded, then tasted the wine. "Excellent," he said.

Dinner arrived. Nicola had ordered scallops in a white basil sauce with baby carrots and summer squash, while Matt had opted for pork tenderloin medallions that were dripping with mushrooms and a Dijon sauce. The bread was hot and yeasty, the butter molded into little seashells, the silverware heavy. But Nicola looked the best of all. Her hair was clasped to one side and fell over a milky shoulder; her eyes, those lovely dark eyes, looked at everything tentatively, and her mouth . . . Each bite she took she tasted carefully, her lips parting for the fork, closing, moving slowly. Forget the food; Matt could have nibbled on those lips all night.

"Is yours good?" he asked.

"I can't fault Went for the cuisine."

"Mine's passable," he teased.

Nicola's dark brows raised. "Isn't it good, Matt? Went's food is usually the very best."

Ah, yes, he had her there; he'd caught her off guard. She still cared. She still looked up to the creep and idolized him. A sharp spear of jealousy knifed through him. What had Went ever done for her?

The man himself finally came popping out of the kitchen. Matt hadn't noticed, but Nicola was a dead giveaway. She seemed to stiffen in her seat, and her cheeks grew rosy in anticipation and apprehension.

Matt glanced over his shoulder. Wentworth Gage was older now, but still just as lean and tall, just as craggy faced and effusive. He was not at all the picture of the fat, jolly cook, being much too hyper to ever gain weight. He'd lost none of his charm, either, as he moved from table to table, just as Nicola had said he would, bowing, exclaiming, kissing a hand or two.

He looked the part. He wore his tall white hat, loose black-and-white checked pants, the white jacket open at the throat and his coveted European chef's badge pinned properly to his breast.

"Oh God," Nicola said, as if poised for flight, "he's coming our way."

"I think it's a little late to run."

"My Lord!" came the man's voice seconds later. "But, can it be? Can it be my *Nicola*?"

The charm and polish oozed from him as if he'd rehearsed it. He held Nicola's shoulders, kissed the air next to each cheek, stepped back and grinned proudly.

"My darling Nicola, *chérie*," he kept saying, "you should have called. You should have asked for the best seat in the house! But this is amazing, finding you here!"

Nicola could not have been more embarrassed by the fanfare. Heads turned in their direction, whispers abounded. "Who *is* she?"

She looked down at her lap. "Dad, you're making such a fuss," she said, flustered. "I wrote you last spring. I said I might come."

"Of course you did! Didn't you get my answer in the mail?" He looked positively outraged.

"Why, no..."

Holy Toledo, Matt thought, suddenly wanting to punch the guy's lights out, she swallowed the old letter-in-the-mail routine—hook, line and sinker!

"But I can't imagine why you didn't get it," Went was saying, the consummate actor. "Now, you must let me take you out tomorrow, Nicola, darling. We'll do the town!"

"Well . . . I . . ."

Matt cleared his throat. "We already have plans," he said, grinning at Went wolfishly.

"Matt . . ." Nicola began, confused.

There was no way he was going to let Went, that phony, French-accented New Yorker, court her for a day and then dump her out in the cold again. No way. "I'm afraid," Matt said, shooting her a look, "that Nicola and I are tied up. Our plans are firm."

A moment of silence stretched out like a thin thread ready to snap. Nicola looked uncertain, Went was gauging his adversary—whom he hadn't yet recognized after so many years—and Matt glared at him with unbending determination and a charming smile.

Went finally sighed. "Well, then, perhaps the next day. I do want to spend some time—"

"I have a flight," Nicola said, and her voice was sad. "I'm off to Colorado again."

"Oh," Went said.

"I have to be there, Dad."

"But this is unfair. It's been too long."

"You could visit her in Colorado," Matt said pointedly as he poured himself and Nicola more wine.

"I'm afraid," Went said, "I didn't get your name."

"Cavanaugh. Matt Cavanaugh." He could have added, *My folks raised your daughter, remember?*

"Of course! I should have . . . And how are Evan and Maureen?"

The atmosphere lightened a bit after that, and Went seemed eager to please. He mentioned always wanting to travel in the West, and wouldn't it be grand if Nicola could find a week sometime to spend in the city? He never mentioned Suzanne, however, and neither did Nicola, who had fallen quite silent, still obviously uncertain, still hurting and sad and adoring and slavishly grateful.

"Well, I must be off to the kitchen before my new *saucier* curdles the hollandaise. You *will* write, Nicola? And you must find that week to visit sometime." He kissed her again and held both her hands in his. Surprisingly Matt thought he detected a slight hesitation, a faint regret, perhaps, in the man's dark eyes.

"Phew," Nicola said, utterly unnerved by the time Went left. "I didn't expect all *that*." Then she seemed to collect herself and looked up at Matt sharply. "Why did you lie to him like that? I could have spent tomorrow in the city." Her tone was accusing.

Matt framed his answer carefully. "I thought I was helping. I assumed that Went would either call and cancel out on you, or he'd have painted the town with you and then let the years pass...."

"But it's my problem, Matt, not yours."

He held her eyes in challenge. "So go on into the kitchen and tell him you're free for the day."

Suddenly there was a feeling of suspense, a wedge forcing itself between them as they sat there, each poised to do battle. It was finally Nicola who relented. "Okay," she said, "you're right. Dad would have given me those hours, then so long Nicola, see you around."

"Mad at me?"

"Yes. Very. You acted like Evan."

"Whoa there! Evan? Me?"

"Yes. Like father, like son. How do you like that?"

"I don't."

It was as if she'd thrown a bucket of cold water in his face. He'd really let himself slide that time. He'd been angry, jealous, stubborn and controlling. Wow.

He couldn't believe it; he'd let his facade drop and hadn't even recognized it. He'd compromised his cover. And for what? To protect a girl he liked, to keep her from getting hurt.

What was wrong with him?

She was watching him across the expanse of exquisite linen and silver and crystal and congealed rich sauces on fine china. She was seeing something unexpected and wondering about it. And it occurred to him to just give up and tell the truth, tell her that he cared about her feelings and that he wasn't a superficial, irresponsible cad. Of course, he couldn't do it.

"Misguided romanticism," he quipped. "Sorry, kid. Just call me Don Quixote."

"Well," she said, mollified, "maybe you were right to do it. But don't do anything like that again, ever. I mean it, Matt. You're not my big brother, you know."

Comically he crossed his heart like a kid. "Never, I swear. Each to his own bad end, I always say. I don't know what came over me."

When the bill arrived, it had Went's note scrawled across it: "Compliments of the house."

"Nice guy," Matt said, "your old man."

But Nicola said nothing; her soft, childish mouth, her pretty, full lips tightened into a line and she frowned slightly.

Outside it was sultry. The city once again oozed the smell of hot pavement and car exhaust, and the carousel it was on vibrated and whirled to a tinkly tune as they walked to the garage to pick up the Ferrari.

"You wouldn't let me drive it, would you?" Nicola asked wistfully as the attendant pulled up, braking with an echoing squeal.

"Sure. You want to?"

"Could I?" Her eyes were shining, those huge dark eyes that he could drown in. He'd do anything to keep that happiness on her face, even let her drive the service's hundred-thousand-dollar toy.

"I'm a good driver," she assured him.

"Get in, kid." He opened the driver's door for her with a flourish. "She's all yours."

Nicola *was* a good driver once she got used to the sensitive clutch and special racing gearbox. She grinned and her long dark hair flew around her head and through the open window, whipping strands across her face as the wind of their passage buffeted her.

"Oh! This is fun!" She gunned it on the West Side Highway, where the traffic thinned out, and the Hudson River flashed by along their left, the battalions of uniform apartment buildings skimming by on the right.

"Take it easy. Cops," he said mildly.

"Oh? Am I going too fast?"

"A little."

He relaxed back against his seat and watched her profile, her open mouth, her black veil of hair. He was giving her pleasure, and it felt good, really good.

Sometime later she pulled into the driveway at home, stopped in front of the door and, reluctantly, turned the car off. "Thanks," she said. "That was a treat."

All the lights were out inside the house by then, and only the yellow porch light guided their way to the door. They both walked slowly, side by side, companionably. Matt wanted to be a decent fellow with Nicola; he wanted her to really like him. Yet if he continued on this path, she'd see right through him to the truth—she almost had back at the restaurant.

"Well," she said at the door, fumbling for her keys in her purse, brushing at the insects that buzzed around the yellow light, "that was nice of you to go along with me tonight. Thanks."

She was adorable, shy and a little uneasy, so young, a world younger than he was. "You're quite welcome."

She found her key and was inserting it into the lock, but he put his hand over hers, stopping her. She looked up swiftly, with a jerk.

"I've got a great idea. Let's go skinny-dipping in the pool," he said, knowing what he had to do, hating it. "I used to do it all the time when I was a kid."

"*Matt.*"

"Sure, come on. It's a hot night. Perfect."

"I don't think so." She was stiffening up; he could feel it in her hand, in the sinews of her arm.

Slowly he turned her to face him. "Why not?"

"Please, this is ridiculous and you know it."

"Then we'll wear suits."

"No, I'm going to bed."

He put his hands on either side of her, leaning against the front door, imprisoning her. "You're chicken, kid."

She had pulled back as far as she could, and he could tell she was trembling a little, trying to put up a brave front, but uncertain and totally unable to play the games that other women did.

"Maybe I am chicken," she said breathlessly.

He let her go, of course. He couldn't hold a woman against her will. "You sure you don't want that swim?"

"No." She slipped away, opened the door and was inside in a moment, closing it in his face.

He stood there, staring at the shiny black paneled door and elegant brass knocker and artful fanlight at the top. He sighed then and turned away to go around the side of the house to the pool. She was something special, something valuable, not to be toyed with like his other ladies. Yes, he'd need that swim, with the cool, soothing water sliding against his hot skin.

He unbuttoned his shirt as he walked in the darkness and yanked it off, angry with himself suddenly. Angry with himself for caring.

CHAPTER FOUR

THE CRACK OF A GUNSHOT split the air, echoing off the walls of the surrounding mountains, repeating itself until, weaker and weaker, it died off. Startled, Nicola looked up from the skillet she was holding over the black iron wood stove.

"A little early, isn't he?" Ron Mitchell remarked dryly.

"It isn't even dawn yet. Is he crazy?" Nicola said. The late elk season this year started promptly at sunup on Saturday, November 3, and a hunter could lose his license if he was caught shooting before that time. Everybody knew that.

"Sure, there're lotsa trigger-happy crazies out there, Nick," Ron said, throwing another piece of wood into the old cookstove.

"Someday a fool like that's going to kill someone," she said, turning back to her home fried potatoes.

She and Ron were the only two stirring in the main log cabin at five o'clock that morning. As guide and owner of the Colorado outfitter service, Ron was checking on the supplies for lunch, the water cans, the ropes in case someone had to drag his kill out, and looking at the topographical maps of the McClure Pass area, searching out new places where he'd locate elk for his customers, who'd paid a bundle to bag a nice trophy this week.

Nicola was, of course, cooking. She had to get up very early to start the fire in the wood stove until it heated up the room and until it reached the right temperature for cooking. No turning the knob to Low or Medium or High. The old stove was a challenge, but once it got going, it cooked like a charm. She had potatoes frying on one burner, a batch of buttermilk biscuits in the oven and French toast stuffed with cream cheese browning in butter in another skillet.

Outside it was still pitch-black, and cold, too. Dawn in the Colorado Rockies, at ninety-five-hundred feet of altitude, often produced subfreezing temperatures. When Nicola arose in the morning in her own tiny, unheated cabin, she threw on long underwear—tops and bottoms—jeans, wool socks, a heavy wool plaid shirt and a bright orange hunting parka before she even brushed her teeth. She made her way across the clearing to the main cabin, where the kitchen and rec room were, and rustled up a huge breakfast for the six hunters who habitually booked Ron's service for this same week every year.

Ron was whistling, feet up, sipping at the coffee in his own personal mug, the one with the lady's face on the side and her nether parts on the bottom so they could be seen when he tipped it up to drink. The aroma of brewing coffee filled the big room, along with the mouth-watering scent of the cooking food.

"I get fat every summer, Nick, you know that? And it's all your fault."

"Sorry." She flipped the French toast adroitly with a spatula. "Just doing what you hired me to do."

"Too damn well." Ron lit up his first cigarette of the day and sighed. He was a middle-aged man, an ex-rancher, who'd found it more lucrative to run a hunting-fishing-guide service than to punch cows. He worked like a demon from June to November, then retired for the winter with his wife on his considerable spread down in the valley near the town of Redstone. He had jug ears, rough features and big gnarled hands, but he could tie a fishing fly to catch the most elusive trout, climb a sheer mountainside, gentle a skittish packhorse, track an eight-point buck across rock or fix a broken Jeep with nothing more than a screwdriver and the roll of duct tape he always carried.

Nicola had been working for him for three seasons. She made a lot of money—two thousand dollars a week during hunting season—but she earned every penny of it, she figured, cooking, washing up, ordering supplies, wrestling with the stove, which she'd nicknamed Old Bertha. and it wasn't easy to cook in high altitudes. Water boiled at a lower temperature due to less atmospheric pressure, and everything took *much* longer to cook: beef roasts an hour longer, a roast chicken half an hour more. Four-minute eggs took six, pasta took half again as long as the directions called for, and all baked goods took longer, too. Carrots never seemed to cook. The first year it had been a guessing game, but now Nicola had it down to a science.

Ron had other guides in his outfit, but this week he was leading the group; he always took his best clients out himself. Most of the six men who were hunting now were old customers, men who came every year at the same time, and they came not only for the hunt and the glorious autumn scenery of the Rockies and the great food, but also for the male companionship, the time to swap stories, see familiar faces and catch up on the past year.

Nicola checked the biscuits. Two minutes more and they'd be done. The checkered oilcloth was spread on the plank table and set with plain, heavy crockery and stainless steel flatware. The coffee was brewed—lots of it. Cream and butter were set out, along with homemade preserves that Ron's wife made: local chokecherry jam, tart and garnet red; clear pink crabapple jelly; wild raspberry. And homemade salsa, too a mixture of onions and garlic and tomatoes and jalapeño chilies, without which no right-minded westerner would think of settin' down to the table.

"Smells good," was Ron's comment.

"You always say that."

"You got those sourdough pancakes on the menu this week, Nick?"

"Tomorrow," she said, covering the French toast and setting it on the warming shelf on the top of the stove.

Ron grunted and stubbed his cigarette out. "Your friend Evan is mighty eager. Is he gonna be one o' them-there angry types if he doesn't bag a bull?"

"Don't worry about Evan. He's hunted all over. He knows the odds." Evan had finally kept his promise and made it out west to hunt, and Nicola was thrilled; she'd been nagging him to do it ever since she'd started working for Ron. There were men he knew who came every year, two of whom had booked the same week as Evan, so he fit in as if he'd been coming regularly. The old boy network reached even to McClure Pass in the high Rockies.

The front door opened then, and Dave Huff walked in. "Gosh darn, Nicola, that smells good! I'm starving." He came right over and kissed her on the cheek, a lighthearted, fair man who lived fifty miles away in Aspen, an old skiing buddy of Evan's. "Um, sweet smelling and a good cook to boot. What more could a man ask for?" Dave always had a kind word for everyone, a joke or a funny story to tell.

The other men were starting to straggle in. Terry Swanson from North Carolina, a hard drinker, a man's man and a very good hunter. Eric Field, a tall, rangy Californian, who claimed he'd been mauled by a bear once. Fred Henn, a businessman from Denver, who was very quiet and did not know the others well. Evan came in then, shook Ron's hand and said pointedly that he hoped they had good luck that week.

Jon Wolff was the last man to arrive. He was the owner of the ski lodge in Canada that Evan and family frequented each January, so they were old friends. He was from Austria originally, a widower of around sixty, weathered but straight as a ramrod, with a hawklike profile. He and Dave Huff were also acquainted, as Dave and his wife met Evan and Maureen at Jon's Bugaboo Lodge every year without fail.

There were, however, no women at hunting camp. Except for Nicola—Nick—who was perfectly happy to be one of the guys, ready with a quip, accepting of bad jokes, a sexless creature who carefully kept her relationship with Ron's clients on a professional basis. Only once had one of Ron's hunters knocked on Nicola's cabin door in the night; Ron had talked to him the next day, and it had never happened again. And Nicola liked it that way.

"Nicola, have you met my old pal, Dave? Of course, he was here last year," Evan was saying. "Isn't she a grand girl?"

"Stop it, Evan, you're embarrassing me," Nicola said.

"And do you know Jon? Jon, come over here. Sure, you know Jon, don't you? How does the season look, Jon? Kept my week in January open for us?"

"Ya, sure, Evan."

Evan rubbed his hands together gleefully. "It's cold as a witch's, uh, bottom out, men. Great hunting, great day."

"There could be more snow, though," put in Terry Swanson. "They'd be down lower then."

"Say, did anyone hear a shot a while ago?" asked Eric Field.

"Yeah," Ron said, "somebody was what you might call overeager. O'course, he couldn't see his hand in front of his blamed face in the dark, much less an elk."

"Crazy," Fred Henn murmured.

"I hope he's long gone when *we* get out there," Evan said.

"Dangerous," Jon agreed, shaking his head.

"There's always one in every crowd," piped up Dave Huff.

"Breakfast," called Nicola, setting the biscuits on the table, then the aluminum coffeepot, a bowl of home fries and a platter heaped with thick, crispy French toast sprinkled with powdered sugar. "Chow's on, men."

They ate quickly, greedily, excited by the hunt to come, gabbing and telling tall tales, bragging, throwing out off-color jokes. Cups of coffee, sweetened with thick cream and sugar—or honey, in Evan's case—were swallowed. Biscuits were split and loaded with sweet golden butter and gobs of jelly. Forks cut into French toast, letting rich, melted cream cheese ooze out. Murmurs of appreciation rose from the table, slurps and "Pass, please" and the clink of forks and knives and "More coffee." The talk was also of the best spots to sit and catch an elk off guard, the times of day that the huge beasts lay down in the protection of the forest, hunting rifles, telescopic sights, the difficulty in packing out a kill without horses handy, how to get a Jeep with a winch in close enough to drag out an animal.

"Not like deer," Terry Swanson said, his mouth full of food. "Elk are some kind of heavy critters."

The talk was all hunting, hopes for the day to come, past experiences. "Damn fool shot himself in the foot trying to load his gun," Ron was telling Eric.

"Dumb horse stepped into a gopher hole and went lame. I almost had to carry him out," Terry Swanson said.

"In Kenya, I got a wildebeest," Evan told Fred Henn, "but I'll bet an elk is as big."

"Have you ever hunted at Tigertops in India?" Fred asked. "Not as many animals as East Africa, but more exotic."

Nicola had heard it all many times. She ignored most of what the men said, busy refilling cups, passing biscuits, pulling another batch out of the oven. The room grew warmer from Old Bertha, and Nicola took off her wool shirt and cooked in her bright blue long-underwear top, sleeves pushed up, neck buttons undone.

The men finished eating, thanked Nicola, gave her outlandish compliments and got ready to leave. It was already 5:40, and the stars still shone, but everyone wanted to be in their spot at first light when the game would be moving around, feeding, drinking, dark shadows against a quickening sky. Opening day.

"We'll take the Jeeps as far as Silver Ridge," Ron said, taking his Winchester from the gun rack, pulling on his bright orange parka and cap. "Everybody got jackets and hats? Jon, give me a hand with the box of lunches, will you? Thanks."

They were ready, each man in heavy walking boots, thick wool socks, heavy pants, long underwear, wool shirts and sweaters. Parkas and hats in fluorescent orange, as prescribed by law to prevent accidental shootings, were greatly in evidence. Nicola followed them outside into the cold morning as they shouldered their favorite rifles, their Remingtons, their Savages, their Weatherbies and Winchesters, checked their pockets for ammunition and checked their sheathed gutting knives.

"Good luck," she said to them all. "Good hunting, guys." She gave Evan a thumbs-up and an encouraging smile, and he grinned back at her like a boy and winked broadly as he climbed into one of the two awaiting Jeeps. Nicola noted the excited chatter of the men, the nervous energy that made them ready to pop. They'd go on like that for a mile or so up the dirt road, the two Jeeps bouncing and lurching, the headlights making crazy, blinding tunnels deep into the forest, then the men would grow quiet and expectant as they neared the spot where they'd wait for dawn in silence.

Elk, Nicola thought as she stood there, were wily and elusive animals. Only hunters with the best guides would even see one this week. In September, though, when it was rutting season, and men could buy a bow and arrow license, the bugle of the bulls could be heard echoing in the valleys, affording a

hunter greater odds of bagging one. It never ceased to amaze
her that a nine-hundred-pound animal could hide so well in the
mountainsides.

Shivering, she went back inside the toasty warm cabin. The
men, hungry and sleepy eyed, had stormed the place, and in the
space of twenty minutes, laid waste to it. She straightened and
stacked dishes, swept the mud from heavy boots out the front
door and restoked the fire in Bertha, as she planned on having
a nice breakfast herself.

Outside, the dark was grudgingly giving way to a mother-of-
pearl glow. The men would all be in their places by now, cigarettes extinguished, hunching down on rocks or fallen logs on
the edge of the cold forest or overlooking gullies, ravines,
streams. They'd be spaced out, the six of them, a couple of
hundred yards apart, waiting, hushed, their hot, nervous
breathing forming white plumes in the frozen air. And then
maybe a branch would be heard snapping deep in the bowels of
the forest, and hearts would begin to pound. At first, in the half
light, an animal would only be a slow-moving shadow merging
from the dark trees, scouting the open meadows. Probably it
would be a female—a cow—because the few bulls lingered
safely behind, rarely showing themselves. And a trophy bull
elk... It was going to take a lucky man to even glimpse one this
trip.

Dawn spilled into the valley while Nicola filled the sink with
cold water, using the single hand pump in the camp. That there
was even one source of running water was a luxury to find in a
cabin in the Rockies. Ron's idea. He'd dug the well out back
himself.

The men wouldn't be cold out there despite the frigid temperatures. No. They'd be sweating, each hoping for a first shot
before the game on the mountainside was spooked. Then
hunting became purely a matter of chance. Oh, Ron knew
where the spooked elk herds would most likely be, running
through the ravines, crashing through the thickets. But to get a
safe shot at a fleeing animal was quite another thing.

Maybe Evan would get a chance....

She put the remaining biscuit dough in the oven for her
breakfast, then slipped back into her parka. In a minute or two

more, she knew, the shooting would start. Then it would sound like World War III out there for an hour, the gunshots bouncing off canyon walls, off rock escarpments, rumbling down through the valleys.

Gunshots like that crazy shot earlier. The fool.

Standing out in front of the cabin, the chimney smoke behind her spiraling upward in a long, thin line, she hugged her arms around herself and turned to take in the panorama around the hunting camp, a view that was familiar to her by now, familiar but still awe inspiring. To the east there were mountains, dark green and gray up close, fading away into the distance toward the white-peaked Continental Divide. The pale morning sun sat on a saddle between two far-off peaks, as if resting there before undertaking its day's work, pinkish, huge, extending long fingers of fragile light to where Nicola stood, touching her with golden warmth.

She turned again, to the north. A long slope of brown grass and spruce climbed away from her, up and up, until she tipped her head back to see the dark hump of the mountain covered with early snow. To the west was a deep cleft that fell away beyond the farthest log cabin in the camp. She couldn't see it from where she stood, but she knew there was a narrow, verdant canyon down there, with a bubbling stream that flowed down over rocks, twisting and turning, to empty into the Crystal River, which emptied into the Roaring Fork River, which finally joined the immense Colorado River, which fed a good deal of the great Southwest before it flowed on into the Pacific.

The south. She turned once more. An alpine meadow spread before her, dissected by the dirt road, studded with brush and shaded by a giant blue spruce, an ancient patriarch. The field was brown now, but in the summer, she knew, it was full of wildflowers: blue harebell, red Indian paintbrush, daisies, tiny purple asters, magenta elephant head, lupine, pink owlclover. A riot of color and variety.

This was her world for half the year, this high mountain beauty surrounded by cool, clear light and sparkling dry air.

The sun had risen a little since she'd been standing there, throwing long shadows across the meadow. It was peaceful, still, utterly silent, and Nicola was the queen of all she surveyed. A pity that the shooting would soon begin.

There was a sound, though, a faint noise, barely perceptible but there—a man-made noise—and it was growing louder, coming closer. A Jeep, grinding up the dirt road. Could Ron have forgotten something? Could Ron's wife down in the valley have sent someone up, a new arrival? But Nicola was positive everyone who'd had a reservation was already there. Well, then, who could it be? Maybe T.J.? Evan had said his son had flown into Denver with him, but T.J. was supposedly staying in the city, a business deal. Well, whoever it was, she'd be stuck with him until the men returned.

The odor of biscuits, on the verge of burning, stirred her out of her reverie. Oh, darn! She hurried back inside, snatched up the pot holder, pulled down the heavy oven door, grabbed the pan and blew on the golden tops.

In the nick of time, she thought.

The cabin door swung open then, and she turned around, cocking her head. The light was behind him, and his face was in shadow. But something in that carriage, in that stance...

"Hey, kid," came a familiar voice, "smells good. Got enough for me?"

"*Matt?*"

He unslung the rucksack he was carrying over his shoulder and tossed it on the plank floor. "Who else?"

"But what on earth are *you* doing here?"

"I paid my fees, rented a Jeep, followed the map Mrs. Mitchell gave me..."

"You know what I mean." She could still hardly believe it. Matt, here.

"If you'd fix me up with some coffee and maybe one or two of those biscuits, I'll tell you my life story, anything. I'm tired and I'm hungry."

"Well, sure." Nicola hesitated, still wondering, barely over her surprise, then put down the pan and fetched him some leftover coffee. She set it down on the table. "There you are. Sit. I'll get you some biscuits."

"Thanks, Nicky," he began, when abruptly the war started in the distant mountains, gunshots splitting the air, one after another. "Um," Matt said, "the boys are certainly having a good time."

She wondered momentarily at his mocking tone, then dismissed it. Good old Matt, sharp-tongued, too quick with a clever remark.

He ate like a starving man, she noticed as she sat down opposite him and folded her arms on the table. Once in a while he talked with a mouthful, then swallowed coffee, then took another huge bite of biscuit laced with jam and butter.

"Great rolls," he said at one point.

"As soon as you're done feeding," Nicola said, one eyebrow arched, "I'd just *love* to hear why you've come."

"Sure, sure."

Well, he hadn't lost any of that seductiveness, she saw, or his good looks. It had been almost six months since she'd seen him. But she remembered that night after dinner at Sansouci as if it had been only yesterday. He'd put his two hands on the door at either side of her head, and he'd leaned close, imprisoning her, making his play, his blue eyes all soft and sultry, sending an undeniable message.

Nicola sat there feeling heat prick the back of her neck as he ate and watched her intently. Was he remembering, too?

Oh yes. She'd almost, *almost*, let him kiss her. She'd let him move in on her like a wolf on its prey, press himself against her dress lightly, but just enough so that there was no doubt as to his condition. Her eyes had locked with his, and her lips had parted, and she'd felt wildly, insanely dizzy with a powerful, awakened need.

Oh, brother.

But it had been Matt who'd moved away from her, saying something like, "You sure you don't want that swim?" Yes. And she'd felt mortified, and afraid, because she'd darn near let him con her. Well, it wasn't going to happen again.

"More coffee?" she asked, rising abruptly, hiding her face.

"Sure. And the rolls were wonderful."

He'd been gone that next morning. Maureen had told Nicola something about his finding a place to live near the city and a job. Then Nicola had left for Colorado. Six months, and now this. Out of the blue.

"Well," he said, patting his lean, muscled stomach over the yellow-and-brown wool shirt, "bet you never expected me."

"No, I didn't. Does Evan know?"

Matt shook his head. "Mom told me he was up here this week. You know, I'm working down in Crested Butte right now."

"Crested Butte?"

"Right. I told you I might be out in Colorado this winter."

"How long have you been there?"

Matt took another sip of coffee, then shrugged. "Not long. A couple weeks."

"You have a job?"

"At a bar. But it's still off-season, so my boss gave me a few days to get acclimated."

"Crested Butte's a ski area, isn't it?"

He nodded. "That's right. It's only a few miles from McClure Pass here, as the crow flies. An hour's drive."

"I see."

"No more questions?" Matt gave her a crooked grin.

"Oh, sorry. I was just curious. I mean, you're the last person on earth I expected to see here." And she wondered at the reception he'd get from Evan.

"Well," he said, "I made an effort to see Mom and Evan at home last summer when I was in New York, and I thought I might join him up here in camp. You, know, father-and-son hunting trip. Spend some quality time, and all that, with each other."

"Come on, Matt," Nicola said sarcastically.

"Hey! I'm a changed man. Why the third degree, anyway? It's a free world."

She eyed him warily. "Yes, it is. Well, I guess I better show you the spare bed. You'll bunk in with Dave Huff."

"I've met Dave. Funny guy. I skied with him one winter up in Canada."

"You did?"

"Many, many moons ago, kid . . . Nicky."

"Um." She walked outside while Matt shouldered his pack and followed. "It's next to the last cabin," she said, pointing.

Then, turning to him, she asked, "Say, didn't you bring a gun?"

He smiled. "I never shoot anything except with a camera."

"Then why are you here?"

"To have that quality time with Evan. I told you." He walked on ahead, carrying his rucksack easily, his strides long and self-assured. Nicola watched that jaunty male sway, the tight buttocks beneath the faded blue jeans.

"What a waste," she breathed.

Doing the dishes in cold water was impossible, Nicola had learned, so she habitually boiled a big pot of water, soaked them in it, then scrubbed and rinsed with cold. It took forever. She filled the big kettle from the pump at the sink, took a deep breath, then lifted it, starting toward the stove.

"Here, jeez, that's too heavy for you."

Oh, swell, he was back. But any man who wanted to help with the dishes...

A few minutes later, Matt rolled up his sleeves and stuck his hands in the hot water and scrubbed away. Nicola rinsed and dried.

"Hot in here," Matt said, and she saw him wipe his brow on his forearm. She pushed open the window. "Thanks," he said, shooting her a quick smile. "That's what I love about Colorado. Freezing in the morning, hot by noon."

"Not always," Nicola said, taking another dish from him. "You know you don't have to help. I'm used to it."

"I like helping. Well, helping you, that is."

"Really?" she replied dryly.

The dishes were stacked and put away in no time. And all due to Matt's good-natured assistance. And she really didn't have to peel potatoes or anything till two or so. The beans were soaking...

"Hey," Matt said, "want to take a hike?"

"With all those gun-toting maniacs out there?"

He was standing in the doorway, a casual shoulder against the frame. "Sure. We'll wear our orange and stick to the clearings. Come on, it's a glorious day."

"I don't know," she said doubtfully. She wasn't sure she wanted to go anywhere with him. A girl could lose herself in those laughing blue eyes or want to smooth down those stubborn curls around his ears. He should have brought a lady friend with him if he didn't want to find the guys and go hunting. Why pick on her? And then she wondered as she stood there, uncertain, and eyed him, was this how Went behaved with women? Helpful, gentlemanly, *friendly*? Was this how her own dad lured them into his trap?

"Well?" Matt said.

"I guess . . . just an hour or so. I have work to do." *You idiot!*

Matt carried a water bottle and two ham-and-cheese sandwiches in a small day pack, and they headed out across the south meadow toward a sloping hillside that was spangled with dark firs. It was a glorious day, just as Matt had said, and she was perfectly content to follow his footsteps through the brown grass and the wet patches of snow. Over logs they went, across rivulets and marshy ground.

"Watch it," Matt said, indicating a muddy pool beneath a clump of skunk cabbage. "Here, give me your hand. Okay, now jump."

She came up against him, her hand still gripped in his tightly. The sun, warm on her parka, was in her eyes, and she couldn't see his face, but she knew her cheeks were flushed, and she was breathing a whole lot harder than she should have been. He seemed reluctant to let her go, but then an errant gunshot somewhere off to their left intruded on the moment, and Matt dropped her hand. "Let's go," he said.

Puffing, Nicola followed him up the steep hillside, along a deer trail, across a field of boulders. At the top of the rise, they could see the tall, white-capped mountains beyond them, and the valley below seemed minuscule.

"Phew," Nicola said, "my legs are tired."

"Mine, too. Let's rest a minute."

The earth smelled of autumn that day, of snow melting on dead brown leaves and marshland, fecund. There was another odor, too, mingling with the soft decay—a male odor, sweaty yet sweet with soap. Matt's odor. Why was it, Nicola wondered while she glanced at him, that some men smelled so sensual while others left her cold?

She'd been resting on a log near him, nibbling on her sandwich, silent, when suddenly Matt went "Sh," reached over and put a finger to her lips. "Over there, across the valley. Sh." He moved closer to her on the log, put his arm over her shoulder and pointed, sighting her eyes down his arm. "See him?"

"No," she whispered, all too wary of Matt's nearness. "What?"

"Bull elk. A trophy size, too." He edged closer. "Look, see that outcropping of rock? There?"

"Yes . . ."

"Okay. Now, about a hundred yards down. Just in that stand of aspen. A little to the right."

"Yes!" Nicola gasped. "I see him. He's looking right at us!"

"You bet he is," Matt said in a hushed voice, his arm still extended over her shoulder. "He knows we're here. He's downwind and can smell us. But he thinks if he moves, he's dead."

"But elk don't *think*."

"Sure they do. Not like us, but they're damn smart animals."

The huge beast, a splendid bull with six points on his rack, stood in the golden light with his head held high and still, alert, his neck massive, swollen, and he carried his antlers parallel to the hump on his back, as if poised for flight. He blended right into the background, his tan-and-dark-brown hide a perfect camouflage against the trees and rock.

"Beautiful," Nicola said.

"Magnificent."

"I hope none of the hunters spot him."

Matt looked very somber and very intense. "That old boy's been dodging them for years. He'll make it."

"But if we had a gun?"

"We wouldn't have seen him, then."

Nicola did not question that curious statement. There was something magic, mystical, in the idea.

The big beast stood there unmoving for a full ten minutes before he turned slowly and calculatingly and vanished into the dense forest on the far hillside.

It was a time before Nicola spoke. "I never thought I'd see one," she said. "I mean, the guys all talk about the big old bulls. But you know if they'd seen one, they'd have shot at it. Wait till I tell them."

But Matt shook his head. "Let's not. Let's keep the old guy our secret." And something in his voice, some uncharacteristic, singular need to share, stirred her so deeply that it was almost a physical pain.

It became one of those silly things—who's going to make the first move?—when either of them inched apart. It seemed the most natural thing in the world to sit there with Matt's arm around her shoulders, natural and comfortable, and yet there was a charge there, a current that Nicola felt flowing between them. Oh yes, it was just like that night six months ago. It seemed that all he had to do was touch her, smile at her, acknowledge that *kid's* existence, and her limbs turned to jelly and her head began to grow light.

"Well," Nicola said, "that was exciting." She stood up and stretched. They started back.

He lazed the afternoon away, or so she surmised, because he'd disappeared into his cabin, and she had not seen him since. Maybe he was out on another walk. Maybe he was reading.

She shrugged and bent back over the pile of potato peelings and scraped away. He'd acted that morning as if her company were the most important thing in the world to him. He'd done dishes, helped shake out bedrolls in the sun, gone on that hike. He'd even made the grandfather elk their own special secret. He'd held her hand walking back to camp after she'd tripped once, and he'd smiled and laughed, tipping his head back, the strong cords in his neck working. Yes, he'd behaved as if she mattered. And then he'd simply vanished. Oh well.

Darn him! Why did he have to ignore her like this? Disappointment settled in her stomach like too big a meal.

It was five-thirty by the time the Jeeps came lumbering into camp. Over the front of one of them, strapped to the hood, was a young bull. Someone had been lucky. Evan, she hoped.

And speaking of Evan, Nicola thought, where in the devil *was* Matt? What if the two of them began that one-upmanship routine and the battle raged? Everyone's week would be ruined.

The hunters were dog tired and starving, dusty and scratchy eyed, but undaunted by the long day.

"Hey, Nicola!" Dave Huff's voice. "Come and see what the greater white hunter here bagged!" It was Dave's elk. They strung it up in between the trees—tradition—and told tall tales as to how Dave had tripped over it sleeping in the woods. "Don't believe a word of it," Dave told her, and patted her so hard on the back she jumped. "Oops, sorry," he said. "I forgot you were a girl."

Where was Matt?

Should she warn Evan?

The men tromped inside the main cabin, put their feet up, lit cigars—three of them coughed—and poured themselves stiff brandies. If they behaved like this all year long, Nicola knew, they'd all be dead of strokes.

"Great animal," Evan said to Nicola. "Did you see it? Damn, but I'm jealous. Tomorrow's my turn, boys," he said, brandishing the cigar. "You bet it is."

"Want to put a hundred on it?" Terry Swanson asked, his hunter's eye challenging.

"Sure," Evan said. "A hundred it is."

"Long day," said Eric Field. "My back hurts like crazy."

"I have some liniment," Jon Wolff suggested. "Goot for the muscles."

"I'll try anything."

"Yup," Evan said, "it was a good opening day. We passed a couple other camps on our way back, and no one had a thing hanging. Good work, Ron." He saluted the guide with his drink. "Here's to tomorrow. Cheers."

Down went the brandies, fast.

Where *was* Matt?

She'd have to warn Evan. This wasn't fair, to either of them. She'd pull Evan aside and tell him that... The door opened then, and in he strode. Oddly, Nicola noticed, his boots were muddy. So he hadn't been napping, then....

"Hiya, Evan. That your elk outside?"

"Why," Dave said, "it's Matt! Well, I'll be damned! Matt Cavanaugh!"

"Matt," Jon exclaimed, "goot to see you again. Such a surprise."

"Hello," Ron said, "I'm Mitchell. I take it my wife sent you up? I wondered about the Jeep out back."

"Well," Evan said finally, the wind gone out of his sails, "this *is* a surprise."

Matt nodded. "I couldn't call or write, so here I am."

Evan looked at Ron. "Is there room?"

"He's got the spare bunk in Dave's cabin," Nicola said from the kitchen. "I hope that's okay."

"Glad to have him," Dave said.

"Well." Evan put the cigar down in an ashtray. Clearly he was no longer feeling his oats. "I hope this trip isn't jeopardizing a job or anything like that, Matthew."

"Naw. I took a few days off."

"You going to hunt?" Evan asked.

"Now, Evan," Matt said, picking up the brandy bottle, eyeing the label, "you know I'm squeamish about that stuff."

"You gotta be kidding," Terry Swanson said under his breath, disgusted.

The atmosphere had changed dramatically just since Matt had entered. She'd expected something like this. It wasn't that the guys minded the new face or a nonhunter, really. No. It was the tension, a palpable thing, running like a high-power line between father and son. Everyone felt it.

Nicola could hear a chill wind kicking up dust outside. She threw another log on the fire while the men began to talk among themselves once more. But Evan was silent now. Wary. And Matt was unusually quiet, as well.

She brushed off her hands and caught herself glancing at Matt. Gone was the jaunty, carefree demeanor. Instead, she saw a grimace on his face when he stared at his father, almost as if he were in pain.

Why, she asked herself, had he really come here?

CHAPTER FIVE

THE NEXT MORNING at five-thirty, over the sourdough pancakes, it started.

"So, Matt, how're things going with you?" Dave Huff asked jovially, helping himself to more maple syrup.

"Pretty good."

Nicola poured Fred another cup of coffee and checked the diminishing pile of pancakes in the middle of the table.

"You been working anywhere interesting lately?" Dave winked. "Oh, you young kids, footloose and fancy-free."

"Well, I was working at—" Matt began.

"*Kid*. He's no kid," Evan snorted. "And he hasn't *worked* a day in his life."

Nicola felt her heart contract in her chest. *Oh no.* She bustled over. "More coffee, Evan?"

But he was glaring at Matt, tight-lipped, and only shook his head at her query.

"Oh, come on, Evan," Dave said, one of the only men in the world who could josh Evan Cavanaugh and get away with it. "I'd like to hear where he's been."

Matt was looking down at his plate, his expression hidden, but Nicola could see a muscle in his jaw tighten.

"Now, where were you, Matt?" Dave pressed, seemingly oblivious to the tension between the father and son.

Matt raised his head, and Nicola could see that his expression was bland. She whispered up a silent prayer of thanks. "Oh, you know me, here and there. I worked at Haig's Point until last June. It's a great place. My golf game sure improved."

"I'll have to try the courses there sometime," Huff said.

Evan muttered something under his breath.

"Und so, you are verking out here in Colorado now?" Jon asked. When Matt nodded, he said, "You vill not find so much powder skiing as ve have in Canada."

Matt laughed, his carefree self once more. "Maybe not, but I've got a job and a place to live. And Crested Butte's a small, friendly town. I think I'll have a good winter."

"Go on," Evan interjected, "ask him about his job."

Jon looked uneasily from Evan to Matt. He was quite aware of the enmity between the two men, having seen their act on their ski vacations years before. "Und vat is your job?" he asked.

"I'm a bartender at this place called the Wooden Nickel. They say it's real busy during the season. Good tips."

"*Good tips,*" Evan said scornfully.

Nicola went over to him and, under the guise of refilling his cup, laid a hand on his arm gently. Evan switched his eyes up to hers and saw the message there. He looked away quickly, and she hoped he understood her silent plea.

"Hey, Fred," Terry was saying, "you hear the one about the traveling salesman who stopped at a farm? Well, see, this farmer's got three daughters..."

Then Eric had one of his own. "Now wait, fellas, I've got one. Now, let me see, I have to remember the punch line. Oh yeah.... Well, see, there was this traveling salesman stopped at a farm, and there was this crippled pig..."

They all laughed at that one, too, even Evan, and Nicola relaxed. The Coleman lantern hissed and the cabin smelled of freshly brewed coffee and wood smoke and bacon frying, a masculine, congenial atmosphere.

"Well, Dave, my good man, are you gonna let someone else bag a critter today?" Ron asked, blowing smoke across the table.

"You bet your butt! It's somebody else's turn. Who's gonna be the lucky guy?" Dave asked, grinning.

"I feel lucky as hell," Evan said. "I even dreamed about an elk last night. I could see him in my sights, a big buck, turned sideways so I could get a perfect head shot off. You bet, I'm as good as a hundred dollars richer." He sighted along an imaginary rifle barrel and squeezed an imaginary trigger. "Pow."

"Let's go, men," Ron said, heaving himself up, "and see if we can get Evan that elk. Good breakfast, Nick."

"Great pancakes," Dave said warmly.

The others agreed, complimenting her, and she liked their polite, gentlemanly ways with her. She liked cooking for people who appreciated her efforts; it must be her need for reassurance, she guessed, that made her work so hard to get those compliments.

"You're an awfully good cook, Nicola," Matt said. "I didn't realize how talented you were."

"Thanks." Flushing, she looked down. "But it's not talent, it's just hard work."

He looked at her and smiled. "You would say that, wouldn't you?" He pulled on his orange parka. "You take care today and don't work too hard."

"Oh, I'll be fine, don't worry. Enjoy the hiking today."

He started toward the door, ready to follow the other men, then turned back to her.

"Sorry if things got heated up just now."

"Oh, you mean you and Evan," she said after a second. "I guess it was bound to happen, and, uh, don't mind your dad too much. He's just surprised to see you."

"Sure, Evan's surprised. I saw you give him a look at breakfast. Thanks, but I can fight my own battles."

"Maybe the rest of us would rather not have those battles fought in front of us," she said quietly.

"You've got a point there." His curved, guileless grin came back then, and he seemed to swagger a little as he went through the cabin door into the predawn darkness.

Some of the men returned early that afternoon, while Nicola was putting the last ingredients into the beef Bourguignonne: the wine and chopped onions sautéed with bacon, the mushrooms and tomato paste. But they only grabbed some snacks and went to their cabins for naps. A solid week of hunting was grueling business.

Dinner was another round of off-color jokes, cigars and liquor and a detailed discussion of a near miss by Eric Field. "Goddamn, I had him in my sights! I was waiting until he turned just a bit, then he musta heard something, and just as I squeezed the trigger he jumped and took off. It was so close!''

"Sometimes it's good to wait, sometimes it ain't," Ron said. "Those're the breaks."

"Yeah, tough break," Eric agreed.

"There's always tomorrow," Jon pointed out.

"Sure, tomorrow."

"Yeah."

After dinner, Evan paid up on his bet good-naturedly, and they sat around the fire, stocking feet up, balancing brandy snifters on full bellies. Nicola heated water on Old Bertha and washed up. As she was finishing, Matt got up and started drying dishes.

"You don't have to do that," she said.

"I know." But he kept on drying.

"I'm used to doing it."

"I like to keep my hands busy. Bartenders have to wash and dry glasses all night, you know." He held a glass up to the light, squinted and rubbed a spot over again.

"I guess they would," she said. His hands were lean, like his body, capable, dexterous, his movements sure and efficient. She watched him work out of the corner of her eye. His red plaid shirtsleeves were rolled up; his forearms, swelling from strong wrists, had cords in them that stood out as he reached for a bowl and dried it.

When she was done, she turned away from the sink, leaning back against it, still holding a dish towel. "Thanks," she said.

"My pleasure."

Laughter burst from the group around the fire. Terry stood up and began pantomiming some funny happening. "And then he..." Nicola heard him say. The fire crackled in the old stone fireplace and spat a spark up into the darkness.

"This is a great place," Matt commented.

"It is, yes. Ron does a good job."

"So do you."

"Matt..." She hesitated, looking down at her feet, which were thrust out in front of her, crossed at the ankles.

"What?"

"Well, I was just wondering . . . why you came up here. Really."

His gaze met hers steadily. "For a little camping and hiking. R and R."

"Oh."

"You don't sound convinced."

"I'm not."

He shrugged. "Why else would I come up here?"

"I don't know."

"Don't be so serious. I'm here to have a blast, to hear a few new jokes, to enjoy the mountains. And now, kid, I'm one beat guy. I'm going to bed. That cold and lonely bed in my cold and lonely cabin."

She frowned. "See you in the morning, Matt."

"That was an opening. You were supposed to take me up on it."

"I'm just one of the guys, remember?"

He raked her with an outrageous leer. "Not in my book, kid."

The next morning was blintzes, tender crepes wrapped around a cheese and cinnamon and vanilla mixture, topped with sour cream. And blueberry muffins and home fries again. It had snowed a little in the night; Nicola had walked through the light dusting on her way to the main cabin.

Fred, losing his reserve finally, was hopping with delight. "They'll be easy to track this morning! Oh boy, it's my day! I can taste success already. How sweet it is!"

"If it snows too hard, we'll have to come back early. These storms can be real bad. Somebody gets caught in one every year," Ron said.

"Let's hurry then," Fred suggested.

"Chow's on," Nicola called.

It didn't snow that day, and Nicola got some hand laundry done in the sink with water she'd heated up. She also washed her hair, then sat with her back to Old Bertha to dry it and read a little more in the novel she'd brought along, not that she'd had much spare time to read.

That evening the hunters returned empty-handed once again, but they'd seen a herd of cow elk in a secluded valley and were going back the next day in search of the bulls. Dinner was pork loin, roasted and stuffed with prunes, and a linzertorte for dessert: ground nuts and butter and sugar in the crust and Mrs. Mitchell's raspberry jam baked in the center.

"Oh God, I'm going to burst," Eric Field said, and everyone laughed at him enviously because he was so skinny.

Matt pushed himself back from the table and set down his coffee cup. "Nicola, that was great. Worth walking twenty miles uphill and freezing all day."

"I'm taking you home to Aspen with me," Dave teased. "Ruthie won't mind. She'd love not having to cook."

"I might ask you for some of your vunderful recipes," Jon said. "So delicious. I could serve them at the lodge."

"I'd be glad to give them to you," Nicola said, flattered.

"For a free week of skiing," Evan advised jokingly.

"Maybe ve could verk something out," Jon replied, not seeing the humor, and everyone laughed again.

"You going into town tomorrow?" Ron asked Nicola.

"Yes, I think so." Town was the tiny, picturesque hamlet of Redstone, fifteen miles away in the Crystal River Valley. "I'm getting short on a lot of things."

"Can you get me a carton of Marlboros? I'm about out," Ron said. He glanced at Jon. "Some of these ex-smokers this week have been bumming my packs. Right, Jon?"

Jon grimaced.

"Sure."

Everyone was tired that night, sitting around sipping drinks, talking desultorily. Terry dozed off, jerked awake, swore, got up and said he was going to bed.

Nicola was checking her supplies and making a shopping list for her foray to the grocery store.

"So, Matthew," she heard Evan say, "doesn't your new boss expect you back at work?"

"Oh, I have the whole week off," Matt replied easily.

"You just started, boy. How can you have the whole week off?"

"It's not busy yet, not until Thanksgiving, when the skiing starts," Matt said evenly.

Nicola looked up. Evan had been tolerating his son for the past couple of days. Things had been going along relatively smoothly—until now.

"Some sense of responsibility! I can tell you, no employee of mine would take a week's vacation when he'd just been hired."

The other men avoided one another's eyes.

"And that job last spring. You got fired. Probably for drinking too much, if the truth be known."

"Lay off, Evan," Matt said lightly. "No one wants to listen to family quarrels."

"You can't keep a job."

"My boss at Haig's Point was a jerk."

"They all are, according to you."

Nicola closed her eyes.

"Boy, am I bushed," Eric said, rising. "See you in the a.m., guys."

Carefully Nicola wrote: butter, milk, parsley, lasagna noodles, oh, and cigarettes for Ron. Her back was bowed to the inevitable onslaught.

"I suppose you've gone through your trust fund," Evan continued. He was like a bulldog; once he had his teeth into something, he couldn't let go.

"Oh, there's a little left," Matt replied offhandedly, as if he hadn't a care in the world, as if his father's argumentative abuse didn't faze him.

He was disappointed in Matt, Nicola told herself. He was hurting and he couldn't help taking it out on his son, but oh, he *could* wait until they were alone.

"Well, Evan," Matt drawled, getting to his feet, "I think we've provided enough entertainment for the evening. Good night, all."

"Take it easy, Matt," Dave Huff said kindly.

"Guten Nacht," Jon said.

"Goddamn kid," Evan muttered when the door was closed behind his son.

"Ah, let him be, Evan," Dave said. "You're not going to change him at this late date."

"I guess not. But, hell, the least he could do is pick up a gun and hunt with it."

Nicola pulled her parka off a wall peg and threw it over her shoulders. "See you in the morning."

"See you, Nick."

Once in her chilly room, she turned on the Coleman lantern, debated whether to build a fire in the potbelly stove but decided not to. She was too tired. She stripped down to her long underwear, shivering, ready to crawl under the down comforter but realized she'd forgotten to turn off the lamp. She stepped gingerly across the cold floor, up to the dresser where the lamp stood, and happened to glance out the window.

She froze. There was a man across the way, leaning against a wall of the main cabin. She only saw him because the moonlight glistened bone white off his face, casting gaunt shadows on his handsome features. She drew in her breath and totally forgot the cold floor.

He looked so different out there alone, stripped of his insouciance, his clever remarks, his dazzling smile. Had the argument with Evan affected him more than he'd let on?

If he was not enjoying himself, why was he here? Why had he come in the first place? He could have hiked around Crested Butte. But if he came to bug Evan, he should be pleased—he'd certainly done *that*.

She studied him as he stood there in the darkness, and she knew it was a terrible thing to do, to intrude on a person's privacy, but she couldn't stop herself. There was something so lonely about the figure out there in the cold, something she recognized, as if he were suffering the same sort of bereavement she herself had so often felt.

Without considering the consequences, without her usual caution, without her promise to herself to be wary, Nicola pulled on her jeans, stepped into her boots and shrugged on her parka. Letting herself out of her cabin, she went out into the cold night and moved silently across the clearing.

The stream in the canyon burbled, muffled male laughter came from the main cabin, and he must not have heard her approach.

"Matt?"

He stiffened, startled, and whirled to face her.

"Sorry, I didn't mean—"

"What are you doing out here?" he asked.

"I meant to ask you that."

"Just getting some fresh air."

"I thought you might be...upset at Evan," she said carefully.

"He's quite a bully, isn't he?"

"Not to me."

"No, not to you."

"There's good in Evan, really there is. I just wish... I mean, why is it that you two are always at each other like that?" She searched his face in the darkness, but the shadows hid any expression that might have enlightened her.

He gave a short, bitter laugh. "What can I say? Evan is so damn competitive, he feels threatened by his own sons. One he chased away, the other is his slave. Poor T.J."

Poor Matt, Nicola thought. Aloud she said, "It's a shame."

"Thanks for the thought, kid," he replied nonchalantly.

"I just wondered...when I saw you out here... Well, I guess I shouldn't have bothered you."

There was a pause then, a split second of awareness between them that held Nicola immobile. Matt shifted forward, reached out to touch her cold cheek with a finger, and she felt a tremor of excitement, bright and breathless, rippling outward from his touch. He dropped his hand, started to say something, then gave up and strode away into the night shadows.

TUESDAY MORNING'S BREAKFAST was whole-grain waffles covered with sliced bananas, chopped walnuts and maple syrup.

"Sorry, no home fries today," Nicola said. "I've got to buy more potatoes."

"We'll forgive you this time," Dave said, his pale blue eyes twinkling.

"Let's get going," Evan said impatiently. "We only have a few days left."

Matt leaned back in his chair and stuck his thumbs in his belt. "I don't think I'll go out hiking with you guys today. You mind, Ron?"

"Suit yourself."

"Too tough for you?" Evan asked, prodding.

"Too intense," Matt replied, shooting him a glance. "I think I'll get a ride into Redstone with Nick here."

She looked up, surprised.

"Is that okay with you?" Matt asked her.

"Sure. Why not?" But there was hesitation in her voice.

The other men were on their way out. "Maybe he's got the right idea," Eric said. "Warm and cozy and good company."

"I'd rather bag an elk," Evan muttered.

"See you later, kids," Dave called over his shoulder.

There was silence when the hunters left except for their voices outside and the growl of the Jeeps starting, then dying away. Nicola stayed deliberately busy, filling the big pot with water from the pump, starting to lift it.

"Here, let me," Matt said at her shoulder, very close behind her. She was afraid to move, afraid she'd touch him, but he stepped in front of her and lifted the pot onto Bertha.

"Ron'll have to start paying you," Nicola said too brightly.

"Perhaps we can *verk* something out," he replied, imitating Jon so comically that she couldn't help laughing.

"You really want to go into Redstone?" she asked, looking at him.

"Well, to tell the truth, I have to check in with my boss. I promised." He leaned close to her and whispered conspiratorially, "I just didn't want Evan to find out I really am responsible. It would ruin my image."

"Oh, I see." She stood there, hands on hips, dishrag in one fist, studying him. He meant it; he really meant it. He wanted his father to think the worst of him. He wanted to punish Evan. "Won't you two ever grow up?"

He grinned. "Hey, where would the fun be then?"

She began to clear the table, wiping at the spills of sticky syrup, turning her back to him. *Men.* They never grew up, not any of them. They never seemed to suffer any sort of sadness for long. They just used women and important words but meant nothing by those words. They didn't even know the real meaning of them. If Nicola ever found a man who meant what he said, who didn't play juvenile games, she'd probably fall in love on the spot.

"You're mad at me," Matt said from behind her.

She shook her head silently, piling dirty dishes up.

"You are, I can tell. You think I'm immature and irritating, like Evan does."

She carried the dishes to the old tin sink and checked the water on the stove. "What if I do?"

When she turned to retrace her footsteps to the table, he was there in front of her, blocking the way. "Don't be mad. It's not worth the effort, kid." Then he tilted her chin up and stared down into her eyes. He was so close she could feel his warm breath and smell the fresh scent of him. His expression was serious for once, his mouth a straight line instead of a curve, his dark brows drawn together. They stood that way for too long, and her heart pounded in her chest as if it would fly through her rib cage. She could feel her cheeks flushing and heat crawling up her neck.

"Matt," she finally whispered, her mouth dry.

"You're as pretty as a picture, Nicky," he replied softly.

"Matt, don't."

He dropped his hand, then gave her an impudent smile. "And a damn good cook, besides."

The spell was broken, and maybe he'd meant that to happen. She cleared the table, scrubbed it clean, soaked the dishes, all in silence. And she washed them while Matt dried, in silence, too, except that he whistled popular tunes while he worked, leaning one buttock against the counter, casual and lazy and much too good-looking.

More than an hour later, her chores done, Nicola checked her shopping list, added a few things and took her coat off the peg. "You ready?" she asked.

"Sure. We can take my Jeep. Or would you rather drive?"

"You drive." That'd keep his hands and his eyes busy, she figured.

It took thirty minutes to reach Redstone, a two-block-long village down in the valley, a tiny place right on the banks of the Crystal River, its main road overhung by giant cottonwood trees. The stores and houses were all fixed up in quaint Victorian style, and up on a hill overlooking the town was the famous haunted mansion called the Redstone Castle, built by coal baron John Cleveland Osgood at the turn of the century. Redstone had been planned originally to house workers for the old coke furnaces just outside of town, but it was now mainly a tourist haven.

"Where can I find a phone?" Matt asked as soon as they turned off the highway and crossed the river on a rickety old bridge that gave onto the one and only street Redstone boasted.

"I guess the tourist information building would be the easiest." It occurred to Nicola momentarily to wonder at this uncharacteristic single-mindedness of Matt and his telephone call, but she directed him to the small log building that was also an art gallery and souvenir shop. It was open because of hunting season but would close soon, as no one ventured to Redstone in the winter, preferring the opposite end of the valley, where the ski resort of Aspen was located.

He parked in front and they went in. "There's the phone," Nicola said, pointing.

"Oh, good, I'll just be a second."

She nodded to the girl behind the counter. "Nice day," she commented.

"It's been a good fall." Which Nicola took to mean lots of hunters buying beer and ammo and postcards.

Idly she looked at the postcard displays. Matt had his back to her, but he was dialing a number on the old-fashioned black wall phone. She could hear the dial whirl, and it whirled too many times, as all of western Colorado used the same area code, 303, and you didn't need to dial that code at all to reach Crested Butte.

She kept looking through postcards, not even seeing the scenes of the Maroon Peak or Redstone Castle or the Hot Springs Pool in nearby Glenwood Springs. She wondered who Matt really was calling and why he'd lied to her, why he'd *bothered* lying to her. So maybe it was a girl, not his boss. Did she care? *Big secret.*

She listened to his voice, low and urgent, and couldn't help straining to hear. He was probably trying to convince this femme fatale to come out and meet him here, or something like that. And Nicola bet he could be persuasive, very persuasive. However, he had a hand up to the receiver, muffling his voice, and she couldn't really hear a thing. Not that she'd wanted to.

He hung up finally, looking a little thoughtful. Probably the woman had turned him down. Smart girl. "Okay, that's done," he said. "I'm not needed yet."

"Hmm. Well, that's good." She'd better play along. No sense embarrassing them both. Still, the idea that he'd lied to her, the notion that he'd just been talking to another woman, was more unsettling than she cared to admit.

"So, onward to the grocery store, right?" he was saying.

"Right."

She bought five big bags full of groceries, paid with one of Ron's signed checks, and they carried them all out and wedged them in the back seat of the Jeep.

"There," she said, "that'll be it for the week."

He shut the flimsy Jeep door, latching it after three tries. "Now, after all that hard work, how about a beer?"

"A beer? Isn't it a little early?"

He checked his watch. "Hell, no. It's after eleven. Tell you what, you get a beer *and* a burger for lunch. What do you say?"

"Well, I have to get back and start . . ."

"Come on, take a break. I'm starved myself."

"Okay, a quick one."

There was only one saloon in town, in the Redstone Inn. They sat at the bar, and Matt ordered two draft beers and two burgers with the works. And French fries.

"Not as classy as your cooking," he explained, "but you need a break from time to time."

They could see themselves in the mirror behind the bar, the only customers in town this time of day: a handsome man in a hunter's plaid shirt who looked utterly at ease, and a dark-haired girl who was a little tense, a little distracted, halfway between laughter and tears.

Why did I agree to this? Nicola thought, switching her eyes away from the mirror. *What's wrong with me?* Matt was not the kind of man she liked or wanted to like. Why did fate keep throwing them together? Or was it fate? And why was he pursuing her when it was that woman on the phone he really wanted?

But Matt was talking to the girl behind the bar, a snazzy blonde dressed in tight jeans and a satin cowboy shirt. "Oh, it sure does liven up in here come evening," the girl was saying. "All those hunters away from Big Mama and rarin' to go."

"I'll bet. And you're the belle of the ball. You work here all winter?" Matt asked, turned on his charm like a well-oiled motor.

"No, I work in Aspen in the winter."

"You don't say. You know, I'm bartending in Crested Butte myself. Are the skiers big tippers?"

The blonde rolled big blue eyes. "Are they ever!"

"Maybe I'll come up to Aspen skiing this winter. I'll look you up. Where do you work?"

"The Red Onion."

"Sure, I've heard of it."

The girl leaned on the bar, her satin-sheathed breasts resting on the polished wood. "Hey, you do that. Ask for Sunny."

"I'll do that . . . Sunny."

Oh boy, Nicola thought. She was getting to see him in action. And as far as Sunny was concerned, it wouldn't have mattered if Matt had been with a girl or alone. All's fair in love and war was Sunny's motto, obviously. Nicola sipped at her beer and ate the hamburger, which wasn't at all bad. Matt ate and drank, still talking to Sunny. He did draw Nicola into the conversation, she had to admit, but the blond girl behind the bar barely noticed her existence. Not that it mattered.

Sunny was sending off signals, loud and clear, embarrassingly clear.

"Matt, we have to go," Nicola said quietly. "I have dinner to fix."

"Oh, sure. Well, Sunny, it's been fun. My sister here has to get back. Take care."

"See you on the hill this winter," Sunny cooed coyly.

Matt waved, stuck a bill under a plate and turned to go, but not before Nicola noticed two things: the bill was a ten-dollar one, and his beer glass was still half-full.

Strange, for a lush. The large tip, on the other hand, wasn't a bit odd.

"What was with the sister routine?" she asked once they were outside.

"I didn't want to hurt Sunny's feelings," he said. "I didn't want her to realize I like you better."

"Oh, Matt."

"There I go being immature again, right?"

She got into the Jeep and folded her arms across her chest, and he climbed in beside her. "Nicola, I was just being friendly. I like to talk to people."

"Your *sister*."

"Jealous, kid?" he asked impertinently.

She whirled to face him. "The only thing I might have to be jealous of were her oversized mammary glands!"

"Yes, they were considerable, weren't they?" Chuckling, he started up the Jeep and rumbled toward the highway.

They bounced in silence for a time, until Nicola felt foolish and unfolded her arms. "Let me ask you one thing, Matthew Cavanaugh."

"Sure, anything."

"Why do I keep running into you? I mean, I have barely seen you since I was ten, and all of a sudden, wherever I turn, there you are."

"Coincidence."

"No."

"Luck?" He laughed, then and laid a hand on her knee. "Didn't I say we should get to know each other better? I think I said that."

"Why?"

"Because I like you."

His hand was on her knee, warm and solid, but then he had to steer around a large pothole on the road and took it away. The spot still felt warm, though.

"Come on, Nicky, relax. Aren't I allowed to like you?"

She was confused. It would be easy to believe him, pleasant and flattering, and what harm could come of a simple friendship? On the other hand, her instincts, her experience, told her that he was dangerous. He could hurt her. Better safe than sorry.

"Well, can't I?" he pressed.

"You can if you want to," she said flatly, "but it may not do you a bit of good."

He laughed at that, throwing his head back, a free laughter that made her want to laugh with him. But she didn't.

They climbed up the highway to McClure Pass, and Matt turned off onto the dirt road to the hunting camp. It was cooler up here; a few clouds were scudding in from the west, but the good weather still held. Matt maneuvered the Jeep over rocks, around potholes, up hills, jouncing along the rough terrain. Nicola was thinking of what she had to do first: boil the rice, as it took forever at this altitude. Stuff the capons. *They'd* take all afternoon. It was a moment before she realized that the Jeep was at a standstill. She glanced over at Matt only to find him turned toward her, his left arm resting on the steering wheel, his right arm resting on the back of her seat.

"Is something . . . I mean, is the Jeep broken?" she asked.

"No."

"Then . . . ?"

"Nicola." He said it caressingly, and abruptly she was afraid. She froze, holding her breath, knowing what was coming, terrified but knowing and perversely longing for it. The moth flying into the flame.

His right hand moved a little, going to the back of her head, creating a small, insistent pressure that she gave in to. Closer. Their lips met softly, then, harder. Inside Nicola was a new sensation, a wonderful, wild sensation, as if she were for the first time in her life free of all restraint, feeling pleasure in a purity she never knew existed, a white-hot shaft of wonder that scalded her all the way to her belly. She felt a frantic desire to touch every part of him, to pull him close, to fuse herself with him, to lose herself in the sensations, in him, for a moment of oblivion.

They broke apart finally, and reality came flooding back to her. Her breath came in great, shuddering gasps, and she felt dizzy.

"Nicola," he said again, his hand still on the back of her head.

She wanted to run, to hide from him, from her own response. She felt the desperation of a hunted creature, the deathly confusion of the prey, but she could only sit there rooted to the spot, held there by pride and Matt's knowing blue eyes.

CHAPTER SIX

THE ACCIDENT HAPPENED at dawn.

Most of the men, all but Evan and Eric and Fred, had already gone up in the first Jeep to their hunting spots, but the second Jeep, it was discovered, had a flat. The three men quickly changed the tire.

Nicola saw it happen. She was out in front of the main cabin, waving goodbye to the men. "Too bad about the flat," she said, lifting her hand to see them off, when abruptly and without warning there was a whooshing sound, and a puff of dust kicked up in the dirt right next to Evan's foot. An instant later came the crack of the gunshot echoing through the valley.

The tableau remained stationary for a split second—everyone paralyzed in whatever position the shot had found them, like one of the lifelike dioramas in a natural history museum. The pause seemed to last forever, yet it was over in an instant, the very instant Eric shouted, "Hit the ground! Holy—"

They all reacted immediately and mindlessly, dropping to the earth, covering their heads, waiting for another shot to whistle by and plow itself into a solid object.

Nicola lay there, too, stiff, her skin quivering, waiting for that shot, that high-powered bullet that would rip into Evan or Fred or Eric or her. It was an endless wait.

Eventually someone let out a pent-up breath, someone else moved, someone whistled, a long, low, shaky sound.

"I think it's okay," Fred said. "We can get up now. God, that was close." He climbed to his feet, dusting himself off, staring in the direction from which the shot had come.

"Evan," Nicola breathed, still shocked and breathless, "are you all right?" She hurried to his side and took his arm.

"Hey," he said, trying to laugh, "that was a close one. I'd like to get my hands on the idiot who fired that rifle."

"How in God's name," Eric was saying, "could someone mistake a man—a man in bright orange standing next to a Jeep in the middle of camp—for a goldarn elk?"

No one had an answer to that one.

Nicola gave the near miss a lot of consideration that morning as she worked, but another subject kept intruding into her musings, too: Matt and the Jeep ride back from Redstone. What a blind, pathetic thing she'd done, letting him see her out of control, panting after him, clinging to him, mindlessly in need. Stupid, stupid, stupid!

Yet she had responded. And where there was smoke, there was fire. Darn him with those magic blue eyes and that all-knowing grin of his. For a moment, she'd really felt that Matt cared about her, that he was trying to tell her something, or show her something, by that kiss. For a moment ... Darn, he was a puzzle to her! Why, why did he keep turning up like a bad penny?

She shook her head and sighed and went back to work. Evan. He was the one she had to think about. Eric Field had, of course, put it in a nutshell. Evan had been climbing into a Jeep, the main cabin directly behind him, his orange coat and hat on. How had that hunter mistaken him for game?

Or maybe, just maybe, it had not been an accident.

She was folding cloth napkins, sitting at the table, when suddenly she stopped cold and dropped the linen.

Hadn't it been only days ago, around November 1, that Evan had announced to the press that he was definitely calling in those Costa Plata loans? And the political experts had given the president of that country, Cisernos, just a short time at the outside for his junta to collapse. Had someone from Costa Plata panicked? Was someone seeking revenge?

She recalled with utter clarity Reynaldo Reyes's threat: call in those loans and Evan was a dead man.

Come on, Nicola, that's crazy.

But was it?

Anyone could have found out Evan's whereabouts this week. And wouldn't a hunting "accident" be convenient?

Everyone who'd been in camp when the shot had narrowly missed Evan, knew the general direction from which it had come. She wondered, as she began to fold napkins again, if the hunter, the would-be hunter, had been sitting in his spot just waiting. And if so, wouldn't there be evidence, like broken branches or flattened down grass, a discarded Styrofoam coffee cup, a chewing gum wrapper, *something*? If a man had been there for a long time, waiting, then maybe he'd left some kind of evidence behind—especially after missing his target. He'd have run, and quickly. And he could have been careless.

Nicola knew she was really reaching when she laced up her heavy boots and put on her parka and gloves. She'd never find the spot. She didn't even know what exactly she was looking for. Nevertheless, she headed out of camp on foot and hiked to the northwest, having sighted a couple of high spots where a man might have waited and watched, staring toward the camp.

It was slow going. Hiking around in the meadow was one thing, but the path she took, a sort of crisscross game trial, led her through unbroken territory. Lots of thicket and buck brush, lots of hidden holes she turned her ankles in, lots of fallen logs. And she was climbing, to boot.

Figuring that a hunting rifle with a good scope could have an accurate range of a couple hundred yards, she pushed on up the steep mountainside, zigzagging the area, her eyes to the ground. It was not only tedious walking, but seemingly futile, as well. Sure, it was easy standing in front of the cabin and looking up, deciding where the shot might have originated, but actually searching the rough terrain...

This is useless, she thought, breathing hard. Maybe it had been an accident, after all. And even if it hadn't been, she wasn't likely to find a darn thing.

She was ready to head back to camp, when she crossed an old mining road that hadn't been used in years. Brush and weeds had inched down the embankment over time and obscured the way, and a part of the road had even slid over the cliff, probably in a spring mudslide. Curious, she followed it, finding the way much easier than breaking ground through the woods. If she followed it downward long enough, she thought, it might even bring her out in the meadow somewhere, and she'd be home free. What a waste of an hour this had been.

She'd been following footprints for nearly thirty yards before the fact even registered in her head. The old road was muddy from the recent snowfall, and the prints were as fresh as some of the deer droppings she was seeing.

"Wow," Nicola whispered, realizing that she might just have come across the intruder's path. "You don't suppose...?"

She followed the tracks for a few more yards, then lost them. Backtracking, she could see where the man had left the trail and headed off into the woods. She glanced at her watch. It was getting late, and dinner still had to be prepared. But she might be onto something here.

She trudged through a dark stand of firs, the pinecones crunching beneath her boots, the fallen needles smelling fresh and damp. Then she broke out into a clearing, a small, steep hillside, at the bottom of which were some rocks. Was this the spot she'd viewed from the cabin? Trying to keep from breaking into an uncontrolled run down the hill, Nicola stepped carefully, keeping her balance. In an unmelted patch of snow, she saw a single footprint and her heart began a rapid beating. *Someone* had come this way. And recently.

The rock escarpment, three massive boulders balancing on a perilous cliff, kept its secrets. There were no prints, no signs of anyone having ever been there. She looked around the area, careful to stay away from the edge, and was disappointed to see nothing whatsoever. Shrugging, figuring she'd been following a perfectly innocent hunter, and angry that she'd wasted so much time, she turned around sharply, ready to beat a quick path home.

She saw it then. The sunlight bounced off the metal and struck her squarely in the eye. Nicola walked over to the grassy spot, leaned over and picked up the shell casing. She was no rifle buff, but it sure looked like a 30-06, a very common caliber of ammunition. Excited, she scoured the area. Yes! There were some depressions in the grass. Someone could have been sitting or kneeling right there...and, oh wow, a cigarette butt. No, three of them! On the paper just below the filters was stamped the name Marlboro.

Several thoughts invaded her mind at once. First, to smoke three cigarettes took time. Whoever had been there had been there for a while. Waiting for a clear shot of Evan? And secondly, hadn't she just bought Ron a whole carton of Marlboros? He'd said something about people bumming his cigarettes... But who? Who had he meant? They were all smoking cigars every night, but who was smoking cigarettes?

"It's amazing," came a voice that made her jump out of her skin, "the people you find roaming the woods."

Nicola's hand flew to her heart. "Damn it all, Matt Cavanaugh, you scared me out of my wits! Darn you!"

"Sorry," he said, smiling, striding up to her. "But I didn't see you."

"I bet."

"Honest. I came along the ridge. Anyway, what in the devil are you doing up here?"

Nicola eyed him carefully. "I might ask you the same thing."

"Now what does it look like I'm doing—swimming?"

"Ha, ha." She watched as he took a long drink from his water bottle, then passed it to her. "Thanks." She drank, thirstier than she'd realized, and wiped her mouth on her sleeve. "Well," she said, gazing up at him boldly, holding her own, "you left with the first Jeep this morning, so I guess you haven't heard yet."

"Heard what?"

While he rocked back on his heels and listened, hardly believing, she told him the whole story. Then she stuck out her hand and unfolded her fist. "A shell casing," she said, "and these cigarette butts. They're Marlboros," she concluded, satisfied.

"Right you are, Marlboros," he said, taking them from her. "This *is* Marlboro country, Nicky. Plenty of people smoke the things."

"You aren't taking this one bit seriously, are you?"

"An assassination attempt on Evan?" he said, trying to hide a smile. "Come on, kid, that's kind of farfetched, isn't it?"

She shot him a disgruntled look. "You were there when that Reyes character threatened Evan. And don't you think it's a

little too coincidental that Evan nearly gets shot just days after
he tells the world he's calling in those loans?"

"So he is going through with it?"

"Don't you read, Matt?" she asked.

"Hey, Crested Butte is one laid-back town, Nicky. We hardly
get up in the morning and run out front to get the *New York
Times*."

"So you don't even care about Evan's safety, do you." It
wasn't a question. "And here I've got evidence, right in my
hand, and you ignore it."

"Really," Matt said, trying to sound contrite, "I just don't
see what's got you so fired up."

"I don't suppose you would."

They hiked back to camp in silence, and Nicola could not
help but question his complacent attitude. How could a son
possibly be so unfeeling, so out of touch with a parent's troubles? She glanced at him several times, then shook her head in
wonder.

NICOLA WAS LATE putting dinner on the table, and the men,
some of them, at least, were in a foul mood. Two had missed
shots at a bull elk, and one had sprained his ankle, Terry
Swanson, the avid, gung ho hunter from North Carolina.

"How am I going to hunt like this?" he said, chewing on his
cigar in disgust, his swollen ankle up on a chair.

"You could find a good spot and sit there," Eric suggested.

"That's how much you know," Swanson spat back. "Cali-
fornians."

Jon Wolff was quiet, as well, barely exclaiming over Nicola's fare; evidently he'd spent the whole day hiking the harder
terrain and had been one of the men to miss a shot.

"There's tomorrow," Ron suggested, casting Nicola a helpless glance. "We'll hang another in camp tomorrow. I can feel
it. Weather's turning, too. Snow in the air. Right, Nick?"

She was serving up second helpings of creamed carrots. "You
bet. We're in for a real blow. That'll move the animals around."
She caught Matt's eye then, inadvertently, and looked away too
quickly. How *could* she have kissed him? But worse, far, far
worse, he knew she'd responded like a lovesick spinster. He

probably felt sorry for her. *Here, let's throw the lady a bone or two, it doesn't have to mean a thing. Do her a favor.* Oh God.

Where had those promises she'd made herself gone? How could she have done that? A time machine, that's what she needed, a way of getting another chance. Given that second chance, she'd repel his advance, say all kinds of right-on things and ease out of the situation like a pro. But he knew she was insecure and hopeless around men. Sure he did. And he'd taken advantage.

"Carrots?"

"What?" Nicola said, shaken from her reverie.

It was Dave. "I asked for more carrots, Nick. Earth to Nick, come in Nick." He got a laugh from the group.

"Very funny," she said, spooning Dave a heaping pile. "Eat them. They're good for your eyesight. Maybe you'll hunt better tomorrow."

"Got me!" Huff said admiringly.

How could Matt take everything so casually? How could he not care about Evan's safety? No matter their relationship—and half the fault was Evan's—Matt should at least have responded with . . . with alarm, with worry, at least with concern when she'd told him about the shot. She fixed him with a dark glare.

So far, Nicola had kept secret her find up in the woods that day. She'd been planning to show everyone immediately, but something held her back, an invisible hand of warning. All evening she kept thinking about those cigarette butts and about the other Jeep having left at least a half hour before Evan's. Anyone could have hiked to that place on the escarpment, and some of them were smokers, too.

Eric, the Californian? No one knew much about him. Was he a . . . a hit man? Oh my gosh. . . .

Or that Terry Swanson, the drinker who never got too drunk, with his thick, North Carolinian accent. He'd had plenty of experience with guns. How had he really sprained his ankle—running from that spot after he'd missed? Nicola glanced over at him from the kitchen, eyeing him speculatively.

It was Jon Wolff, though, she suddenly remembered, who'd been bumming cigarettes. She looked at him, at his sharp,

German features, his tall, lean build. Maybe Jon had taken that potshot at Evan. For money? For political reasons? There certainly were a lot of Austrians who had emigrated to Central America, maybe to Costa Plata. Did Jon, or someone close to him, have interests there?

Whoa, Nicola thought. She was sure letting the old imagination fly. Next thing, she'd be thinking Ron did it—a prearranged payoff from a Costa Plata source. *Sure, Nick.*

Regardless, she had to get Evan aside and show him what she'd found. He had to be warned. Just in case.

The men were, needless to say, discussing hunting safety when she served dessert. No one had forgotten the near miss that morning, apparently. And maybe it was just that, after all, an accident—a stupid, half-blind hunter, a bullet that had ricocheted.

Casually she tapped Evan on the shoulder and nodded toward the door. No one paid him any mind when he stood, stretched and put on his coat. Nor did anyone think about Nicola's departure, or so she thought. What neither she nor Evan saw was Matt's somber gaze following them out the door.

"My, Nicola," Evan said, zipping up his parka, "you're looking awfully mysterious."

Nicola, too, zipped up and thrust her hands in her pockets. "I had to talk to you alone," she began, pacing back and forth in front of him, stomping her feet in the cold. "It's about that accident this morning."

"Come on," Evan said, shaking his head, "that's all I've listened to today."

"Well, I'm sorry," she said, "but you have to listen again. There's something I've got to show you."

The cabin door opened and closed then, and one of the men stepped into the shadows toward them. "What's going on?" It was Matt.

Darn. He'd only make light of everything. "I'm having a private conversation with Evan," she stated, wishing he'd go away.

"Don't tell me," he said, "it's about 30-06 shell casings and Marlboros."

"That's right," Nicola said, "and I intend to have my say."

"What's this all about?" Evan asked.

"Oh, Nicky here'll tell you," Matt replied. He looked her in the eye then and nodded. "Go ahead."

Nicola produced the casing and cigarette butts from her pocket and handed them to Evan. She told him how she'd found them and gave him a detailed summary of her theory. "It's just too coincidental," she said, "your calling in those loans, that Reyes's threat, and now this."

Evan sighed. "Nicola, I appreciate your concern, honestly I do, but the whole thing's preposterous." He handed the things back to her.

"It's not!" she insisted.

"Television," Evan said, scoffing, "and all those thrillers you kids read. It's making you confuse fantasy and reality."

Nicola shook her head in frustration. "Why are you so stubborn, Evan?"

"Me? I'd call it sensible. Some nut made a mistake this morning. That's all. Hunting accidents happen every day."

"I'd tell you I think Nicola's got a point, but you always know best, Evan," Matt said sarcastically.

"Well, well," Evan said, turning to him. "I'd almost think you give a damn."

"Don't read too much into a simple statement," Matt replied.

"Come on, you two, *please*. This is serious," Nicola begged, but they were ignoring her.

"Look, Evan, I'm really not in the mood to argue. Do whatever you want, stay and get shot, it's none of my business."

"You know what you are?" Evan said. "You're a coward, boy. It would be just like you to turn tail and run when the going got tough. You're a wet-behind-the-ears kid, not to mention a bum. Don't tell *me* what to do when you can't even get your own act together."

They faced off like two snarling dogs, neither giving ground. Nicola, afraid to move, stayed in the shadows and felt utterly helpless. Evan's face, turned to the light from the cabin, was diffused with red, and Matt's profile, partially obscured, looked pale and ghostly.

"Well?" Evan was saying, "none of your smart-alecky remarks, boy? Nothing to say?"

"Oh," Matt replied coolly, bitterly, "I have plenty to say, Evan. But now's not the time or place."

"I think the timing is perfect, boy. This has been coming."

Matt folded his arms across his chest. "You really want to hear it, don't you?"

"Please," Nicola tried, her voice a whisper. Oh God, why did they have to do this to each other?

Neither seemed to have heard her plea. Evan thrust his face toward Matt's. "Why don't you get what's eating you off your chest, boy?"

"Okay, fine. I don't mind at all telling you what a lousy father you are, Evan. You drive me out of the house every time I see you. You always have. Even when I was a kid, you pushed and pushed. 'Say, Matt, a B's decent, but let's try for an A next time.... Oh, Matt, I know you won that swim meet, but you could extend your arms more.' Yeah, Evan," Matt said, boiling now, "you're the reason I'm a bum. And as for my brother—"

"What about T.J.?" Evan was in a rage. "What right do you have to criticize him?"

"Plenty. You've driven the guy half out of his mind. You've held the presidency of the family bank over his head for ten years now, dangling it like a carrot. And Mom, she's been in the middle of it all. Just look at how T.J. has to cling to her skirts because he can't talk to you. You're driving them both nuts, Evan!"

"Go to hell."

"Maybe I will. But I'll see you there, Evan, you can bet on that." Matt stormed back into the cabin abruptly, his face ashen, his hands held at his sides in white-knuckled fists. Seconds later he emerged, a bottle of Wild Turkey tucked under his arm, and strode toward his own cabin.

"Go ahead," Evan yelled after him, "get drunk! You couldn't possibly act like a man, could you?"

All the while Nicola was standing there, hugging herself with her arms, shaking, trying not to cry. The door of the main cabin was open, a rectangle of light spilling out onto the ground, silence coming from within. They'd heard. They'd heard it all, and to a man, they were embarrassed. How could Evan and Matt have done such a cruel thing—not just to themselves, but to everyone?

Dutifully, quietly, she went in and cleaned up the kitchen. Slowly the men began to talk again, their voices low, their eyes avoiding Evan, who sat apart from them, brooding, still hot under the collar. And all the while, she kept seeing Matt's face, pale with rage, beyond frustration. Why did she feel so badly for him? He'd get over it, probably already had, in fact. Why, he probably wasn't even as upset by the fight as *she'd* been. But he'd been so pale; she'd never seen anyone white with fury before, she'd only read the term in books.

Oh Lord....

Dave Huff was talking to Evan. He didn't look as if he were ready to turn in yet. That meant Matt was alone in the cabin, alone with a bottle of Wild Turkey and his thoughts. Alone with the aftermath of a terrible anger and no one to talk to. She took up her parka again, said good-night and headed out along the line of cabins.

"Matt?" She rapped lightly on his door. "It's me. Can I come in?"

"Suit yourself."

She pushed open the door and found him sitting on his bunk, his back to the wall, his knees up, arms hanging loosely over them, the bottle in one hand.

She forced an encouraging smile. "You aren't going to drink that whole thing, are you? I mean, it won't help."

"Don't play shrink with me," he said tightly. "I'm not in the mood."

She sighed, still poised half in the door, half out. "Okay, I won't. But I think you should consider that Evan is probably frightened. But you know how he is."

"Oh yes, I do know that." He took a long swig. At least, when he tipped up the bottle, she could see that it was still nearly full.

"Well," she said, shifting her weight to the other foot, "do you want to talk?"

He hung the bottle over his knee again, negligently, but his face, for once, looked all of his thirty-eight years. For a long, uncomfortable moment, he stared at her, as if deciding. Finally, when she was crawling with tension, he spoke. "Come here."

Tentatively Nicola closed the door and walked to the bed. She sat down gingerly. Her back was to him, and she could sense his reaching out, his fingers touching her long hair lightly—she could feel the need oozing from him like blood from an open wound. Where was the carefree Matt now?

Slowly he pulled her back until she rested in the crook of his arm, her head against his chest. She could hear the heavy beating of his heart. This was how it should have been between a man and a woman, she thought, open and honest, sharing the good and the bad.

Nicola knew he was going to kiss her. The long, corded muscles in his chest and arms were tightening, rippling, anticipating. He'd press her to him, turn her face to his and cover her mouth with those warm lips. She could almost taste him, and she prepared herself.

"Nicky," he whispered, his arm flexing, his hand rubbing her fingers, "this isn't going to help."

Her heart squeezed. Did he think she'd come there to offer herself as if she were some kind of a pill or something?

Sensing her alarm, he laughed lightly. "Said that badly, didn't I? What I meant, what I should have said, is that I need to be alone right now."

"Oh."

"Hey—" he ruffled her hair gently "—I know I must be nuts. I'll get over it, and I'll rue the night I let you go so easily."

"Will you, Matt?" she asked, easing away from his hold. "Will you?" But she never got an answer.

THAT NIGHT, sleep, which normally came to her quickly, was elusive. She couldn't help lying there beneath her down quilt in the cold darkness and wondering about the parallels of their lives. At times, hers seemed worse. At least Matt didn't have a mother who was unable to cope with life, an unhappy woman who had nothing left to offer but tears. And sometimes she'd have given anything to have a good, sound argument with Wentworth. *Something* was better than nothing. But she had her work and her independence, and maybe someday Went would slow down and have time for her. There was always hope.

But Matt. Half his life was already gone, and he'd made nothing of it. And one thing was for sure: a man did not so easily find opportunity in his middle years. He had to already know how to go out into the world and make things happen. Matt had no experience with success; he deliberately avoided it.

Conflicting emotions buffeted her every time she envisioned him. She'd felt wonderfully alive in his arms, trembling with awakened sensation and need. And yet the very pleasure he'd brought her also scared her half to death. To be so dependent on someone else, on a man, when previously she'd stood up, strong and self-sufficient, facing life unencumbered—it was frightening.

She decided that night in the cold silence of her room. She decided that this game she was letting herself be drawn into—the male-female game—was no good. She didn't know how to play it, nor did she want to. She'd made a dumb mistake going to him that night, playing the expected role, but she wouldn't repeat it. A moth might fly into a flame and die, but *she* had another chance.

The next morning she made her way through the cold darkness to the main cabin and lit the Coleman lamps, determined. She wouldn't have lost anything—there hadn't been anything between them to lose. This was it. They were only acquaintances, after all. It wasn't too late.

She lit the wood in the stove, pulled out her pots and pans and then saw it: a small, folded, white piece of paper propped on a burner. She opened it, a hand of foreboding brushing her heart.

Nicky,
Sorry, but I had to get back to work. Say my goodbyes, will you?

Matt

She looked at the note once more, staring at it, blinking away the moisture in her eyes. Then she crushed it in her hand, pulled open the door of the firebox and tossed it in.

CHAPTER SEVEN

MATT BOUNCED ON THE SEAT of the Jeep. It was still dark out, and he was driving too fast, but he felt the powerful urge to put the hunting camp behind him as quickly as possible.

A hideous thought prodded his mind as he steered: his old man deserved everything coming to him. Yet a part of Matt loved Evan; a part of him still remembered when he'd been a small boy and his father had taken him riding and skiing and camping and they'd had great times, father-and-son stuff. So what had happened?

Things must have degenerated during Matt's teenage years, the time a boy had to struggle to rid himself of his father's control. The old king against the young one. In primitive societies, the young king had to kill the old one. In civilized ones, they were only allowed to quarrel. Some fathers, Matt guessed, were able to accept the independence of their sons, but Evan never had. He wanted to run their lives. He *did* run T.J.'s.

Matt pulled the steering wheel sharply to the left to avoid a deep rut. He wondered what Evan would think if he knew what Matt actually did for a living. Would he respect his son then? Or would his present censure merely attach itself to this new information?

Ah, hell, Matt mused, *who cares?*

But then he recalled, without a bridging thought, as if so many years had not gone by, the pain and wild frustration of being powerless against his father, the injustice of it. It was an old story, a cliché, but that didn't lessen the suffering a boy went through. His estrangement from his family had begun long before Ned Copple had gotten his hooks into Matt. What bothered him was that it still hurt so much.

It was well past first light when Matt made the summit of Kebler Pass. Crested Butte was a nice little town, hidden away from the hustle and bustle of the real world. Too bad he'd be leaving it so soon.

Matt had gotten a room in an old painted Victorian bed-and-breakfast place called the Brass Horse. It was inexpensive and strictly for transients, young college types taking a semester off to work and ski in the Rockies. He made his way up the steps quietly and turned the key in his lock, letting himself into his room, tossing his duffel bag onto the bed. He picked up the phone and dialed without even taking time for a much needed shower.

The call was answered on the second ring. "Copple here."

"It's Matt. Listen," he said, kicking off his muddy boots, "we've got real problems."

"Your father?"

"Exactly. Someone took a shot at him yesterday morning, and I couldn't get to the guy before he took off."

"Damn. I take it Evan's all right?"

"Fine. The person missed. Trouble is, Evan's not taking it seriously."

"He wouldn't."

"I had to leave the camp and get in touch with you. And I'm going to have to dump this cover and head back to New York, pronto."

"I don't like it, Matt. Evan's going to catch on."

"I don't have a choice, Ned. It's bad enough that he's up there in that camp unprotected as it is."

"You're in Crested Butte?"

"Right. And tomorrow I'll be in New York. I don't have the slightest idea *what* I'm going to tell my folks, either. I just know that Evan's going to be in twice the danger there, and plenty hard to cover twenty-four hours a day."

"I'll put a couple guys on the case to spell you."

"Do that."

"But what about the next few days?"

"I don't think the man'll try again, Ned. A second attempt would look too coincidental. Whoever took that shot is probably gone."

"And the group of hunters?"

"Could be one of them. I want you to check out a few names for me. You never know. Got your pencil?" Matt gave him everyone's name at the camp, their home cities, anything and everything he'd noted in his head. He never mentioned Nicola, though; it just didn't seem right to even share her name with Ned.

"Okay," Ned said, "call me the minute you get back to New York. Oh, and don't forget to leave your job there in the usual manner. Evan, God bless his determined soul, might just pick up a phone one day and check on his son."

"Got ya." He hung up and went straight to the shower.

Evan sure had gotten into a pickle this time. It had only been a few days since he'd made his announcement on the Costa Plata loans, but Matt was betting on that finance minister, Reyes, having taken immediate action. With Evan dead, the World Bank might take a new, less hard line, on those loans. Just the possibility would have been enough to cause Reyes, with Cisernos's blessing, to act quickly.

What excuse was Matt going to use when he got home? And just how in the devil was he going to stay close to Evan—especially after that fight last night?

Showered and changed he bundled up his dirty clothes and shoved them into a plastic bag—they'd get washed in New York. Then he packed up his few belongings, checking the room for anything he might have forgotten, and headed back down the stairs and out into the bright autumn morning.

Crested Butte was a small, funky ski area, an old mining town with only one paved street, the century-old mining shacks and false-front stores only recently spruced up with new paint. It was a town that had seen its share of battles between labor and management in the old days, and battles between the huge AMAX mining conglomerate and environmentalists in the more recent past. It was cozy and charming, and its inhabitants were stranded back somewhere in the idealistic, freedom-loving sixties.

Matt had only just come to this mountain retreat, and now he was leaving. He'd known all along it wasn't going to last, but he'd needed a cover job, an excuse to be in Colorado to show up at hunting camp. And while Evan had been brooding over his oldest son's latest bartending job, he'd been too busy to see through the cover and to question why Matt had been comfortably working in a restaurant in New York then suddenly up and gone to Colorado. No, Evan wouldn't possibly suspect anything fishy, because he'd been too mad at his son. But then, that was the whole idea of a cover in the first place.

He ambled on down the main street and felt his stomach growling. It was well past ten now, and a bite or two would hit the spot. He eyed a favorite locals' spot, Penelope's, a two-story fern-and-stained-glass eatery in one of the old false-front buildings still left standing. The house's famous tenderloin hash sure would hit the spot.

Matt knew a couple of the employees there; they were regulars at the bar where he worked. He took a seat at the counter, pushed aside the menu and smiled up at the waitress. "Hi, Suzy. Tenderloin hash, please, and a couple of eggs, sunny-side up. Coffee, too."

"Where you been?" Suzy was twenty at the outside, blond, short and round and sassy; her old blue jeans beneath the apron were faded and torn in spots—suitable for Crested Butte.

"Hunting," he said.

"Catch anything?"

"You don't *catch* the game, Suzy, you shoot at it. And no, I'm not really much of a hunter."

"I'm glad," she said, then bounced off to put in his order.

Suzy, he thought, like several of his other acquaintances here, was going to be buzzing with the news tomorrow. He could just imagine it. "Hey, did you guys hear about Matt? He got fired. Poor old drunk."

Matt drank his coffee and let his thoughts settle themselves. And as soon as he had a perspective on what he needed to do in the next few days, he took a moment to think about Nicola and the cool, impersonal note he'd left. He sighed. If he closed his eyes, he could see her black swatch of hair swinging over her shoulder as she leaned over the monstrosity of a stove. Ah yes, her cheeks were flushed, her dark eyes bright... Too bad there hadn't been time to unpeel all her layers, every lamination she'd built up to protect herself. Too bad he couldn't have come clean about himself, but then, would she—like Evan—merely shrug and think, so what? The knowledge of his real job didn't change a thing about his personality. Was that what she'd think?

Nicola. An amazing woman. He'd been nosing around on that ridge yesterday morning, looking for the spot where the bullet had come from, and he'd run into her. Uncanny. And too close for comfort. He hadn't been able to tell her that he'd hiked back to keep his eye on Evan and heard the shot, so he'd come up with some lame excuse for his presence.

Nicola.... She was even more appealing in jeans and a plaid shirt than in her city duds. A woman of the outdoors. Lean and hard muscled, competent. But sweet and vulnerable, too. A combination that was irresistible. It was uncanny how she'd found that spot. Uncanny, as well, how she'd gotten under his skin and muddled his thoughts. It was a new experience, at his ripe age, to feel like that because of a woman. He'd felt like that in high school, even in college once or twice, but not since. He stayed too tightly in control to ever let himself feel like that about a female.

"Tenderloin hash and eggs sunny-side up," came Suzy's voice, and she plunked the plate down on the table. "Get you anything else?"

"Just some more coffee."

So why, he wondered as he broke the yolk of an egg with a corner of his toast, hadn't he found the right woman? Was it really because of his unusual line of work? Maybe. Or perhaps he *was* a coward, hiding all these years behind his cover. Nasty thought, that.

Okay then, Matt decided, maybe he was a chicken at heart, but he still had this job to complete for the service. He could hardly march into Ned Copple's office and announce that he was through, at least not until the Costa Plata Caper was over.

"Hey, Cavanaugh!" came a voice from across the aisle, an old-timer who was fond of calling everyone a flatlander.

"Hi, Gary."

"Ya got anything to show for yer huntin' trip?"

Matt shook his head. "I got skunked, old buddy."

"Told you ya would. Now if you'da let me guide ya..."

Matt barely listened, although he nodded at appropriate moments as he chewed pensively. What a lousy assignment this had turned into—watching his own father. Normally Ned would have handed this one over to the FBI or even the National Security Agency, but since Matt had the expertise and the inside edge, it had fallen to him. Here he'd been, hanging around his parents since last summer and having to come up with the wildest stories as to why he'd taken a job near New York, why he'd moved on to Colorado just a couple of weeks ago, and now, why he was going back to New York. Ned was really going to owe him for this one—retirement from Section C, maybe. Although, Matt recalled grimly, Ned was fond of saying that you never retired from the field, you only got buried.

"Yessiree," old Gary, the plumber, said, "I got me a six-point trophy bull back in '52, I did. And I ain't hunted since. Course, I could find ya a big ol' bull if I wanted, mind ya."

"Sure you could, Gary," Matt said.

A picture of Juan Ramirez flew into his mind. The rebel leader was sitting behind his desk, his yellow eyes alight with the fire of reform and revolution. It wouldn't be long now, Matt guessed, before the hopeful and idealistic Juan readied his guerrilla troops to free the downtrodden people of Costa Plata from Cisernos. And then the good-hearted U.S. Congress would vote on aid to that war-torn country, to Ramirez, its new president, and on it would go, the cycle of idealistic young men replacing the older, jaded, corrupt ones. And maybe, just maybe, this one would turn out to be a good guy.

"So, ya wanna take a ride on up to Harvey's Ridge there, Matt?" Gary grinned, showing darkened teeth. "Might jist get ya an animal today."

"Say," Matt said, "that's really nice of you, but I probably have to work."

"Yer misfortune," Gary said, shrugging.

Evan, Ramirez, Reyes—the images flew around in Matt's mind as he paid his check and headed back out to the street. And who *had* taken that lousy shot at Evan? An amateur, that much was evident. Would Reyes have sent an amateur, though?

And Nicola. Oh yes, she was whirling around in Matt's head, as well. One thing was sure, he'd been an idiot to have kissed her. Everything had been just fine after they'd left the bar in Redstone; that was to say, Nicola had been plenty put off by his flirtation with the buxom Sunny. Then he'd gone and spoiled it and kissed her.

Why did she always have to be around, complicating matters?

Nicola, tall and lean, graceful, competent. *And smart*. But on those sad, melancholy eyes, those questioning, judging eyes that made him look deep inside himself despite all the warning sirens in his head. Nicola. . . .

ALTHOUGH MATT WASN'T DUE BACK to work at the Wooden Nickel till the end of the week, it was no trouble switching shifts with one of the guys so he could work that night. He kept a beer on the bar next to the cash register, taking drinks from it in full sight of the handful of locals who patronized the place that quiet Thursday evening.

The talk ran to the usual stuff: gossip, what kind of ski season it was going to be, who was getting married, who was knocked up, who'd gotten arrested for driving under the influence last Saturday, and, because the snow hadn't flown yet, how the hunting season was going.

"So, how was the hunting?" a steady customer of the bar asked Matt.

"Didn't see a damn thing."

"Too many guns out there nowadays."

Matt nodded, agreeing, taking a swig from his glass. "Too darn many easterners, too."

"It's not a sport anymore. It's a freaking shooting gallery."

"Ah, shut up, Abner," someone else called over. "You been sayin' that ever since I kin remember."

Matt laughed with the rest of them, maybe a little louder, and tilted his glass again, then served a new couple at the bar, mixing their cocktails adroitly.

"I can see you been a bartender a long time." This was from an older man with a familiar face, who sat at the bar next to Abner.

"Yeah, I've been around." Matt shrugged.

"Where you from?" The man pushed his beer glass toward Matt, who refilled it automatically.

"Lots of places."

"Crested Butte ain't a bad town. You might like it here."

"It's as good as any. I hear the tips are great during ski season."

"That they are."

Matt drank again, then knocked over an empty glass when he reached for it. "Slippery," he said to the older man, winking broadly.

By the end of his shift, he was slurring his words and spilling drinks. When he ambled out at 2:00 a.m., the bar was three-deep in dirty glasses, and he'd left the cash register jammed.

The following morning he awoke at ten, eyed his already packed duffel bag, showered and brushed his teeth. Afterward, carefully, he poured the bathroom glass full of bourbon from a bottle he'd borrowed from the bar and gargled with it, grimacing and spitting it out. Then he slapped some bourbon on his unshaved cheeks, dressed and, whistling jauntily, went to work.

He arrived at the Wooden Nickel at eleven, just in time for the day shift. Someone had gotten there before him, though, and had cleaned up the mess. The barroom smelled of stale smoke and flat beer, but the bar was clean as a whistle now. The manager, Jay, sat on a stool, counting last night's take and making out a deposit slip. He looked up when he saw Matt.

"Hello, hello, hello, Jay buddy," Matt said, approaching the bar. "Up with the birds, I see."

Jay looked him over and sniffed, wrinkling his nose in disgust. "Hell, Cavanaugh, you smell like a brewery. I like you, man, but you've only worked here a couple of weeks, and you can't stay sober. This place was a disaster area when I got here."

"Sorry, it was a busy night."

"Busy?" Jay tapped the pile of bills he was counting. "With this take?"

Matt stood there, waiting.

"I'm gonna have to let you go, Cavanaugh. I hate to do it, but business is business. Pick up your check. I'll take your shift. Sorry, man, but that's the way it's gotta be."

Matt grinned carelessly and shrugged. "It's been fun."

"Yeah, I'll bet," Jay said bleakly.

Only ten minutes later, Matt threw his stuff onto the back seat of the rented Jeep and swung into the front seat. By the time he was halfway to Denver he'd forgotten all about the check, the job and the humiliation he always felt. He was thinking only of his assignment—protecting Evan Cavanaugh—and furiously trying to think up some half-baked excuse for arriving, yet again, at the old Westchester homestead.

CHAPTER EIGHT

NICOLA COULDN'T have been more surprised or pleased when she'd opened up an envelope from Evan and Maureen and found a round-trip airline ticket to New York.

> Hope you'll have time to use this. We'd love to see you at Thanksgiving this year. Consider the ticket an early birthday present.
>
> Love, Evan and Maureen

Her job with Ron's outfitter service had been through for the year, and the job she hoped was still available in Wyoming was not due to start until close to Christmas, so she had decided to go ahead and fly east. And, Nicola had thought as she'd packed, the employment at the ski lodge near Jackson, Wyoming, was no real plus in her life—it didn't pay very well. Maybe she'd stay in the East this winter, find a good-paying position and tuck a little money away in her savings account. One thing was for sure, she'd learned, and that was that good, dependable cooks were hard to find. All she'd had to do was look through the want ads in the papers to discover that.

In fact, she was sitting in the kitchen at the Cavanaughs', talking to Lydia and leafing through the *New York Times* help wanted section discussing just that.

"You know, Lydia," she was saying, "I could find a place to hang my hat in the city right here and have a job in a day." Nicola ran her finger down a long column. "It's tempting."

Lydia sipped from a coffee mug that read This Is My Kitchen, Find Your Own, and snorted in derision. "Sure you could, Miss Nicola. Jobs in the city are a dime a dozen. But finding a place to live, now, there's the hitch."

"Um." She flipped the page.

"Always been that way in New York. Take Mr. T.J., for example. He still has to live at home and commute."

He doesn't have to, Nicola thought. He lived at home because of Maureen and because he intended to stay highly visible, so that when the time came for Evan to retire from his spot as president of the family-owned bank, T.J. would be readily on hand. The trouble was, Evan was still going strong.

"Here's one," Nicola said, tapping the page. "'Assistant chef for large hotel, East side. Excellent pay, benefits plus. Send résumé.'"

The kitchen door swung open and Maureen walked in. She looked positively radiant in a shimmering green robe and matching slippers. "Good morning, Nicola, Lydia. Is the coffee ready?" She ran an affectionate hand across Nicola's shoulder and sat down. Morning routine at the Cavanaughs' never varied. Breakfast was served at eight, promptly, in the formal dining room, but Maureen and T.J. habitually invaded Lydia's territory every morning early and read sections of the paper—T.J., finance, Maureen, the society page—then disappeared to shower, dress and prepare for the day. Evan never showed his face until fully dressed, at eight sharp.

"You know," Nicola said, "it's tempting to try and find a place to live in the city and snatch up one of these jobs. It would be different, anyway."

Maureen raised a thin brow. "Now, you know you wouldn't be happy, dear, unless you could hike or ski or do something outdoorsy."

"I could do all that on vacations and on days off. Same as I do now."

"Well, I suppose you could. It would be wonderful having you close. You could even live here."

Nicola's head came up from the paper. "And commute? Ugh. What I should probably do," she said lightly, "is tell Went that I'm moving in with him."

Maureen made no comment. It was understood that the subject of Nicola's relationship with her parents was best left alone. "My, the coffee's strong," Maureen said. "Have you switched brands, Lydia?"

"Twenty years ago I did," Lydia replied pertly, and went about her work, squeezing fresh orange juice using an old-fashioned metal contraption with a handle.

T.J. came in. "Morning." He still looked drowsy and shuffled his slipper-clad feet. His light brown hair was mussed.

"My," Maureen said, "but you look like something the cat dragged in." She accepted his kiss on her cheek. "Sleep badly?"

"Not great." He fetched himself a coffee mug and sat down, pulling out the financial page, burying himself in it.

"So, Nicola," Maureen said, "I'd love to take you shopping today."

Nicola had confessed that she hadn't a thing to wear for the Thanksgiving gala—tomorrow night—and she'd been putting off the search for two days. She sighed, grimacing. "I guess I better take you up on it. It's either that, or I show up in jeans."

"This afternoon, Dave and Ruthie Huff are due in. So we'll have to make it this morning."

"Okay." The prospect of shopping with the exacting and untiring Maureen was intimidating. Of course, Nicola was thinking, she'd like to look her best. Went was catering the affair, as always, and, much as she hated herself for it, Nicola would love to impress him, make him really notice her.

"The Huffs are coming?" T.J. rattled his paper, hunching his shoulders over it.

"Yes. And they'll stay in the yellow room. They missed their shopping trip last year, and Ruthie insisted on coming early."

"Old Dave probably went duck hunting, instead," T.J. commented.

"Something like that," Maureen put in. "And, Lydia, if Nicola and I aren't back by noon, you tell Margaret to dust the yellow room, won't you?"

"Margaret," Lydia snorted, still squeezing oranges, "wouldn't know a dust rag from a mop."

Maureen went back to the society page, and Nicola held in a giggle.

It took them the entire morning at the Scarsdale Mall to find just the right creation for Nicola. Maureen rarely did her shopping in the city, preferring the small, exclusive local boutiques. It was always embarrassing shopping with Maureen, because she insisted on buying Nicola gifts, with Nicola protesting futilely. Generally there came the moment of compromise: Maureen paid half, a future Christmas or birthday present, and Nicola picked up the tab for the rest. This trip was no exception.

"This way I'm only half as mortified," Nicola said, putting her credit card back in her wallet.

"I don't know why you won't let me just buy you something."

"You took me in, you fed me and cared for me all those years. It's enough."

"Well, I got a daughter that way, didn't I? And I skipped the diaper stage. It was my pleasure, I assure you."

Yes, Maureen got her daughter, ready-made, eager to please. And, Nicola supposed, she got a mother.

Suzanne's face popped into Nicola's head unbidden. That sad, ethereal face that was still unlined, the dark, bottomless eyes. For many years, Nicola had prayed that one of the drugs her mother was given would be the miracle cure. Other people's depression had been controlled so that they led normal lives. But one drug reacted much the same as the next for Suzanne. If the medication kept her mother from weeping at the drop of a pin, then it made her drowsy or caused unbearable headaches or some other insidious side effect.

Oh yes, Nicola knew all about the antidepressants on the market. She'd read everything written, kept up on the latest pharmaceutical research—she still did. But what she'd discovered was that for every action, there was a reaction. There was no complete cure for clinical depression, not for Suzanne, anyway, but she kept hoping that a new drug would work or that her mother would wake up one day cured. She couldn't stop the hoping or the pictures in her mind of her and Suzanne doing things together. Like shopping for a dress. Considering everything, though, she'd been fortunate. She had Maureen's love, and Evan's—and how many people had been given a second chance like that?

Maureen was driving, heading back home, taking the curves slowly and cautiously. Cars kept passing; one driver behind her beeped.

"Oh, bug off!" she said under her breath.

Nicola laughed. She herself would have been doing the speed limit or better, but then Maureen had never been a confident driver. Evan, she knew, was terribly impatient with his wife in the car, refusing to understand that some women of Maureen's generation were still a bit behind the times and that they preferred it that way.

Yes, Evan could be a bully. The way to handle him, though, was to let him vent his steam, then regain lost ground when he was in a more receptive mood. His bark, at least to Nicola, had always been worse than his bite.

Curious, she wondered if Evan had mentioned to Maureen the near miss up in hunting camp. Probably not. And she wondered, too, if Maureen knew about the fight between Evan and Matt and Matt's sudden departure.

"Heard from Matt lately?" she ventured.

"Why, yes, in fact I did. A couple of weeks ago. He called to say he was back in New York, of all places, and job hunting again. I don't know why he hasn't been out to visit. My, but he moves around so much I can't keep track." She sounded blasé, but Nicola knew better. Nicola wondered if Maureen even knew that Matt had been to hunting camp at all. Maybe it was best she didn't.

The memory of Matt's visit still hurt Nicola. It seemed that every time Matt breezed in, he left behind wounded hearts. Hers was no exception. But then she'd let it happen, hadn't she?

So Matt was somewhere nearby. That great winter he was going to spend in Colorado had obviously turned sour. Had it been the fight with Evan? Or had Matt lied about having time off from his job? Maybe there never had been a job. She wouldn't put it past him....

In the East. He'd made that long-distance phone call from Redstone, she remembered. Had he telephoned a lady and the woman had convinced him to leave the West for a visit? Maybe

he'd left camp so abruptly because he had made other arrangements.

It killed Nicola to be constantly plagued with thoughts of
Matt, with mental pictures of his sparkling blue eyes and that
easy, dimpled smile. It killed her to know that she'd pegged him
right all along—a man too much like her father to be safe—and
yet she'd fallen for his charm, just like all those other women
before her.

"Flight gets in at three," Maureen was saying.

"What?"

"Dave and Ruthie get in at three. Knowing Dave, it'll be
Chinatown tonight. He *always* wants Chinese. Can you imagine, driving all the way into the city just for a cheap dinner?"

"I like Chinatown," Nicola said. "It's . . . funky."

"Um. Well, I'd rather eat locally, thank you, but Dave, bless
his heart, is always insistent. And he's one of the few men who
can hold his own with Evan."

"They go back a ways, don't they?"

"Twenty-five years. This winter is the anniversary of our
first trip to the Canadian Rockies, in fact. We met Dave and
Ruthie that year, and Dave hit it off instantly with Evan.
They're like kids together, always challenging each other.
Someday—" Maureen shook her head "—one of them is go-
ing to overdo it."

"Is that why Jon's coming to Thanksgiving dinner this year?
Is it a kind of reunion?"

"I suppose. Jon's got family in New York. He's got family
all over the place. He visits us every so often."

Family all over the place, Nicola thought, remembering her
notion about Jon and those cigarettes. Casually she asked,
"Does he have family in South America?" She would have said
Central America, but then Maureen might have gotten too curious.

"Now, that's a funny question. I'm not sure I know. He
might. Why do you ask?"

"Oh, no reason." But Nicola filed the information away in
her mind. *He might. . . .*

As so aptly predicted, Dave bounced into the Cavanaughs' house that afternoon insisting that everyone dress casually. "It's the annual trip to Chinatown," he announced cheerfully.

"Must we?" asked Maureen as she and Ruthie embraced.

"Did you ever try to say no to Dave?" Ruthie made a face.

Like Dave, Ruthie Huff took excellent care of herself. In her mid-fifties, she didn't look a day older than forty-five. She wore her brown hair short, but not old ladyish, and she had it frosted regularly. Her five-foot-five figure was trim and fit; she skied, hiked, bicycled—one of Aspen's beautiful people. In many ways, Ruthie reminded Nicola of Maureen. The difference was, Ruthie held her own with her husband—and then some.

"Well, hello, Nicola," Dave said, turning to her in the living room. "I didn't know you were going to be here."

"Neither did I."

"Oh, Ruthie," he said, "you remember Nicola from years ago, when she lived here. Say, is Went, that old charmer, catering the *grande affaire*?"

"I hear he is," Nicola said easily.

"The way you cook, kiddo, he's a fool not to put you right in his own kitchen."

Dave, Nicola thought, was never one for tact. "Oh, he's got a stable of sous-chefs already. Who knows, maybe someday." She shrugged. *Sure.*

It was a Wednesday night, a work night, and Evan had gotten tied up in the city, something about an African diplomat and a World Bank loan to see the man's country through a drought crisis. They were all to meet Evan in Chinatown.

Somehow, Nicola got dragged along, as did T.J. She'd have preferred to have spent a quieter evening at home, maybe to have had dinner with Lydia in the kitchen and then to have curled up with a good book by the fire. But when Dave was persistent, Ruthie was right: he just would not take no for an answer.

They all ate at Dave's favorite restaurant on the edge of Chinatown, on Canal Street. And did they *eat*. The six of them ordered the whole gamut, the Imperial Dinners. There was Mandarin lobster and Szechuan beef, hot and spicy, and twice-cooked pork, sweet-and-sour shrimp, Oriental vegetables and chicken lo mein, mountains of steamy hot rice, delicate pots of fragrant tea. Everyone exchanged dishes. Dave and Evan, of course, had to bite into the red peppers, both exclaiming emphatically that they weren't hot in the least. And then T.J. tried one and nearly choked.

"There's steam coming out of your ears," Nicola teased.

It *was* a good time. But somehow, Nicola had gotten paired up with T.J., and—she hated to be so critical—he was his usual, quiet, boring self. He watched his father and Dave and all their silly, boyish antics, and he looked as if he were somewhere between disapproving and jealous. She wondered if he had any real friends, male friends, or if there was a woman in his life. If so, he sure kept her a secret. Now, Matt, on the other hand...

Oh, brother, there she went again, letting him crop up in her thoughts at the most unwanted times. And yet if he was there at the table, he'd be holding his own with Evan and Dave. He'd be dropping those hot peppers into his mouth like oysters and telling everyone that they weren't as bad as some he'd had. He'd make his mother smile and irritate Evan, and he'd woo Nicola, catching her off guard, making her laugh with his good humor and spontaneous remarks. She'd feel all glowing and warm inside, and her cheeks would get flushed. If he was there, that was.

"More tea?" T.J. asked her.

"Oh, sure, thanks."

They walked the twisted streets of Chinatown after dinner, slowly, complaining about eating too much, laughing about how they'd all feel after Thanksgiving dinner tomorrow. Ruthie bought a silk kimono with brilliantly colored parrots on the back, and Dave got them all paper fans with dragons on them, made in Taiwan.

"Now, what am I going to do with this junk?" Evan asked.

"Oh," Dave said, "use it when your temper flares, Evan. Although, God knows when I can recall anything like that happening to you."

They were easy people to be with, and they laughed a lot, the men cracking terrible jokes, making even worse puns. All but T.J. Around Evan, he paled.

The city, the lights and sirens and exotic odors, the myriad people, the thousands of shops and restaurants and street hawkers, delighted Nicola. New York was exciting, vibrant, *alive*. There was a pulse to the city, a beat like a steady drum, unique, compelling. It wouldn't be so bad to work there. She could see shows and walk the streets, leap into the melting pot of the world. And on days off, she could drive up into the mountains; in the summer she could hike and in the winter, ski. She'd see Suzanne more often that way, and maybe even Went—if he could spare the time. Then, of course, Evan and Maureen were nearby. And maybe she'd run into Matt once in a while. . . . *Do yourself a favor, kid, and forget him.*

They got home late; it was past eleven, but Dave and Evan stayed up in the living room and chatted over brandies. Nicola said her good-nights and headed to her room, yawning. Country girls hit the sack by ten. Lord, but bed looked inviting. The bag from the boutique was still sitting there, however, the shiny, dusty-rose bag with twisted ribbon handles. She'd better hang up her dress.

Idly Nicola wondered if Went would even notice her tomorrow. Would he make his rounds through the throng of guests? When everyone was served, would he sit down to a glass of wine? She'd be in her dress, with its calf-length swirling skirt of dark green velvet and its draped top. A little old-fashioned, not daring or anything, but elegant. And expensive—Maureen had seen to that. And maybe Went would put a hand over hers and tell her how terrific she looked. Then maybe he'd say, "Gosh, Nicola, honey, I wish you'd stop by more often. I really meant it about showing you the town. I know I've never been there for you, darling, but I've changed. Give me a chance. Let me show you. I love you, baby, I always have."

Nicola changed into a nightgown, turned out the lights, frowned into the dark and crawled into her warm, safe bed.

THE ROLLS-ROYCES AND MERCEDESES and long black limousines started arriving at 6:00 p.m. but by then everything was ready.

Went had been in the kitchen since early that morning, so early that Nicola had still been asleep, and when she'd finally gone downstairs, she'd been afraid to do more than poke her head in and say a quick hello.

When Went worked, he *worked*. He'd brought two helpers with him, and all day long there were rattles and bangs, arguments and swearing in French and English, coming from behind that swinging door.

"It's always like this," Maureen said, waving her hand. "Don't pay any attention."

Just before six the Huffs and T.J. and Nicola and the Cavanaughs gathered in the living room to drink a glass of bubbly and toast the holiday. The men were all dashing in their tuxedos; even T.J. had a kind of flair in his formal clothes. The women were lovely—Maureen in gold lamé and Ruthie in a suede skirt and elegant beige sweater of feathers and angora.

"You look beautiful," Maureen whispered, leaning close to Nicola. "I wish Suzanne could see you. She'd be so proud."

Nicola had twisted her hair on top of her head. Her neck was long and white and graceful, the dark velvet of her dress showing up its smooth texture, and she wore a cameo her mother had given her. She flushed at Maureen's words, noting the men's appreciative glances, ill at ease under the attention, unaccustomed to it. It was a heady feeling, being dressed up and glamorous—flattering but discomfiting.

Then the guests began arriving, and the entire, sparkling house was filled with beautifully dressed women, men in dinner jackets, chattering, waiters circulating with champagne and hors d'oeuvres on silver trays.

Nicola was introduced to so many people her head spun, and she gave up trying to remember who and what they were, or which sensationally dressed woman belonged to which distinguished man. There were many faces that looked familiar, either because she'd met them before at the house or because their visages had graced the pages of *Fortune* or *Time* magazine.

There were Wall Street magnates, World Bank officials, the head of the Federal Reserve Bank, even a senator from the Midwest and his wife. Jon Wolff was there, wearing a rusty old tuxedo that must have seen performances at the Staatsopera in Vienna before World War II.

Maureen was gracious, Evan jovial and avuncular, T.J. quiet, as usual, nursing a glass of champagne in a corner, watching the gathering silently.

Dinner was announced. At each setting was a card with a name. Maureen had worked for hours arranging the seating, worrying about who was having an affair with whose spouse, who was quarreling, who would be comfortable with the rather strange wife of Nigeria's World Bank representative, and who spoke French or Italian or German. Nicola was seated to the right of Evan, at the head of the long table, and to *her* right was an empty chair with a card in front of it. She looked over at the attractive woman sitting beyond it, the wife of the Midwest senator, she thought, and they both shrugged and smiled at each other. But Nicola knew who had been meant to sit in that empty chair; she knew whose name was on that card. Matt. Probably he'd had to work that night, or perhaps he'd simply chosen not to come.

The feast was worthy of Wentworth Gage. Roast turkeys, each stuffed with a different dressing: pine nut, oyster, old-fashioned bread and egg. Yams in brandy and butter, trays of relishes, whipped potatoes, five different vegetables to choose from. Cranberry jelly, orange-cranberry sauce. Rolls hot out of the oven, celery sticks stuffed with caviar, cranberry bread. And each dish had Went's touch—a shade of difference in an herb of a spice or a texture, a special, mouth-watering flavor that made even the most jaded palate crave another taste.

Nicola was proud of her father's expertise. He was more than an expert, he was a genius. She was proud and almost jealous. If *her* reputation matched Went's, would he notice her then? Or did he simply not care?

Did he consider Nicola at all? Was he ashamed that he spent time with other women instead of his daughter? She rolled his delectable yams over in her mouth and wondered at the mystery that was her father's mind. She'd tried everything to get him to notice her. So far nothing had worked, not even following in his footsteps. Damn him.

He emerged from the steaming kitchen when dessert was being served: pecan pies, pumpkin pies, pumpkin chiffon cake. Oh, he was charming when he wanted to be! He was tall and

lanky, elegantly slouched, his face rawboned with a big nose.
But his expression made his homely features attractive in a
quirky way. He was smiling now, grinning, bowing to the long
tableful of guests. Applause greeted his bow, and he accepted
the homage due him with regal modesty.

"Thank you, thank you. I hope everything has been satis-
factory. No one's going to leave with an empty stomach, I assume?" he said.

Laughter greeted this sally, and groans and pats on many full
bellies.

"There is someone here tonight... Oh yes, there she is!"
Went said, searching the crowd. Then he stalked, long legged,
straight to Nicola. She stared up at him openmouthed as he
reached down and tugged at her hands, pulling her upright. "I
want to introduce my daughter to you all, my beautiful daughter," he said, smiling warmly at her. "And, ladies and gentlemen, this child of mine is a talented chef in her own right! My
daughter, Nicola Gage!" And he drew her close, his arm
around her as the entire assemblage oohed and aahed and
clapped.

She blushed; she hung her head; she laughed in embarrassed pleasure. At that moment she adored her father. "Thank
you," she said, her cheeks burning, but her voice was too low.
She cleared her throat and spoke up more loudly. "Thank
you." And Went squeezed her tight.

He finally let her go and waved to everyone, disappearing
back into the kitchen. Nicola sank into her chair, half laughing, half crying. Oh yes, Went could be charming.

The senator's wife leaned across the still empty seat between
them and said, "I'm Irene, Nicola. I had no idea you were
Went's daughter. How proud you must be."

"Oh yes, of course," Nicola replied.

Nicola wasn't certain exactly when she became aware of a stir
at the entrance to the formal dining room. Maybe it was when
Evan turned in his seat to look, or maybe it was the eyes of the
secretary's wife, which lifted to the door. Whatever. A few
more heads turned, curious, as waiters walked around unobtrusively, serving coffee and liqueurs. A voice could be heard.

"Well, well, Clyde, I'm late again, as usual, aren't I? Happy Thanksgiving!"

And the butler, Clyde, came into the dining room, ushering in the new arrival, ushering him directly toward the empty seat next to Nicola. She heard Evan grumble something under his breath, and the crowd buzzed and whispered. Heads bent, people wondering, guessing.

But Matt was oblivious to the quiet commotion he'd created. He was self-assured and roguishly handsome in his tuxedo as he strode toward Nicola, his smile perhaps a bit too broad. Or maybe she was only imagining that.

"Nicola? Well, fancy finding you here," he said a touch too loudly, and she wondered, for a split second, if he'd had a few too many drinks before arriving. "Has it been a wonderful Thanksgiving dinner?" he asked insolently, raising a goblet of wine as soon as he sat down.

"Yes, delicious."

He leaned across Nicola and spoke to his mother. "Sorry I'm late, Mom." Then he nodded to T.J. and his father, raising his glass as if in a toast to them.

It was quite an act, Nicola thought. Errant son, wastrel, ne'er-do-well. Debonair but irresponsible. Why had he come? Why had he bothered? And did anyone else but Nicola notice that it *was* an act? She wasn't quite sure how she knew, how she recognized the falsity of his routine and knew it wasn't the real Matt.

"I'm Irene," the woman on Matt's right was saying, holding her slim, beringed hand out to him.

"How delightful to meet you, Irene. Better late than never, as they say."

Nicola had time to catch her breath, to steel herself. Matt, unexpected, his black-clad thigh touching hers as he leaned toward Irene. And then he was turning toward her, his head bent close. "Nicola, you look gorgeous. I didn't know you were going to be here."

"Maureen sent me a plane ticket."

"Well, isn't that nice?"

The food in Nicola's stomach felt like lead. Her heart pounded too hard. She was irritated at her reaction; Matt only had to appear and she fell apart. But his head was still bent toward her, and an invisible current flowed between them, so intense that it would begin to spark in a moment....

"Quite a collection," he whispered sarcastically.

"Yes." Her heart fluttered ridiculously, and that awful, exquisite slow melting began in her stomach as his breath fanned her cheek. He'd kissed her, this man, pressed his lips to hers. And his hands had stroked her body, moving on her skin, the same hands that turned the crystal wineglass right now, letting the light sparkle on its facets.

She felt trapped, frightened, her senses sharpened to fever pitch but concentrating on one thing alone. She raised her coffee cup, drank, tasted nothing, felt Matt's eyes on her, and she knew she was defenseless.

There was dancing after dinner. A five-man combo played old tunes, Lester Lanin style, danceable music. It was better then, away from him, and she relaxed a little, tapping her foot to the music. T.J. took her for a requisite dance. "Moon River," she thought it was.

"Don't move too fast," she said. "I'm so full I'll pop."

But T.J. didn't laugh at her attempt at humor. "I'll be careful," he promised, utterly serious.

Then Dave Huff grabbed her for "Chances Are," hummed in her ear, made absurd, lewd suggestions that she laughed at. Then Evan took her for a spin, leaving Maureen in the grasp of the vice president of the World Bank. "What's that son of mine up to?" he asked her. "Did he give you a hint?"

"'Up to'? What would he be up to?" she asked innocently.

"I don't know. Showing up late like that. Why'd he bother to come at all?" muttered Evan.

"Forget it. Have fun. Are you having fun, Evan?" she asked.

"Sure, *fun*. When this crowd goes home, I'll have fun," he groused good-naturedly, and she was glad to have nudged him out of his bad mood.

Then an official of Evan's family bank, whom Nicola already knew, asked her for a dance. He was a nice man, only a little shorter than she was. Oh well. But he danced like Fred Astaire, and he made Nicola laugh and blush with his compliments. Oh, this glitzy life could become a habit, she thought. And then she felt like Cinderella, disguised as a beautiful princess, with the clock ticking closer and closer to midnight.

When the band broke into "On the Street Where You Live," Nicola was talking to Maureen, the flushed and successful hostess. A hand touched her arm, a voice said, "Excuse me, Mom," Nicola turned, and Matt pulled her out onto the floor.

"I've been patient," he said, looking down at her.

She couldn't breathe. He was holding her too close, one hand at the small of her back. His breath was wine sweet, his blue eyes held her hypnotized, seeing into her innards, unlocking all those carefully controlled emotions.

"Patient?" she asked faintly.

"Your dance card was full. I was getting into a jealous snit."

"Matt."

"I wanted to apologize for leaving hunting camp like that."

"You don't need to apologize."

"I thought you might be insulted."

"Why?"

He laughed, his dimple deepening, and pulled her close, whirling her around. "You're the best-looking female here." He grinned down at her. "Not the richest, not the oldest, but the best looking."

They spun by Evan, who scowled at Matt, then past T.J., who stared wordlessly, his face a mask, unreadable. Did T.J. ever *enjoy* anything? She felt light in Matt's arms, and she wondered whether he could feel her trembling. She wanted to go on forever in his embrace, but at the same time she couldn't wait until the music was over, the dance ended, her gown turned back into rags.

"Matt, my dear boy," came a voice, "vill you please let me have the pretty lady for a minute?" It was Jon Wolff, looking a bit like Count Dracula in his rusty black.

Thank heavens. She was saved. But when Matt reluctantly handed her over to Jon, she felt suddenly cold and naked. Ridiculous.

"Later," Matt whispered huskily, and then Jon was stepping around the floor with her, stiff and formal and so very proper.

"I am so glad to find you, Nicola," Jon was saying, and she had to force her mind back to reality. "I have a problem up at the lodge, the Bugaboo Lodge, you know."

"Oh dear, is it serious?" she replied politely.

"Yes, very serious. My cook has left me. He got married and his vife must live in Calgary, so there I am. It is Thanksgiving and I have no cook."

She looked at him quizzically.

"Would you be interested?"

"Me?"

"I pay very well. Christmas to April. The verk is very hard, long hours, but sometimes you can ski, too."

"Are you really offering me the job, Jon?"

"I am begging you, Nicola. You see before you a desperate man."

A crazy thought skimmed through her brain: a desperate Jon, bending his face to her neck, with his vampire fangs bared. She stifled a giggle.

"Vill you consider the offer, at least? I have put ads in the Calgary and Edmonton and Vancouver papers, but it is very late for a fine chef to change plans," he was saying.

"Do you want my résumé?" she blurted out.

"Ah, no, Nicola. That veek at hunting camp was résumé enough."

"I'll take the job," she said impulsively.

"Just like that?"

"Yes, why not? I'd love to."

Jon had stopped and was regarding her in utter amazement. "You vant to know the details? Now?"

"Tomorrow. I'll call you tomorrow. All right?"

"Fine, perfect. *Gott in Himmel*, I am a happy man."

"And I am a happy woman, Jon!" Nicola said, delighted.

"Come on, Jon, tear yourself away from Nick. I've got to tell you about these new powder skis I just bought!" Dave Huff said, coming up to them. "You don't mind, do you?"

"Tomorrow. You vill call?" Jon said as Dave grabbed his arm.

Nicola laughed. "Don't worry, I'll call you."

The band was taking a break. Nicola wandered across the floor, smiling automatically, nodding, returning comments. But her mind was busy. The Bugaboos! She'd heard Evan talk about helicopter skiing in Canada for years. There were no ski lifts out in the wilderness of the Bugaboo Mountains of British Columbia, only helicopters to transport the skiers to snowy peaks, then pick them up at the bottom and spirit them away, up to another untouched piste.

Jon's Bugaboo Lodge had been one of the first places established for that kind of skiing. Oh Lordy, but she had a million questions for Jon tomorrow! She didn't even know how to *get* there or how many people she'd be cooking for or where the supplies came from! What an adventure! What an opportunity!

She had to get away somewhere and think. Questions teemed in her brain. Wow. The patio. Slipping to the far side of the room, to the French doors, Nicola let herself through. It was cold and damp out, with a breeze whirling dead leaves into corners. She hugged her arms and walked back and forth, smiling to herself in the moonlit darkness.

The Bugaboos. She knew a few things about Jon's lodge, from Evan. It was very expensive to spend a week there, about two thousand dollars per person. It was totally isolated in the winter, except for the helicopter and a radiotelephone. The food, he'd remarked often enough, was superb. Uh-oh, better get out the old recipe books.

She marched back and forth, planning, thinking, excited. Oh yes, she'd have to ask Evan what kind of skis were best in that bottomless Canadian powder.

"Nicola." The voice startled her, and she turned toward it, stopping in midstride. A shadow detached itself from the dark bulk of the house and approached her. "I saw you come out here."

"Matt."

"Who else? What're you doing, marching around in the cold?"

"I've been thinking." She laughed, wanting to share her news. "I've had the most wonderful offer! Jon wants me to cook up at his lodge this winter!"

"Does he?"

"Yes. Isn't that wonderful?"

"I suppose so."

"Well, it is." She wouldn't let his casual attitude spoil her happiness. "Just think, I'll be able to see Evan and Maureen when they come up in January. Won't it be fun?"

"It's pretty isolated up there," Matt said.

"I'll be so busy, I won't even notice."

"Will you?"

"Aren't you glad for me, Matt? This is the opportunity of a lifetime!"

"Hmm. Right. Come here, Nicola, and stop talking so much."

"Why?"

"Okay, I'll give in." He moved close to her, so she could see his face and his formal white shirt in the moonlight, then he took her hand and held it, playing with her fingers. "I don't want to talk about your new job."

"What do you want to talk about?" She longed to snatch her hand back, but she couldn't. Her mouth suddenly went dry; heat radiated up her arm from her hand, and that awful, help-less melting started once more.

"You. You look beautiful tonight, but I told you that al-ready." His voice was soft, soothing, and he wouldn't let go of her hand.

"Why are you doing this?" she asked in a low voice.

"Doing what?"

"Playing with me."

"I'm not playing with you."

"Then what do you call this act of yours?" She finally pulled her hand away.

"It's no act, Nicky."

"What do you want from me?" she asked, trembling, knowing but not knowing at all.

There was an awful moment of silence, as if they were both frozen in their stances, Nicola poised as if for flight, Matt steady, cocksure, compelling.

"I want this from you," he finally said in a whisper, and he pulled her to him, his mouth coming down hard over hers. She forgot everything, all her inner warnings, her self-promises. Their flesh spoke for them, the only reality she knew at that instant, the only reality she wanted to know. Her body leaped in a sweet agitation that wouldn't be denied, and a slow, hot flame kindled in her, warm and throbbing. She felt his lean, hard body against her, flattening her breasts, and his arms were like iron bands holding her, and she wanted to be held.

Then he lifted his head, and the cold touched her face. "I'd like to do that again. What do you say, Nicky?" He was smiling, holding her lightly.

"No," she said, realizing how she'd been taken in. "I don't think so." She was breathing hard, her heart thudding in her chest as if she'd run a race.

"You didn't like it?" he asked.

She backed out of his embrace, shivering suddenly from the cold. "Yes, I liked it."

He reached out for her once more. "You're cold. Want my coat?"

"No, I don't want your coat. I don't want your kisses, either."

"Nicola, I swear..." He sounded sincere, but she knew how good he must be at *that*.

"No." She held up a hand. "Don't touch me. You're like my father. I know about men like you. You don't mean a thing you say."

"Don't equate me with your father." His voice was tight.

"Why not, Matt?" she asked breathlessly, turning and moving toward the French doors, toward the light and heat and noise inside.

But he had no answer; he just stood there, a slim, straight figure in stark black and glistening white. And Nicola hurried away from him, hurried inside to mingle and smile and drink another glass of champagne, to compliment Maureen and tell Evan the news about her new job.

And all the while she felt the pain of leaving Matt, the pain of his dishonesty, the pain of his agonizing similarity to Wentworth Gage.

It struck her suddenly, like cold fingers running along her spine, and she stopped in her tracks in the middle of the crowded room. She was afraid of what Matt represented, and she distrusted him just as she did Went—yet didn't she love her father with as much passion as she hated him?

CHAPTER NINE

IT WAS SATURDAY. That meant it was the day that the old guests left, spent, sated with skiing and good food and conversation—and the new guests arrived. A crazy day, what with the Bell helicopter buzzing between the helicopter pad in Spillimacheen, fifteen minutes over the mountains, and the lodge, taking out the old, ferrying in the new.

It was the day, too, that Jon Wolff turned into an old lady, fretting and worrying and checking the supplies that came in on the helicopter, checking the guest list, the linens, the menus, the thousand details that made the Bugaboo Lodge run smoothly.

This job had turned out to be the most challenging of Nicola's life. She cooked for around twenty people per week, connoisseurs all, wealthy folk for the most part, who knew the difference between beluga caviar and fish eggs, and what year was the best one for Burgundy.

That Saturday in January was special, though. The Cavanaughs were coming for the week. Evan always came, Maureen sometimes, but this week both T.J. and Matt were making the trip, as well.

"All of them?" Nicola had asked Jon.

"Yes, they haven't all come together for years. Isn't that nice? But I vill have to put the young men in the same room."

Matt and T.J.? Here? Was this some sort of attempt at family reconciliation? It smacked of Maureen's doing; she wanted her sons to get along with their father so badly.

Matt. Why? He knew she was there, but she didn't flatter herself that she constituted reason enough for him to suffer the proximity of Evan for an entire week. And how would he react when he got there? Would he be his usual flippant self? Would he treat her casually? Would he pursue her again?

Well, she would stop that, just as she had at Thanksgiving.

She prepared the beef tenderloin that would be the main course for dinner that night, readying it for the oven. Her kitchen was a dream—no Old Bertha to stoke up. Electricity from the lodge's own generator, the best in commercial stoves— a Vulcan—and a huge refrigerator and even a walk-in freezer. She kept a week's worth of supplies on hand—a lot of food— but the fresh produce came in on Saturdays the same way the guests did: by bus from Calgary to Spillimacheen, two hundred miles, then by helicopter to the lodge.

The Bugaboo Lodge was isolated. In the summer there was an old logging road that connected it to the outside world, but in winter the road was closed by snow and by the very immediate danger of avalanches that regularly slid off the slopes above the road. The place was linked to the outside world only by the radiotelephone set to Banff, where the Canadian Helitours' main office was, and by the helicopter—tenuous links, especially when bad weather prevented the chopper from flying. None of these facts, though, kept people from all over the world paying top dollar for a week of blissful skiing and gourmet meals.

There were two girls who helped in the kitchen, the helicopter pilots, who doubled as mechanics, three guides for the skiing, several maids and Jon and herself for staff. And they were busy every day from Christmas to mid-April, working hard and skiing when there was room in the helicopter. Nicola was given a week off once a month, when Jon's former cook would fly in and take over, and she needed that week.

Matt. She hadn't heard from him, but then she hadn't expected to. Maureen wrote that he was working in a bar in Tarrytown, nearby, and that she saw quite a bit of him. *How nice for Maureen.*

Her first reaction to Matt had been correct—he was dangerous. He was too attractive, too much fun, too free and easy. He tugged at her emotions in a way against which she couldn't defend herself. And he'd be here soon, right here in the lodge, and she'd have to see him every day, talk to him, be polite. Well, maybe she could stay extremely busy right here in the kitchen.

Jon bustled in. "*Mein Gott*, Nicola! Vill you have enough raspberries for tonight? You ordered a lug, didn't you?"

She smiled to herself. Jon was always like this on Saturdays. "Yes, don't worry."

He poured himself a cup of coffee and sat down hunched over the kitchen table. "I need a rest—I am exhausted. I have made ten beds this morning. Those lazy girls."

They weren't lazy, and Jon didn't need to make beds, but you couldn't tell him that, not on Saturdays.

"Vat a veek! It is the vorst. *Mein Gott*, I mean the best. Such a mixture, so many important people." He sighed and gulped half the coffee. "The Huffs and the Cavanaughs, you know them. But the others. Do you know the name Helga Gantzel?"

"No."

"Ach, you young folk. A once famous actress. So beautiful. Of course, she's my age now, sixty or so, but ven I vas young she vas the toast of Germany, of all Europe. And she's coming with Werner Bergmann. He is young, very young, but vith a voman like Helga..." He snapped his fingers. "And there's a Japanese man, a Mr. Yamamoto, and Carlos Santana, who is from Spain. A financier. It's no coincidence those two are coming this veek. They snatched up last-minute cancellations, to talk to Evan, you know."

"Why would they want to talk to Evan? Do they know him?"

"No." Jon leaned forward. "These two have set up an auto plant in Central America, in Costa Plata. You understand vat's going on there? Evan has told you?"

"Yes, I know. But how would you know about these men and their auto plant?"

"I have family in Managua. Nicaragua is so close. You see, my cousin has been so vorried about the political problems there. Such a nightmare for him. And he tells me these things. He is thinking of moving his family to Canada, even."

"Oh, I see."

"These men, they vill lose everything when Cisernos falls. And Evan is here this veek. They vant to talk to him."

"Oh Lordy, how awful. Evan will have a fit. He hates to be bothered by business when he's on vacation."

"I know, I know. Vat a week this vill be." Then he bounced up and put his cup in the sink. "So? Everything's okay here, Nicola? Dinner vill be fine?"

She smiled reassuringly. "I've got it all under control, Jon."

He went out mumbling under his breath, *"Gut, gut. Mein Gott."*

There wasn't much to do until later. Nicola checked everything once more, then let herself out the kitchen door. It was a clear, bright day, sunny and cold. A beautiful day. Thank heavens the chopper could fly to bring the guests in. There had been Saturdays when the old guests had been stuck here while the new ones were twiddling their thumbs in Spillimacheen, a tiny crossroads boasting nothing more than a general store, a post office and the helipad. But, still, the skiers who insisted on untracked powder put up with the inconveniences to get it.

She walked along the snow-packed path toward the building where the staff lived, which was separate from the main lodge. Nicola was lucky; as chef she had her own bedroom, which was very nice, but not in the least luxurious. And she shared the bathroom.

Even the main lodge was not fancy. It was a plain square edifice of stucco and wood and windows, two stories high, but its setting was spectacular. It faced a glacier and the famed rocky Bugaboo spires. A long mountainside flowed upward from the building, covered with snow-laden spruce, and all around rose the peaks of the Bugaboo range, sharp and white and pristine under the sun.

Nowhere else in the world was there skiing like this, Nicola thought, letting herself into her room. She'd been up, oh, maybe a couple times a week since December, whenever there was room in the helicopter. Paying guests, of course, came first, but sometimes a skier was injured or too tired or wanted an afternoon off. Then Nicola could go skiing—and it was heaven. Into the chopper, crowded, everyone laughing and excited. Up to the top of a mountain, the chopper's blades kicking up a whirling maelstrom of snow as it landed and disgorged its anxious passengers. Then on with the skis, the goggles and following the guide down, carving turns in the untouched snow until her legs were as weak as jelly and her heart was content.

She combed her hair and redid her ponytail, put on mascara. She tucked her bright pink turtleneck into her corduroy slacks and thrust her face closer to the mirror, clucking her tongue at the white "racoon eye" marks on her face—from wearing goggles while skiing. Everyone who skied had them all winter long.

She sprayed perfume behind her ears. Oh yes, she knew why she was doing it. For Matt. But she couldn't help it. A girl had her pride. She wanted to be attractive; she wanted him to notice her. She wanted to have the choice of saying no.

Or was she just playing games with herself? That night on the terrace... She shivered again, right there in her toasty-warm room, remembering. Sometimes she thought she'd been cruel, turning him away like that. Sometimes, as she lay in bed awake and wondering, she questioned whether Matt might not have meant what he said. Maybe he *did* like her. Maybe he was old enough to want more than a one-night stand. There were times—isolated moments—when she thought there was a sadness behind Matt's mocking blue gaze and curving smile. A loneliness. But maybe she was just kidding herself, wanting him to have a weakness, wanting him to be a nice guy deep down inside.

She gave one last look at herself in the mirror, felt her heart give a thump, then she turned and went outside just in time to see the helicopter landing on the pad, returning from Spillimacheen.

Jon was there to greet the group. He was dressed in his usual Saturday outfit: his wool knickers and hand-knit knee socks and a boiled wool Bavarian jacket. He greeted everyone graciously, with heavy, Germanic courtesy, clicking his heels, bending over the ladies' hands, shaking the men's somberly. Nicola stopped at the corner of the lodge, watching, wondering, preparing herself for the sight of Matt.

A young honeymooning couple got out of the helicopter, then an older man—most of the guests were male. No one she knew. A pair of college boys on break. Then a woman. Oh Lordy, she was wearing a full-length sable coat, and she dripped with jewels. It had to be Helga Gantzel. Was she going to *ski* in that coat? Helping Helga down was a gorgeous young hunk—blond, pale blue eyes, shoulders like Hercules and a smile like the Cheshire cat. Werner.

Then a slim, dapper Japanese man got out. The one Jon had mentioned? And a swarthy, handsome fellow. The rich Spaniard?

She waited, but no Cavanaughs were on that trip. She sighed with relief, feeling as if she'd had a stay of execution. But it was only for a few minutes more, until the chopper made another flight.

She should go into her kitchen, but that would be hiding. She couldn't let Matt govern her actions, and she did want to see Maureen and Evan. So she stood there in the sunlight with Jon, chatting with the new arrivals, introducing herself, answering questions, acting the part of the hostess, which Jon liked her to do.

"Oh yes, wonderful skiing this week," she said, answering one of the college boys. "We've got ten feet of snow so far this year."

"Awesome," he said. "When do we start?"

The helicopter was returning, floating toward them through the clear air, glinting in the sun. Then it was settling down on the pad, causing a whirlwind, whipping Nicola's hair into her eyes. The small blizzard died down, the snow settled, the door slid back. Oh yes, there was Maureen! And Evan. She waved and grinned. T.J. got out, looking around as if assessing the place, comparing it to his memories. His face showed no emotion; he smiled at Jon, but it never reached his eyes. Poor T.J.

The three Cavanaughs ducked under the rotors, and Jon greeted them. Nicola hugged Maureen, kissed Evan's cheek, then impulsively kissed T.J.'s, too. "I'm so glad to see you!" she said.

Other people were ducking and moving toward them—strangers, a couple of young women obviously on the prowl, another pair. Oh, it was the Huffs!

Matt was right behind them. Nicola kept up her facade, joking with Dave Huff, saying hello to Ruthie, asking questions, answering dozens of queries about the skiing. But something inside her sighed and rolled over, and she had to take a deep breath.

He wore a bright blue parka and jeans; he moved so well, so fluidly. The smile was on his face, telling the world that he refused to bow to the rules, that he didn't care what anyone thought.

"Hello, kid," he said.

"Hi, Matt." She kept her voice even, unaffected.

"Don't I get a kiss, too?" He mocked her, challenged her.

"Sure." She stepped up and brushed his cold cheek with her lips, but even that brief touch was like fire. The memory of his taste and smell came rushing back to her. "That okay?"

"For now," was all he said.

The Bugaboo Lodge was done on the inside in cheery cuckoo-clock, Bavarian-style knotty pine, with utilitarian furnishings. There was a cozy bar by the huge stone hearth, and that was where everyone met before dinner for wine and hors d'oeuvres and animated conversation. All the guests there naturally wanted to size up their companions for the week, the people with whom they'd be skiing all day, drinking and eating at night, their best friends for the charmed time they spent in the lodge. Introductions flew around thickly, as did questions. "Where are you from? Oh, do you know the Johnsons?" And offhand remarks of other places visited, backgrounds, jobs, the vital facts they needed to know about the strangers they were with to place them.

Nicola came out of the kitchen for a while before dinner, having promised Evan to have a drink with them.

The first person she saw when she walked into the room was Helga, leaning against the fireplace in tight black velvet pants and a shiny gold sweater. Her shoulder-length blond hair, still glamorous, fell over one eye, and Helga had a habit of pushing it back behind an ear. Diamonds flashed from her lobes, her wrists, her fingers. She was holding a glass and smiling up at Werner, smiling tightly and a little desperately.

"There she is!" Evan called. "Come over here, Nicola."

"All settled in?" Nicola asked brightly.

"Oh yes, Jon always gives us the same room," Maureen said. She looked wonderful in tan slacks and a pale pink ski sweater, but then Maureen always looked that way.

Evan thrust a glass of *Gluwein* into her hand. "Oh boy, it's just like old times. I can't wait. Hope the weather holds."

"So, how is your job?" Maureen asked.

"Wonderful. Lots of hard work, but I've skied quite a bit."

"You going to ski with us this week?" Evan asked.

"I hope so."

T.J. came over. "I haven't been here in years. It's all the same, Dad, isn't it?"

"The cook's new," Evan said, "and that's what matters."

"You better tell me if the food's good," Nicola said. "I mean it. You're the only ones I can ask."

Maureen pointed at the tray of appetizers on the bar. "Well, those were delicious."

"Better than Went's," Evan agreed. "Everyone was saying how good they were."

Nicola blushed. She never wanted to be *better*, for goodness' sake. She only wanted to be noticed by her father. "Don't tell him that, please," she said, treating the whole thing like a joke.

A burst of laughter made her turn her head. The college boys had latched on to the single ladies. They must have been telling naughty stories. She noticed Matt then, in the corner with the dark Spaniard; he was listening to the man, his eyes bright, the curved smile on his face. Was he avoiding her deliberately? Or was it Evan he was avoiding?

He noticed her looking at him and held his glass of wine up in a brief salute, then turned back to the Spaniard. Nicola was angry at herself suddenly and ashamed that he'd caught her watching him. *He* obviously didn't wander around mooning over *her*, craving a word of greeting, wondering, hoping, despising his own weakness. No, he kissed a girl, flattered a girl until her insides melted and her head spun, then he forgot her.

"Nick! What's up?" It was Dave, slapping her on the back, full of fun. Her spirits rose instantly.

"Beef tenderloin and new powder," she said.

"Oh, I'm going to gain weight," Ruthie moaned. "I know it."

"No, you won't. You'll ski it off," Nicola said.

"Unfortunately, I can eat more than I can ski," the woman replied.

"Hey, Evan, old buddy. You up to the steep and the deep?" Dave asked, poking Evan in the gut with a finger, taunting. "Can you keep up?"

"Don't worry, Dave, my boy. I just had my yearly physical. I'm fit as a fiddle, 110 percent. You just better watch your tail."

The conversation was light and easy, the guests bubbling with expectancy, geared for having the best week of their lives, lubricated by Jon's famous *Gluwein*. On everyone's mind was the same anticipation, the same excitement, a togetherness that crossed international barriers—the love of powder skiing, the thrill of that first glorious untracked run in the morning.

Nicola and two helpers served the meal family-style in the dining room. Everything had turned out well, and even Jon relaxed for an hour, joining the guests at dinner.

There was cream of asparagus soup, butter-lettuce salad with Nicola's special vinaigrette, thinly sliced beef tenderloin in mustard sauce, lightly seasoned zucchini and wild rice with pine nuts.

"Oh my God, I'm going to just stay here and eat all day. Forget the skiing," said one of the guests, a man from Toronto.

"This is *wunderbar*," Helga said. "Don't you think so, *Liebchen*?"

"Excellent," Werner said.

"Marvelous!" someone else agreed.

Dessert was raspberries, the ones Jon had been worried about, in peach liqueur.

"Sit down for a moment, Nicola," Jon said. "Everyone vants to meet you."

So she joined the entourage for a small glass of brandy.

"To our wonderful cook," Ruthie Huff said, raising her glass.

Nicola was embarrassed at the praise, liking it, but discom-
fitted by the attention. She sipped the smooth brandy and felt
her cheeks grow hot as the roomful of people toasted her.

She smiled, and she must have replied something witty, because the group responded with laughter. And when she looked
across the table, there was Matt, gazing at her. It seemed to her
that the laughter and conversation died away and the room was
empty except for the two of them. They stared at each other
that way for an unending moment, for too long. Then the world
jerked back into place, and Nicola heard the buzz of conversation again, the clinks of forks on dishes, and she excused
herself quickly, too quickly, and beat a hasty retreat to the
kitchen.

The drinking and introductions and conversation continued
after dinner, after Nicola had overseen the cleanup and the
breakfast preparations. She could have gone straight to her
room; she considered it seriously, but Evan and Maureen would
have wondered. They expected her to spend some time with
them.

The flames undulated and hissed and spat in the big fireplace. Conversation eddied and flowed, jokes were repeated,
stories compared. Skiing was discussed, fervently, intently,
knowledgeably. What kind of skis were best in warm heavy
powder as opposed to cold light snow. Which ski boots were
warmer or gave more support. When the weight should be
shifted in a turn. Whether to keep your weight equally on both
skis in powder. Whether to make big swooping turns or tight
ones. What kind of wax to use.

Nicola sat by the fire, surrounded by the guests, the strangers who were already getting to know one another, gravitating
into cliques, feeling one another out, just as they did every week
all winter long.

She was tired from her long day, on edge, feeling Matt's
presence too keenly despite the fact that he was ignoring her.
She could see him across the room, talking to the Japanese
man, Rei Yamamoto, and to the Spaniard again. Then Jon,
ever the perfect host, joined them, introducing the three men
to Werner and Helga at the bar. Helga seemed always to be at

the bar. She didn't even ski, Jon had told Nicola; she was there to be with Werner, and young Werner adored powder skiing.

Helga liked Matt immediately, Nicola saw. The woman moved her shoulders provocatively under the glittering gold sweater, and the blond hair fell over her eye as she talked animatedly to Matt. She still had charm, a trim body and a carefully nurtured beauty—from a distance—but it must have been her life's work to keep herself that way. Nicola felt the bite of jealousy as she watched Helga zero in on Matt. Werner must have felt the same way, because he was glowering, but then Matt said something to the young German and Werner smiled, was charmed, gave in to Matt's friendliness.

"Great group, isn't it?" Evan asked her. "Some good skiers."

"Gee, Dad, I sure hope you don't get anyone in your group who'll hold you up," T.J. said.

"Oh, Jon will see to it that nothing like that happens," Maureen was quick to say, "won't he, Evan?"

"Sure, he'll put me in the fast group. We have to get our vertical feet in, you know," Evan replied complacently. Every skier was promised one hundred thousand vertical feet of skiing for the week. If they went over—a feat to brag about—they paid extra for the privilege; if they didn't make enough runs to reach their hundred thousand, they got credit for their next visit. It was set up that way, because the largest expense in the operation was the helicopter—the more it flew, the more it cost.

"Señor Cavanaugh," came a voice. "I am Carlos Santana. May I introduce myself?" It was the swarthy Spaniard, a handsome man in his mid-forties, dressed in stunning Continental style, wearing a cashmere turtleneck sweater and pleated wool trousers.

"Mr. Santana?" Evan shook his hand. "My wife, Maureen, my son T.J. And you know Nicola."

Carlos bent over Maureen's hand, then Nicola's. He smelled of brandy and cigarette smoke and heavy male cologne. "A dinner fit for the gods," he said to Nicola. "*Absolutamente perfecto, señorita.*"

He turned to Evan again. "Imagine my surprise at finding you here in this remote spot, *señor*. Perhaps you would have a *momento* sometime? I have a small point I wish to discuss with you." He took out an ostentatiously ornate cigarette case and lifted a cigarette from it.

As he searched in his pocket, T.J. held his own lighter up. "Let me," he said.

"Please have one," Santana offered, holding the case out to T.J., then to the rest of them, but only T.J. took one, lighting Santana's cigarette, then his own.

"'A small point'?" Evan repeated dryly.

"I assure you, it is nothing. Just a moment of your time." Santana waved his cigarette negligently.

Darn him, Nicola thought. *Can't he leave Evan alone? The man's on vacation.* She should warn Evan about Santana and Yamamoto, but Jon would already have done that, she was sure.

Helga was leaning on the bar, her mascara smudged, her voice growing thicker. When Nicola went to the bar to get herself a soda water, she could hear Helga talking to Werner and the man from Toronto. "I've been around," Helga was boasting. "I speak five languages, did you know? Yes, Werner, *Liebchen*, you know, but Harold didn't know. And I have made films in twenty countries, yes, twenty. Once I was dubbed in Chinese. And I'm telling you both something. *Bitte*, darling, can I have another drink? What was I saying? Oh yes. That man, Santana, that oh-so-elegant Spaniard. From Madrid, he tells me." She leaned conspiratorially toward Werner and Harold. "I *know* Madrid. He is no more *madrileño* than I am. His accent is Central American, pure Central American. He thinks he can fool me, Helga Gantzel? I lived in Madrid for three years with my fourth husband, who was the Count of Salamanca."

"Is that so?" Harold asked.

"Yes, dahling. It would be like Paul Newman pretending to be English, you understand. So, Señor Santana is an imposter. I'll bet my last mark on it."

A Central American, Nicola thought, abruptly alarmed. Was he from Costa Plata? Was he only pretending to be a European investing in that country?

She glanced over to where Santana stood talking casually to T.J., both of them puffing on their cigarettes.

And then Nicola recalled the cigarette butts she'd found at the hunting camp. Whoever had tried to shoot Evan was a smoker. But lots of people smoked. Many Europeans still seemed to. And so did T.J., for that matter. Even Maureen had smoked once, but Evan, the health nut, had made her give it up. She still stole a puff or two from T.J.'s cigarettes occasionally.

Was there any significance to Santana's pretending to be from Spain? He had his reasons, she was sure. But what were they? And what was the "small point" he wanted to discuss with Evan? Something related to the World Bank, she'd bet.

She glanced back across the room at Evan, who was talking to one of the helicopter pilots, Junior. Evan loved all that technical stuff: lift and horsepower and fuel consumption and RPMs. He noticed her gaze and mimicked her troubled frown and smiled at her, then went on asking Junior about the chopper.

Well, she wasn't going to let Evan ignore this new information she had. She took her glass of soda water and went over to him.

"Hi, Junior," she said, "mind if I talk to Mr. Cavanaugh for a minute?"

"Go ahead," Junior said, "I was just on my way to the bar. See you tomorrow, Mr. Cavanaugh."

"What's this serious look of yours?" Evan asked. "Someone criticize the menu?"

"Evan, I really think you should get serious yourself for a minute and listen to me."

"Go ahead, whatever it is." He rolled his eyes and upended his glass.

"Did you know that Santana and the Japanese man, Mr. Yamamoto, have an automobile plant in Costa Plata?"

"Jon told me. It figures, doesn't it? You just can't get away from them. Don't worry, I can handle it."

"But I just heard Helga saying that Santana's accent was Central American, *not* Spanish. What if he's from Costa Plata? What if that awful Reyes sent him here to hurt you?"

Evan shrugged.

"Are you sure he's just a businessman, Evan?"

"Listen, Nicola, I'm here on vacation. Frankly, I don't care if he's Elvis Presley returned from the dead. I'm here to ski powder."

"But, Evan, what if he's here to influence you or threaten you . . . or even worse?"

Evan patted her head with affection. "Now, don't you worry about those kinds of things. Tell me, how's the skiing? That's what I'm really interested in."

She sighed. "Oh, Evan, I wish you'd take this less lightly."

"Not this week, Nicola." And he patted her head again, smiled and went over to join Dave Huff, who was telling a group the story of the time he'd been caught in an avalanche just above the lodge on a steep run.

"It was like swimming. I couldn't breathe," Dave was saying to his spellbound audience. "All I thought was, 'this is it, Dave, old boy.'"

"And who pulled him out?" Evan broke in, slapping Dave on the back cordially. "Yours truly!"

"Were you hurt?" one of the college boys asked.

"Banged up a bit. But I got in my hundred thousand vertical that week, anyway," Dave bragged.

"Sure, if you count the distance he slid in the avalanche," Evan retorted.

They made a great pair, those two, Nicola thought. Old friends, good buddies. They'd hunted together for years, skied together, visited each other. It was a good thing they had no business interests in common; where business was concerned, Evan had no friends at all.

She was aware of something then, as if there were a cold draft on her back. She turned, thinking to find a window open, but she met Matt's gaze from across the room. He was watching her, a glass in his hand, his dark brows drawn together.

She was suddenly uncomfortable, too hot in the smoke-filled room, her skin prickling. The allure was still there; she couldn't escape it. What did he want from her? Why did he run hot then cold? Why did he alternately pursue then ignore her? It wasn't fair.

She turned away deliberately and sat down, nursing her soda water, listening to Dave's funny stories. She wished she could just leave, go to her room, go to bed, forget Matt Cavanaugh and his games. But she'd turned stubborn; she'd outwait him. She'd sit there until everyone was gone, and then she'd confront him. She rehearsed the confrontation in her mind. *What is your problem, Matt? Pick on someone else, will you?* Oh yes, she could be stubborn and determined when she wanted to be!

People were starting to drift away to their rooms. Bedtime was early in the lodge. Breakfast was at seven, and then the chopper fired up, and the first group had to be ready to go. And almost everyone, except Helga and Maureen, wanted to be in shape to hit the slopes tomorrow.

The fire still crackled, the college boys had their women pinned into corners, Helga swayed out of the room on Werner's arm, waving a glass around. *"Guten Nacht,"* she said to everyone graciously, slurring. *"Guten Nacht, my friends."*

And then Nicola turned to face up to Matt, to toss him the gauntlet. She'd make him leave her alone; she'd tell him just where he stood in her book. She'd tell him.

She swiveled around, ready for the challenge. She searched the room, her heart pounding. But he was gone.

CHAPTER TEN

THE LODGE, which had been silent and expectant that Sunday afternoon, burst into life. Suddenly there came the sound of ski boots thumping outside, the front door banged open, and the living room and bar swelled with happy, flushed, animated people, with high-pitched chatter and laughter and a lavish amount of boasting.

The day of skiing was over, the guests had returned home from the hills.

"What'd you think of that new bowl we did today?" Dave Huff slapped Evan on the back. "Now, that was a run!" He was weary but elated, his blue eyes dancing.

With the help of one of the maids, Nicola set out trays of hearty snacks: cheeses and thin, crispy Finnish crackers, wedges of her own pizza bread, cut vegetables and dips. Everyone crowded around the bar, where Dave was standing mixing drinks, his enthusiasm spilling over into the crowd. Helga and Maureen, the only two who had stayed behind that glorious day, awakened from their naps and appeared downstairs clad in après-ski attire: wool slacks, hand-knit sweaters and ankle-high boots of soft suede.

Maureen touched Nicola on the arm. "Noisy, aren't they?"

She nodded. "But happy as larks. Oh, what I wouldn't have done to have been up there in that fresh powder."

"Will Jon let you ski?"

"It's up to me, really. If I have my work done and there's room in the chopper..." Nicola shrugged.

"Ah," Evan said, joining them, "there you are." He gave his wife a kiss on the cheek.

Even Maureen looked mildly surprised, and she smiled warmly. "You must have had a good day."

"Wonderful." He beamed. "And don't listen to Dave. I outskied him every inch of the way."

Yes, Nicola could see, everyone was cheerful, though exhausted. But it was a good tiredness, a healthy one, and it glowed on the red-cheeked faces.

She glanced around the room. There was that young honeymoon couple, off in a corner by the fireplace, totally lost in marital bliss. And T.J., over there, chatting quietly with the Japanese man, Rei, and his pal Carlos. An odd couple, she thought again, wondering at their true motive for this skiing vacation. And there, near the bar, was Ruthie, taking a glass of wine from Dave, casting around for a place to sit, flushed and pretty in her bright pink one-piece suit.

Nicola checked the trays of food, set out some more crackers and wiped up a spill. Idly she looked around the room, telling herself it was to see if anyone needed anything, but knowing that she was really searching for Matt.

Why did the mere knowledge of his presence in the lodge make her stomach feel hollow with excitement?

She thought back to that time she'd seen him last June, stepping out of his Ferrari, the easy, ironic smile on his lips, and she recalled the way the morning sun had struck his hair, lighting it. She'd been unable to keep her eyes off him since. And if she was being thoroughly honest with herself, she'd have to admit that her thoughts were constantly invaded by images of him, by the little nuances of caring she'd caught him at, by his mannerisms, his walk, the sway of his hips and shoulders.

"Here." It was Evan, handing her a glass of wine. "I feel so bad, up there all day having a ball, and you down here cooking in a hot kitchen. Have a wine, relax a bit."

"Thanks," Nicola said, taking it, trying to collect her thoughts. "But I'll just *bet* you were thinking of me while you were up there." She nodded toward the peaks outside.

"Well . . ."

Matt appeared finally from upstairs, and Nicola watched him out of the corner of her eye. He'd showered and changed into jeans, a white turtleneck and a dark green sweater. His hair was still damp, combed back over his forehead and ears, and he looked around the room briefly as if checking out the lay of the land.

"So Dave fell right above me," Evan was telling her and Maureen, "and I swear, I thought the snow was going to give."

"A slide?" Maureen asked, alarmed.

But Evan shook his head. "Oh, I don't really think it would have slid. That guide of ours today, Hans, was real careful. And can he ski! You should see him in the bottomless stuff in the bowl."

"Are you going to ski tomorrow, Maureen?" Nicola asked, trying desperately not to follow Matt with her gaze.

"Tomorrow, yes. A few runs."

"Good, good," Evan said. "The snow's dynamite." He leaned against the wall, eyeing the roomful of skiers. "Look at that kid," he said, gesturing toward Matt. "Fits right in, doesn't he? But I guess he's had lots of experience in resorts."

"Evan," Maureen warned.

Matt sauntered over. "Hi, folks." His greeting was general. He did not look at Nicola.

"Did you have a good day?" Maureen asked.

"Great skiing," he answered.

Nicola glanced down at her wine. She wished she could escape to the kitchen, but Evan would make a remark about it, and Maureen would beg her to stay and . . .

"I've seen you ski better," Evan said abruptly to his son.

"I guess I'm out of practice. Give me a day or two," Matt replied easily.

"You just don't understand about taking care of your body," Evan began.

"Sure, I know, the body's a temple." Matt gave a short laugh.

Evan bristled. "Well? It is, and if you'd take better care of yours—"

"Please," Maureen began, but Matt had already turned his back on the three of them and was heading toward the bar.

At least Matt hadn't risen to the bait tonight, Nicola mused. In fact, he seemed distracted, as if Evan could have said just about anything and it would have rolled right over him.

"That boy's just downright rude," Evan said, disgruntled. "He didn't even say hello to Nicola."

"He's tired," Maureen said doubtfully, as if she herself knew that wasn't quite it.

"Tired from doing *what*?"

Finally Nicola was able to make an excuse. She edged her way through the crowd, picking up empty glasses, soggy cocktail napkins, broken crackers. She disappeared into the kitchen, stirred the pots, checked the oven and the bread that was rising on the shelf above the stove.

Why did Evan continually hound his children? He treated her so kindly, but with his boys he was relentlessly hard and controlling. Sometimes, she thought, she could shake Evan. But he'd never listen to her.

Nicola's pity for Matt was short-lived, however, when she returned to the throng and saw the act he was putting on. Only minutes before he had been distracted and remote, but now he was the epitome of the garrulous barkeep, serving drinks from behind the bar, talking to two people at once, laughing, toasting the great day on the hill with Dave. What a charmer!

She stood in her tracks and watched him from across the room. *Was* it an act? Or was this the real Matt Cavanaugh? How thoroughly, disarmingly attractive he was. No one could resist him. He was busy telling an acceptable, mixed-company joke, something about a mouse and an elephant, and leaning close to Helga's ear. Helga was lapping it up, holding her glass high for Matt to refill, smiling broadly, her makeup a touch too loud for the rustic setting.

On and on the joke went. The elephant fell into a pit, and the mouse rushed for help. "Oh," Helga exclaimed, "the dahling little mouse!" And as the older woman pushed her heavy blond hair off her face, Nicola could see that her eyebrows were raised as if she were permanently surprised.

The crowd thickened around the bar, and all Nicola could see now was Matt's handsome head, still bent toward Helga, while his hand, seemingly with a mind of its own, poured drinks with a flourish. He was laughing and talking a mile a minute; his eyes shone with joie de vivre. His lips curved in that smile she was growing to know so well.

He'd pressed those lips to hers ...

So the mouse returned to the pit where the elephant was stuck, but he hadn't found a rope. "Well, how are you going to get me out?" Matt asked in his deep elephant's voice. The mouse squeaked, "I've been keeping this a secret. I didn't want to hurt your feelings." Suddenly the mouse produced his male adornment, dropping it over the edge ...

The crowd roared its approval. Nicola folded her arms across her chest tightly.

"He's incorrigible," Maureen said at her ear, but she was smiling. "I don't know how Matt does it."

"Years of practice," Nicola said coolly.

"He was an outgoing little boy. It seemed as if he got all the charm in the family...." She paused, uncertain, then went on. "T.J.'s so serious-minded. I just wish he'd relax."

"Maybe here he will," Nicola put in.

"Ah! There you are!" Jon hurried over to Nicola's side. "I vas vorried...."

"Dinner's all set."

"Of course it is." He mopped at his brow. "The beginning of the veek is always so tense."

"Everything is wonderful," Maureen assured him, winking at Nicola.

"Oh yes, yes, I know, and my poor dead vife, Greta, she used to say I vorried too much. Maybe she was right."

"I think she was," Nicola replied. "Have a glass of wine. Dinner will be on the table at seven sharp. I promise."

Jon nodded distractedly and headed off into the group again.

"Phew," Nicola said, smiling ruefully.

"Is he always this bad?" Maureen asked.

"Always. Until Friday, then he calms down. But Saturday morning it starts all over again."

"I never noticed."

"You never knew anyone who *verked* for him before," Nicola said, and the two of them laughed.

One by one the skiers climbed the steps to shower and change for dinner. A few of the hard hitters, though, stayed at the bar, where Matt continued to tell amusing stories and pour stiff drinks. Ruthie dragged Dave away, while Evan went up with

Maureen in tow. T.J. hung around, leaning against the fireplace, and the honeymooners stayed where they were, entwined and oblivious. The college boys stuck around, pumping one of the guides on how he skied the powder. Carlos left, but Rei had another drink and sat down next to Werner on the couch. Werner wasn't paying any attention to the man from Japan, though. No. Werner was watching Helga with an acute eye.

Now, if I had drunk all that liquor, Nicola thought of Helga, *I'd be facedown on the bar.* But old Helga was going strong. Only that veil of hair that hung over her eye had slipped a notch or two.

Matt held up a bottle of schnapps. "One more?"

"Oh," Helga said, breathless, "I mustn't. Well . . . perhaps a wee bit on the ice here." She batted false eyelashes.

Red-hot jealously spurted through Nicola. Quickly, unable to bear another moment of Matt and Helga, she went into the kitchen, picked up the nearest thing in sight, a pot holder, and threw it against the wall.

Dinner was a success. Like hunters and fishermen, the skiers ate huge amounts of food. The difference was, Nicola tried to lay off the butter and cream sauces, the high-cholesterol items.

Jon popped into the kitchen when the tables were cleared. "Excellent," he exclaimed, "excellent!"

"Thank you."

"I don't know vat I would have done this season vithout your expertise."

"Oh," Nicola said modestly, "you'd have found someone."

When she returned to the living room, Hans was counting heads for the after-dinner activities—cross-country skiing and snowmobiling—for those who still had the energy.

Rei Yamamoto and Carlos chose the snowmobiles, and T.J. opted to join them. At least, Nicola thought, T.J. had made some new friends, even if their motives were a bit questionable. She wondered if those two had befriended T.J. just because his father was head of the World Bank. Oh dear, maybe they were going to try to get at Evan through his son. Or

IN FROM THE COLD

maybe, she thought, ashamed of her cynicism, they just en-

"Come on, Nicola," Evan coaxed. "Come cross-country
skiing with us. Get some exercise."

"Come on, you'll sleep like a log!"

It wasn't a bad idea, she decided. It'd take the edge off, chase
the weariness from her bones. It would also spare her the sight
of Matt playing games with Helga.

Several of the other guests were getting ready, trying on the
low leather boots, propping skis from the storeroom against the
walls in the living room, choosing long poles.

Nicola hurried over to the bunkhouse and pulled on a pair of
knickers and long woolen socks, a heavy turtleneck and an
oversize Scandinavian sweater. Grabbing a hat and warm
gloves, she rejoined the group.

"Oh, good," Evan said, seeing her attire, "you're going."

There was Evan and a guest from California and Dave.
Werner was tugging on his boots and surprisingly so was Helga.
Nicola would have thought the woman too inebriated to stand,
much less ski. The guide was that cute young man from Ver-

Yes, it would feel good to work out the kinks, push herself a
little, get some fresh air. She felt better already.

It was just then that Matt clattered down the stairs, with his
parka and cross-country ski boots on. Her heart sank.

It occurred to Nicola to back out of the deal then. Enough
was enough for one evening. But she wasn't going to let Matt
spoil everything for her. She wasn't going to cower or run away.
She'd just ski ahead of him—or lag behind. She didn't want to
play his game anymore; she'd be darned if she could figure out
his rules, and the stakes were much too high for her.

The moon was full, sitting lightly on a jagged peak, as they
all pushed off from in front of the lodge. It was surprisingly
bright out, but all the color was leached out of things, so that
the scene was akin to an old black-and-white film, all silver and
jet and shades of gray. Skip led them toward the summer logging road, which was well packed for a few miles from previous cross-country skiers.

Behind them, heading out from the lodge, were the snow-mobiles. Their engines growled and whined as they approached the skiers, then passed them, disappearing around a bend ahead until they could no longer be heard.

"I don't know why T.J. likes those things," Evan said, puffing along beside Nicola. "Too damn noisy."

"They're fun," Nicola said, "once you get the hang of them."

"No exercise involved, though," he said critically.

The group moved in a line now, silent for the most part, following the silvered path through the pines. It was a beautiful night, the stars diamond sharp in the black sky, the air fragrant with pine and wood smoke from the chimney of the lodge. She was aware of Matt behind her; she could hear his breathing as he slid across the packed snow, one ski, then the other, his poles moving in even rhythm with his legs. It was a nice evening, true, but she'd have preferred to go it alone.

Up ahead of the column was Skip, keeping an easy pace. Directly behind was Werner, then Helga, Dave, Evan, and in front of Nicola was the Californian. Matt held up the end. If she could drop behind a bit, wait a few minutes, then she'd follow on her own. It would be peaceful. . . .

Nicola skied over to the side of the road and stopped, bending over as if to retie her boot. She could feel the smooth rise and fall of her chest, her even breathing, the dampness on her brow under the wool hat. In a minute or two they'd all be around that curve that led into a steep-sided canyon. Matt had said nothing when she'd pulled aside, merely taken up the slack and gone on with the others. Good.

She waited, gazing up at the heavens, tipping her head so that the face on the moon righted itself. There was nothing in the world like a night sky in the mountains—sharp, crisp, utterly delineated from the horizon. She was immensely glad she had decided to go along.

She pushed off after a suitable time, moving from side to side to gain momentum, poling, pushing, pulling, pumping. She kept a comfortable pace, listening to her breathing, feeling that perfect rhythm and the slight burn in her arms and thighs. She was really going to sleep like a baby tonight.

He came at her from beneath a tall pine, a shadow detaching itself from the forest. At first she was startled, then irritated.

"Can't you take a hint?" she said, skiing on.

But Matt quickly closed the gap she was purposefully creating between them. "I thought maybe you had trouble with your skis," he said, breathing hard.

"Well, I didn't."

He was abreast of her now, slowing his pace to match hers. "Great night, isn't it?"

"It *was*."

"Come on, Nicky. We're here to have fun, aren't we?"

"You're the one paying for fun. I just work here. Look, Matt, you don't have to be nice to me. Go play your games. Go on, catch up with Helga."

He chuckled. "Why, Nicola Gage, you're jealous."

She flushed and was glad he couldn't see it in the dark. "Don't be ridiculous."

"I'm flattered, kid."

"Don't be."

They skied in silence for a while then, until they could make out the group ahead.

"We may as well catch up," she said.

"I kind of like it back here."

That was the only excuse she needed. She knew it was spiteful and childish and that he'd probably laugh at her, but she did it anyway, forcing her pace, pushing herself to the limit.

But he kept right up, as if he'd anticipated her move. "You're mad because of Thanksgiving," he said, sucking a lungful of air. "You're mad because I kissed you."

Nicola was really panting now. She wouldn't give him the pleasure of an answer; she'd just keep skiing until he left her alone.

But he kept up, and she could hear his hard breathing behind her, close behind. Darn him!

"Will you slow up?" he finally said.

Nicola felt sweat dampening her back and chest, and her hair beneath her hat was wet. Still, she shook her head. "Just leave me alone, why don't you?'' But her pace slowed inevitably, and soon he was beside her.

She heard it then, ahead of them, an angry voice, no, more than one. Matt had halted and was listening.

"What?" she said, sliding to a stop.

"Someone sounds like they're ticked off," he said lightly.

Still breathing hard from their skiing, they came upon the group moments later. And they both stopped short at the tableau that presented itself, a black-and-white picture etched into the pale silver snow.

Helga was stamping one ski, furious, not altogether sober, and Werner was by her side, his square jaw thrust forward pugnaciously, his features harsh in the moonlight. And Evan faced them, his expression hard. The others stood around in stiff discomfort, unwilling spectators.

Skip cleared his throat. "Say, uh, we better be going back."

But Helga was livid with rage.

"What's going on?" Matt said, catching his breath.

"Ah!" Helga hissed between her teeth, lifting a pole and brandishing it dangerously close to Evan's face. "This man, this father of yours is a cheat! A liar!"

"Now, see here, Helga," Evan said, his face as contorted and pallid as hers, "put down that pole. It was just business, for God's sake."

"Business!" she shrieked. "I came to you for help and you . . . you insulted me!"

"Helga," Evan said, "what do you want from me? Put down that damn ski pole."

Nicola watched it all, caught somewhere between wonder and embarrassment and fear for Evan. What in heaven's name was Helga talking about? And shouldn't they get that pole out of her hand before she really did hurt him?

It was Matt who made the first move. "Helga," he said, his voice demanding and hard, "give that to me. You're acting like a child."

But Helga swung around abruptly. "You stay out of this!" she cried, poking at Matt, almost catching his thigh with the sharp tip of the pole. "Everyone is trying to destroy me!"

"Helga," Evan said, "you've gone crazy."

"Ha!" she cried, beside herself.

The group held its breath collectively. Finally Evan tried to maneuver his skis backward, and Nicola could see he actually was taking the woman quite seriously.

"Yes," Helga said, her voice as shrill as fingernails on a blackboard, "someday you will pay for this, Evan Cavanaugh. Someday I will kill you!"

CHAPTER ELEVEN

"Nicola! Ach, *Mein Gott*, Nicola!"

She rubbed her face and tried to rouse herself. "What is it?"

"Ve are in terrible trouble!" Jon's face was drawn; he was jumping with nerves. "Did you know half our food order vas missing? From Saturday. Did you know?"

Nicola sat up and tried to think. "I had Jenny check the invoices. She said everything was okay."

"Ach, *Mein Gott*. She knows nothing, that girl. Half the lettuce is missing and only one lug of tomatoes came in. And the case of Riesling I ordered to go vith the salmon!"

"Oh Lordy."

"This is vat I have nightmares about. Maybe I should go to Calgary and run a normal hotel. *Gott in Himmel*, then I could go to the store myself or phone the delivery people! This place, I am getting too old for it, Nicola."

"Look, we can manage. We'll have vegetable salads, instead."

"No, no. That is not good enough. And the vine. And the salmon, too! No. But I have fixed things, I think. That is vhy I'm getting you up so early. I have persuaded Junior to fly you to Spillimacheen in a few minutes. Then you vill see, probably the stuff is still sitting at the bus stop. Or, if it isn't, then you call Nobel Food in Calgary and have them ship it on the next bus, so ve'll get it tomorrow."

"Oh. But who'll do breakfast and pack the lunches?"

"I vill. Me and Jenny, that careless girl. You vill be back soon, anyway. How long can it take? As soon as the groups stop for lunch, Junior vill pick you up in Spillimacheen."

"Darn," Nicola said, "I *knew* I should have checked those invoices myself."

"Yes, yes," Jon said, agreeing. "The other cook before you always did."

She felt a stab of guilt. This was so different from her previous jobs, so isolated here, and she should have realized... In Colorado, of course, you could always drive to a grocery store and pick up missing items locally. But not here. Jon was probably wishing his former cook hadn't married and moved to Calgary—he'd probably double the man's wages at this point to have him back.

"Now, you hurry to meet Junior. He vill have to make this a fast trip."

"Sure," she said, looking down at herself, "but I better get dressed, Jon."

"Oh yes, of course...."

She dressed quickly, pulled on her parka and ran along the snow-packed path to the back door and into the kitchen. Jon and Jenny were already busy cracking eggs and brewing coffee.

"It's omelets this morning," Nicola reminded them, feeling that awful guilt again. "With coffee cake. Figure three eggs per person."

"Okay, ve do fine. Just get that stuff for us."

"And for the lunches, I've got it all written down in my book. Don't put bananas in the lunches. Sometimes they freeze and turn black."

"I know, I know. Go get in the helicopter so Junior can get back quick."

Reluctantly Nicola left the kitchen. She should have reminded Jon about the honey for Evan's coffee, but Jon knew, she was sure. And a hundred other details. She *should* have suggested Jon go to Spillimacheen, but under the circumstances, she'd best let him work off his agitation in the hot kitchen.

The big Bell helicopter was sitting on the helipad, its rotors drooping. Junior was leaning against it, smoking a cigarette. He stubbed it out in the snow when he saw her coming and waved, then headed toward the cockpit door.

"Thanks, Junior, this is a big favor." Nicola said as she reached him. "Jon's going nuts."

"I know. He almost cried when he woke me up this morning. The guy needs a course in stress management," the pilot said over his shoulder.

She climbed in. Surprisingly there was another person there, sitting in the middle of the forward-facing row of seats. She blinked and stopped short, half in and half out.

"Hello, kid."

"Matt?" She pulled herself in hesitantly and sat on the bench facing him. "Are you leaving or something?" she asked, busying herself with the seat belt.

"No, just going along for the ride. I have to make a phone call," he said casually.

Another one of his mysterious phone calls, Nicola thought, remembering the one in Redstone, the one he'd lied about.

"It's for a bartending job in Palm Beach. I was supposed to call last week, but I forgot," he was saying.

Junior started the helicopter, and snow flew around in a white cloud outside, obscuring the lodge. The engine whined, warming up, and quivered, like a creature coming alive.

"All set, folks?" Junior called back to them, lifting his earphones, and Nicola raised her thumb.

The chopper rose straight up, defying gravity, tilted crazily and turned east, toward Spillimacheen. If Nicola twisted around, she could look through the Plexiglas bubble and see where they were going, over the Bugaboo Mountains, straight east, down into the Spillimacheen River Valley. The morning sun filled the interior of the machine, lighting Matt's face but leaving hers shadowed. He looked tired, as if he'd been up late. Maybe he had—with Helga or one of the single ladies. She switched her eyes away from him, looking out of the side window, watching the white peaks flit by below.

Matt's eyes were still on her, however. She could feel them, touching her like fingers. She wouldn't look; she wouldn't. It wasn't far to Spillimacheen, fifteen minutes over the mountains. She would just sit there and take it, and then they would land and she could get away from him.

The mountains fled below, giving way to lower peaks, then foothills, and then she could see the river, winding black and shiny along the valley floor. Almost there.

"Not having much of a week, are you?" Matt said over the noise of the engine.

She didn't take her gaze from the window. "No. Frankly, I'm tired of trying to figure you out."

"I know."

His reply surprised her, and she turned her gaze to him. He looked sincere.

"Mom begged me to come on this ski trip. I wouldn't have been here otherwise. And T.J. She wants us to be friends, all her menfolk. Believe me, it's not much fun for me, either. Evan rags on me and humiliates T.J. He won't meet either of us halfway. Hell, Nicky, I'd rather be lazing on the sand in Palm Beach."

He meant it. No joking, no devil-may-care pretenses, no sarcastic cover-up. He felt *something* then.

"Nicky, can we call a truce? Just be friendly for this week?" he said.

"I'm not at war with you," she said carefully.

He gave her a rueful smile. "I wonder." Then he leaned across, took her hand from where it lay on her lap and started playing with her fingers. "You have pretty hands," he said. "Small and pretty."

She pulled it out of his grasp. "I thought you wanted to be friendly."

"I *was* being friendly."

The chopper was descending, tilting, vibrating.

"Too friendly," she said.

"A guy can't win."

She sat quietly for a minute, gathering her thoughts. This was the perfect time to bring up the subject. "Matt, can you be serious for a minute?"

He looked at her questioningly.

"It's Evan. I'm really worried about him. There was that business with Helga last night. What on earth was that all about?"

Matt laughed. "Helga. Evan's known her for years, ever since she was a big star. Our bank helped her finance an apartment building in New York years ago. Then she came to him last year and wanted him to invest in a movie. She would be the star, of course. Her comeback. He wouldn't. Part of the trouble was she was going to play the part of a thirty-five-year-old. You know Evan. If he thought it was a bad investment, he would have told Helga so—brutally."

"Oh."

"I knew all that. So does Mom. It's no coincidence Helga's there this week. She's still trying to convince Evan. She's harmless. Sad, but harmless."

"Are you sure? Isn't it awfully odd that she's here this week? She doesn't even ski. And those two smoothies, Yamamoto and Santana. Did you know they have business interests in Costa Plata? Santana wanted to talk to Evan. Jon told me all about them. They stand to lose a lot of money if Costa Plata goes bankrupt."

"Jon? How does he know all that?"

"He has a cousin in Nicaragua who's worried, too. So worried he may move to Canada."

"Jon? A cousin in Nicaragua?"

"That's what he said."

"Small world, isn't it?"

Nicola looked at him sharply. He wasn't the least bit surprised about Jon's cousin—it was as if he already knew. She furrowed her brow. "I'm really concerned. What if one of those men is working for Reyes? Do you remember that threat? Oh, and I forgot. Carlos Santana has a Central American accent, not Spanish. So that could mean—"

"Since when are you an expert on Spanish accents?"

"I overheard Helga say that. She had a Spanish husband—she speaks the language. I mean, *you* could tell that Laurence Olivier was English and not American or Canadian, couldn't you?"

"You're in earnest about this, aren't you?" he asked.

"Yes, darn it, I am. I tried to tell Evan, but he pooh-poohed it. He's on vacation. He refuses to pay any attention to it."

"Little Nicky, you're really getting worked up, aren't you?"

"Don't patronize me, Matt. I think you should be concerned, too. He's your father."

He was studying her, watching her too closely, a strange expression chasing itself across his features, a narrowing of his eyes, but then, as if he thought better of it, he wiped his face clear and grinned roguishly. "Don't worry, kid, Evan can take care of himself."

Spillimacheen was a tiny crossroads. There wasn't much snow on the ground here surprisingly, not like in the mountains. Junior let them off on the curiously incongruous helipad.

"I'll be back whenever they take their lunch breaks," he said, leaning out of the cockpit door. "You better stick around and watch for me. Around one, maybe. And I'll be in a hurry."

"Okay, thanks. See you." Nicola waved at him as he pulled his head in, closed the door and took off, rising, tipping, blowing snow at them, buzzing away toward the mountains like a busy insect.

"So, business first?" Matt asked.

They walked to the general store, whose plate glass windows were so cluttered with dusty displays that they were opaque. Spillimacheen, B.C., read the sign over the door. Bus to Calgary Loads Here.

"A thriving metropolis," Matt said as he opened the door for her, and the bell that announced customers tinkled in welcome.

The man behind the counter was smoking a pipe. When they entered, he took it out of his mouth and studied it intently as he spoke. "I heard the helicopter. You folks from the lodge, eh?"

"Yes," Nicola said. "I'm checking on our produce shipment that came in Saturday on the bus. We're short several things, and we wondered if they got left off the helicopter." It was somewhat disconcerting, talking to the man while he directed all of his remarks to his pipe.

"I don't think anything got left. You go on and check around here. I'll ask my wife. She's in back." He gestured with his pipe.

They looked around the store, but there was nothing except the usual stuff sold there: cans of food, guns, fishing rods, kerosene lamps, gasoline cans, axes and hand tools, snack foods. They looked outside, but there was only the bench by the door and a hitching post, presumably for horses in the summer.

"They never sent it," Nicola said to herself.

"Does this happen often?" Matt asked.

"Not since I've been here. Let's go see if his wife found anything."

She hadn't.

"Darn," Nicola said. "I'll have to call Calgary. What a hassle. And the helicopter will have to come pick it up tomorrow. Oh, is Jon going to have a fit."

The public phone was outside, an open booth that was very chilly in this winter weather. Nicola called Nobel Foods in Calgary and, in her sternest voice, demanded to know why three cases of produce, fifteen pounds of pink salmon on dry ice and a case of Riesling had been left off the bus to Spillimacheen.

"We'll have it up there tomorrow," the man promised. "On the bus that gets in at two. Okay?"

"Not really, but we can't do anything about it. Are you sure it'll be here tomorrow? We can't just phone and ask, you know."

"I'll put it on myself, first thing in the morning," he assured her.

"Inefficiency," Matt commented when she hung up.

"You'd think by now, after all these years of dealing with the lodge, they'd be more careful, wouldn't you?" She gestured to the phone. "Go ahead. Your turn."

He reached for the receiver, then hesitated. "While I make this call, maybe you could see if the fellow inside sells coffee. I didn't get any this morning."

"Me, neither. What do you take?"

"One sugar. Please."

It was pretty obvious that Matt was trying to get rid of her. Who was he calling? she wondered, opening the door and tinkling the bell again. If it was a man about a prospective job, why would he care if she heard or not? She'd bet his call wasn't about a job. What she couldn't figure out was why he bothered acting so mysterious about it, as if everyone didn't already know his reputation with the ladies.

"Sure, we have coffee. The machine's right over there. Help yourself, young lady," the store owner said to his pipe.

When she got outside again, Matt was leaning against the wall of the building, hands in pockets, shoulders hunched against a stiff breeze. He took the Styrofoam coffee cup from her. "Thanks. This'll really hit the spot."

"Did you reach the man?" she asked deliberately.

"No, he wasn't there. I'll have to try later."

"Um. Too bad."

"So." He looked at his watch. "What now?"

Nicola turned full circle, taking in all of Spillimacheen, what there was of it. She gave a little laugh. "We've got until at least one this afternoon."

"Can we take in a quick movie? An art gallery? Botanical gardens?" he asked dryly.

She had to smile, even though being stuck for several hours in Spillimacheen with Matt Cavanaugh was not her choice of a way to spend her morning. And they *were* stuck together; there was nothing to do, not even any place to sit and wait inside where it would be warm. It was as if Matt had planned it that way. "We can wait here, I guess," she suggested.

"Or we could take a walk." He slapped his arms. "Warm up a bit." He finished his coffee and tossed the empty cup into a trash can.

There was absolutely no choice unless she wanted to wait there all alone. "Okay. Where to?"

He pointed down the country road. "That way."

They set off at a good place, attempting to warm up. The road followed the floor of the river valley, and mountains rose on both sides of it. The wind blew on and off, chilly gusts that picked up dead leaves and dust devils where the ground was not covered by snow. A farmhouse, white and Victorian square, sat back from the road to their right. Brown stubble poked from the light dusting of snow in fields on either side of them.

They marched in silence, side by side, a fair distance between them. Nicola tried to think of a safe subject, but everything that came to mind seemed artificial and forced, so she just let the silence continue. And so did Matt.

They passed a barbed wire fence enclosing an empty field in which some sort of livestock had once grazed; it was bordered by a line of tall, denuded oak trees, planted long before as a windbreak by the pioneers to this remote valley. A farm dog, shaggy and bristling, raced, barking, to the end of his territory bordering the road.

"Quiet, Spot," Matt said.

"He isn't spotted."

"But does he know that?"

They continued on, leaving Spot watching after them suspiciously. "Do you like dogs?" Matt asked.

"Sure, I like dogs. I never had one, though." She kept her eyes straight ahead, determined to appear neutral in all ways.

Matt pulled the collar of his blue parka up and stuck his hands in his pockets. "There's a lot I don't know about you."

She shrugged.

"And finding out is like pulling teeth."

She said nothing.

"A hard nut to crack, is that it?"

She kept walking, lifting her hand to push back a strand of hair that was blowing into her eyes.

"All right," came Matt's voice, "I apologize. I'm duly punished. Now you can let down and answer my questions."

"I thought we were going for a walk," she said mildly.

"We are. Damn it, Nicola." He stopped short, right in the middle of the road, took her arm and pulled her around to face him.

She stumbled, her forward motion stopped too suddenly, and put a hand out to steady herself, touching Matt's arm. She drew it back as if stung, then stood there, breathing hard, held face-to-face with him.

"I'm not your enemy," he said finally, softly.

"Then let me go, Matt," she said quietly.

He dropped his hand. His eyes were sad. His dancing blue eyes . . . She focused somewhere over his shoulder, knowing he was still staring at her. A gust of wind ruffled his hair and batted at her parka. She sniffed, her nose dripping and red from the cold.

He made an angry gesture, a cutting motion with his hand. "Okay, you win. We'll play your game—"

"I'm not playing a game," she interrupted swiftly.

"No," he said, eyeing her from under dark brows. "I forgot. You don't know how to play games."

"Can we continue our walk now?" she asked coolly. Inside, she was exulting at the power she had over Matt when she was cold to him. Exulting and a little scared, and then it came to her that she *was* playing a game. She'd lied and not even known it. Because what she really wanted to do was to go to him and feel his strong arms around her, his mouth on hers, his hard, lean body pressed against her. She wanted to rest her head on his chest and feel his hands stroke her and calm her fluttering heart and whisper into her ear that he'd be so very careful with the delicate love she offered him.

Matt turned and strode away, his shoulders tense. She kept up, apart from him, hating what she was doing, but knowing no other way to protect herself.

An old pickup truck came toward them, the only vehicle they'd seen. It slowed, then stopped, and an elderly man stuck his head out of the window. "You folks got a car broken down out here, eh?"

"No, we're taking a walk," Matt replied. "Thanks anyway."

"A walk? Saints alive. A walk, eh?" The man shook his head. "It's going to snow, don't you know? This afternoon. My old knees told me. Don't be out walking too long."

"Thanks," Nicola said. "We won't."

"Snow," Matt repeated when the truck had gone on. "You think he's right?"

"Oh no. If it snows, the helicopter won't be able to pick us up," Nicola said in a worried tone. "Oh wow, that'd be awful. Dinner..."

Matt searched the sky. "It isn't bad yet. Junior will be back before any weather rolls in."

"I hope so," she said fervently. Stranded in Spillimacheen with Matt, not only for the morning, but until a storm blew past? She *couldn't*. She couldn't bear being around him all that time, fencing and parrying and having to watch what she said and did. And wanting him all the time, craving his touch as a person dying of thirst craved water. Oh no. It couldn't happen, it would be intolerable. Junior would have to make it back!

They reached a curve in the road and an old apple orchard. A split rail fence ran alongside the trees, and a flock of pretty birds with cherry-red heads were pecking at the few withered old apples still clinging to the gnarled branches. Matt stopped, put a foot up on the lower rail of the fence and leaned crossed arms on the top one.

"Cute birds. Do you know what kind they are?" he asked, as if nothing had happened, as if she hadn't made him angry.

"They're called pine grosbeaks in Colorado."

"I like birds. They're so uncomplicated," he said idly, watching them. They twittered and flapped, busily eating the apples, hopping from branch to branch, scolding one another.

She stood beside him, feeling foolish, cast in the role now of sulking youngster. "I like birds, too," she said.

"You see?" he said, turning, leaning his elbows against the fence. "We do have something in common."

"That we like birds?" she asked.

"It's a start."

CHAPTER TWELVE

MATT RIPPED OPEN THE CANDY BAR, shoved half of it in his mouth, then dialed Ned's private line in Washington. He was well aware of Nicola standing close by, chewing on her own snack from the general store, eyeing him.

Had she seen the numbers he'd dialed?

He swallowed, took another mouthful and turned slightly in her direction. Not only could she have seen his hand, but if she'd wanted, she could have made out the numbers, as well. He gave her an innocent grin.

The phone rang and rang. No answer. At this point he had two options: either stall the helicopter pilot somehow and try again later, or dial directly into the Foreign Service switchboard, using an unscrambled line, and give his instructions to Ned's secretary. He opted for choice number one. Wait. Choice two would have Ned murderously furious; an agent only used the open lines in case of a dire emergency.

"No one home?" Nicola asked from her spot leaning against the wall. She was suspicious. Oh, Nicky hadn't clue one as to what he was up to, but just the fact that she was curious was enough to tell him that he'd started making mistakes.

So what? He was fed up with his line of work, anyway. Either Ned brought him in, or Matt was going to take his chances and quit. They wouldn't really, ah, terminate him, would they? Heck, Jennings, one of the other Section C agents, had been brought in after thirty years in the service, and now he had a cushy job, working for the Paris office as a translator. Naw, Ned wouldn't give Matt too hard a time....

"Well," Nicola said, sighing, "guess we both struck out today."

"Looks that way." He noticed the sarcastic note in her voice—she thought he'd been trying to get a lady, no doubt, but he couldn't tell her otherwise. He watched as she crumpled up her candy wrapper and tossed it, a basketball-style bank shot, into a nearby trash can. "Good eye."

"For some things."

Dust was kicking up across the road and swirling around the building. It was going to be a hairy ride back to the lodge. "You want to go inside and wait?" he asked.

"Sure, why not?"

What really hurt, what twisted his gut into knots, was how much he cared for Nicola. He wanted to plunge into that bottomless pool of sensations with her, delve into his true feelings, really live, for once. But that meant coming clean. And even if he told her everything, even if he showed his real face, what would that face be? He had no way of telling; he'd lived this charade too long. He was a coward, he guessed, afraid that there was no real Matt Cavanaugh behind the cover identity, or afraid that if there was a real man there and he spilled the beans about himself, he'd find out that she didn't like him, anyway.

Now *that* was a scary proposition.

Nicola leaned her elbows on the counter inside the store and chatted with the owner. "It's really starting to blow out there," she said.

"Looks bad," the man agreed, staring gravely at his pipe.

"I sure hope the helicopter makes it here soon," she said.

"Bad" was an understatement. Matt could see outside from where he stood, resting a shoulder against the front window. The dust was now mixed with icy pellets of snow, dashing itself against the glass, obscuring the street. During the moments between gusts, he could see dark and threatening clouds scudding across the peaks to the west. They were in for a real storm. The prospects of the chopper returning to pick them up were getting dimmer by the second.

He turned, folded his arms and watched Nicola. She tossed her head, laughing at something the shopkeeper said, and he could see the long, delicate line of her neck. He wondered vaguely if they were stuck here for a night, where they would sleep.

"Getting worse out there, eh?" the man was saying.

Nicola turned and glanced out the window, looking straight past Matt, as if he didn't exist. "Darn," she said, frowning, "the helicopter will never fly in this now. Darn."

Not that she wanted his reassurance . . . "Look," Matt said, "I'm sure Jon can handle things. This isn't your fault, Nicky."

She only stared at him, then turned away again, stiff, upset. "Well," she said to the man, "can you put us up somewhere for the night if we have to stay?"

"Not here," he replied. "But the bus is due in at two. You could catch a ride to Radium Hot Springs, about an hour away. There're a couple of hotels there."

She let go of a breath. "What do you think, Matt?" Her eyes didn't meet his.

"I guess we'll have to if Junior doesn't get here by two," he replied distractedly. *Swell.* Now Evan was left totally without protection. Murphy's Law. First he couldn't get hold of Ned to have the guests checked out, now this. And what if one of the guests—Rei, or Carlos, most likely—made an attempt on Evan's life tonight? The thought chilled him, almost made him physically sick. And there was only that damn radio contraption back at the lodge, a tenuous link with the outside world in the event of an emergency. Matt had no control of the situation; he was stranded, without even a radio link to the lodge from here.

"You don't look too pleased about this," Nicola was saying.

"I'm not. Sorry," he added quickly, "I meant about being stuck here." That didn't help, either.

The trouble was that he was worried sick about Evan, and just being near Nicola made him feel vulnerable, unable to trust his own reactions, his own judgment. His carefully constructed world was crashing down around his ears, and there wasn't a thing he could do to stop it.

They waited until two, unable to do a thing, both ill at ease—for vastly different reasons, Matt knew. Poor Nicky, stuck with him. He wondered just how much she disliked him, just how strong her antipathy to men like her father really was. And yet she still loved Went, didn't she?

"Bus is here," the man said, startling Matt out of his dark reverie.

Of course, they sat together in the nearly empty bus. But it was a silent ride. He tried to make small talk with her; he tried not to notice her thigh pressed up against his on the narrow seat.

"Really coming down hard out there now," he said, staring out the window as the daily bus sped along the country road.

"Yes," she said. "I hope it stops by morning."

"Me, too."

All so polite, so careful, as if one of them might shatter the precarious wall of civility that had gone up between them. What he really wanted to do was spend his precious, difficult time they had together pouring out his problems to her, telling her about his confusion, his disillusionment, his gut-wrenching concern for Evan. He could, for instance, tell her that he'd been living at home since Thanksgiving, a thankless chore at best, and bartending at a glitzy steak house in nearby Tarrytown. And all to keep an eye on Evan. There were the other agents Ned had sent; Matt usually checked in with whoever was watching the place at night on his way to work in the evening.

Maureen had been bewildered at the rather weak excuse he'd given her—"I couldn't find an apartment, Mom"—but happy to have him around. Evan growled and grumbled about his no-good bum of a son, but so far had let him stay. Oh, how furious Evan would be if he knew Matt was his bodyguard!

And T.J. wasn't real happy about having big brother on the scene, either. He never said a word; he held whatever jealousy or resentment he felt about Matt inside, but Matt sensed those pent-up feelings, close under T.J.'s skin, ready to erupt someday. He just hoped he wasn't around when T.J. let loose. He pitied his younger brother. Yes, he pitied him, but he didn't really love him.

He could push the limits of security and tell Nicola all that, or he could tell her just enough to wipe that barely expressed distrust off her face. He could. But, damn, the very notion of baring his soul like that was unthinkable.

"I hope one of the hotels has a room, *rooms*," she said, correcting herself.

"Me, too." *That is, if we get there at all,* he thought to himself as he glanced out the window into the worsening storm. He knew it would be even worse up in the mountains at the lodge, a real old-fashioned blizzard.

Radium Hot Springs, down the river from Spillimacheen, wasn't much larger, but it did have a couple of hotels and restaurants and, naturally, the popular hot springs. There were shops for tourists, gas stations, a post office—the essentials.

They got off the bus and stared up and down the street through the sheets of falling snow. About a half a block away, right in downtown, was a small, clean-looking hotel.

"Shall we try it?" Matt asked.

"It's as good as any, I guess."

They got rooms, but they were lucky, the desk clerk told them, because this time of year was popular with the tourists from Calgary. "On a weekend," he said, "we'd be full up." Then he glanced at their empty hands.

"We got stuck up in Spillimacheen. We're at the Bugaboo Lodge," Matt offered in order to save Nicola any embarrassment. He heard her laugh at his shoulder. Well, at least *she* hadn't lost her sense of humor.

"Thanks," she said as they climbed the steps.

"Oh, that. Yeah, well, I forgot we took two rooms, and all I could see was that guy staring at our empty hands."

They dined around eight but might not have eaten at all if Nicola hadn't phoned his room and suggested it. He'd been lying on his double bed, staring at the unmoving ceiling fan, brooding, feeling frustrated and helpless. How unlike him. But then, he'd never been assigned to watch his father before. And he'd never had to lie to a woman he cared about before, either.

"I think there's a restaurant right down the street," Nicola had said. "I'm really hungry, and I thought you might want to join me."

He'd leaped at the opportunity to be with her again, to take in that special, honey-sweet scent of hers, to forget those bugaboos hiding in the recesses of her mind. "That sounds great. I'll be in the lobby in three minutes."

The restaurant they ate at was strictly Western in flavor, right down to the sawdust floor. Wagon wheels hung on the walls, the lighting was old, converted oil lamps, the tablecloths red-and-white checked oilcloth. Country-and-western music drifted through the air from a jukebox. Nicola ordered salad and bar-becued chicken; he settled for a steak, on the rare side.

"You want it practically walkin', eh?" the waitress said.

"Well, not quite."

They both had Canada's own Moosehead lager, and then there was nothing to do but wait for Nicola's salad to arrive. She gazed around the room; he gazed at her face.

"Would you stop that?" Nicola finally asked.

"Stop what?"

"You know, staring at me."

"Oh, sorry."

Silence. And then they both said something about the Willy Nelson song that was playing, and they both shut up and smiled self-consciously. He picked up the glass sugar dispenser and turned it slowly in his hands; she straightened her silverware for the fourth time.

"Um," he said, "snow's letting up."

"Yes, it is." She poured the rest of her beer into her glass.

"You want another one?"

She shook her head. "Booze makes me say things I regret."

"Like what?"

Nicola laughed. "Oh, you know. You've probably seen your share of tipsy women."

"Oh, I've seen plenty. But you're not like that."

She seemed to be deciding something as she sat there with her brows drawn together. Finally she sighed, as if giving up. "Okay," she said, dropping her gaze, "if I'm not like the la-dies you meet in bars, what am I like?"

She'd opened the door a crack, albeit reluctantly, but he was ready to go in. *Take it slow. You're both new at this trusting stuff,* he cautioned himself.

"Well, for one," he said, his voice low and sincere, "you don't play games."

"Go on." She picked up her fork and turned it over in her hand.

"You know what you don't want...but then again, and maybe I'm dead wrong, you don't know what you really *do* want."

"Very observant."

"You aren't mad yet?"

She smiled and shook her head. "Not at all, I'm fascinated. I didn't think you ever thought about this kind of thing."

"Well, I know what you think about me," he remarked dryly. Then he said, "I think you idolize your dad, and I know you love your mother, but I think you put too much stock in your hopes that she'll recover someday."

"Um."

"Phew," he said, smiling broadly, "I thought you might have slapped me by now."

"Not me."

"Good enough. Well, I honestly believe that you think I have it better with Evan and Maureen than you do with your folks. Let me clarify that." He cleared his throat and swallowed some of his drink. "You need to take a good, hard look at Went and Suzanne and accept reality. The way it is, I think maybe you scare Went off."

"What?" Her salad had arrived, but suddenly she wasn't very interested in it.

"Well," Matt said, "with your dad, it's got to be slow and easy. He ran away from family commitments years ago, and if you really want his friendship, you'll have to prove to him it won't be a demanding relationship."

"You know," Nicola said, picking up a lettuce leaf thoughtfully, "maybe you're right. Maybe every time I see him, I'm too eager. You might have something there."

"Maybe there's more to me than meets the eye," he ventured.

Her glance came up sharply.

"Anyway," he said quickly, "I have my intuitive moments, I suppose. For instance, I think you're real vulnerable with men...."

"Oh?"

"I do, yes. And I was rotten to have taken advantage of that."

"I'm *not* afraid of men."

"I never said 'afraid.' But you are sensitive. Oh, I see yo‸
holding your own with the old boys, like at hunting camp, bu‸
it's different with me, isn't it?"

Matt sat there with his elbows on the table, his fingers stee‸
pled in front of his face. He watched her and he waited. He
watched her duck her head, not so much in embarrassment a‸
in thought. And he saw the delicate curve of her neck where he‸
hair was swept back, and her capable, slim white fingers hold‸
ing the fork. Her lips were parted, expectant, lovely.

"I think I went too far just now," he said as much to him‸
self as to her. Did he really want to continue this probing o‸
their souls? Yet, to let these moments pass, to dodge the risks‸
was equally reprehensible.

Finally her eyes came up. "You hurt me, Matt. I thought ‸
was ready for you, but obviously I was wrong."

The food arrived; the waitress was talkative and lively. Bu‸
Matt barely noticed her. He felt as if he were on the edge of a‸
abyss, ready to either step back out of danger or to plunge in.

The waitress left, returned to fill their water glasses,
shrugged, then disappeared for good.

He took a very deep breath and pinioned Nicola with an in‸
tent gaze. "If I hurt you," he said, "I'm sorry, more sorry than
you know or will even believe."

She shook her head, wondering. "What's with you, Matt?
One minute you're Mr. Playboy, the next you're like this....
You're thoughtful and caring and...and, I don't know. That'‸
the trouble, I keep thinking you're someone else. You confuse
me."

"*You're* confused!" he said, then laughed ruefully. "I'm the
one in the fix, Nicky."

"What fix?"

He cut into his steak, took a bite, tried to find a way out. He
could tell her everything, but that was just not possible consid‸
ering the oath he'd sworn those many years ago. And yet he felt
cheated. If only he could somehow convince her that he wasn'‸
the useless jerk he appeared.

"Look," he said, "there are some things about me you don'‸
know. Let's just say that things aren't always as they appear."

"You're talking in riddles, Matt." Her dark, melancholy eyes held his.

"I know I am, but it's the best I can do. I care for you, Nicky, really do."

"I wonder."

"Hell. What more can I do? I'm not lying. I want you, kid. I want you in every way. And I've wanted you since that day last summer, since we went riding. Remember?"

"Oh yes," she replied carefully, "I remember."

"So that's it. I haven't cared about a woman this way for a long time, Nicky. Maybe never. Either you believe me or you don't."

Like him, she sliced into her chicken and took a bite, but she swallowed hard, nervously, and then had to wash it down with half a glass of water. He waited, having no idea whatsoever how she was taking this revelation of his or if she was even believing it. He could hardly believe it himself.

Finally, in midbite, she stared at him in earnest. "What do you really mean, Matt?"

"I mean forget the dinner, forget the lodge. Let's take tonight and grab it. I can't promise you more than that, Nicky, but I can promise there'll never be another one like it. Not for me, anyway."

"Just like that?"

"Just like that."

"And if I want more? If I become a clinging, jealous, screaming harridan?"

"It won't change the way I feel."

"So...it's a proposition. Plain and simple, isn't it? No, don't answer that. I get the picture. We both want to...to go back to the hotel together. But there are no strings attached."

Matt leaned back in his seat, slumping. He'd blown it. He couldn't promise her more than tonight, and he'd blown it.

"Okay."

"What?"

She was looking at him, her face pale and dead serious. She put her napkin on the table. "I said, okay. Let's go."

It was as cold as ice outside. The snow had let up, but the night sky was inky black and a bitter wind swirled down the nearly deserted street, slashing at them as their boots crunched in the newly fallen snow. He walked close to Nicola's side and hunched into his coat. "Cold?" he asked.

"Freezing."

But not for long, he thought, toying with a smile.

They walked up the hotel steps holding hands, and Matt could almost feel the flood of her conflicting emotions streaming through her fingertips. She was understandably on edge. Nicola obviously had never made a habit of this. In her touch was anticipation; she was wondering if she'd be any good at it, if she could live up to his expectations. He could help her with the nervousness, but as for the rest, she'd have to discover for herself that he wasn't some kind of international bed hopper who slept with every pretty lady he could get his hands on. There was warmth at the tip of her fingers, though, and that came from desire, from need, from the bottled-up wellspring of love deep inside her. He'd have to nurture that, treat her like a precious treasure. The last thing on earth he wanted to do was to see her hurt.

But don't ask for more, Nicky. I'll give you all I have while I can. Would there be a way of holding back the dawn?

He tried to lighten the situation, squeezing her hand, smiling down into her eyes. "Your room or mine?" he asked softly as they approached their doors.

"Oh," she said, "mine."

He took her key, pushed it into the lock, swung open the door. She seemed hesitant.

She took a deep breath. "I'm a wreck, Matt. Isn't that ridiculous?"

"No. In fact, it's part of what makes you so special to me, Nicky. Just never change, promise me that."

Kicking the door closed gently with his foot, Matt caught her arm and pulled her to him, imprisoning her against his chest while he locked his fingers together at the small of her back. He kissed her then, slowly, moving his mouth over hers, carefully parting her lips, exploring, tasting. He pressed against her and felt the tautness below her waist straining against him, and his own need, a red-hot bar of desire. He pushed his knee between her soft thighs and felt her quick, indrawn gasp. Finally, with his lips still on hers, he reached up and unfastened her long dark mane and spread it lovingly over her shoulders.

And then he smiled with his mouth pressed to hers. "I've wanted to do that for so long," he whispered.

Nicola put her hand against his stomach and nudged him away a little. "Would you mind if I, you know, take a quick shower? It's been a really long day and, well . . . Don't laugh at me."

"I won't," he replied, and ran a finger across her chin lightly. "But I could use one, too."

She looked puzzled for a split second, then shook her head. "Oh no. I know exactly what you're thinking, Matt, and . . ."

"Why not?"

Nicola looked completely ill at ease, in a quandary. "I, ah, I've never . . ."

"Then now's the perfect time to start."

She was difficult to convince, but in the end he won out. With only a small lamp turned on by the bed, she let him unbutton her shirt and toss it aside. Then, while he undressed, she unzipped her pants and stepped out of them. But he got to take care of the bra and her panties, grabbing her hand and pulling her toward him, even though she protested all the way. She was lovely, all long, lean limbs and slim, curved hips, her breasts small and firm. Yes, she was beautiful to him, just as she'd been that time on the diving board when he'd studied her from afar. But now she was his, and it was all he could do not to have her instantly, right there on the bed, quickly, without preliminaries. But he held himself back; it would only make it that much more pleasurable when they finally joined.

Before they even stepped into the shower stall, Matt turned her around and crushed the full length of her body to him, feeling those small breasts against his, the length of her hips and thighs molded to his own, her breath hot and quick now, full of expectation but a little uncertain still.

Finally he reached inside the stall and turned on the water. "Warm enough?" he asked.

She stuck her hand in. "Perfect."

"I want my back scrubbed," he said.

"No way, me first," she replied as she stepped in, laughing, the spray from the shower head striking her dark head and her slender shoulders.

Matt moved in and faced her, blinking away the water, spanning her waist with his hands. She was all soft and warm and slippery, and his desire to know her fully quickened.

He rubbed the bar of soap along her spine and kissed her thoroughly, deeply, bringing his head up once to shake off the water before his tongue probed the moist inner warmth of her mouth again. And all the while he ground his lips to hers, his hands lathered her back and hips, her soft belly up to her breasts. Oh yes, those wonderful, pert breasts, whose crests grew hard at his touch.

Nicola leaned back against the wall of the shower and raised her arms, running her fingers through her hair, pushing the heavy, slick mass back over her shoulders. But he caught her hands and held them to either side of her head, then lowered his mouth to her bosom, flicking his tongue from one breast to the other, over and over, drinking in the shower spray again and again, until she moaned and twisted and bent to put her mouth to the top of his head.

"Oh God, Matt...."

He moved lower, tasting the underside of her breasts, her stomach, making her squirm when he nibbled on a hipbone. She tried to stop him when he lowered his head further, but his mouth and tongue were strong persuaders, and he savored her, sinking to his knees, until she twisted her fingers in his hair and cried out, her whole body rocking, sagging, clinging to him.

Barely toweled off, he led her to the bed and pressed her dripping wet body onto the sheets. She must know, of course, that he had yet to find his own release, and she took the time to run her hands along the ridges of muscle on his back and chest, his thighs, until he groaned, almost losing control. He rolled onto his back, breathed deeply and asked her if she was ready.

"Yes," she said softly, running a finger down his chest until he quivered. "I can't believe it," she said, "but I am."

Matt stayed on his back. He wanted Nicola to remember this night, to find the greatest fulfillment possible. With his hands he positioned her above him, her knees straddling his hips, and then he guided her to him, feeling the soft, warm flesh enfold his hardness. Moving his hands from her hips to her waist, he entered her fully and deeply, and they both gasped together at the hot, pulsing pleasure of the union. Thrusting upward to meet her movements, Matt caressed her breasts with his hands, kneading them as she arched her back and her head lolled from side to side.

"Oh God, Matt, oh God," she whispered, and he spoke as well, unintelligible things, endearments, encouragement, until they were both panting and clinging and thrusting, harder, deeper, their flesh pounding and grinding. He let himself float on the cloud of white-hot passion, knowing that her desire was reaching a crescendo, waiting for her, pacing himself. Their movements became frenzied as they sought the same moment of release. It built and it promised, beckoning; it built into a fever pitch of gasping and thrashing, and then finally, they both cried out into the night and shuddered, holding each other and trembling.

At three in the morning, Matt awakened, and he touched her cheek with his lips, half thinking to awaken her as well, to begin the odyssey anew. But she was sleeping so peacefully, so beautifully. In the darkness he could just make out her profile, and he smiled to himself. She'd said their lovemaking was the most wonderful thing she'd ever known, and he'd kissed her and said the same. Amazingly it was true. And now there was no doubt left in his mind that this was the woman he wanted to share his life with. Yet, lurking like a shadowed creature in that corner of his brain was the knowledge that the time wasn't right. There were things to be done, ends to be tied up. And there was his father, over that tall ridge of snow-clothed mountains, in danger. How could Matt forget that fact and wallow in this newfound love? In the morning he had a job to do, a commitment to fulfill. And Nicky wasn't going to like it. No matter what she'd said last night, they both had known it was all sweet lies—there were *definitely* strings attached.

If only, Matt thought as wind rattled at the windowpanes, the dawn would never come. . . .

But it did. Scratchy eyed, he slipped out of bed and dragged the telephone into the bathroom, closing the door as far as he could without pulling the wire out of the wall. He switched on the light quietly.

"Be there, Ned," he said in a low whisper as he dialed.

On the third ring, Ned answered. "Matt, for God's sake, what's going on?"

"Things are getting sticky. Here's a list of possibles." Matt rattled off the names of those he wanted checked out. "Got it all?"

"Yes," Ned said. "But when will you be in touch again?"

"Damned if I know. It's not so easy. All there is in the lodge is the radio telephone to the Helitours office in Banff. I could use it, but only in an emergency. And when I'm gone from the lodge, Evan is left unguarded."

"You should have talked him out of this trip, Matt."

"Sure. Ever try to reason with Evan?"

"You want some backup?"

"There's no way to get them here. No, I'll handle it."

"Okay. I'll get right on this list," Ned said. "Later."

"Sure, later." He hung up and sat for a moment, thinking, rubbing the stubble on his chin. What if something had gone down last night?

But he couldn't consider that. *Stick to the facts, Matt.*

He rose from where he'd been sitting on the closed toilet seat, snapped off the light and opened the door carefully, trying to keep it from squeaking. In the darkened room he didn't see her at first, though, not until he was putting the phone back in place.

But she was sitting up in bed, the sheet pulled up to her chin. Their eyes met and locked, and in that instant he knew, undeniably and irrevocably, that he'd compromised his cover.

CHAPTER THIRTEEN

MORNING BROUGHT WITH IT a pale winter sun, but gray clouds still clung to the surrounding peaks. They caught the bus back up the valley to Spillimacheen, but the highway was icy and the going was slow. Matt's body was there on the seat next to her, his thigh in the faded denim touching hers, rubbing against it with every jounce of the vehicle, but his feelings and his attention were elsewhere.

Nicola wondered who he had been calling so early in the morning. Who was so important that he'd missed one—now two—days of skiing to fly to Spillimacheen to use a telephone? A prospective employer? No, not likely. A woman? No, not really. She just couldn't believe he'd go to all that trouble for a woman.

Who, then?

She turned her head slightly to study his profile. He wouldn't notice, because he was looking out the bus window at the gray-brown river valley sliding by. His brows were drawn, his mouth curved down at the corners, so unlike his usual expression. Something was on his mind, an all-consuming problem that had to do with that illicit phone call this morning.

It certainly wasn't Nicola he was worrying about.

She felt betrayed. This wasn't the same man who'd loved her in the night. That man had been warm and passionate and giving, intent on her pleasure, caring about her. She felt a hard lump of pain in her belly, and she wanted to double over with it, curl up and hug the ache to herself. Nausea rose in her throat, and she turned her head away quickly to hide the burning tears in her eyes.

She'd let herself in for it; she'd done exactly what she'd sworn not to do. Like a moth, she'd flown directly into the

flame, eyes wide open, wings fluttering in an ecstasy of fulfillment. Why, then, was she so surprised to be burned?

He'd been withdrawn all morning, neither the insouciant
playboy nor the rebellious son nor the happy sportsman nor the
tender lover. He was an entirely new person, one she couldn't
touch, not even physically. He'd given her a lame excuse for the
phone call, the bartending job in Palm Beach, but it was such
a manifest lie that he'd barely even tried to convince her.

The phone call was the key to Matt Cavanaugh. The phone
call. She had to know about that, then she'd understand him.
That was what she focused on as the bus rumbled up the valley
of the Spillimacheen River toward the distant mountains. She
could bear it, she could function, if she just held on to that one
idea: the phone call.

Matt shifted in the seat, inadvertently pressing a shoulder
against her as the bus lurched around a curve. "Sorry," he said.

"Um." She couldn't fit her brain around the reality of his
detachment. He'd loved her last night. His lips had loved her,
his hands, his whole lean, hard body had worshiped her.

"The ride seems longer than yesterday," he remarked idly.

She looked at her hands. He'd said he liked her hands once.
Last night she had touched him intimately, held him, stroked
him with them. "Matt." Her voice was very low, and she didn't
even know what she was going to say, but she needed some sort
of communication with him, some proof of her own self-worth.

"What?" He turned his head, as if noticing her for the first
time.

"I just said your name."

He sat, politely expectant and maybe a little impatient,
wanting to get back to his private thoughts.

"Matt, I...uh... I think I should... I think you owe me an
explanation...."

He waited.

She plunged in. "Who were you calling this morning?"

His faced changed, chameleon-like, lighted up by a jolly,
slightly embarrassed smile, punctuated by his adorable dimple. "I told you, the man in Palm Beach. For the job, you
know."

"That's not good enough, Matt. It's a lie."

He changed again, his mask turning to one of utter neutrality, mild, sincere. "Okay, so it wasn't anyone in Palm Beach. But it wasn't important. It has nothing to do with you, Nicky."

"Yes, it does. It changed you, that phone call. You're different. It's as if I don't exist anymore. Something happened," she said in a low, harsh voice, not looking at him. Then she noticed that one of her hands was clenched into a fist.

"Look, I have some problems. Nothing serious, but I can't talk about it." Now he was peeling down through another layer to the nice guy, the affable, thoughtful pal.

"Matt, you can tell me. Please, whatever it is, you can tell me."

He put a hand on her fist, stroking her fingers so they relaxed. "Take it easy, kid. There's nothing to tell."

"Is it another woman?" she threw out, knowing he'd deny it even if it was. "All those calls? Redstone and now here. Where does she live? It must be on the East Coast if you call from here so early...and she's never home, is she? Is that your problem, Matt, that your girl is cheating on you?"

Then he did the first genuine thing he'd done all morning—he laughed.

"Don't laugh," she said brokenly.

"Oh, Nicky, I'm sorry. Is that what you think? Another woman, oh my God."

"Well?"

He took both of her hands in his; his expression was earnest, and she knew it was the real Matt now, the one she loved. "No, there's no other woman."

"Then tell me about the phone call. What's going on, Matt?"

"I can't." His face was sober; it suddenly struck her that there was a look of Evan about him—in his eyes and in the lines that bracketed his mouth—a look of a man who carried a great responsibility and had learned to live with it.

"Matt?" she whispered, frightened by this revelation, this truth she'd just seen.

He squeezed her hands. "I can't tell you, not now. Trust me."

"Matt, what is it? Is it . . . is it something about Evan?" The words had flown into her head; she didn't even know where they'd come from. "I don't know.... It seems that you've been around him so much. Is he in danger, is that it?"

"Nicola." His eyes were shadowed as he searched her face. "Please, Nicola. I love you. Please trust me."

Her heart leaped at his words, and joy burst within her. *He loves me*. And then, in the same breath of time, the joy whirled inward upon itself and turned cold and hard and dropped like a stone to her feet. "That's probably what my father says to all his women, but they make the mistake of believing him," she said.

"I'm *not* your father."

"No," she said miserably, "no, you're not." For the rest of the ride, Nicola could only stare out of the window feeling a knot of uncertainty grow in her chest.

It was the other helicopter pilot, Bernie, who picked them and the food up later that afternoon at Spillimacheen. If he wondered at the bleak silence between Nicola and Matt, he said nothing about it. "Guess you were stuck pretty bad, huh? What a mess. Jon was going bananas, you can imagine. Will he be glad to see you!"

"Everything okay at the lodge?" Matt asked casually. "Good skiing today?"

"Great. There was a foot of new powder this morning from yesterday's storm."

"Sorry I missed it," Matt said, not sounding very sorry at all.

THE NEXT DAY the weather was perfect: cold and clear, with a blue sky and all that new powder that everyone had been skiing the day before.

Jenny, who'd tweaked an already bad knee skiing in the previous day's fresh snow, offered to clean up after breakfast and take care of the box lunches so that Nicola could go skiing—if there was room in the helicopter. She said she'd get Cindy to help her, so Nicola didn't feel too guilty.

"Oh, be quiet, you two," Ruthie said. "Hans knows where he's going."

Werner was there and T.J. and Carlos Santana and Helga. Was she going to ski? But no, Nicola saw, she didn't have ski boots on; she was just going along for the ride.

Nicola clumped up to Bernie. "Is there room for me?"

Bernie looked over the skiers and counted heads. "Sure. There're only seven here and you. I think there's one more coming."

"Great."

Evan was making a boisterous comment to Werner. "You young kids, you could probably ski all day and you-know-what all night! I envy you!"

Even Werner had to crack a wintry smile at that. "I am not so very young, you know," he replied modestly.

"He's just the right age," Helga said defensively.

"I'll bet," Ruthie said, winking at Dave.

"Nicola! Great! You're coming along," Evan said. "It's too bad you were stuck in the valley."

"We've had wonderful skiing," T.J. offered. "Haven't we, Dad?"

"*Fantastic.*"

"All right, folks. Is everyone here? I think we're ready," Hans was saying. "Oh, here comes the last one."

Nicola looked and bit her lip. Darn it. Matt was hurrying along the path, skis over his shoulder, looking as if he didn't have a care in the world. He was so handsome and debonair in his bright blue parka, which matched his eyes perfectly, his goggles pushed up on his forehead and his tight ski pants with bright red racer's padding on the knees and shins.

"Sorry," he panted, "sorry I'm late."

"For God's sake," Evan grumbled.

"Okay, let's go," Hans said.

They all climbed in the door of the helicopter, arranging themselves on two bench seats facing each other. Bernie stuck his head in, counted them all, then pushed the door shut.

"It's going to be cold up there this morning," Dave said.

"Then the snow will be lighter," Carlos said. "Much better than warm sun."

"He's right," T.J. put in. "It'll be good this morning."

Nicola had managed to sit as far away from Matt as possible, in the corner opposite Hans. She would pretend he wasn't there, that's all. She'd have her day of skiing and enjoy it.

The helicopter let them off at the top of a shining white peak. Hans unloaded the skis and poles, everyone took his own and put them on, stepping into bindings with neat clicks, gloved hands grasping poles, pulling goggles down. Everyone stamped and took a deep breath, getting ready.

"Skadi check," called Hans. Skadis were the electronic rescue beacons that every skier wore on a cord around his neck. They sent out electronic beeps that could be detected by a receiver, so that if someone was buried by an avalanche, that person could be found rapidly. No one was allowed to ski the untracked Bugaboos without one turned on to send a signal. Hans had each person move past him while he listened for beeps in his earpiece to make sure the Skadis were working. "Okay, all set."

The group was poised, expectant, at the top of the run. Below them was a glistening, pure white bowl of powder snow, a blank piece of writing paper, and each skier was desperate to inscribe his own perfect message upon it, his own gracefully carved words, linked one after the other, endlessly, down the face of its purity, until the wind covered the tracks or new snow filled them in. Above was the clear, cold blue sky to witness their descent and the yellow sun that cast their elongated shadows ahead of them. The chopper was gone now, its faint thumping still audible, returning to the lodge to pick up another group and deposit it, also, on the top of the world.

"Oh my God, heaven!" Dave breathed, sucking the thin air into his lungs.

"Let's go," Evan cried, stamping his skis.

"You will all stay behind me," Hans cautioned.

"Yes, yes," they chorused, impatient.

"Be careful of the cliff there." He pointed with his pole, a compact, fair Canadian, young and wiry, sober with his responsibility. "We'll stop and count heads just above the trees, there."

"Come on!"

War whoops split the air as Hans aimed his skis downhill
first, sliding off easily, relaxed, then Evan and Dave, T.J. and
Matt, Carlos and Werner. Nicola watched them go for a second. She and Ruthie would ski together, the buddy system being in effect. The men were all marvelous skiers, carving round
turns down the fall line, leaving their twisting trails behind to
testify to their passage. They flew like brightly colored birds,
rooster trails of snow streaming behind them, only their arms
and heads visible in the snow churning around their bodies.

Nicola pushed off with Ruthie. Ah! She felt the resistance of
the snow, shifted her weight, turned to the left, rose, then
shifted again, sensing the inert acceptance of the snow under
her pliable skis. She was free, skimming down, swooping, the
cold wind hitting her face, her chest heaving like a bellows. Left
then right, the snow boiling up around her; she sucked it into
her lungs and felt like coughing, as if she were breathing in
dust, ducked her chin to breathe more easily. Down, down, her
legs aching, but she couldn't stop—that would be a betrayal of
herself and the mountain.

Pure sensation engulfed her, a perfection of movement and
balance and strength that drove all thought from her except the
next turn and the next. And then she was aware of the group
stopped in front of her above the line of trees that stood like old
women in snow-encrusted shawls, and she leaned on one ski,
came around in a perfect curve and stopped.

"Oh Lordy!" she cried, full of joy.

"That was great!"

"Terrific!"

"¡Fantástico!"

"My poor legs!" somebody lamented.

"Okay, everyone here? So now we'll make our way through
these trees. Carefully. There's another snowfield below. Try not
to fall into any tree wells, please," Hans said.

Tree skiing was another story entirely. You needed to make
tight, perfectly controlled turns, and you needed a good eye for
choosing your path, snaking between the trees without hitting
any. It was slower, more demanding, but requiring greater skill.

"Oh boy," Ruthie said, "don't leave me to climb out of a
tree well by myself."

"Okay, we'll stick close together," Nicola replied, pushing off with her poles. The air in the belt of frozen trees smelled of pine, fresh and cold, and the snow was stippled with shadows. Nicola dodged under an overhanging branch, brushed it and felt it release its load of snow onto her. The pitch was steep; she had to work her legs harder, make quicker, more complete turns to keep her speed under control. She felt the dampness of sweat on her skin under her suit, felt her chest going in and out, her legs working, shifting, weight to one side, lifting then shifting to the other.

She came out into the bright sun below the trees, Ruthie right behind her, and stopped by Hans. Beyond them stretched another snowfield, thousands of feet in altitude.

"What's this run, about four thousand feet altogether?" Evan was asking.

"That's about right, Dad," T.J. said.

"Okay, so four or five runs like this, and I'll make my quota for the day." He meant that his week would add up to the promised hundred thousand vertical feet, Nicola knew.

"Too bad you missed those two days, Matt," Evan went on. "We did twenty thousand vertical each day."

Matt was leaning negligently on his poles. "Those're the breaks, I guess," he said carelessly.

Then they were off again, slicing down on the smooth, white, flawless surface, letting out inadvertent cries and shouts of pleasure at the precision of movement, breathing in the tickling crystals. Pole plant, lift to that perfect moment of suspended weightlessness between turns, pressure the snow, lean into it, carve the turn, pole plant, lift again to hang above the powder, shift to the other side, *press*.

Nicola pulled up to a stop halfway down the slope to help T.J., who'd taken a tumble. "You okay?" she asked, handing him his hat and snow-packed goggles.

"Sure, I'm fine." He untangled his skis and stood up, slapping his hat against his leg to dislodge the snow.

"That was a good one!" Ruthie said, laughing, as she stopped beside them.

"When you do it, you should do it right," T.J. said, smiling for once.

They all arrived down at the spot in the valley where the helicopter was going to pick them up and stepped out of their bindings, waiting.

"Let's do that again," Ruthie said.

"Yes, we will. If we all go to the right a little, we'll have another untracked run," Hans agreed.

Bernie came for them shortly, the thump of the rotors announcing his approach.

"Good run?" he called, leaning out, pulling his headphones away from his ears.

"*Wunderbar,*" Werner shouted back, grinning widely, waving a ski pole.

"We're going to do that one again," Hans said. "Can you meet us right here with the lunches?"

"Sure thing."

The skis and poles were loaded, they all climbed in and the chopper tilted, beat at the air, surged, and they were up, on their way to the top of the mountain again.

Matt was sitting next to Ruthie, teasing her. Nicola looked away, but she could hear what he was saying. "You've lost weight, Ruth, you know that? You look terrific. And you haven't forgotten how to ski, either."

"Oh, shush, Matthew. I have sons almost as old as you!" And she poked him in the ribs with her elbow.

Helga sat next to Werner. "*Liebchen*, was it good? But I like the scenery so much better from up here. And Bernie is such a gentleman." She held Werner's arm, clinging to him, wearing too much makeup to withstand the revealing light of day. She was deliberately rude to Evan, turning her back on him. Was Nicola being as obvious as that in her snubbing of Matt?

Everyone talked, joked, complained about tired legs or shortness of breath. Nicola could have been with a group from the week before or the week to come. Everyone was red cheeked, red nosed, stimulated by the thrill of adventure.

"Oh, Werner," Helga said over the loud din, "you are enjoying yourself, yes?"

And he smiled, replying in German.

"Well," she said, snuggling against him, "it was hunting in the autumn, and now skiing. Perhaps we shall fly to a beach in Mexico next month."

But Nicola only heard the part about hunting. In Colorado? she wondered, her brow furrowed. "So, Werner," she began, leaning across the aisle, "you're a hunter, too. Tell me, just where do you like to—"

"All right!" Dave cried. "At the top of the world again! Everyone ready?"

Bernie let them off in the same place. They clicked into bindings, grabbed poles, looked to Hans for direction. Then down they went once more, on the other side of the bowl. Werner and Carlos crossed each other's tracks in figure eights, a long precise line of connected loops. Down, down, until their legs burned and they had to sniff back the cold drips from their noses.

Nicola and Ruthie were in the middle of the group, off to one side. The white slope lay ahead, seamed by a gully. Nicola turned aside to avoid it smoothly, putting pressure on her ski, totally forgetting about Werner and hunting, loving the pleasure of the power, the exhilaration, the challenge. The hill dropped off suddenly in front of her skis, a ten-foot cliff, but she was going too fast to stop. She sailed off the cliff, horrified, her heart lurching, but she landed softly, easily, with a whoomp. "Oh Lordy!" she cried to no one in particular, stopping to catch her breath.

Ruthie appeared around the side of the cliff. "God! I thought I'd find a wreck," she said.

Nicola laughed in relief and triumph. "I did it! I jumped that cliff! Did you see that?"

Over lunch she told the others the story of her surprise flight.

"You're lucky you didn't break your neck," T.J. admonished, blowing a stream of cigarette smoke out into the pristine air.

"Aw, she can handle it. Who taught her, after all?" Evan said. "And will you put that cancer stick out, T.J.?"

"Sure, Dad," T.J. said, stubbing his cigarette into the snow.

"Take it easy, Nick," Dave said. "If something happens to you, our gourmet delights are finished."

Matt watched her closely while she replied to these remarks. She was too aware of his scrutiny, oversensitive. It probably meant nothing. But her mouth was dry, and she couldn't seem to swallow her sandwich. Hans opened a bottle of wine, handing plastic glasses around to everyone, and they toasted the day, one another, the runs, Bernie, Hans, anything and everything.

"Oh, look," Helga said. A Canada Jay was stealing a crust of bread from Werner's fingers. "Even the birds love you, *Liebchen*."

The afternoon went too fast. Nicola wanted it never to end. It flashed through her mind briefly that Jenny should be cooking the rice, but the thought fled just as quickly. The only reality was turning and turning, writing her story on the snow, breathing and flexing and descending flawlessly, feeling the mountains, knowing them. She wished suddenly that her mother could share this pleasure with her. Maureen could share it with her children. So could Ruthie, whose sons and daughter often came to Canada with her. Suzanne would come alive under the influence of the immense sky and the mountains and the clear, cutting air. Maybe she should write Suzanne's doctor and ask if her mother could come up to visit her at the lodge. Yes, she'd have to do that....

They were on their last run, a thousand feet above the valley where Bernie would pick them up, when Nicola saw that Evan had stopped below her. He was leaning forward on his poles, head down. Evan *never* stopped; he prided himself on his endurance, she knew. She halted just above him, sinking up to her knees in soft snow. "You okay?" she asked, panting.

Evan looked up. He appeared tired, the color drained from his usually ruddy cheeks. "Yes, sure, I'm fine. Just catching my breath."

"You sure?"

"Go on, I'm fine. Where's that son-of-a-gun Huff? He left me, didn't he?"

"Up ahead, I guess. Are you sure..."

But Evan was getting angry. *"I'm okay."* Then he pushed off with his poles, turning nicely, easily, without any problem.

Nicola decided to keep him in sight. He'd be furious if he knew she was watching out for him, but he hadn't looked well.

Altitude sickness, possibly. It could come on very suddenly. She skied behind him, keeping well back. They were almost down. The helicopter was already there, waiting for them, a silver bug squatting on the snow, its antennae circling idly.

Maybe Evan was tired, maybe he'd had too much wine at lunch, she thought.

Five hundred feet above the valley, Evan careened forward, sprawling in the snow. Nicola felt her heart catch, then she was racing down to him, snapping off her skis, kneeling in the snow next to him.

"What happened?" she heard, and looked up. It was Matt, stepping out of his own skis. "I saw him fall. Is he hurt?"

But Evan was sitting up, growling something. "Damn binding was loose." He stood, brushing off snow, swearing under his breath.

"You all right, Evan?" Matt asked.

"I'm..." began Evan, then abruptly, as if alerted by some internal alarm, his eyes grew huge and knowledgeable, and he fell over backward into the snow, unconscious.

CHAPTER FOURTEEN

NICOLA CRADLED EVAN'S HEAD in her lap as the helicopter's right ski touched the landing pad, the big machine tipped crazily, and then the left ski settled down hard amid the crowd gathered there, waiting anxiously. She fought the panic welling up inside her. Panic wasn't going to help Evan.

Matt, who sat across from Nicola, looked at her gravely. For a brief moment she saw a flood of emotions flickering across his face: fear, helplessness, anger, regret. So much turmoil seething inside him, she thought, just like her. So he was human, after all. *Oh, Matt,* she wanted to cry, *what's happened to Evan, what's happened to us?*

Jon was the first to open the sliding door, and Matt leaped down to the pad.

Then Jon was up inside the helicopter, beside Dave. "How is he, Nicola?" Jon asked, stooping over.

"He's still unconscious," she said, putting her hand to Evan's brow. "I just don't know."

Maureen climbed into the helicopter then, and Dave put his arm around her shoulders. "He'll be okay," Dave was telling her. "I think he overdid it today."

"Oh God," was all Maureen could get out.

"Vat if it's his heart?" Jon turned to Dave.

But then Matt was back, issuing orders, dragging in the stretcher. He worked with amazing efficiency considering it was his own father lying there ashen-faced and unconscious, and in moments Evan was being carried across the snow toward the lodge.

"He ought to go straight to the hospital," Ruthie Huff said to Nicola.

Maureen, who was walking with them, her hand clutched in Ruthie's, wasn't so sure, though. "I don't know," she said. "What if he's only got altitude sickness?" She looked at the two of them for help. "It couldn't be his heart. Evan's so healthy."

"Of course not," Ruthie said reassuringly. "I only meant that he should be checked out by a doctor. He's as strong as a horse."

Inside the lodge, everyone seemed to be talking at once, offering opinions to Maureen, who was trying to follow the men with the stretcher up the stairs.

"Too much exertion," Rei said, rushing up, bobbing his head.

"The flu," said another.

"I don't think it's his heart," came the guide's voice, "I've seen heart attacks before. Their lips turn blue."

"Look," Nicola finally said brusquely, making a path for Maureen to the stairs, "let's just let Mrs. Cavanaugh go on up and see. Excuse us."

The men had gotten Evan from the stretcher onto his bed, removed his boots and parka and put a blanket over him. Nicola stood in the doorway and tried to see if Evan was any better, if he'd regained consciousness yet.

"Fill this, will you, T.J.?" Matt handed his brother the water pitcher and turned back to Evan, bunching a pillow under his neck. "Hey, Evan," he said in quiet voice, "Dad. Feeling any better? Hey, come on."

Jon rattled into the room then, nudging past Nicola, carrying a portable oxygen bottle. "I think he needs air, yes?"

Then Matt began to place the mask over Evan's mouth and nose, but Evan stirred, pushing the contraption aside. "Get that . . . away."

Nicola's heart leaped. For a brief moment the grouchy old Evan had reappeared.

T.J. moved past her then to Maureen, who was sitting on the edge of the bed, and handed her the pitcher and water glass.

"See if you can get him to take in some fluid," Matt suggested.

"What's all this?" Evan was drawing up his knees and trying to throw off the blanket.

"Oh, darling," Maureen said, reaching out to still him, "do lie there calmly, won't you? You've had a terrible time."

"That's right," Matt agreed, hovering over the bed, "do what Mom says. We don't even know what happened to you yet."

Within a very few minutes, Evan seemed much himself again, grumbling, complaining about all the fuss, insisting that he'd gotten a little light-headed and taken a bad spill. "Huff's probably laughing his head off," Evan said angrily.

Oh, but it was good to see him like this again! Never had Nicola welcomed more gladly one of Evan's irritable moods. Everyone seemed relieved, too, and smiled at his comments.

Jon put away the oxygen. "Ve von't be needing this, I think."

"You didn't eat enough breakfast," Maureen declared. "I warned you, darling."

"I ate plenty."

Within twenty minutes of returning to the lodge, Evan's color was better, and he seemed completely lucid, if tired and complaining of nausea.

"Dad's going to be fine," T.J. said, putting a hand on Maureen's shoulder.

"Of course he is," the woman breathed.

Nicola felt her heartbeat settle into an even pace finally and went out unobtrusively, letting her breathing return to normal, remembering that she had work to do. She answered questions from the guests who were waiting below. "It looks like he'll be fine.... Yes, that was a close one.... No, he's talking and sitting up.... No, he says there's not any pain." She made her way into the kitchen and hurriedly pulled out pots and pans, checked the cooked rice, turned on the oven, grabbed things out of the fridge and tossed them on the cutting board. How long would the salmon take?

"Is everything all right here?" It was Jon, standing in the door, his brow furrowed.

"All's well. Dinner will be at the usual time. Not to worry," she called over her shoulder.

"That Evan," he said, "a strong man, yes? But still, I think maybe he should be seeing a doctor."

"He insists he's fine."

"Ah, yes, he vould. But everyone is still very vorried, you see." He mumbled something else and then headed back to the guests.

Everyone was worried, Nicola thought to herself as she reached for the wire whisk and a bowl. But *was* everyone? Or was there one guest who was merely berating himself?

She called the maids to serve dinner at seven then returned to the kitchen and began to clean up. Evan was reportedly doing much better, resting comfortably, and Matt and T.J. had come down to dinner while Maureen had taken hers in the room with Evan. Probably, Nicola told herself, Evan had overdone the skiing. He was no spring chicken, after all. And yet his boast to Dave the day they'd all arrived nagged at her. Evan had bragged that he'd just had a complete physical and was as fit as a fiddle. It seemed unlikely to her that he would have just collapsed like that.

Too many coincidences, she thought, becoming unsettled all over again. First Reyes making that threat, then that near miss in hunting camp, then Helga's tirade, and now this, a perfectly healthy man keeling over for no apparent reason.

Was Reyes behind all this? Or how about those two, Rei and Carlos, both heavily invested in Costa Plata? They'd practically jumped Evan the minute he'd arrived. She remembered her thought about Reyes having sent them.

Then again there was Helga. Nicola pictured the woman's expression when Evan had been carried in on the stretcher. Not surprisingly, she'd looked awfully smug. And Nicola guessed it would be a mistake to underestimate her. Of course, her lover, Werner, with those frigid pale eyes of his, might be protecting Helga's interests. Or *was* he a lover? Maybe she'd hired him to come along and—

"Hello, am I disturbing you?" It was Maureen, poking her head in. "I wanted to get Evan some tea."

"How is he?" Nicola opened a cupboard and pulled down a box of herbal tea and a jar of honey.

"Thanks," Maureen said. "Oh, he's his usual self, grouchy. But he still feels sick to his stomach. I thought some tea . . ."

"Poor Evan," Nicola said, thinking. "Maureen, could I come up and talk to you and Matt and T.J. for a minute?"

"Why, of course." She looked at Nicola suspiciously, then smiled. "I'll tell the boys to go on up to Evan's room. Is everything all right, dear?"

"Oh, probably," was all she said.

The atmosphere in the bar was hushed that night when Nicola walked through. Everyone was still up and about, but conversation was low and lacked the usual animation. They were all subdued, each wondering about the isolation of the lodge, questioning his or her strengths and weaknesses, probably wishing there was a doctor handy, just in case. On her way up to Evan's room, Nicola spoke to several of them, giving reassurances that Evan was going to be fine.

"You know," Dave said, stopping her on the bottom step, "Evan's never been sick a day in his life. Try to persuade him to fly into Banff in the morning, will you, Nick?"

"I'll try."

She found the Cavanaughs already there, Maureen and T.J. both in chairs, Matt lounging against the dresser. Evan was propped up in bed, looking tired and drawn but alert.

"I feel like a complete fool," he said to Nicola when she closed the door behind her. "I'm not an invalid."

"We know you aren't," Nicola was quick to say. Already she knew Evan was not going to like her little speech, not one bit.

"Well," she said, coming to sit on the foot of the bed, forcing a smile, "I guess everyone's wondering why I wanted to see you all." She glanced around at the faces nervously; they all looked as troubled as she was feeling, all but Evan, that was.

"What's on your mind?" Maureen asked softly. "You can tell us, dear, we're family."

Nicola sighed. This wasn't going to be easy. "I don't think Evan's sick," she began, and looked them each, one by one in the eye. "What I'm saying is, I believe someone here at the lodge is responsible for what happened to him today." She met Matt's intent gaze and held it for a long moment. "I think someone's trying to . . . kill him."

Maureen was the first to react by gasping, her hand flying to her throat. And then T.J. let out a long whistle and fumbled for his cigarettes.

"Now see here," Evan began, pushing himself up.

"*Listen* to me," Nicola said, feeling Matt's eyes scrutinize her, "this can't be a coincidence." She turned to Evan abruptly. "You've got to tell Maureen about hunting camp, Evan. You have to now."

"What about hunting camp?" Maureen asked.

They told her then, and T.J. as well, because he hadn't been there.

"Damn, Dad," T.J. said, "you should have told us before! Are you *trying* to get yourself killed?"

Maureen was practically in tears. "Oh, Evan," she said, clutching his hand, "darling, what if Nicola is right? This Costa Plata business. And that horrible man, Reyes, who threatened you. And now you're telling me someone took a shot at you? Evan, how could you have kept that from me? What's happening to us? Maybe you should listen to Nicola."

"Ridiculous," Evan said, storming. "She's got one hell of an imagination."

"No," T.J. put in, "she's right. Something strange happened to you today."

"Like what? I fell. Big deal."

"You passed out," Nicola said, getting frustrated, "and you know it."

"And how did someone make me pass out?" Evan snorted in derision.

"I don't know," Nicola said. "Poison, something."

"Poison!" Now Evan was really angry, red suffusing his cheeks and neck. "Are you crazy, Nicola?"

"Now, wait a minute," T.J. said, stepping forward, taking his mother's hand, "maybe she's not so crazy. I think you should fly into Banff first thing in the morning and get some tests taken."

"The hell I will!"

"Evan," Maureen said, "*please*, listen to the children, they might be right. Oh God."

"I'm not going anywhere! You've all lost your minds!"

T.J. put a hand up as if to silence his father. "What about Rei and Carlos? Don't they have a joint venture in Costa Plata? An auto plant?"

"So what?" Evan asked, steaming. "I already talked to both of them. They admitted they came here this week to find out exactly where I stood on those loans."

"Well," T.J. said, "there you are. You told them face-to-face you were going to be the instrument of their financial ruin."

"He's making sense," Nicola said. "Please listen to him, Evan."

"Hogwash."

"And Helga," Maureen said. "I wouldn't put anything past that...that *woman*."

"There's Werner, too," Nicola added. "We only have Jon's word for it that he's her lover. And in the chopper today, Helga mentioned that Werner had gone hunting this fall."

Evan laughed harshly, but the act seemed to drain him. He sagged back onto his pillows. "Next you'll be telling me that Werner is a hit man," he said, trying to sound amused. He waved his hand in the air. "You're all letting your imaginations run wild," he said. "I could tell you about Jon's family, too, you know. He's got relatives in trouble in Central America. They stand to lose a lot. The problem is, my concerned family, everyone could be after my hide. It's not the first time, and I assure you, it won't be the last."

"But Evan..." Nicola protested.

"*Enough.* I was perfectly fine until you started all this tonight, young lady, and I won't hear another word. Men in my position make enemies. It's the name of the game. Now, why don't you all disappear and let me get some rest. Tomorrow's going to be another fabulous powder day."

Disheartened, worried, Nicola rose to her feet. She looked around for help, but none was forthcoming. Evan, as usual, had had the last word. She noticed then, as she stood with her hand on the doorknob, that Matt was still there, half in the shadows, leaning against the dresser. He hadn't moved a muscle the whole time. Nor had he spoken a single word.

Evan, too, must have just realized the same thing. He swiveled his head and glared at his son. "I must say, Matt, you do have a knack for staying calm. Nothing to say?'' There was challenge in Evan's voice, and pain.

Slowly Matt unfolded his arms and stepped into the lamplight. His face looked surprisingly old and haggard. ''You're right, Evan,'' he said, his voice mocking, ''why should someone want to kill a nice, harmless old guy like you?'' And with that, he pushed past Nicola and strode down the darkened hallway.

Nicola made her way downstairs and stood in the middle of the kitchen feeling restless and afraid. Something was terribly wrong. It wasn't just Evan's predicament, either. Oh, that was a nightmare all by itself, but there was something else. It had been in that room, in Evan's room, an unseen entity, a disquieting force. Everyone had seemed himself, of course, and they'd all been genuinely concerned, but underlying that concern had been a sense of loss, as if at one time they had truly cared for Evan, but now they were just going through the motions. What had Evan done to them through the years? Why was there this holding back, this fear of loving, of being hurt? Didn't he see what this ruthless, stubborn attitude of his had done?

Standing there, lost in her troubled thoughts, Nicola had not heard Matt enter the room. It was only his shadow falling across the tiled floor that alerted her and made her spin around, startled.

''Oh,'' she breathed, ''it's you.''

He stood there, looking tall and handsome, yet strangely like a man who no longer found life's bad joke so amusing.

Another side to Matt, she thought, a distressing side. Her heart squeezed unaccountably, and she was almost overpowered by a need to rush to him and comfort him.

''I want to talk to you,'' he said, ''away from here.''

Something in his voice told her this was no game. He was in deadly earnest. She nodded, took her parka off the peg by the back door and followed him out.

The night sky was brilliant, crystal clear and diamond sharp. But on those perfect winter nights, it was always cold, a dry, biting cold that groped at her face and numbed it instantly.

Yet Nicola barely noticed. She knew only that something was awfully wrong with Matt, and she sensed, too, that he was not going to share it with her. *Who are you, Matt Cavanaugh? Who are you, really?*

They strode side by side in silence, out across the shadowed field of snow toward the helicopter pad. Their feet crunched in the white stuff, and their breath froze on their lips. She shoved her hands deeper into her pockets but thought only of this man walking close by her, this man whose body had filled hers and made her cry out in a fevered frenzy, this man who calculatingly kept himself from her, who lied to her, this man whom she loved despite it all.

"Nicola," he said softly, so softly that she wasn't certain she'd heard. "I don't know what to say to you. All I know is that you had to go it alone upstairs tonight, and I couldn't be there to help."

"You were sarcastic enough," she said.

"I know. Evan does that to me. He gets to every one of us, I guess."

"Then you are worried."

"Sure, I'm worried. I just can't find it in myself to let him see it."

"Afraid it will weaken you in his eyes?"

Matt smiled crookedly. "Something like that."

They'd reached the pad, and Nicola stopped, leaned against the cold metal of the big machine and faced him squarely. It hurt to be alone with him, to want to reach out and touch his face but not to have the time and permission to love him. How could she have let herself care so deeply?

"Nicola," he said, and leaned against the chopper, too, his body so close to hers that she could almost feel its warmth. "Look, I know I've hurt you."

Oh, how she wanted to deny it!

"And I'm sorry. It's partly my fault, but not all of it. I just don't know what words I can use to convince you that I care, kid. There *aren't* words to tell you how much."

"Really?" she said airily, her stomach wrenching. "I think you know the words, Matt. I just don't think you're capable of feeling them."

"So smart, aren't you?" He laughed lightly. "Maybe you're right. Maybe I knew at one time." He shrugged. "I guess I'm getting old and jaded."

"You could try," she whispered, looking up at his face. "You could let yourself feel. You could try being honest."

"Right. And I could tell you everything, Nicky, and get myself in a whole lot of trouble."

"There you go again."

"Yes, here I go again." Abruptly he moved and took her shoulders in his hands, fixing her with those eyes. "I'm asking you to trust me, Nicky, for a little while longer. Call it blind faith, I don't care. I can't answer your questions, not yet. But I swear I will, and you'll understand."

"Damn you," she breathed, uncertain, knowing that if he didn't let her go in a moment, she'd come apart at the seams. But paradoxically if he did let her go, she'd cry. "I don't know what to think or do or say. You keep talking in riddles. Oh, Matt," she said with a sigh, unable to look him in the face, "I want to trust you. I do. But for me it's so hard. I've been burned so bad."

"I know. Went."

"Yes. I have to protect myself. You see that, don't you?"

"Yes."

"Then how can you ask me to trust you? You sleep with me, lie to me, I don't even know who or what you are."

"I'm the man who cares about you very much, who'd kill any other guy who even looked at you. You believe that much, don't you?"

"Yes...no...I don't know. Oh, Matt, you've really torn my walls down, haven't you? And I don't even know if you care at all that I...that I love you."

Suddenly the world seemed to close in on her as if the night sky had fallen and the earth were swallowing her up. She felt the blood rush into her cold cheeks, and her knees were about to buckle. If he didn't say something, do something, in a moment she was going to scream. How could she have admitted her love to him?

Carefully he put a finger under her chin and lifted her head. "Nicky," he said, his voice deep and concerned, "I don't have the right to take your love, not yet. But maybe someday, someday soon, I can give you back as much." He bowed his head toward her, his mouth so close she could feel his warm breath fanning her lips. "Is it enough, for now?" he whispered.

"Oh, Matt, oh yes, as long as you do care." She felt his mouth cover hers, tenderly at first, and then with force, parting her lips, his arms encircling her, molding them together. She wanted to cry and laugh and pull his parka open right there and feel the hard corded muscles of his back against her fingers. She wanted him, all of him, and in any way she could have him. It no longer mattered that she knew nothing about him; she knew everything she needed to know, and strangely she *did* trust him—she had to, she was out of choices and wholly head over heels in love.

They went to the bunkhouse, tiptoeing down the hall so that none of the staff heard them. Then in her tiny room, he pulled her around to him and his mouth closed over hers hungrily, and she could feel his urgent arousal pressed into her belly.

Breathless, he lifted his head up and whispered, "Are you sure? I never want to hurt you again."

She could only nod, closing her eyes. Yes, she was very sure.

Parkas fell to the hard floor, and boots were tugged off. Then she was lying on her narrow bed and he was pushing up her black turtleneck, unsnapping her bra, lowering his head until his lips brushed her breasts. Their passions awakened like the wildness of a winter storm.

Nicola gasped at the instant warmth that coiled in her stomach and spread downward. She twisted her fingers in his thick, curling hair, along the soft skin at the back of his neck, and then she was pressing his head to her bosom, impatient, yet wanting his caresses to go on forever.

Matt responded with equal need, tasting her nipples, his head coming up to trace the line of her collarbone with his tongue, their eyes meeting briefly before he took her mouth in a hard, greedy kiss.

They shed their clothes hastily, all quick movements, their breathing sharp and shallow. And then he was next to her on the bed, his nakedness brushing hers, playing with her, teasing, tantalizing. She ran her hands along the steel hardness of his thighs and buttocks and up his spine, touching all the vertebrae, glorying in the feel of his tight muscles, his maleness.

While Nicola boldly explored his body, Matt had the leisure to move his hands along the curves of her thighs and hips, the swell of her stomach. He kissed her, running his lips across her shoulders, down her arms, tasting her flesh. He ran his tongue down her side, over her ribs to her waist, and shock waves darted into her hips and she laughed, pulling his head away. He seemed to know all the little places on her body that, once touched by artful hands, sent pulses of white-hot pleasure coursing through her.

"Oh, Matt," she breathed, "make love to me."

Smiling, his eyes heavy lidded, purposeful, he poised himself above Nicola and entered her slowly, moving his hips in a circular pattern until her movements beneath him quickened, became wild, impatient, their bellies slapping together in the age-old ritual of fulfillment.

When it was over and they lay side by side, their breathing becoming even again, he reached up and ran his fingers through her damp hair. "Thank you," he said, his voice wholly sincere, "thank you for putting your faith in me."

She lay there for a long moment, her head turned to him, her eyes fastened on his. She could tell that love did that to a person, it took over all reason and logic and led a soul down an unknown path. She could tell him that, but Nicola sensed he already knew how deep her commitment was. She merely smiled instead, contentedly, and said, "You're welcome, Matt Cavanaugh."

CHAPTER FIFTEEN

"I SUPPOSE I'LL GET chicken soup and Jell-O for lunch!" Evan said truculently the next morning.

"Now, Dad," T.J. said soothingly.

"Damn it, I want to go skiing! I'm on vacation!"

"Darling, you know you don't feel well enough to do that. There's always tomorrow," Maureen said.

Evan subsided, muttering angrily, like a child denied a treat. He sure could be a pain in the neck, Matt thought once again. But the fact that Evan hadn't gotten up, dressed and gone skiing meant that he really didn't feel very strong. It shook Matt to the core to see his father in bed, circles under his eyes, looking pale and old. Evan had never been sick, never weak, never uncertain, and to watch him in the role of a petulant invalid rattled Matt more than he liked to admit.

Had Evan been poisoned? Matt had already considered food poisoning but had instantly rejected the idea. Everyone at the lodge ate the same meals; someone else would certainly have been sick, too, if it was the food.

Poison. Matt was no expert, but there were dozens and dozens of lethal substances available in chemical supply houses, in pharmacies and, horror of horrors, in local grocery stores all over the world. Heck, every woman alive had a ready supply of them under her kitchen sink! He wanted to believe Nicola had leaped to conclusions, but then he'd been thinking the same thing from the moment they'd gotten Evan in the chopper.

Poison. There were so many types—fast acting as well as slow. Two scenarios were possible: either someone had been dosing his father over a long period of time, or that someone had administered a large dose quite recently.

But who had gotten to Evan?

Matt leaned against the wall of his father's room, arms crossed, watching the drama unfold: T.J. was solicitous, Maureen fussy and anxious, Evan irritated.

Evan had been served toast and tea for breakfast and was complaining all the while. "I'll bet Nicola cooked up something delicious for everyone else," he growled. "And I get this." He flicked at his tray contemptuously.

"It was blueberry pancakes and eggs and sausages," T.J. said artlessly.

Dumb, Matt thought.

"See? See what I mean? I love her pancakes!" Evan said.

"But you felt so sick to your stomach," Maureen said. "And we've all been worried about poison."

"Poison! You people *are* crazy. Do you think Nicola's been poisoning me? Why can't I have her pancakes and sausages?"

"Evan, stop giving us a hard time. You know Mom's right," Matt said.

Evan glanced at Matt. "Since when do I need advice from you, wise guy?"

Matt shrugged. *Since I'm responsible for your safety,* he wanted to say. Instead he offered another suggestion. "I really think you ought to be flown to the hospital in Banff, just to be checked out."

"I told you to forget it. I'll feel better tomorrow. It's the last day of skiing, and I'm going up in the chopper come hell or high water," Evan insisted.

Matt had never had such an impossible assignment. He was alone in an isolated ski lodge, trying to protect a man who obstinately refused protection, and he didn't even know who the enemy was. But worse yet, there was Nicola—sweet, worried, innocent Nicola—in the middle of this predicament running around talking about poison and Evan being in danger. Good Lord, how was he supposed to protect her, too? How many people had she voiced her suspicions to? If she'd told the wrong one, or if word got back to that particular guest of the lodge, then she'd be in danger, as well.

And Matt had to stay flippant and carefree and unconcerned to keep his cover intact. He prayed it was holding firm—with everyone else, that was. With Nicola his cover was definitely compromised. Ned would murder him; he'd told her too much already. Nicola Gage knew more about him than his own mother.

"Stop hovering over me," Evan snapped at T.J.

"Sorry, Dad, I'm just worried."

"We're all worried," Maureen said, "aren't we, Matt?"

He nodded dutifully.

"Well, I wish you'd all go worry somewhere else and leave me in peace. Go skiing, all of you. I paid for this farce of a holiday, so you better get your money's worth. Go on, get out of here," Evan said.

"Dad, will you be all right?" T.J. asked. "I think someone should stay with you."

"I'm staying," Maureen said. "I'll go downstairs, and you can take a nice nap."

"You'll check on him, Mom?" T.J. asked.

"Of course."

"Oh, for God's sake!" Evan blustered.

"I, for one, think he's right. If he's too damn stubborn to go to Banff, then we should at least enjoy ourselves," Matt stated easily, but inside his gut churned. How was he supposed to handle this now, with Evan refusing to fly to Banff? And if he hung out in the lodge with Maureen, hovering over his father all day long, everyone was going to notice. Too bad he couldn't come up with a bum knee or a sprained ankle. Too obvious, though.

Okay, Matt thought, he'd go skiing; he'd pretend he couldn't care less about his old man. Maureen was going to watch Evan anyway, and only Helga would be around. Maureen could handle that one, all right; she wouldn't let the woman within fifty yards of her husband.

Maureen. Should he discount his own mother as a suspect? She had plenty of motive to rid herself of a husband who had caused her emotional anguish for years. And who had a better chance to use poison?

He looked at his mother, petite and trim, every inch a lady. He studied her expression and the nervous fluttering of her white fingers. No, it wasn't Maureen; all of his training and instincts for deception told him that.

To be fair, he should consider T.J. Poor T.J. Everything he craved was in his father's hands: money, power, position, the family bank, Maureen. Oh yes, he could see how T.J. adored his mother and tried to protect her, how much he strived for her approval.

Matt studied his brother, too, the expressionless features, the slightly receding hairline, his gawky height and his tenseness. But that was because T.J. needed a cigarette and wouldn't dare light up in Evan's room. It couldn't be T.J., the downtrodden. No, he had no guts at all; they'd been beaten out of him. Maybe, Matt thought fleetingly, he'd think more of T.J. if he stood up on his hind legs and *did* try to kill Evan.

There was a knock on the door. "Can I come in?" Nicola asked.

"Sure, send everyone in, why not?" Evan said caustically.

She went right over to Evan and kissed his cheek. "I'm so glad you're better today." She still had her apron on from breakfast, and her silken black hair was pulled back into a ponytail. Her cheeks were flushed from working in the hot kitchen. She looked beautiful. His palms tingled with the sudden memory of how her skin had felt, smooth and cool, and he recalled with complete clarity the way the soft, dark cloud of her hair had looked drifting on her pillow after they'd made love. He had to blink and force his mind back to reality.

"Did you eat breakfast?" she was asking.

Evan waved his hand. "That baby food. I wanted your blueberry pancakes."

Nicola put her hands on her hips and turned to Maureen and T.J. "Has he been like this all morning?" she asked.

Matt stepped forward. "He sure has been. Cranky as hell."

She couldn't acknowledge him or what had gone on between them, he knew, nor would she ever show her feelings in front of the family. He wanted to put an arm around her and tell them all proudly, "This is my woman and we love each other," but he couldn't do that, either. Not yet. For now, he had to pretend indifference when his body quivered with the awareness of her, and watch her faint awkwardness, her discomfort, which nobody noticed but him.

Studiously she avoided meeting his eyes, turning to his father, instead. "Evan, you're sick. You're supposed to rest and eat lightly. Are you going to behave?"

"Probably not." Evan had a twinkle in his eye. Nicola could always do that to him. It was a talent that the rest of his family, sadly enough, lacked. "What's on the menu for tonight?"

"My lasagna, you know, the northern Italian recipe. You've had it."

"Yes, and I'll have it tonight, Nicola, or else," Evan said sternly.

"We'll see," she replied lightly.

Nicola was untying her apron. "Well, I've left soup and crackers for your lunch. Maureen, you can find everything, can't you?"

Evan groaned.

She ignored him, unperturbed by his grousing, and turned to T.J. "Are you skiing today?"

But Evan answered. "They're both going. I want them out of my hair."

"Oh, good," Nicola said unconvincingly. "I'm going, too."

"Great, get out of here, all of you," Evan said, waving his hand.

"Oh, be quiet, you big grouch. You're just jealous," Nicola teased.

"You bet your bottom I am. Huff is going to top my vertical feet, and it gripes me."

She patted his arm. "I've got to get going now, or else Junior will have to wait. You take care."

"Yes, we better get ready, too," T.J. said, edging toward the door.

"See you this afternoon," Matt said as if he hadn't a care in the world.

"Have fun, all of you," Maureen called after them.

The rest of the guests at the lodge had recovered with astonishing rapidity from the unpleasantry of Evan's sick spell the day before. The group that gathered at the helipad that morning was in the usual high spirits. They all asked after Evan as a courtesy, but they were more intent on their day of skiing. T.J. was there, along with Nicola, Werner, Carlos and Rei. Even Jon was taking a morning off from worrying. Dave and Ruthie Huff and Hans completed the party.

"So, how is he?" Dave asked Matt. "A bear, I bet."

"You got it."

"He's a little better," T.J. added.

"Poor Evan, it must be killing him," Ruthie said.

Someone hopes so, Matt thought.

A few minutes later the helicopter shuddered above the peaks, and Matt studied the faces of the people packed shoulder to shoulder on the benches, facing one another. He studied them and matched motivations and used every ounce of experience and instinct he had to try to feel out the guilty party. Surely the man or woman—never forget women, who could be cleverer and more diabolic than men—was in that helicopter, pretending, as Matt was, to be something he or she was not. Rei the enigmatic Oriental, Carlos the volatile Latin, Werner the stolid Aryan, Dave the joker, Ruthie the capable wife, Hans the guide, Jon the old friend, T.J. the put-upon son and Nicola.

Nicola was an innocent, but she was also a catalyst for the evil going on around her. She saw the danger Evan was in, but she couldn't seem to make anyone believe her. Matt wished he could tell her *he* believed her; she must be going half out of her mind, thinking she was crazy or paranoid. She sat in the corner seat, next to Hans, very quiet, a little pale, and beneath her sad, dark eyes were the fingerprints of weariness. He wanted to hug her, to hold her close and kiss each pale, blue-veined eyelid and erase that slightly harried expression she wore. He wanted to feel her long body relax under his hands, to comfort her, to tell her how very much he cared about her.

"Now, listen up," Hans was saying. "The weather reports we got from Banff this morning were not great. There's a front heading our way. It may fizzle out over the West Coast or it

may not. But you can see it's windy out." He gestured toward
the window of the chopper, and all heads turned to take note.
It was overcast, with wind blowing plumes off the high peaks.
"So," Hans continued, "we'll be extra careful today. Wind
makes the snow unstable, and it can slide. We may end up skiing in the trees lower down, where it's safer."

"Oh, come on," Dave wheedled. "Just one little bowl?"

"*Sí*, this morning, before the wind gets bad," Carlos said.

"What do you think, Jon?" Rei asked.

Jon raised a restraining hand. "I am not the guide. Hans
decides vat to do."

They landed at the top of a snowfield. Everyone piled out,
collected skis and poles and stood ready while Hans skied a few
yards down the slope, checking the snowpack.

"I think it's okay," he called up to them as he sidestepped up
the hill. "It's protected from the wind here. Let's have a Skadi
check."

They filed by him, one by one, knowing the routine. But today Hans was a little more cautious than usual. He stopped
Werner. "Is yours turned up?" he asked. "I'm having trouble
hearing it.

Werner unzipped his parka and pulled his Skadi out. He
smiled ruefully. "I had it turned to receive," he explained.
"Sorry."

They paired off. If it wouldn't have embarrassed Nicola,
Matt would have taken her for a partner, but Ruthie was already at her side, jabbering away about men and Evan and how
could Werner have been so thick, so he let it lie.

"If it snows tonight, we'll have fresh powder tomorrow," Rei
was saying.

"And if it *keeps* snowing, we'll be stuck in the lodge," Matt
added. "The helicopter can't fly in the snow. It's happened
before."

"Well, then we better get a lot of skiing in today," Werner
said. "Just in case."

"I agree," Rei said, shuffling his skis in the knee-deep snow.

Hans tilted his head back and checked the snow blowing off
the peaks around them. "Follow me," he said. "Please stay

within sight of your partner. Today you really must stick to the rules, or we'll have to return to the lodge."

Groans and hoots met his words, and Matt complained along with everyone, as if he wouldn't like to return to the lodge.

Hans pulled his goggles down and took off, Jon following, skiing in the old-fashioned Austrian style, standing straight up, rotating a shoulder to initiate each turn. The rest followed, two by two, spreading out to find an untracked path in the wide bowl.

"I'd feel better staying behind," T.J. said, "just in case anything happened."

"Sure, fine with me," Matt said. It was common for the strongest skiers in the group to bring up the rear, for safety's sake, and Matt knew T.J. was right. On a marginally safe day, he and his brother were good choices to be the tail gunners.

Matt loved to ski. He loved the freedom of it, the power, the speed, the beauty of using finely tuned equipment to perfection. He'd been brought up skiing, and he wished he was having the fabulous time he was supposed to be having. He wished he could joke and cavort in the snow without care; he wished he could love Nicola without restraint and have a grand old time with his dad. As it was, he had to look as though he was having that grand old time, but he had to be on his guard each second, assessing people, judging whether they were as saturated in deception as he was, deciding who the enemy was.

He followed T.J. down, staying alert to the feel of the snow. He aimed over to his brother's right, toward a slightly steeper pitch than the center of the bowl, traversing to get to it. He felt it then, that sinister hollow whomp of the snow settling under his weight, and froze. He'd felt it before in touchy places. It meant that the snow had released its tension and wouldn't slide—this time. Drawing a deep breath, reveling in the risk and the closeness of the call, Matt made tracks down the steep side of the hill, turning, turning, breathing in the frozen crystals that swirled up around him.

And all the while he watched the skiers below him: Ruthie in purple, Dave in blue, Rei in black, Carlos in yellow, Nicola in bright, cheery red. She was a graceful skier, smooth and controlled. A good all-around athlete. She was good at a lot of things. Unfortunately, trusting was not one of them. If he wanted Nicola, he'd have to prove himself to her. He'd have to tell her the whole truth; nothing else would suffice.

He came to a stop at the bottom of the open bowl, next to Hans. Everyone was huffing and puffing and talking at once.

"Great run!"

"Did you see that turn?"

"It was *deep* on my side!"

"Damn, but that was good!"

The group wanted to do the bowl again. Hans wasn't sure. Gray clouds were scudding in from the west, blowing steadily toward them as the front pushed in off the Pacific Ocean.

"Sure, once more, before it gets bad out," Dave urged.

There was a chorus of agreement, everyone begging, suggesting, pushing. "Come on. It's safe now, we've already skied it. Then we'll ski lower down."

"Okay, it should be all right for one more run," Hans said, and everyone cheered.

The chopper came in, thudding, causing the snow to foam up around them, and it flew them up to the top once again. Dave wanted to ski with his wife this time, "Just for a change," and the couples rearranged themselves as they flew, T.J. with Carlos, Rei with Hans.

"I'll go with Nicola," Matt said.

She shot him a look that lasted too long, a questioning, probing glance that turned into an uncertain smile. "Sure," was all she said.

Someday he'd explain everything to her, every cruelty, every deception. He'd tell her why they had all been necessary and how he'd gotten himself into this nasty situation in the first place. He'd make her understand. This was the last time, he promised himself fervently, clenching his jaw as he watched Nicola turn her head away to stare out the window, rejecting him. The last job.

Soon the snow lay before them once again, tracked on one side of the bowl, untouched on the other. The group was poised above the clear side, savoring the pleasure to come, picking lines.

"Whoo-eee!" yelled Dave, shoving off behind Hans, Ruthie following. The others started, carving their lines, shouting their joy, racing, crossing one another's tracks to make figure eights. Matt and Nicola went then, and she took a line far over to the left, below the steep chute Matt had done last time. He followed her, aware that Jon and Carlos and some others were behind him. Maybe he should have warned everyone about that unstable steep spot, maybe he should have told Hans. But surely it was safe now; he'd already skied it.

His thought was scarcely completed when it happened. He was watching Nicola's red back one second, then there was a whoosh and a roar and an explosion of snow, and she vanished in the foaming avalanche the next. It happened so fast; he had time only to shout and race after her, panicking, helpless, seeing her head disappear, feeling the stinging pellets of the snow cloud hit his face.

He was there first, kicking his skis off, aware in a corner of his consciousness that utter silence prevailed for a split second before voices were yelling up to him, but he was so out of breath he couldn't answer. He saw a patch of red, a broken ski, a hat lying defenselessly on the churned surface. He ran, scrabbling over the rough avalanche path, reached the red patch. Her suit! He dug with his hands, cursing the hard-packed snow. Voices approached, shouting, but he was too busy to answer, clawing at the snow. Then there were people helping him, and they uncovered her face.

"Thank God!" someone said.

"*Gott in Himmel.*"

"*Gracias a Dios.*"

"Is she alive?"

"How did it happen?"

They pulled her out. She was white-faced but breathing. Her eyes opened, and she stared blankly at Matt as he chafed her hands.

"You're okay," he said softly. "You're safe."

"What . . . ?" she began.

"An avalanche. A small one, luckily, a surface slide. It caught you."

She shut her eyes and shivered.

"Does anything hurt?" Hans asked.

"I . . . I don't know." She moved her shoulders, her legs. "I think I'm all right."

"Mein Gott!" Jon shouted. "My partner! Werner! He is not here!"

Hans swore. "Okay. Matt, you stay with her. Everyone else, listen up. Take out your Skadis, turn them to receive. Got it? *Receive.* Put in your earpieces." He did it along with them. "Stay calm. Listen carefully. He's got to be below us. We'll spread out, an arm's distance apart. Walk slowly. When the beeps get louder, we're closer to him. You all know the routine, we've gone over it before. Start right now. I'll radio Junior immediately. The helicopter has rescue equipment. Any questions?"

They started, a line of brightly clad skiers, walking downhill, their heads cocked, listening avidly. Matt turned back to Nicola. She was trying to get up. "I'll help, too. Matt, I'm okay now. They need us."

He pushed her back gently. "Relax, kid. They'll find him."

Her eyes were huge, frightened. She sank back weakly. "I almost . . . I can't remember . . . It was so fast. I thought I fell and then . . . and then . . . I . . ."

He put an arm around her shoulders. "You're okay now. It'll pass."

"Oh God. Werner. What if he's . . . you know . . ."

"They'll find him," he repeated.

She turned her face into his shoulder and gave a short sob.

He stroked her dark hair; it was wet and tangled. "It's all right," he soothed. "The helicopter will be here soon. You'll be back at the lodge in no time."

There was a shout from below. Hans was holding up his hand, then everyone converged on the spot, digging with hands and the avalanche shovels that Hans carried in his backpack.

"They've found him," Matt said. "Everything's going to be fine."

She was clinging to him, staring down as they dug Werner out. "Is he . . . ?"

But Dave Huff was making a thumbs-up gesture and calling up to them. "He's alive! He's okay!"

"Thank God," she whispered.

The helicopter flew in then, landing a hundred yards away on a flat spot. The men carried Werner to it, and Matt helped Nicola, supporting her as she walked, because she was tottering a little.

"Oh, honey," cried Ruthie, hugging Nicola, "I was so scared!"

"We were all lucky," T.J. said. "It could have been any of us. Thank heavens it was only a small slide."

Werner was coming to, pale, his face scraped and bleeding. "What . . . ?" he mumbled.

Then they were all in the helicopter, and Junior was on the radio to the lodge, reporting to the group of skiers that had been waiting on the helipad what had happened. Matt sat next to Nicola, still grasping her cold hand. Everyone talked at once, relieved, guilty it had not been him, scared or exhilarated by the danger, each according to his own inner voice.

"How did that happen?" Hans kept saying. "I figured it was safe."

"Fate," Carlos said. "It was not their time."

"Never again," Ruthie breathed.

"Poor kids," Dave mumbled, sober for once.

"Ach, everyone will cancel their reservations," Jon muttered. "The newspapers . . ."

"They're okay, Jon. No one was killed. Hey, it's happened before."

"Yes, and I am grateful no one has ever been killed, so grateful."

"It is the risk we take," Rei said, "for the pleasure of skiing."

"It's always a risk. We know that, Jon," T.J. agreed.

The voices eddied and flowed in Matt's head, keeping him from thinking, from remembering. He leaned back against the vibrating wall of the chopper and shut his eyes for a moment, listening to the whomp-whomp of the blades over his head, trying to clear his thoughts. It came to him grudgingly, the memory of that snow settling under his skis on the first run. It had been stable. Then, too, the fracture line had been off to the side, way above where Nicola had been skiing.... It shouldn't have happened that way. No. Not unless ...

His eyes flew open, and his heart felt suddenly like a cold stone beneath his ribs. Slowly his hand tightened on Nicola's, and his gaze came around to meet hers, and in that instant he saw the same question in her eyes. Had someone intentionally set off that slide? And, if so, had it been meant specifically to annihilate her?

CHAPTER SIXTEEN

NICOLA WRAPPED THE BLANKET around her shoulders more tightly and gazed into the fire. Around her in the living room the guests who had given up skiing for the day were talking, offering her and Werner more hot tea, a bite of lunch, recounting the events of the morning nervously.

But no one was more upset than Hans. "We never should have gone down the slope," he kept saying to the others, with a guilt-ridden expression on his face. "It looked stable, though, honest it did. It *should* have been stable. I just don't get it."

Matt, who was pouring a couple of drinks at the bar, met Nicola's eyes meaningfully for a moment, then went back to the drinks.

The guide shook his bowed head. "It *shouldn't* have slid like that."

It shouldn't have, Nicola thought, but it had.

She shifted on the sofa and readjusted the blanket. Her left ankle hurt, and so did her left hip. And her elbow. She could just imagine the bruise on her upper arm; by tomorrow it would be a doozy. But she was alive. That's what mattered. And so was Werner.

As she sat there she wondered over and over; had the slide been meant for her, and had Werner only been caught in it by accident?

She shouldn't have opened her mouth as she had with her theory about Evan's sudden illness. She'd mentioned it to a couple of the maids and Jon, of course, and who else? Dave, yes. And when she'd told Dave, there had been others around. Who? But really, it didn't matter. Anyone could have blabbed—the whole lodge had probably known by that morning that she thought Evan had been poisoned.

Nicola dragged her eyes from the mesmerizing flames and glanced around the room. A few of the skiers looked troubled over the slide, especially those gathered around Hans, listening intently. Others had sidled up to the bar and were making hapless jokes. Matt had them well in hand, of course. Amazing how he could put on an indifferent face while her own was a dead giveaway—she knew she looked downright scared.

Over there was Jon, his head bent toward Dave in serious conversation. Were they discussing the slide, her, Werner? Were they talking about Evan?

"I feel much better, and you?" It was Werner, speaking to her from an easy chair where he, too, was wrapped in a blanket.

"Oh," Nicola said, "I'm still a little dazed. I'll be all right by tonight."

"Yes, me, too. Tomorrow I'll be ready for the mountain again, yes?"

"Sure," she said, distracted.

An unfocused fear seemed to fill her, as if she were a child intimidated by a faceless monster in a dark closet. She wondered if there would be another attempt on her life or on Evan's. And if so, from which direction would it come? And when?

Matt was pouring Helga a drink, another drink, Nicola noticed; the woman must have consumed half a dozen in the past hour. And she was showing the effects. One false eyelash was hanging slightly askew, and she was wobbling on her high-heeled boots. She kept tossing her head back, the swath of flaxen hair falling across her nose.

"Oh, my poor Werner! My dahling! What if I had lost you?"

"He's okay," Matt said. "Here, let me refill your glass." He winked at T.J., who, like most of the group of skiers, had given up for the day, disheartened.

Well, Nicola decided, the slide had accomplished one thing: Werner was crossed off her list of suspects. It would have been unbelievably careless of him to have set off that slide and then gotten caught in it. Of course, things like that had been known to happen. Maybe she was discounting too quickly the tall, muscled German with those cold blue eyes. Maybe Helga had more than one reason to be getting drunk: she'd almost lost her lover boy, *and* she'd failed to silence Nicola.

Who else had been above Nicola on that slope? Rei, the smiling, suave Japanese man? His buddy, Carlos? They both skied expertly, and either one of them could have kicked off the slide on purpose. And what was more, they'd gone off skiing again, obviously unconcerned.

Jon had been up there, too. Jon, with his relatives in Central America, who were worried about the repercussions of a bankrupt Costa Plata. And she shouldn't forget, Jon had also been at hunting camp. Even as she mulled over the facts in her head, Jon lit a cigarette, holding the match for a long time, as if lost in thought, until he burned his fingers. Those cigarette butts on that hillside . . . The trouble was, there were too many people around, and most of them seemed to light at least an occasional cigarette.

Her head was swimming. She looked up and saw a glass of wine being offered to her. "Here," said Matt, "you look like you could use it."

But Nicola shook her head. "What I need is an aspirin, and to get into the kitchen and get my work done."

"You're not cooking this afternoon?"

"Of course I am."

"Come on, Nicky, you've got to rest."

"What for? So I can drive myself bananas trying to figure out who's the bad guy around here? No thanks." She sighed. "I'd rather be busy."

Casually Matt put aside the drink, then squatted in front of her. "Listen," he said quietly, "I don't want to hear another word out of you about poison and hunting accidents. You're to keep quiet." He said it kindly enough, but there was an authoritative edge to his voice.

"I think I've learned my lesson," she said, looking down at her folded hands, all too aware of his scrutinizing gaze.

"Matt," she said then, "when are you going to tell me what's really up with you? And what about Evan? I'm really upset."

He said nothing, merely patted her knee, then headed on back to the bar. She felt a spurt of exasperation. *Patience, Nicola, patience,* she told herself.

After a short nap, the routine of cooking dinner did calm her somewhat, and the aspirin she'd taken helped the ache in her muscles. Yet even as she chopped the onions, carrots and celery and diced the smoked ham to make the *soffritto* for the lasagna, her thoughts kept circling back to the guests, one by one, each face imprinting itself on her mind's eye. Which one of them had tried to kill Evan . . . and *her?*

"I don't know," Jon said, coming up behind her from his office, "you should be in bed, maybe. This is bad business, this avalanche. Only a few still ski today. They are all very nervous."

"I don't blame them," Nicola said. "But things like this happen."

Jon bowed his shoulders. "Yes, yes, it is awful."

Nicola held the knife poised above the ham. Yes, she thought, Jon, of all the skiers up there, would have known how to get a slide moving down that chute. He knew every inch of the mountain, knew every unstable slope, every tree and rock and angle of pitch. And he was a high-strung sort. Intense, worried, perfectly capable of going off the deep end if it involved money. Was Jon going to have to help his relatives financially?

"Be careful there," Jon said, nodding toward the knife, "you'll cut yourself. You should be resting."

"I'm fine," Nicola said, eyeing him.

It was midafternoon when Matt strode into the kitchen looking like a man with a purpose, or perhaps, she thought, a messy task confronting him. His hands were jammed in his trouser pockets, and his face was pulled into tight lines around his mouth and brow. The spark was gone from his blue eyes.

"Look," he said, "I need to see you up in Evan's room for a few minutes."

Nicola glanced at the clutter on the cutting board. "I've got dinner to finish—how about later?" she asked.

"*Now.* I want to see you now. This is a whole lot more important than your noodles there."

"Well, in that case," she said, shrugging, taking off her apron.

She was curious as she followed him out and across the living room. Maureen and Ruthie were the only two there, having wine by the fire. Matt stopped for a moment when his mother waved him over.

"Darling," she said, "what are you two up to? If you're thinking of disturbing your father, he's trying to rest."

"No, no," Matt was quick to say. "We're, ah, headed to my room. There's this ski wax I wanted to give Nicola."

"I see. And Matt, when Evan wakes up, I'd like you to try to talk to him about seeing a doctor. He won't listen to me, and frankly, I don't think he looks any better this afternoon."

"I agree," Ruthie added. "Talk to him, Matt. Dave's already tried." She shrugged. "Men."

"And how are you feeling?" Maureen called to Nicola.

"Oh, fine. Much better," she replied, wondering why Matt had just told his mother a lie. Ski wax?

Evan did not look well. He was pale, and she could see he had left most of his lunch on his tray.

"What d'you want?" Evan asked irritably, putting down the *Powder* magazine he'd been reading.

"Just a little chat," Matt said, taking charge. He made Nicola sit in the rocking chair beside the bed, lifted the magazine from the bedclothes and set it aside.

Why did he want her there? Nicola wondered, and she began to feel a sense of urgency in the room, as if the air had become charged.

"Okay," Matt was saying, "I want you both to listen to me. And what I have to say doesn't leave this room. This is on a need-to-know basis, so Mom and T.J. are to be kept out of it. Is that understood?"

Evan grumbled "most ridiculous thing I ever heard," while Nicola stared at Matt in mute fascination. She'd never seen him like this: determined, commanding, a muscle ticking in his jaw. *He's Evan, younger, but the spitting image....*

Matt walked to the door, opening it and checking the hall before closing it again, and Nicola rubbed at her bruised elbow and felt her heart begin to pound. What was going on?

"Okay," he said, beginning to pace the room, pinning his father with a hard gaze.

"'Okay,' what?" Evan demanded.

Matt stopped abruptly. "Try to listen, Evan," he said. "Just this once, try to listen without interrupting. Will you?"

"Sure, sure." Evan glared at his son suspiciously.

"There *have* been attempts made on your life, Evan. That was no accident at hunting camp, and this isn't any flu you've got."

"Who the hell do you think you're talking to?" Evan began.

Matt ignored him. "I'm breaking the rules telling you two this. I'm breaching security, but you're too damn stubborn to listen otherwise." Matt paced, his face drawn. "I'm an agent of the U.S. Foreign Service, Evan. I'm on a job, right now, here."

"Ridiculous," his father scoffed.

"No, Evan," Nicola said softly, putting a hand on the older man's shoulder. "Listen to him."

Matt glanced at Nicola, then turned his full attention back to Evan. "I'm sure this is not exactly news to you," he said, "but the United States government has a vested interest in protecting the head of the World Bank. You, to be exact. And—"

"Look," Evan interrupted, "this is a pretty bad joke here, boy, and I fail to see any humor in the situation, so why don't you and Nicola just go—"

"I'm dead serious," Matt said.

"He's telling you the truth," Nicola put in, as all the pieces of the puzzle finally came together. "Listen to him. Please."

"Evan," Matt said, "Dad, why do you think I've been hanging around you? Because I like it?"

Evan was silent, his face pale and haggard, old suddenly.

"Do you understand," Matt was saying, his voice softer now, "that you're in grave danger here? You refuse to leave the lodge, and you've left me with no choice whatsoever but to blow my cover."

"Your 'cover,'" Evan said to himself.

"That's right. I've been working on this case since last May. It's in the interests of the service to see those loans called in, Evan, to see the present Costa Platan government topple. And it's in our interests to see that no harm comes to you as the instrument of that downfall. Are you following me?"

"Of course I am," he replied, but gone was the heavy hand; it was almost as if he'd been defeated. "How long?" he asked then. "How *long* have you been with the Foreign Service?"

Matt let out a breath. "Since college."

Evan sat up straighter, his black brows, so like Matt's, drawn together. "All these years? And you never told us? And here you are, without my permission, without consulting the World Bank, *protecting* me?"

"I'd say you need it," Matt replied coolly.

"But you can't do that. You can't just take matters into your own hands like that!"

"It's not my hands. The Foreign Service gets its directives from the secretary of state. I only follow orders. You know that's how governments work."

"My God...."

"I wouldn't be telling you this if there was any other way to get the job done. And now Nicola—" he shot her a glance "—is in danger. Maybe you're not worried about yourself, but think about her. That slide today was no accident."

Evan sat there motionless, trying to assimilate everything, his guard down, while Nicola could only stare in utter wonderment at the man she loved, Matt Cavanaugh, agent of the Foreign Service, a spy, a complete stranger to her.

She watched Matt intently, knowing the truth at last, yet still unable to fit her thoughts around the reality. Matt, footloose, fancy-free Matt, a spy. But then, what else would Evan's son be but some kind of a hard-core professional? Why hadn't she seen it all before? Yet she had; a part of her had sensed the disparate sides of this man.

"Since college?" Evan was asking, the confusion in his face giving way to frustration. "You're telling me that you've been gallivanting around the world as a bartender for damn near twenty years, and it was all a smoke screen?"

"You could put it that way," Matt answered.

"All these years!"

Uh-oh, Nicola thought, looking up.

"Yes," Matt said, "that's about it."

"You couldn't have told us?"

"That's right. I'd have been useless to the service if I had told anyone."

"But your mother... and me? We went on hoping, believing, praying, for God's sake, that someday you'd settle down and... and..."

"And come into the family business? Be a yes-man to you, Dad? Sorry, but I had my own route to go."

"Give me a minute," Evan said under his breath, and Nicola could see that he was sweating now, a cold, clammy sweat.

"Matt," she whispered urgently, nodding toward Evan.

I know, his eyes told her, *I know.*

"All these years," Evan kept repeating, the anger draining from him, "all this time."

"I am sorry," Matt said, intruding gently on his father's thoughts. "I was young, Dad, and rebellious. The job gave me a way to vent that wild streak in me. What can I say? And then the years just slipped away."

"But you hurt us," Evan breathed. "Oh, brother, did you hurt us! You have no idea what it was like to think that your only... your oldest son," he said, correcting himself, "had turned out to be a spoiled little..." He looked up into Matt's eyes. "I suppose you blame me, don't you, for pushing too hard? Maureen always said I drove you away."

"I don't blame you. I don't blame anyone," Matt replied softly. "We all do the best we can." And then, a mocking smile touching his lips, he said, "Hey, we could write a book together on lousy father-son relationships. We'd make a fortune, Dad.''

Nicola caught Matt's eye. "Listen," she said, "you two can hug and make up or tear each other to shreds at a later date. I think, though, that we better concentrate on getting Evan out of here safely.''

Matt turned to his father. "She's right, as usual.'' He gave a short laugh. "You'll agree to fly to Banff, Dad?''

Evan sighed, giving in for once. "I'll go. I don't like it, but I'll go. And Matt," he said, "you've got to tell your mother.''

"I can't just yet. But soon. I promise.''

"What,'' Evan said, his old self again, "in *another* twenty years?''

They left Evan to rest, although Nicola doubted he could. She felt sorry for him, only just now discovering that his son was someone else entirely. And could Evan come to terms with that? Could she?

As they stood in the hallway outside Evan's door, Nicola put her hand on Matt's arm tentatively. "You really threw him for a loop in there just now,'' she said.

"I know.''

"What did you expect? Did you think he'd leap for joy and take you right back into the fold?''

"Hey,'' Matt said, "what about my feelings? That man lying sick in there treated me like an idiot for years. Me, my mother, T.J. He's no saint, Nicky, you know that. He's hard, and he can be ruthless. And ask yourself this—was anyone surprised that someone was trying to kill him? Hell no.''

Of course, Matt was right, and his anger was justified. Still, there was hope, wasn't there? And certainly Matt was not without blame. "I saw something in there," she said, "I never would have dreamed it, either. But the two of you are alike, really alike. Oh, I know Evan can be a tough cookie, and he sure has a lot to learn about being a father, but you're hard, too, Matt. I think you enjoyed shocking him like that. It was as if you were throwing those wasted years in his face, saying, "'Here, Dad, if you'd been a better father, you would have seen me for myself.' That's true, isn't it, Matt?''

"Maybe. I don't know." He took her hands in his then, and faced her. "But you saw through me, didn't you, Nicky?"

"I don't know."

"You trusted me. And you gave everything you had, even when it was hard."

"You make me sound like Joan of Arc or something."

"And you aren't even that shocked by what I do," he went on.

"Oh, I'm shocked. I can't even get it all straight right now."

"But you're not mad, are you?"

She shook her head, and that was when he caught her chin in his fingers and tipped her face up to his. He placed his hands on her cheeks then, and his mouth covered hers. It was not a long kiss, nor even a passionate one. Rather, Nicola thought dreamily, it was a kiss of trust, of sharing, of promises to come.

He moved then, slightly, his mouth beginning to leave hers, their lips still trying to cling until the touch was feather light, an ending, a beginning. Her stomach rolled involuntarily as she looked up through half-closed eyes and met his gaze.

"We better get Jon to radio the chopper about Evan," Matt said in a whisper.

"And tell Maureen," she replied.

"About Dad going to Banff," he said, running a finger down her cheek, "not about me."

"Okay."

"Okay." He reached around and gave her fanny a pat. "Let's go. I'll give Mom the good news, and you find Jon."

Happily, feeling as if she could whistle, Nicola headed straight to Jon's office, where the radio was located. The chopper could unload its last skiers and then fly Evan out. And once in Banff, at the hospital there, whatever was wrong with Evan would be discovered. He could mend, and there wouldn't be anyone around to harm him.

"Oh, Jon? You in here?" She opened the door and found him hunched over his cluttered desk, shuffling papers absently. "Listen," she said, "Evan's agreed to fly on into Banff and see a doctor."

"Ah," Jon said, straightening, looking pleased, "good. Ve'll radio Junior and have him come straight here to the lodge. Good, good." He switched on the set, waited for it to warm up, tapping his fingers on the top of the desk. Matt came in then and stood in the doorway.

"He's calling Junior," Nicola told him.

"Jon here. Come in, Junior. Over." He released the button on the hand microphone.

Crackle. "Yeah, Jon, I read you. What's up? Over." Crackle.

"Vat is your status? Over."

"Just picking up the last of group three and bringing them home. Over."

Crackle, sizzle.

"Good. Now, I vant you to vait on the pad and transport Mr. Cavanaugh to Banff. You understand, Junior? Over."

There was a long string of static, and several crackles interrupted Junior's words. "We got . . . problems. Storm moving in . . . west. Winds at . . . forty-two knots and . . . real bad up here, Jon . . . in morning. Over."

"You sure? Over."

"Sure . . . maniac would . . . fly . . . over."

"Over," Jon said, pressing the button, "and out."

Slowly, her heart beginning a rapid beating, Nicola moved to the window and pulled aside the ruffled muslin curtain. She sensed Matt's presence behind her, and she could feel the frustration emanating from him. Outside, the sky was black, there were twisters of snow coming out of the trees, and streaming plumes of white blew off the forbidding spires of the Bugaboos.

CHAPTER SEVENTEEN

THE *BESCIAMELLA* came to a boil as Nicola whisked it, and she took it off the stove, stirring salt and nutmeg into the rich white sauce. The routine of cooking soothed her; the kitchen was warm and secure, and she had time to consider a new reality while her hands were occupied.

Matt. She would never, never in a million years have thought . . . But it all made so much sense now. Everything fit together. She was buoyed up with joy, besieged by amazement, pricked by guilt that she hadn't recognized his worth. All those wasted years, all those hard words from Evan and the passive sadness from Maureen. All the disappointment. How had he stood it?

She searched her inner self. Had Matt's revelation changed her love for him? A spy. How did one love a spy? She supposed the same way she'd love anyone else, but wouldn't he always have to keep secrets from her? And, dear Lord, when would she ever see him again?

Things always work out, Nicola told herself firmly. Nevertheless, this predicament she'd gotten herself into promised to pose some awfully big problems. She'd just have to talk it all over with Matt; they'd figure something out.

She began to layer the lasagna noodles, the *soffritto*, the *besciamella*, the Parmesan cheese. Until now, she knew, she'd always been so afraid of love, so afraid to sip the magic elixir. But that had all changed. He'd said he loved her. . . .

She stopped short, a long lasagna noodle dangling from her fingers. Was she truly free of fear now? She searched within, searched the hidden crevices of her mind and found a small, noxious shadow still cowering in a corner, asking, Does he mean it? Will he always love me? Can I trust him?

So, she'd have to deal with that; she'd tell Matt, she could tell him anything. But, she suspected, he already knew that about her anyway.

He was upstairs now, with Evan. She wondered what they were saying to each other. How difficult, how awkward. But they were, at least, talking. Suddenly she wanted to tell her mother that she was in love, really in love, and what a fine person her man was. "Mom? You remember Matt, don't you? Yes, Maureen's son. We're in love, Mom. I'm so happy. And do you know what he's been doing all these years? You won't *believe* it." She wanted to share it. She wanted her mother to be happy for her, to laugh and cry and tell her not to rush into anything.

And Went. Well, he would say something polite if she told him, but he wouldn't really care. He'd be glad if some man took Nicola off his hands—not that she'd ever been on his hands, not really.

Maureen would be thrilled, more a mother to her than her own. And Evan... How would Evan react? She grimaced, wondering as she slipped the two large trays of lasagna into the oven. Would he be thrilled, furious? She just didn't know.

Snow tapped against the kitchen window, begging entrance. The storm had come roaring in, a full-blown blizzard, with howling winds and snow so thick that from the lodge you couldn't even see the helicopter tied down on the landing pad. Jon had called Banff on the radio, telling them of Evan's condition and asking for a doctor to be kept handy in case his situation deteriorated. It wouldn't be much help, but a doctor might be able to give some advice over the radio.

Nicola felt the isolation of the lodge, a fragile island in a whirling white ocean. No one could get out, no one could get in. And Banff had reported that the weather service was calling for at least twelve hours of heavy snowfall.

Nicola thought about tomorrow; if the storm held fast in the mountains, the lodge would be full of frustrated, restless skiers, playing checkers and ruing the waste of their last precious day.

It had happened before, and it always made Jon doubly nervous, but somehow everyone survived. *What an odd choice of words,* she mused.

Dinner was a success, despite Werner's obvious discomfort from his ordeal and Helga's drunken doting on him. The college boys, each paired up with a lady now, couldn't hear enough about the avalanche. "What a rush!" one of them commented with fervor.

When everything in the kitchen was tidied up, Nicola sat by the fire talking to Maureen, worrying about Evan and the fact that he was still complaining of nausea.

"If only we could fly him to Banff," Maureen said more than once.

Nicola sipped on a blackberry brandy provided by Jon. She tasted the strong, fruity alcohol and wondered, before dismissing it as ridiculous, if Jon had slipped something into her drink. A person could go nuts thinking about the whole crazy situation.

Finally T.J., who'd been talking at the bar, went up to Evan's room to spell Matt, and Nicola couldn't help but train her eyes on the staircase, waiting for Matt to appear, knowing that he'd come over to them and say something reassuring. If only she could tell Maureen how she felt, share the wonderful news. And she would, soon, when all this terrible business with Evan was behind them.

Matt did appear, and he did crack a joke or two, taking Maureen's hand and squeezing it while his gaze held Nicola's.

"Well, Evan tried to eat some dinner," he told his mother, "and I think he's looking much better." But Nicola wondered. Evan's plate had been returned to the kitchen, his favorite lasagna all but untouched.

And then Matt turned to her. "Say, I wonder if you wouldn't run on up to my room for a sec," he said. "I'll find that *Powder* magazine I promised."

Of course, he'd promised no such thing, but Nicola got the hint. "Oh, sure, thanks."

Maureen seemed not to notice their departure, nor did anyone else, yet Nicola climbed the steps feeling every muscle in her body ache and was certain that all eyes in the room were watching them. She wondered what he wanted.

Upstairs the hallway was dim and silent. Matt stopped her short and held a finger to his lips. "Sorry about that," he whispered, "but I wanted to see you alone. I've been going over and over that slide today in my head," he said, "and I just can't figure it."

"*You* can't."

"Then you haven't any idea who might have set it off?"

Nicola shook her head. "I just can't believe someone would try to... to kill me." She shivered, hugging herself.

"Poor Nicky." He reached out and tucked her loose hair behind an ear. "It's been hard on you, I know. I just wish I had a clue to go on."

"I just wish Evan was out of here," she said.

"Yes."

"You know," Nicola said, "I'd search every inch of every room in this place if I thought I'd find anything."

"You mean poison?"

"Exactly. And I did think of doing it, but I really doubt if anyone would have a bottle with a skull and crossbones on it just lying around." She looked up into his eyes. "I mean, do you think we should?"

"Search the rooms?"

"Well, yes."

He shook his head. "I'm embarrassed to say that I don't know the first thing about poison. I wouldn't even know where to begin."

"I thought you were a spy."

"This is the first job like this I've ever had, and I'm only doing it because I was the obvious choice to stay close to Evan."

"So we're at a dead end."

"Until someone tries again, I'm afraid."

"Oh God," Nicola said, "you're right. We're all stuck here in this storm, and—"

"Hey, don't think like that, Nicky. Evan's being watched every second of every minute, and I'm not about to let you out of my sight, either."

"Really?"

"Really." He ran a finger along her jaw. "I don't give a damn what people think. Do you?"

"No. Not if you're here with me. Oh, Matt," she said, but suddenly the door to Evan's room opened and T.J. came out. He saw them down the hall and seemed a bit surprised.

"Oh," he said, "I thought I heard something. I'm glad it's just you two. I'll tell you, I don't like this whole thing."

"Neither do I," Nicola said. "How is Evan, anyway?"

"Okay. He keeps asking for a cup of tea, but I told him I wasn't leaving until someone came up to spell me."

"I can get it," she offered.

"Oh no, that's okay. I know my way around the kitchen. If you'll just sit with Dad . . ."

They found Evan dozing fitfully, licking dry lips. Nicola sat by the bed on a rocker, watching him, fretting, wondering if they shouldn't radio that doctor in Banff and see if there wasn't something, *anything*, that could be done here at the lodge.

"Oh," Evan said, opening his eyes, disoriented, "where's T.J.? I didn't hear you two come in."

"He went to get you your tea," Nicola replied, and she rose and began straightening Evan's pillows.

"Where's Maureen?"

"Downstairs."

"Is it still snowing?"

"Like crazy," Nicola said.

"Good. Old Huff won't be able to get in his vertical feet tomorrow."

"That's mean," Nicola put in.

"But honest," Evan said, turning his head to study Matt, who was standing, looking out the window. "Don't you think honesty is important, Matt?"

"What?"

"I said, don't you—"

But T.J. came in then and set the cup down by the bedside. "Here you go, Sleepy Time. I hope that's okay."

"Sleepy Time. How clever of you," Evan said, pushing himself up, grumpy.

"Sorry, Dad," T.J. said. "I only meant to be cheerful."

"Well, I don't feel cheerful."

"Evan," Nicola admonished.

"Hell," he said, "I hate being fussed over."

"I know. Well," she said, "I'll say good night. I can see you're in good hands now. I hope you feel better in the morning."

"And by the way," Evan said, his brow creasing, "are *you* all right?"

"Just sore." She smiled crookedly, shrugging.

"You take it easy, Nicola," he said, and she left, catching Matt's glance, knowing that in a few minutes he'd come downstairs again, looking for her.

She went through the bar, where Bernie was playing his guitar for the assemblage, and headed toward the kitchen, intending to take out the loaves of banana bread from the freezer to thaw for morning. The room was spotless, reflecting back to her a dull gleam of stainless steel. There was a tea bag lying on the counter by the stove, though. T.J. He always had been sloppy. Maureen spoiled him. Maureen and Lydia.

She picked the damp, limp thing up and threw it into the trash can, then automatically reached for the sponge to clean the counter. Out in the bar the guitar was twanging, and everyone was singing the chorus to "Ramblin' Rose." Nicola hummed along as she wiped at the counter. Wind-driven snow rattled the window. Idly she wondered if Matt would appear soon, and would he want to go to her room? She hoped so. It was awfully cold out, though, and they'd have to run, but then they'd be warm soon....

The sponge grated against some granules on the counter. Oh, that T.J. He'd spilled sugar all over.

Sugar. Boy, was Evan going to be furious when he tasted sugar instead of honey. T.J. knew better than that....

It came to her reluctantly. It didn't want to come, but it did, a suspicion bordering on knowledge, oozing up out of the mire. Slowly, barely in control of her actions, Nicola wet a finger with her tongue and pressed it into the granules, raising her finger back to her mouth. The stuff was tasteless. Utterly tasteless....

Abruptly the blood left her head. She reached for the counter, faint with horror. A thousand wild thoughts whirled through her head, circling like bats, flitting, terrifying. T.J. Sugar. Poison. T.J.! As if she were awakening from a nightmare, the room began to come back into focus, and finally a rush of adrenaline surged through her veins. She raced out of the kitchen, mindless of her stiff muscles, and pounded up the stairs, her heart thumping, her chest sucking in air. She flung herself against Evan's door, fumbling at the knob, twisting it, bursting through into his room.

"No!" she cried. "No!"

She lunged for the teacup that Evan held, lunged and knocked it aside, flinging hot tea everywhere, still crying, "No, no!"

"What the...?" Evan gasped.

But she couldn't explain. Horror fueled her body. "It's you!" she breathed, whirling on T.J. "Oh God, it's *you*!"

"Nicky..." Matt began, stepping toward her, looking from her to T.J., bewildered.

But T.J. was backing toward the open door, his face frozen, drained of color, backing away stealthily, slowly.

Comprehension was dawning on Matt. He stepped toward his brother, held a hand out. "Wait, T.J.," he started to say, but his brother lashed out, lizard quick, and knocked Matt aside. Then, with an inhuman wail of anguish, T.J. turned and fled.

Matt stumbled, holding his jaw. Evan was climbing out of bed, his face a mask of pain, of knowledge. "Nicola, is Matt all right?" he asked first, reaching shakily for her.

"I'm okay," Matt said. "Nick, how did you...?"

"It was the sugar," she breathed. "There was sugar on the counter, but it wasn't sweet, and then I knew!"

"Oh no, oh no," Evan whispered, sinking back onto the bed. "Not T.J."

"Take it easy, Dad," Matt said, sitting on the side of the bed, holding his head. "He can't go anywhere."

But Evan shook his head. "Go after him. Matt, go after him. Help him."

Nicola was frozen, paralyzed. T.J. a murderer. Evan...her... Oh God, he *had* been above her today. Poison. He could have been giving Evan poison all along. Why? Why?

"It's my fault," Evan whispered, white-faced. "I pushed him too far. I knew he was weak. I knew."

"Evan." Nicola put a hand on his back. "He can't go anywhere in this storm. We'll find him. There must be some explanation—there must."

Matt stood, carefully working his jaw, feeling out the damage. "Let's go, Nicky. We better look for him. There's no telling what T.J. will do."

She glanced at him, alarmed. What? What did Matt mean? Their gazes locked, and Matt made a quick movement with his head toward Evan, a negative gesture, as if to tell her, *Don't worry Evan about this. He's too weak.*

She followed Matt out and down the stairs. What did he plan to do? Talk to T.J.? Reason with him? Murder. T.J. had tried to murder his father and her. The shot at hunting camp. T.J. knew exactly where Evan would be that week. Oh no, the cigarette butts, the Marlboros.

Matt was cursing under his breath. "I should have known," he said harshly. "I should have seen it."

"You couldn't have," she replied. "He's your brother."

"I should have seen it," he repeated.

The fire was crackling cheerily in the bar, and everyone sat around singing while Bernie played his guitar. It was a scene from a brochure for a ski lodge: comfortable, happy, fun, full of camaraderie. A few guests looked up as Matt and Nicola came into the room.

"Have you seen T.J.?" Matt asked casually.

"Yeah, he went out. Thataway." One of the college boys stabbed a thumb toward the front door, then put his hand back on the knee of his lady friend.

"In this storm? He must be nuts," Nicola remarked.

"He must have a hot date with one of the maids," the boy said, winking.

"Thanks," Matt said.

"Where could he be going?" Nicola asked as they hurried out of the room. "There's no place. The storm—"

"We need our parkas and a flashlight," Matt said tightly. "God knows what he's thinking."

"The kitchen."

While Matt fetched his jacket, she grabbed her own coat off its hook and found the flashlight, then opened the back door. The cold hit her face, and the wind howled in her ears. Snow filled the air, thick and cloying, an impenetrable white veil in the narrow beam of the flashlight, melting into slush on her skin instantly.

Matt was alongside her shortly and pulled at her arm, trying to tell her something, but the wind snatched his words away.

"Tracks!" he yelled louder. "We've got to find T.J.'s tracks!"

Six inches of new snow had already piled up; it had been falling more than an inch an hour. Prime conditions for avalanches, Nicola thought as Matt led her through the snow and darkness toward the front of the lodge.

The light over the door showed shallow dimples in the snow, nearly filled in already. They followed them with the flashlight through the roaring blackness toward the maintenance shed. The doors of the shed were open, yawning like a gaping mouth in the face of the blizzard. And there were tracks, much clearer than the footprints, leading out of the shed.

"The snowmobile!" Nicola shouted so that Matt could hear her. "He took one of the snowmobiles!"

Matt tugged her into the shed, and together they yanked the doors shut. Nicola pulled the light cord, and abruptly there was quiet and illumination and they could talk.

"He's taken the snowmobile," she panted.

"Where? What's he thinking?"

"The tracks went toward the old logging road. That's the only possible way out of here, but it's—"

"He's crazy," Matt said grimly. "He can't think straight."

"Matt, he'll freeze to death! He can't get away. It's miles, I don't know how far. He doesn't have enough gas to get any-

where. And, oh my God. The road crosses avalanche paths,
dozens of them. In this storm, they'll slide. Matt.''

"We'll have to follow him. Can you drive one of those
things?''

"Yes, but—''

"Let's go. He's already got a head start.''

"Wait.'' She grabbed his arm. "We have to wear suits. We'll
freeze otherwise. We won't do T.J. any good, then.''

The padded snowmobile suits, bright orange and stained with
grease, hung on hooks on the wall. They dressed, pulling on
thick gloves and helmets and goggles. Then, with Matt's help,
she lifted the lighter back end of the machine, and they swung
it around to point out of the shed. Nicola pulled the hand
starter, a lawn-mower-type cable, once, twice, three times until the engine sputtered and roared to life. Quickly she pushed
the choke knob back in so it wouldn't flood, then depressed the
accelerator on the handlebars until she was sure the growling
machine wasn't going to stall.

"Open the doors,'' she called, swinging herself onto the seat,
pulling down her goggles.

Snow blew into the shed in fitful gusts as Matt pushed open
the doors. The snowmobile's single light pierced the darkness,
cutting a hole in the night, a hole filled with thick, swirling
snowflakes that reflected back to Nicola's eyes like a blank wall.
Matt got on behind her; she felt his hands at her waist, holding on to the quilted fabric of her suit. The rapidly vanishing
groove that T.J.'s machine had made lay in front of her, but
only to the extent of the reach of the headlight. What lay beyond? Only darkness and cold and wind and a sad, crazed human being running for his life.

"Ready?'' she shouted.

"Ready!'' Matt said into her ear.

She gave the machine gas, and the engine screamed and
lurched forward. She followed the line in the snow as fast as she
could, bouncing and sliding, her ears filled with the engine
noise, her body tense, her hand controlling the gas feed. The
snow was piling up, ever faster, splatting onto the windshield,
sticking there, making it hard to see. She was afraid to go too

fast, even more afraid to go too slow and get bogged down in the deepening snow. There were drifts across the logging road, and when she hit them too fast with the two front skis, the machine skewed sideways, trying to rip the handlebars out of her grasp.

T.J. was up ahead somewhere. How far? The mountain loomed to her right, a dark, unseen bulk. She was aware of Matt, his body pressed against hers, and his very presence steadied her.

How far had T.J. gone? He wasn't even dressed warmly. He'd freeze or he'd get stuck in the snow or run off the road or get lost in the trackless wilderness or be buried in an avalanche.

The headlight threw crazy shafts of light ahead into the driving snow and against the dark tree trunks that popped up at her like ghostly sentinels. She had to catch up—she had to.

She hit a snowdrift then, at the wrong angle, and the handlebars were wrenched out of her hands. The snowmobile flopped onto its side, the track still moving, and tossed them in the deep snow. It was a nightmare, then, of heaving and gasping and sinking to their hips in the snow, to right the machine. Thank goodness Matt was there. Wrapped in a cocoon of whipping snow, they stood for a minute to catch their breaths before getting back on the snowmobile. He grasped her arm, and she knew there was so much they had to say to each other, but they couldn't, not then.

They must have traveled five miles along the old logging road, the extent to which it was safe for cross-country skiing from the lodge. Beyond that there was acute danger of slides, and even one place where there was a permanent pile of avalanche debris that blocked the road all winter, she suddenly recalled. T.J. wouldn't know about it. He would be barreling along at top speed, half out of his mind, and there would be this wall of snow in front of him . . .

She felt her heart leap in fright, and she wanted desperately to tell Matt about it, but when she turned her head and shouted, the wind whipped her words away, sucking them out of her throat and flailing them on the storm. And then she could only hope and pray and depress the throttle as hard as she could.

Suddenly there it was, the solid barricade of snow across the road, faintly seen through the blizzard. But then, she had been looking for it. T.J. would never have....

Simultaneously Matt stiffened against her back, and she saw T.J.'s machine, a shadowy blur on the snow. It was on its side, and a dark hump, almost covered with snow, lay motionless beside it.

CHAPTER EIGHTEEN

EVERYTHING HAPPENED QUICKLY during the next few days, so quickly that Nicola wondered if she was still in charge of her own destiny.

Jon had come to her the morning following T.J.'s accident and insisted that Nicola go with the Cavanaughs to help them through this difficult time. He'd get his former cook to fly in right away. She'd agreed on the spot, relieved, thankful that she wasn't leaving Jon in the lurch. She'd flown home to New York with the family, the *whole* family, and she'd been glad to be there, ready to share the bad with the good, ready to sit between Matt and his silent, withdrawn brother, ready to give what comfort she could.

Everything had gone smoothly under the circumstances, yet she felt as if her life was in the hands of a puppeteer. Despite the fact that she wanted to be with the Cavanaughs, she couldn't help but wonder where she would be going from there. She'd cook, of course, but where? Nicola hadn't changed, but everything and everyone around her had.

Upon returning to New York, Evan had refused to press charges against his son. He'd accepted full blame for T.J.'s aberrant behavior, an uncharacteristically humbled man. They'd quietly driven T.J., who had only a dislocated shoulder from his accident, to an upstate New York mental hospital, a very exclusive hospital, where only the wealthy could afford the long healing process.

And Evan. He, too, had entered a local Westchester hospital and been given a clean bill of health with mild reservations: no overexertion for several weeks, watch the alcohol and caffeine. The remnants of the arsenic would be in his system for a while yet, although recovery eventually would be complete. T.J. had come clean immediately, admitting that he'd purchased the poison through a chemical supply house in New York and had only begun to slip the tasteless arsenic into Evan's tea just before the trip to the Bugaboos.

Evan had grumbled royally over the doctor's advice, especially the taking-it-easy end of things. "What am I supposed to do all day long," he'd said, "lie around in bed?"

But Maureen had stepped in. "I think," she'd replied, "you could afford to take a few months' leave from the World Bank. You *should* do it, dear, and maybe this family can pull the shreds of our lives together."

There hadn't been much Evan could say to that.

So now Nicola sat at the dinner table with Maureen and Evan and Matt, a part of the troubled family, each member of which was trying in his own way to make the necessary adjustments.

T.J. had inadvertently brought them together, given them this chance to open all the old wounds and let them finally heal. What a devastating shock it had been to Evan to find out that neither of his sons was what he appeared—and it had all happened in the space of a day. The strange thing was, Evan held no malice toward T.J., none whatsoever. Oddly he almost respected his younger son for the attempts on his life, although Evan was well aware of just how disturbed T.J. was.

Yes, Nicola had made the decision to be there with her adopted family. So why, then, was she still feeling as if someone else were pulling her strings?

The answer should have been obvious. It was Matt, naturally, trying to manipulate those strings. Matt, the man who was finally showing his true colors—Evan's colors—and who was gently but firmly trying to run Nicola's life. She wanted to be with him every second of every day, and it was clear to Maureen and Evan what was going on even if Nicola and Matt kept separate bedrooms. The Cavanaughs approved, and underlying the anguish and recriminations there was happiness for the love that had blossomed in the midst of so much turmoil.

But Matt had become, well, not pushy exactly, Nicola decided, but intent upon getting his own way.

"Matt tells me you're going to Washington with him," Evan said to her during the meal.

"Well, I don't now if I—"

"Of course you're going," Matt said, interrupting. "Don't you want to go? It's only for a few days."

"I wish someone would clue me in," Maureen interjected.

"We will, Mom, on everything, just as soon as I get the go-ahead from my boss."

Maureen frowned. "Your boss. You won't even tell me who you work for." She looked at Evan. "But you know, don't you? It makes me so angry...."

He gazed at his wife with understanding. Amazing what a terrible shock could do to a person, Nicola thought. "Listen," he said, "in a few days Matt will tell you everything and you'll understand. Right, Matt?"

"Right, Evan."

"So are you going to Washington, dear?" Maureen asked Nicola.

But Nicola couldn't decide. She wanted to go; she wanted to be there when Matt told his boss he was through with field-work and wished to be stationed in the home office. She wanted to support Matt in this decision and be there for him if his boss gave him any trouble. But she also knew in her heart that Matt, given an inch, would snatch away her independence. By not going, she would be making a statement. *Give me room to breathe.* Oh yes, Matt was definitely Evan's son.

There was another matter, too. Marriage. Maureen had hinted at it to Nicola in private; Evan expected it. But no one had told Matt. And somehow Nicola couldn't see herself traipsing around Washington, or wherever, for the rest of her days as Matt's doting mistress. Besides, she couldn't afford to sit around forever, sponging off the Cavanaughs. She needed to find a job and keep busy, but she was so uncertain about the future that she just kept hesitating, unable to make a commitment to an employer.

"I think I better stay here," she finally said, catching Matt's sharp glance. "Maureen wants me to drive her up to see T.J.'s doctor."

So, angry and disappointed, Matt took off for Washington, and Nicola drove Maureen north to visit the doctor; even though she ached for Matt's company, she at least felt free to think again and to make her own choices. And then, too, she could be there for Maureen.

T.J.'s doctor didn't look anything like Nicola had expected; he wasn't white haired and bearded and stooped like Sigmund Freud. He was tall and freckled and strongly built and young.

"Call me Dr. Stan. Everyone does. My last name is unpronounceable. So good to meet you, Mrs. Cavanaugh, and I'll bet you're Nicola. Thomas has told me about you."

"Thomas?"

"When we make a complete, therapeutic break with past behavior, we often change our names. So he's no longer T.J., he's Thomas," Dr. Stan explained.

"How is he?" Maureen asked shakily.

"Physically he's fine. Mentally he has a ways to go. But then, that's what he's here for."

"Can I . . . can I see him?" Maureen asked.

Dr. Stan put a hand on hers. "Mrs. Cavanaugh, I'm afraid that would be counterproductive to Thomas's well-being. He first has to learn to live with himself, then he may be able to move back into society."

"May?" Maureen asked faintly.

"Mrs. Cavanaugh, I won't lie to you or jolly you along. Your son has severe problems with self-esteem and with repressed rage. There's no magical cure, no pills. It will take time and hard work, and Thomas may never be able to live with you again."

"Never, oh God. . . ."

"We have a forty percent cure rate here. That's very high, so his chances are excellent."

"Is there anything I can do . . . we can do?"

"I'll let you know when it's time to see him. There may be some family therapy called for."

"Anything, Doctor, anything. We love T.J. . . . I mean Thomas."

"You *keep* loving him. That's vitally important, Mrs. Cavanaugh."

They drove home in a thoughtful mood. Maureen cried a little and dabbed at her eyes and then said, in an uncharacteristically forceful voice, "If we need to go to family therapy, Evan will go, Nicola. I don't care what he says."

And Nicola believed her.

The new, if unspoken, rule around the house was openness and honesty, a difficult goal for the Cavanaughs to achieve, but they tried—even Evan.

But was *she* being open? She wanted Matt, she loved him, her whole being ached for him, yet she didn't quite have the guts to tell him that the bottom line was marriage and kids and her own career. She was afraid he'd buck her at every turn.

Matt came home on a weekend in early February, rocking the house with his presence, grinning from ear to ear. He announced to the family that Ned had given him a post in the home office and that his Section C days were history. "Hell, I even got a raise!"

Evan put down his Sunday newspaper and took off his reading glasses. "I want you to come into the family bank," he said. "I need you there, Matt."

Matt put his arm around Nicola's shoulders. "Not a chance, Evan. I've got my own gig going, and I'm happy as a lark."

"I'd give you a free hand."

"Easy to say now. But face it, Dad, you're no more capable of that than I am of pushing pencils in a bank every day."

"But won't you be in an office with the Foreign Service?" Maureen asked, looking up from her book.

"Most of the time, I will. But there'll still be trips to Paris, Rome, you know." He squeezed Nicola's shoulder. "Come on outside," he said, winking at her. "I want to talk."

It was a cold day, gray and blustery, the wind soughing in the bare tree branches, dead leaves stirring on the tarp over the swimming pool. Nicola felt her cheeks sting with the raw dampness as they walked, bundled close together, along Maureen's garden path.

"How was T.J.?" Matt asked, looking straight ahead.

"The doctor was guarded. Optimistic but guarded."

"I wonder if he'll ever be well again."

"Who knows?" she said. "He spent so much of his life hating Evan. I guess all he ever thought about was being left out of the family business and worrying that you'd inherit everything."

"Crazy."

"Yes, it is. But if he can get over that hatred, if he and Evan can ever talk, really talk, that is . . ."

"How is Evan doing?"

"Oh," she said, "good, considering everything. He talks a lot to Maureen about what a fool he was trying to run his sons' lives. He's beginning to get it, anyway. And Maureen's been the Rock of Gibraltar. I think she's reveling in the role of Evan's sounding board."

"I guess we'll all make it through," he said. "It's been hard, though."

"Worse," Nicola said, pulling the open collar of her sweater closed while they walked, each thinking separate but oddly similar thoughts as the wind whirled dead leaves up into a spiral, then let them drop.

"I did some thinking," Matt said then, "while I was gone. I guess you were right to stay here."

"I thought so."

"Look, I know I've got a crazy life-style, and Lord only knows, I'm too much like my dad for comfort. But, Nicky, I can learn. You only have to tell me to back off, and I will."

"What're you trying to say, Matt?"

"I'm saying that I love you so damn much I'm willing to do anything to have you. I was scared half out of my mind that I'd get back here and find you gone off to some wilderness somewhere."

"Me?" She laughed. Was he kidding? Surely he must realize that she'd been putting off going back to work, halfheartedly reading the want ads, because she knew there had to be a confrontation between them, an honest examination of their feelings. "No wilderness for me," she said. "It's the wrong season, anyway."

He stopped and pulled her around to him roughly, playfully, his mouth searching for hers. "Oh God, Nicky, you taste so good. I swear, I'll turn into a lap dog if you'll let me."

"I doubt *that*."

"You're probably right." He grinned that old, wicked grin of his, and his blue eyes danced in the gray winter light. "I don't know how good I'll be at settling down, kid. But I'm getting old, and nature is starting to do the trick for me. I want you, I do know that, and I want kids and dogs and cats and all that stuff."

"Are you...proposing?" She felt her stomach roll over, and her knees were threatening to give out on her.

"I guess I am. You wouldn't consider living in sin, would you?"

"Stop teasing."

"Okay. But will you marry me, Nicky?"

"There'll be rules," she said, hardly believing her own temerity.

"Oh?" He brushed her hair off her shoulders and put his hands on her arms.

"Yes. I've had to be too self-sufficient, Matt, you know that."

"Still don't trust men."

"Not entirely, I don't. I'll be honest."

"But I already knew that. And it's a part of what makes me love you so much. I want to spend my life with you. I want to be the man you trust the most."

He kissed her thoroughly then, pressing the length of her body to his, a long, white-hot kiss that made her feel as if her life force were draining right out of her toes and pooling at their feet.

Breathless, she wedged her hands between them and laughed. "Wow," she said, "I guess we *better* get married."

"You mean it?"

"Absolutely. But we're equals in this, buddy, and none of this Evan-style bulldozing. Okay?"

"I'll put it in writing."

THE DAYS OF FEBRUARY slipped away. There was so much to be done, arrangements to be made, invitations to be sent out, a larger apartment to be found in Washington—not an easy task. And then there were the weekends when Nicola insisted on going skiing or hiking or something. Living in the city was certainly going to have its drawbacks, but if she was going to be with Matt, then that was okay.

They'd just gotten back from Washington, having found an adorable, if expensive, Georgetown apartment, when Maureen tapped on her door. "You'll probably be furious with me," she began, then went on to tell Nicola that Went was going to cater the March wedding and that he insisted on seeing Nicola immediately about the arrangements. So Nicola had to turn around, after just driving up from Washington, and head into the city.

What Maureen had not told her, though, was that good old Went had a surprise for her.

They sat in his hot, cramped office behind the kitchen. In the background, pots and pans clanged furiously as the dinner hour approached. Matt had offered to come along with her, but Nicola had known in her heart that she had to go this alone. It was time to tell Went the truth, time to be honest with him and herself. She sat there readying her speech in her head, prepared to tell him what a jerk of a father he'd been, and how, because of his neglect, he'd botched up her life, made her angry and insecure, darn near made her run from Matt. Oh yes, she was all ready—no more games.

But then Went popped his surprise on her.

"I've been thinking," he began, nervously folding and refolding a kitchen towel. "I'd like to open another restaurant."

"Oh, really," Nicola said. He didn't have time for anyone but himself—and a woman or two—as it was.

"Yes, Nicola, another French restaurant. And I've been thinking about Washington."

"Washington?" A faint bell rang in her head.

"Another one like Sansouci, but smaller, more intimate. There's a spot for sale, in fact, not far from where you and Matt will be living."

"How do you know where I'll be living?" Nicola was beginning to smell a rat.

He waved a hand eloquently. "Oh, I had a chat with Evan the other day."

"I see."

"Well, yes, and you know, I'll need a right-hand man in Washington, a good manager, and a good chef, too."

"Dad..."

"And I was thinking... Here I have this beautiful daughter, family, you know, and she's always working for someone else."

"Are you suggesting...?" She couldn't believe it. This *wasn't* happening.

"If you say yes," he said, shifting his eyes away uncomfortably, "then we could see each other once in a while, Nicola. Look, I haven't been much of a father, have I? And if I can do this one small thing, well, maybe we could get together from time to time."

"Yes," Nicola said, her resentment melted, barely able to hold in her joy, "oh yes, Dad! It'll be the best restaurant in Washington! You'll see!"

"I'm sure it will." He smiled, embarrassed, happy, proud of himself. "There's one other thing, though. When I have grandchildren, I want to visit often. I missed so much of your growing up. Anyhow, we'll make it a great success, you and me. We'll call it Sansouci et Fille."

Nicola wanted to laugh and cry and hug him. Oh, she wasn't so blind as to think he was going to change overnight—no doubt he'd only make it to Washington a couple of times a year at best—but it was a start. And Went had gone the whole nine yards for her this time. Incredible.

"Thanks," she said, choking on the word despite herself. "Thank you, Dad."

The house in Westchester began to swell with expectancy as the date of the wedding neared. Matt was gone a lot, getting acclimated to his new work, flying to London once on the Concorde for an overnight. But when he was home, it was heaven between them, laughter and kisses and breathless long nights stolen in her room. They took the time to visit Suzanne and invited her to the wedding. Surprisingly Suzanne was delighted, nervously putting aside her depression for once and declaring that she would be there, and was there anything she could do to help Maureen?

When they were outside in Matt's car, however, Nicola frowned. "She won't make it. I already know that. Oh, she'll send a lovely gift, but it will be too much for her to actually come. And then she'll get depressed because she can't."

"Maybe she'll make it," Matt said softly.

Suzanne sent her regrets that March morning as the house in Westchester was turning inside out for the affair. Nicola clenched her teeth and stood it, though, because life couldn't always be perfect. She'd accept her mother's condition, and she'd try only to think of the good times and never the unhappy moments with her mother.

The house looked beautiful. Flowers rose from delicate vases everywhere, and the air was scented with hothouse blossoms and the singular musk of old lace. Went gave the bride away, and Nicola stood next to Matt in front of the minister and repeated the solemn vows. When it was done, and he lifted the veil, there was a moment, a pause, and a reverent hush filled the room.

"We'll go see Suzanne tomorrow," Matt whispered, his eyes holding hers. "We'll tell her all about it, and she'll be happy. Okay?"

"Okay," Nicola breathed, her heart filling with love, "but now it's time for us."

"For us," Matt said as his head descended toward hers, and the first moment of the rest of their lives began.

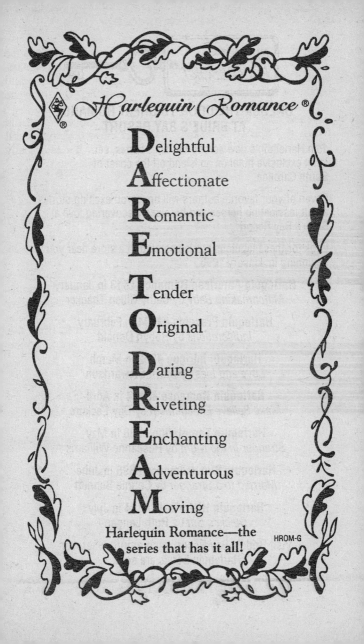

Harlequin Romance ®

Delightful

Affectionate

Romantic

Emotional

Tender

Original

Daring

Riveting

Enchanting

Adventurous

Moving

Harlequin Romance—the
series that has it all!

HROM-G

BRIDE'S BAY RESORT

UNLOCK THE DOOR TO GREAT ROMANCE AT BRIDE'S BAY RESORT

Join Harlequin's new across-the-lines series, set in an exclusive hotel on an island off the coast of South Carolina.

Seven of your favorite authors will bring you exciting stories about fascinating heroes and heroines discovering love at Bride's Bay Resort.

Look for these fabulous stories coming to a store near you beginning in January 1996.

Harlequin American Romance #613 in January
Matchmaking Baby by Cathy Gillen Thacker

Harlequin Presents #1794 in February
Indiscretions by Robyn Donald

Harlequin Intrigue #362 in March
Love and Lies by Dawn Stewardson

Harlequin Romance #3404 in April
Make Believe Engagement by Day Leclaire

Harlequin Temptation #588 in May
Stranger in the Night by Roseanne Williams

Harlequin Superromance #695 in June
Married to a Stranger by Connie Bennett

Harlequin Historicals #324 in July
Dulcie's Gift by Ruth Langan

Visit Bride's Bay Resort each month wherever
Harlequin books are sold.

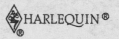

HARLEQUIN ®

New York Times Bestselling Author

PENNY JORDAN

Explore the lives of four women as they overcome a

CRUEL LEGACY

For Philippa, Sally, Elizabeth and Deborah life will never be the same after the final act of one man. Now they must stand on their own and reclaim their lives.

As Philippa learns to live without wealth and social standing, Sally finds herself tempted by a man who is not her husband. And Elizabeth struggles between supporting her husband and proclaiming her independence, while Deborah must choose between a jealous lover and a ruthless boss.

Don't miss CRUEL LEGACY, available this December at your favorite retail outlet.

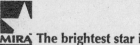

MIRA **The brightest star in women's fiction**

MPJCL

Harlequin® Historical

If you're a serious fan of historical romance,
then you're in luck!

Harlequin Historicals brings you
stories by bestselling authors, rising new stars
and talented first-timers.

Ruth Langan & Theresa Michaels
Mary McBride & Cheryl St. John
Margaret Moore & Merline Lovelace
Julie Tetel & Nina Beaumont
Susan Amarillas & Ana Seymour
Deborah Simmons & Linda Castle
Cassandra Austin & Emily French
Miranda Jarrett & Suzanne Barclay
DeLoras Scott & Laurie Grant...

You'll never run out of favorites.

Harlequin Historicals...they're too good to miss!

HH-GEN